Bid Time Return

Donna Baker

HEADLINE

First published in 1993
by HEADLINE BOOK PUBLISHING

First published in paperback 1994
by HEADLINE BOOK PUBLISHING

10 9 8 7 6 5 4 3 2 1

ISBN 0 7472 4325 5

Typeset by
Letterpart Limited, Reigate, Surrey

Printed and bound in Great Britain by
HarperCollins Manufacturing, Glasgow

HEADLINE BOOK PUBLISHING
A division of Hodder Headline PLC
338 Euston Road
London NW1 3BH

O! call back yesterday, bid time return
Shakespeare, *Richard II*

For PETER, with love

ACKNOWLEDGEMENTS

Much of my information on Furness and the mining of haematite there comes from the following books, to which I am much indebted: *THE IRON MOOR* by Alan McFadzean, and *THE DIARY OF WILLIAM FISHER OF BARROW* edited by W Rollinson and B Harrison. I must admit to some licence in local detail — Pennington Moor itself is a figment of my imagination and Ulverston does not have a Mayor. But there are also many places that can still be found and the gravestone headings in Pennington churchyard are (apart from those of the 'family') authentic. There is still a good deal of evidence of the old mines left in the now rural landscape of Furness, and my own home was once part of the offices of the mining company on Lindal Moor. Anyone who wants to experience for themselves the reality of an iron mine can visit the Florence Mine, near Egremont in northern Cumbria, and such a trip should be combined with the fascinating museum of mining at Caldbeck.

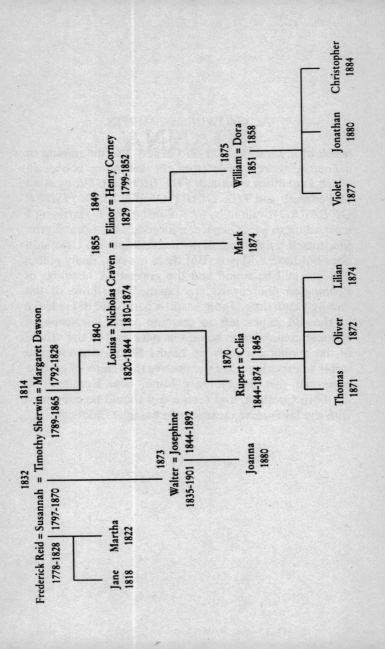

JOANNA

Chapter One

My first sight of the country of Furness filled me with dismay.

With the wind blowing in my hair – a wind that I was to learn seemed always to be blowing across this broad and rolling peninsula – I stood on Pennington Moor and gazed around at a landscape that seemed to speak of nothing but devastation. I supposed it had once been green and hilly, with secret valleys and running streams, but now it lay torn and bleeding, with water running crimson from the gashes in its flanks. It seemed a million miles, rather than a few thousand, from the clear white mountain peaks I knew so well; its murky skies a world away from the shimmering distances to which my eyes were accustomed.

If this was the country where my father had been born, I was not surprised he had left it. And the thought of spending the rest of my own life here, among these small and ravaged fields, crowded with clanking machinery apparently intent on devouring what natural scenery was left, lay cold and heavy on my heart.

Why had I come here? Why hadn't I stayed in the country where I had been born and spent all my twenty-one years? Penniless though my father's death had left me, was there nothing I could have done? No work, no employment that could have given me even the most slender of livelihoods to enable me to remain where I felt myself to be at home?

I had asked myself that question many times, and each time had been faced with the same stark answer. There was nothing. In this year of 1901, there was no living to be made by a young woman of my so-called 'station' among the British families in India. I had soon given up seeking work as a governess. Those who had young children employed an *ayah* to look after them; older ones were sent back to Britain to school. And I knew that no other course such as cooking or needlework would be open to me, even if I could have brought myself to accept so tedious a life.

'You have a family at home, don't you, Joanna?' my father's friend George Ledger had asked me. 'Can you not go to them?'

'I suppose I'll have to.' I looked despondently out through the windows of his airy bungalow. It was April and the *chota bursat*, the 'little monsoon', had begun. Torrential rain hammered on the roof and turned the garden to a quagmire. It rained in England, they said, but never as hard as this. There were times when I had longed for that land of softness, of gentle rain and cool winds, of sunshine that didn't sear the skin from your face. But now that it seemed close, a reality, I drew back from the pictures in my mind. 'But the thought of being dependent on others, on *strangers* . . .' I shuddered, picturing the young women I knew, the vapid existence they led, fluttering from one ball to another, flirting with young civil servants or subalterns, waited on hand and foot by obsequious servants. To have to live that sort of life, with people I didn't know, in a cold, strange country . . .

'But they're not strangers. They're your family.'

'They're strangers,' I insisted. 'I've never known them. My father hardly knew them – even those that are left. He hasn't seen England since he was twenty; he left home in eighteen fifty-five. Forty-six years ago! Of course they're strangers. And they may not want me.'

4

My voice quivered a little and I frowned, angry with myself for my self-pity. I wasn't normally prone to weeping. But since my father had died, tears had overcome me on the most inappropriate occasions.

Perhaps it was because I had not cried enough when my mother had died. I was only a child then, but the three of us had seen death more than once on our travels together, and my father's grief had been so intense that I could not inflict my own upon him too. And perhaps there had been a strange, painful pleasure in knowing that I was now the most important person in his life.

If that were so I was paying the price, for all the pent-up sorrow of the past nine years was welling up in me now and refusing to be suppressed.

George Ledger looked embarrassed, as men always did when confronted with emotion. British men, anyway. The Indian men I knew, like Chanden Singh and the Tibetan lama, Rimpoche Tayang, were not afraid of feelings, either their own or those of others. But people like George Ledger believed in the stiff upper lip, and although they acknowledged that 'the ladies' might be prey to vapours, they preferred not to be forced to witness them.

'Not want you?' he said gruffly. 'Why shouldn't they want you? You're family, ain't you? Of course they'll want you – only natural they should. As for being dependent on them, you've inherited a house, haven't you? You can live in that, or sell it. Anyway, I don't see where else you're to go.'

Neither did I. And I understood that George Ledger would not have welcomed any further discussion, with its awkward overtones of penury and the necessity for employment. In his view, a young lady should be content to remain at home, and consider herself fortunate to have a family who could enable her to do so. He thought I should have been doing so long before this anyway; he had never approved of the ramshackle life I had led with my father.

As soon as the monsoon was over I packed my bags, bade a sad farewell to my friends and departed on the train for Calcutta.

Leaving India had been like tearing a tree from the ground in which it had grown, wrenching the myriad tiny roots from the earth to which they clung for nourishment. I felt the pain of each one, adding to the almost intolerable pain of losing my father, and it was not until the steamer was within a day or two of reaching England that I could begin to look forward to my new life.

After all, I thought, I was quite accustomed to travel, to arriving in strange places and adapting myself to local customs. Only a few days before his death, my father and I had been planning a new adventure – a trip to South America, where he could make new discoveries for his books and I find new flowers and trees to draw. Could I not look on England as a foreign country – which indeed, as far as I was concerned, it was – and treat this journey as the first part of a new adventure?

And once I had sold Pennington Hall, the house my father had inherited and passed on to me, together with a small income from the family mines, I would no longer be poor or dependent. I could choose my own life. I could go to South America, just as we had planned.

Now, after further travelling which seemed more tedious than any of the days at sea, I was in Furness and gazing about me at the place that was to be, for a while at least, my home.

It was May, but where was the golden sunshine I had been promised? Where the soft blue sky, the temperatures that would have been pleasantly cool to skin more used to the searing heat of northern India?

As I stood on this windy upland, staring across the raw, broken hills to a grey, sullen sea, I felt cheated. The people I had talked to back in India, people who had grown up in England and had a nostalgic memory of it, had told me that England was beautiful, that although it rained often, the rain was soft and gentle, making a landscape green with grass and bright with flowers. They had not told me that it was like this.

I turned my head. Mark was watching me.

'Are you disappointed?'

I hesitated. Perhaps I should be tactful. But my face must already have answered him and the tactful words would not come.

'Not disappointed, no. I knew it was a mining area. I know the family mine haematite and I've seen plenty of mines in India – antimony mines, mostly. But somehow I'd expected it to be different here. My father used to talk of green hills and valleys, and mountains in the distance.' I looked up at the hovering clouds, the smoke-filled sky. 'It all looks so grey. So hopeless. And this is spring. What must it be like in December, in January?' I turned back to him. 'I'm sorry. I think it will take me a while to get used to it.'

He inclined his head. He was, I guessed, about seven or eight years older than I, tall and well-muscled with dark hair that sprang in a strong wave from his forehead. His eyes were very brown, almost as dark as those of the Indians I had known, but without their liquid quality. They were eyes that could be warm but might also be cold and hard, like stones found on a riverbed. They were neither particularly warm nor cold now but were watching me thoughtfully. I returned his look. There was something passing between us, some communication, but I could not quite interpret it. I turned away again. Perhaps I did not want to interpret it. After all, I wasn't intending to stay in Furness. There was no need to make either friends or enemies of the people who just happened to be my family.

Not that Mark and I were related by blood. He was the son of Elinor, about whom my father had been able

7

to tell me very little – he had left England soon after her marriage to Nicholas Craven, so he had not known much about her, only that she was Nicholas's second wife. The first had been Father's half-sister Louisa, the one who had died in childbirth. And that child, Rupert, now being dead also, they had no interest for me.

'You've had a long journey,' Mark said abruptly. 'Let's go home.'

I turned and climbed back into the motorcar. I had been surprised and impressed to find such magnificent transport awaiting me at Ulverston railway station. I had seen only a few motorcars in India, owned by such people as the Viceroy and other high Government officials, or one of the rajahs, and I had never ridden in one. As Mark drove through the streets of the old market town I looked about, half expecting to see more, but there were none.

'Most people still use horses,' Mark said when I asked him. 'There are one or two other motors in the area, but modern ideas take a long time to reach us in Furness.' His hand rested proudly on the dashboard. 'This little beauty came from Scotland – the Argyll, she's called, made by Hozier's in Bridgetown. They produced five hundred cars last year.'

'Five hundred! But they must be very expensive.'

'I suppose they are. But worth it for the convenience.' A cart, dragged by a sweating, mud-caked horse, came round a corner and with much yelling and shoving the carter managed to force it close against the hedge so that the motor could pass. Mark glanced back and frowned a little at the mud left on the car's painted sides and I hid a smile. Clearly, it was a new and very precious toy.

We drove slowly through the narrow lanes. It was a difficult journey, for there was a steady stream of carts being dragged from the mines to the railway sidings. They were loaded with iron ore, great bulging rocks of haematite that gleamed round and knobbled, like petrified kidneys.

8

The horses that hauled these heavy loads were caked in the same crimson mud that turned each road into a mire, and the carters themselves were streaked and spattered with the raddled stain, their faces like those of painted warriors under their battered caps.

'But some of them are women!' I exclaimed, turning in my seat. 'Do women do the same work as men?'

'Some of it. Ore-dressing, carting, jobs like that. Not underground, these days.'

He spoke casually enough, as if it were commonplace for women to do hard manual labour. In India I had seen plenty of women labouring in the fields, but they had always been women of the lowest caste, and never white. Somehow, never having known any other than those of my own class, it had not occurred to me that white women might do such work. I was shocked, yet at the same time ironically amused. Suppose I were to write to George Ledger and tell him I had found employment in a mine . . .

'You mean they used to work in the mines themselves? Below ground?'

'Oh yes. That was stopped quite a few years back – women and children working underground. We know better now. And the new tramways mean there's much less carting.'

Another cart passed us, drawn tightly against the high bank. I looked into the face of the carter and saw an old woman, grey hair straggling under the grime, who glanced at me with sullen indifference and then turned away. Her back was bent, her feet shuffled in broken boots, and the clothes she wore looked as if they relied upon their caking of ferruginous mud to hold them together.

My amusement vanished and I fell silent. Had this woman been leading carts all her life? Was this all she had ever known – as a young girl, as a mother with children tagging at her heels, as the crone she had become? Had she seen nothing but these narrow lanes, the twisting ways from mine to furnace?

'Where does the ore go?' I asked. 'Where are they taking it?'

'To the furnaces, or to the quays at Ulverston or Barrow. Some of it goes to Scotland to be smelted, some of it stays here at Hindpool or one of the other furnaces. There are still one or two old bloomeries at Coniston and Nibthwaite and Newland – quite a few, really.'

The names meant nothing to me. I tried to remember if my father had ever used them in his reminiscences. But he had not spoken much of the haematite mining and I had not been interested enough to press him. Now I wished I had. Dismayed though I was by this first sight of Furness, I was already aware that its history was my history too, and I felt a sense of deprivation that I knew so little of it.

Even of my own family, I knew little more than names. Not until I had met them, seen their faces and heard their voices, would I begin to think of them as real people, as my own family. Did they feel the same about me, these shadowy figures? Did they look forward to meeting me, to growing to know me? Or did they accept my arrival with no more than a grudging sense of duty, a sigh of resignation and a hope that I might as soon depart again?

The car grumbled its way out of the narrow lanes and along the moorland road. I sat up straight, suddenly interested. The sky had begun to clear – perhaps the wind was blowing the clouds away. And the views had begun to take more definite shape.

We were heading due west, away from Ulverston with its busy canal and quays, its cobbled streets. And before me, stretched almost at my feet, I could see the broad, dun-coloured sands of an estuary, carved with winding channels, while beyond them rose a hummocky hill, shadowed with black, and away to the north were the

10

craggy outlines of dark silhouetted mountains.

'Stop!' I exclaimed, and stared at the spaces that had so abruptly opened before me. 'Can we stop for a few minutes? I want to look at it.'

Mark drew the car to a halt and I stared at the expanse of sand with its pattern of channels stretching like fingers towards the open sea. The sun had thrust aside the clouds now and was sending shafts of brilliance down to the dancing water. On the sand itself I could see people moving about, digging, leading small carts, pushing barrows. The edge of the water was fringed with birds and on the far side, at the foot of the great round hill, there was a town, with ships moored alongside a quay.

I had seen larger estuaries in India, and more people. But I had never seen quite this quality of light, this aspect of sun gleaming capriciously on pewter water, this darkening of hills. My mountains had all been glimmering white peaks, reaching high into harsh blue skies, the colours of trees and flowers a brilliant foreground. Here there was a subtlety I longed to grasp, and my fingers itched suddenly for my paints.

'That's the Duddon estuary,' Mark said. 'You can walk across the sands, if you're careful. But I don't advise you to try it. The tide comes in very fast, and there are quicksands.'

'Have you done it?' My eyes were still on the scene below them.

'A few times. I know the way.'

'Will you take me sometime?'

He glanced at me in surprise. 'It's not an afternoon stroll. You can be up to your waist in water in places, even at the lowest tide.'

'And so?' I asked with some amusement. 'There are no other dangers, are there? No crocodiles or water snakes?'

Mark laughed. 'No, of course not! But it's still hardly a jaunt for ladies.'

11

'Oh, *ladies*,' I said dismissively, and turned to him. I searched his eyes. Could I trust him? Could I tell him how I felt without risking scorn or censure? There was something there, surely, a warmth, an openness, that told me he might understand. Or if not understand, at least accept my feelings. 'Mark, please help me. I've lived such a different life from the people you know. I don't know how I shall settle to the life of an English lady. I don't believe I *want* to settle to it, not if it means being very quiet and genteel, paying calls of an afternoon and sewing in the parlour. I've never done that sort of thing.'

Mark looked surprised. 'But surely in India the ladies live much the same sort of life as they do here?'

'The ladies, yes. But I don't believe I ever was a "lady". My father was an explorer, he travelled all over northern India, even into Tibet, carrying out surveys. And I went with him. My mother died of malaria when I was twelve and there was no one to take care of me. He wouldn't have left me anyway. He had very strong ideas about how parents should look after their children.' I looked down at the estuary again, thinking of the many journeys we had undertaken together, the dangers we had faced – and the sense of security I had always known in his company and now so sorely missed. 'We would have crossed something like that, not knowing any of the dangers, charting it as we went. It was his job.'

'And you enjoyed that?' He sounded unbelieving and I laughed.

'It was my life! I never thought about enjoyment. But yes, I enjoyed it – I must have done, since it's what I want to go on doing.'

He looked more than surprised now. 'But how can you? Ladies don't—'

'I told you,' I said. 'I've never been a "lady". I've never sat in drawing rooms with my mother, making polite conversation with other women. She wasn't interested in that sort of life – she wanted to be with my father. She had no family of her own, her parents had both died when she was quite young and she'd been taken in by an officer and his family as a companion for their daughter. Then, when the daughter was sent to England, she stayed on as a companion to the officer's wife. But they always treated her as if she were a servant, and she hated the tedium of all the afternoon parties where she was only supposed to speak if spoken to, and never given credit for any intelligence. Life with my father must have seemed like being let out of prison.' I paused, thinking of the tales she had told me, of her constant encouragement to think my own thoughts, to treat my life as my own, as something precious.

'I've spent my life travelling, and not the kind of travelling you know, either. We would hire a couple of yaks and a native porter or two, and just set off across mountains higher than those,' I nodded towards the craggy hills that lay to the north, 'and with no cosy villages to put up for the night. We camped on bare, stony ground, made fires from the dung our yaks dropped, and lived on what we could carry. Sometimes we managed to acquire horses and could ride, but that was a luxury. Once or twice there were nothing but sheep to be used as pack animals, and that's a slow, painful business. And sometimes we simply had to carry our own loads.' I smiled at his astonished face. 'One soon forgets about being a "lady" in such conditions. No large trunks or travelling cases, no ball gowns or fashionable dresses. Most of the time, I went dressed as a boy – it was easier and safer.'

'And you enjoyed it?' he asked again.

'It was my life,' I repeated. 'And I think I want no other. To exchange it for the kind of life women have to live in England . . . How would you feel, Mark, if you had lived wild and free and were suddenly put into a cage?'

13

'That's different,' he said. 'I'm a man.'

'No,' I answered him, 'you are a human being. And so am I.'

He climbed out of the driving seat and went round to the front of the car to start the motor again. As he swung the starting handle, I could see that his brow was furrowed in concentration. He hadn't understood, but he was trying to. And at least he hadn't sneered at me.

The engine coughed a bit then stuttered into life and he got back into the car.

'So what do you plan to do?'

I shrugged. 'I don't know. Travelling is expensive – my father could do it because he was paid for the surveys he undertook. It depends on how much the income is from the mine, and what Pennington Hall is worth—'

'You mean you'll *sell* it?' The car had begun to move forward, but now it jerked to a standstill as if it were as startled as he, and the engine stopped again. He sighed and climbed down to go through the starting procedure once more. This time, we both waited until we were well under way before continuing the conversation.

'Yes, I suppose I'll sell it,' I said. 'After all, what else can I do with it? I don't want to live there.'

'How do you know? Until you've seen it, how can you tell?' He sounded quite dismayed, I realised with surprise. 'You can't make decisions like that without seeing all the evidence.'

'And Pennington Hall is part of the evidence?' I shook my head. 'No. It's just a house. A house that has had no part in my life. It means nothing to me, Mark. Furness means nothing to me. Whereas India, Tibet, Peru – those are all exciting. Foreign countries with everything to be discovered. New sights to see, new people to meet, new experiences—'

'You'll see new sights, meet new people and have new experiences here,' he interrupted. 'And the house *is* part of your life. It helped make your father what he was and

14

so it had its influence on you through him. The people who lived there – some of them living there still – had their influence as well. They are all part of you.' He turned his head and met my eyes. 'Unless you know them, you'll never know yourself, Joanna. And whatever experiences you encounter through life, you'll never be able to realise their true value if you don't know yourself first.'

I stared at him. There were echoes of Eastern thinking in his words. But what could Mark, an English solicitor not many years older than myself, know of such things?

I turned my head away. I was not ready for this. I wanted still to live by the rules I knew, the freedom I had grown up with.

'How far is it to Pennington Hall?' I asked abruptly. 'I think I've had enough of travelling for the time being anyway.'

He smiled and we drove on in silence. But I knew we would talk more, when the time was right.

Pennington Hall was a long, low, stone-built farmhouse, its uneven walls limewashed white under a grey slate roof. Square windows looked out from each side of the stone porch and a whole row of them from the upstairs rooms. The porch itself was festooned with climbing roses and the walls almost hidden by creeping plants – wisteria, honeysuckle and a shaggy lime-green ivy.

I stared at it. My father's descriptions had never prepared me for this, the picture he had painted in my mind was of stark grey, a grim-fronted, frowning house planted firmly in a bare yard. It must have been since his time that someone had turned that empty yard into a garden, bright with a profusion of plants and flowers. Who had done it? Susannah? Timothy? It seemed unlikely.

My Aunt Martha was at the door to greet us as we drove up and I looked at her with interest. My father had told me about her, and her sister Jane. They were the daughters, by her first marriage, of his mother, Susannah, who had married his father Timothy Sherwin after his first wife Margaret had died. It was all so complicated, I had barely listened to him, but since his death I had looked out many of his letters and drawn up a family tree, to fix them all in my mind.

Martha was seventy-nine, I knew, but she hardly looked it. Bundled up in scarves and woollen jumpers, for the wind was spitefully cold, and with rosy cheeks and bright, inquisitive eyes, she looked more like a middle-aged farmer's wife than a genteel maiden aunt of advancing years. I tried to relate her to the plump, giggling girl my father had described to me and failed. But I knew he'd been fond of her. As a baby, she and her stepsister Louisa had played with him and taken him for walks. Jane, the eldest, had had little time for him and neither, it seemed, had his mother.

And now Jane and Louisa were dead and only Martha was left, to live alone here at Pennington Hall while my father spent his life thousands of miles away. Had she ever wondered what would happen to her if he came back? Had she expected him to come back – perhaps when he married? And what would he have done? I could not believe that he would have turned her out.

'So you're Joanna!' she was upon me the moment I stepped from the motorcar. 'After all this time!' She came barely to my shoulder, but she hugged me tightly nevertheless and I felt an unexpected emotion at the warm contact. I had experienced so little such contact since my mother had died. A brief kiss of greeting or parting from my father, a light, impersonal touch from the wives of some of his Civil Service or Army friends – no more than that. Sudden tears were hot in my eyes and I dashed them away, afraid of their being seen.

Aunt Martha stepped back and looked me up and down. 'Oh yes. I can tell you're Walter's daughter. You

16

have his look – his eyes. *So* much like dear Louisa and Papa. In fact, with the right dress and your hair done a different way, you could almost be Louisa . . . Rupert was quite different, much more like Mark.' Her eyes rested for a moment on the man who stood beside me, dark as a gipsy. 'They take after the Cravens, of course, though Nicholas is quite fair . . . But don't let me keep you chattering in this cold wind. Come inside and have a cup of tea. You must be parched after your journey.'

I followed her indoors, curious to see the house, the first English one I had been in. I had stayed in a hotel in Liverpool after leaving the ship, but hotels were impersonal and nothing like a private house. And this house was something special, for it was mine.

My house. I stood in the hall, gazing about me. It was wide and spacious, but crammed with furniture – hall-stands, whatnots, a heavy dresser made of some dark, glowing wood with mirrors on top, a scatter of tables each bearing a collection of enormous-leafed plants in ornate china bowls, and two or three chairs with worn upholstery, striped in cream and gold. The walls were papered with a dark red, embossed paper, though little of this was visible between the multitude of pictures and mirrors hung upon them. The whole effect was crowded and stuffy, as if the hall were in fact much smaller than it was, and I thought of the airy lightness of the bungalows of my father's friends in India. How different this would look furnished with chairs and tables of bamboo, with a few graceful plants instead of these heavy creatures that looked as if they were ready to swallow you, and the walls painted white.

Well, I could do it if I wanted to. It was my house. I could do with it whatever I liked.

Aunt Martha was leading us into the drawing room off the hall, a large room that could also have been airy and spacious but was equally crammed. I gave up looking at each separate piece of furniture and instead resigned

17

myself to seeing them as a mass, without individuality, although I was sure that many of them were very fine. Many others were quite hideous, though, and I determined to get rid of them as soon as it was decently possible.

'And now we'll have tea,' my aunt said, and rang a little bell. The tea soon appeared, brought in by a maid who stared at me with unconcealed curiosity – as if she expected me to be black or have two heads, I thought with amusement. Aunt Martha's teas were something I could certainly approve of – muffins, scones, plenty of sandwiches, and at least two kinds of cake. I was hungrier than I had thought and had eaten several platefuls and drunk three or four cups of tea before I could really pay attention to conversation again.

'. . . and so William has invited Julian to stay for a few weeks,' Mark was telling my aunt. 'He's very keen for the Millom company to amalgamate with Sherwin and Craven, and I believe he thinks that if this friendship between Julian and Violet comes to anything, old Mr Barlow will be more willing to agree terms.'

'No doubt he would,' Martha agreed. 'It's always been common enough for businesses to benefit from such a marriage. I don't say I approve of it myself, mark you. To my mind, a marriage entered into for any reason other than love is bound to come to grief. But there's no doubt it happens.'

'Well, perhaps they are in love,' Mark said, sounding amused, but my aunt shook her head positively.

'No. I've seen them together and they're not. Oh, good enough friends, I'm sure, but that's all. And don't tell me that's enough, Mark, I've seen too much unhappiness and pain in my lifetime to believe that any reason other than love can make a marriage. Don't think that because I've never married myself I know nothing of these things. The looker-on sees most of the game, you know.'

I glanced at her with interest. Until now, she had impressed me as a warm-hearted but perhaps rather naive woman, welcoming enough but full of inconsequential chatter and probably a gossip. Now I began to wonder if she were not more perceptive than I had given her credit for.

'Well, I'm sure William wants the best for Violet,' Mark observed. 'Though opinions might vary as to what the best is. Julian's considered a very good catch, you know, and Violet's keen enough.'

'That's the danger of it. Violet's like all young girls, sees wealth and good looks and thinks that's the whole man. But you know as well as I do, Mark, that that's very far from the truth.' She sighed. 'Well, we shall see. Perhaps I'm wrong. They may be very well suited after all.' She turned to me. 'And what of you, Joanna? I daresay you've left a good many young subalterns swooning on the quayside at Calcutta?'

I laughed. 'Not that I know of! Father and I were too busy travelling to move much in society. He had plenty of friends, of course, in the Civil Service and the Army, but we knew just as many Indians, Nepalese and even Tibetans, and on the whole they were much more interesting.' I thought of some of the young Army officers I'd known – the 'subalterns' of Martha's romantic fancy. Vapid yet arrogant, filled with the vanity of their Britishness which they seemed to imagine gave them some kind of superiority over the people whose country they had commandeered, yet in my view totally dull and devoid of interest. No, I would not have wanted to become attached to a subaltern, or indeed to any of the young British men I had met.

The conversation changed then, with Mark and Aunt Martha both asking me about my life in India and telling me about Furness. I knew a certain amount, of course, from Father and from the letters written him by the family – mostly Aunt Martha herself, who had been a tireless correspondent – but there was much more to know.

Where was the Louisa mine, for instance? It was a name that had intrigued me ever since I had first heard it, as a small child. How had my Aunt Louisa come to have a mine named after her? But when I asked Martha, she only shook her head and gave Mark a strange glance, almost of complicity, as if it had been agreed, or perhaps always tacitly understood, that the subject was one of those not discussed in the family.

Within the family? Or only with me?

I sipped my tea and looked out of the window at the garden. The trees and hedges were green, and flowers were blooming in the borders, small but bright and clear, unlike the luscious blooms of the rhododendrons and other plants of northern India so familiar to me. Beyond the garden, the hill rose towards the moor and I could see the golden blaze of the thorny bushes Mark had told me were gorse. Always in flower, he had said, and with a touch of mischief in his eye quoted me an old rhyme: 'When gorse is out of season, kissing's out of reason'.

I turned my head and looked back at him. He was listening to Aunt Martha, his dark head bent courteously to hear what she was telling him. I wondered why the task of meeting me had fallen to him when it might have been more conventional for one of the women of the family to do it. Not Aunt Martha, of course, for she was too old, but Celia, my cousin Rupert's widow, might have come, or her son Thomas and his wife. Perhaps they were too busy, I thought. Or maybe convention wasn't as strict here as in India, where protocol seemed so vitally important. With the Victorian reign over at last and a new, freer age beginning with the new century, many of the old, hidebound rules were beginning to be relaxed.

Mark glanced up and our eyes met; the promise of warmth and understanding that I'd glimpsed in them

20

earlier was more marked now. Here, I thought, was one friend at least. And my Aunt Martha another. I felt grateful to them both. I had changed my mind about my stay in Furness. In this strange, wrecked landscape, I felt as if I was going to need friends.

Chapter Two

Mark departed soon after tea on that first day and I was left alone with Aunt Martha. Now, at last, was my chance to find out more about the family. But Martha seemed less inclined to sit and chat. She was anxious instead to show me round the house and, remembering that she had been acting as caretaker for what had been her home since she was a child, I realised that it would be unkind to show a lack of interest.

Not that I had any lack of interest to show. This was the first house I had owned, and although until now I had seen it merely as a means of providing myself with an income, I couldn't help feeling a sense akin to awe and pride at suddenly being the owner of such riches. For riches there certainly were. The house itself was much bigger than I had realised, with large rooms, and the grounds stretched to two or three acres, with a walled kitchen garden containing peach, apple and plum trees as well as soft fruits and vegetables, a rose garden which was just coming into bloom, wide lawns, a delightfully tangled shrubbery and a pond. The stables contained two or three horses who all poked their noses over their doors to greet Martha as soon as they heard her step, and at one end of the house was a fine conservatory.

'Papa built that five years before he died,' Martha told me. 'It leads off the morning room.' She had insisted we look at the garden first, while there was still light, and it was clear that the outside of the house interested her far more than the inside (I was introduced by name to almost every plant growing), with the exception of the conservatory, which was filled with exotic and tender plants.

I exclaimed with delight at recognising some of my own favourites. There, blooming as happily as ever they had on Himalayan soil, were the Asiatic primulas which I had drawn and painted so many times. The drumstick, *Primula denticulata*, which my father and I had found in upper Nepal, here in both its natural pale lilac and its cultivated colours – pink, red, violet and, prettiest of all, pure ivory, like a cluster of snowflakes. *Primula rosea* too, almost over now but still delightful with its soft pink flowers. Martha had them in great clusters, along with the yellow eyes of *edgeworthii* and the azure blue of *sonchifolia*.

'Are these all grown from the seeds we sent?' I asked, for one of Father's tasks had been to collect new seeds and plants for growers in England, and we had often sent a few to Martha.

'Oh yes. And there are lots growing in the garden too – at the edge of the orchard mostly. But I grow them in here because I like to experiment with new varieties. They've been a great interest for me over the years.' She gave me her happy smile. 'I can't tell you how grateful I've been to you and your father for sending them.'

I looked round the conservatory. It was clear that my aunt spent a great deal of time either in here or in the garden. As well as the Asiatic plants, there were varieties I had never seen before, from other continents – cacti and succulents, some grotesque but fascinating, smothered with vicious spines, others brilliant with gaudy flowers. And there were others, plants that were more like small trees, which Martha told me came, along with the cacti, from the Americas; some tall and stately with great oval leaves, and one quite magnificent specimen, like a great bush with its leaves slashed as if someone had been using them to practise origami. *Monstera deliciosa*, my aunt told me this was, so called because it grew very large and would in ideal conditions produce an aromatic fruit. 'But mine have never managed to do so,' she said a little sadly.

'It's a beautiful conservatory, all the same,' I said, gazing about me at the luxuriant foliage. 'Why, you have everything one could wish for here. I can see I shall want to spend hours in here, drawing and painting. And what a splendid Wardian case!'

'It is lovely, isn't it,'she said, evidently pleased by my appreciation. 'I've had it for a number of years now and it's very well established. See, there's a *Hoya carnosa* and a *lycopodium*, both doing very well. And . . .' She enumerated the plants she was growing in the closed glass case with its ornate framework. It was the most ornamental I had seen. I knew how effective they were, and how plants could be safely transported in them even on long sea voyages; many of the specimens Father and I had sent back to collectors in England had been put into Wardian cases, and if such an invention had not existed I doubt whether many of them would have survived the journey.

At last our tour came to an end and with supper over I was able to go to the room Martha had prepared for me. It was my father's old room, she said a little shyly, but of course if I wanted to change it, I must say so at once. The room my grandparents had shared was all ready for me if I preferred it, and so was dear Louisa's. But I was happy enough with father's room, and glad to be where he had spent so much of his boyhood. It gave me a sense of familiarity which was as comforting as it was irrational, considering he had not set foot in the house for forty-six years. But there were still little touches that reminded me of him – a few shells on the window sill, a childish picture on the wall, a fishing rod standing in one corner and a small regiment of lead soldiers ranged on a desk.

'I always thought he might come back someday,' Martha said a little wistfully as we stood together by the window which looked out towards the broad reach of Morecambe Bay. 'I wanted him to find his things here and know that I'd looked after them.'

I felt sudden tears sting my eyes. All those years, she had waited and hoped. I pictured her, coming into this room with a duster, taking as much care of his shells and his soldiers as if they had been valuable *objets d'art*, looking forward to the day when he would come back and find them here.

But he never did. And now I had come in his place.

No, even if I had loathed his room I could not have hurt Aunt Martha's feelings by rejecting it.

After she had left me and I had begun to unpack the small case I had brought with me – my other luggage, such as it was, was arriving separately – I realised that the situation was more complicated than that. It wasn't a question merely of hurting my aunt's feelings by objecting to her choice of room. There were other ways in which I could hurt her far, far more. By selling this house, for instance. By taking away the home she had known for almost seventy years. By tearing her from her beloved garden and conservatory. What recompense was that for the loving care she had given the house all these years, knowing all the time that my father might return and reclaim it? Of course he could have sold it at any time and forced Martha to find somewhere else to live – with her sister Jane, perhaps, or with Celia or Elinor. But he never had.

And why not? There had been times in plenty when the money would have been welcome. Yet never for an instant, to my knowledge, had he considered turning his half-sister out of her home. It was as if he had felt a moral responsibility towards her. And I supposed he was right.

And if she were his responsibility, did that not also make her mine?

I stared out of the window. The moon was climbing high in the sky, turning the landscape below into a patchwork of blues and greys. At home, the same moon would have lit on peaks of shimmering white but although there were mountains here a few miles to the north, they were less than the foothills I was used to and there would be no snow on them at this time of year. I suddenly felt unbearably homesick and pressed my forehead against the glass, fighting to control the tears in my aching eyes.

The only consolation I had found in leaving India was that, with the money gained from selling Pennington Hall, I would be able to realise the dream my father and I had shared and go to South America. If I had never come here, that was what I would have been able to do. But curiosity had brought me to Furness, to see where my father had been born and grown up. And so I had met Aunt Martha. I had seen her feelings for the house and the garden. I had even shared in them, for the garden was beautiful, the conservatory a jewel, and I would no more have wanted to give them up if they had been mine than she would.

If they had been mine? I thought with ironical amusement. But they *were* mine. Mine, to do with as I liked.

Immediately, the other part of my mind, that part which was more closely linked to my heart, answered no, they were not mine. In law, they might be so, but in truth they were hers.

Aunt Martha had tended the garden as if it were her family and each plant in it her own child. She had dug and raked and sown the seeds, she had taken cuttings and pushed them into the earth with her own hands, she had created this beauty herself. Tearing her away from it would be like tearing away one of the very trees or

26

shrubs she had so lovingly nurtured. And I could not do it.

I sat staring out of the window for a long time until I grew cold and crept into bed, where I lay huddled, wondering what I could do now, where I could go. And my heart ached, both for the India I had left and the South America of my dreams. For it seemed to me at that moment that I had lost them both.

'Of course,' Elinor said, 'Mark doesn't *have* to live in Ulverston. He knows that perfectly well. And as soon as William and Dora have their own household he'll come back here to be with me.'

I caught her glance as she said these words and wondered what she was thinking. William, her son by her first husband, had stayed in Green House when he had married Dora, and brought up his children there. It seemed a little odd to be expecting him to find another household at this stage, when the children were grown up and ready to leave home.

'Or I'll go and live in Ulverston to look after him,' Elinor added, with another glance at me. And again, I wondered. Wouldn't Mark be marrying one day? Would he, or his wife, really want his mother living with them, especially when she had a perfectly good house of her own?

Elinor seemed old to be Mark's mother, but I knew that he had been born when she thought her childbearing days were over. She was still handsome; her hair, which Martha had told me used to be like spun gold, was now pure silver and her skin was still soft and almost free of lines. She must once have been very beautiful, I thought, and I wondered how she had ever settled down here in quiet Furness, coming as she had from a busy city like Liverpool.

Elinor had already told me that Mark had inherited his house in Ulverston from the elderly solicitor who had taken him into partnership. The old man had shown an interest in him ever since he was a baby, losing his father so tragically on the very day he was born. There had been a legal tangle to sort out then over property, and by the time the business had been completed, old Humphrey Littlecote had become something of a surrogate father to Mark. He had overseen his upbringing and education and finally taken him into the firm with him. Two or three years ago he had died, leaving Mark everything.

'Would you really want to live in Ulverston?' Martha asked. 'It's so peaceful here. I've always loved Green House.'

'You may call it peaceful,' Elinor retorted. 'I call it dull. I never see a soul these days. Dora has her own friends, who have no time for an old woman, and as for the children, why, they fly in and out as if it were a hotel.'

'Well, Jonathan's away most of the time anyway, isn't he?' Martha said, and turned to me. 'Jonathan's the one at medical school; I think I told you about him. He's studying to become a doctor.'

I nodded. During the past day or two Martha had told me all about the family in Furness. I knew that William had stepped into the breach when Rupert had died and taken over the management of the mine, much against Elinor's wishes since she had always looked down on the mining industry. Her first husband, Henry Corney, had been a banker or something of the sort in Liverpool, and the Cravens, Nicholas's family, were merchants; Elinor had expected both her sons to follow in one or other of these sets of footsteps. But she could not complain that the mines had not been prosperous; as I looked round the room I reflected that William had done very well.

'Jonathan's away, yes. But Violet isn't, and I see very little more of her. She's forever rushing out on that precious bicycle of hers.' Elinor sniffed disapprovingly.

'Girls have far too much freedom these days if you ask me.'

We were sitting, the three of us, in the drawing room of Green House and at this point we were interrupted by the arrival of Rupert's widow, Celia. As yet I had not met her, or any of the rest of the family; Martha had thought I needed a day or two at Pennington to recuperate from the journey, and I was surprised to find that I did, in spite of my experience in travelling. Long sea voyages and a train journey could, it seemed, be much more exhausting than trekking through Nepal and Tibet with a couple of yaks. But today it had been arranged that we should all come to Green House where I could be introduced to the whole family.

Celia came in with her daughter Lilian, who at the age of twenty-seven was still unmarried and lived at home. Celia was a few years short of sixty, a small, plump woman with hair that looked as if it had once been bronze but was now salted with white. She had a smiling, china-doll face, but there was a cold look about her eyes, as if her smile never quite reached them. Her lips spoke welcoming words, yet I felt uneasy, as if the truth behind them was something quite different. Celia, I thought, despite her soft voice and smiling face, could be a dangerous person to cross.

Lilian obviously took her colouring from her mother, though in every way she seemed a paler copy. She was a tall, rather lanky, woman with sandy hair and a thin, horsey face peppered with freckles. Her eyes were a pale, indeterminate, greenish-blue and she had a sharp nose. She looked down it at me as we were introduced and held out a limp hand which felt damp and cold.

'Is Violet here?' Celia asked. She had come into the room in time to hear Elinor's disapproving remark about girls and their freedom (Freedom! I thought. An afternoon riding the lanes on a bicycle!) and her voice made the question, innocent enough, sound barbed. I wondered what the relationship was between the two of them. I had noticed the tension in the air the minute Celia and Lilian walked in, as if it bristled. 'I would have thought she could have stayed at home to greet Joanna,' she added with a sweet smile in my direction.

'Oh, she'll be home in a minute,' Elinor replied carelessly. 'We have Julian staying here at the moment, you know. I daresay they've gone walking together and forgotten the time. You know what these young lovers are.' Her glance rested a moment on Lilian, who looked as if she had never had a lover in her life, young or old. 'I expect you've done the same many times, haven't you, Lilian?'

Lilian's pale, freckled face flushed an unbecoming red and I felt sorry for her. She didn't seem an attractive person, but she could still feel humiliation as deeply as the next.

Celia tightened her lips. 'I'm glad to say that Lilian has never given me a moment's worry,' she said sharply. 'I must say I agree with you, Elinor, girls these days are given far too much freedom.'

The conversation looked as if it would develop interestingly, but any further exchange was interrupted by the arrival of the two people in question. At least, I supposed that was who they were for nobody volunteered to introduce them to me for several minutes.

Violet was as fair as her grandmother must once have been but would never be as beautiful. Her eyes were too small and too close together. But she had a certain prettiness, and a coquettish manner which I knew would be attractive to some men. I wondered if her companion were one of them.

He saw me immediately. Presumably he knew that I would be there, for as soon as he came into the room his eyes roved about, as if looking for someone, and when they lighted on me they paused and I saw that little rise of the eyebrows that often serves as an acknowledgement. I believe he would have come across to me there and then without waiting for an introduction, but the others began to talk to him and Violet at once, asking how they were and where they had been on their bicycles, and he was forced to pay attention to them.

I watched him, surprised and a little disturbed by my own reaction. After all, I had seen plenty of handsome and attractive young men in India. But none of them had looked at me with quite that instant acknowledgement, almost recognition, and none of them had given me the same feeling. As if we did not need introduction. As if we already knew each other, had known each other – and known each other well – for a long, long time.

Chanden Singh, the teacher who was my father's closest friend in Darjeeling, would have said that this was indeed the truth of the matter. That perhaps all of us – Celia, Violet, Elinor, Martha, the whole family – had been together in lifetimes past and forgotten, and that every now and then some fragment of memory was bound to break through and startle us with that brief flash of recognition. He would have talked of *samsara* and of *karma*.

I still did not know whether I believed his words. But when such a moment came to me, a moment of feeling that this had happened before, that I almost knew what would happen next, that the stranger I had just met was no stranger at all, then I began to think it was true that the spirit was eternal, living from body to body, moving slowly up the ladder to *nirvana* or, more rapidly perhaps, down to one of the many hells.

I became aware that Martha was speaking, and that Julian was standing before me.

'. . . dear Walter's daughter Joanna,' she said. 'You've heard of my brother Walter, of course – our explorer.'

'Indeed.' He had a deep voice. 'I've even read some of his books.' He took my hand and held it, not tightly but

31

caressingly, his fingers moving very slightly against my palm. His eyes, looking into mine, were a very dark blue though his hair was as fair as Violet's, swept back in a loose wave. 'I'm honoured to meet you, Miss Sherwin.'

I inclined my head slightly. For the first time I could remember, I felt tongue-tied. I could think of nothing to say, so I merely smiled and murmured something conventional, wondering if I was a disappointment to him. No doubt he had been told how outrageous I was, with my odd clothes and wild way of life, and here I was dressed as unobtrusively as anyone could wish and behaving as modestly as a girl just out of the schoolroom.

Violet came across and stood beside him, taking his arm possessively. I caught a flicker of amusement about his lips and he glanced at me ironically, as if inviting me to laugh with him. I felt an immediate repugnance, but to my annoyance this didn't stop him being attractive to me. It was as if there were some bond between us, some invisible cord which held us together. I could not laugh with him at Violet, but neither could I turn away.

'So you're Joanna,' she said in her babyish voice. 'All the way from India. Tell me, is it really true that they still eat people there?'

'No, nor ever has been,' I answered shortly. 'The Indian races are generally very gentle, and not violent at all.'

'I'm sure they know their place now, at any rate,' Julian said smoothly. 'The British have been there for a long time now, quite long enough to teach them the right way to live.'

'They have a good deal to teach us,' I said. 'Some of the Eastern ways are much more enlightened than ours.'

Violet stared. 'Oh, surely not! Why, half of them aren't even Christian.'

'Exactly,' I said dryly, and a stunned silence fell on the room. I glanced round, realising for the first time that everyone had been listening to this exchange, and realising too that while I had been talking to Violet and Julian, Mark had come into the room. He stood at the door now, his dark eyes upon me. I sent him a silent message of appeal, but he did not respond. I would have to deal with the situation myself. And why not? I had said nothing amiss.

'Some of the Eastern religions are every bit as advanced and as civilised as Christianity,' I said. 'And more ancient. The Buddhists, for example . . .'

But I had evidently trodden on forbidden ground. Martha, her face pink, fluttered towards the door, murmuring something about tea. Elinor forestalled her by sharply ringing the little bell that stood on the table beside her. And Celia began an animated conversation with Lilian about some friends who had called that morning while Lilian was out.

Religion, it seemed, was not to be discussed in the drawing room, especially a strange, exotic Eastern religion such as Buddhism. Like death, it was a taboo subject in polite society.

I glanced at Julian. The amusement still played about his mouth and he gave me again that little signal of recognition, the minute lift of the brows. I wanted suddenly to laugh and looked quickly away, knowing that this would be an even worse breach of manners than I had already committed.

Mark was still leaning against the door jamb. He was watching me, his dark face shadowed, his eyes veiled. I wondered what he was thinking. But he looked remote, distant, as if thinking of something quite different.

I could not read his expression as I could Julian's.

The cold wind had abated and the sun shone more warmly as I left the house next morning and walked across the fields to Pennington church. The banks were starred with primroses, yellow as butter, and here in the village it was possible to believe oneself far away from the clatter and dust of the mines. I looked up at the sky, so gentle a blue, and thought that if England could be like this all the time it would be a pleasant place after all.

As I walked, I reflected on the tea party yesterday. After Julian and Violet had arrived, conversation had been general, the kind of conversation one would expect at a family tea party. Everyone had shown polite interest in me and had drawn me into the circle – not far, but far enough to make me feel that I was part of the group. I had sensed certain undercurrents of tension, but these were normal in most families, so I had taken little notice of them.

I had been forced to take notice, however, of Julian. He had sat by me the entire time, passing me plates of sandwiches and cake and insisting on refilling my cup with tea. Violet, on his other side, had been restless and fidgety, constantly endeavouring to claim his attention but without much success. At first amused, I had become embarrassed by it. I knew quite well how such behaviour could make me unpopular if Julian were already earmarked for Violet. And it was obvious, too, that Elinor was displeased by it. Her glances were cold and she twice interrupted when I was answering someone else's question, once with a query about Celia's comfort and once with an exclamation of feigned surprise about the time.

I reached the churchyard and went in through the gate. Martha had told me where to find the graves I sought. She had offered to come with me but I declined, saying I wanted to walk alone, and left her in the garden, grubbing up weeds.

I walked between the gravestones, looking at the names. Local names such as Ashburner, an old family of charcoal-burners – Mark had told me that charcoal had been an important factor in smelting the iron – Salthouse and Benson. There were couples who had died within a short time of each other, like James and Dorothy Fell,

34

only a year apart. And some like the Ashburners, Jane who had died in 1846 and Thomas who had waited another thirty-two years. Many of them had lived their allotted span and were in their seventies. One, tragically, had been killed at twenty-one by an engine on the tramway at Lindal Moor.

In the corner, I found the ones I had been looking for. A little group of them, close together. Three were ornate constructions of marble, with angels standing over them, wings outspread and hands folded, and the usual panegyric extolling of the dead person's virtues, of which I took little notice. The names and the dates were what I had come to see.

TIMOTHY SHERWIN 1789–1865
SUSANNAH SHERWIN 1797–1870

And next to them:

LOUISA CRAVEN 1820–1844

Then two others, which struck me by their difference. No ornate marble here, no angels or cherubs with pious expressions and open books; no fulsome praise. Just two plain headstones, carved only with the names and the dates, which stood out all the more for being so bare.

NICHOLAS CRAVEN 1810–1874
RUPERT CRAVEN 1844–1874

I stared at them. Rupert and Nicholas, dead in the same year. What had happened? Had it been merely coincidence? Deaths in the same year could still be months apart and nothing to do with each other. Or was there something more to the story?

It could have been an epidemic. Had there still been cholera in England then? Or perhaps smallpox, or some other disease ravaging the country? Prince Albert had died only a few years earlier, of typhoid, or there was diphtheria or consumption – any number of causes. Perhaps it had been an accident in which both had met their deaths. Or two separate accidents.

The fact that neither my father nor Martha had ever mentioned it made it all the more mysterious. Perhaps he had never known – he relied solely on my aunt's letters to keep him informed of family events, and by the mid-eighties he had lost a good deal of his interest in people he barely knew. But he'd been fond of Rupert when they were children; surely he would have been affected by his death at so early an age, thirty, and leaving a widow and three children. One of them, Lilian, must surely have been no more than a baby. Hadn't she been born in that very year?

If there had been a double tragedy, why had he never told me? And why hadn't my aunt mentioned it to me? She had told me so many family stories in the past two days. Wasn't this one just the kind of fascinating, though tragic, event that she loved to talk about?

I sat down on the grass by the graves and studied the headstones as if they could give me a clue. But they stared back at me, impassive, keeping the secrets of the graves they guarded. They imparted nothing except their plainness, so unusual in this age of elaborate decoration. What did it mean? Why had they not been given any kind of eulogy? And why, if they had not died together and in unusual circumstances, had they both been given the same stark treatment?

I turned back and examined the others. Such a sad little story, I thought. Louisa, only twenty-four years old when she died. And her son Rupert only six years older. He had never known his mother, just as his own daughter Lilian had never known him.

As I sat on the grass, the warmth of the May sunshine seemed to dim and the soft air turn cool. A shiver prickled across my skin. Before my eyes, a mist seemed to descend, blurring the scene before me. I felt a strange disembodiment, as if I were being lifted from myself and held aloft, above the graveyard, above Pennington, above Furness itself. I seemed to hear, in the whisper of the wind, voices calling to me in tones of entreaty.

I closed my eyes, feeling suddenly afraid. What was it? What was happening to me? Was it all imagination, this sense of being swept out of my body, this drift of voices that called yet could not clearly be heard? Or was there something – some strange, unearthly contact, some knowledge that hung about these graves and whatever tragic secret they guarded, that had importance for me and my own life?

I clung to the grass as if the earth were rocking beneath me, yet I barely felt its strands between my fingers. I was swept by the sensation of being afloat. If I opened my eyes, what would I see? Would I look down at a landscape far below, torn and scarred by the mining that had given my family its livelihood? Would I see below me a truth that had meaning for my own life?

Was this why I had come – been *brought* – to Furness?

In India, in Tibet, such things were easy to believe. The air there pulsed with mysticism. But here, in down-to-earth England, in the brutally ravaged landscape of Furness?

I felt myself sway and knew that I was falling. And then a hand touched my shoulder and I jumped and opened my eyes to find Mark beside me, concern in his face. I was back – if I had ever left it – in the churchyard at Pennington with the family graves around me and the soft May sunshine stroking my skin.

'Joanna?' he said. 'Are you all right? You looked as if you were about to faint.'

Perhaps that was all it was, I thought as I smiled and nodded. Perhaps I was still just tired from the journey.

But when I looked back at those stark headstones, I was less sure.

I felt certain that there was something here for me to find out, to be told. Something of importance.

I could ask the family. Martha, Celia, Elinor, they had all been here in that year of 1874. But I sensed that none of them knew the whole truth, or would be willing to impart it. And to each one it would look different, distorted.

It might have begun long before then, anyway. Perhaps when Louisa had died; perhaps even earlier than that.

Who can tell where truth begins?

Chapter Three

'Are you feeling better now?' Mark asked solicitously.

He had taken me into Ulverston, to his own house. At first, he had intended to take me home to Pennington Hall, but I had begged him not to. Kind though Martha was, I didn't feel able to cope with her fluttering concern. Neither did I want to be taken to Garth House and thrown upon the mercy of Celia and Lilian. In fact, I said, I was perfectly all right, but Mark had insisted that I needed rest and refreshment. And it was no more than a few minutes by car.

'You just like being able to show off,' I said teasingly as he tucked me into the passenger seat, and he laughed and said perhaps that was it. But he was quite right; within ten minutes or so we were in Ulverston, the car parked in the drive of his house near the square, and he was settling me in a pleasant, sunny room and sending the little maid for tea.

I drank half a cup and nodded my answer to his question. 'Much better, thank you. I don't quite know what came over me. I'm not at all prone to fainting.'

'You're probably still tired,' he said, just as Martha would have done. 'It's a long way from India, every-thing's very different here and you must still be missing your father.'

I glanced at him quickly, surprised by his perception. But I wasn't quite convinced that it was merely tiredness and grief that had caused the strange sensations I had experienced at the graveside. I still felt an inexplicable pull, as if someone was reaching out, as if there were some message being transmitted to me.

But fatigue could, I knew, cause some odd effects. And perhaps if I had not grown up in India, if I had never talked with Hindus and Buddhists, such ideas would not have entered my head. Perhaps I would have thought of ghosts instead. Of restless spirits, rather than rebirth. Of—

My thoughts stopped, took a deep breath and started again, like Mark's car when it stalled on a hill.

Samsara. Could it be true?

'Joanna!' Mark's voice seemed to come from a long way off. 'Joanna, what is it? Are you feeling faint again? Here, put your head down.' He laid his arm across my shoulders, pressing gently so that I bent forwards. For a few seconds the roaring continued in my ears, and my head whirled. My mouth filled with saliva and I swallowed several times; then the nausea began to ebb and I reached half blindly for the cup of tea he was handing me and took several sips.

'That's better. I'm all right now.' Cautiously, I sat up. I gave him a shaky smile. 'I'm sorry to be such a nuisance.'

'You're not a nuisance at all.' He was looking at me with concern. 'I really think I ought to take you home, Joanna. You'd be better off in bed, being properly looked after.'

'No. No, I don't want to be fussed over. I'm sure there's nothing wrong. As you say, I'm probably just tired. A little over-strained, perhaps. If I could just stay here for a while . . .'

'Of course, if it's what you want.' But he still looked worried. 'I don't like to leave you on your own, though.'

'Then stay with me,' I said, and wondered if the words sounded flirtatious. It was just the kind of thing Violet would have said, and if I had said them to Julian he would certainly have taken them in that way. But Mark was not Julian. He hesitated, then sat down beside the couch where I was sitting, my feet up and covered by a light rug.

'All right,' he said, 'so long as you promise to rest properly. Sleep for a while.'

But I knew I could not do that. The moment I closed my eyes, the images would start to appear. Images of Louisa and Rupert. Images of Buddhist temples and the statues inside them. Images that were barely formed, of mysterious beings, gods and half-gods; of spirits born and reborn, of lives lived and lessons learned – or unlearned.

Chanden Singh would have said that I was being shown something important and that I must not ignore it. But so many of his lessons were obscure. How, without help, was I to recognise what I was being shown? How could I learn a lesson I did not understand?

When the pupil is ready, the teacher will appear. How often had I heard that aphorism? But was I ready? And who was to be my teacher?

Teachers could come in strange guises. Perhaps Martha, or Julian or Celia – any one of them; perhaps all of them.

I wondered what Rimpoche Tayang would have said, and knew the answer to that. *Follow your instincts, for they are your inner guide.* I looked at Mark and knew what I wanted to do.

'I don't want to sleep,' I said. 'I want to talk. Tell me, Mark, have you ever heard of *samsara*?'

He shook his head. 'Never. Is it some kind of dance?'

'No. It's the Buddhist word for cyclic rebirth. The idea that each of us is reborn, over and over again, into a different body, until we have learned enough to attain *nirvana* and need never be born again.'

He looked at me thoughtfully. This was one of the things I had first noticed about him and I liked it more

41

each time I encountered it, this capacity he had for listening, for paying attention and not discounting a new idea simply because it sounded bizarre.

'You mean that we might both have lived before? Not once, but many times?'

'Yes. And not necessarily as the same sex each time, or even in the same country. You might have been a Chinese woman or a Red Indian chief, or even an animal – a dog, a cat, a fish. Every living thing is somewhere on the scale, and what we will become in our next life depends upon how we behave in this. In fact, everything we do has a consequence, and whatever happens to us is because of some action we've taken in the past. That's called *karma*.'

'It's not so very different from the Christian ethic,' he said. 'If we follow the Ten Commandments on earth, we'll have a good chance of going to Heaven after we die.'

'Except that Christians have only one chance. Buddhists believe that we have as many as we need. However low we sink – and there are some hells that even Satan would dread – there is always the chance of lifting ourselves up again. And it is our own responsibility; nobody else can do it for us.'

'It's a tough philosophy,' he said.

'And a very gentle one, too. We don't know whose spirit may be reincarnated in any living body, so we must be careful of all creatures. Our dead fathers may be those rabbits we saw in the meadows on the way here. Or we may ourselves be their reincarnations.' I hesitated. The lama had always warned me against speculating too deeply on these lines. 'But it doesn't really matter. Our duty to the spirits we carry within us is to give them the best chance possible of rising a little higher. If we don't, we shall be the ones to suffer, in this life or the next. And it may take several incarnations to recover from some acts. At least, that's what they say.'

'And do you believe it?' he asked. 'Are you a Buddhist, Joanna?'

Again, I hesitated. 'I don't know. Sometimes, I could believe wholeheartedly. I felt I *knew* that it must be right. But some of the concepts were so difficult . . . When I talked to Buddhists about it, they could never quite answer my questions. Or perhaps it would be more true to say that I could never quite understand their answers. It was as if I needed to be told in some other way.' I stopped again. Was that what had been happening to me at the graveside? Was someone, something, trying to answer my questions?

'I've had such a different life from yours,' I said at last. 'I've grown up so differently. Unless I tell you just what it was like, I don't think you will ever be able to understand.'

Mark settled himself more comfortably on his chair.

'Then tell me,' he said.

'Takorwa!'

The cry was set up by a small boy watching goats on the outskirts of the *daba*, and soon it had spread throughout the whole village. As we approached, tired and dishevelled from our long journey, the people began to come out of their flat-roofed huts, staring at us. Their broad, dark faces were unsmiling and we half wished that we had kept some of the stones we had picked up as soon as we came in sight of the buildings. But they had all been thrown at the scrawny dogs which had run snapping at us.

Not all Tibetan villages were as unwelcoming. In some, we had been quickly drawn into the hut of the *deba*, or head lama, and entertained with butter tea. But occasionally, in wild and lonely places, we came to a more suspicious community where we were probably the first white faces ever seen.

It was always necessary to be careful. Foreigners were

not officially welcome in Tibet and there was always the danger of our being denounced to the authorities. Even in remote parts, where villages seemed to be almost inaccessible, allegiance was paid to some overlord. Because of this, we travelled in heavy disguise, wrapped in the same layers of clothing that the Tibetans themselves wore, our faces tanned by the sun.

George Ledger, my father's friend, had urged him to leave me behind. 'It isn't safe to take a young girl with you on these journeys,' he had said. 'It's bad enough when you stick to the known regions, but when you go off into the wilds . . . Leave her at home, Walter. Emily and I will look after her.'

I watched Father anxiously and to my relief he shook his head. 'Joanna and I stay together,' he said firmly. 'Since Josephine died, we only have each other. What use is it to be apart? As for going into the wilds, what kind of an explorer would I be if I stuck to the known regions, as you suggest? What kind of surveys could I undertake, what information could I discover that is not already known?'

George sighed and shrugged. He had argued this point many times before and always lost, but I suppose he felt he ought to try again, especially when my father had begun to talk of going into Tibet.

Tibet. The name itself was enough to set a thrill running through me. We had talked, again and again, of making a journey into that murderous land. The city of Lhasa was one of our main objectives, but what we most longed to see were the sacred lake, Manasarovar, and the holy mountain of Kailas which guarded it.

Kailas was sacred not only to the Tibetan Buddhists but to their Hindu and Brahmin neighbours as well. Each sect saw the great four-armed mountain as the navel of the world, the spiritual centre of the universe, and believed that the four greatest rivers of Asia sprang from its slopes. This belief was considered by many to be mythical and was one of the questions Father and I hoped to answer during our journey.

Manasarovar, the Victorious Lake, and its neighbour Rakas Tal, the Demon Lake, were also full of legends. The waters of Manasarovar, it was believed, would redeem the sins of a hundred lifetimes and deliver a bather to paradise. And, as befits such a holy place, it was said to be reached only after the most difficult pilgrimage in the world. It was certainly long enough – over a thousand miles from the city of Lhasa. And before reaching it we must also visit the great Buddhist monastery of Samye.

We made our preparations carefully, for we knew that travel in Tibet was so precarious that any plans were certain to be changed almost hourly. It was essential to travel discreetly, even secretly. Generally, we felt fairly confident of being welcomed by the ordinary people, but in a country like Tibet one never knew who was one's friend and who one's enemy.

When we finally set off, I could scarcely contain my excitement. At last we were to see those fabled sights! And even the hardship of the road to Lhasa – the heat of the days, even in spring, and the bitter cold of the nights, the bare, rocky tracks that sometimes disappeared altogether across the stony plains, the scarcity of water and the difficulty of finding fuel with which to make a fire – none of it was enough to dampen my enthusiasm.

The sights we saw along those hard mountain ways were enough to make up for a good deal of discomfort. Broad, empty plains have a stark beauty all their own, and the tracks often led into lush valleys, thick with rhododendrons and watered by clear streams. On the mountain passes we would stop, entranced by the clarity of a view that seemed to stretch for a lifetime across gleaming, untouched peaks. Often on these passes we would find a cairn, or *la-dzay*, of stones and our porters would drop three more stones on top of it as a votive

45

offering, calling '*Lha! So-so-so-so!*' as thanks to the mountain spirits for our safe passage. We soon learned to do the same; as my father said, it never did any harm to propitiate the local gods. And on some of the more well-trodden routes the gods must have been well propitiated, for the *la-dzay* was so high that it was necessary to throw the stones to the top.

Lhasa was fascinating, but we did not stay long, for it was hard to maintain our disguise in a city and we felt safer out in the wilds. After a few days which we used to replenish our supplies and employ new porters, we set off again on the thirty-mile walk to Ganden. My father had a letter of introduction from Chanden Singh, back in Darjeeling, to the head lama of Ganden, and he hoped to obtain from him a similar letter to the next monastery on our route. By this means we might be assured of safe travel all the way to Kailas. We were not so enthusiastic about danger that we would refuse any such help.

At Ganden we had been welcomed with evident pleasure. The head lama was a youngish man, eager to hear about the outside world, and he and my father spent many hours in conversation during the two or three days we were there. I also was welcomed and made to feel at home, and I was allowed to wander quite freely around the monastery and the village that lay beneath its walls.

'I don't think I have ever seen such a beautiful place,' I said to Father on the first evening as we stood looking out from the edge of the great amphitheatre on which it was built, across the valley of the Lhasa River towards the mountains beyond. 'The old hermits certainly knew how to pick a good site for a monastery.'

'They did,' he agreed. 'The lama has been telling me something of its history. It's one of the four great centres of Tibetan Buddhism. It was founded in fourteen hundred and nine by a hermit they call Je Rimpoche, one of their most revered holy men. We must go to see his tomb, the Ser Dung, covered in gold, and the Serthri – the Golden Throne.' He looked around the silent walls of the monastery. 'Why do we consider such people a backward nation?' he asked. 'They built and created civilisations equivalent to ours and often greater. Yet because they preferred to maintain a simple way of life and didn't go out to conquer other lands, we look down on them.'

'And think we must convert them,' I added. 'It's no wonder they don't want to admit foreigners when they see what we've done to other countries – repressing their religions, destroying their way of life and taking over their land as if we had some kind of divine right to rule the world.'

'And warring with other countries for possession,' he agreed. 'Well, let us hope that war never comes to this place. To think of such majesty being razed to the ground as so many of our own buildings have been . . .' He shook his head, as if the vision were beyond words, and we continued our walk without speaking. We passed courtyards where sculptors were carving yet more sacred images, carpenters and masons were busy with repairs or new building, and groups of monks were holding forth in noisy debate, for one of the Tibetan monks' favourite occupations was discussing religious matters. These discussions frequently turned into arguments, sometimes so heated that the debaters would come to blows, which always amused me, since they were supposed to be such peaceful people.

'They're human beings just the same,' my father said, sharing my amusement. 'Being religious and a monk doesn't stop you having a temper, or being over-sensitive, or just waking up with a headache one morning. And living all together like this, with no women, no relief, it must be difficult.'

I enjoyed roaming the alleyways between the colleges and gazing at the great temples painted in the Tibetan tradition of white with black and red ornamentation, dramatic yet pleasing to look upon. Inside, the walls were brilliant with painted images of the many deities of mythology – fearsome gods with dragon heads and a multitude of arms, gentle ones with hands raised in graceful blessing, and the broad-faced, smiling Buddha presiding over all.

The chapels were dim, lit only by flickering butter lamps or the light that filtered in through the few skylights. Some of them were so small and dark as to be not much more than caverns – but every one, large or small, was covered with painted images and as often as not draped in the white scarves offered by pilgrims, gleaming like ghosts in the shadows.

We could have stayed longer, for my father was becoming deeply interested in the Tibetan culture, but after a few days we were on our way again and relying for hospitality on villages like the one we had just come to, or camping alone out on the wild plains.

We had left Ganden with two porters and two yaks. One of the porters had abandoned us two days before and gone home, but the other had stayed. Now he went forward and spoke to the villagers, who listened impassively without once taking their eyes off us.

'He's telling them we're undertaking a holy pilgrimage,' my father said. 'He says we have a message from the head lama of Ganden monastery to the *rimpoche* at Samye and must be allowed to pass unharmed.'

'Do we?' I asked. 'Do we have a message?'

'Only the one that tells the lama about us,' Father answered with a twitch of his lips. 'But it's enough to mention the names. The monasteries have a great deal of power.'

The porter finished speaking and the villagers drew together for a muttered consultation. Their dark eyes slid sideways to look at us again and then the one who seemed to be the *deba* stepped forward.

He spoke to us but his dialect was strange and guttural and my father understood only a few words. The porter translated.

'You are welcome to stay in this village tonight. There is a hut you can sleep in. The *deba* wishes you to give his respects to the *rimpoche* lama when you arrive at Samye.'

My father bowed. 'I shall be pleased to do so. Thank him for his kindness and the kindness of his people.'

'He invites you into his house for butter tea,' the porter continued, and my father looked pleased. The villagers parted to make a way for us and we followed the *deba* to the largest of the huts.

We had to duck our heads to enter and, like most Tibetan homes, it was dark inside. A stone platform ran along the wall, covered with yak-hair rugs. We sat for a few moments letting our vision adjust and gradually I became aware of a group of small children, all staring at us unwinkingly. I smiled and put out my hand, and it was instantly grabbed by a dozen smaller hands, my fingers examined and my sleeve stroked, smelled and even licked.

The *deba's* wife was stoking the fire and presently she lifted off the huge kettle which was a permanent feature of every Tibetan home, and poured tea into a large can. She tipped a few lumps of yak butter from a battered metal plate into the can and mixed it thoroughly before pouring it into the cups that we had already taken from our packs.

We had already been entertained many times in this way on our journey through Tibet and knew the social niceties. Accordingly, we accepted the *tsampa*, roasted barley flour that was one of the main staples of Tibet, and mixed it into a porridge with some of the tea, and when a lump of dried goat meat was passed round we hacked off a slice and ate it. To have refused either would have caused offence.

The night we passed in this village was typical of many such nights. We slept in a corner of the hut, our belongings between us and the wall. 'They're human beings,' my father said again, 'and even though we don't carry much, we're rich in comparison with them.' But we never did have anything stolen; whether because we were careful or because the Tibetans were in fact completely honest, I never quite knew.

Our way to Samye led first along a bare ridge, with only a few plants covering the rocky ground. I saw a few alpine cushion plants, their thick-petalled flowers growing in spongy green mounds, like sphagnum moss. At this altitude they were shorter, stumpier and thicker than those I had seen down on the plains. There were a few other plants – a kind of cinquefoil and something that looked as if it might be related to the carnation – and I sketched them quickly whenever we stopped, but apart from the lizards that basked among the rocks there was little other wildlife.

The valleys, however, were by no means empty. From the high paths we could see herds of yak and the tents of *drogpa*, the nomads who spent their lives wandering the countryside, gathering a living wherever they could and trading in the markets. The green carpet of summer was spreading over the lower ground and from here it looked a smiling land, prosperous and almost lush. But we knew that winter in these parts was indescribably bitter, with blizzards raging across bleak, treeless plains.

Our last night was spent at Nyango, and we rose early next morning for the final walk to Samye. Already the Tibetan spring was turning to summer, and the heat of afternoon was becoming uncomfortable. The track here was sandy, and I found my feet sinking in at every step, which made it all the more tiring. But ahead of us, across the valley, we could see the golden roof of the monastery, gleaming like a fallen sun, and by midday we were there, standing in a willow grove to the south of the town and looking up with awe at the first great Buddhist monastery of Tibet.

'It was there that I met the lama,' I said to Mark. 'Chanden Singh, who lived in Darjeeling and was probably my father's greatest friend, told me a good deal about the religions of the East and their way of life – and they're much more devout than you are here in England, for all your churchgoing and morning prayers for the servants – but it was the lama who gave me real insights into Buddhism. He had travelled himself and spoke good English, so he was able to explain things much more clearly. I used to listen while he and Father were talking and when he saw that I was interested, he would take endless trouble to help me understand.'

'And he told you about *samsara*?' Mark asked. 'And the other – what was the word?'

'*Karma*. Yes. I'd heard the terms before, of course, but never properly understood them. He made them seem simple, though the Eastern mind is so profound, I'm sure the meanings are really much deeper. But he didn't seem to think that mattered. He felt it was enough that I should understand in my own way.'

'But you're still not quite sure you believe in it,' he said, smiling.

'I don't know what I believe in,' I said. I thought of my feelings at the graveside, the sensation that some truth was there for me to find. Something that was important to me, to my life. Louisa, Rupert, Nicholas – the names circled about in my brain, as if their owners were calling to me.

I sat up abruptly. The mystical side of the Eastern religions, of any religion, had always given me some discomfort. That was why I found it difficult to accept any of them. The idea of invisible spirits, whether Buddhist or Christian, gazing down at me from some position of all-seeing power was one which I automatically denied.

51

Perhaps, the lama had gently suggested, because I knew I was guilty. Otherwise, why should I care?

But guilty of what? Like anyone else, I was riddled with a hundred small guilts, but were these enough to cause the anger of all-powerful gods, or bring into action forces like *karma*? The transmission of a soul, or spirit, from one body to another, travelling endlessly through life, I could almost accept – it made as much sense as any other theory of life – but that my actions today could affect an incarnation many years in the future seemed too much.

My head was spinning again. Mark and Martha were right, I was exhausted from the journey. Tiredness always affected me like this, making everything seem very sharp and clear when in reality my thoughts were distorted. I knew I was best left alone, to rest and sleep before trying to talk again.

'Will you take me home now?' I asked, and Mark was on his feet at once. He held out his hands and I put mine into them so that he could raise me from the couch.

For a moment we stood there, hand in hand. I saw his eyes darken and felt a strange movement somewhere deep inside me. Then he let my fingers drop and stepped back.

'I'll go and start the car while you get yourself ready,' he said. 'I hope you'll come again, Joanna. I'd like to hear more about Tibet.'

And I would like to tell you, I thought. For there was no one else in the family who would listen with such attention. And I could not cut off that period of my life as if it had never existed.

I had thought, when leaving India, that I was leaving Eastern mysticism behind as well. But I had been wrong. Here in Furness, the East was still reaching out to me. And here, where my father was born, I would find my destiny.

Chapter Four

'So you see,' William said, 'you have in fact quite a substantial share in the mine. Not a majority holding, of course, but enough to bring you a perfectly adequate income.'

'Provided the mines continue to prosper,' I said.

He gave me a sharp look. 'Do you imagine that they won't?'

I shrugged. I'd been in Furness for two or three weeks now and was beginning to find my feet. I'd spent quite a lot of time roaming around the area by myself, walking over the fields and on to the moors, borrowing Violet's bicycle to go further afield. I'd visited the mines and even talked to some of the men and I'd begun to form a picture of what sort of future haematite mining had.

'You've got problems with flooding,' I said. 'It seems an antiquated way of dealing with it, pumping out one pit at a time with old engines. Isn't there a better system?'

William flushed a dark red. He was a heavily built man, rather florid, with a rapidly balding head. He had managed the mines well, Martha said, since Rupert had died, but he struck me as something of a bully and he obviously didn't care for his methods being questioned by a young woman recently arrived from foreign parts.

I objected to his patronising manner and wanted him to know that I had a mind of my own. Who was he to decide what income was 'perfectly adequate' for me?

What did he know of my needs, my plans?

'We're about to instal a centralised pumping station,' he said coldly. 'Most of the pits will be interlinked, with flood doors in case of a sudden inrush, and water will be taken out through Pennington number one pit. The plans have been drawn up, if you'd care to inspect them.'

I smiled at his sarcasm. 'No, that's quite all right. I'm sure you know far more about it than I do. After all, you've been working in haematite all your life.'

'Not quite,' William said. 'I went to Oxford University and travelled a great deal first. I'm not quite the country bumpkin you seem to think me, Joanna.'

Our eyes met and I knew that he liked me no more than I liked him. But we were part of the same family, and he had my income under his control. There was no point in antagonising him.

The library door opened and Julian came in. He was spending a few days at Green House, as he had been doing when I first arrived; he seemed as much at home here as if he were a son of the house. He looked surprised to see me and started to back out of the room again.

'It's all right, Julian,' William said, as if glad of the interruption. 'Joanna and I have finished our talk.' He began to put away the books and ledgers he had been showing me. 'Was there something you wanted to ask me?'

'I was looking for Violet,' Julian said. 'It's such a beautiful afternoon, I thought she might enjoy a walk on the shore. But she doesn't seem to be about.'

'I think she and Dora have gone to Ulverston to do some shopping,' William said. 'They decided to go while you were playing tennis. I don't suppose they'll be long.'

Julian smiled. 'On the contrary, I should imagine they'll be gone the whole afternoon. We both know what those two are like when they get near shops.' He turned to me. 'Perhaps Joanna would like to come instead. It's too good an afternoon to waste indoors.'

I hesitated. I still felt wary of Julian, though I'd met him only once or twice, for soon after my arrival in Furness he had returned to Millom. But there seemed to be no reason not to go for a walk with him and I had nothing else to do now that I had been through the accounts with William and knew just what my financial position was.

We set off down the narrow, sloping lane that led to the shore. To our left I could see the shining spire of Bardsea church on top of its little hill, with the village clustered about it. There was a definite air of the seaside about Bardsea, with its sturdy little cottages, very like the pictures of Cornwall one of the officers' wives in India had once shown me. Ahead of us I could see sails beating up the bay, while grey smoke puffed from the funnels of steamships.

Julian strode at my side, talking easily of what he had been doing since we last met. He led a sybaritic kind of life, it seemed, with visits to friends and relatives punctuated by parties and trips abroad. France was a favourite venue, and he seemed to have plenty of friends with yachts who were only too pleased to have his company for a cruise around the Mediterranean, or simply to ride at anchor in some small, sunny fishing harbour.

'You'd enjoy it, Joanna,' he told me. 'After all your travels, it would seem like luxury.'

He was right about the luxury, I thought, but I wasn't so convinced that I would enjoy such a life. For a holiday, it might be all very well, but as a way of living? It sounded rather empty to me.

We wandered along the beach and I thought of all the people who had walked here before me. All those members of my family – my grandfather Timothy, Nicholas and my aunt Louisa, their son Rupert . . . I wondered what thoughts had passed through their minds as they walked here, what worries had pressed upon them, what joys and fears they had experienced.

Why did I feel so close to them, these people whom I had never met? True, their blood ran in my veins, yet I had known nothing of them other than the scraps of information my father had given me during our journeys into the wilderness, as we sat under the great jewelled canopy of the Asian sky. All were dead before I was born, so why did I feel this kinship, this bond?

Their blood ran in my veins . . . Rimpoche Tayang would have said it was not a matter of blood. That was merely physical. More important was the spirit that was housed in the body. Flesh was ephemeral; the spirit eternal.

Did I believe it?

'. . . arranging a tennis party for tomorrow,' Julian was saying and I brought my attention back to him with a guilty start. 'I hope you'll be able to come, Joanna. You do play tennis, I suppose.'

'Oh yes.' There had been many tennis parties in Darjeeling and the other cities where we had lived, moving from the rough hospitality of the nomads' camps and the mountain villages to the society of the British civil servants and Army officers. In fact, tennis had been one of the more enjoyable aspects of city life. 'I'm supposed to be quite good.'

'Marvellous. You'll partner me, then.' He smiled at me with boyish charm. 'We'll murder the others.'

'Oh, but won't you be partnering Violet?'

'I'll play with Violet for some of the time,' he said carelessly. 'But it wouldn't be polite to neglect you, would it? After all, you're a stranger here and yet part of the family too. You're special.' He turned as he said this and looked down into my eyes. I met his glance and felt an odd quiver inside. His eyes were very dark and his hair gleamed like newly harvested corn in the afternoon sun. His smile revealed white, even teeth.

'I don't think there's anything special about me,' I

protested, but my voice sounded weak in my ears and I felt myself blush.

Julian laughed. 'And that's one of the reasons why! You're different, Joanna – refreshing. Most of the girls I know are so affected – they simper and flutter their eyelashes, and never give a straight answer. It's all coyness and pretence. But you speak your mind. You're not afraid to be yourself.'

'I wouldn't know who else to be,' I said. 'Though since I've been here, I sometimes feel I ought to try. Violet's mother and grandmother, for instance – I'm quite certain they don't approve of me. They think I'm very odd and unconventional. Celia, too. She and Lilian look at me as if I've just arrived from another planet. Which I suppose to them I have. Nobody here seems to know or care a scrap about India, or any other land.'

'That's because they've never lived anywhere else,' he said. 'Look at old Mark, stewing away in that dusty solicitor's office! William's the only one who has been anywhere, and he's done nothing much. You and I are different. We've seen a bit of the world. We know there's more to it than Furness.'

'I'd like to see more,' I said restlessly. 'I'd like to travel to South America. I'd like to see Peru and the Andes, go to Galapagos where Charles Darwin saw the giant tortoises. I'd like to go up the Amazon and draw the plants and flowers there.'

'Well, why shouldn't you?' he said, surprising me. 'What is there to stop you?'

I stopped and stared at him, and then felt a smile begin to spread slowly across my face. It seemed as if it would never stop, and must surely have been almost touching my ears when I broke into an excited laugh. 'Why, nothing!' I exclaimed. 'Julian, you're right. There's nothing to stop me!' I clapped my hands, gazing up at him. 'Do you know, until this afternoon it seemed as if I would never be able to do the things I'd always dreamed of but now I know that I can! I thought I was penniless, except for Pennington Hall, but William tells me I own a large share of the mines. I've more money than I thought!'

'Really?' He spoke lazily enough, but there was a trace of increased interest in his tone. 'How very nice for you. Very much more?'

'Oh yes,' I said, and laughed a little. 'Quite a lot more. I can go anywhere I like!'

I laughed again with excitement. And Julian, catching my mood, began to smile and laugh with me.

'Joanna, that's wonderful!' he exclaimed, gripping my fingers in his. 'Peru, the Andes, the River Amazon! The world is your oyster. And, listen, I've got an even better idea.' His eyes were gleaming, his fingers warm around mine as he looked down into my face and said slowly, as if he meant every word, 'Why don't we both go? I've always wanted to see those places too. Let's go and explore together, Joanna. Let's leave Furness to sleep while we see the world!'

'. . . pleasant enough, I suppose,' said Elinor's voice from the other side of the hedge. 'But no idea of how to behave in company, of course. What would you expect when she's spent all her life in the wilderness.'

I lifted my head, suddenly aware of the voices. They had been approaching for some minutes but, unable to pick out the words, I had scarcely registered them. Now, with dismay, I realised that the speakers were settling themselves on the seat just behind me on the other side of the hedge and there was no way I could slip away unnoticed.

The garden at Green House was a charming one, full of secret corners and hidden nooks. Whoever had first designed it – Louisa, perhaps? – had understood the delights of bowers and sheltered corners, and there were several small suntraps and shady places to please all desires. It was a garden where it was easy to be alone, and I had wandered off from the tennis party as soon as my own game was over, needing a breathing space away from the noisy crowd around the court. I wanted time to think. I had settled myself on a mossy stone seat, surrounded by a hedge of honeysuckle, but now Elinor and her companion were seated only a foot or two away, on the other side of the hedge.

I half rose, but they were talking again and I sat down, knowing that already I had heard too much. If I showed myself now, they would think me guilty of eavesdropping; if I stayed, I would certainly be, but I might as well know what they really thought. No one was likely to tell me to my face.

'I always thought these colonials were inclined to put on airs,' the other woman said. I recognised her voice. She had been introduced to me as the wife of some dignitary in Ulverston and had come this afternoon with her daughter and son. 'You would think that it was some sort of honour to have lived in India. Nasty, dirty place, by all accounts, full of ignorant foreigners. I'm not surprised she has no manners.'

A painful indignation caught me like a blow to the stomach, and I had to press my hand against my mouth to prevent myself from exclaiming aloud. No manners? What had I said, or done, to cause offence? And as for 'ignorant foreigners', I thought of the many Indians I had known who were gentle, cultivated people.

'Well, it's to be hoped she won't stay long,' Elinor said. 'William tells me she's better off than any of us had realised. He's not pleased, of course, to think that she might take the money out of the mine – it's been very useful all these years. But it will be worth it to see the back of her.'

'I didn't realise she owned Pennington Hall,' the other woman said.

'Oh yes. It was left to Walter when the old man died.

It never should have been his, of course. What did he ever do but go off and leave the whole place to others to take care of?' Elinor's voice was sharp, as if she, too, were indignant. 'It caused nothing but trouble, that bequest. Celia always thought it should have gone to Rupert since he was more or less managing the mine when his grandfather died. So by rights William ought to have it now. After all, he and Dora have never had a home of their own, whereas Rupert built that very nice house at Loppergarth where Celia still lives. But no, she says it ought to have been Rupert's and then gone to Thomas.'

'That's Celia's elder son, the one who works with William now? The rather nice-looking young man with auburn hair.'

'That's right. And perfectly well provided for – his wife had her own house when they married, a place near Broughton Beck that she'd inherited from some relative. No, if anyone should have Pennington Hall it should be William and certainly not some interloper who would never have bothered with us at all if she hadn't had something to gain.'

I felt my face burn scarlet. Elinor's words were so unfair, yet I had to admit that she was right in one thing: I wouldn't ever have come to Furness if it hadn't been for my inheritance. Or would I? The house could have been sold without my presence. Surely family feeling had played *some* part in my decision.

'Well, she seems to be welcome enough in some quarters, anyway,' the other woman said a little slyly, and I heard Elinor snort.

'You mean Julian? Yes, she's fairly setting her cap at him, isn't she? And of course he, dear boy, is far too well-mannered to make it clear to her that her attentions aren't wanted. Did you see how she made sure they were paired in the tennis? And she knows he's more or less engaged to Violet. But I daresay she saw at once what a good catch he would be – her share of the Pennington mines put together with his father's business at Millom would make a very fair income.'

'I suppose there's no chance of Julian being influenced? She does have a certain attraction for a man who likes that rather wild type.'

'No chance at all,' Elinor said, her voice sharp again. 'Julian has far too much sense. He knows quite well that his father and William are in absolute agreement over the match between him and Violet. They've worked out a very generous settlement. It will be worth it to join the two businesses together. No, our colonial is due for a disappointment, I fear, and I for one shall be delighted to see her face when she realises it.'

I could bear no more. I got up, intending to reveal myself so that they should know I had heard them. But before I could step round the hedge that divided us, I heard another voice and shrank back again.

'Mrs Craven! I've been looking for Joanna.' Julian sounded cheerful and slightly out of breath. 'It's our turn to play again and she's disappeared.'

'Well, she isn't here.' The two women were evidently getting up and moving away. 'Perhaps you'd better see if any of the other young men are missing, Julian. She does seem very fond of walking on the shore . . .' The voices faded as they moved away and I was left once more alone.

And that's a hint to you, Julian, I thought, trying to collect my thoughts. Elinor is aware of our walk yesterday and she doesn't like it.

I had known from the start that any friendship between Julian and me would be frowned upon, and I had kept clear of him for that very reason – though I'd also felt a certain wariness. But now that was gone and I felt a reckless desire to let him cultivate me; yes, even court me, if that was what he wanted. After all, we were both free to lead our own lives. And until any formal engagement was announced between him and Violet, he was still eligible.

Elinor's words burned in my ears. So I was due for a disappointment, was I? And she would be delighted to see my face when I realised it? Well, we would see about that. I wondered what her face would look like should we ever announce our intention of going to South America together . . .

I had not had a chance to talk to Mark again since the morning when I had visited the cemetery. He had been away on a difficult case, and I had found myself suddenly inundated with invitations to visit people all over the area, from Grange and Arnside to Kirkby and Broughton. Some of them had known my father and I found it fascinating to hear stories of his boyhood, and to tell them of some of his journeys. But I never told anyone else about the spiritual beliefs he and I had encountered, or the strange mysticism of the East.

I had tried to forget the strange feelings I had experienced that morning. But the day after the tennis party, Martha had to go out alone on some errand and I found myself at a loose end. I worked for a time in the garden, but the June sunshine was hot and I gave up after a while and went indoors. I could not settle to anything inside, so after luncheon I put on a broad-brimmed hat and went out for a walk.

I didn't mean to go to the churchyard – I'd avoided it lately. But it was there that my footsteps took me, and as I walked through the gateway and along the path, I decided to stop fighting the urge to see the graves again. Perhaps it was meant that I should go there; perhaps I should take notice of the strange feeling that they held some message for me, some truth that was important for me to know. Perhaps I should listen to what they had to say.

Timothy. Louisa. Rupert.

They lay there beneath the turf, silent, unspeaking. And yet the feeling was there, as strong as ever.

What *was* it they were trying to tell me?

I stared at the grey headstones. And as I gazed, they seemed to dissolve before my eyes. In their place, I saw faces. An old man's, heavy with sorrow and guilt, his eyes dark with suffering. A girl's, first pale and taut with terror, then softening into love. And that of a young man, dark as a gipsy, who seemed to be reaching out for something he could never have, something that was to be denied him for ever.

With a swift movement, I was on my feet. I cried out, and the sound of my voice echoed strangely, frighteningly, around the empty churchyard. I backed away from the graves, staring at them as if hypnotised, half expecting their long-dead occupants to rise and reach out for me.

'No!' I cried. 'No! I won't listen. I won't. I don't want to know. You shan't tell me!' And I turned and ran as if pursued by demons, past the marble angels, past the cherubs and across the grassy mounds to the churchyard gate.

I would never go there again, I told myself as I leaned against the wall, fighting to catch my breath. Whatever was going on in there, whatever they wanted, I would never go near them again.

'And did you ever reach Lake Manasarovar?' Mark asked.

We were walking up the slaters' road to Kirkby Moor. Mark had called at Pennington Hall to invite Martha and me out for a drive in the motorcar. But Martha had just begun some gardening and was clearly reluctant to leave her grubbing, so I agreed to go with him alone.

He had stopped the car at the bottom of the road and suggested we go for a walk. The air was clear and the views of the mountains sharp, their silhouettes rugged against the sky. To the south we could see past Barrow and across the estuary and Morecambe Bay, as far as Lancaster on the green hills opposite, and down the coast to Blackpool. There was just enough breeze to prevent the heat becoming uncomfortable and I lifted my face and looked about me, remembering that first day when I had arrived here and stared about me in dismay. This was the England I had expected to see!

'Oh yes, we reached Manasarovar.' I thought of the day when we had finally come within sight of Tibet's sacred lake, its waters as clear as crystal, reflecting the icy blue of the sky and the snowy peaks of the holy mountain of Kailas that loomed above. The trek had taken us a hundred days, and we were weary, hungry and dishevelled. But the sight of the lake restored our spirits at once, and I felt suddenly convinced of its magical qualities. How else could a mere stretch of water fill me with such elation? Why else should I feel suddenly strong again, as if I were at the beginning of my journey and not the end?

It wasn't the end, of course; before turning to go home my father had to make his survey, which involved many days of measuring and map-making. And we found ourselves thrown suddenly and unexpectedly into the midst of a market town of several hundred people, which was magical enough in itself for normally the whole area was completely deserted. But for two or three months each summer, we learned, Tibetan nomads for miles around would come to this place to set up a bazaar and barter their goods – yak tails, wool and butter for cotton cloth, sugar and grain – with merchants who came over the Himalayas. As well as the merchants and nomads, the market was filled with pilgrims making the holy journey round Mount Kailas, and the whole place had a carnival atmosphere which was the last thing we had anticipated in what we had thought to be a wild and lonely region.

Eventually, however, we turned to make our journey back to Lhasa. Without the anticipation of the lake to spur us on, it seemed a long and wearisome trudge across the trackless wastes and the hardships seemed somehow worse. I remembered the day when we had to ford a river in icy torrent, struggling with animals, packs and luggage in water that swirled about my shoulders and almost swept me off my feet. We were too cold and exhausted to collect dung for the fire we so desperately needed and spent a miserable night shivering on the riverbank. On another occasion we were threatened by bandits and forced to give them our yaks; we had to carry what luggage we had left (fortunately they saw no value in my father's maps and papers) and when we reached the next village we were able to buy only a pair of sheep to act as pack animals. If there was ever a time when I wished my father had been content to remain a civil servant in Darjeeling, it was then. But the feeling didn't last. The next day dawned bright and clear, the next village we came to was welcoming and hospitable and we were able to exchange our sheep for a donkey, which was better than nothing, and when we reached Lhasa we found our friend Rimpoche Tayang from Samye there. We stayed for two weeks, safe under his protection, and the three of us spent hours in discussion.

'He told us more about Buddhism,' I said to Mark as we reached the top of the moor and gazed down at the two estuaries, one on each side of the peninsula. 'Father was very interested by this time. For years he'd been developing a much more spiritual attitude to life, and it was as if this journey was something of a pilgrimage for him too. I think he came to believe quite deeply in the whole concept and would have stopped exploring in order to study religion, but we'd only been back in Darjeeling for three months when he died. It was quite sudden – a heart attack. And totally unexpected.'

'Perhaps he was ready to go on to the next life – a little

higher up the ladder,' Mark suggested, half seriously.

I considered this. 'Perhaps he was. If there was no way to learn more in this life . . . Chanden Singh would say he was probably already incarnated – a Tibetan baby, perhaps, destined for the monastery.' I glanced up to see if Mark was taking this seriously. I wasn't sure that I was myself. 'We don't *know*, do we? Any more than we know about Christmas, or the Resurrection. We just have to believe whatever seems most likely to us.'

'And to those brought up in a certain religion, that's the one easiest to believe,' he agreed. 'Until we begin to question it. But if you've been exposed to more than one school of thought—'

'– it's very difficult to decide which one is true. Or even if any of them are true.' I looked out across the Duddon estuary, towards the hump of Black Combe and the town of Millom at its base. Julian's home was over there. 'There must be hundreds of different religions in the world. How do we know?'

'Without studying every one, we can't,' he said. He sat down on a rock and clasped his knees. 'Still, it seems to me that there's a common thread through most of them. The idea of an afterlife, a heaven and a hell, the morality of a fundamental goodness . . .'

'But most of them seem to attribute it all to some god,' I said. I chose a rock near him and settled myself on it. 'Some creator who must be obeyed and propitiated. Only Buddhism seems to believe it stems from natural law, like evolution. A fundamental moral order, which doesn't come from any being, but just is. And believing that gives us total responsibility for ourselves. It's all up to us. We can't simply plead forgiveness. We can't escape the consequences of any of our own actions because we'll be born again and again until we wipe out all our bad *karma*. And in every life we'll suffer, because life itself is suffering.'

'I can't accept that,' he argued. 'I'm not suffering. I don't think I ever have.'

'But you will,' I said simply. 'Because you've done what every human being does – you've become attached to certain people, certain things. And attachment means suffering.'

'Attachment? You mean love?'

'Yes, if you like.' I hesitated. 'Look, I was attached to my father. We went everywhere, did everything, together. I loved him. And now he's dead.'

'And you're suffering,' he said quietly. I nodded, suddenly unable to speak. He reached out and took my hand, holding it gently between both of his. 'But isn't it worth the suffering, to have known the love?'

I gave him a wavering smile. 'I think it is – most of the time. But when he died . . . Have you ever lost anyone close to you, Mark?'

He shook his head. 'Not knowingly. My father died when I was a baby.'

'It hurts,' I said simply. 'It hurts a lot. Then you wonder if it would have been better if you'd never known the love. If they hadn't mattered quite so much.'

He was silent for a while. Then he said, 'But it does get better. Time does heal, surely.'

'Yes, it does. The wound never quite disappears, there's always a scar, but one can function again.' I brought my thoughts back to the principles we had been discussing. 'Suffering, to Buddhists, is one of the Four Noble Truths, on which the whole philosophy is based. In fact, it's the first of those Truths. The second is a list of the causes of suffering, which none of us can avoid, including birth, ageing, sorrow, pain, grief, despair—'

'Birth?' he interrupted. 'But without birth we wouldn't be alive.'

'Exactly,' I said. 'And if you don't believe that birth is suffering, ask any woman who has borne a child. I've seen plenty of babies being born, Mark, but I haven't seen many women who haven't suffered. The babies don't seem to like it much either,' I added.

Mark laughed. 'True! So what are the other two Noble Truths?'

'The third is the cessation of suffering – the reasoning that there is a cure if only we are courageous enough to take it. The fourth is the cure itself, the path leading to the cessation of suffering.'

His brow was furrowed. 'I don't quite see the difference.'

'I found it difficult too. And it's hard to explain.' I thought for a moment. 'All I can say is that understanding comes only after a great deal of meditation, not emptying the mind but sitting in deep, profound thought, working through the reasoning for ourselves. There are certain prescribed concepts for meditation. Death, for instance, which will make us value life.'

'Value it? But surely you've been saying we don't want it!'

'Oh, we want to be liberated from it, yes.' I smiled at his bewildered face. 'But while we've got it, we value it as something very precious. Because it's our chance, you see. We're not fish or lizards or cats or dogs, which are much lower forms of life. We have an enormous advantage, we're human beings. And we have the chance to hear the Truths and to meditate on them. We have the chance to practise compassion, which is very important. We have the chance to find enlightenment and liberation.'

'And if we don't take the chance?'

'We slip down again. In any case, we're bound to go through a lot of lifetimes, hundreds, perhaps even thousands. Only a few spirits attain enlightenment in one lifetime. I don't think even the Buddha himself claimed that.'

'You know a lot about it,' Mark said thoughtfully. 'Yet you're still not sure you believe in it.'

I stared at the stretching sands, rippled from the outgoing tide. From here I could see that it was possible to walk across them to the far shore. But Mark had told me that there were hidden dangers – deep gullies filled with water, impossible to climb out of, quicksands, a tide that could sweep you out to sea in a matter of minutes. Like life, it seemed an easy journey to begin with, but how many people accomplished it without risk?

'I don't know,' I said slowly. 'In Tibet and India, it was commonplace, everyone understood to some extent and believed what they were told. But the monks still found a lot to argue about. That was what made it so interesting, I think. There is such a depth to it.'

We sat in silence for a while. I wondered where Julian was, and what he was doing. He had suggested another walk but I had declined, knowing that he was expected to spend the day with Violet. Not that I had been influenced by any feeling of good will towards her – neither she nor her mother or grandmother had shown me anything but the barest necessary civility – but if I were to antagonise any of the family by snatching Julian from under her nose, I wanted it to be because I was serious about it, not simply for spite.

I felt certain that I could, if I liked, take Julian for myself. It was a strange feeling, for I had never wanted or even had much opportunity to attract a man before, especially one already clearly spoken for, but there had been a message in his dark blue eyes all through the tennis party, which I could not mistake. And even if I had chosen to disregard it, I could not have ignored the way he sat down by my side at tea, kept my plate filled and laughed at every little remark I made.

Nor could Violet. Or Dora, or Elinor.

Did I want Julian? I wasn't sure. Nor was I sure that he had been serious when he'd suggested we go off together, travelling the world. Surely it had been just a spontaneous joke, a rather daring flirtation. And yet . . . underneath his laughter and teasing I thought I detected a thread of intent. An invitation, at least, to try. Clearly he was not so enamoured of Violet that he wouldn't be prepared to look elsewhere if the attraction were strong enough.

Be careful, a small voice warned me. You're treading on dangerous ground. But I was still seething with anger over the gossip I had overheard between Elinor and her crony. Although I had determined not to take Julian out of spite, I couldn't help feeling that it would be very pleasant indeed to wipe the condescending expression from their faces. And Julian was a free man, after all. If he chose to turn his attention to me . . .

'Look,' Mark said suddenly. 'There are the gipsies.'

I followed his pointing finger. He was looking down at Duddon sands, at the stretch past the grassy point he had told me was Dunnerholme. And I saw, setting off across the broad estuary, a trail of people, carts and wagons. There were horses, too, drawing the wagons, being ridden or simply led, and more than one of them seemed to be mares with foals at foot.

'Gipsies?'

'Yes. They come every year. They camp here and sell pegs and broomsticks and tell fortunes. They go to all the fairs hereabouts. They're going over towards Ravenglass now and up the coast, but they'll be back in a few weeks for Charter.'

I stared at them. I had heard of gipsies but these were the first I had seen. I had a sudden longing to be with them, to travel wild and free beneath the sky.

And with that longing came a rush of sensation so powerful that it seemed to shake the very rock on which I sat. I put my hands down beside me and clung to the heather. I looked up at the sky and saw it reeling above me, the feathery white clouds swirling in the heavens. I heard the roar of blood in my ears and felt the light-headedness that precedes a faint. I let my head fall down towards my knees and felt the warmth of Mark's hand upon my shoulders.

'Joanna?' he said and I could hear the anxious note in his voice. 'Joanna, are you all right? Joanna?'

I could not answer. I knew only that it was no ordinary faint. It was brought on by the sight of the gipsies.

The message was becoming more insistent. It was determined to be heard. And I could not escape it for much longer.

Chapter Five

The summer was hot, but to me, accustomed to the heat of India, it seemed pleasantly temperate, warm enough day and night yet never without the fresh, cool breeze that came in from the sea. Surrounded on three sides by the sea, as Furness was, there was always somewhere one could go to feel the air, and I spent a good deal of time wandering on the moors, finding quiet spots away from the mines or strolling along the shore.

Duddon sands was my favourite place. Time and time again I found my way there – on my own bicycle now, for I had begun cautiously to spend some of the money William had told me was mine – and walked along the broad expanse to Dunnerholme. Often I took my sketch-book and paints with me and set myself up on the grassy promontory to try to capture again the rippling fawn sands and the lacy border of the lapping waves. I sketched the people there too – the cockle-gatherers, the men digging for bait, the pedlars coming across the sands. And I kept a look-out for the gipsies; their wild way of life fascinated me and I longed to talk to them, to learn their ways and compare them with the nomads of the East. But I never saw them.

'Your Aunt Louisa used to do just the same,' Martha told me once, seeing me returning home with my paints. 'In fact, there used to be a picture somewhere, one that she painted at Dunnerholme.' She studied the one I had brought back with me. 'Very similar to this one, except

72

that she had more people crossing the sands. A whole group, with horses and carts . . . I wonder where it is now. I seem to recall Papa giving it to Rupert. Perhaps Celia has it at Garth House.'

If she did, I wasn't likely to ask her. And I doubted if she had kept it anyway. She had completely refurnished the house after Rupert's death, throwing out a good deal of the furniture and furnishings, and when I visited it I felt nothing of his presence within its walls. He'd left it, I thought. There was more of him in the graveyard.

All the same, I'd have liked to see that picture, to hold it in my hands and know that Louisa had painted it, perhaps sitting in the very spot where I liked to set my own easel. And I'd have liked to know who the people were that she had painted. The gipsies, perhaps, members of the same tribe Mark and I had seen. Had she, too, envied them their life and longed to run away from the constrictions of Victorian girlhood and live free and wild under the stars?

There was a bond between us, I felt convinced of it. Between Louisa, her son Rupert, and myself. It had drawn me to this place and I could feel them calling me, crying out to me.

Perhaps if I knew more about them, if I understood what their lives had been, if I could solve the mystery of their deaths . . .

For there was a mystery, of that I was sure. At least about Rupert's death. I thought of the gravestones again, the year in which he and Nicholas had both died. Separately or together? Through accident, illness or some other cause?

And Louisa – her death had been, by all accounts, no more than an ordinary tragedy. Yet no one talked of it. It was all a long time ago, and who was there now to remember or care? Yet it was a part of the family history, after all. And I, who had never known any of them until these past few weeks, I cared. I wanted to know.

As the days went on, I wanted more and more to know. But how was I to find out? Who should I ask?

Martha was the obvious choice. She was the only person alive who could remember those days. She had lived in this house since before my grandfather Timothy's marriage to my grandmother Susannah – Martha's own mother. She had been Louisa's stepsister, no doubt a maid of honour at her wedding; she had known both my father and Rupert from birth.

She must know. But when I asked her, she shook her head and looked so sad that I could not find it in my heart to press her. There must, I thought, be some other way of finding out.

I asked Mark. But he, too, shook his head.

'I've never been able to find out the truth,' he said. 'I've always thought there must be some shameful secret about it all, but what could it be? And how could it involve Louisa as well as Rupert and my father?'

'Your mother must know something,' I said. 'And Celia. Whatever it was, they were both widowed by it.'

'We don't know that there was an "it",' he said. 'It could have been two quite separate occurrences. It probably was. But you won't get either Mother or Cousin Celia to talk about it. I used to try, but I gave up long ago.'

'Other people?' I hazarded, but again he shook his head.

'No one will discuss it. I've tried them all – the old vicar, the doctor, some of the miners. It's as if there's a conspiracy of silence. I suppose there are documents – parish registers. But I would have to ask to see them, and I've never done it. It feels wrong, somehow, as if I were prying into a secret. And I wonder if I really do want to find out, after all. I'm afraid you'll have to resign yourself to never knowing, Joanna. It's probably best forgotten.'

I said no more. I would have liked to take his advice and forget it. What use would it be to know what had happened here twenty-five years ago, still less fifty-five years ago? How could it possibly have any relevance to my own life, to my own problems?

But that was the British, the Western, way of looking at things. In the broader view of the East, fifty years was no more than the blink of an eyelid. Every breath drawn had relevance.

The feeling of the presence of other beings was about me more and more now. At first, it had been confined to the graveyard. Then there had been my experience up on Kirkby Moor. Fearful of repetition, I had for a while avoided both places. But I could not do so for ever, and besides, there was nothing malign in those presences. I had no feeling that anything, or anyone, wished to harm me. My fear was simply the fear of the unknown, the unexplainable.

And I felt drawn to go back, either to the graveyard or to the moor. Only there, I thought, would I be able to give myself up to the voices that called so insistently and ask them to answer my questions.

'And do you really mean to tell me,' Julian asked, 'that there's no young officer languishing in India? No diplomat? Not even a commissioner?'

I laughed. I was sitting in a wicker chair in the orchard and Julian was lying on his stomach on the grass, his head near my feet. His fingers were idly tracing small circles on my instep. The light touch was like thin fire.

'Nobody at all,' I said, wishing I had the strength to move my foot away. But if I did, he would know he was disturbing me. Better to leave it there and pretend I didn't notice. Besides, it was an extremely pleasant sensation. 'I told you, I didn't have much chance to get to know young men. And I wasn't really interested anyway.'

'I know, you were always off exploring with your papa.' He rolled over and looked up at me, shading his eyes against the sun. 'What a strange life you've led, Joanna. Roaming about the desert, dressed as a man. Didn't it ever occur to you that it wasn't a normal way of life for a girl?'

'Oh, I knew that perfectly well. Obviously I could see that other girls of my age were living quite differently.' I thought for a minute. 'But actually, there weren't that many. Most people sent their children home to England to be educated. The climate wasn't considered suitable for children and I suppose most people felt they'd be better off here. And once they'd grown up, they usually stayed here. The boys would go to university or start their own career and the girls generally got married. A few came out to India, but usually only for a holiday. The ones that came to stay were mostly married already, or looking for a husband.'

'And you didn't want to do that?' His fingers were lightly encircling my ankle. I wondered where Martha was. She had been weeding the primula border at the edge of the orchard, but now she seemed to have disappeared.

'Find a husband? No, I didn't.' I thought of my feelings about marriage, or at least the kind of marriage that seemed to be most women's lot. Putting aside one's own life to adapt to a man's. Setting aside one's own interests and desires to serve his. 'I was quite happy with my life with my father,' I said a little sharply. 'I suppose if I'd met someone like him, someone who would take me on the same kind of journeys—'

'You mean you didn't want to stay at home, being the dutiful little wife, tempting her husband with dainty dinners and pretty ways? You didn't want to float about in silk and lace, looking decorative? You didn't want—'

76

'No, I didn't!' I stopped his teasing and changed my position, moving my feet away from his straying fingers. 'Do I look the sort of person who'd want those things?'

Julian laughed again. 'No, I have to admit that you don't.' He didn't at all seem to mind the fact that I'd shifted my feet out of his reach. He sat up, rather closer than I had expected, and reached out for my hands which lay in my lap. He laid one of his over them and I felt its weight, pressing lightly but insistently on my thighs.

'You don't look that sort of girl at all,' he continued, his fingers stroking mine. 'You look far more interesting. You look the sort who would want to be out there with her husband, sharing his adventures. Travelling through forests and over deserts, climbing mountains, cooking under the stars. Now there's real romance, Joanna, don't you agree? How can sophisticated soirees and tennis parties compare with that? I don't wonder you find Furness deadly dull.'

I glanced at him suspiciously, wondering if he were still teasing. But his face was perfectly grave. He was studying my hand – tanned and thin, not at all like the soft, well-cared-for hands of young women like Violet and Lilian. He shifted a little closer, and looked at the fingers one by one, touching them as if they were made of fragile and precious glass.

'I don't find Furness dull,' I said with an effort. 'It's quieter, of course, and different, but it's interesting.'

'Like exploring a new country,' he said with a smile, and I nodded.

'A little. Except that here there's a more personal interest. I was never particularly aware of it before I came here but I feel I belong in a strange way. I feel that this is where I came from.'

'Even though you were born in India?'

'Yes.' I looked around the orchard. 'I think of my father playing here. And my aunts, when they were girls.' I stopped suddenly, certain that for a brief moment I had seen them, girls in pinafores running across the lawn. A baby boy, lying in a bassinet beneath the trees. An old man, his face oddly twisted, stumping across the grass . . . I felt breathless, giddy. Were they pursuing me here now, the voices, the messages?

'What's the matter?' Julian asked curiously and I was back with him in the present. 'You look quite pale.'

I gathered myself together. Somehow I didn't feel I could talk of mystical matters to him as I could to Mark. Julian was so very much of the earth, his concerns those of the flesh – I was once again aware of his fingers on my hand, stroking and caressing, almost but not quite touching my thigh – and I felt instinctively that if I talked to him of *karma* and *samsara* he would stare, laugh uneasily and change the subject. And go away thinking that I was more than odd – perhaps a little mad. 'Touched' by the Indian sun.

'I'm all right,' I said. 'Just a little hot.' My broad-brimmed hat had slipped off my head and lay on the grass. Julian reached over for it and handed it up to me. With my face shaded, I felt a little more comfortable.

'Suppose,' he said casually, still inspecting my fingers, 'someone were to ask you to marry him who did want you to go travelling. Would that make a difference?'

I glanced down at him, but he was examining my thumbnail as if it were the most interesting thing he had ever seen. I decided to treat the conversation as a game.

'Oh, I expect so. It would depend where he wanted to go, of course. I'm not very interested in the North Pole, or Antarctica. But—'

'The Andes,' he said, smiling at me. 'Or Peru. Or even Africa, perhaps. Don't you long to see lions, Joanna? And giraffes? And baboons and chimpanzees and gorillas?'

'Oh yes.' I lay back in my chair, eyes half closed, imagining the jungle. The huge trees, the climbing plants, the exuberance of flowers. Africa, home of Table Mountain, the scarlet *Disa grandiflora* and the *Hypoestes stellata*, pink and white but with peacock eyes so changeable it was impossible to tell if they were blue or green. How would one paint such a chameleon colour? And there were the scarlet heaths, the polygala, the golden sundews, the asphodels, the tritomas, the watsonias . . . I thought of climbing the great crags, far from the petty civilisation of Furness, standing on the plateaus among springs and streams to gaze out across plains where only animals roamed, where tribes of people still lived close to the earth, undisturbed, unconverted, of wandering among the plants and flowers, sketchbook and paints in my pack, a lifetime ahead of me to follow my dreams.

And South America. The coral tree of Brazil with its gigantic orange flowers, the poinsettia with its scarlet bracts, the oddly named flannel flower, its delicate white petals contrasting with its woolly covering. And the drooping white flowers of angel's trumpet, where hummingbirds with whirring wings and long thin tongues fed on nectar.

'Yes,' I said, smiling, 'I might marry a man who would take me to those places. But where would I find such a man in Furness?'

He looked up at me. His eyes were narrowed, perhaps against the sun. But he had shifted position since he had last had to shade his eyes, and the sun was behind him now.

'You might not have to look as far as you think,' he said. 'Don't you remember our talk on the beach the other day? I'm a little tired of the Mediterranean and yachts.'

I stared at him. I was acutely aware of his hands over mine, his stroking fingers, the weight of them in my lap. Our position seemed all at once uncomfortably intimate.

I had the sensation of standing on the brink of

something. One step and I would be over the edge. I had stood on many such brinks in my travels, on top of a cliff that had to be climbed down, on the edge of a river that must be forded. It hadn't always been possible to see what lay ahead, we had simply had to take what risks there might be. But they had always been calculated risks, taken in the light of experience.

In this situation, I had no experience. I did not understand the risks. But the caressing fingers, the intent, dark eyes, the smiling mouth were deeply persuasive. And I could not ignore the fast beating of my heart or the tingling of my blood.

My lips parted slightly. I hardly knew what I was going to say. But to my intense relief, before I could utter a word, Martha reappeared. She was an odd, almost laughable figure in her untidy collection of clothes, her blouse half out of her tattered skirt, her straw hat frayed, but to me at that moment she was more welcome than an angel. She was pushing a wheelbarrow and she saw us and came over.

'I've brought you some tea,' she said, and I saw that in the barrow were a teapot, a jug of milk, three cups and a few plates of cakes and sandwiches. 'Rose looked tired to death, poor girl, she hates this heat, so I told her to stay in the cool and rest.' She lifted the tray from the barrow and set it on a low wicker table. 'Isn't it heaven under these trees? Now, tell me what you've been talking about. You both look very serious.'

Julian smiled. 'We were talking about India. I was telling Joanna how much I'd like to travel, as her father did. But it's difficult for a married man who must leave his wife at home.'

'Oh, much too difficult,' Martha agreed, pouring tea. 'I'm sure most explorers must be single men. Or have very understanding wives.'

'Or wives like Joanna,' Julian said with his eyes on my face, 'who would come along too.'

I said nothing. I had been drawn back from the edge of the cliff on which I had been so precariously balanced and given respite. I might find myself standing there again, but I had time to collect my thoughts, to look around and see if I really wanted to take that dangerous path.

I was also aware of another sensation, one which had so often accompanied that sense of danger. The thrill that had drawn both my father and me into the unknown. The wish to see round the next corner, over the brow of the hill. The desire to *know*, to experience . . .

I looked under my lashes at Julian, now accepting a cup of tea and a slice of fruit cake from my aunt. I felt again that odd little quiver of excitement. And at the same time I caught from the corner of my eye that fleeting, shadowy glimpse of three girls walking in the orchard and a boy who had once been my father.

They were following me everywhere now, it seemed. I was never free of their presence, the uneasy sensation of spirits around me, voices calling, hands tugging insistently at my sleeves. Sometimes, as in the orchard, I was almost convinced that I could see them; sometimes it was as if they were just out of sight, no more than shadows at the edge of my vision, vanishing when I turned sharply as if in a strange game of Grandmother's Footsteps. And always, always there was that feeling that I was receiving a message I did not understand, a message that grew ever more urgent. As if the past were trying to speak to me.

I had still not decided what to do next. From the beginning, it had been clear that I could not sell Pennington Hall, at least not while my Aunt Martha lived. But now that I knew from William that my income from the mines was not insignificant, there was nothing to stop me travelling, provided I was careful, and I was accustomed to that. So why didn't I go? Why did I linger here in Furness, walking on the hills, striding along the sands, roaming about the meadows and fields, the broken hills and the mineworkings?

There was something, some bond, which had drawn me here in the first place. And now that I was here it was like a chain, bound tightly round my heart. The landscape meant more to me than I knew. It was as if there was a familiarity about it, like a place I had visited when I was very young and almost, but not quite, forgotten.

That sense of knowing what was about to happen, what lay round the next corner. That sense of having been here before . . . *Samsara*.

I shook such feelings away impatiently. They belonged in the East, not here. Of one thing I was certain. Drawn though I was by the voices that called to me, I did not want to know what their message was. The closer it came, the more uneasy I grew. My initial curiosity had gone; in its place was fear. Whatever it was, whatever it had to do with my father, with the deaths of Rupert, Nicholas and Louisa, I would prefer it to remain a mystery. Knowledge, I felt instinctively, would bring suffering – the suffering they had known. What use would it be to feel that pain again? Wasn't it enough to have suffered it once? Wasn't it the blessing of *karma* that the spirit could forget?

Not, I thought, if the lesson still remained to be learned. But couldn't I learn it some other way, if indeed there was such a lesson to learn?

Restless, tormented by my thoughts, I roved about the house and garden, looking for places where the ghosts could not follow me. But it seemed that there was nowhere free of them. Finally, in desperation, I left the house and went up the lane that led to the moor. Perhaps it was just the heat. Perhaps I was still exhausted by the events of the past year, my father's death, the months of indecision, the journey to Furness and the strangeness of it all. Perhaps all I needed was fresh air and exercise.

I walked up the steep, narrow track. It was quiet now, for the mines on this side had been worked out and abandoned while new pits on the far side of the moor were dug. Nobody was about. And yet, faint on the afternoon air, I seemed to hear the clatter of machinery. Not the clatter I had become used to, for there was no sound of steam, only the steady clop of horses' hooves and the creak of winding gear. And the voices of men as they came up from the pit in kibbles that clanked against the rock . . .

I caught my breath and looked about me, seeking the cause of the sounds, but there was nothing, only a glimmer in the afternoon air, like a mirage in a hot, dusty desert. A glimmer that seemed to resolve itself into something solid yet transparent, vague shapes that drifted almost invisibly across my consciousness.

I saw a girl coming up the track behind me. She was walking fast, as if trying to escape something, as if afraid of being called back. Her hair flowed behind her, a rich chestnut brown, and her eyes were fixed on the hilltop above me.

I waited till she drew level and looked into her face. With a shock, I saw that I knew it, had always known it. Her eyes looked into mine, a deep blue of the kind that can also, in the right light, look green. But she gave no sign of acknowledgement. It was as if I were not there. She passed by and went on.

But when I turned to watch her go up the hill, I saw that she had not passed me at all. There was no hurrying figure ahead, climbing the track that led on to the moor. Instead, I felt as if her body had blended with mine, as if her thoughts were circling in my own head, as if I knew just where she had come from and where she was going. And, in one brief, agonising second, as if I knew all that was going to happen to her.

I made one last frenzied attempt to escape. And then I was hurrying up the hill, a part of that girl as I had always been, as I had known I must be. And then I was no longer Joanna, but wholly completely Louisa.

LOUISA

Chapter Six

Breathless, panting from the climb, Louisa breasted the hill above Carrkettle and stood with a hand on her side looking down into the valley, past Marton, over Lindal Cote and the Henning Valley towards the little sea-wrapped town of Barrow. Looking at the deep gashes in the flanks of the hills, at the mud that ran red and loose like crimson gore, at the horses straining to drag carts of ore along the narrow lanes.

Near her was the main shaft of her father's first haematite mine, begun soon after he had married her mother in 1814 and so gained control of the farmland. Like most of the pits in the area, it was worked by a horse gin, the big cob plodding endlessly about a capstan and hauling up iron kibbles full of lumpy ore. She watched for a few minutes and saw the bucket, stained with red mud, rise slowly to the surface.

Instead of red and black ore, it contained men who stepped out, their faces raddled, eyes bloodshot and blinking in the hot sunlight. One of them glanced over, saw Louisa and came across, wiping his forehead with the back of his wrist to leave smears like wounds across his brow.

Louisa smiled. Jacob Rigg, pit captain, was one of her friends. She had visited his small, crowded cottage often, playing with his children and talking to his wife Carrie; she felt as much at home amidst the turmoil there as in her father's big, quiet farmhouse.

But there was silence in the farmhouse no longer, and she came to the mines for comfort.

'Hello, Jacob.'

'Now then, Miss Louisa,' he greeted her. 'What brings you here? Isn't it the wedding tomorrow?'

Louisa made a face. 'Yes, and you wouldn't believe the fuss that's going on. The servants are running about like chickens with their heads cut off, fetching this, carrying that, and the kitchens are in uproar. There isn't a moment's peace to be had anywhere.'

'Don't tell me you came here for peace!' he grinned. They were having to raise their voices to be heard over the creaking of the chains that hauled the kibbles to the surface and the rumble of ore being transferred from iron buckets to carts, ready to be taken to the furnaces at Ulverston or the quays at Barrow. With pits scattered about the moor like a pox, each one worked by a horse gin or jackroll, there was indeed not much peace in the scene.

Louisa laughed. Her eyes, blue like her father's, were suddenly alive with merriment, and she lifted both hands and swept back the dark brown hair that had blown about her face as she climbed out of the valley. It hung in thick waves below her shoulders and she wondered yet again if she might be able to persuade her father to let her pin it up tomorrow.

'Certainly not,' he had answered when she asked him. 'You're barely a month past your twelfth birthday. Do you want to be thought forward?'

'But it's so hot! All this hair around me!' She caught it in both hands, lifting its weight away from her neck. 'You don't know what it's like, Papa.'

He stared at her and for a moment she felt uncomfortable and dropped her hands away from her neck. But before the heavy hair had settled about her shoulders again he was shifting some papers on his desk, clearly indicating that the conversation was over.

Louisa had sighed and gone softly from the room, to find Jane in the corridor. She stopped abruptly.

'You were listening!'

Jane gave her a scornful look. 'Listening? Why should I want to do that? I don't suppose you have anything interesting to say. Anyway, why shouldn't I hear it? It wasn't secret, was it?'

'I was talking to my father,' Louisa said. 'It was private.'

'Private! Asking him if you could put up your hair?'

'You *were* listening!'

'I wasn't. I *heard*, that's all. Anyway, he won't let you,' Jane stated. 'You're only twelve – much too young.' With exaggerated nonchalance, she lifted her own thin mousy locks. 'I shall put mine up, of course.'

'Why? You're only two years older than me. Why should you put your hair up when I'm not allowed to?' Louisa knew she shouldn't rise to the bait Jane cast, but her indignation drove her on. That and the feeling that if she always allowed Jane to win, her life was not going to be worth living.

But Jane always did win. She did now, with an unanswerable retort. 'Because my mother says I can, and my mother's going to marry your father and then she'll be mistress of the whole house.' She stared at Louisa, her small eyes gleaming with triumph. 'I'm putting it up for the wedding – Betsy's going to dress it for me. Besides, I shall be fifteen in September, that's nearly three years older than you.' She gave Louisa another malicious glance. 'You're not really much older than Martha – just a child still.'

She turned and whisked away down the corridor, leaving Louisa burning with annoyance. She looked at the closed door of her father's study, half inclined to go back and seek his sympathy. But it would do her no good. She had tried before, when Susannah had first come here with her two daughters, and for the first time she could remember, he had been deaf to her complaints.

'Please, Louisa, stop behaving like a spoilt child. Jane and Martha are delightful girls, quiet, modest, well-behaved. You would do well to follow their example. In fact, I think it's a very fortunate thing for you to have a stepmother like Mrs Reid, willing to take on your upbringing. You've been allowed to run wild for too long.'

'*She's* told you that!' Louisa burst out. 'You've never said such a thing before. She hates me, Papa, can't you see? Oh, why did you have to bring her here?' She reached out and caught his hands, gripping them tightly. 'We were happy enough. You don't need anyone but me.'

He disengaged his fingers. His face was shuttered and cold. 'You don't understand, Louisa. A man needs more than a daughter to go with him through life. One day I shall be alone—'

'I'll stay with you! I'll never leave you.'

'You will,' he said. 'You'll grow up and marry one day.'

'No! I won't.'

'You will,' he repeated. 'And then where will I be? All alone in this great house. Would you have me lonely in my old age, Louie?'

But Louisa shook off his attempt at winning her over. Again she denied that she would ever marry, ever leave him alone. 'At least wait until I do,' she begged him. 'You don't have to marry her *now*.'

'And you think she'll wait ten years, until you're grown?' He smiled and shook his head.

Louisa didn't think anything of the kind, nor did she want it. She wanted her father to herself, for always. At this time, she didn't even visualise herself as growing up; she would have preferred to go on indefinitely in exactly the way they had since the death of her mother Margaret

90

four years ago. The idea of Susannah Reid growing tired of waiting for her father Timothy to marry her was a very appealing one to Louisa.

But it hadn't happened. In spite of her protests, her father had gone ahead with his plans and now the wedding was looming near. And Louisa, to escape the flurry of last-minute preparations, had slipped out in her oldest clothes and come up to Pennington Moor.

Up here, she was free from chatter about gowns and flowers and wedding breakfasts. Instead, the air was filled with the clatter of machinery and the earth was red and slippery with slurry and water pumped from the pits. Men and women worked without pause, loading the carts with ore and leading them away through the maze of lanes that criss-crossed the rolling hills of low Furness. The kibbles rose to the surface and were lowered again in endless rhythm; mostly they brought a load of ore to the surface, sometimes miners coming off shift.

As Louisa watched, a fresh crowd were descending the mine from which Jacob had just emerged. Men, brawny from the hard work of gathering ore below ground; women, dressed like men in rough breeches and caps; children from six or eight years upwards, skin and hair stained red from the dust and mud in which they spent their days.

One of them was Jacob's own son, Billy, barely a month older than Louisa. He had been working in the mine for only a few months; as mine captain, with extra pay, Jacob had been able to keep his children above ground for longer than most. But now, with seven other children and a new baby on the way, he could afford no idlers and Billy had been put into the pit where he spent his days at the base of the shaft loading ore from a wheelbarrow into the kibble. Later, when he had grown a bit, he would become a hurrier, manhandling the heavy barrow along the tunnel from the workings. But whatever he did, his life would now be the same as that of every other mineworker, revolving round the pit. For six days a week, it would be all he had time for, the only world he knew.

'I see the gipsies are back again, over Askam way,' Jacob said, wiping his face again. 'I suppose they'll be round the doors with their bits and pieces, selling this and that and asking to tell our fortunes.' He gave a short laugh. 'Fortunes! That's a fine word for such as us. Well, it's time I were off home, get a bit of dinner inside me. Will you be coming round to see the new babby when it arrives?'

'Yes, of course. And before then too, once this wedding's over.' Louisa sighed. 'I must be a very selfish person, Jacob. I seem to think only of myself and how hard my lot is, and then I come here and see how you work, and watch your Billy going down the mine, and I wonder what I have to complain about. My life is so easy, yet it doesn't seem to be when I'm at home.'

Jacob nodded. ''Tis always the way, Miss Louisa. We can always find things to moan about, and we can always find folk worse off than ourselves. My Billy's had it easy enough, working in the fields scaring crows and picking up stones, but he knows he's too old for that now. He's got to learn a man's trade, aye, and proud to. There's nowt to be ashamed of in working the pits, Miss Louisa.' He gave her a sidelong glance. 'Mebbe your life's none so easy after all. Having nowt to fill your days makes 'em long, good or bad.' He nodded again and turned away, trudging off down the hill to Marton. Louisa stood for a few minutes longer, watching the men come and go, watching the old horse in its ceaseless plodding and the constant rise and fall of the kibbles.

The sun was dipping slowly down the sky now, casting a sheen of beaten copper over the distant sea. Above her, seagulls wheeled on dark grey wings, their cries like laments on the shifting air. They came inland at the end of the afternoon, heading for the tarns where they settled for the night. If they arrived earlier, local people knew a storm was approaching; wives brought in their washing early from the bushes where it was spread, and those who crossed the sands at Duddon kept a careful eye out for higher tides.

It was time for Louisa to go home. By now, she would probably have been missed and although no one would worry about her, they would certainly be annoyed. There would doubtless have been a hundred and one tasks for her to do, from keeping Martha occupied – a job Louisa thought more properly Jane's than her own – to dancing attendance on Susannah Reid. And none of them congenial.

She walked down the hill more slowly than she had climbed up. Jacob's words were busy in her mind. The gipsies had come back. If she walked across the moor to Askam, she would see their tents and smell the wood smoke of their fires.

Louisa had always been intrigued by the gipsies. From the day when she had caught her first brief glimpse of their camps, she had longed to meet them, and her longing had been increased by the tales she had been told of their roving lives. With no settled homes, travelling from place to place with their baskets and pegs, their brooms and lace, they seemed as free as the air that swirled around Furness. Where had they come from? she would ask. And where were they bound? What had they seen and learned as they strode free along roads that led to places that were no more than names to her?

Such tales would surely be even better coming from their own lips, and her head was filled with questions. What must it be like to live as you pleased, travelling from place to place as the fancy took you, eating food you had caught or gathered yourself, and sleeping under the stars? What must it be like to live as one family, men and women and children mingling freely with no master, no mistress, no servant?

She had never had the chance to ask such questions. The cook and kitchenmaids who were her principal informants had impressed upon her that the gipsies were a wild, rough lot who would snatch children from their homes and carry them away, stain their skins with walnut juice to hide their fair looks, and sell them as slaves. It was dangerous to approach them, dangerous to be out alone while they were near. And besides, they spoke a strange, foreign language; they weren't properly English at all.

Louisa came within sight of Pennington Hall. Her father was in the yard, just climbing up into the small carriage, and Susannah Reid and her daughters were there too. Going back to the house he had rented for them nearby, no doubt – and going back for the last time too, for tomorrow Susannah Reid would be Susannah Sherwin and never leave again.

Louisa cast a final longing glance at the hills, the sky and the glimmering sea. The life of a gipsy seemed more attractive than ever.

'So here,' Timothy said, preening his whiskers a little, 'is your new mother, Louisa.'

Louisa looked up at him and did not speak. She had known this moment would come, known it for months, and dreaded it. Even yesterday, she had hoped that something would happen to prevent it – a call from Susannah Reid's own family perhaps, or some disastrous accident which would wipe Susannah and her daughters from the face of the earth.

But that thought made her feel guilty. Better still if God could somehow arrange it so that they had never even existed . . . Her hopes and prayers had gone unanswered. Susannah, Jane and Martha had continued to exist and her father had evidently seen nothing wrong in bringing a new wife to Pennington Hall to replace Louisa's own mother. The wedding had taken place as

94

inevitably as sunrise and now, barely half an hour from the altar, he was expecting Louisa to be pleased about it.

'Well, give your new mother a kiss then,' he said, a shade impatiently, and laid his hand on Louisa's shoulder to draw her closer.

Louisa stiffened, but she could not refuse. Lifting her face, she dutifully received her stepmother's kiss and knew it to be as cold as her own. For a moment they stood close, the woman and the twelve-year-old girl, and then stepped back, each relieved to have the encounter over. If she never kisses me again, Louisa thought, it will be no loss to either of us. And looking into Susannah's eye, she read the same thought.

But her father seemed satisfied enough. With a bellow of laughter, he clapped Louisa on the shoulder as if she were a boy and then turned to the wedding guests.

'See this! Half an hour's work and I've added three beautiful women to the one I already had, though Louisa's as good as a son to me, and has been ever since my dear Margaret died – son and daughter both.' Louisa felt her skin redden as he drew her against his side, and wondered what his second wife thought of such mention of his first. As if Louisa herself weren't reminder enough . . . She stole a glance at Susannah and saw that although her lips were stretched into a smile, her face was set and her eyes cool and remote, as if she had no thoughts at all.

Her daughters' faces did not conceal their thoughts. Jane, looking very grown up with her hair pinned high, was staring down her nose, haughty and disapproving. And dumpy little Martha had on her sullen expression. But perhaps it was nothing to do with Louisa at all; perhaps she was merely sulking still about not being allowed to carry what she considered the best posy.

The rest of the guests were crowding round now to give their congratulations. They were mostly local people – ironmasters like her father or farming folk like the Dawsons, relatives of his first wife. The mine workings ran under Dawson land as well as Sherwin; Timothy had acquired the lease with the farm when he married Margaret and by adding it to the royalties he already rented he had become one of the largest individual mine owners in Furness.

Louisa knew them all. Any strangers present must therefore be related to Susannah and she eyed them warily, wondering what they knew of her. Possibly nothing at all. She was already aware that to Susannah she was no more than an irritating encumbrance, an appendage that came with Timothy rather as a favourite dog or cat might do, to be tolerated rather than loved.

Except that Susannah did not tolerate her. Susannah disliked and disapproved of her, and Louisa felt exactly the same about her new stepmother. The less they saw of one another, she thought, the better.

But it is not easy to avoid a stepmother when you are only twelve years old and the stepmother is determined to mould you into shape – her shape. The only way Louisa knew was to leave the house altogether for periods as long as could be managed, and at this she was adept. It was, after all, what she had spent a good deal of time doing ever since her mother died.

'Poor, motherless scrap,' Cook had commented one afternoon when Louisa was sitting under the kitchen table, having stolen in to beg some cake. 'Losing her ma like that and only eight years old. And not a soul to take proper care of her now that Nurse has gone.'

'I'm sure I do my best,' sniffed Tilly, the upstairs maid, affronted. 'But I've still got all me own work to do and looking after a headstrong little madam like Miss Louie I never did bargain for.'

'Nor's anyone saying any different,' Cook said hastily. No one wanted Tilly to leave. They were all fond of Louisa and ready to give a hand with her whenever necessary, but no one wanted to take full responsibility.

On the other hand, they all rather enjoyed the relaxed regime of a house without a mistress and weren't at all keen to see a permanent governess or, worse still, a new wife installed and wanting changes.

Louisa, munching cake beneath the table, understood this perfectly. She knew that if she played her part, the servants would play theirs. Consequently, she minded her manners, as laid down by Cook and Mrs Huddle, the housekeeper, and when called into her father's presence, she behaved as modestly as any parent could wish. For their part, the servants made sure she was fed and had clean and tidy clothes to wear and said nothing about the long periods she spent out of the house.

With such connivance it was easy for Louisa to roam at will about the fields and on to the moor; she knew every footpath and narrow lane for miles around and she had playmates in every cottage. The rest of the time, she spent as much as possible with her father. He took her about with him a good deal, seeming almost to forget at times that she was only a small girl, treating her as a boy, almost as another man. And Louisa had learned to be a chameleon and be whatever she thought he wanted her to be.

Since Susannah had arrived on the scene, all that had changed. Visits to the mine had abruptly ceased – 'no place for a well-brought-up young lady'. A governess was being installed to teach the three girls. A new regime was being drawn up: long days spent in the schoolroom, hours spent at the pianoforte or with a needle and, on fine afternoons, ladylike walks or perhaps 'calling' with Susannah.

Louisa moved restlessly to the window and stared out. From here, she could see the jagged silhouettes of the mountains that lay a few miles to the north. Sometimes her father had taken her with him when he visited the blast furnace at Nibthwaite on the shores of Coniston Water, and they had spent hours walking on the wild and

97

lonely fells. She thought of the wind blowing through the bracken, the ripples on the surface of the tarns, and longed to be there now, away from this hot, stuffy room and this crowd of people who seemed to have come to do nothing but talk trivialities and fill their mouths with food.

How was she going to tolerate the life that lay ahead? The pianoforte she didn't mind too much; she would quite enjoy it if she could learn to play some real tunes. Painting was interesting too, though she preferred to try to paint a landscape rather than the flowers Susannah said were more appropriate subjects for a young girl. But to sit on fine afternoons embroidering samplers with their mass of different stitches, to go out with her stepmother, dressed in stiff, uncomfortable clothes, to call on the wives of other manufacturers – why, she would be driven mad before Christmas came! Somehow, she would have to find a way of escaping.

The guests were filing into the large dining room where the servants had been busy for days laying out the long tables. There were two stretched down each side and another across the head; they were spread with snowy linen cloths and decorated with displays of roses. Each setting was elaborately laid with silver cutlery, brought by Susannah from her old home in Liverpool, and fine china that was Timothy's wedding present to her. The glasses that sparkled by each place were heirlooms from the Dawson family, and Louisa saw one of the cousins pick his up and eye it covetously. But that's mine! she wanted to cry, and had to bite her lip. It was the only thing in the room that she knew for certain, now that her father had married again, would one day belong to her, and she felt a hot resentment that it should have been used on this day.

She took her seat at the top table with her father, stepmother and new stepsisters. What ugly words they were – *step*mother, *step*sisters. You knew at once that they would never be a real family, never hold for you the abiding affection that a true mother or sister would hold. Old fairy tales came into her head, stories of wicked queens, poisoned apples, children abandoned in forests or shut out of the house to fend for themselves. She tried to imagine herself turned away, friendless, with nowhere to go. I'd go to the gipsies, she thought, and her heart skipped as she dreamed of roaming the countryside by day, sleeping under the stars by night.

The tables groaned with food. As well as the hot dishes that were brought in in seemingly endless succession – the roast meats and fowls, the pies and puddings that had kept the kitchen like a steam bath for the past three days – there were spectacular centrepieces: cold poached salmon, a good three feet long, glazed with aspic, stretched upon silver dishes; arched oxtongues; a huge platter of salmagundi to accompany the meat. And for dessert there were crystallised fruits, jellies and spun sugar.

Grandest of all was the wedding cake, five tiers of gleaming white icing, frosted as ornately as Cook knew how. It towered on the head table, admired by everyone, and although enough food had been consumed to last for several meals, each guest found room for a piece of cake once the ritual of cutting it was over. When the edifice was borne with much ceremony out of the room, each glittering glass was filled once again with champagne, and the toasts began. It seemed that everyone wanted to propose a toast; everyone wanted to make a speech.

Louisa, seated at the end of the table, had been aware for some time of a dull throbbing in her head. The noise, the heat, the stuffiness of the room, the smell of the food, all combined to produce a nausea that she was afraid would cause her to disgrace herself. She looked round for a way of escape and saw that one of the side doors leading to the kitchen was open.

Everyone was listening to an interminable speech

being made by old Dr Robinson who had brought Timothy into the world forty-three years earlier and seemed to feel it necessary to tell the full story. He was seated at the far side of the room from Louisa and all faces were turned towards him. Now was her chance to slip away unnoticed.

Of course, she might have known that Martha would notice. Probably equally bored, she happened to be looking round and Louisa caught her eye just as she vanished through the door. But there was nothing she could do. In the midst of the speech, even Martha could not attract her mother's attention, and by the time the old man sat down and the next speech began, it would be too late. Louisa hardly cared anyway. What did it matter what the consequences were? From now on, she must take her opportunities where and when they arose, or life would be nothing but a cage.

She met no one as she ran quickly up the back stairs and into her room. Thank goodness the house was large enough for them each to have their own room so that she had not been forced to share with the other girls. Swiftly, she unbuttoned the blue silk gown made specially for the wedding – each girl dressed alike and carrying flowers – and let it fall to the floor. With relief, she pulled on her old brown holland shift, almost too small for her now and as comfortable as an old friend, and then ran down the back stairs again and out through the little side door.

Again, she met no one. The servants were still occupied in the kitchen, clearing away uneaten food, washing huge piles of dishes, and preparing their own wedding breakfast, plainer but equally hearty and washed down with beer and porter rather than champagne. None of them saw Louisa as she passed the open kitchen door. And if they had, what matter? They all knew Miss Louisa and her ways.

Outside, Louisa ran across the lawn to the shelter of the shrubbery and then stood still, taking deep breaths of fresh air. She felt as if she had just been let out of prison, and she had a sudden vision of her life henceforth, with escapes like this becoming more and more difficult to manage. This might be the last she could ever accomplish.

The last chance! she thought with a sudden feeling of both despair and excitement. The last chance I'll ever get to go and see the gipsies.

There was no question in her mind as she ran through the shrubbery and out into the narrow lane. No fears of the long walk there and back, no thought of the lateness of the hour before she could be home again. She could not look forward, for the future was too bleak, and she could not look back for the past was too sad. All she had was today, perhaps her last chance of making her dream come true.

And if the gipsies stole her, stained her brown and sold her as a slave? At this moment, Louisa could not fear such a fate or even care that it might happen. All she could think of was travelling the country roads and sleeping under the stars. And being free.

Chapter Seven

Martha was not the only person to see Louisa slip away. Timothy, listening with some embarrassment to the old doctor's reminiscences, caught the movement from the corner of his eye and turned his head very slightly, just enough to see the whisk of her blue skirt as she slid through the door. He sighed, but turned back again. He did not want to draw Susannah's attention to his daughter's defection.

Where was the minx off to now? He felt a quickening of anger. Couldn't she at least stay by his side for these few hours? Was it so much to ask, that she should behave as a daughter while there were guests in the house? Wedding breakfasts didn't happen every day, after all. A little longer sitting at a table wouldn't have hurt her, and she could have gone walking with her new sisters afterwards. They could all have gone together – a new family, getting to know each other, settling down together.

He was roused by a sudden burst of laughter and some applause. Startled, he looked around and realised that everyone was looking at him and smiling. Clearly, he was supposed to react in some way; all he could think of was to smile back rather foolishly, but it seemed to be all right because everyone laughed again and turned their attention back to Dr Robinson.

He felt Susannah's elbow dig sharply into his side.

'You're not listening,' she hissed. 'And where's

Louisa? She was sitting at the end of the table.'

'I suppose she had to slip out,' he murmured. 'It's been a long day, after all.'

'It isn't too long for Martha to behave herself,' his new wife snapped, still in a whisper. 'And she's two years younger than Louisa. That child needs some discipline, Timothy.'

'She needs a mother's hand,' he answered, 'and I'm sure you can give her that, Susannah. Your own daughters—'

'*My* daughters understand the importance of good manners,' she said grimly. 'Louisa's been allowed to run wild for too long. I shall have something to say to her about this.' She turned her attention back to the speaker, who was now in the throes of a story about Timothy's father.

Timothy sighed. Why did everyone feel it necessary to make such long speeches at weddings? He could hardly blame Louisa for wanting to escape. Perhaps it would have been better to let all the children go before this part of the reception began. But probably Susannah was right, they had to learn to mind their manners. And although he'd never noticed anything wrong with Louisa's behaviour, he could see that it was different from that of Jane and Martha.

Louisa, for example, did not sit for hours with a needle, embroidering samplers. He wasn't quite sure of the importance of these scraps of fabric with their texts and alphabets, but Susannah seemed to set great store by them. She also considered it essential for girls – 'young ladies', as she preferred to call them – to have *accomplishments*. These, as far as Timothy could see, involved being able to do a great many things like painting, playing the piano, singing (whether or not the 'young lady' concerned had a voice worth listening to) and being able to 'converse'; but not necessarily doing any of them particularly well.

Louisa could do all of these things, but not in a way that Susannah approved of. She could thump out a tune on the piano, paint a glorious orange sunset, and talk for hours as he took her about the countryside with him. But thumped-out tunes, brilliant sunsets and, most of all, her conversation were not what Susannah deemed proper for a young lady.

'She talks of nothing but the *mines*!' Susannah had exclaimed in horror when she and Louisa had first met. 'Surely you don't discuss such things with her, Timothy?'

'Why not? She's interested, and she already knows a good deal. And the men like to see her about the place.'

'You mean you take her with you? To the *mines*?'

'Yes.' He looked at her appalled face and felt a qualm. 'Shouldn't I?'

'Of course you shouldn't! Why, those mines are no place for a young lady. Dirty, noisy, rough – goodness knows what language she must hear, what ideas she must pick up. I only hope she won't pass them on to Jane and Martha.' Susannah shook her head. 'I shall have to have a serious talk with Louisa.'

'I don't think you'll find her a bad influence,' Timothy began, feeling a need to defend not only Louisa but himself. But Susannah lifted a hand and stopped him.

'Timothy, she can't be an influence for good left to herself the way she has been. Why, it's worse than I thought. You gave me to understand that she'd been properly looked after by one of the more superior maids. Now it seems she's been allowed to bring herself up. I only hope it isn't too late.' She spoke as if Louisa were already too far down the slippery slope for any hope of redemption. Timothy felt a twinge of irritation.

'Susannah, don't you think you're making too much of this? Louisa hasn't been left to herself, she's spent a good deal of her time with me. And the men mind their manners when she's about. I doubt if she's heard any language worse than she might hear in your drawing

104

room. I know she might be lacking in some of the finer points you think so important, but remember, she lost her mother when she was only eight years old. And she's been a good companion to me these past four years.'

Susannah sniffed. 'I don't doubt that. And that's the trouble, Timothy, if you don't mind my saying so.' By her tone, he understood that she wasn't really concerned about whether he minded her saying so or not. 'You've taken her about with you as if she were a boy, as if she were your son. And that's—'

'But she's been as good as a son to me! I never expected to have another child, son or daughter. Until I met you, I never thought to marry again. After Margaret—'

'Margaret is in the past,' Susannah said quickly. 'And Louisa is not a son, Timothy, and shouldn't be treated as one. Why, whatever hopes will she have of marriage if she grows up wild and independent, thinking she can go where men go and do as men do? No one will give her a second glance, and she won't know herself how such things should be managed.' Susannah came closer and laid a hand on his arm. 'I'm sorry to be outspoken, Timothy. I know you've made Louisa your companion and I can see the temptation to do so. But it isn't wise, and it isn't fair on the child herself.'

'You think I've done badly by her?' He stared at Susannah. 'I thought that having lost her mother . . . I tried to replace Margaret for her—'

'And used Louisa to replace Margaret for yourself,' Susannah said shrewdly. 'But you'll have a wife now, Timothy. You can let Louisa go, let her learn to be a young lady, as she should. Now, don't worry about it any more. I'll see to it that she has the education she needs. And if it's a little hard at first, if she needs rather more discipline than she likes, why, I know you'll both thank me for it in the end. And for the beginning, there must be no more visits to the mines.'

No more visits to the mines. No more days out, walking the fells. Timothy, only half aware that the old doctor had sat down and one of Susannah's relatives had taken his place as the focus of attention, knew that he was going to miss Louisa's company badly.

Ever since Margaret had died, leaving that great, yawning gap in his life, he had taken Louisa about with him. As an eight-year-old, herself bereft and bewildered, she had clung to him and it had seemed a cruelty to push her away from his side when she could as easily ride in the trap.

She was the only company he had in those first bleak days and her affection all the love he knew. He had never got along with Margaret's family – her cousins had expected the farm to go to them when old Jeremiah Dawson had died and never ceased to resent Timothy's success with the mine. And after his marriage he had seen less of his old friends, for home life had been enough for him and he had never liked to stray far from his own fireside.

After Margaret died, he had come to depend on his daughter for company. And soon enough, no longer content with waiting for him in the trap, she had climbed down and begun to roam about the pitheads, talking to the men first in a childish way, then beginning to ask questions. Questions that had surprised him with their intelligence, questions that he had sometimes been hard put to answer.

'What's a ginnel? What's black powder? Why are the buckets called kibbles? Why are those boys winding the kibbles up, don't you have enough horses?'

Jacob Rigg, who had been standing by one day as she fired such a salvo, laughed. 'You've got a bright one there, Mr Sherwin. Why, she'll be takkin' ower t'whole mine and givin' us all our orders!'

Timothy laughed too, but he had looked at his daughter and felt a sudden pride. This must be what it was like to have a son. It was from that moment, he thought, that the companionship between himself and Louisa had really begun, and the sorrow he had felt at not having a son had begun to diminish.

But all that had come to an end. Susannah had decreed that Louisa must stay at home and learn to be a young lady. There must be no more jaunting about the countryside. No more neglect of the education a girl should have, the *accomplishments* she must acquire. No more evenings spent by the fireside poring over mine accounts, discussing a new vein, making plans.

Well, perhaps Louisa hadn't been quite so interested in that anyway. But she'd sat with him, listening faithfully, her bright chestnut head nodding, her face glowing in the candlelight. And sometimes he'd found himself looking at her and fancying Margaret was back with him again. He'd almost reached out to her once or twice, thinking to touch her hand – and then drawn quickly back, startled and half afraid.

Perhaps it was just as well that Susannah had come along. She would take over Louisa and do all the things he had, it seemed, so shamefully neglected.

And she would give him a son.

His attention returned to his surroundings. Susannah's uncle was drawing to the end of his speech – thankfully, the last. People were applauding politely. Susannah turned back to Timothy.

'Why are you looking at me like that?'

He smiled at her, thinking of all that she would do for him, all that was to come.

'I was simply thinking how very fortunate I am, my love.' He raised his glass to her and the guests laughed and applauded again.

And for the time being, Louisa was forgotten.

Louisa's steps took her rapidly across Pennington Moor and Ewe Dale to the valley above Askam where the gipsies traditionally had their encampment.

As she came nearer, she slowed down. Her first exhilaration at escaping the wedding party was turning now to a nervous excitement. Suppose it were, after all, true . . . She saw herself snatched up, thrust into one of their tents, bound and gagged so that she could not escape and then sold.

Sold to whom? Who bought slaves these days? What were they used for? She knew that in fashionable circles it was considered quite the thing for ladies to have a little black boy to dance attendance on them. But now there was a movement to make it illegal to own slaves in Britain and her father had told her that a law would probably be passed in the next year or two. Perhaps gipsies would stop stealing children then – if it was really true that they did – because it would be impossible to sell them. Or perhaps they would sell them in America instead.

She wondered what would happen to all the little black boys when people were no longer allowed to own them as slaves. Would they be simply turned out of doors to fend for themselves on the streets with the rest of the beggars? Wouldn't they feel the cold?

The sides of the valley were thickly covered in gorse bushes and low, stunted hawthorns; large trees did not flourish on the windswept uplands of Furness. Louisa crept down through them, not wanting to be seen. The gipsy encampment would, she knew, be in the clearing at the bottom where a shallow stream ran down to the sea, and already she could hear the sound of voices floating up through the branches, calling to one another in words she did not understand, singing, laughing. A shiver of excitement ran across her skin.

At the edge of the bushes she crouched down, cautiously parting the prickly branches with her fingers.

The tents were there, just as Jacob had said. About a dozen of them, like a cluster of long, low canvas cottages

108

filling the little valley. Before them burned a fire, its embers spread wide but burning low so that any flames were invisible in the bright sunlight and what smoke it emitted was faint against the blue sky. Blackened iron cooking pots set round its edges sent out appetising smells and Louisa, who had thought herself sated by the excesses of the wedding breakfast, felt a sudden hunger.

But she dared not venture out from her hiding place. The sight of the gipsies, moving about their camp, gathered round the fire, was a more daunting one than she had expected. Big, dark men and boys with rough clothes and bright scarves whittled pieces of wood with flashing knives while others came striding down the valley with rabbits and fish swinging in their fists. Women, more loosely clad than Louisa had ever seen outside of a bedroom, stood with babies balanced on their hips as they gossiped; some squatted on the grass bending withies to make baskets or tended the pots on the fire.

There were children too, plenty of them, but none of them looked as if they had been stolen. All were as dark as the men and women, but they were naturally dark and not, Louisa was sure, stained. And they seemed happy enough, rolling and fighting on the ground, and healthy too, though their bodies were not plump like the children of Louisa's acquaintance; rather, they were lean and wiry, as if their bodies used every scrap of food they came by and had none left over to build fat.

No doubt there is enough to eat now, she thought, watching as one of the older boys came carrying a fresh-caught rabbit and sat a little way apart from the others to gut and skin it. But what of the winter, when there is little enough to catch alive and the trees are bare? Did they have supplies in those flimsy tents, as Cook had in her storehouses, where meat and vegetables could be kept fresh during the cold, dark months of the year's tail? How could they carry enough to feed themselves? How could they light their fires when the wind blew rain into every corner, when snow spread its icy blanket over valley and hill?

Without thinking, she had been edging forward through the bushes. Suddenly, the boy near her glanced up and Louisa froze. His dark eyes seemed to be staring straight at her. She felt her heart hesitate then kick against her ribs before beginning to thump uncomfortably. Could he see her? Was she still hidden among the thorny branches? And if he did see her, what would he do?

Thoughts of being captured, kept in one of those dingy canvas tents and sold for a slave were suddenly rather frightening.

Very cautiously, Louisa began to wriggle backwards. Her one thought now was to get away. She had seen what she came to see, the gipsy camp and its inhabitants, and now she wanted to go home. Or at least to somewhere safe, among people she knew and trusted. Jacob Rigg's cottage, perhaps – the new baby might have arrived by now. Or one of the other miners' homes where she would be made welcome. There would be little enough chance from now on if Susannah had her way.

The boy was still staring at the bushes but she was sure now that he couldn't really see her. Perhaps he had some kind of sixth sense – didn't they say gipsies had 'second sight' – which told him there was someone there, watching. Louisa felt panic grip her heart again. In another moment, he would come to investigate and she would be discovered. All at once beyond caution, she moved more quickly. Her foot slipped on some loose stones and, twisting round to save herself, she felt her hair catch on some thorns.

Her squeak of pain and dismay was quickly suppressed but when she tried to free herself, she only tangled her hair the more in the spiky twigs of the hawthorn.

Desperately, she twisted this way and that, her fingers catching painfully on the prickles while tears of frustration welled up in her eyes. She felt a sob forming in her throat and tried to swallow it, but it would not be swallowed. In a moment it would force its way out and the boy would hear her. And *still* she couldn't get her hair free from that hateful branch!

'Here, hold still a minute. Let me do it.'

The voice was close beside her and she froze in terror. He had seen her after all. Or at least he'd probably heard her struggles. She shut her eyes and felt his fingers in her hair, moving quickly and carefully to release her. Then the pulling ceased and with relief she knew that she was free. She opened her eyes and looked up at her rescuer.

He was two or three years older than she was, a good bit taller and well built. His skin was tanned, his hair almost black and his eyes so dark a brown that it was impossible to differentiate between iris and pupil. They were laughing at her now and she felt a spurt of indignation.

'Don't do that! Don't laugh at me.'

He glanced quickly down towards the camp and put his finger to his lips. 'Shush! Not so loud, they'll hear you. You don't want to be kidnapped, do you?' There was an odd note in his voice, as if he were still laughing, but Louisa was too shaken to analyse it. Fear knifed through her again at the word 'kidnap'. So it was true, gipsies *did* steal children! Here was one actually admitting it, actually *threatening* her. For the first time in her life, she found herself wishing fervently that she had taken notice of what she had been told. And wishing what she had never dreamed of wishing, that she had stayed at the wedding breakfast, listening to interminable speeches, bored almost to the point of screaming, but *safe*.

'Come up this way.' The boy had her hand now, holding it tightly so that she couldn't escape. Moving quickly, he dragged her up the bank, through the overhanging trees, to the head of the valley. Here there was a grassy ledge, hidden from the camp. He sat on a little hummock and pulled her down beside him.

'So.' The dark eyes surveyed her, still glimmering with laughter. 'Spying on us, were you?'

'I was not!' Indignation momentarily overcame her panic. 'I just wanted to see. I heard you were here, I've always wanted to see a gipsy camp.'

'So you were spying.' He repeated it quite flatly. 'Hiding in bushes, watching, what's that but spying?' He shook the hand he still held, and laughed out loud. 'It's all right, I'm not going to do anything to you. Why shouldn't you spy? I've spied on you often enough.'

'On me?' Louisa stared at him. 'Don't be ridiculous! How could you have done?'

'Easily,' he grinned. 'By hiding in bushes, watching you in your garden and in the fields. Only *I* don't get caught.'

Louisa lifted her chin. Her fear was beginning to ebb. He was only a boy, after all, no older than her cousin Richard Dawson. What could he do to her? He couldn't keep her by force, not all by himself.

'I don't believe you,' she said with dignity. 'You can't have been spying on me. You've only been here a day or two.'

The boy laughed again. 'I've been here twice a year ever since I can remember. And I've seen you often.' He paused, teasing her with his eyes. 'Shall I prove it to you? Shall I tell you how much I know about you?'

'You don't know anything,' she began, but was silenced as he lifted one hand and laid it against her mouth.

His fingers were warm and hard. She tried to speak again but felt her lips move against his rough skin, almost as if in a kiss. Heat flooded into her cheeks and she twisted her head away sharply. The boy grinned.

112

'You're Louisa Sherwin,' he stated. 'You live at Pennington Hall and your father owns the big mines up on the moor. You go there with him a lot. And now your father's getting married again and you're going to have a new stepmother and two stepsisters.' He frowned a little. 'Isn't it today he's getting married? Shouldn't you be there?'

Louisa gazed at him in astonishment. 'How do you know all that? How *can* you know?' The stories of second sight came back into her mind and she shivered. 'I'd better go home. I shouldn't have come.' She tried to draw her hand away from his.

His fingers clasped hers more tightly. 'Go home? Just when we're getting to know each other? Why? You're not trashed, are you?'

'Trashed?' She gave him a bewildered look.

'Scared – frightened.'

'No, of course not!' Her response was immediate and vehement but rang false even in her own ears. 'What is there to be afraid of?'

He smiled slowly. His teeth were white against his tanned skin, his lips curving upwards, his eyes narrowed. She felt something move inside her and her fear returned.

'What is there to be afraid of?' he repeated, as if considering his reply. 'Why, nothing at all. Only the stories you've heard about us – how we capture *chavvies* and sell 'em to America for cotton-picking. Or maybe *eat* them.' He spoke the last words with a little lunge and snapping movement, and Louisa recoiled with an involuntary gasp. 'And how we can do magic, of course, and cast spells and fly on broomsticks – no, there's nothing to be scared of, nothing at all.'

Louisa recovered herself a little. 'You're talking nonsense,' she said with spirit. 'You can't do those things at all. There's no such thing as magic.'

'Why, exactly,' he said. 'I told you, there's nothing to

113

be afraid of. They're only stories you've heard.'

She stared at him for a long moment and he smiled. A real smile this time, not a grin, not teasing her, just smiling. And really, she thought with some surprise, he looked quite a nice sort of boy. Friendly, with merry eyes and a mouth that looked as if it smiled a lot. Not cruel at all. Not wicked. And he hadn't actually hurt her, only held her hand rather tightly.

'Isn't it true, then?' she asked at last. 'Any of it? About – about taking children, that sort of thing?'

He shrugged and shook his head. 'How should I know? Some may do it, perhaps. We don't. We've got enough *chavvies* about the place already!' He laughed again and this time, after a small pause, Louisa laughed with him. A little tremulously, a little uncertainly, but a laugh nevertheless.

It made her feel better. She looked away, then peeped back at him and the look on his face made her laugh again, though she could not have said what she was laughing at now.

'So how do you know those things about me?' she asked.

'I told you. By spying on you.' His grin broadened. 'Don't get conceited, it's not just you. We know all about everyone around here. We need to know whose land we can camp on without being sent on our way. We need to know who'll turn a blind eye to a bit of poaching. We need to know who'll buy the things we sell at doors – pegs and ribbons and such. And who'll tell us all the local news. If a new baby's expected, we can go along there with a few pretty things to bring the baby luck. If someone's ill or dying, well, my old grandmother's got a stock of potions, she can cure just about anything.'

'I thought you just came for the fairs,' Louisa said. 'The Charter Fair in Ulverston and that sort of thing. I've seen the stalls there and the cheapjacks. There's a man who pulls teeth.' She shuddered.

'That's my dad,' the boy said cheerfully. 'He can set bones too. So if you fell down our bank and broke your arm . . .' He gave it a sudden little twist and Louisa cried out. 'Go on, that didn't hurt you.'

'No, but it might have done!' She tried again to pull her hand away. 'Why don't you let me go? I told you, I have to go home. I shouldn't have come out at all.'

'But you did. So you didn't really want to be there at your dad's grand wedding. And I reckon you'd rather stay here.' His eyes danced. 'You came to see us, after all. Why not have a proper look?'

'No!'

He was half on his feet, tugging at her hand. Louisa resisted. It was one thing to be caught by this boy, quite another to be forced into the camp with all those hard-faced men and wild-looking women. 'No, I don't want to.'

He looked down at her as if assessing whether or not to persist, and then dropped back on to the grass. He lifted her hand and began to play with the fingers.

'Let me go,' Louisa said, feeling slightly shaky.

He glanced up at her from under long dark lashes. 'Why? You'll run away if I do.'

'And why shouldn't I?' she demanded haughtily. 'You've no right to keep me here. You say you don't kidnap people.'

He laughed. 'I'm not kidnapping you. I just want to talk, that's all. I want to find out about you.'

'You said you already knew all about me.'

'I know your name and where you live, that's all. I want to know more than that. I want to know all the things you wanted to know about me.'

Louisa caught her breath. 'Who says I want to know anything about you?'

'You did. You came here to find out. You came to spy.'

Again, the word made her feel uncomfortable. 'I wanted to see your camp, that's all.'

'And now you've seen it, so you'd like to go home?'

'Yes.'

'You just wanted to see our camp, watch us for a while, and then go away and forget all about us.' His hand tightened on hers, more cruelly this time so that she had to bite her lip. 'What do you think we are? Animals in a zoo? A sideshow at the fair? Do you think that just because we live in tents it gives you the right to come and stare – something to amuse you when you're feeling bored?'

Louisa was silent. She stared at their entwined hands, feeling the tears prickle behind her eyelids.

'Tired of your miners, are you?' he said. 'Looking for some new amusement to pass your idle life?'

Louisa flung up her head. 'Don't speak to me like that! You've no right—'

'I can do anything I like,' he said coolly. 'I'm free. I don't answer to any man. You won't find me going underground to work twelve hours a day to make men like your father rich.'

'The miners are free. They can work for anyone they like.'

'To do exactly the same thing. Twelve hours a day underground, day in, day out, for as long as he wants them. If they want to spend a day in the open air, can they do it?' He shook his head. 'If they want to up sticks and go and live somewhere else, can they do that? No. They're slaves, Louisa, slaves. Just as much as those children you thought we'd steal and sell to America. And the miserable wage your father pays them don't make a scrap of difference to that.'

'They have homes, they don't live in tents. And they eat—'

'You've been in those cottages,' he said. 'I'd rather have a tent any day. And eat the good food the land

116

provides.' He dropped her hand suddenly. 'Ach, it's no use talking to you. Go back to your fine house and your fancy food and clothes. Forget you ever came here. We live in different worlds, you and me.'

Louisa stared at him. Her fingers, released from the warmth of his clasp, felt cold. She saw the scorn in his face, heard it in his voice, and felt the ice creep through her body, bringing a strange loneliness.

'What have I done?' she asked, and her voice sounded desolate.

The boy laughed, a short, unamused laugh. 'Done? Oh, you've done nothing. You can't help being born the way you are. But you'll do plenty; you'll do the same as all your kin. You'll hide your eyes from what's real. You'll pretend everyone's happy and comfortable although if you only opened your eyes and looked you would see they're not. You'll turn gipsies away because it's what your kind do, without even thinking whether it's right or wrong. Without even wondering where we'll lay our heads that night. And to make yourself feel better you'll tell stories about us, stories about stealing children and robbing houses and killing sheep and pigs. It won't matter if they're true or not, and it won't matter why some of them *are* true.' He met her eyes. 'Yes, we'll pinch rabbits and chickens and whatever we can get because a lot of the time we're *hungry*, Louisa, hungry and cold, and if a farmer turns us off his land we'll take what we can with us and who's to blame? Wouldn't you steal for your children if they were starving? Well, wouldn't you?'

Louisa could bear no more. She jumped to her feet, tears streaming down her face. She stared down at the gipsy boy, still lounging on the grass, and shouted her words at him.

'Why do you tell me all this? Why is it all *my* fault? I can't do anything about it, it's nothing to do with me. I just came to – to see, that's all. I can't help it if people

117

turn you away.' She shook her head, angry with the tears that threatened her vision.

'Oh, what's the use, I'm going home. And don't try to stop me!'

She turned and ran, half expecting him to leap up and follow her. But there were no footsteps behind her and when she reached the top of the hill and looked back, there was no sign of the gipsy boy on the little grassy bank, no sign that there had ever been anyone there. And of the camp itself, hidden in the valley bottom, there was only the faintest wisp of smoke curling into the sky to betray its presence.

More slowly, Louisa made her way home. She felt depressed, lonely, somehow unfinished, as if something important should have taken place but had not quite happened.

She tried to wish that she had never gone to the camp, but somehow it didn't seem true. It had been right for her to go, even if it left her with this strange feeling of incompleteness.

She wondered if she would ever see the boy again, then wondered if she wanted to. What could they have to do with each other, after all? He was right when he said they lived in different worlds; those worlds could surely never meet.

It was only then that she realised that she did not even know his name.

Chapter Eight

His name was Kieran. Kieran Matthews. He was three years older than Louisa and he had never been to school, but he could reckon in his head while Louisa was still writing the figures down on a piece of paper. He was sharp and quick, and when she offered to teach him to read he snatched the opportunity eagerly. Not many travellers could read or write, he said, and he devoured the books she smuggled out to him.

'Do you always call yourselves "travellers"?' she asked idly as they lay on their backs in the heather on Kirkby Moor, staring up at the sky. 'Not gipsies?'

He scowled. 'People call anyone on the road gipsies. We aren't gipsies. We earn our living – we make baskets and pegs and brooms. We make toys that cottage folk can afford to buy, not the grand things you've got in your nursery, but dolls made of wood and rags that *chavvies* like to play with. We sell dogs and horses and whatever we can come by, and we make folk laugh and sing at fairs.' He squinted at her and grinned. 'Mind, we live off the land as well. It's only common sense. If a rabbit runs in front of you he's asking to be tonight's supper.'

'But you never take work. You never do farming or harvesting, or pick up potatoes.'

'We work for ourselves,' Kieran said shortly. 'Why should I call any man master?'

They had known each other for some time by now; it was the end of August, when the heather spread a carpet

119

of brilliant amethyst over the high moor. Louisa was supposed to be at her lessons but with the sun shining so gloriously outside, she had pleaded a headache and been allowed to go and 'rest'. Whether anyone knew that she had slipped out in her oldest clothes instead of going to lie down in her bedroom, she had no idea. Nobody ever checked. Perhaps they didn't want to know.

Since Timothy and Susannah's marriage, six weeks earlier, Louisa had found all her worst fears coming true. The first had been the governess, Miss Barrow, imported to give the three girls lessons each morning and take them for walks or sit with them, sewing or sketching, in the afternoons. She also took luncheon with them and was expected to be available in the evenings for games or conversation. All of which left very little time for Louisa to spend either alone or with her father.

From the first day, she had begun to plan her escape. Only small escapes at first such as lingering overlong on a visit to the privy, which caused Miss Barrow to enquire solicitously as to the state of her health. Or remembering some message she was supposed to give Cook, which involved an urgent visit to the kitchen. At first, these excuses had been accepted but soon enough the governess had realised that Louisa was looking for, or manufacturing, reasons to avoid lessons, and inevitably there had been a tussle of wills over it.

'But Jane and Martha are so slow,' Louisa complained. 'I can do the work in half the time they take. Why should I have to sit and wait when I could be doing something else?'

'You could do extra work,' Miss Barrow said. 'You're an intelligent girl, Louisa, you could learn a great deal.'

'And would that please my stepmother? If I were to know more than Jane?' Louisa gave the governess a challenging stare. 'Perhaps it would be better if I do badly. It's what they all expect of me, after all.'

'Don't be silly. Of course you won't do badly.' There

was a nervous note in Miss Barrow's voice and Louisa realised that the governess was actually afraid. The knowledge gave her a feeling of power, a sensation she had never experienced before.

'Of course!' she said. 'If I do badly in the tests, my stepmother will be angry with you, won't she?' She saw the look in the governess's eyes and felt a guilty kind of triumph. It wasn't fair to torment the poor woman; a governess must have a poor enough life, and Louisa didn't envy her the task of teaching Jane and Martha. But she couldn't afford to be kind, or even fair, not when her own freedom was at stake.

Miss Barrow had argued a little more but soon seen that it was futile. As long as Louisa was allowed her freedom, she was prepared to do the work required of her. If forced to spend the whole day indoors, she simply stopped working and did badly in the tests that Susannah imposed each Friday afternoon. And this, as Louisa had foreseen, brought trouble not only for herself but for Miss Barrow as well. After one such incident, the governess realised that her job depended on all the girls passing their tests and said no more about Louisa's absences.

Jane and Martha were a little more difficult. Louisa's poor results on that first Friday had convinced them that she was dull, stupid and idle, and they set upon her the moment they were back in the schoolroom.

'Even you should have known what Istamboul used to be called,' Jane had sneered. 'Mamma was appalled.'

Louisa shrugged. 'What does it matter? It's five hundred years since it was called Constantinople. What good does it do us to know that now?'

'It's *general knowledge*,' Jane said impatiently. 'If you don't have some general knowledge, geography and history, what are you to talk about at soirees?'

Louisa laughed. 'But we don't go to any soirees.'

'We will, when we're older. And ladies have to have

121

some conversation or the gentlemen will think them dull.' She gave Louisa a contemptuous glance. 'Not that any gentleman is likely to give you a second glance anyway. You don't seem to care how you look. Your hair's in a tangle now, and your pinafore's torn.'

'Well, I doubt if I'll wear a pinafore to soirees,' Louisa retorted. 'Anyway, I thought it wasn't expected that ladies should have anything in their heads apart from the latest fashions. Not that one can make much conversation out of the capital of Turkey changing its name five hundred years ago.' She put on a high, falsetto voice. '"My dear, have you heard? *Turkey* has decided to change the name of Constantinople to Istamboul? Can you *imagine* it? Yes, only *five* hundred years since – I had it *straight* from the latest papers." I should think that will have the gentlemen agog.'

'You don't have to be more stupid about it than you can help,' Jane said coldly. 'But if you don't pass the tests, Miss Barrow will be dismissed, and we don't want that, do we?'

'Why not? You don't seem particularly fond of her.' Privately, Louisa considered the governess a vapid, lukewarm sort of creature. She wished her no harm but she was curious to know why Jane wanted her to stay.

'One doesn't get *fond* of a governess. But as governesses go, the Barrow isn't bad. Martie and I have had some absolute fiends – one who made us sit with backboards every single afternoon, one who used to hit our fingers with a ruler if we made the slightest mistake and one –' she stopped. 'Well, take my word for it, the Barrow is a lot better than most of the ones we've had. And she's terrified of losing her position here, so we can do more or less as we please with her. So do better next time, see?'

'I see perfectly well,' Louisa said coolly. 'I can pass the test easily as long as I don't have to sit indoors all the time. It makes my head ache and that makes me dull. If I can go outside, I'll remember much better. And you can have your precious Miss Barrow all to yourselves.'

'Just so you can do what you like and go off on your own?' Jane said indignantly. 'What do you suppose Mamma will say about that?'

'How will she know? She never comes into the schoolroom.'

'I could tell her.' Jane gave Louisa a sharp glance. 'Then what would happen?'

'You've already told me, Miss Barrow would be dismissed.' Louisa shrugged. 'Well, it's up to you, but I don't see why she has to know. After all, she doesn't know about the sweets Miss Barrow gives you and Martha. Or the novelettes she lends you.' Louisa turned away, as if no longer interested. 'I wonder what she'd say if I did better than you in the tests. Perhaps she'd wonder if it's you who were not studying.'

'*You* do better?' Jane laughed scornfully. 'Why, you probably can't even *spell* Istamboul.'

Louisa smiled. And for the next two days, she spent every spare minute at her books so that when the girls gathered in the schoolroom on Monday morning she was already ahead of the other two in their lessons. As the day wore on, Jane grew more and more disgruntled as Louisa answered every question first. When she made an excuse to go outside on Tuesday afternoon and didn't return until just before tea, no more was said.

That Friday, Jane did just a little better than Louisa in the test and everyone seemed satisfied. Although Susannah naturally found a good deal of fault with her, Louisa knew that she would have been less happy if there had been no fault to find. From then on, Louisa came and went more or less as she pleased; as long as she neither outstripped Jane nor lagged behind Martha, nobody interfered. Apart from a few grumbles which seemed as routine as Susannah's fault-finding, Jane and Martha seemed more than content to have Miss Barrow to themselves.

Louisa could not, of course, spend the time with her father, for Susannah would have known about it at once. But while Kieran was there, it didn't seem to matter.

Every afternoon, having mastered her work for the day, she would make her escape, running like a wild thing released up the green slopes to the moor. It hurt her a little to be forced to avoid the mines; she longed to roam about the torn red earth again, to watch the horse gins and the jackrolls winding their loads to the surface and to talk to the men she had looked upon as friends. But she dared not risk word of her truancy getting back to Susannah. And besides, there was Kieran.

He waited on the rim of the valley, hidden in the shelter of a clump of hawthorns, watching as she climbed the slope. When she came up to him he said nothing, only threw away the grass stem he had been chewing and uncoiled himself. Then he would set off, walking fast, and Louisa would hurry along beside him, not knowing where he might be taking her but content to follow wherever he led.

Today they had come up the slaters' road to Kirkby Moor. High on the top, out of sight of the quarries, they could look out in all directions, from the mountains of the north to the ridges of the Yorkshire Dales and the flat top of Ingleborough. To the west lay the dark whale shape of Black Combe, above Millom, and past that they could sometimes see the cliffs and crags of the Isle of Man. And on either side of the Furness peninsula stretched the wide, sandy estuaries of Morecambe Bay and Duddon.

'It's like being on a magic carpet,' Louisa said, touching the purple heather spread around them. 'I feel as though we're flying.' She lay back again and stared at the small, racing clouds. It made her feel dizzy, as if the

124

whole earth were wheeling about her. 'Can people really fly on broomsticks?'

Kieran laughed. 'What do you think?'

'I don't know. Sometimes, on days like this, or on nights when I look out of my window and see a full moon, I could believe anything.' She rolled over suddenly. 'Teach me to catch a rabbit, Kieran, will you?'

It was like that with Kieran. A mixture of magic and down-to-earth practicality. He seemed to be able to do anything – catch food and cook it, chop down trees to make toys and utensils, keep a fire going even in the rain, mend a torn tent or a broken chair. Things that the boys and men Louisa knew could never have done. Her father might know all about mining but he had probably never lit a fire in his life, even indoors. Even the servants could not do all that Kieran did. And nobody she knew had the ability to bring into her life the colour and the magic that came with him.

He taught her not only to snare rabbits but to clean and skin them. Together, they lit a fire in one of the places they had made their own, a small, hidden valley riddled with burrows, and cooked their dinner. Louisa had already eaten luncheon at home and would not have thought herself hungry; but the smell of the meat and the onions she had stolen from the kitchen mingling with the scent of wood smoke on the summer air had sharpened an appetite she had never known she had. Nothing had ever, she declared, licking her fingers afterwards, tasted as good as that.

'What about all that fine food you eat at home?' he asked, stretching himself out on the grass. 'Fancy stuff, all prettied up and covered in jelly and icing.'

'It doesn't taste half as good as this.' Louisa found another bone with some meat still on it, and picked it up to chew it. 'Do you know what we had today? Fish, boiled to death, and mashed potatoes and peas with all the colour cooked out of them. It tasted like three

125

different kinds of cottonwool. Father won't eat such stuff – we never used to have it – but Susannah says it's good for growing girls. Ugh!'

'I had fish last night,' Kieran said idly. 'Some of us went up Blawith way and guddled a few trout in the beck. We cooked them straightaway – they're no good if you make them wait.'

'Any fish we have,' Louisa said, 'has got tired of waiting.' She looked at Kieran, lying with his eyes closed. 'I wish I could learn to guddle trout.'

'I'll teach you,' he said, still with his eyes closed. 'Next year.'

Louisa stared at him. '*Next* year? Why not now?'

'Because we're going,' Kieran said. 'We're moving on.'

A cloud moved across the sun. Louisa felt its chill, the first touch of autumn. 'Moving on? But – where? When?'

'Tomorrow perhaps, or the next day. When Scarth says.' Scarth was the leader of the travellers, the one they all respected and obeyed. If he said it was time to move on, they would move on. 'Time for the fairs,' Kieran said. 'We've had our summer.' He opened his eyes and looked at her. 'What's the matter? You knew we'd be going.'

'Yes, but . . .' Louisa hesitated. She had known, of course, but she'd pushed the knowledge aside. She hadn't wanted to think of Kieran moving out of her life. 'I didn't think it'd be so soon,' she finished lamely. 'When will you be coming back?'

'For the Ulverston Charter, I expect. And then we'll be going south.' He grinned suddenly. 'Maybe you'd like to be kidnapped after all!'

Louisa flushed and looked away. She was still self-conscious about those early fears. And she was discon-certed by the odd feelings inside her now. A kind of longing, but what for? She envied the gipsies their freedom but did she really want to share the hardships Kieran had described to her? The winters in nothing but a tent, with rain soaking the canvas and wind gusting the sides, with snow piling up all around and perhaps actually burying the tent?

'You'll forget all about me,' she said despondently. 'Next time you come back, you won't even remember me.'

'After knowing you for so long?' His dark eyes teased her. 'Don't forget, I've been watching you for years. Why should I forget you now?'

Why should you want to remember? she thought, but dared not ask. She had never understood why Kieran bothered with her at all. He had plenty of company in the camp – boys of his own age, girls of hers, all of whom knew just as much as he did about guddling trout and snaring rabbits. At first she had thought he simply wanted her to teach him to read and write, but those skills accomplished, he still waited for her in the bushes at the top of the valley, still seemed content to spend his time roaming the hilly fields with her.

When he returned next year, would he still want to be her friend? People changed, and going away made them change faster. She felt a foretaste of the loneliness she knew awaited her.

With Kieran gone and her father separated from her by Susannah, how would she live through the long, bleak days?

Timothy rode his cob down the hill from Pennington Moor and into the yard. Joseph, the stable boy, came out to meet him and took the bridle as Timothy dismounted.

'The mistress was here a while since. Looking for Miss Louisa.'

'Looking for Louisa?' Timothy stared at him. 'But surely she's been at her lessons.'

127

Joseph shrugged. He knew, as did most of the servants, that Louisa was rarely at her lessons in the afternoons but he judged it wiser to say nothing. He had only told Timothy about Susannah because the master was sure to run into her and it was best he should know what temper she was in.

Timothy went into the house through the side door, stopping to take off his boots and jacket. He padded through to the parlour and found Susannah there, just about to drink tea. She looked up at him, frowning.

'Timothy. I wish you wouldn't come in here in working clothes. You're all over red mud. And you've no shoes on!'

He looked down at himself. It was true that his trousers were streaked with red slurry, but it was dry and unlikely to come off on the furniture, provided he didn't sit down. 'I took my boots off so as not to bring in mud,' he said defensively.

'And then came in here! Couldn't you have washed and changed first?'

'I shall, directly. I just wanted a cup of tea and to ask you—'

'I might have had *visitors*. What would they have thought, to see you march in here like a common workman?'

Timothy felt a smouldering of anger. 'Any visitors you might have, Susannah, would be likely to be friends of mine also. And they all know how I earn my living. Why, some of them do exactly the same. They know mines are dirty places.'

'They probably also know that parlours are not,' Susannah said acidly. 'And *my* visitors are likely to be women, not men accustomed to being out on the pit-heads. I'm afraid you've grown very lax over these past years, Timothy. No wonder Louisa—'

'Ah yes, Louisa,' he interrupted, reminded of his purpose in coming to the parlour, a place he normally avoided at this hour for the very reasons Susannah had just given. 'You've been looking for her, I hear. Why isn't she in the schoolroom?'

He hadn't meant to say it like that. He'd meant to put it as a simple question, the sort of question any concerned parent might ask on hearing that his daughter was apparently missing. But the slightly acrimonious tenor of the conversation caused it to sound aggressive and accusing.

Susannah bristled immediately. 'You may well ask! That young woman is fast becoming a hoyden. I'm not at all sure she's not beyond control, Timothy, and I blame you for it. It's no wonder she's turning out the way she is.'

'And what way is that?' Timothy was beginning to feel irritated. 'Louisa has always seemed perfectly all right to me. A pleasant, intelligent companion—'

'She does not behave as a young lady should,' Susannah said tightly.

Timothy thought of his daughter, so eager and alive as she'd accompanied him to the mines or walked with him on Coniston Fells, her eyes bright and brown as autumn bracken, her hair glinting like new horse chestnuts in the sun. His irritation grew. Couldn't Susannah see anything good in the child?

'That depends on what one requires of a young lady,' he said sharply. 'For myself, I dislike drawing-room airs and graces. I'd far rather have a companion who can converse on interesting, everyday matters than one whose head is filled with fashion plates and empty gossip.'

'I see. So presumably you'd prefer me to put on my oldest clothes and come with you to the mines? You'd like to see me tramping about in the mud, hobnobbing with a lot of rough working men, rather than making a pleasant home for you.' She looked around the drawing room, recently redecorated to her own taste. The walls were covered in cream paper striped with gold and red and the floor was covered with a carpet of dark crimson. Two chaise-longues and several elegant chairs, also striped in cream and gold, were artistically placed about the room, with small polished tables nearby. 'I suppose you do find this pleasant?'

Timothy heard the sarcasm in her voice but decided not to respond to it. More and more, in the past few weeks, he had found Susannah's remarks grating on him and he was disturbed by the feelings they engendered. Surely one ought not to feel like this about a wife so recently acquired? He could not remember ever having been irritated or annoyed by Margaret. And she had made a pleasant home without making him feel he had no right to be in it.

'I never said anything about what I would prefer you to do, my love.' He sat down and took her hand. 'You must do exactly as you wish. I only—'

'Timothy!' Susannah snatched away her hand. 'You're sitting on my best chairs. They'll be covered in that horrid red mud!'

He leapt up as if he had been stung and looked down at her in despair. It was impossible to talk to Susannah in this room. It was her room now, not his; her territory, where she was mistress and he not much more than a serf. He tried again.

'Susannah, please tell me about Louisa. Did you find her? And why was she not at her lessons?'

Susannah sniffed. She lifted a teacup with fingers daintily crooked, and sipped. Timothy wondered whether there was a chance she might offer him some tea, but decided he'd prefer a real drink of good ale from the cellar instead.

'Louisa,' said Susannah disapprovingly, 'does not appear to have been at her lessons very much at all this week. In fact, when I questioned Miss Barrow, it seemed that she makes a habit – a *habit*, mark you – of disappearing soon after luncheon and not returning until teatime, if then. Goodness only knows where she goes to. Perhaps you have some idea?'

'I? Of course I have no idea! Why should you think that I have?'

'You were in the habit of taking her about with you – to the mines, to the furnaces, to all kinds of unsuitable places.'

'But not since our marriage. I've missed her company a good deal, I won't deny that, but I've never flouted your wishes in this, Susannah, nor in anything else,' he added, thinking of the many alterations he had been obliged to make in his life. Changing his clothes for dinner, attending church twice on Sundays instead of the token appearance at morning service, often coming home early from the mine for some tea party of Susannah's. Not that she had actually compelled him to do any of these things, but she had managed to make it very clear that she expected them. And he, anxious always to recapture the happiness he had known with Margaret, had been only too willing to comply. But somehow the happiness had eluded him and he could not think what more he could do to attain it, nor in what way he was acting wrongly.

'But where is she now?' he asked, striving to get the conversation back to where he had intended it to begin. 'Did you find her?'

'I can't say that I actually *found* her, no. She simply reappeared. Came out of her room looking as if she'd been there all afternoon – which she certainly had not, for I looked there three or four times.' Susannah made no attempt to conceal the annoyance in her voice. 'She stared at me as impudently as you please, trying to pretend she'd never been out of the house.'

'Perhaps she hadn't.'

'And I suppose you'd have me believe there are secret passages here. A priests' hole, perhaps, where she conceals herself?' Susannah gave him a contemptuous glance. 'Timothy, the child had quite clearly been out for hours, and up to heaven knows what mischief. There was grass in her hair. Now tell me how she could have come by that, lying on her bed with a headache!'

Timothy sighed. 'I've no idea, my love. But she wasn't with me, nor anywhere I've been. And I'd be ready to swear she hasn't been near the mines for weeks. The men keep asking after her – they miss seeing her.'

'And that's exactly what I mean!' Susannah cried. 'Timothy, don't you see how disgraceful that is? Men, *working* men, having the temerity to ask after your daughter. Why, that's putting her on a level with them. You might as well send her down the pits to work and have done with it.' She lifted the silver teapot and poured herself a second cup. 'Something will have to be done. I knew the situation here had been unsatisfactory before we married, but if I'd been aware of the extent of the problem, well . . .'

'Well what?' Timothy was beginning to feel really angry. Why should he be kept standing here in his own parlour like some outdoor servant while his wife drank tea – *his* tea – and harangued him? And about his own daughter, too. No doubt the minx had been naughty – she shouldn't have played truant. But on a day like this, with the sun shining outside, who could blame her? 'What are you saying, Susannah?'

She looked up, perhaps warned by something in his voice, and stopped whatever she had been about to say. 'Oh, nothing. But something really must be done about Louisa. Her behaviour is quite unacceptable and it's beginning to affect Jane and Martha.'

'How?' he asked. 'Have they been slipping out and coming back with grass in their hair?'

'Indeed not! They both know better than that, I'm glad to say. But their lessons must be suffering with all this coming and going, it's bound to be unsettling. I must say I'm very disappointed in Miss Barrow. I thought her a very good class of person, well qualified to have charge of my daughters. But this laxity—'

'Well, I daresay that now it's been discovered she won't allow it again.' Timothy decided to wait no longer to be invited to drink tea in his own parlour. He poured himself a cup. But he did not sit down to drink it. 'She'll be much more careful from now on.'

'Oh no,' Susannah said. 'She'll not have the chance. I've told her to go.'

'Go? You mean you've dismissed her?'

'Certainly. I know you think Louisa is capable of bringing herself up, Timothy, but I mean to be more careful with my own two daughters. I don't propose to have them running like gipsies around the countryside and having common labourers asking after their welfare. Whoever is in charge of them must be trusted to see that they grow up as young ladies and not as madcaps.' She looked pointedly at his muddy clothes. 'And if you want your daughter to be a young lady too, you might think about setting her a good example yourself.'

Timothy's temper erupted. He set down his cup. 'And not come into your elegant parlour in my dirty clothes, reminding you that I have to work for a living?' he said, his voice low and angry. 'It must be painful to you, Susannah, to think that the tea you don't offer to me and the chairs you won't allow me to sit on and the wages for the governess you want for your daughters all have to come from haematite, from these dirty clothes and the muddy boots that I did at least remember to take off before I dared come in. It must be a matter of shame for you to have to admit that I go to the mines every day instead of pursuing the idle life of a *gentleman*. Well, I'm sorry for that, but I can't hide it, however much you may like to pretend.'

He looked at the little table, so daintily laid. The tea

had hardly satisfied his thirst at all. He still wanted a mug of good strong ale.

Susannah stared at him, her face white but for two red spots of anger on her cheekbones. 'Timothy! How dare you speak to me like that, and in my own—'

'Your own parlour?' he cut in. 'But I've just pointed out to you, Susannah, that it's *my* parlour. And I wonder how *you* dare to speak to *me* in that way. Telling me my daughter's a hoyden, hinting at even worse when all she's done is take herself out for a walk in the fresh air and sunshine, which would have been a much better task for all three girls than whatever that colourless mouse of a governess has been doing with them. Why, if you want my opinion—'

'I don't,' Susannah said frigidly.

'— Louisa is the only one who's shown any sense at all. Whatever she's been doing this afternoon, it's done her more good than a week's worth of lessons, I'll wager.' He turned and strode to the door, regretting now that he was not wearing a pair of good thick boots that would have made a clatter on the floorboards. Still, at least he could slam the door, hard.

He did, and felt the better for it. But he knew that the quarrel was by no means over.

'And it's all your fault!' Jane concluded. 'If you'd been in the schoolroom this afternoon when Mamma came—'

'She never usually comes to the schoolroom,' Louisa countered. 'How was I to know? And you didn't have to tell her I often go out in the afternoons.'

'I don't tell lies to my mother,' Jane said haughtily. 'Anyway, why should you do just as you like? Martha and I have to stay in and do lessons, why shouldn't you?'

'Well, you'll have to now,' Martha put in. 'We'll be having a new governess as soon as Mamma can find one, and until then she'll teach us herself,'

The despondent mood in which Louisa had returned

to the house, knowing that it would be months before she saw Kieran again, deepened. It was bad enough to have lost her best – her only – friend. But to be condemned to spending every day caged indoors, doing tedious lessons with a hatchet-faced governess determined not to let her out of sight – and, worse still, with her stepmother before the new governess was engaged – seemed to her to be at least as bad as the fate worse than death that was continuously and mysteriously mentioned in the novelettes that Jane read so voraciously.

'Well then, let's hope she finds a governess soon,' Louisa said bluntly. 'It's bad enough having to sit in the schoolroom with you two all day without having your mother glowering at me and biting my head off every time I speak.'

The girls gasped and Jane exclaimed, 'I'll tell Mamma you said that! I'll tell her!'

'Go on, tell her,' Louisa said recklessly. 'I don't care. I don't care what you do, or what she does either. She can't do any worse than she has already.'

Jane made a lunge at her, catching a handful of hair and jerking it roughly. Louisa gave a cry of pain and fought back. Her hands clenched into hard fists, she pummelled her stepsister, hitting indiscriminately wherever she could reach. In another moment they were on the floor, rolling over and over as they grappled with each other. Jane gave another sharp tug and an agonising tearing sensation told Louisa that some of her hair had been pulled right out, it seemed in great clumps. Tears of pain and rage stung her eyes and she twisted round, using her teeth as well as her hands, uncurling them now to scratch with her nails wherever she could find bare skin.

She could hear Martha screaming, but she took no notice. All the disappointment and misery and loneliness of the past months, together with the despair that had come with the loss of Kieran, welled up inside her and

135

turned to a raging fury at the unfairness of life. Why did it have to be *her* mother who had died? Why did her father have to marry again? And if he must, why choose Susannah? And why, why did the only friend she possessed have to leave her just when she needed a friend more than anything else in the world?

I wish I had gone with them, she thought, rolling on top of Jane and getting her own fingers tangled in the other girl's hair. I wish I'd been kidnapped.

She gave a savage jerk that brought away a handful of mousy hair. Jane let out a howl of agony, and at that moment the door opened and Louisa heard Susannah's horrified voice.

'*Louisa*! *Jane*! What in heaven's name is going on here? What are you doing? Stop it! Stop that dreadful fighting and get up at once. *At once*!'

The two girls stopped. Louisa gave Jane a brief glance, saw with unholy glee that her face was scratched and tear-stained, and rolled away. She scrambled to her feet, brushed her dress and gave her stepmother a defiant glance.

'Jane started it, but I don't expect you to believe me.'

Susannah ignored her. She stepped across to her daughter and took her in her arms. 'My poor little girl! What has she done to you? Look at your face, all over blood.' She turned on Louisa, her mouth working with rage. 'You little shrew! You spitfire! Why, you're nothing but a savage, you're not fit to be in decent company. I shall see your father about this. A good beating is what you need and if he won't give it to you I'll do it myself. Go to your room at once.'

Louisa stood her ground. 'And leave Jane to tell lies about me? I told you, she started it.'

Susannah let go of Jane and grabbed Louisa roughly by the shoulders. Her face was scarlet with rage and her fingers dug cruelly through the thin fabric of Louisa's dress. She shook Louisa violently. Louisa's head went back and jerked forward again, sending pain shooting through her neck, and she felt her teeth clash together, catching the edge of her tongue. She tasted blood and felt tears once again in her eyes.

'I said *go to your room*!' Susannah hissed. 'And stay there until you're sent for. Better still, I'll lock you in. I'll put a stop to your antics for once and for all, you little hussy. And I'll see that your father hears about this. I'll make sure he gives you the beating you deserve.'

'He won't do it! He won't touch me,' Louisa retorted as she was hustled along the passage to her room. 'He's never beaten me, never.'

'More's the pity. You might have grown up a little more civilised if he had. But he'll do it now, or I'll know the reason why.' Susannah wrenched open the door of Louisa's room and thrust her inside. 'Now, stay there. And perhaps by the time I let you out again you'll be ready to apologise.'

'No!' Louisa yelled through the closing door. 'No, I won't! I'll never apologise because I'm not sorry. You hear that?' As she heard Susannah's footsteps tap rapidly away, she let her voice rise to a scream. 'I'm *not sorry*! I'm *glad*! Glad, glad, *glad*!'

But there was no answer. After standing trembling in the middle of the room, Louisa turned and flung herself on her bed.

Chapter Nine

Life was never the same again for Louisa after that day.

For the rest of her life she would remember it as the day she grew up, painfully and unhappily. And remember it also as the day she first began to build the barrier between herself and her father, a barrier that was only once to be broken down, and that in a way more shocking than she could have imagined. Perhaps the barrier had its roots in the past, when her mother had died, but it became inevitable when Timothy married Susannah.

'It makes me very sad to hear such things of you, Louisa,' Timothy said when he came to her room at last. She had lain on her bed long after the storm of weeping had subsided, able to hear only faint sounds from below. She heard the clattering of hooves in the stable yard outside and the voices of the outdoor servants. But within the house there was nothing save the occasional sound of a door closing and, once, raised voices.

Perhaps her father and Susannah were quarrelling over her! With some hope, Louisa raised her head but the voices faded and she heard no more. Later, there was a tap on the door and she heard Tilly's voice asking if she wanted any supper. 'It's only bread and milk,' the maid's voice whispered, 'but Cook sent me up with it. Open the door, Miss Louie, there's a lamb.'

But Louisa had refused to move. The door was locked from the outside, but nothing would have made her

138

admit that to the maid. Instead, she pretended not to hear. If her stepmother intended to starve her, let her do so. Then perhaps her father would be sorry for what he had done. Perhaps he might even turn Susannah out of the house, and her two hateful daughters with her!

Tilly had gone away, probably afraid of being caught bringing Louisa food against orders, and the house had fallen silent again. Louisa wondered what was happening. Were Jane and Martha telling her father their version of the story? She had no hope that they would tell him the truth. She felt a shaft of indignation and pain that he should hear the story from their lips before hers.

Footsteps sounded on the stairs and she started up, certain that he must be coming for her. But they died away again and she sank back on to the bed, despair settling over her like a dark grey cloud. Perhaps he wasn't going to come at all. Perhaps nobody would ever come again. Perhaps Susannah meant to leave her here for ever, to die of starvation and thirst, to be forgotten by all . . .

She was jerked awake by the sound of the door opening softly. Half sitting up, she realised that it was almost dark. She brushed hair out of her eyes and saw her father coming in, carrying a candle.

'All in the dark?' He set the light down on her washstand and turned to survey her. 'What is all this I hear about you and Jane fighting?'

'She started it,' Louisa said sulkily. 'She pulled my hair.'

'And you pulled hers, I gather.' He looked serious. 'It makes me very sad to hear such things, Louisa. Why can't you and Jane be friends? I thought you would settle down so happily as sisters.'

Louisa tossed her head scornfully. 'I, settle down with that sly little prig? Papa, you don't know what she's like. She'll do anything to get me into trouble, and Martha's as bad. Well, no, she's not *quite* so bad,' she acknowledged fairly, 'but she will be soon.'

'What were you fighting about?'

Louisa could hardly remember now. What had they been fighting about?

'Oh, because of Miss Barrow leaving. They say it's all my fault for going out in the afternoons.' Her eyes flashed indignantly. 'Papa, I *can't* stay indoors all day doing nothing but study. It does make my head ache and I'd have to go out then, so why not go out *before* I get the headache?' She gave him an appealing glance, the one that had so often won him over in the past. But although she was sure his lips twitched a little, his voice was stern as he replied.

'No, Louisa, it won't wash. You must do as your new mamma says. She knows what's right for little girls, she has two of her own, after all. And I'm afraid she's right when she says I've allowed you to run wild. It won't do any good in the long run. You have to learn to behave as a young lady should.'

Louisa stared at him. 'But I haven't run wild! I've come with you. I've been learning about the mines. I know more about haematite than Jane or Martha ever will. That's far more use than knowing what the capital of Turkey was five hundred years ago! That's the sort of thing Miss Barrow was teaching us. How does that make me a young lady?' She paused, and then added vehemently, 'And she's *not* my new mamma, nor ever will be!' She came close to him, laying a hand on his sleeve. 'Papa, why don't you send her away? Let it be like it used to be. We were happy, weren't we? We liked being here by ourselves, we don't need anyone else.'

Timothy looked down at her hand, then back into her face. He shook his head. 'Louisa, don't be childish. Of course I can't send her away. She's my wife. You're talking nonsense.'

'And I suppose it's nonsense that I'm unhappy – that doesn't matter, does it! No, what matters is that *she* gets

140

what she wants. Never mind that my life's been ruined, never mind that she's cruel and spiteful and Jane and Martha hate me. Never mind that I'm cooped up here like a bird in a cage.' She stared at him, the tears hot in her eyes. 'Why is it so wrong to want to go out on the hills?' she demanded passionately. 'Why is it so wrong to want to be outside instead of shut up indoors? Why can't I go about with you as I used to? *She* doesn't want to.' Her voice trembled and broke as she added, 'Don't you even miss me, Papa?'

He shook his head, bemused. 'Louie, what can I say? Of course I miss having you with me. I liked having you there beside me, chattering away and asking your questions. But your stepmother's right, it isn't good for a young lady to go tramping about the countryside hobnobbing with rough working men and getting herself dirty. You're growing up, Louisa—'

'Am I? Only a few minutes ago I was a "little girl"!' She pulled her hand away. 'Oh, never mind. It's easy to see you just don't care about me any more. Ever since you met her, you've been different – you haven't wanted me at all.' She turned away, bitterness welling up inside her. 'Perhaps it would be better if I went right away. Or better still if I'd never been born. If it had been me who died, instead of Mamma. You'd have been glad if—'

'*Louisa!*' Timothy's hands shot out and gripped her by the shoulders. She gasped, reminded painfully of her stepmother's treatment – and of her threats. For the first time, it seemed possible that her father might indeed lay violent hands upon her. 'Don't you dare speak to me like that!' he growled, and she was suddenly afraid. 'Don't ever let me hear you say such things again.' He released her abruptly and she saw that he was trembling. His voice was suddenly harsh. 'I see it's no use talking to you. I had hoped to make you see reason and not have to punish you. I told your stepmother that beating you would do no good, that talking was best. But now I see that I was wrong.'

His shadow loomed huge on the wall behind him. Louisa gazed at him in terror. He was suddenly no longer her father, so dear and beloved, but a frightening stranger. He bent to pick something up. She saw the cane in his hand, and shrank back on the bed.

'You're not going to *beat* me?' she whispered.

'Believe me, Louisa, I don't want to. But if it's the only way . . .' He reached forward and drew her up from the bed turning her round as he did so. 'Lift up your skirts, Louisa.'

'No!' This could not be happening. Not her gentle father, who had taken her about with him everywhere he went, who had talked to her and told her stories and taught her nursery ditties. 'Papa, *no!*'

She heard the swish of the cane only seconds before she felt it, stinging her buttocks. The stroke was not hard, but the indignity of it brought tears to her eyes. She bit her lips, determined not to cry out. For all she knew, her stepmother and the two girls were out there on the landing, listening, waiting to hear her screams. Well, she would never give them that satisfaction, never!

He struck her six times, each a light, tingling stroke that quickly faded but caused her a pain more intense than any mere physical sensation. When he had finished, he turned her round again to face him. She realised that they were both trembling, and looked at him with eyes made huge by tears.

'Papa,' she whispered brokenly, and he caught her suddenly in his arms. 'Oh, Papa . . .'

'Louisa!' he muttered into her hair, and she felt his arms like iron bands around her, holding her tightly against him. 'Oh, Louisa. My poor, poor love. My lamb.'

She clutched his shoulders and buried her face against his neck. For a few more moments they held each other;

and then Timothy stiffened suddenly and pushed her away.

'Papa?' She stared up at him, frightened anew by the strange expression on his face. 'Papa, don't leave me.'

'That's enough, Louisa!' His voice was a stranger's, hard and angry. He picked up the cane and backed towards the door, almost like a circus lion-tamer leaving the cage.

'You'll stay here till morning,' he said curtly. 'Those are your stepmother's orders. And when you come down to breakfast, I trust you will be ready to apologise and to do exactly as you are told.'

He was through the door as he spoke the last words. For a second, she saw his face, pale in the glimmer of the candlelight, staring in at her. In the devious shadows his expression changed and shifted, making him a stranger yet again. And then he closed the door and she heard his footsteps rapidly fading down the stairs.

Louisa stood quite still for a moment longer. Then she sank back on to the bed.

But she could not weep again. Her tears had gone and in their place was only coldness.

Deep in the heart of the red earth, Timothy followed Jacob Rigg through the newest pit. It was the deepest they had yet sunk on Pennington Moor, and the horse gin had wound many hundred kibbles of muck and slurry to the surface before the miners could begin driving in on the level. Now the working stretched for almost half a mile under the green fields, while at the far end men laboured with pick and shovel to force their way even further.

'It's ower rich, this one,' Jacob said as they trod through the tunnel, keeping their heads bent for fear of striking them on the craggy roof. The light from their lamps danced on the rough walls, creating a pattern of light and shade. Limestone, host rock to the haematite, glimmered pale and grey, and Jacob stopped to point out the darker shadow of the ore.

'Good kidney there. We'll rob that out later, but there's finer stuff further in. Ginnels the size of half a street, and we reckon there might even be a good-sized sop where they're working now. And there's summat else I want to show you as well.'

Timothy bent his head lower. A good six feet tall, he had often envied the mine captain his shorter stature. Where Timothy was cramped and stooping, Jacob could walk upright, his short body and legs, bandied from constant crouching, giving him a grotesque, gnomic appearance in the flickering lamplight.

As they dropped lower down the steep slope, the temperature dropped with them, striking chill against their faces. There was a damp, dusty smell but no danger here from firedamp, scourge of the coal mines, and therefore no singing of the canaries which were taken down coal mines to warn the miners of bad air. The air in a haematite mine was, if not fresh, normally quite breathable; there was no risk of its taking fire.

They came to a larger space. Men were working here, hacking away at the veins which stood like rich doors to a fortune in the shaly walls. Already they had stripped out an entire ginnel, and Timothy stepped into the vertical gap that remained, holding up his lantern to try to see the extent of the void.

'It's enormous,' he said with awe. 'Why, I could fit my whole house in here.'

Jacob came to stand beside him. 'Aye, it's good enough. And plenty more to come. We haven't finished this 'un yet, not by a long chalk. But there's more.' He led Timothy out of the great crack and through a branching tunnel. 'We reckon there's a girt big sop through the end here. See, the whole floor's kidney, and it stretches three or four hundred feet in all directions and maybe as far beneath us.' They paused and Timothy looked at the men working all around, pushing the cavern out further and further. He knew that a really good sop of haematite was like a basin filled with ore, as deep as it was broad. If they were indeed standing on top of such a deposit – as experience told him they almost certainly were – there must be millions of tons here, just waiting to be mined out and brought to the surface. A fortune at their feet.

'And this as well as the ginnels,' he said. 'We were right to drive this level, Jacob.'

'Aye.' The little man nodded, his shadow dancing on the walls. 'It could turn out to be flats, of course, but I don't reckon so. This goes down a long way. But come and see this.' He turned away, leading Timothy through yet another narrow tunnel.

Timothy thought how easy it would be to get lost down here. As the workings increased, so they became more and more like a maze, twisting and turning deep underground, with vast caverns created where sops and ginnels had left their hollows. Shafts opened suddenly in the floor, a deathtrap for the unwary; others ran off into the darkness, perhaps to end in a blank wall, perhaps to join up with another cavern deeper still.

Their lamps gave the only light down here, feeble in blackness that seemed almost solid. Timothy thought of how he had come down here as a small boy, terrified when he had dropped his candle and for a few moments found himself in pitch darkness. Suddenly, the walls had seemed to close in on him and he was horrifyingly aware of the thousands of tons of rock above him. He opened his mouth to scream, but the darkness seemed to be crushing him, suffocating him. And then his father had appeared with his own lamp, laughing, and Timothy had been too relieved to speak. Nobody ever knew just how frightened he had been in those few moments.

He thought of this experience whenever he saw the children down in the mines, boys and girls no older than

145

he had been, pushing the barrows and kibbles from the workings to the bottom of the big shaft – hurrying, they called it. The children certainly worked hard, but there was no 'hurry' about it. Shoving and straining at the big heavy buckets, it was slow, hard work for small bodies. Timothy wondered if they ever felt the fear he had experienced.

Louisa, he knew, hated to see the children going down the pit in the big iron kibbles. But what could he do? Their parents worked in the mine, their cousins, aunts, uncles – it was their way of life. And without their earnings, their families would be much the poorer.

The thought of Louisa weighed heavy on his mind. He was still uncomfortable whenever he remembered that scene in her bedroom. He had never struck her before, never wished to; she had always been biddable enough when it mattered and the rest of the time as bright as a bird about the place. But these days she was a changed creature, listless and heavy-eyed, sulky where once she had been full of chatter, her voice silent when once she had laughed and sung.

He and Susannah had made up their quarrel – or, more true to say, he had apologised and Susannah had graciously accepted his apology. It made life more comfortable, to be without her icy silences and disapproving glances. But he did not feel more comfortable about Louisa.

What was amiss with her? Was it just her age? He knew that girls of Louisa's years were often temperamental. So many changes were going on in their bodies as they grew to adulthood, and they scarcely knew themselves whether they were child or woman. And it was well known that children often found it difficult to accept a step-parent. But he had thought it would be so easy. Susannah's girls were meek enough, answering politely when spoken to and quiet the rest of the time. They behaved with the decorum he had been assured was appropriate in young ladies; they did not rush about and let their hair fly loose, they were never found clambering about in trees in the garden or playing mud pies with the cottagers' children.

He sighed a little. Louisa had seemed much happier, it was true, when allowed to do these things. But if Susannah said they were unsuitable occupations for a well-brought-up young lady . . .

'Here,' Jacob said, stopping where two or three men, naked to the waist, their sweating torsos streaked with mud, were swinging their picks at the wall. 'Look at this.' He bent and indicated a large block of ore lying on the floor of the tunnel. Like everything else down here, it was covered with red slime but as Timothy bent his light towards it he saw what Jacob was pointing at.

'Why, surely it's pencil ore!' he exclaimed.

Jacob nodded. 'I've heard tell of it, never seen it before. See them little rings? That's the ends of spikes of ore, set in there like marlins. Give it a blow with summat,' he took one of the men's picks and struck the block sharply with its head, 'and bob's yer uncle, out they comes!'

Timothy caught the end of one of the spikes with his fingertips and pulled. The entire rod drew smoothly from its bed, a 'pencil' of perhaps eight or nine inches long and almost an inch thick. Some of the others were of like size, some thinner, and he had no doubt that each one could be drawn forth as easily.'I reckon,' Jacob said, 'this is the best vein we've ever struck.'

'I think so too,' Timothy said, and thought how delighted Louisa would be with this. If only he could bring her down to see! She had been begging him for some time to let her come down one of the mines, but Susannah would never countenance it.

'We'll give it a name,' he said with sudden decision. 'A pit as promising as this ought to be specially known.

We'll give it a name that everyone knows, so that it will always be famous.'

'Aye, happen,' Jacob said in his non-commital way. 'And what'll we call it, then?'

'Louisa,' Timothy said. 'We'll call this pit Louisa.'

The news that Louisa had a pit named after her was received with less pleasure than Timothy had expected. 'Louisa?' Susannah echoed. 'You're calling it *Louisa*?'

'Yes. Why not? It seemed a good idea. She's been so downhearted of late, I thought it would cheer her up.'

'The only reason that young woman is downhearted is because she can't have her own way all the time,' Susannah said grimly. 'This will undo all the good work I've done, Timothy. She'll think she can twist you round her little finger, just as she used to do.'

'She never did that,' he protested. 'And she's never been a temperamental child, Susannah, not until these past few months.'

'Which is another way of saying it's all my fault, I suppose! Timothy, I refuse to be blamed for Louisa's shortcomings. She's a self-willed, headstrong and unruly little hussy. I suspect that she was spoiled ever since she was a baby.'

Timothy took a deep breath. Susannah's increasingly disparaging comments about Margaret, coming more and more frequently, had the power to induce in him a rage that made him fear what he might do to her. It took all his self-control to remain calm.

Dimly, he knew that he was angry because she was attacking memories that had grown dearer with each year that had passed since Margaret had died; she was attacking the love he had borne for his first wife. That was why she made such difficulties for Louisa, Margaret's daughter, why she disliked any reference to his past life.

But Margaret was dead. It was Susannah he had to live

with. As he had told Louisa, he had chosen her to be his wife, and he was committed.

'My love,' he said placatingly, 'it's only a mine. I thought it would please her to have it named for her and be of no matter to you. Why should you mind, after all?'

'Why? I suppose it never occurred to you that I might like to have it named for myself?'

He stared at her. 'For yourself? The mine named *Susannah*? But you hate the mines.'

'I've no wish to go near them, it's quite true,' she said, 'but I realise that it's where our livelihood must come from, and if shipowners' wives can have ships named after them . . .'

'So that's it,' he said slowly. 'One of your friends in Liverpool has had a ship named after her, and you want to be able to flourish your own pride. I'm right, aren't I?'

'It isn't a matter of pride,' she said stiffly. 'Simply a gesture, a courtesy towards your wife. I would have thought that was quite apparent.'

'Well, I'm sorry, but I never thought you would want such a thing. But the next time we sink a shaft—'

'Oh no,' she said, turning away. 'I don't wish to come second to your daughter. If this mine is as good as you say it is, I think it should be this one.'

'That's out of the question,' he cut in brusquely. 'I've already named the pit and told the men.'

'They can be told again, can't they? You are the master, aren't you?'

'I told you, it can't be done. Someone may already have mentioned it to Louisa herself.'

'Oh well, certainly we must not interfere with *that*!' Susannah exclaimed in a huff.

'Susannah, I can't change it now. Louisa would be sure to find out, and she'd be so hurt.'

'And it doesn't matter if I'm hurt?' The two red spots were burning on Susannah's pale cheeks. 'No, don't touch me, Timothy! Don't try to win me over with soft words and kisses. They mean nothing, they're gone in a moment. It's *things* that matter – money and clothes and furnishings. Things that other people can see. And naming things, so that other people know.' She stared at him. 'Don't you understand? Don't you *see*?'

'No, I don't see. Things are not important. They are what can be gone in a moment. It's people who matter, Susannah, people and their feelings.' He reached towards her again. 'Loving is what matters. Don't you love me, Susannah?'

Susannah moved impatiently under his touch. 'We're married, aren't we? Isn't that good enough for you?'

'Does marriage mean love?' As he spoke the words he knew that he had believed that it did. Between him and Margaret, marriage and love had gone together, as closely intertwined as the two of them had been as they lay in bed together at night.

He tried to recall his feelings about Susannah when they had first met. It had been at a dinner party at a house on the shore of Windermere. A good many industrialists from Manchester and Liverpool had built grand houses in that area to spend holidays in, sometimes for the whole summer. They entertained lavishly and Timothy, meeting a mill owner at some local function, had been invited for a weekend. Susannah had been present with a lady companion, but he had scarcely noticed the friend. Susannah, dark like Margaret and wearing a gown of her favourite shade of green, had caught his eye at once.

Was that all it had been, that she bore a fleeting resemblance to Margaret – he could not see it now however hard he gazed – and by chance wore her favourite colour? Susannah didn't even like the colour much. Once, when he had asked her to wear that gown again, she had looked down her nose and said, 'That old thing? I've thrown it away.' And Timothy had felt shocked, almost betrayed.

By then their engagement had been announced and Susannah wore his diamond ring – though not the one he had given to Margaret; that would one day belong to Louisa. He had visited Liverpool and met her family, and he had scarcely had time to wonder whether she loved him.

But if she did not, why marry him? She had a satisfactory income. What other reason could there be?

Perhaps that was why their love did not seem to flower as it had between him and Margaret. There was no eager response to him in bed, no whispered words of love, no ardent stroking or touching or kissing. Susannah simply lay there, quiescent in his arms, and he was never quite sure whether her sighs were of pleasure or impatience.

Was it good enough, that they were married? Was that all the expression of love that was needed?

'I do my duty,' she said sharply when he tried to put this into words. 'I have been married before, Timothy. I know what a wife must do.'

And I have been married before too, he thought, and I know what a wife *can* do.

But there was nothing he could say. In this matter, as in so many others, he and Susannah were a world apart. He felt the distance between them as a yawning chasm, slowly and treacherously opening at his feet, a chasm into which he could easily fall and be lost for ever.

He had a sudden sharp recollection of that childhood experience down in the mine, and knew again the terror of the thick, suffocating darkness and the overwhelming dread that he might never see daylight again.

The idea of having a mine named for her would, only months ago, have given Louisa a pleasure more intense than any she had yet known. But now that delight eluded her. When her father gave her the news, she could only stare at him and think of how it might have been.

151

'Well?' he said with an impatience born of nervousness. 'Aren't you pleased?'

'Yes, of course I am.' But she spoke listlessly and avoided his eyes. The thought came to her that this was his way of trying to make up for beating her. A sop to her injured feelings, like giving sweets to a child to make it smile again.

Once, it might have worked. But there was that cold, hard lump in her breast now where her heart used to be, and it would not melt.

Timothy made a gesture of exasperation. 'Louisa, what in heaven's name is the matter? I thought you loved the mines! I thought you'd be pleased and excited to know that one was named for you, and that the best we've ever had. Don't you care at all? Doesn't it mean anything to you now?'

While he was speaking, she had moved slowly away, her gaze directed out of the window. From here she could see across the broad estuary, past Grange and Arnside and the huddled roofs of Lancaster, as far as the flat top of Ingleborough in the Yorkshire Dales. But her eyes were not on the sandy bay, nor on the distant hills, and at his last question she whirled round, her eyes flashing.

'Mean anything? What could it mean? I'm never allowed near the mines these days. I'm not even allowed to talk about them. I haven't seen any of my friends there for weeks – they must think I don't care any more – and you never take me out without taking Jane and Martha too. And that only for Sunday afternoon walks, with *gloves* on!' She moved closer, looking up into his face, meeting his eyes with a directness that caused him to drop his gaze. 'If you had thought for months about how you could be most cruel to me, Papa, you could not have thought of anything better than to name a mine after me and never let me go to see it.'

For a moment, she caught a brief flash of understanding, of regret, in his eyes. Then it was gone, and she wondered if she had imagined it. She saw him gather himself together, as if physically thrusting away ideas he did not want to hear.

'You're being childish again,' he said coldly. 'I have no intention of being cruel to you, I simply wanted to do something to please you.' He sighed and his face grew heavy. 'I'm afraid your stepmother is right, Louisa. You've become self-willed, spoiled and ungrateful.'

'Spoiled?' she cried. 'When I am never allowed to do a thing I want to do? When I have to spend all my days with stupid girls and a stupid governess, learning stupid things that are no good to anyone? When I see you going out day after day without me and I know you're seeing people who are my friends and going to places that I love as much as you do, maybe even more, and I know I can never go there again? At least, not till I'm grown up, and what use will it be to me then? Nobody will know me, nobody will remember me.' Her words burst out of her, flung themselves at him, then ended on a note of desolation. She clenched her fists and brought them up to her head, angry with both him and her stepmother, angry with the tears that stood in her eyes and brimmed over on to her cheeks; most of all, angry with her own impotence.

'There's nothing I can do,' she said bleakly, turning back to the window. 'I'm caught here. And you say I'm spoiled and ungrateful. What do I have to be grateful for, can you tell me that?'

He said what she had known he would say. 'You have a good home. You have warmth, food, comfort, everything you need. Of course you should be grateful.'

'And don't you *have* to give me those things?' she demanded, wheeling back. 'Did I ask to be born? Did I ask to be your daughter and such a burden to you? Perhaps you'd rather I just wasn't here any more.

153

Perhaps you'd rather I'd never been here at all. My mother was the only person you ever really cared about, and now you don't even care about her. You can't, or you would never have married—'

'I told you,' his face was like thunder, 'never speak to me like that! Whatever happens to us is God's will, and to question it is blasphemy. I won't have it in my house. And I won't have any more of these scenes either. You're not thirteen years old yet, you've a deal of growing up to do and you'll do it the way your step-mother and I want you to do it. And if that's sitting at your studies instead of gallivanting around the country-side, so be it.' He turned and strode to the door. 'I should have named the mine after Susannah instead.'

'Then do so!' Louisa screamed as he shut the door. But his footsteps were already stamping away down the passage and whether he heard or not, she never knew.

The mine remained in her name. But it was a long while before anyone took any pleasure in it.

Chapter Ten

Walter Sherwin was born on 20 August 1835; the day of the earthquake.

It was fitting enough, Timothy thought afterwards. The child had been conceived in a turmoil of guilt and anger, the months of pregnancy had been a misery for all concerned and the birth itself a nightmare and no one sure who would survive it.

'Surely it ought to be easier for her,' Timothy had said when Dr Robinson arrived. The midwife had already been in the house for a week, making ready, but once the labour had begun it was clear that she was going to need help. 'She's had two children already.'

'Not always the case.' The doctor was rolling up his sleeves as he spoke. 'Complications can set in with any birth, and it's thirteen years since your wife gave birth to her second child. She's no longer a young woman, Timothy.'

The words brought fresh guilt, and as Dr Robinson went upstairs to Susannah, Timothy turned away and stared out of the window.

If only he could have forgotten his desire for a son, if only he had left Susannah alone and not insisted on his rights as a husband . . .

If only things had been different between himself and Louisa.

Restlessly, aware of the struggle going on upstairs, he roamed about the room. Like the rest of the house, it had been completely refurbished in the three years since he and Susannah had married, and there was little left now of the rather plain room he had shared with Margaret. Instead, there were thick carpets on the floor, new tables and chairs, fine pictures hanging on the walls and heavy curtains at the windows.

It was exactly the kind of room a man in his position should have. And it suffocated him. He flung open the window and leaned out, breathing the sultry August air. Three years wed, and his child about to be born.

Leaning at the window and finding the air outside as suffocating as that within, Timothy's thoughts went back yet again to the day he had taken Louisa to the mines.

He'd known it was a foolish thing to do. For too long now he had found himself more aware of Louisa than a father should have been. Perhaps it was her increasing resemblance to Margaret – but wasn't that common enough? Many girls grew to look like their mothers, surely, without their fathers looking on them with the same desire. Perhaps it was all the stronger because he had lost Margaret when they were still at the height of their passion. It was as if Louisa had been sent to torment him. And the wife he had taken to ease that torment had only increased it.

He knew now that this was why he had married Susannah. The desperate loneliness, the need for the love, both physical and emotional, that his wife had given him, the craving for relief and the sudden appalling realisation that Louisa was beginning to replace Margaret in his mind, that he was beginning to be obsessed by her, by her dark blue eyes, her glossy chestnut hair and her developing young body, had driven him into Susannah's arms. 'Better to marry than to burn', St Paul had said; and Timothy had been burning, on fire with frustrated desires and loneliness and guilt, and marriage had seemed to be the only answer.

But St Paul had never been a married man. If he had,

and if he had been married to a woman like Susannah, he might have spoken otherwise.

It was all so different from what he had expected. His first thought was that Susannah was disappointed in him, that he didn't measure up to Frederick Reid, her first husband. That first night, their wedding night, she had lain in his arms unmoving, permitting only the minimum of caresses. He had touched her breasts, smoothed his hand over her stomach – flatter than Margaret's, thinner, and delineated by hipbones that stood out sharply against his hand. This she had tolerated – he was sure now that it was just that, toleration – but no more. When his fingers reached down towards the thin, silken skin of her thighs and the delicate creases that lay between them, she had pushed his hand sharply away and he, afraid that he had hurt her, thinking that perhaps she was more sensitive than Margaret had been, had kissed her and proceeded instead with his own penetration. And this she had permitted, so perhaps she was as eager as he, perhaps she did not need the caresses that Margaret had so much enjoyed.

But he must stop thinking of Margaret, he had told himself on that first night, and on many others since. Susannah was his wife now; he must not make comparisons or pretend that it was Margaret who lay in his arms now, returning kiss for kiss, moving against him, whispering and sighing, crying out his name. Indeed, it was a poor pretence, for Susannah did none of these things. She simply lay there, submitting to him. And when it was over and he longed to lie a little longer, kissing and touching as he had done in his first marriage, Susannah merely turned over, as if thankful to have done with it.

She needed time, he thought. Time to grow accustomed to him. Perhaps she, too, was remembering her first marriage, thinking of her first husband. They both needed to erase those old memories, to bury and forget the past. But the months had gone by and nothing had changed. Susannah's body lost any attraction it might have had for him; there was none of the pleasure he had found in loving Margaret. Instead, he felt soiled and diminished afterwards, as if he had betrayed that love; and his only excuse was that he was a man, that this was marriage, and that he desired – was entitled to have – a son.

It was then that he had begun again to notice Louisa. Sometimes he thought it had always been there, this feeling he had for her. When she was a small girl, nestling on his lap, when she had crept into his and Margaret's bed in the early mornings and he had felt her warm, plump young body snuggling against his. But there had been nothing sinister in that, surely. It was nothing more than the delight any father might take in his child. This flesh came from my flesh, this skin and bone and hair sprang from my love. He had thought it beautiful, had seen nothing shameful, and neither had Margaret.

Nor could it be wrong that as Louisa grew he had begun to notice how much she resembled her mother. Those blue eyes, like cornflowers in the fields, that hair like new-split chestnuts. It was natural, surely, that his eyes should see again the girl he had wooed and wedded, that, lonelier than ever in a marriage that had proved so arid, he should long for the woman who had been his helpmeet. Perhaps it was merely his misfortune that his treacherous body should be aroused by hers in a way that a father's should never be. But it was not his misfortune that he had allowed himself to be overcome by it on that day a year ago. That was his fault, his lack of self-control, his wickedness, and for that there could be no excuse.

Timothy leaned his head against the windowframe. The air was more stifling than ever, the sky heavy and threatening. There was thunder about, and he wished it would come and clear the air, but there was more than that, a kind of menace, an ominous waiting as if the earth were holding its breath. He shook his head impatiently and listened to the moaning from above. If only this child would get itself born!

Perhaps it was retribution for his behaviour. Perhaps both his wife and child were about to die. If they did, he would be to blame. He had forced himself upon Susannah that night, forced himself on her in an attempt to assuage his guilt. If she died now, he would have killed her. And if the child died too, he would be doubly a murderer.

The memory of that July day with Louisa haunted him. His daughter, sitting beside him once more, bright-eyed and eager, delighted to be with him, happy simply to be in his company and going to the mines. And he, knowing the obsession that had been growing in him over the past months as he had watched her budding womanhood, had allowed himself to be swayed. He had relinquished control and taken his own delight in watching her, in feeling her arm against his, in listening to the music of her voice.

They had talked about the miners, about slaves – he barely remembered what they had discussed. He knew that he had been startled by Louisa's thinking; when they had last ridden like this, she had been a child still and accepted all she saw. Now she was beginning to think, and in what Susannah would have described as a very *unladylike* manner. But Timothy had enjoyed her thinking, even though he didn't agree with all she said. It was like breathing fresh air to hear her stating her opinions.

And then she had laid her hand on his arm, the hand that was so like Margaret's; she had looked up at him with eyes that could have been her mother's and made some trembling remark that was filled with the same yearning that echoed in his own heart. And he had forgotten everything, all his caution, all his sense of right

159

and wrong, all his awareness of who this really was beside him and of the taboos that must exist between them. All was swept away, and he was with Margaret again, Margaret and yet not Margaret, and all he could think of was how much he loved this strange, other-worldly being and how much he had missed her and how he longed to make her truly his.

For a few moments he had tasted delight. For a few moments he had been transported to the stars. And then, with a fall so violent he scarcely expected to recover from it, he had known that he was for ever damned and that nothing could expiate the sin he had committed.

Since that day, Timothy had been racked with guilt. He had taken care never to be alone with Louisa again. How could she trust him? How could he trust himself? Knowing that she must regard him with disgust, he had avoided her company as much as possible, kept his eyes turned away from hers. Sometimes, giving her a covert glance, he had fancied that she looked sad, that she would have welcomed his affection, but when he had gathered up courage enough to approach her, she had warded him off with an iciness that froze his unhappy heart all over again and convinced him that he had lost her for ever.

For a few months after that, he had lived in aloof misery, unable to take comfort from anyone. His wife cold, his daughter alienated, there had been nothing in the world to give him pleasure, and he had absorbed himself in his mines, in making money. But that had never been enough; Timothy Sherwin needed more than that and eventually he turned back to the only person who could give it to him.

He turned back to Susannah. And Susannah had scorned him.

'Really, Timothy! I thought you were past all that.'

'Past it? But we've been married only a little above

two years. I'm a young man still—'

'You're forty-five years old. And I am thirty-eight. Do you think I want to risk having a child now?'

He stared at her. A child! In the misery of the past few months he had forgotten, or discarded, his desire for a son. But perhaps that was his only chance of finding happiness now – in a son, in a fresh start. A son he could love normally, bring up in his own way, who would be able to go with him to the mines, learn the business, be ready to take it over when he was too old. A son . . .

'I married you to have a child,' he said now in low, tense tones, and saw the ugly flush run up Susannah's neck.

'Then you were a fool,' she answered crisply. 'You should have chosen a younger woman.'

'I chose you,' he said, reaching for her in the bed. 'And precious little return you've given me for all the comfort you've had.'

He scarcely heard her stifled gasp. He barely noticed her struggles, her anger, the scratching fingernails or the twisting body. Inflamed with anger and a certain savage pleasure in her protests, he caught both wrists in one of his hands, ripped her nightdress from her body with the other and thrust himself into her. There were no kisses, no caresses, no care for whether or not he hurt her. There was no love; only a sense of punishment, a cruel revenge for all the misery he had suffered, for all the humiliations she had dealt him here in the bedroom and in every other area of their lives.

But with the knowledge that in this he was master, that nothing Susannah could do would stop him from having his moment of triumph and planting his seed in her, he knew an equal sense of loss. A knowledge that this union had nothing to do with love but more with hatred and revenge. A battle from which neither of them would emerge the victor.

Timothy, leaning his head against the open window

nine months later, felt that painful climax all over again, and all the others that had followed it during the next few months as he thrust himself, night after night, into his wife's reluctant body. Like a man obsessed, as if driven by a black, desperate and totally overriding urge, he had endeavoured to grasp that moment of triumph, to master for ever the woman who had so cheated him of the happiness he had sought. But always it eluded him; even when, exhausted by her struggles, Susannah lay submissive beneath him and endured the savagery of his thrusts, he never felt that he had conquered. And always, as he fell spent beside her, came the dark shadow of guilt and self-disgust.

What sort of a man was he, after all? How would his loving Margaret have viewed such behaviour?

As he leaned there, his weary eyes caught a strange, faint glimmer in the landscape. At the same moment, he heard a low, ominous rumbling deep within the earth. It approached through the hills, shook the house beneath his feet, ended with a crack that he was sure must have damaged the foundations beneath. He caught at the wall, as if afraid he would fall, and gazed out, startled, at the trembling hills.

For a few moments there was nothing. Then it came again: a low, approaching rumble, as if the thunder had gone underground, ending in that final deep crash, as if somewhere far below a cavern had collapsed.

And in the silence that followed, he heard Susannah's last scream and the thin, wailing cry of a baby.

Louisa, sitting at the head of the valley near Ireleth, heard the same trembling roar somewhere deep below her. Her first thought was for the mines and the people – the children – trapped underground. She did not know until much later that it was in that moment that her half-brother Walter had drawn his first shivering breath.

With the new baby due to be born, she and the other

162

two girls had been sent over to a neighbour's house at Tytup. But Mrs Alcott, who had known Louisa since she was a baby, had seen nothing wrong with the girl going off for a walk alone. Like everyone else in the area, she had been accustomed to seeing Louisa riding in the trap with her father or roaming the fields by herself. And it had not escaped her notice that since Susannah's arrival these jaunts had become rare.

No harm could come to the child, she thought. Why not let her have a little freedom for once?

Louisa set off at once up the little valley beside Poaka Beck. She ignored Martha's pleas to be allowed to come too. 'I'll be walking too fast for you,' she said, and it was true, for Martha at thirteen was as plump as ever and seldom moved with any speed. In fact, it was difficult sometimes to believe that she and Jane were sisters, Martha's round face and fair curls were so different from Jane's thin, horsey features and straggling mouse-coloured hair.

They were different in nature, too. Over the years Louisa had learned to recognise their moods and read their expressions and behaviour. She knew that when Jane's small pale eyes were narrowed, spite lurked close behind them, and that taunts, sarcasm or even lies would come from those tightened lips. She knew that Martha watched her sister for guidance, and that if Jane were occupied with something else, she would sometimes dare to smile at Louisa, a real smile, albeit somewhat timid. It made her face look quite different and Louisa thought sometimes that had it not been for Jane, she and Martha might have become friends.

But Martha never dared risk her sister's temper. Nor did Louisa make much effort to penetrate the barriers of hatred and spite. Instead, she went her own way as much as possible, attending the lessons she was forced to attend, sitting meek and silent at meals, and slipping out whenever possible to roam her beloved hills and valleys.

163

Sometimes it was only possible at night. But a full moon can show the way as well as a hidden sun, and Louisa could slip like a shadow along the paths and byways she knew so well.

She would return from these expeditions feeling released, able to breathe again. But there was always a certain hunger too, as if she were seeking something she could never find. A fulfilment that would ever elude her.

Often on these moonlit nights, she would roam as far as the little valley near Ireleth, and there she would think of Kieran and wonder where the travellers were. And why they had never returned.

But today she was out in full sunlight, free for as long as she desired, for Mrs Alcott had given her a small parcel of food to take with her – a piece of bread and cheese, an early apple – and she could go wherever she liked. To the mines, perhaps, her own mine, the one named after her, which she had visited only a few times. Or up the slaters' road to Kirkby Moor, where the heather would already have spread its purple carpet. Or over the meadows to Askam and along the sands to the abandoned quarries at Dunnerholme, with Black Combe like a big dark whale across the estuary and the frieze of the mountains ahead.

She went, of course, where she had known all along she would go: to the hidden valley where the travellers had camped and where she had spent her father's wedding day with a dark-eyed, teasing gipsy boy.

As always, her heart began to beat faster as she came up the last grassy slope to the valley rim. As always, a wild hope filled her mind; and as always, when she came breathlessly to the top and looked down at the silent, empty space, the hope died bitterly and left her yearning.

She had never overcome the pain of loneliness that this moment invariably brought. But neither could she overcome the hope, the thought that this time they might be there, this time she would see the fires burning and the children playing, the women tending their cooking or making baskets, the men swinging into the camp with a bunch of rabbits in their fists. And Kieran already halfway up the slope to meet her, eyes bright with wicked laughter.

The day was hot, almost airless. The sun, brilliant at sunrise, was now a pale disc hanging behind a gauzy pewter sky. It was not exactly cloud, more a thickening of the air, a drawing in of the suffocating humidity that had grown over the past few days. There was no breeze at all; not even a blade of grass stirred. And there was no sound of birdsong, not even the wild lamenting cry of a gull.

Louisa sat down. After that first moment of piercing disappointment, so often experienced, she ceased to think of Kieran. Instead, her mind went back to Pennington Hall, and Susannah.

Louisa knew that Susannah was having a baby, and that it would be born today. She knew that the pregnancy had been a difficult one – Susannah had made sure that everyone knew that – and from listening to the servants in the kitchen, she knew that the birth was likely to be difficult too. Susannah might even die, and the baby with her.

Louisa tasted the thought. She cared for her stepmother no more now than she ever had – rather less, in fact; but did she actually want her to die? Wasn't it a sin, akin to murder, to wish someone dead?

But then if Susannah had never come here, she wouldn't be in this situation now, she wouldn't be lying in the big bedroom upstairs groaning and crying, with the midwife looking grave and Louisa's father at his wits' end, so it was her own fault if she died, wasn't it?

And perhaps without Susannah, Louisa thought, as she had so many times before, she and her father would be able to get back on their old footing. There would be nothing then to stop her driving out with him to the mines, visiting *her* mine, accompanying him on trips to the bloomeries and the furnaces, walking the fells. Nothing to stop them being the companions they had always been. Except . . .

As it had done so often in the past year, that one memory, pushed firmly down beneath the surface of her mind, thrust its way to the top and caught her unawares. With a little moan, Louisa closed her eyes and put one hand to her forehead.

Why had it happened? What had it meant?

And what exactly *had* happened? She had thought of it so often, and tried so often to avoid thinking of it, that the memory had become hazy and distorted. She had hoped it would vanish altogether, leaving her in peace, but it hadn't. At odd moments it would reappear, striking like a soft, heavy blow against her heart, and she knew that until she confronted it there would never be peace.

She sighed and gazed out across the little valley towards the village of Askam and the estuary beyond. The tide was out and the river made a broad network of twisting channels across the sands. A few people were crossing the sands, most on foot but one or two in horse-drawn carts. The way was clear enough if you knew it, but the sands were treacherous and the channels shifted from day to day. It was common enough for people to be caught by quicksands and swallowed up alive, and the incoming tide advanced so rapidly that more than one traveller had been swept away and drowned.

The still air shimmered, so that the sands looked like water even where Louisa knew they must be dry. Across the estuary, Millom was sunk in a haze of heat, and Black Combe was almost invisible against a sky of gathering darkness. A storm was coming, and a bad one. But it was coming slowly.

Louisa thought again of that day a year ago, when she had snatched the opportunity of a rare few hours alone with her father.

Where had Susannah and her daughters been that day? Louisa could never recollect. All she could remember was watching from her bedroom window as Jane and Martha followed their mother into the carriage and the three of them disappeared down the drive.

Louisa stared after them. All at once she was aware of the house around her, empty for once of their stifling presence. She closed her eyes for a moment, imagining that they had never been there, that Susannah and her father had never married, that it had all been a dream. Everything was as it had been; just she and Timothy alone together, comfortable, with all the old closeness and affection that had been so sadly lost.

A great gush of sorrow filled her heart and when she opened her eyes again they were full of tears. She looked down at the drive once more. The carriage was out of sight. And then she saw Timothy, walking slowly and heavily round the house, coming from the stables. His shoulders were bowed, his head bent and he looked as if he carried a burden almost too heavy to bear.

In that second, Louisa knew that there need be no barrier between them. It had all been false, engineered by her stepmother to drive the two of them apart, culminating in the beating that Timothy had no wish to administer and Louisa had seen as the final betrayal. And there had never been a chance to redeem their loss.

But now we can, she thought with sudden exultation. They're all out, and Papa and I are here by ourselves. We can do whatever we like and they can't stop us.

Timothy had entered the house and she heard his study door open and close. She could still remember her elation as she ran down the stairs to her father's study and burst in, as she had always been accustomed to doing, without knocking.

167

He had looked up from his papers, frowning. Startled, Louisa came to a stop before his desk and for several moments they stared at each other. Almost like strangers, she thought, and the idea was heartbreaking.

'Papa?' she said at last, tremulously, and suddenly he smiled. He reached out across the wide desk and laid his hand palm upwards on its green leather top. Her heart skipping a little, Louisa laid her own hand against it and their fingers curled together.

'Oh, *Papa*,' she said, and came round the desk to sit on his knee.

It was so long since she had done that. Since the day of the beating there had been no open affection between her and her father, nothing apart from the dutiful kiss of greeting and parting.

Now with his arms warm about her and her body close against his, Louisa felt herself back in those happy days of the past, when they had been companions and there had been nobody to tell them it was wrong.

It *wasn't* wrong! she thought passionately. Fathers and daughters *should* love each other. And she lifted her face for his kiss.

But instead of laughing and ruffling her hair, as once he would have done, he stared at her. And there was something in his expression, a darkness in his eyes, that made her draw back.

'Papa—'

'Let's go out,' he cut in. 'Let's go to the mine. Jacob's been asking after you, and Billy too. Put on some old clothes, Louisa, and let's go out as we used to.'

The moment of discomfort was past and she laughed and slipped off his knee. In half an hour they were in the trap, setting out through the narrow lanes. It was a cool day, and one of the few dry ones that summer, for rain had fallen almost continuously since the winter.

'The farmers are having a bad time of it,' Timothy commented as they drove along. 'Sheep shearers

168

costing four shillings a day, the wheat crop disastrous. Why, in Walney it was almost all washed away back in the winter. And any that did survive looks like rotting on the stalk.'

Although it wasn't raining, the lanes were full of the red, slippery mud that came everywhere from the mines. Only in the driest weather did the mud turn to deep red dust, clogging the hedges and creating a crimson haze over the landscape as the carts and trucks taking ore to the furnaces stirred it into clouds. Then the women driving the carts drew their shawls across their faces, trying to keep the grit from their eyes, and the hedges themselves looked as if they were rusting under a coppery sky.

Mostly, however, the red earth was wet and sticky. It clogged the wheels of carts and clung to the horses' hooves, it filled the narrow, twisting lanes that criss-crossed Low Furness and made the carts heavier than ever to drag, so that sweat ran like blood down the horses' straining sides. Clots of slurry out of the pits dropped from the piled ore, adding to the thick slime that coated road and hedgerow, and flew up again from plodding hooves to spatter the carters and transform them into figures from nightmare with eyes gleaming in raddled faces.

From the high ridge that ran along the top of the moor, Louisa could see across the Levens estuary and the bay to Poulton-le-Sands. Once a simple fishing village, it was becoming known as a seaside holiday resort, with plenty of boats to take people out on the water and a regatta in July. Tradesmen from Manchester, not yet able to afford one of the grand houses being built in the Lake District, would take their families there for a few weeks every summer, to play on the sands and enjoy prawns and cockles collected by the nobbies – huge nets, dragged by heavy horses through the shallow tides.

People crossed the bay on foot, as they did the Duddon estuary, but the sands were just as treacherous and it was dangerous to go without a sand pilot to guide the way.

That day, as Louisa and her father drove along the moor, the tide had been high and the view only slightly obscured by the smoke from the furnaces at Ulverston. The bay was alive with sail, great spreading sheets of white and brown canvas that bellied out in the wind and caught pale fingers of sunlight poking down through the clouds. Tall ships forged steadily towards the mouth of the Ulverston canal, bringing a variety of supplies – rum, sugar, tobacco – to be replaced by cargoes of pig iron or copper. Louisa knew that down on the banks of the canal, shipbuilders were busy, for Ulverston ships, built to handle heavy ore, had a reputation for fine workmanship.

'The sun's coming out,' she said, gazing out over the scene. 'Look, the clouds are breaking up. I love to see the bay like this, so busy with all the sails.'

'Aye, it looks pretty enough today,' Timothy remarked, reining the horse in to allow a cart to pass. 'But it's taken a deal of lives over the years. Not just people trying to cross without knowing the right ways, either; it's swallowed whole villages in its time, and who's to say it won't take more?'

'Whole villages?' She turned to look at him. 'Do you mean to say those stories are true?'

'Some of them, without any doubt.' He pointed across the sweep of water. 'Down there, past Bardsea, there used to be villages nobody knows about these days. Sometimes bits of Low Scales can be seen even now at low tide, but the others – Rosse, Crimleton – they've been gone for centuries. My father could remember when the best part of Aldingham got washed away – sixty years ago, that was. He was a boy of eleven when the great storm blew up and took half the parish. The church was at the centre of the village then, now it's almost at the water's edge.'

'I thought they were just tales,' Louisa said, straining her eyes to see across the wide bay and trying to imagine the cottages and churches that perhaps still stood somewhere beneath the waves. 'It's so shallow at low water.'

'Oh, there'd not be much left of them now. Torn to pieces by the water and scattered. It'd just look like so many rocks and stones by this time.' The cart had passed them and he flicked the reins on the horse's back. 'Walk on.'

They were among the mines now, the land on either side of the road torn and gashed like wounds in the flank of some great stranded beast. In the open levels, Louisa could see the men labouring with picks, hacking the ore out from its surrounding limestone, while at the heads of the deeper shafts horse gins and tumbletrees wound steadily to bring the kibbles to the surface.

It was so familiar, she wanted to weep. And yet there was something different even in its familiarity. Nothing had changed in the two years since she had been allowed to come here, yet everything was different. Or perhaps the difference was in herself.

'Those little children,' she said, staring at a large kibble just about to descend, 'what are they doing?'

'Why, going down to work, of course.' Her father glanced at her. 'You've seen them before, Louie. Don't tell me you've forgotten how a mine works.'

'No, of course not. But they look so small. Surely—'

'They're the same age they always were,' Timothy said indifferently. 'You've just got bigger. You've grown a lot these past two years. Why, you're almost a woman.'

She looked at him then, catching his glance as it moved over her body. His eyes had darkened a little and she felt a sudden, not quite comfortable, warmth. She turned quickly back towards the mine.

The kibble was full now of small bodies, their ages

ranging, she guessed, from eight years to fourteen, though even those looked small for their age. She thought of Martha, plump and well fed, comparing her with these pale and weary-looking children. Why, they didn't even look like children, some of them, more like old men and women with wizened faces and eyes that were sunk in dark hollows in skull-like faces.

Was this what working in mines did to little children?

'They look terrible,' she said, 'starved and tired. Papa, it can't be right.'

He stared at her. 'What's got into you, Louisa? They look no different from what they ever did. You've seen them before often enough, these and others like them. They always look like this. They're miners' children. You mustn't compare them with our sort, Louie.'

She looked at him doubtfully. Was it true that miners and their families were somehow made differently, stronger than they looked, able to toil below ground at heavy tasks without taking harm from it?

'You've forgotten,' Timothy said again. 'You never used to worry your head about these things.'

But I was just a child then too, she thought. Since then, I've learned to think, to look at life and wonder. I've learned to doubt.

I've learned to doubt you, Papa.

But that thought was too painful, too frightening, and she pushed it away, refused to let it into her mind. Instead, she slipped her arm through her father's and rested her head against his shoulder.

'It's good to be here with you, Papa. It's been too long since you brought me. I've missed it.' She looked up into his face. 'I've missed you.'

His expression softened and he lifted his other hand to touch her cheek. For a moment, as his fingers lingered against her skin, Louisa felt a sensation of complete rapport, of a closeness she had not known since she was a small child, cuddled between her parents as they lay in

172

their big bed. She remembered creeping in early in the mornings, wriggling her body between theirs, snuggling in the warmth. It was a special kind of warmth, encountered nowhere else, a warmth made by human bodies in loving sleep, and Louisa had revelled in it. Until now, she had never realised how much she had missed it.

'Oh, Papa,' she said, 'I love you.'

She felt her father's arm tighten, holding her hand firmly against his side, and his hand cupped her cheek, turning her face again towards his. Briefly, they looked into each other's eyes and for a moment she thought he was about to kiss her. Then, sharply, he drew back.

'Here comes Billy Rigg,' he said, looking past her towards the pithead. 'I daresay he's grown bigger too since you saw him last.'

Louisa turned quickly, and felt a shock. She had not met Billy since the day before her father's wedding and in her mind he had remained the same rather small twelve-year-old that she had seen going down in the kibble. But the boy coming towards her now was sturdy and well grown, halfway to manhood, his body hardened and muscled by strenuous work. If Timothy had not told her this was Billy Rigg, she might not have recognised him. His face had changed too. It was almost adult, hardened like his body, unsmiling.

'Miss Louisa. Don't see you much these days.'

'It's good to be here.' But even as she said the words, she was uncertain of their truth. Yes, everything was as it had been two years ago. There were more pits – her own, the Louisa, the newest and largest of all – and more trenches dug for day levels, but these did no more than expand the scene; they did not alter it. Yet the place was no longer friendly. It was familiar still, but there was a savagery in that torn and bleeding landscape. And she could not close her eyes to the misery in the faces of the children as they descended into the depths of the mine. It was of no use for her father to say that they were different from other children, that they did not feel the hardship. She could not believe it. She had played with those children, with their sisters and brothers, and she knew that they were not different. She could not look into those hollowed eyes and believe that they did not suffer.

'How are you, Billy?' she asked, unable to put her feelings into words, unable even to express them to herself at this moment.

He grunted. 'Well enough. You've heard my father's been ill.'

'No!' She turned to Timothy. 'You never told me.'

Timothy shrugged and she understood that there had never been a time. Mining talk was forbidden at table or on their Sunday afternoon walks as a family, and when else did she and her father have opportunity? But Jacob had been mine captain for years; would it have been so amiss to have mentioned his illness?

'What was wrong? Is he better now?'

Billy grimaced. 'Better as he's likely to be. He's got consumption.'

'I'm sorry.' Louisa looked at him helplessly. Consumption was one of the scourges of the miners' cottages, running like wildfire through families during the damp, raw winters. Men coming to work on foggy mornings were often racked with coughs, and children commonly declined during their early years and died almost before they could walk.

When she had travelled about with her father, Louisa had frequently encountered the symptoms of the disease and had heard Dr Robinson talk of the conditions which encouraged it. Poor housing, he would say, and poor hygiene; together, they were killers. And the dank, suffocating air of the mines did not help. People must get out into the fresh air more, spend their Sundays in their gardens or on the hills, and then they would remain healthy.

But the Riggs lived well enough, in a dry cottage with plenty of garden produce to keep them fed. Louisa had been there many times, though not in the past two years, and she had seen the fire burning in the grate, with the pots simmering for Jacob's supper. She had seen his wife working in the garden with the children, even the youngest able to do some small task, and she had met them on Sundays out walking, their faces made rosy by sun and wind. Jacob should not have caught consumption.

'I'll call and see him,' she said to Billy. 'Is there anything he needs, anything I could take him?'

'Not much. He's not in his bed, he's about and talking of coming back to the mine soon.' The boy began to turn away. 'But he'll be pleased enough to see you. He often talks of you and the days when you came here regular.'

Louisa felt guilty, though it was not her fault that she had been unable to come. She felt as if Billy were reproaching her for her neglect. And perhaps that was how it seemed to him, for how was he to know?

Her father had moved away to talk to some of the other men. She reached out and touched Billy's sleeve.

'Billy, don't go. Tell me about the rest of the family. How are they all? How's the baby – little Tom? I haven't seen him for so long.'

'He's not the baby now.' Billy's voice was terse. 'There's been another since you were by, Miss Louisa. Lottie, we call her. And Tom took a knock on his head six months since and ha'n't been the same since.'

'Oh, Billy.' Louisa's eyes filled with tears. Tom had been the brightest of all the Rigg children, active and inquisitive even at a few weeks old, struggling to sit up, his eyes following his mother as she worked. Louisa had missed him more than anyone else when she had finally been banned from visiting the cottages as well as the mines, and had longed to see his progress and hold him in her arms. 'Did you ask the doctor to look at him?'

'With Father sick as well? Doctors cost money. Anyway, there's nowt to be done. He slept a bit when it happened and he walks a bit crooked now and don't talk so well, but he'll still be able to work in t'pit. And that's what matters, after all.'

The note of bitterness in his voice struck Louisa to the heart. She gazed at him, her helplessness increasing. What could she say to this boy who had once been her friend and now believed she had abandoned them? How could she make him understand?

And did it matter anyway whether he understood? With a sick father, a damaged brother and several others younger than he was, Billy was very nearly head of the family, breadwinner for them all. Did it matter what he thought of her?

Only to me, probably, Louisa told herself. But oh, I would like to take that anger from his voice and that tight bitterness from his mouth and eyes.

'I'll come and see you all,' she promised rashly. 'Soon.' There must be some way to escape from Susannah and the new governess, the third since Miss Barrow had gone. Surely now that Father had brought her here again he would not let her go back to the old regime. 'I'll not let them stop me coming again, Billy.'

But he was already turning away. The kibble was waiting, filled with men and boys, their picks and shovels in their hands; with no more than a nod he was gone, ready to start the day's work. Twelve hours below ground, with dusk falling as he came back to the surface. And in winter, never a sight of daylight from one Sunday to the next.

Louisa climbed back into the trap. She felt saddened by her visit, and wondered how she could have come so often in the past, so blithely, without seeing the reality that was before her eyes. I was too young to understand, she thought. I'd been coming ever since I was small, it all seemed normal to me then. But after a gap of two years . . .

176

Timothy swung himself up beside her and took up the reins. The trap moved away, back to the road.

'Well?' he asked after a few minutes. 'Is it good to be back at the mines?'

'In some ways. I know now just how much I've missed it all, even more than I'd thought. But,' she looked up at him, her dark blue eyes bright with tears, her lashes glistening, 'it doesn't seem right that people should have to work like that. All those children going down the mines. Jacob ill with consumption, little Tom hurt on the head.'

'That didn't happen in the mine. Children are getting hurt every day in their own cottages. It's nothing to do with mining.'

'But the cottages, they're so small and damp, it must be horrid to live in them. If—'

'They're no worse than any other workman's cottage.' Timothy was frowning. 'Louisa, you mustn't be sentimental. These people are different from us. They've always lived like this and they always will. What do you suppose would happen if we gave them better houses to live in, with good furniture? Would they appreciate it, take care of it? Of course not! It doesn't mean anything to them. Why, if they had such a simple piece of furniture as a washstand they would probably use it to store firewood!'

'That isn't fair!' Louisa exclaimed angrily. 'I've been in Jacob Rigg's cottage. It's tidy and clean, and they do have furniture. Probably even a washstand. They aren't savages, Papa.'

He glanced at her and inclined his head. 'No, I know. I'm sorry, Louisa. I was being flippant. But you must realise that Jacob and his wife are a better type of person than most of the miners. Whatever Susannah may say, I haven't let you mix with the rougher kind, and I'm afraid that's the kind most workmen, be they miners or other labourers, are. And many of them do live like savages. They know nothing better.'

Louisa was silent. She thought of the cottages she had known, the bright fires, the clean-swept hearths. Poor enough they were, and simply furnished, but comfortable in their rough way. She had thought that all the miners' cottages were like that.

Did they really live so badly? Jacob Rigg's family had always seemed healthy and strong to her, but the children she had seen this morning, packed into the kibble as if they were about to be boiled for some cannibals' feast – well, they hardly looked worth cooking! Thin, pinched faces, arms and legs like sticks; how did they have the strength to do the hard work she knew awaited them below ground? What kind of homes had they left, and what breakfast did they have inside them? Could it really be true that these things didn't matter so much to them?

They know nothing better. But how could they know better if never given the chance? And did it necessarily mean that they didn't suffer?

'Perhaps they *should* know something better,' she said suddenly. 'Perhaps if they earned more money—'

'It would be spent on drink. And how could they earn more money anyway? I pay them well enough for what they do.'

Do you? she thought. Is a few shillings an hour enough for a man, a woman or even a child to spend a lifetime tunnelling underground?

Only a year ago there had been slaves still working in the Lancashire mills not far away. Louisa herself, out for a drive with her stepmother, had seen a shipload disembarking at Greenodd, bound for the rich houses in the Lake District, and she remembered Jane and Martha's excitement and how Susannah had ordered the carriage to stop so that they could watch the black men and boys shamble in chains down the gangway. Her two stepsisters had talked of little else for days and Susannah had demanded a blackamoor of her own to parade before her

178

friends, a demand that Timothy, to Louisa's relief, had utterly refused.

'Slavery's finished in this country, and about time too,' he declared roundly. 'It'll be against the law in a few months and what do we do with our blackamoor then? Turn him out to fend for himself on the streets? That's what's going to happen to most of these poor unfortunates, mark my words.'

And he had been right, for slavery had been abolished very soon after that last shipload, and although some of the longer established slaves had learned to be useful servants, many more were turned out to roam city streets or drift towards the docks, perhaps with a last faint hope of finding their way home again.

At least the miners were free, Louisa thought as the trap turned homeward. They had their own homes, however poor, and they had money in their pockets, however little. They could choose other work if they desired, and other places to live. They didn't have to stay here and be little more than slaves.

They were back on the moor road again, heading towards the mountains which stretched before them from east to west on the horizon. Louisa knew a good many of their names – the Old Man of Coniston, the Langdale Pikes, Helvellyn. She had walked with her father on the fells of High Furness, revelling in the wildness of it, longing to explore further, and he had promised her that one day they would. She turned to him now, her face suddenly alive.

'Can we go for a really long walk, Papa? Somewhere far away, somewhere near Grasmere or Keswick? It's so long since we've done anything like that and we always said we would.'

Timothy looked at her and smiled. 'There isn't time now. Your stepmother will be home by teatime and I promised—'

'Not today. Sometime soon. We could leave early in

179

the morning, take all day.' Her voice was eager, she was a child again, the miners forgotten. Impulsively, she laid her hand on his sleeve, looking up into his face. 'Please, Papa.'

Timothy stared at her. The lane they were travelling was a quiet one, off the route taken by the carts of ore. Its surface was dry and the banks of the hedgerows grassy and pink with willowherb. Beside them, a stream ran down a narrow gorge and ahead was a small pack-horse bridge with a space of grass where camp could be made.

With one hand on the reins, Timothy checked the horse. The trap stopped at one side of the road and the horse began to crop the grass. The clouds had almost all dispersed now, letting sunlight through, and it was warm down here in the hollow, out of the unseasonable wind.

Louisa sat very still. Her heart was beating quickly, though she did not know why. Her hand was still lying on her father's arm; she looked at it but did not take it away.

She had not felt so close to him for over two years. She had been starved of the warmth and affection there had been between them, and she knew that it was Susannah's fault. Susannah had come between them, had through her jealousy kept them apart. Susannah hated her, and Louisa knew and returned that hate. But nothing had happened to the love between her and her father. Being together today, doing all the things they had been used to doing together, had shown her – shown him too, surely – that nothing Susannah had done, nothing Susannah could do, could really harm them. And now that they had rediscovered their closeness, surely he wouldn't allow it to be lost again.

She raised her eyes to his, saw in them the strange darkening that told her he must be thinking the same.

'Oh Papa,' she said in a trembling voice, 'why can't it always be like this?'

Timothy covered her hand with his. He, too, was very still. And then he lifted his fingers and touched her cheek.

'Margaret . . .' he said in a low voice. 'You could be Margaret, sitting there . . .' And his hand cupped her cheek and lifted her face towards his.

The kiss was not like one Louisa had ever known before. His lips touched hers gently, delicately, at first, little more than a brushing movement from side to side. Almost without knowing it, she let her own lips part a little and then felt the tip of his tongue flick against the inner skin, graze lightly against her teeth and then insert itself into her mouth, touching her own tongue, playing with it, teasing it a little . . .

Louisa's head swam. A surge of sensation, of thoughts, of feelings, swept through her body. She wanted to draw back, yet could not. She wanted the kiss, yet her soul cried out against it. She lifted her hand, meaning to push him away, and found herself touching his hair, stroking it.

Timothy groaned, a deep groan that she could feel throbbing through his body, vibrating against hers. And then the kiss changed, became harsh, passionate, demanding, and his hands were hard and tight on her body, his arms crushing her, and she felt fear invade her and struggled against him, trying to turn her head, trying to cry out against that assaulting mouth. It was no longer the kiss of a father, nor ever had been; she understood, instinctively, that this was the kiss of a lover, that the desperate yearning she heard in her father's groan and felt in his crushing body was the result of a different kind of loss and deprivation from that which she had known. A deprivation she feared but could not yet understand.

Timothy bent his head to kiss her neck, to push away the bodice that covered her shoulders, to reach down for her newly budding breasts. Her mouth was free at last but shock caught her throat and for a moment she still could not speak.

'Papa! No, *please*!'

He was still at once. For a moment they were both frozen in the horror of what was happening. And then he lifted his head and stared at her.

'My God, Louisa. What have I done?'

She wanted to reach out to him, to comfort him, to reassure him. But she dared not touch him, dared not let her fingers near him again. Instead, shuddering, she withdrew into the furthest corner of the seat, gazing at him with eyes that were dark and troubled in a whitened face. Her hair was dishevelled, her bodice pulled open, and she put up trembling fingers to draw it together. Tears spilled from her eyes and ran scalding hot down her icy cheeks.

Timothy half lifted a hand, then let it drop again. His eyes were black, his mouth slack. He shook his head once or twice, as if to clear it, wiped his mouth with a hand that shook, turned away. He picked up the reins, then let them drop. He turned back at last, and reached out for Louisa's hand, but she drew sharply back.

'No,' she whispered, 'don't touch me again. Not yet . . . Oh, Papa . . .'

'What have I done?' he asked again, still in that low voice filled with terrible desolation. 'Louisa, my dear, dear child, what have I done?'

But she could not answer him. She did not know what he had done, did not know how much of it was her own fault. If she had not touched him so, not let her hand lie on his sleeve, not looked at him in that way . . .

And what had happened, after all? Why did it feel so wrong?

They had never gone out alone since that day. Never driven to the mines, never had their long walk on the fells. They had never even stayed long alone in the same room.

From that afternoon, her father had withdrawn from her and she knew that it must be because he blamed her for what had happened. I must be a bad person, she thought over and over again. A really, truly bad person. It's inside me, part of me, and can't be changed. All I can do is not let it happen again – not let it be possible to happen again.

And when Timothy, with pleading, sorry eyes, approached her, when his hand touched her hair or his lips moved against her cheek in one of his duty kisses, Louisa would move away, her glance cool, her face averted. If she was bad, if it was something she could cause by looking at him, touching him, speaking to him, then she would not do those things again. She would not look at him. She would not touch him. She would not even speak to him unless there were others present and it could be seen to be innocent.

And she would not think about it. She would push it to the back of her mind as an unpleasant animal, a rat or a snake might be pushed into a cage and thrust hard against it if it ever dared to rear its head again.

After that, quite quickly it seemed, her father lost interest anyway, and she wondered if after all she had imagined the whole thing. Perhaps they had never gone out on the moor that day, never visited the mine, never seen the kibble full of little children. Perhaps she had never talked to Billy and heard about Jacob and little Tom. Perhaps it had all been a dream.

Certainly, Timothy never referred to it. And from that day, Louisa detected a change in his attitude to his wife. He was conciliatory where once he had been sharp, his words were soft when once they might have been abrupt. It was as if he was trying to make up whatever quarrel there had been between them, as if he was trying to prove to Susannah, perhaps to Louisa too, that their marriage was normal and happy. It was only a few months later that Susannah had begun to show signs of her pregnancy.

But the pregnancy did not seem to have been welcomed, at least by Susannah, and the months in between had been difficult for them all. And now, on a sultry August day with the throbbing air filled with the threat of thunder, the baby was being born and Susannah, perhaps, about to die.

And then what? Louisa wondered. With two spoiled stepsisters and a baby in the house, who would even notice her?

It was at that moment that she heard the first low rumble of the earthquake and felt the trembling of the earth beneath her.

Chapter Eleven

There were only a few small roof falls in the mines on the day that Walter was born, and no collapse of the high, deep ginnels or the great empty caverns left by the digging out of a sop. The earthquake had been much deeper underground than these, although it had been felt as far away as Broughton-in-Furness and perhaps further than that. Two or three pit props, already shaky, cracked and had to be replaced, and possibly some of the disused tunnels, in levels never visited now, might have caved in. But little more. All the same, it had been very frightening down there.

The earth tremor stopped everyone. Underground, it was loud, its rumble growing to a roar and filling the dark, foetid passages with its threatening growl. Rock and earth shook all around, and each man put out his hands, partly as if to ward off the trembling walls, partly for support. Some of the girls and women screamed and the small children squealed in terror and clung to each other.

Billy Rigg had moved on from hurrying. He was among the men now, hacking at the ore and dumping it in trucks for the hurriers to push or drag to the bottom of the shaft. They had chains fastened round their waists and down their thighs to their knees, so that each movement took the weight of the truck. Some of the older children were strong enough to drag it alone, but mostly they worked in groups, one in front taking the strain and the rest shoving from behind.

Pieces of ore and rock fell from the roof in some places. One of the pieces hit Billy Rigg on the head. He wasn't killed but, like his little brother Tom, he would never be quite the same again.

There was no other damage.

'Well, you've got your son,' Susannah said, when Timothy was at last admitted to see her. 'I hope you're satisfied.'

She was lying in the big bed, pale and flat, and her voice was thin. Her damp hair straggled around her face, her eyes were dark hollows of exhaustion.

Timothy looked at her and felt a strange mixture of emotions. There was shame, for hadn't he deliberately brought her to this state, deliberately risked her life? There was concern, for Dr Robinson had told him she was not yet out of danger and although he knew now there was no love or even affection between himself and Susannah, he did not want to see her die. And she was, from today, the mother of his son, and that thought brought further strange emotion.

He looked into the crib where the baby lay sleeping. He was a good weight, the doctor said, in spite of Susannah's difficult pregnancy, and there was no reason why he shouldn't thrive. But to Timothy, who had not seen a newborn baby for fifteen years, he looked frighteningly small, his face squashed and red. He had dark hair, curling with damp, and his head, turned sideways on the little lace pillow, looked slightly elongated.

'Pretty, isn't he?' Susannah said bitterly. 'All those months to be endured, just to bring forth a monster.'

Her words kicked at Timothy's heart. A monster! How could a mother describe her own baby so?

'He's not a monster. All newborn babies look a little crumpled. He's had a hard time too.'

'He's given *me* a hard time.' Susannah sounded as though the baby had done it deliberately. 'And he looks more than *crumpled*, Timothy. Look at him properly. Look at his head.' She turned her face away, as if in disgust.

Timothy stared at her, still feeling the shock of her reaction. Then he reached a tentative hand into the crib, cupped it under the baby's head and lifted it gently from the pillow. And felt what she meant in the split second before he saw it.

The head was more than elongated. It was misshapen, uneven, with ugly bulges. Over the right ear, the skull was distorted to a heavy lump almost half the size of the head itself, and on the left side was a similar, but smaller, distortion.

There was no disguising it. The head was deformed.

Timothy's heart sank. This, then, was to be his punishment. Not merely the years of loneliness that stretched ahead, not just the misery of living with a woman who despised him, but this – this grotesque creation, this travesty of a child.

This was what happened when you used the act of love for revenge. This was retribution in its most devastating form.

Dr Robinson was out of the room and the midwife was busy in the dressing room leading off the main bedroom, which was to be a night nursery. Timothy stared at the baby, then at his wife.

'The doctor didn't mention any damage. What's caused it?'

'Who knows?' She sounded as though she didn't care, he thought. But perhaps that was just because she was tired, exhausted by her ordeal. And he felt a sudden, unexpected tenderness for her. She had, after all, just borne his child, and the disappointment was as great for her as for him.

'Susannah,' he said gently, 'don't fret about it. Just

187

sleep now. I'll talk to the doctor and see what is to be done.'

Her eyelids, which had been drooping, flew open. 'Done? There's nothing to be done. It's God's will, a judgement on us. A judgement on *you*.' Her voice gathered a strange, frenetic strength. 'You forced this child on me, Timothy, and look at what you've made. A monster, a *gargoyle*. It will be an idiot, there to remind us all its life – to remind *me*.' The two red spots were burning in her white face as they always did when she became angry, and she half raised herself on one elbow and pointed a shaking finger at him. 'You'll regret this for the rest of your life, Timothy Sherwin. What you've done to me, to him, will follow you to your grave – yes, and beyond.' Her voice rose shrilly, the eyes she fixed on him were wild and burning. '*The sins of the fathers will be visited on the children, yea, even unto the third and fourth generations*. Your sins will be visited on your children, Timothy, and on your grandchildren's children, and bad cess to you all!'

Timothy recoiled. Her voice had risen to an eldritch screech such as he had never heard before. It went on and on, a shriek that rose and fell as if it had taken on a life of its own, as if it no longer came from a human throat but issued instead from the depths of some unnatural being, a she-demon, malevolence incarnate. It pierced his mind and drove black fear deep into his heart.

This was more than the feverish raving of a woman who had only just survived a terrible ordeal, more than the natural grief and disappointment of a mother who finds her child imperfect. Susannah, who had never wanted another child, who had submitted to him only out of wifely 'duty' and not submitted at all during those last guilt-ridden encounters, had become something different. It was as if she were calling up supernatural powers, drawing them to her aid, using them to inflict on him all the damage she could conceive in revenge for the conception he had forced upon her and which had been his own revenge.

She was laying a curse on him.

Half mesmerised, he backed away from the bed while Susannah reared up, her distorted mouth screaming words he had never thought to hear from his wife, words he would not have thought she knew. They came pouring from those twisted lips and the baby woke in the crib beside the bed and began to cry, a thin, keening lament. There was a flurry as the midwife rushed in from the dressing room.

'What's goin' on here?' She caught Susannah by the shoulders, forcing her to lie back on the bed. 'Be still now, you'll do yourself an injury carryin' on that way.' Holding the panting figure still, she looked over her shoulder at Timothy. 'What started her off like this, sir?'

Timothy passed a shaking hand across his brow. He was trembling and feeling sick. 'I think she's upset over the baby.' The words sounded inane, trivial, after the horror of Susannah's outburst.

'Upset? Why? He's a fine lad.'

Susannah was sobbing now, harsh ugly sobs that tore her body. The midwife held her firmly. 'Calm yourself, madam. You've no call to carry on like this. You've got a lovely baby, bonny as ever I saw.'

'Bonny?' Timothy felt outraged, as if something vital had been ignored, counted as of no importance. 'Have you see his head?'

The midwife gave him a look, as if to comment on the stupidity of such a question. 'Aye, I've seen it.'

'Well? What do you have to say about that? Is that bonny?'

'Sir, there's no call to fret—'

'No call to fret? When our child's born deformed, and in the most grotesque way? When it's obvious he's going to be an idiot—'

'You don't know that, Mr Sherwin—'

'How can he be otherwise, born so misshapen? Perhaps my wife's right, perhaps it is a judgement on us.' He paced to the cot and stared down. The baby was sleeping again, his eyes tightly closed, long dark lashes fanned out over the red cheeks. From this angle, he looked perfectly normal, no more squashed than any other baby. It seemed to make the reality all the more tragic.

Susannah's bout of hysteria seemed to cease almost as suddenly as it had begun. Exhausted, she stopped sobbing and thrashing in the bed and lay still, shuddering. Her eyes closed.

The midwife soothed her into sleep and came to stand beside Timothy and look into the crib. She touched the baby's chin with the tip of one forefinger and his mouth began to move at once, in a sucking motion.

'You see? There's nothing wrong with him at all. He knows what he's supposed to do.' She sighed. 'I'd have liked to put him to the breast straightaway, but madam wouldn't have it. We'll try again when she wakes up – she needs her sleep now.'

'But his head—'

The door opened and the doctor came back into the room. Timothy turned to him with some relief. 'Look, I want the truth. What's the matter with my son? What's caused this deformity?'

The doctor cast a quick look at the bed and drew Timothy over to the window. There, with the August afternoon drawing towards an evening as sultry as the afternoon had been, they looked out towards the green hills with their gashed mines and the silhouettes of gin and jackroll on the skyline. The sky was heavy, the clouds that had been thickening all day now forming giant thunderheads; the dying sun coloured them copper and a brooding silence hung in the air as if the earth tremors of the afternoon were only the beginning of some cataclysmic upheaval.

'I don't believe there is anything seriously wrong with the baby,' the old doctor said quietly. 'This misshaping of the head happens sometimes. The bones slip about to make the birth easier.' He demonstrated with his hands, holding one over the other and sliding them back and forth. 'Sometimes they get rather more pushed about than they should and it just takes longer for them to return to normal. I've seen it before, once or twice.'

Timothy looked doubtfully at him. 'And you know this to be the case? It couldn't be any worse damage?'

The doctor hesitated. 'Well, I can't say for certain. He'll need watching for a few weeks, and we shan't really know until he begins to develop – sitting up, walking, talking. By about three or four years old we should be able to tell—'

'Three or fours *years*? But you can see the state my wife's in!'

'There's nothing I can do about it. There's no way of telling whether the brain's been damaged, apart from waiting.' Dr Robinson glanced across towards the bed where Susannah now slept. 'Your wife has had a difficult pregnancy and a bad labour. She naturally feels exhausted now, and she'll need care. But once she recovers from her first shock . . . She's the child's mother, Timothy. She can't help but have normal maternal feelings for him, whatever his condition. In fact, she'll probably devote more attention to him rather than less.'

Timothy said nothing. He gave Susannah and the baby one more glance, then took the doctor down to the library and poured them both a glass of whisky. They drank together, making abstracted, desultory talk, avoiding all further mention of the baby, and then Dr Robinson rose and took his leave.

'Remember what I said. Mrs Sherwin will soon recover her spirits and the baby's head will almost certainly be quite normal within a few weeks. As for his

191

future development, as I said, we shall have to wait and see but I feel quite confident that there will be no permanent damage.'

As he went out to his pony and trap, the first rumble of thunder sounded and a few heavy drops of rain fell from the lowering clouds. The two men looked up at the sky.

'Well, this should freshen things up,' Dr Robinson remarked. 'Make everyone feel better. And we haven't had any repetition of the earth tremors. I wonder if there was any damage caused anywhere.'

'My mine captain came to see me while you were busy with my wife,' Timothy said. 'There were a few rock falls, nothing serious. One or two minor injuries. No more than that below ground, at least in my pits. A good deal of hysteria in the kitchens, I gather.'

'Well, we don't have many earthquakes in these parts.' Dr Robinson smiled and held out his hand. 'Goodnight, Timothy. And congratulations on a fine, healthy son.'

Timothy watched him go and then went back indoors. The doctor's last words sounded in his head. A fine healthy son. Was that really what he had? The son he had dreamed of, longed for, the son who would follow him in the business, make the name of Sherwin known and respected throughout the mining industry?

Or would the baby who lay sleeping upstairs turn out to be the monster that Susannah had called him? A simple-minded deformity, living testimony to Susannah's hatred and her curse?

The storm raged through the night, filling the air with blinding flashes of lightning and the furious crash of thunder. Louisa sat at her window for a long time, watching it. She saw the whole sky split by a jagged pattern of white light, counted the seconds – one, two, three – before the thunder broke, and knew the storm must be very close indeed. The next time it was closer still, and the third brilliant splintering of the sky was accompanied by a simultaneous explosion that seemed to shake the house.

Louisa jumped. Surely something must have been struck! She glanced nervously about her, but the room seemed normal and there was no sound from the rest of the house. Some of the maids, she knew, would be down in the kitchen, cowering under the stairs. She looked out of the window again and saw a tree on fire, over on the side of the hill.

It was like a torch, blazing gold against the dark, tumultuous sky, and even the rain that was falling so heavily seemed powerless to put it out. Louisa watched, fascinated, and then thought of the baby upstairs. What effect might it have on him, being born during an earthquake and with such a thunderstorm to welcome his first few hours?

She had not yet seen her new half-brother, and neither had Jane or Martha. The baby needed sleep, they had been told, and although Martha had pouted and sulked and promised complete silence, Timothy had been adamant. Both Susannah and the baby needed complete rest and nobody was to be allowed near them until he gave the word.

'It's not fair,' Martha said. 'I wanted to pick him up and change his clothes.'

'He's not a toy,' Jane told her sharply. She seemed least interested in the new arrival and had treated her mother's pregnancy with a disapproval that bordered on disgust, though the disgust had been aimed at Timothy rather than Susannah. 'Anyway, you'll have plenty of chances. He's going to be here a long time.'

'You don't think there's anything wrong with him, do you?' Martha asked. 'Papa looks very anxious.'

Louisa had noticed that too but attributed it to the earth tremors which had frightened everyone. An earthquake, they were calling it, though no great cracks had opened in the ground and no houses had tumbled in a heap of stone and dust. But everyone had their story to tell, from one of the kitchenmaids who had been in the act of lifting a kettle of boiling water from the range and spilt some of it, scalding her foot, to the stable lad who had found the horses panicking in the stables and, in trying to soothe them, had been kicked sharply about the body and had three ribs broken. But not many people, it seemed, had been hurt, even in the mines for which Louisa – and surely her father too – had felt most fear.

Sitting on the rim of the little valley, clutching at the earth that rocked beneath her, she had thought at once of the mines, of the people working deep below. She had thought that the shaking and rumbling must be mines collapsing, vast caverns caving in, tunnels crushed beneath the weight of splintering rock. In her mind, she had seen horrific pictures of men smashed to a pulp, their torn flesh and blood mingling with the red slurry of the pits; of women and children choking and suffocated by rock and dust and thick, glutinous mud.

She remembered nothing of her flight away from the valley, back across the moor to the mines. But when she reached the pithead of her own mine, the Louisa, she had found a knot of people at the top of the shaft and had thrust her way through them.

'What's happened? Was there an explosion?'

The men and women, their faces streaked and grimy with red mud, looked round at her.

'Nay, 'tis nowt to do with t'mines,' one of them said. 'Not unless it was summat over at Lindal. But nowt much has happened here, only young Billy took a knock.'

'Billy? Billy Rigg?'

'Aye, they're bringin' him up now.' The man nodded to where a kibble was rising slowly to the surface. Louisa

pushed her way over and saw three men inside support-
ing a limp body. She looked at the grey face, at the blood
already caking on Billy's head, and caught her breath.

'Is he – is he dead?'

One of the men with him shook his head and stepped
out of the kibble. Together, the three of them lifted Billy
out and laid him on the grass.

'Bit of rock fell on him, but he's breathing still. We'd
best get him home.'

Louisa watched as they brought a field gate and laid
Billy on it. His face was devoid of all colour, a trickle of
congealed blood standing out in dark red clots. His
breathing was heavy and laboured.

'Oh, poor Billy.' She leaned over him, touching his
head with gentle fingers, stroking back the hair. 'Will he
be all right?'

'Happen he will. It were a tidy knock, but folk have
got over worse. Bit of a headache for a day or two and
he'll be right as rain, likely.' The men lifted the gate and
bore it away. Louisa followed, not knowing what else to
do; simply to have gone home would have been unthink-
able. But there had been nothing for her to do at the
cottage. Although Carrie Rigg already had her hands full
with looking after her sick husband Jacob and the rest of
the family, there were neighbours and friends in plenty,
gathering round to offer sympathy and advice. Anxious
and helpless, Louisa had come home, forgetting that she
was supposed to be with Mrs Alcott at Tytup. But for
once, nobody had noticed. Her brother Walter had just
been born and the household was in a flurry of delight,
pleasure, and a lingering fear that the earthquake might
strike again.

Louisa stared out of the window into the night, watching
the tree burn like a torch against the backcloth of black sky
ripped apart by searing white flashes. The thunder was all
around now; each separate clap merged into the next to
form one long, continuous reverberation, like giant drums

195

being beaten somewhere in the clouds. She thought of the baby again, and then of Billy Rigg, wondering if he had woken up yet, if he knew what had happened. If he knew why it had happened.

It wasn't anyone's fault that Billy Rigg had been knocked on the head by a lump of rock. It was what they called an 'act of God', which Louisa supposed meant a punishment of some sort.

But why should Billy Rigg be punished when he had done nothing wrong? And why should those who had done wrong go unscathed?

Perhaps Billy had committed some sin during his short life. Perhaps his punishment was, in the eyes of God, justified. And perhaps her punishment, too, would come, her punishment for whatever she had done that had caused her father to commit his own sin.

She looked out at the sky and saw a web of lightning crack it in a hundred places. As the thunder crashed about her ears, she saw all their sins like that web of lightning, one leading from another, mingling and entwining so that no one could be free of them; each followed inexorably, inescapably, by its own dread punishment, as the lightning itself was followed by the thunder that crashed and echoed about the splitting sky.

There's no escape for any of us, she thought with a dark sense of doom. Not for Billy Rigg, not for Papa, not for myself. Not even for that baby upstairs, so tiny and new. Even for him, who had as yet committed no sins at all, punishment would come.

In the days that followed Walter's birth, Louisa was allowed more freedom. Without the mistress up and about the house, likely to appear at any moment, there was a sense of holiday. The servants seemed to relax and Louisa found herself welcome in the kitchen, as she had been before her stepmother had frowned upon such 'hob-nobbing'. The new governess, too, was more lenient and Jane and Martha disappeared on escapades of their own, without bothering about how Louisa was spending her days.

Jane, at seventeen, was fast becoming a young lady. Her hair was 'up' almost all the time now and she was beginning to curl her lip at the idea of lessons. During Susannah's pregnancy she had begun to spend her afternoons with her mother, sitting with her in the drawing room reading or sewing. It seemed unlikely that she would return to lessons now that the baby was born; she talked of clothes and dances and parties, even possible husbands. Childhood, for Jane, was over, and she was glad of it.

Martha, as always, followed her sister like a puppy, poring with her over fashion plates and practising the latest dance steps. Miss Creary, the governess, encouraged them in this; she was interested in fashion herself and although only possessed of two day dresses and one for evenings, she was constantly finding little ways of decorating them. Her last position had been with a family who held and attended a good many dances, so she knew all the most recent styles.

Louisa scorned such activities. She would rather be out in the open air, walking the hills or down on the sands. And now Jane and Martha, as if tired of tormenting her, took little notice of what she did.

'After all,' Jane observed one day, 'having accomplishments and being pretty isn't important to you. You don't want to get married, do you?'

'How do you know that?' Louisa said at once, though Jane's words were true enough. 'I expect I shall find a husband just as good as yours. That's if you find one at all.'

'I shan't have to look,' Jane said with dignity. 'Mamma will find me one, and he'll be the most eligible man in the area.'

'I shall find my own husband,' Louisa retorted. 'And

197

he will be the most eligible man in the area.'

'And how will you do that, without being able to dance?' Jane sneered.

Louisa did not reply. She had no intention of learning to dance with her two stepsisters, but she had watched them both at their lessons and practised the movements secretly by herself. She felt quite sure that she would be able to dance perfectly well with a partner. As for the other 'accomplishments', she could play the piano as well as either of the other two girls, had a pleasant enough singing voice and enjoyed painting. Often now, on her rambles over the hills, she took her sketchbook and sat for hours drawing.

One of her favourite places was Dunnerholme where the old quarries had made a grassy promontory of green hillocks and little valleys; she could look north towards the mountains of Westmorland and west over the Duddon estuary towards Millom and Black Combe. Here, with the sea washing the foot of the low cliffs, she could sit with her father's telescope and watch the birds feeding at the water's edge: orange-billed oyster catchers stylish as a gentleman dressed for the evening with their black and white plumage; redshanks, long-legged and gawky; and sometimes, darkening the sky as they flew overhead, great flocks of migrating geese.

She loved to sketch the rippling sands with their channels of water flowing out towards the sea, a constantly changing pattern of light, colour and movement, the sands sometimes a subtle shading of fawns and pale sunlit browns, sometimes a deep burnished glow of umber. The clouds above were reflected in the shimmering wet of an outgoing tide so that the whole estuary looked as if the world had turned upside down; while later the sands would dry out and lose their shine, their ripples matt and roughened like the paper used to smooth wood. And on a windy day the finest of the sand would blow like a storm in the desert.

Louisa took out her sketching things as often as possible during those first few weeks after Walter's birth. With autumn fast approaching, she knew that there would not be many more days when the weather was fit to sit outside, and she meant to make the most of this short period of freedom. For it would be short, she was certain of that. Susannah would not allow her to roam about like this once she was fully recovered.

The tide was falling as she came along the firm, wet sands, the edges of the rippling waves clustered with wading birds probing with long bills for shellfish and worms. Across the estuary, at the foot of Black Combe, the masts of the schooners being built in Postlethwaite's shipyard made a tracery of black against the bronze of dying bracken and, although at sea level the air was still, a high wind feathered the sky with thin wafting clouds and the sun's rays were blurred and softened by the haze.

Louisa settled herself on her favourite rock and began to draw. In the past few months she had grown more and more absorbed in this new pastime, using it at first as an excuse to wander the countryside alone – sketching was an acceptable 'accomplishment' – and then finding it a pleasure for its own sake. There was a peculiar joy in setting her favourite scenes on paper or canvas, a further delight in continuing the work at home when she might otherwise be expected to be sewing or reading aloud to her stepmother, both of which she heartily disliked.

Now, from being a pleasant hobby, sketching and painting had become a demanding taskmaster and today she was trying without much success to convey to her canvas that precise quality of light that came from sunshine diffused through high, gauzy clouds. It was made more difficult by the fact that the sands were drying out rapidly, their sheen disappearing as she watched so that it was never possible to compare her efforts with the scene now before her. But the attempt

199

was a challenge rather than a frustration and Louisa lost herself in concentration, seeing nothing but the shifting fawns and buffs of the rippled sands, the dying blue of the receding tide and the gossamer wisps of cloud.

There were, as always, people down on the sands. They dug for bait to go fishing, collecting ragworm, lugworm and other wriggling creatures in pails for the fishing expeditions that kept many a mining family fed. Others searched for cockles or hunted at the water's edge for crabs. And some were already setting out on the trek across the sands, so much shorter than going round the long coast through Kirkby and Foxfield, but also much more dangerous.

Louisa worked steadily, hardly aware of time passing. The tide was disappearing fast and she wanted to catch that last glimmer of light on wet sand. Much of the background could be finished at home, or on another day; but the light would never again be of quite this quality, quite this ethereal faintness. And if she didn't capture it on canvas, how could she recall it in years to come? How would she ever know how it had been?

The last brush stroke was done. The light had changed, deepened with the late afternoon. The sands were now burnished with pale gold deepening to ochre and a soft auburn where the clouds cast shadows over the web of trickling channels. The sun, low in the sky, was a hazy orb of copper and the feathered clouds were tinted with soft apricot.

Louisa laid her brush gently down and sat still, gazing at the scene before her. She watched as the people on the sands began to make their way back towards the shore. A trail of carts, crossing the sands from Foxfield, caught her eye. Curiously, she watched them, aware that they were not the common carts of the local cockle fishers or farmers. They were piled high with what looked like goods, yet they did not look like pedlars or tinkers. And yet they were familiar . . .

The travellers! Her heart leapt. Surely they were the travellers, the gipsies, unaccountably absent for the last two summers. The horse-dealers and fortune-tellers, the fairground showmen, colourful as peacocks, wild and free as deer.

Scarth and his people.

Kieran.

She was half on her feet, her eyes fixed on those carts that came slowly, so slowly, across the sands. A few riders came on ahead and she lifted the telescope to see if she could recognise anyone. But as yet they were too far away and she lowered the instrument in frustration. Travellers they certainly were, but were they the ones she knew? Was Kieran among them?

Louisa sat down again on her rock, biting her forefinger. Her heart was beating quickly and she felt slightly sick. Would Kieran remember the girl with whom he had roamed the hills? Would he care? She was no longer the Louisa she had been then, little more than a child. And Kieran must be almost a man by now.

Feeling suddenly depressed, Louisa began to gather her things together. Memories of that summer three years ago came crowding in, with all their warmth and laughter, and she felt their loss more keenly than ever. Each year she had waited, hoping for the gipsies to return, and each year she had been disappointed. She felt a despondent certainty that this would be yet another such false expectation. And even if they did come, if Kieran should be once more waiting for her at the top of the valley, his dark eyes alight and burning, what use would it be? He was a gipsy, after all, here today and gone tomorrow. He could never be of any real importance in her life.

A dark cloud had crept up unnoticed from behind Black Combe and covered the sun. The warmth had gone from the afternoon and Louisa shivered. She pulled her shawl round her shoulders and started to walk back across the dunes to the road, to begin the climb over the moor.

She would no longer think about the travellers and Kieran. They were part of her past, nothing to do with the present, even less with the future. A childhood game, no more.

Louisa sighed. In spite of her resistance, she knew that her childhood must pass, and pass soon. She had no wish to emulate Jane, but neither did she want to remain a child like Martha. Not that I ever was a child like Martha, she thought with brief humour.

In the past few months, her body had told her that more and more clearly. First, the slow swelling of her breasts, now softly rounded so that Susannah had commented acidly one day that she would need no bust improver sewn into her dresses. The tone had made Louisa feel that she was somehow at fault in this, perhaps because Jane, stick-like and gawky, had had these contrivances sewn into every dress she possessed and made it seem a virtue; however, since the end result appeared the same, Louisa found it difficult to understand why the artificial shape should be preferable to the natural one. Perhaps there was something sinful about a body that grew so wilfully. With shame, Louisa would recall that day when her father had thrust aside her bodice and laid his lips on her breasts. If they had not then been already budding, would he have done such a thing?

It was only a few weeks after that that Louisa had seen the first show of blood that marked the biggest step of all on her journey into womanhood. She had woken to it one morning, finding the sheets stained, and had gazed in horror and fear. Was she ill? Had she been injured in some way while she slept? She felt heavy-eyed and sluggish, and her back ached. She must be ill, perhaps dangerously ill.

Yet with the fear came a shame of the same kind she felt when she remembered that afternoon with her father. It seemed in some way connected, as if this were the punishment she had been waiting for, the retribution for her sin. That must be the answer, she thought, still half dazed with sleep, her head throbbing. I am to bleed to death and nobody will know why.

She heard the other girls get up and knew that she ought to follow them. She would be expected at breakfast, there would be trouble if she was late. But I'm dying, she thought. Surely they won't be angry with me when they know I'm dying.

For several minutes she lay there, feeling the blood seeping from her body, wondering what to do and knowing that if she got up the bleeding would increase, would flow so quickly that she would not be able to go downstairs at all.

The door opened and Tilly, the maid who had looked after her before Susannah's arrival, came in. She looked at her and frowned.

'What's to do? Poorly, are you?'

'Oh, Tilly,' Louisa whispered, with tears coming into her eyes, 'I think I'm dying. Look.' And she pulled back the bedcovers.

Tilly glanced down and grinned. 'Dying? Nay, Miss Louie, you're not dying. That's just your monthlies, that is, and a fine mess you've made with 'em and all. Here, let me show you what to do.'

Since then, Louisa had grown reluctantly accustomed to the bleeding that took place every month. She had learned to reckon the date on which it was likely to begin and knew how to prepare for it. She knew that she must use the strips of folded linen kept in a drawer for the purpose, and that they would be washed, ironed, aired and put back ready for next time. She knew that the bleeding would last for about five days and during that time she must not bathe, wash her hair, go barefoot or take any risk of catching cold. She knew that this burden would be hers probably for the rest of her life.

'Doesn't happen once you're old,' Tilly had told her. 'But how many of us has the chance to get old? Or even wants to?' And Louisa, although still half believing that she was somehow immune from age, agreed.

All the same, she couldn't ignore the fact that she was growing up, nor the strange, restless sensations she was beginning to experience, sensations that she could not identify or understand but which brought their own peculiar shame. She felt awkward and self-conscious, certain that everyone was watching her, that everyone *knew* . . . But what it was that they knew, she had no idea.

It was as if some deep reservoir of emotion had lain hidden all her life and, in the past few months, begun to well up, bewildering her with its intensity. It took her by surprise on soft summer mornings when she woke with the dawn and lay listening to birdsong in the garden; it caught her unaware at sunset when the sky turned auburn and then deepened to indigo, with the first stars making tiny bright pinholes in the gathering darkness. It prowled through her body like a hungry animal and left her filled with a yearning she could not understand.

What were they, these feelings that sometimes lifted her up with elation, the certainty that just round the corner something wonderful was waiting, and at other times weighed her down with the gloomy conviction that nothing good would ever happen, that she would live her whole life like this, caged, restricted at every turn? At those times, heavy with a sense of impending doom, she would sit for hours in her bedroom, staring out of the window and seeing nothing but bleakness in the landscape she had so much loved.

As always, she was happiest alone, out of doors, away

from the mocking eyes of her stepsisters and the disapproval of her stepmother. Away, most of all, from the constraint between herself and her father.

The air had grown cold now as she climbed the steep, rutted track onto the moor. The slaters had already gone and the road was quiet; she was almost halfway up when she became aware of someone coming down.

She could not yet see him over the low stone walls that bordered the track, but the sound of his horse's hooves on the metalled way came clearly through the dusk. Someone taking the moor road over to Askam, probably, or perhaps some pedlar looking for a sheltered spot to spend the night. She could hear the sound of boots as well, so whoever it might be was leading his horse, perhaps because it was already heavily laden.

The track curved up between the walls. At the next bend, she would see him. She could hear the clop of the hooves quite close now. And another sound: a man's voice, talking softly to the beast, encouraging it down the rough, rocky track. A deep voice, warm as velvet but with a hint of roughness, like gravel. Not a voice she knew, nor a local accent. A pedlar, then. But not, from the sound of that soft, gentling voice, someone she need be afraid of.

They rounded the bend together, Louisa and the man with the horse. And stopped simultaneously, staring.

He was taller than she remembered, grown in the past three years. His body, sturdy enough then, had filled out so that he was almost as big now as Scarth. But his dark hair curled over his head in the way she remembered, and his eyes were as merry, even in their surprise.

And the feeling she had for him was still there, flooding through her body; a deep warmth that spread from her heart into her stinging breasts, into her quivering stomach, into her thighs and arms, tingling in the palms of her hands. But it had never been like this; never as intense as this.

'Louisa,' he said in that new, deep voice. 'Louisa . . .'

It was all the greeting she needed. And she returned it, saying his name once, wonderingly, then again, over and over again as if by so doing she could make herself believe it.

'Kieran. Kieran. *Kieran* . . .'

Chapter Twelve

'Why were you away so long?'

Louisa sat on a heathery mound, hugging her knees and staring down towards the smoking furnaces of Ulverston. At the foot of the canal she could see the masts of the tall ships.

Kieran lay stretched out before her, chewing a stalk of grass. He looked up, narrowing his eyes against the sun. 'We've been trying some new pitches, different fairs, over in the north-east and down south a way. Scarth was tired of this area, said it was no use, but he's decided to come back and work it again for a bit.'

'So how long will you be here?' She heard the anxiety in her voice, almost a hunger. The thought of his leaving again was a physical pain somewhere deep inside where she had only recently begun to be aware of feelings at all.

The only pleasures in her life, it seemed, had been her life with her father before Susannah had arrived, and her friendship with Kieran. One had been tarnished for ever, the other taken away. But now it had been returned to her, and she was terrified already of losing it again.

'How long? Oh, till after Charter, I should think.' His voice was lazy, deep and drawling. 'Though Scarth did say we might pitch in somewhere this way for the winter.'

'The whole winter?' She didn't even try to keep the delight out of her voice, and Kieran looked up at her and grinned.

'Aye, mebbe. Think you'll like that?'

Louisa felt her cheeks colour and glanced hastily away. Among her new and strange feelings was an odd shyness that sometimes overcame her. She stared down at the heather for a moment, then looked back at him and smiled.

'Yes, of course I will. You're my only friend.'

'Oh, dordy me! And you so grand. You must have plenty of mates.' His dark eyes teased her and Louisa blushed again.

'I haven't. I hate all my stepmother's friends and now that I never go anywhere with Papa—' She stopped, then went on, 'In any case, the people I used to know – the miners and their wives and their children – they don't seem to like me any more. They think I've deserted them.' Her voice trembled suddenly and she felt hot, unexpected tears in her eyes.

Kieran stared at her. The laughter had gone from his face. Instead, his dark eyes were soft and he stretched out a lean brown hand and took hers. She felt its roughness and curled her fingers in his, the warm contact bringing more tears to spill down her cheeks. How long was it since anyone had held her like this, in friendship and comfort?

She thought of her mother's arms, now little more than a distant memory. And then Papa . . . but his touch was lost to her now, and the memory held only shame. Apart from Tilly, nobody else had ever held her, nobody had touched her unless it were Susannah with an angry slap or Martha and Jane with their sly pinches.

'You ought to have friends,' Kieran said, his voice gentle. 'You ought to have a lot of friends. And you ought to have lovers too.'

'Lovers!' Louisa's cheeks were aflame now. She stared at him. 'I don't want lovers,' she denied quickly. 'Anyway, I'm much too young.'

Kieran laughed. 'Too young?' His eyes moved over

208

her body and she caught her breath, making an instinctive movement to pull her shawl closer about her shoulders. 'What do years have to do with it?' he asked softly.

Louisa turned away. Her heart was beating fast and she was trembling. She could feel an odd spiralling tingle in her stomach, as if something small was twisting inside her. She tried to pull her hand away from Kieran's and he laughed again and held it more tightly. 'You're not too young, Louisa.'

'I think,' she said, and her voice came shakily, 'I think I'd better go home now, Kieran.'

'Home? Why? You've only just arrived.'

'My stepmother will be asking for me.'

'And since when,' he asked, 'have you ever fretted about your stepmother?'

Louisa was silent. He knew too much about her, too much about her home and family, too much about the thoughts that passed through her mind. Looking at him now, she was sure he could read every one, and she turned quickly away again, as if by hiding her eyes she could also conceal her thoughts.

'We're all worried about her. Since Walter was born—'

'Oh aye,' he said, 'Walter. How old is he now?'

'Six weeks. And his head's almost better.' She had told him on that first afternoon, when they had found time after the first pleasure of meeting to exchange news, about the baby. Kieran had told her that one of the gipsy babies had been born in very similar condition, but that his grandmother had bathed the misshapen little head daily and within a month or two it was normal. 'I told Tilly about your grandmother – it was no use telling anyone else. But it seems to be getting better all the same.'

'I told you it would. And he'll be not one whit the worse for it.'

'He seems bright enough now, he's just started

smiling, but nobody will really know until he's four or five years old.'

'Trash! Of course you'll know before then. And if he's smiling already, there can't be much wrong with him.' Kieran spoke with all the authority of someone who had spent a lifetime caring for babies, and Louisa looked at him in surprise. None of the boys or men she knew would have professed the slightest interest in young children, and even her father seemed to look on baby Walter with a kind of trepidation, as if by holding him he might do some damage. Or maybe that was because of his head.

'Anyway,' Kieran said, reverting to Louisa's words about Susannah, 'why are you fretted about your step-mother? She ought to be about again now the *chavvy*'s six weeks old. Our women don't stop in bed above a day or two, and some of 'em are up and about again straightaway.'

'Susannah isn't. She won't get up. She just lies there and won't even look at the baby. She won't do anything for him at all.'

Kieran stared at her. 'You mean she's not feeding 'un?'

'No.' Louisa felt her blush begin again. All she knew on this subject was hazy, and she was half ashamed of knowing even that much. 'There's a – a woman. A wetnurse, they call her.'

'Aye, I know. Someone who's had a baby of her own and lets yourn share the milk. But why hasn't she taken to 'un? Surely not just because he had a bumped head, poor little *chav*.'

Louisa shrugged. 'Why else would it be?'

Kieran looked thoughtful. Then he said, 'There was a *rakli* – a girl – in our camp a few years ago, she had a babby and after he was born she wouldn't have a thing to do with 'un. Turned her face away and wouldn't even look at 'un, let alone hold 'un. And anyone came near her, she'd let fly something terrible, swearing and cussing up hill and down dale, like she'd turned against everyone, even her own *mush*. Seemed like the birth had turned her head.'

'That's just what Susannah's like,' Louisa said. 'She seems to hate everyone. The things she says, the way she looks . . .' She shivered. 'Papa's at his wits' end. I believe he thinks she'll have to go into an asylum.'

'Well, that'd make life a mite easier for you,' Kieran said, watching her.

Louisa gasped. She felt her face flame and put up her hands to hide her shame. The thought had passed through her mind more than once. Were her feelings so plain, showing in her face, her voice, her eyes? Did everyone know that she had sometimes looked at Susannah's wild eyes, listened to her ranting voice and thought, *If you run mad, you'll be put away and then life will be as it was before*? Did they also know that she was invariably consumed with guilt at such a thought, for who could wish such a fate on even their worst enemy?

'That would be dreadful,' she said. 'Asylums are terrible places – I've heard about them, some of the people I know go there on Sundays to look at the poor souls inside. Like a zoo. Papa would never send Susannah into one of those.'

'He might just put her away at home. In a room somewhere, with a nurse. Either way, she'd be out of your road.'

Louisa stood up. She was trembling and felt sick and angry. 'I'm going home now. I should have gone before. I don't know why I came at all. You do nothing but say hateful things!' Her voice was high and shaking. Her breath came quick and harsh, and angry tears seared her eyes. She stared down at him, angered further by his still indolent posture, forgetting how only a few moments ago he had taken her hand and spoken to her with gentleness and understanding.

Kieran's glance met hers. His eyes were dark, unreadable. In a voice that was almost toneless, he said, 'I'm only saying what's in your own mind, Louie. Don't tell me you haven't thought it yourself.'

'I haven't! I haven't thought such things at all. I wouldn't. I *couldn't.*'

'You could,' he stated flatly. 'Anyone could. Why should you be different from everyone else?'

She shook her head blindly and put her hands up to her face again. The tears were flowing now, uncontrollably; they ran through her fingers and down her hands into the wrists of her dress. Her shoulders shook and she was suddenly aware of Kieran beside her, his arms round her, holding her close. With a sob, she turned her face into his shoulder and let herself weep.

'There,' he said when the storm had abated, 'that's better out than in. Did you think there was summat amiss with you, Louie, to be thinking such things?'

'I thought I must be bad all through,' she whispered. 'Whatever may be wrong with her, to think of *anyone* being put into one of those awful places is so horrible. And when I found myself thinking that – perhaps *she* might . . .' She shuddered violently and began to cry again. 'I wanted it to happen, Kieran. I – oh, I must be a wicked person, to think such things. I must be.'

'You're not.' Kieran's arms held her tightly and she could feel the strength and hardness of his body, the warmth of his skin. She clung to his shoulders, her fingers moving convulsively, digging into the rough fabric of his jacket. His hair was against her face and she could smell the rich smell of him, a smell composed of earth and heather and trees, of sweat and skin and blood, a smell that was uniquely Kieran. 'You're not wicked, you're not bad. You're just human.' He turned his head and she lifted hers and met his eyes. 'Look, Louie, we're all bits of bad and bits of good, even your stepmother. Some of us has more good bits and some has more bad, but we're all mixed up. And when someone's been unkind to you like she has, 'tis natural to wish her somewhere else. And if she's running mad, why then the natural place is the asylum. And who's to blame you for thinking of it?'

'But I don't have to *hope* it,' she whispered. 'Not when I know how terrible those places are. Bedlams, they call them, and that's what they're like. I've been told about them. Men and women looking worse than animals, running about filthy with no clothes on, screaming and cursing and – oh, it's too horrible to talk about. How can I wish Susannah in such a place?'

'Because you've no cause to wish her anywhere else,' he said bluntly. 'She's made your life a misery, Louie, and you'll never have back what she's took away. As for hoping, have you tried to make yourself hope – or not hope – for anything? 'Tisn't something you can decide about. You either hope or you don't, and that's all there is to it. And it don't mean you're wicked, either.' He paused, then added quietly, 'I don't reckon you really hope that anyway. It's just gone through your mind, and you can't help thinking things.'

Louisa was silent for a few moments. Then she said slowly, 'You're right, I don't really hope for it. I just want her to go away. But it's all been so awful, with the baby, and her being so – so strange.' She began to cry again. 'I hated myself for thinking those things.'

'Well, you don't have to.' He was still holding her, his rough hands stroking her gently. Again, she was sharply aware of how long it had been since anyone had touched and held her. It was a feeling that was strange, this closeness, this warmth, a feeling she had forgotten or perhaps never really known. Kieran's touch was not like a mother's touch, or a father's – but her mind veered away from that. And there had never been anyone else, no aunt or uncle, no cousin or brother to touch her and hold her and comfort her.

It's like being starved, she thought, though in all these years I never knew I was hungry. Or perhaps it was really that I never knew what it was I hungered for.

She lifted her head again and turned towards him. Kieran's face was close to hers, his breath warm on her cheek. His eyes were almost black, with no more than a narrow rim of earth-brown colour. She caught her breath, scarcely knowing why, and in the split second before his mouth touched hers she knew that he was going to kiss her; knew too that she wanted it.

The kiss was soft and sweet, little more than a brushing together of lips that were just parted. Kieran's mouth was warm and slightly moist, moving against hers with a gentleness that was wholly unexpected and strangely exciting. She felt a stirring inside her, a tiny sparkle of sensation that spiralled through her stomach, making her gasp and tighten her hold; and as she did so, Kieran made a low sound deep in his throat and his mouth hardened and covered hers with a rough urgency that brought the spiral of excitement surging powerfully through her whole body.

Louisa's response was instant and involuntary. Lifting her face to his, straining her body against him, she returned his kiss, delighting in the warmth and strength of him, in the heat pulsing through her veins, in the rapid beat of her heart and the tingling of her skin. She could feel Kieran's hands moving on her shoulders, tracing the line of her shoulder blades, slipping down to her narrow waist and over the swell of her buttocks. His fingertips caressed her gently, but without conscious knowledge of its meaning she sensed the restrained passion in them and tightened her arms about his back, moving her hands over his shoulders.

She heard the quickening of his breath and felt the tautness in his muscles. As his kiss deepened, his hands grew harder, squeezing the soft flesh, pulling her strongly against his body. His mouth was open against hers, his tongue forcing its way between her parted lips, licking over her teeth, thrusting against her tongue. And at the same moment his hands slid up her body again. Slipping under her arms to cup her breasts, the tips of his fingers inserting themselves gently into the neck of her gown.

Instantly, Louisa stiffened. She pulled abruptly out of his arms, her hands still on his shoulders but holding him away now, her fingers rigid where only a moment ago they had been caressing and soft.

'Don't do that!' she gasped. 'Don't . . .'

Kieran stared at her. His face was suffused, his eyes dark. Sweat shone on his brow and cheeks and she could smell the strong animal smell of him and hear his quick, almost savage breathing.

'What's amiss?' he asked, and his voice was like gravel.

Louisa shook her head. Desperately, she sought a reason to give him, but could only say, 'I don't like to be touched like that. I don't like to be kissed. I *hate* it.'

'Don't like it?' he exclaimed. 'Don't talk rubbish, Louie. You liked it as much as I did.'

'No!' she backed away, her heart thumping painfully. 'I didn't like it. I don't want to be kissed like that, I don't want to be touched . . .' Her voice trembled and broke and she turned away from him, her hands covering her face, the tears streaming again. 'I hate it, I tell you,' she repeated through her sobs.

Kieran stood still for a few moments. Then he moved towards her and touched her again, his arm gentle about her shoulders. Louisa twisted away, fear now surging in her as, only a few moments earlier, passion had. Her skin burned where he had touched her, her lips felt swollen, and in place of the delight that had come with his first touch she knew only shame.

'Don't touch me, *please* don't touch me!' She raised her face, still streaming with tears, and she stared at him

215

with eyes that were wild and dark. 'Please . . .'

He stood quite still. His arm, raised to encircle her once more, remained half lifted, then dropped back to his side. His brows drew together in a dark frown and Louisa, gazing at him through a haze of tears, felt a new fear.

She could bear it no longer. With a stifled sound that was half sob, half scream, she turned and ran away from him, through the purple heather and over the rocks, away and back down the valley to Pennington.

But even as she ran she did not know whether she was running towards or away from her refuge.

Slowly, Walter's head took on a normal appearance and, rather more slowly, his mother too regained her usual senses.

'It happens sometimes,' Dr Robinson said to Timothy. 'For no reason at all, a woman will take against her baby and run mad for a while. Nobody knows why it is, and usually she recovers within a few weeks and all is well again.'

'We all know why Susannah did it,' Timothy said sombrely. 'She thought she'd given birth to a monster.' And in his mind he added silently, *And I know why*. There had been times when Timothy had feared that both mother and son would end in an asylum, and all through his own wickedness. But the child's head looked normal enough now, and indeed he appeared to be developing as quickly as any other baby, smiling at the right age, laughing an infectious little chuckle, reaching out for his toys. And Susannah was just as before, a little quiet perhaps, a trifle subdued, but Timothy could not be too sorry for that. But she still did not take to the baby.

'Oh, Beck will see to him,' she would say carelessly, referring to the wetnurse. 'I really have far too much to do. With the inauguration to prepare for – it's an important occasion for Jane as well as you, you know.'

Timothy sighed. Having recently been appointed Mayor of Ulverston, he was forced to spend a good deal of his time attending social functions, which was the part of the job he liked least. Susannah, however, throve upon it and it was largely his appointment that seemed to have brought about her recovery.

The inauguration, she had decided, was to be the occasion of Jane's first public appearance as a young lady. Her coming-out, she called it, though there was no question of a 'season' in London or any presentation at Court. 'We don't move in those circles,' Timothy had told his wife bluntly, and only just prevented himself from adding *thank God*. 'She can attend the inauguration, along with the other two, and if you want to say she's coming out, you can, but to my mind it's pretentious balderdash for people of our kind.'

'Your trouble is you've no ambition,' Susannah said sharply. 'If it were left to you, all three girls would have grown up as hoydenish as Louisa. As for *her* attending the inauguration, I should think even you would see how ridiculous that is.'

'Ridiculous? Louisa? Why?'

'There's no need to sound so indignant. It's simply that I doubt if she wants to. You know how Louisa is in company — gauche, tongue-tied, awkward. She hates occasions, she'd rather stay at home and read a book than put herself out to be pleasant to other people. She certainly won't want to dress up.'

'Nevertheless,' Timothy said, 'she should have an invitation. And if she wants to come—'

'She won't,' Susannah said, and from the look on her face Timothy recognised that about this his wife had made up her mind. Whatever her private inclinations, by the time Susannah had finished with her, Louisa would not want to come.

In fact, Susannah was quite right. Louisa's private

inclinations were just as she foretold. The idea of a grand and very formal social occasion, with all her father's and Susannah's friends present, was considerably less attractive than the promise of a peaceful evening at home alone. Alone! The thought of it was like being shown a gateway to Heaven. Nobody to watch and criticise, nobody to carp, nobody to distract her from her own pursuits. It was like a Christmas present in itself.

The spectacle of her two stepsisters preparing for the occasion made her even more thankful not to be going.

'It's worse than when my father got married,' she told Tilly, sitting in the kitchen one afternoon when the rest of the family were out. 'There was enough fuss then, with all the dresses and gewgaws, but this is worse. Martha thinks herself quite grown up with her fashionable new gown.'

'Well, she's a little copycat, that 'un,' Tilly said. 'Whatever Miss Jane does now, Miss Martha will do tomorrow. Mind, she'd follow you as soon as her sister if you let her. I've seen her lookin' at you sometimes. I reckon if she thought she could get away with it she'd be off with you, up on those moors.'

'Of course she wouldn't! She hates me as much as Jane does.'

'If she hates you,' Cook said shrewdly, 'and I'm not so certain she does meself, then it's because her sister does. Tilly's right, she's a copycat. Don't matter who it is, she just needs someone to copy and if it weren't Miss Jane, it'd be you. Look how often she comes down to the kitchen just when you happen to be here. That's no coincidence, mark my words.'

'Well, I don't want her copying me,' Louisa said in disgust, and looked up in alarm as soft footsteps were heard on the basement stairs. Hastily, she rose and snatched up her bonnet and shawl. 'I'm going for a walk.'

The servants were laughing as she whisked through

218

the scullery, but it was Martha's voice she heard as she slammed the door behind her. Crossly, she made her way across the yard and through to the kitchen garden, from where she could escape to the fields. Surely it couldn't be true that Martha would follow her as slavishly as she followed Jane. And if it were, it was no flattery, simply an irritation.

She looked up at the moor, a dark shadow against the misty sky of late November. Of late, she had been trying to avoid meeting Kieran, trying to push him from her mind. Although her feet longed to climb up the steep little road and her body urged her to turn in that direction, she went instead along the road that led to Broughton Beck. Perhaps there, wandering by the stream that ran through the fields, she could find a little peace.

The meadows were empty, cattle taken in for the winter. Louisa climbed the stone steps that made a stile over the wall and strolled slowly beside the beck. Around her the air was quiet, a faint mist hanging in the hedges, and already the sky was beginning to darken towards evening. Lamps were being lit in some of the cottages and birds were squabbling in the bushes over roosting places.

'Well, this is a pretty sight for a chilly afternoon,' a voice exclaimed. 'And where might you be wandering?'

Startled, Louisa jumped a little. She had been so absorbed in her thoughts that she had not noticed the young man coming towards her through the meadows, and they were almost face to face before he spoke. She stopped and looked up, half surprised, half afraid. And then she chided herself for her fear. Who was there to fear in this place where she knew everyone and everyone knew her?

But this was someone she did not know, a stranger.

He stood a good eight inches taller than she did, looking down at her. There was a challenge in those grey eyes, a twitch of humour about the finely chiselled lips that warned her that he saw this encounter as a source of amusement. With another flicker of disquiet, she remembered stories she had heard in the kitchens of servant girls or dairymaids being caught and ravished by young men of the gentry who considered such girls no more than fair game, a source of entertainment on an idle afternoon.

He was certainly gentry – so much was obvious from his dress, the high, frilled collar of his fine cotton shirt, the fabric of his coat and breeches. His fair hair fell in tousled curls over his high forehead, and his boots gleamed even under the mud with which his walk had coated them. On his face he wore the rather supercilious look that many young men of his class reserved for servants.

Louisa felt an immediate spurt of annoyance. But on glancing down at herself, she had to admit that he had reason to take her for a serving girl. As usual on her walks, she was dressed in clothes that Tilly would probably have been ashamed to be seen wearing out of doors – a shabby gown, an old, much mended shawl and boots that were unpolished and worn. She had removed her bonnet and some of her pins had been lost so that her hair streamed down her back in a tawny wave. She could feel the sting of colour in her face, heating further as she stared at the young man.

'Well?' he said, a trifle impatiently. 'I asked you a question, miss. Don't you have the manners to answer, or has the cat got your tongue?'

Louisa's annoyance grew. 'I don't see why I have to answer if I don't want to. You're not my master.' Out of a mischievous urge to confuse him, she spoke in the local accent, learned since she was a child from the kitchen staff and mineworkers. Let him think her a dairymaid if he liked, why should she tell him any different?

His brows rose. She stared boldly at him. Really, he

did look a very *personable* young man, as her stepmother would have said, and she wondered who he was and what he was doing here.

'So,' he said softly, 'you've got some spirit, have you? Well, it makes a change from some of the mealy-mouthed wenches I'm accustomed to. Too much yes sir, no sir, three bags full sir. Becomes rather a bore. I don't imagine you're ever a bore, hm?' His voice was low and silky, and Louisa stepped back a little. Somehow, without her noticing it, he had come rather nearer than she liked. But she kept her eyes fixed on his and her voice pert as she replied.

'I'm sure I wouldn't know about that, sir, but I like my own company well enough. Especially when I'm out walking.'

The young man's brows rose further. 'Do you indeed? And might that be a cunning way of telling me you prefer my room to my company?'

'Not at all. I'm sure you've a right to walk where you please, same as me.'

'And if I please to walk where you do?'

Louisa shrugged. Again, he had come a little too near and she felt uncomfortable and a little frightened. Perhaps she should tell him who she really was. But he would be embarrassed and probably angry with her, and if he were a tattler the story might well come to her father's ears, and Susannah's. And that would put an end to her solitary walks.

'Can't stop you, I suppose. But it's getting dark – I'll have to turn back any road.'

She turned to walk the way she had come and he fell into step beside her. Louisa's heart sank. Suppose he intended to walk all the way home with her? How was she to shake him off?

'At least tell me your name,' he said persuasively, 'and where you work. Do you get out every after-noon?' She glanced up and caught his eyes moving over her, lingering on the bright waves of hair. 'Perhaps we'll meet again.'

'Oh, I don't reckon that's likely, sir. I only get one afternoon a month, and then I slip across to see me mum.' She bit her lip, realising her mistake and hoping he had not noticed it, but his next words dashed her hopes.

'So was that where you were going this afternoon? No? Then you must have slipped out without leave.' He smiled. 'A naughty girl, eh? Perhaps it's not the only way you're naughty.'

Louisa's discomfort changed abruptly to panic. They were almost at the stone stile and she set her foot on the lowest step. As she laid her hand on the top of the wall, he covered it with his.

'Don't be in such a hurry, little girl,' he murmured, and his face was close to hers. 'Stay and talk for a while. I'd like to know you better. Tell me your name.'

'No!' The pertness had gone from her voice and it was edged now with panic. 'Please, sir, let me go. I've got to get back. If the mistress finds I'm gone . . .' She tried to pull her hand away but his fingers tightened over hers. '*Please*,' she whispered frantically.

'Let you go? But we've only just met.' His smile taunted her. 'Tell me your name. Perhaps then I'll let you go.'

Desperately, Louisa sought for a name to give him, but her mind was blank. 'Jane,' she said widly at last. 'It's Jane – Jane Reid.'

'Jane,' he repeated softly, almost as if licking it. 'But not such a plain Jane. A very pretty Jane, in fact.' He lifted his hand but took hers with it, raising it to his lips. 'And my name's Nicholas – Nick my friends call me. So now we're introduced. Don't say you have to hurry back.'

'But I do!' This was getting worse. It was almost dark now and she had two miles and more to walk home

222

through the lanes. The young man had fast hold of her hand and was moving his mouth over her fingers in a caressing way that was having a very disturbing effect on her. Waves of heat were passing over her body, yet she was shivering as if with cold. 'Please, sir, let me go. I – I'll be dismissed if I'm not back soon.'

He paused and lifted his eyes to hers. 'You really are worried! Well, I'd not be the cause of a maid being turned out of her place – not for the sake of a chance meeting in a field, anyway. Very well, Jane, I'll let you go – on payment of a small forfeit.'

'A forfeit?' Louisa said faintly, and he laughed and drew her close.

'The usual forfeit. Have you never played party games in your kitchen or whenever it is you work? A kiss, pretty Jane, a kiss, and then I'll let you go.'

Louisa stared up at him. His face was pale in the gathering dusk, his hair gleaming as if with its own soft light. She could see the glint in his eyes, hear the laughter in his voice. She could feel the strength in his hand, still holding hers.

A kiss? She couldn't. But he would not let her go without it, of that she was certain. And if she offered her lips, would the kiss be a mere brushing of lips, a token like the forfeits she had indeed paid at party games? Or would it be the kind of kiss that Kieran had given her, that her father—

'No,' she whispered. 'No. *Please*, no . . .'

But Nicholas took no notice. He bent his head and laid his lips on her face. In her terror Louisa stood frozen, unable to move, and felt his mouth stroke slowly across her cheek to find hers. Her lips were slightly parted when he touched them, and the movement of his head gently forced them to open further. She felt his tongue flicker against the soft inner skin, felt the instant fiery response within her body and as instantly felt the shame.

'*No!*' Her sudden twist caught him by surprise and he

let go of her hand and stumbled back against the wall. As quickly as her skirts would allow, Louisa climbed the two stone steps and scrambled down the other side. She looked over the wall, half afraid that he had hurt himself, and saw him laughing at her from the meadow.

'So you really are a firebrand! Well, all the more worth winning for that. But never fear, little Jane, I won't ravish you. I don't take any pleasure from rapine. I like my maids to be willing.' He leant his arms on the wall, smiling at her. 'And you will be,' he said softly. 'You will be willing, pretty Jane.' As Louisa stared, mesmerised, he lifted a hand and reached across the wall to run it lazily down her neck. 'We'll meet again. And next time we'll meet earlier. To give us time to talk, hm?'

Louisa said nothing. With an effort, she tore her eyes away from his and turned. She ran along the little track that led back into the village of Broughton Beck, stumbling a little in the gloom, convinced that he was following her. But when she reached the first cottage and looked back, he was nowhere in sight.

She still did not know who he was or where he came from. And, thankfully, neither did he know anything about her. A bubble of nervous laughter rose in her throat as she thought of him enquiring for 'Jane Reid'. And then she hoped that he would not, for it wouldn't take long for someone to remember that Jane Reid was Timothy Sherwin's stepdaughter, and no time at all to know just who it was Nicholas had really met in the field.

Nicholas. She wondered if they ever would meet again.

If they did, it would not be by her doing.

Chapter Thirteen

When he was four years old, Walter Sherwin stepped out of frocks and babyhood and into the trousers and jacket of a small boy. His curls were cut short and everyone could see that his head was neat and round, with no unsightly bulges; indeed, he had been so clearly normal throughout his short life that most of the family had forgotten there had ever been any concern for him.

Only his mother seemed not to have recovered from her first reaction to that bulging head. Although her early fury had diminished, she still retained a simmering resentment which was directed at both Timothy and her son and created a discomfort throughout the house.

'There'll be no more,' she told Timothy soon after Walter's birth. She was still sleeping alone in the big bedchamber they had shared until her pregnancy had made a double bed uncomfortable for two. 'You have your son now, and I hope you're satisfied with him.'

Susannah developed a habit of calling Walter 'the boy', as if to dissociate herself from him. And she did very little for him; never bathed him, seldom held him on her knee, never kissed or cuddled him or held his small, warm body close. That was left to the nursemaid and the wetnurse, or to anyone else who might take an interest, mainly Louisa and Martha.

'I told you, he's not a toy,' Jane said when she first noticed that Martha was spending much of her time in the nursery. 'It doesn't do babies any good to be cooed and fussed over all the time. Anyway, you're too old to play with dolls.'

'He's not a doll.' For once, Martha had the temerity to speak against her elder sister. 'Or a toy. He's a real, live human being and he's learning something new every day. He smiled at me this morning – such a lovely little smile.'

'Oh well, if it's *smiles* you want,' and Jane bared her teeth in an ugly grimace that brought tears to Martha's eyes. From then on, the younger girl only visited the nursery when Jane was occupied with other tasks, such as accompanying their mother on her afternoon calls. But more and more often, Martha was required to go too, and her visits became rarer.

Louisa was left to play nursemaid. To her surprise she found that she enjoyed it. She liked watching the baby's little milestones of development, his first smile, the first little chuckle which sounded so endearingly deep coming from that tiny throat. She observed his first exploration of himself and the world about him; his discovery of toes which could be sucked, his surprise at finding ears attached to both sides of his head. And his head itself; with satisfaction, she watched as the bumps gradually disappeared and its shape became normal.

By his first birthday, nobody would have doubted that Walter was a normal, intelligent child. In fact, as Dr Robinson remarked when he came to visit and check on the baby's progress, he might well be said to be more intelligent than most. At four months he was sitting up in his crib, at six he was crawling, at nine standing and taking his first steps. He climbed everything that could be climbed and attempted to climb a good many things that could not. He learned new words every day and at eighteen months could hold a conversation. His questions soon exhausted the servants, except for Tilly who had an answer for everything, even if she had to make it up on the spur of the moment.

'No, the moon won't fall out of the sky,' she told him. 'It's held up by a silver rope.' And, 'There's nowt to be frightened of in thunder, it's just God movin' his furniture about.' And Walter would go to the window and stare up at the heavy sky, as if his gaze could pierce the black clouds and catch a glimpse of a white-haired old man struggling with a heavy bookcase or table.

'Why doesn't he have someone to help him?' he asked, and Tilly told him that God had the angels. 'That's what you can see flashing,' she explained. 'It's their halos, catching the sun.'

'But it isn't sunny today, it's raining.'

'Not in Heaven, it isn't,' she said briskly. 'And that's enough questions for today, Master Walter. Time you had your bath.'

So at four, when he stepped into his first trousers, Walter was a mine of information, some of it a mixture of fairy tale and Tilly's own imagination, some of it surprisingly accurate. And he knew quite well who his friends were: his half-sisters Louisa and Martha; Tilly, who had taken over as nursemaid when he was only a few months old; and most of the servants. He regarded his father with awe and longed to be taken out in the trap to visit the mines Louisa talked of. His mother he barely knew; she was a cold, distant figure and in her presence he always felt uneasy, filled with a strange guilt even when he could not think of anything he had done wrong. And Jane he frankly loathed. Her indifference towards him was all too apparent to him, though she concealed it well enough from her mother and stepfather, and she had not grown out of the habit of delivering sly pinches or knocking over the towers of wooden bricks which he spent much of his time laboriously building. Fortunately, she came rarely to the nursery and avoided him when he was brought downstairs for the regulation 'visit' after tea each day.

Walter was not the only one who had changed in those

four years. The three girls had developed and matured too. Jane, at twenty-one, was a haughty young woman, tall and angular, her face still thin and long like that of a superior carriage horse. As if to make up for her looks, her clothes were always of the most fashionable, with the pointed waistlines which emphasised her narrow waist and wide skirts which hid the thinness of her body. Bust improvers and whalebone gave her the shape nature had neglected to provide, and because a low neckline would reveal the boniness of her chest, she wore a chemisette beneath her bodice, or trimmed it with lace frills. Her thin, mousy hair was always tightly drawn into a bun, making her look severe and forbidding despite her fashionable clothes.

Martha, at seventeen, was still half a child. She had lost none of her plumpness which Tilly had called puppy-fat and said would go as she grew older, but instead had added more curves. She had no need of bust improvers and Jane had remarked acidly more than once that she ought to 'strap herself in'. 'When you're old enough to wear necklines as low as mine,' she said, trimming on another lace frill, 'you'll look quite inde-cent.' But there was envy in her voice and although she professed not to care that she hadn't found a husband yet, it was clear that she would be consumed with jealousy if Martha walked ahead of her to the altar.

As she might well do, Louisa thought, for Jane's attractions were sparse despite her finery. Her tongue was as sharp as her bones and she modelled herself on her mother, treating the young gentlemen she met with haughty arrogance. Martha, on the other hand, extended her deferential behaviour to all, paying wide-eyed attention to every word and laughing at each little quip.

Louisa herself found her confusion increasing as she grew out of the schoolroom. Marriage, which seemed to be the only idea in her stepsisters' heads, was one which occupied her mind too, more than she would admit, and she frequently found herself brooding over the young men she met, wondering which, if any, might prove a possible husband.

It was, after all, the only way she could escape from Pennington Hall. Without marriage she would be doomed to spend her life at home, in her father's company and Susannah's. Her relationship with her father was now so cool and distant she could scarcely believe it had ever been otherwise, and Susannah made no attempt to conceal her dislike. The idea of spending a lifetime alone with them filled her with despair.

But did it have to be marriage? Was there no other escape?

Sitting at her window or tramping about the fields as she still loved to do, Louisa would remember how she had once declared that she would make a better marriage than Jane or Martha. She had spoken without thinking, stung by Jane's taunts, but now her words came back to her and she wondered if she could make them come true. How angry Jane would be. How angry Susannah would be!

It was a tempting idea. But the implications of marriage, the mysterious rituals that even now were little more than a hazy idea in her mind, disturbed her with their hint of guilt and shame. There was still the memory of the day her father had taken her out to visit the mines and had kissed her lips with a lover's kiss and touched her breasts with a lover's hand. There was still the picture of the sunlit day on Kirkby Moor when Kieran had kissed her, and the November afternoon when in the gathering dusk she had met the man who called himself Nicholas.

She had never seen him again. Nor had she seen Kieran, for shortly after that the gipsies had disappeared again, driven out of the area by a brawl that had taken place one night during Ulverston Charter and ended with a man's death. It was as likely to have been the fault of a local man as of the gipsies, but travellers were always used as scapegoats and they had not come back again. Louisa was strangely relieved, even though she missed Kieran sorely every day; but after the kiss, their friendship had altered and she was afraid of the road she had been about to travel.

Since then, she had spent her days alone whenever she could escape Susannah's eye, roaming about the countryside and visiting the miners' families since she still dared not go near the mines themselves. Among the local people, even those not connected with the mines, she was well known, and she often took shelter from the weather at one of the farmhouses or spent a few minutes gossiping with the dairymaids or ploughmen she met along the way. If compelled to stay at home, she took refuge in the nursery with little Walter, or took him for walks.

Sometimes she would look at him and think wistfully of the son she would never have if she refused to marry. But memories of Susannah's pregnancy would come to her mind then, and she remembered well her father's fear that neither his wife nor the baby would survive the ordeal of birth.

No, she thought as her nineteenth birthday came and went and Susannah began to make even more acid comments about her appearance and behaviour, I shall never marry. I'll find some other way of leaving home.

But as what? As a governess? A lady's companion? Both offered lives of little more than drudgery, hampered and restricted even more than her life was now, and she knew her father would never agree to such a thing. If she defied him, ran away from home, how would she live? The few pieces of jewellery she possessed would bring only enough money to keep her for a very short while. Besides, most of them had been her mother's.

Oh, Mamma, she thought as she had done so often in her life, if only you were here now to help and advise me. Or just to comfort me, to hold me, to give me warmth and love . . .

The door to her bedroom crashed open and Martha came tumbling in. Today was one of her childlike days; indeed, she was more like a large, boisterous puppy as she flung herself on the bed. Louisa glanced at her with a faint irritation mixed with an almost unwilling fondness. Just lately, perhaps hurt by Jane's increasing jealousy, Martha had been turning more to her stepsister. At first, Louisa had been suspicious, but her own hunger for warmth and affection soon overcame her and she and Martha were, albeit cautiously, becoming friends.

'You'll never guess!' Martha cried, rolling over on the bed. 'You'll never guess what's going to happen.'

'You'd better tell me then.' Louisa could hear foot-steps on the stairs and knew that Jane was following her sister. Aware of a growing intimacy between Martha and Louisa, she seldom allowed them to be alone together for long.

Martha sat up. Her curls tumbled down around her plump, rosy face and her eyes sparkled.

'There's going to be a ball! A Christmas ball. It's to be at Tytup and all sorts of people will be there. The Rawlinsons, the Ainslies – everyone who matters. And we're to be invited, all of us.' She hugged herself with glee. 'Think of it, Louie! We'll have to have new gowns and dancing slippers and *everything*, and we may even meet our future husbands there!'

Jane came into the room as she spoke the last words and stood just inside the door, her face frozen with disapproval. She was still wearing her outdoor clothes, her thin body hidden by a dark brown cloak of padded silk with a short cape over the shoulders. In her hand she carried her bonnet and kid gloves as if she had not had time to put them down on entering the house. She was breathing quickly, as if she had hurried up the stairs.

'I told you not to come rushing in here,' she said angrily to Martha. 'You know Louisa isn't interested in balls and things.' She slipped off her cloak and dropped it carelessly on Louisa's bed. 'Or in husbands. Hasn't she said often enough that she intends never to marry?' She moved over to the little mirror on the washstand and studied her reflection. 'I shall certainly need a new gown, though. I've nothing fit to wear at all.'

'You've got your green silk,' Louisa said, unable to resist the barb because Jane's green silk had been a disappointment. She had chosen it only because Louisa had said she liked the material, but its vibrant colour had quite overwhelmed Jane's colourless looks. Martha, forgetting to be tactful, had remarked that the dress seemed to be wearing Jane rather than the other way about and Louisa, though desperately envious for she knew that the dress would have suited her tawny hair and strong features, had laughed. Jane had been furious with both of them and never worn the dress.

She gave Louisa a look of dislike. 'You know I hate that dress. It's such a vulgar colour. I can't think why I ever chose it. Not at all fashionable.'

'I'll have it then,' Louisa said at once. 'I don't care about fashion.'

'That's easy to see,' Jane retorted. 'I'm ashamed of the way you go about. You look like a gipsy girl in those awful clothes you wear and that dreadful shawl. Why, it must be years old.'

'It is,' Louisa said quietly. 'It was my mother's.'

'Well, there you are then.' Still staring into the mirror, Jane tilted her head this way and that. She began to unpin her hair. 'I think I'll try a new style for the ball.' A faint gleam appeared in her pale eyes. Her momentary irritation had disappeared and she was clearly as excited as Martha. 'You're right, Martie, there will be all kinds of people there. We must make sure our dresses are the latest thing, with the best lace and ribbon trimmings.'

Louisa gave her a contemptuous glance. 'That's all you think about, gewgaws and frippery that you believe might catch you a husband. Well, I'd rather be taken for a gipsy girl than a silly miss who thinks of nothing but lace and ribbons.'

'Well, be a spinster all your life if it suits you,' Jane said carelessly, throwing back her mousy hair and twisting it on top of her head. 'I wonder if this style would suit me . . . They tell me Sir Stanley Craven's son will be at the ball. I'm longing to meet him, aren't you, Martie?'

'Oh yes,' Martha breathed. 'They say he's the handsomest man in Furness. And so romantic. He's been living in France these past three years with his mother's family. Everyone says he's fascinating.'

'That's just because he's new,' Louisa said scornfully. 'He's someone different, so all the fond mammas in the district will be hunting him for their daughters. Thank heaven I don't care for such nonsense.'

'Thank heaven I do! I shall do my best to catch his eye, you may be sure. He's the most eligible bachelor for miles around – you know his father's building that great house down near the shore at Bardsea? Imagine living there. Imagine being *mistress* of such a house.'

'You imagine it – I can't be bothered.' Louisa snatched up her bonnet and shawl. 'I'm going for a walk.'

'Looking like that?' Jane said in a scandalised tone. 'Suppose you meet someone?'

'Then they'll simply take me for a gipsy girl, won't they?' Louisa said. 'So no one need be embarrassed by me.'

She stalked out of the room, seething with impatience. All this talk of eligible bachelors and husbands! What was so wonderful about marriage, after all? She could not see that either her father or Susannah were happy in their union. When not arguing, they were silent, and their silence had none of the quality of companionship that she had experienced with Kieran as they roamed together over the hills. And if the feelings that she had known had anything to do with it, they must be no more than some trick of Nature, to entice girls to give themselves to a man so that babies might be born and the human race continue. Happiness, love – these had nothing to do with those dark movements somewhere deep inside, those hungry yearnings that led only to guilt and shame.

Yet if she didn't marry . . .? Her earlier thoughts came back to her mind and turned again in their endless circling. There was no other escape. Without a husband, without income of her own, there was no way in which she could break free of the cage that her home had become. Without a husband, she was doomed to a life at Pennington Hall with a father who had become a stranger and a stepmother who hated her.

She remembered again what she had said to Jane and Martha, quite soon after Walter was born. *I shall find my own husband*, she had told them. *And he will be the most eligible in the area*.

Words spoken in haste and temper, it was true. And yet . . .

Suppose she did marry, wouldn't it be the ultimate blow to Susannah and her daughters if she were to be the one to snatch the prize? If she were indeed to marry the most eligible man in Furness? And if it were to secure her freedom also . . .

Perhaps I should go to the Christmas Ball after all, she thought. And perhaps I should make sure that I catch the eye of this new young man everyone talks of – the fascinating son of Stanley Craven.

Her mind so busy that she hardly knew where she was heading, she walked swiftly through the grounds and out to the lane that led to Whinfield. Her sketchbook was in her pocket; perhaps she would walk up to Lindal Moor and draw the scenes there. The silhouette of a tumble-tree, etched against the sky, had a drama about it that appealed to her in this frame of mind, when the tranquillity of undisturbed landscape was somehow unsatisfying.

The mine manager's house stood on the crest of the hill, together with the offices and the stables where the horses were kept. From here, ore could be loaded in traps and taken straight down to Ulverston, or to the quays at Barrow. The hills and valleys around it were a mish-mash of deep shafts and heaps of spoil brought up in kibbles and dumped beside the pitheads, and the road down to Lindal village from Marton was deep in cold red mud.

Louisa leant against a stone wall and observed the scene. These were not her father's mines, they belonged to the company of Harrison and Ainslie, and she knew only a few of the men who worked there. But most of them knew who she was and gave her a nod as they went about their business, and nobody took much notice of her sketching. Miss Louisa was well known for being a bit odd but that was her business and no one had reason to interfere.

She stayed there for a while, drawing with the piece of charcoal she always carried about with her. The sun was going down now, sinking with a copper flame into the glowing sea. The strong lines of the rigs stood out harsh and black against the blazing sky and the men working around them were transformed to shadows, moving like black demons in a mysterious ritual dance as they wound up the tumbletrees. The horses, too, endlessly plodding round the windlasses as if working out some ancient rhythm, were creatures from myth, horses no longer but stark black shapes that came from some other world, as if the shafts of the mines led down into Hell and these were its denizens come to the surface.

The afternoon was still, drawing into evening. In the deep fold of the valley, the village of Lindal was beginning to spark with light as cottagers lit their lamps, and past the low hills Louisa could see the dusky haze over the little town of Barrow, burnished by the glow of the dying sun. Below, to her left, the spreading sands of Morecambe Bay were turning from buff to pewter as the sky darkened, and across the sands she could see the windows of buildings at Grange and Arnside, lit gold by the last few rays.

Soon it would be dark. With a sigh, she rolled up her sketch and slipped it into her pocket. She turned to walk back through the lanes to Pennington and saw, coming up the hill towards her, a figure.

There was something familiar about him, something she recognised. She had met him before, she was sure of it, yet he was not a local man. As he came nearer she observed his tall, slender figure, his fair hair falling in curls over his forehead, and suddenly she remembered.

It must be a good four years since they had met by the stream down in Broughton Beck, not long after Walter was born, in that overheated summer when Kieran had turned into a man and she had fought against becoming a woman. She remembered the November afternoon, a damp, raw afternoon, not like this glowing evening, when she had wandered by the stream rather than climb to the moor where Kieran might be waiting, and had met the fair-haired stranger who called himself Nicholas. She could remember his kiss still, and she put her fingers to her face as if to wipe it away.

They had never met again. She had made sure of that, keeping away from Broughton Beck as she had begun to keep away from Kirkby Moor. But after a while, irked by her self-imposed restrictions and telling herself that he had probably only been staying for a short visit, she had begun to return to Broughton Beck. With the gipsies gone too, she had soon resumed wandering freely wherever she pleased.

The young man was approaching closely now. She felt

a moment of panic, then chided herself. Of course he wouldn't remember her – why should he? He had taken her for a serving girl, and had probably forgotten her within moments of their parting. There was no need even to speak to him. As they came close, she kept her eyes down, looking at the muddy road as if taking care to pick her way.

The young man stopped. Louisa made to pass by but, aware of his eyes fixed on her, she glanced up reluctantly.

'It's you,' he said and the sound of his voice gave her a jolt. 'It's Jane. Jane Reid. A few years older, a good deal riper, but Jane Reid nevertheless.'

Louisa gasped. She had forgotten that she had given him her stepsister's name. She shook her head quickly. Surely he could not remember her so well! Not after four years in which she had done a deal of growing up. If she simply denied ever having seen him before . . .

'No, sir, you must be mistook. I'm not Jane anyone. My name's –' she cast about wildly and picked a name out of the air, '– my name's Moll.'

'Moll, is it? And not Jane at all?' His grey eyes crinkled a little. 'So you never were at Broughton Beck on a winter's afternoon a few years ago?'

'Broughton Beck?' Louisa said innocently. 'Is that over High Furness?'

The man laughed outright. He stood regarding her, hands in his pockets, and Louisa smiled back, suddenly enjoying herself. What was the harm, after all, in a little sparring? He didn't know who she was, never would know. Even if they were to meet socially, he would never recognise the serving girl, be it Jane or Moll, in Louisa Sherwin.

'What game is it you're playing, you minx?' He asked softly. 'And why is it you and I meet whenever I come here? Do you know, I've never been back since that visit four years ago, but every now and then I've caught a

237

glimpse of a girl who reminded me of you. A curve of the cheek, a turn of the head, that impish look in your eyes. And the feel of your lips in a kiss . . .' He moved closer and Louisa glanced about her, suddenly nervous. 'I've thought of you often, Jane Reid,' he murmured.

'I told you,' she said, 'I'm not Jane Reid. I've never even heard of her.'

'And that I do believe!' he said with another laugh. 'I wonder who has, around these parts. Do you have a different name for each day of the week? Jane for Fridays, Moll for – what's today? – Tuesdays? Who will you be if I meet you tomorrow? Who will you be on Sunday?'

'I'll be Moll. I'm always Moll.' Louisa took refuge in bewilderment. 'I don't know what you're talking about. Anyway, I've got to go now, I'm late already.'

'And always in such a hurry,' he said. 'It was the same before, I recall. But you found time to give me a kiss.'

Louisa stepped back. The road was deserted and they were hidden from the fields and mines by high hedges. The sun had disappeared now and the moon not yet risen. Darkness was gathering about them.

'Maybe you should tell me your name, if you reckon we've been such friends,' she said boldly. 'It might help me to remember too.'

'Am I so easy to forget?' His teeth gleamed white in a smile. 'Does the name Nicholas mean nothing to you any more?'

'Nicholas?' she repeated, trying to sound as if she had never heard it before. 'No, I can't say it does. Nicholas what? Maybe it'd help to hear your other name.'

'I doubt if I told you that. But since you ask, and since we're to be neighbours, I'll tell you. It's Craven, Nicholas Craven.'

'Nicholas *Craven*?' Surprise shook Louisa out of her charade and she stared at him. So this was the most eligible bachelor in Furness, the fascinating stranger who was half French and had just returned from a long stay in his mother's country. Whose father was a rich merchant, building a grand house on the shore at Bardsea . . .

Who was going to be attending the Christmas ball.

Jane already had her mind set on becoming Mrs Nicholas Craven. So, probably, did Martha and every other marriageable young woman in Low Furness.

Was this her opportunity to revenge herself on her stepmother and stepsisters? If she could snatch this prize from under all their noses, wouldn't it prove once and for all that Louisa Sherwin was as capable as any young woman of finding a husband? That finery and accomplishments, small talk and empty chatter were not the only ways of ensnaring a man?

And then her heart sank. What chance had she now? She had masqueraded as a serving girl, had lied twice about her name, had spoken in the accents of a cottager. She had met him dressed, as Jane had said, like a gipsy girl. What would he say when he met her in her stepmother's drawing room? What would he think?

He probably won't even recognise me, she thought. He'll probably not even notice me. How will I ever catch his eye, when Jane means to do so and Martha too, and both have their mother to help them? How can I ever capture his interest when all Furness will be yapping at his heels?

Chapter Fourteen

By the time the date of the Christmas ball arrived,
Louisa and Nicholas knew each other well.

She was still 'Moll' to him when he felt like teasing
her. And she had kept her secrets well; he still did not
know where she lived or what she was, though his
guesses were many. Not a housemaid, he said, playing
one day with her fingers for they were too smooth, too
soft. Nor yet a kitchenmaid or cook, for her arms were
too slim and had no muscle. He had never yet seen a
cook without arms like a prizefighter.

'It comes from all the hard work they do, sir,' Louisa
said, wondering if he ever sensed that she was teasing
him too, simply by giving him that title. 'Beating eggs,
rolling out pastry, kneading dough. It's as hard as any
man's work.'

'And you know all about men's work too, don't you?'
he scoffed. 'Kitchens, parlours, mines – you know about
them all, of course.'

'Yes, I do,' Louisa said in some surprise, for she had
never thought herself especially knowledgeable. 'I've
grown up with it all, you see.'

He stared at her. It was a mild afternoon, wanting a
week yet to Christmas and they were sitting on rocks
down on the shore near Bardsea. Louisa had walked out
as far as the Urswick road and he had met her there on
his horse and swung her up in front of him before she
could protest. The tide was far out and the sands firm

and shining. The flat rocks where they sat were smooth and white, sloping gently towards the sea under an overhanging canopy of trees.

'I wish I knew more about you, Moll,' he said slowly. 'There's something strange, something different from other girls. Why won't you tell me your true name? Why do you have so many secrets?'

'Maybe I don't have any. Maybe you know all there is to know.'

'How can that be true when I don't even know where you live, where you work?' He stroked her fingers gently and Louisa shivered. Softly, he went on, 'How can I know all there is to know when you never allow me more than a kiss?'

'I've told you, sir—'

'You're a "good girl",' he finished for her. 'I know, I know, and I've heard it all before. But none of the others meant it as you do.' He lay back on the rock and reached up, his fingers trailing gently down her arm. She could feel them through her sleeve and again she shivered. I ought to stop this, she thought, I ought to say it's time to go. But it was pleasant to be stroked like this, so gently, so slowly. It was like being a kitten, fondled by a kind owner. She wished she could purr, to show her pleasure.

'You're special, Moll,' he said. 'And you have secrets. It maddens me, not knowing the truth about you.'

Louisa looked down at him. For a moment they were both still, meeting each other's eyes. She saw the darkening of his pupils, caught the expression that passed across his face. She felt the brief tightening of his fingers on her arm.

Her heart gave a painful kick. With a jerk, she pulled herself away from him and scrambled to her feet. She was breathing rapidly as she stood on the rock and then she set off along the beach, striding fast, almost running. But the shifting shingle caught her steps, slowing them down so that she felt almost as if she were in the grip of a nightmare, using all her strength to run from some hideous pursuer yet unable to move.

'Moll!' Nicholas was on his feet too, running after her. 'Moll, wait. What have I done? What have I said? Moll, don't run from me like this.'

He was upon her now, his hands at her shoulders. Louisa gave a little scream of pure terror and his hands dropped away as if he had been stung.

'Moll, what's amiss? You know I'll never hurt you.'

She turned and faced him, her eyes wide and dark as the evening sky. She looked up at him, half afraid of what she might see, and then gave a gasping sob of relief. For his face was not the face of nightmare that for a moment she had dreaded, but the face of Nicholas, fair and open and concerned.

'Don't fear me, Moll,' he said gently, and gathered her into his arms. 'Don't ever fear me.'

Louisa leaned against him and let him hold her. Her terror had passed and she felt safe again. And when she felt his kisses in her hair, on her cheeks and finally upon her lips, she knew that she was still safe, for he would do no more than that. No more than hold her and kiss her with gentle, tender kisses.

'What was it, Moll?' he asked after a while. 'What were you so afraid of?'

But she shook her head. It must remain one more mystery. For how could she ever tell him that when she had looked down into his face and seen that darkening of his eyes, he had reminded her of another man?

How could she ever tell him that he had reminded her of her father?

'Of course Louisa won't want to go to the ball.'

The invitations had come and everyone was in a flutter. Jane and Martha had already reached such a pitch of excitement that it seemed they could go no

242

further, though it expressed itself in different ways. Jane grew haughtier than ever, behaving almost as if she were already engaged to the eligible Nicholas Craven – though she had still to meet him – and Martha spent hours in front of her mirror, prinking her hair and demanding the services of her mother's maid to help her try out new styles. She also spent a good deal of time gazing out of the window or drifting about the house with a dreamy smile upon her face.

'He'll never look at you,' Jane said crossly. 'You're much too young. Isn't she, Mamma?'

'Of course she's not.' Susannah was so desperate to capture the prize that she hardly cared which of her daughters actually carried it home. 'Plenty of girls are betrothed at seventeen. And Martha looks at least twenty when she's dressed for company.'

'I don't suppose he'll be interested in either of us anyway,' Jane remarked dispiritedly. 'There are lots of girls richer than we are.'

Louisa hid a smile, thinking of Nicholas and his pursuit of the 'maid', Moll. 'Perhaps he's not interested in riches. He might rather marry a milkmaid.'

'Oh, you *would* say something ridiculous like that!' Jane snorted. 'Well, there's one thing certain, he won't look at *you*!'

'Are you coming to the ball then, Louie?' Martha asked.

Before Louisa could answer Susannah said sharply, 'Of course Louisa won't want to go to the ball. You know she dislikes such occasions.'

'I'm invited, am I not?' Louisa said, glancing at the little pile of cards with their pretty scalloped borders and gilt printing. 'Then I think I'll go.'

Susannah glared at her. 'I don't think you'll enjoy it,' she began, but Louisa smiled coolly.

'I think perhaps I may. After all, Stepmamma, you've been trying to persuade me to go to such affairs. And

243

you're quite right, I'll never find a husband unless I go about more.'

'You needn't think you can set your cap at Nicholas Craven!' Jane said furiously, and Louisa laughed.

'I shan't set my cap at anyone. I'm not interested in a husband who has to be caught. If I marry, it will be because the man has pursued me, not the other way about.' She glanced at her stepmother. Susannah was looking as put out as her daughter. Clearly, she did not want Louisa to go to the ball and was seeking a reason to prevent her.

'You've nothing to wear,' she said at last. 'Nothing fit for such an occasion. And it's too late to have anything made now, the dressmaker's far too busy with our gowns.'

'No matter,' Louisa said lightly. 'I'll wear Jane's sea-green silk. It only wants a little altering and the colour suits me perfectly.'

'Your sister's cast-offs!' Susannah said scornfully, but she could not refuse. The dress had never been worn and with a little letting out here and a few stitches there it would fit perfectly.

The day of the ball drew nearer and it seemed that the whole of Furness was in a flurry over it. Every day there was some fresh piece of news to discuss, some extra item of clothing to be obtained. Jane wanted a new cameo brooch for the occasion and Martha would have pink ribbons threaded through the neck of her gown. Both declared that the shoes they had been fitted with pinched their toes, and Martha lost one of the kid gloves that had been bought specially. They were of the new, shorter length and her pride and joy, and she pouted and sulked when told that she would have to wear her old ones instead.

'The're perfectly good,' Susannah told her sharply. 'We haven't time to go jaunting about now looking for replacements. Perhaps it will teach you to be more careful.'

244

The preparations gave Louisa more opportunities to slip out of the house. Her own gown was ready and she had little concern for the fripperies that went with it; she was free whenever her stepsisters were being fitted or occupied with poring over the latest fashion papers. Fortunately, the weather was fine and clear and nobody thought it strange for her to be out; it had come to be expected that on fine days Louisa would be nowhere to be found.

In the last week, she saw little of Nicholas and supposed that he too was caught up in the fuss of preparations. But on the day before the ball, when she had begun to think that he had given her up, she saw him strolling in the meadows near Broughton Beck where they had first met.

'Now you'll have to tell me the truth,' he said, smiling, as she came close. 'You are Jane Reid, aren't you?'

Louisa looked at him. His grey eyes were dancing, his mouth twitching with laughter. For a moment, she was tempted to tell him the truth. What would he say, she wondered, if she told him that they would be meeting at the ball on Friday evening? But as she looked into his eyes, panic suddenly caught her throat. Until now, she had given hardly a thought to that meeting, seeing it as some fairytale happening somewhere in the future. Now it was almost upon them and the reality of it struck her like a blow from a miner's pick.

He was going to recognise her! Somehow, she had overlooked that fact, vaguely believing in Jane's derisive prophecy that no one would connect the 'gipsy' Louisa with the well-brought-up daughter of a mine owner. And if her meetings with Nicholas had been confined to that first one, four years ago, and the second when they had encountered each other on the Lindal Moor road, perhaps he never would have made the connection. But now he knew her too well. He had been given time in plenty to study the curve of her cheek, the way she turned her head, the wave in her chestnut hair. He knew the touch of her fingers and the slenderness of her arms; he knew the way her body felt in his arms, held close against him.

It was not possible that he would not recognise her.

It would be better to tell him now. She *should* tell him now. But then he would know she had lied to him, lied about more than her name.

He's going to know that anyway, she told herself. He'll know the moment he looks at you, the moment he takes you in his arms for the first dance.

'Well?' Nicholas persisted. 'Are you going to tell me?'

Louisa met his eyes, saw the glint of laughter and knew that she could not do it. She could not spoil this last meeting, this last cold winter's afternoon with the sun dying in a blaze of glory in the western sky.

Instinctively, she knew that she and Nicholas would never meet again like this. Too many fond mammas were hoping to ensnare him for their daughters – it was scarcely conceivable that he would remain unattached by the end of the ball. From next week, he would be occupied with courtship, with a wedding in the offing. Lonely walks around the countryside and flirting with serving girls would be a part of his past.

Whether it would be Jane or Martha who caught his eye, or one of the other young ladies who lived in the area, Louisa had no idea. All she knew was that whatever happened at the ball, this last afternoon must be hers.

The hall at Tytup was the largest in the district and on the night of the ball was richly decorated for Christmas. Holly sprayed from behind every picture, ivy trailed from every ledge, and garlands of both framed every mirror and picture. Great candles glowed on sconces and in the middle of the ceiling hung a huge kissing bunch made of two large hoops set to make a sphere, covered with greenery and dangling with apples and oranges. The pearly berries of mistletoe and the scarlet of holly glowed amidst the leaves and as the dancers swirled about the floor, the great sphere moved gently above them, its rich colours gleaming in the light of candles and lamps.

Like every other lady present, Louisa was given a dance card. This was in the form of a small booklet made of card, embellished with trailing ivy and holly designs and printed in swirling letters of gold. Each dance was listed and numbered, with a line next to it on which the gentlemen could write their names with the tiny pencil attached to the card by a silver cord.

'I hope someone will want to dance with me,' Martha said nervously as they took off their cloaks in the room set aside for that purpose. 'I can't bear the thought of sitting with Mamma and the other mothers all evening.'

'Of course someone will dance with you.' But Jane spoke absently. As they went down the broad staircase her eyes were everywhere, seeking the mysterious Nicholas Craven. Martha, too, was quivering with excitement and almost dropped her programme when a young man, a shipowner's son from Ulverston, approached her and asked for the first dance.

Louisa followed them slowly. She was still afraid of meeting Nicholas, and for once would have welcomed the chance to sit with the mothers in a corner. She wondered if he would recognise her; her mirror had shown her that she looked very different in the sea-green silk, with her hair piled in chestnut curls on top of her head. Gone was the wild gipsy that Jane and Susannah so disliked; in her place was a stranger who took everyone by surprise.

'Why, Miss Louie, you look beautiful!' Tilly had exclaimed when she was ready at last. 'You really suit that colour, it brings out the green in your eyes. And the shape's better for you than it ever was for Miss Jane – shows off your figure.'

Louisa stared at herself. Tilly was right, she had never noticed those green flecks and shadows in her eyes before. Neither had she realised just how much her shape had changed over the past year or two. Her waist had narrowed down, so that the dress had not needed to be let out at all, and above it her breasts, though not as full as Martha's, filled the shot silk tightly and every stitch was pulled to its limit. The low neckline revealed a soft swell of white and against it lay a necklace of tiny emeralds set in silver.

Timothy had brought it to her less than half an hour ago. Looking critically into the mirror when he knocked, she had been startled to see him entering her bedroom; he had not been inside it since the evening he had beaten her, after her fight with Jane. Her eyes met his in the glass and she knew that he was remembering it too. A hot blush ran up her bare neck and into her cheeks.

Timothy stopped just inside the door. He was staring at her and she was even more disturbingly reminded of that other day, the day when he had taken her to the mines and kissed her. She felt her fingers clench themselves into fists, the nails digging into the soft pads at the base of her thumbs. She dragged her eyes away from his and then turned slowly to face him.

'Don't look at me like that,' he said quietly. 'I'll do nothing to harm you.' Oblique as it was, it was the only reference he had ever made to that afternoon. 'I came to bring you this.'

He held out his hands and she saw the necklace lying across his palms. The silver gleamed in the lamplight, the emeralds glowed a deep, piercing green.

'It was your mother's,' he said. 'I'd like you to wear it tonight, Louisa.'

Slowly, Louisa reached out and touched it. She lifted it from his hands and held it up to the light. She gazed at

248

it, at each separate stone, and as she thought of her mother wearing this, the tears came into her eyes.

'It was my wedding present to her,' Timothy said.

Louisa turned back to the mirror and reached behind her neck to fasten the clasp. But she had not looked first to see how it worked and for a few minutes she fumbled. Her father came closer and, with hesitation, put up his own hands.

'Let me do it for you.'

Louisa stood very still. The touch of his fingers against her bare skin was cool, yet felt like fire. The roughened skin scratched gently on the nape of her neck, sending little shivers through her. She closed her eyes, unable to look into the mirror and meet his glance, and then she felt his fingers fall away and opened her eyes again to see the necklace in place.

Timothy had stepped back, away from her. His face was pale and she could see that he was breathing quickly. For a moment, she felt again the old panic, the fear, and then he was looking at her with a father's eyes, with pride and wonder. He shook his head slowly, as if finding it difficult to believe what he saw.

'You've grown up, Louisa. You're a woman, and a beautiful one.'

Louisa felt the tears sting her eyes and looked down so that he shouldn't see them. She felt his hands on her shoulders once more, the fingertips brushing her bare skin as he laid his cheek momentarily against hers. His skin was slightly rough, coarse against her smoothness, and she could feel the scratch of his whiskers.

'Oh, my poor Louisa,' he murmured. 'My poor, poor Louisa . . .'

They stood together, not moving, as if caught in a spell. And then it was broken. Susannah's footsteps sounded on the stairs and her voice could be heard calling peremptorily for her husband.

Timothy took his hands from Louisa's shoulders and

stood away from her once more. As if he expected never to see her again, he let his eyes move slowly over her, taking in the colour and style of her dress, the shining chestnut hair, the gleam of the emeralds at her throat. And then, with an odd look that was half pride and half sorrow, he turned and left the room.

Louisa remained quite still. Her throat was aching with a sudden surge of grief for the years that they had lost.

'*Louisa*! The gentleman's asking you for a dance. Where on earth are you, child?'

Susannah's voice was irritable, though she was doing her best to overlay her irritation with a semblance of fondness. With a little laugh, she said to the man who was standing before them, 'She's such a dreamer. We never know whether she's with us or in some world of her own.'

'I'm sorry,' Louisa said guiltily, and handed the man her dance card. 'Yes, of course you may have a dance. I think there are several left.'

There were in fact a good many left. Louisa had been at some pains to remain as invisible as possible, sitting with her stepmother and the other older women in a corner close beside a large potted palm – almost behind it until Susannah ordered her sharply to bring her chair forward. 'I'll not have any of my girls wallflowers,' she had said, and urged Louisa to accept any request. 'It's not as if you're expecting to find a suitor here, after all.'

And why not? Louisa wanted to ask rebelliously, but she remained silent. She had seen the look on her stepmother's face when she had come into the bedroom to see if she were ready and caught her first glimpse of Louisa in the sea-green silk and emeralds. She had been as surprised as Timothy, as surprised as Louisa herself, and so too had Jane and Martha. All at once, they had seen in Louisa a possible competitor.

'I wish I had kept that dress,' Jane said, looking with dissatisfaction at the new gown she was wearing, which she had been so pleased with. 'It's better than I thought – I must have tried it on in a bad light.'

Now that Louisa had been forced out of her corner, more gentlemen came to claim dances from her. Some were older men, her father's friends and business acquaintances, but there were a good many young men too, and vapid creatures they were, most of them, Louisa thought as she whirled dutifully about the great hall. Conversation was limited to the most tedious of small talk and she looked enviously at other girls, laughing and chattering to their partners. What were they finding so amusing? Was it simply the men who came to dance with her who were boring, or was it that she herself was of no interest? She thought uncomfortably of Susannah's insistence on 'accomplishments' and drawing-room manners. Could she possibly be right? Did her strangeness put people off?

It didn't put Kieran off, she thought with a sudden stab of longing for the gipsy who seemed to have understood her so well. Nor Nicholas . . .

Involuntarily, she glanced about the hall. So far she had not caught sight of Nicholas, either on the dance floor or among the men who stood in groups at the side. Perhaps, after all, he wasn't here.

The evening seemed suddenly flat. It was as if the lamps had dimmed, the colours become muted, the gaiety and sparkle left the dancers' faces. The music lost its tunefulness and when Louisa glanced at the clock she stifled a sigh at the thought of the hours that lay ahead.

The dance ended and her partner escorted her back to Susannah. Louisa thanked him perfunctorily and looked at her card. The next three dances were blank and she sat down on a hard little chair and surreptitiously eased her feet in their satin slippers. Without much interest, she watched as the guests formed for the next dance.

251

'Martha's doing so well,' Susannah said fondly to the other women. 'She hasn't lacked a partner once. And Jane too – the men are positively flocking to dance with her. And how are you enjoying yourself, Louisa dear?' she asked in a solicitous tone, conscious of the other mothers listening.

'Well enough, thank you.' Louisa fanned herself, more for something to do than because she was hot. She stared about the room, watching the swirling colours. If she had her paints with her . . . But she knew she would rather be on the shore at Bardsea, or sitting on a rock on Dunnerholme trying to capture the shades of the trembling sands. Both places seemed a million miles away from this overheated, over-decorated ballroom with its too-loud music and its gaudy dancers . . .

'Mrs Sherwin.' It was the voice of one of the Ulverston shipbuilders. 'May I introduce my nephew? He's expressed a desire to know one of your daughters.' The voice paused. Louisa, still watching the dancers, did not bother to turn her head. It was scarcely likely to be her that the nephew wanted to meet, and if it was, he was probably as tedious as the rest. She wished it were all over and thought longingly of her bed.

'My nephew, Nicholas Craven. Nicholas, this is Mrs Timothy Sherwin, wife of one of my friends.'

'An honour, ma'am.'

Louisa sat very still. The quality of a voice when heard indoors against a hubbub of music and chatter can be quite different from its tones when heard outside, raised above the lament of the wind and the cry of gulls. But it was Nicholas's voice, unmistakably his voice. And she dared not turn her head.

'Mr Craven!' There was an equally unmistakable thrill of excitement in Susannah's voice. 'Of course you may make my daughters' acquaintance – both of them. They're dancing at present, of course, but I'm sure they'll be delighted to make room for you on their cards.

Look, you can just see Jane over there, dancing with the tall gentleman – I believe he's quite besotted with her. And my baby Martha is making quite a success for herself. This is almost her first ball, you know, and she's been so looking forward to it.'

'Delightful, both of them.' Nicholas spoke in a drawling voice that was as artificial as Susannah's affected tones. 'But don't you have a third daughter, Mrs Sherwin? I'm sure my uncle said—'

'Oh, you mean Louisa. She's my stepdaughter.'

'Your stepdaughter, of course,' he said, and Louisa knew he was looking in her direction. 'I think I should like to meet her.'

'Certainly, if you wish.' Susannah's voice had lost a little of its warmth. 'She's sitting just there, by the palm. Not so many partners as my own two – she's rather shy and awkward in company, poor dear.' Susannah raised her voice slightly. 'Louisa, this gentleman wishes to make your acquaintance. Mr Nicholas Craven, this is my stepdaughter, Louisa.'

'Delighted,' he murmured as Louisa turned in her chair and reluctantly offered him her hand. He bent over it slightly, lifting his eyes to look at her at the same time. For a long moment, they looked into each other's eyes and Louisa felt the hot blush mounting into her cheeks.

'Perhaps if you have the next dance free?' he suggested, and she made a fumbling pretence of looking for her card.

'I don't know, I'm not sure—'

'Let me look.' He took the card from her and glanced down the column of names. 'Why, how fortunate, you've got the next two dances free. That means I can put my name against both of them.' He scribbled quickly with the little pencil. 'And since it's only a few moments before this one finishes, I hope I may stay here and wait with you.' He gave her a friendly smile and sat down on the chair beside her.

253

Susannah looked annoyed. 'I'm sure my own two daughters would have been pleased to dance with you,' she began, but Nicholas turned smilingly and lifted his hand a little.

'Oh, but I'm sure their cards are full – didn't you tell me how popular they both are? And perhaps I shall have an opportunity later. Meanwhile I would be foolish to allow this charming young lady to escape me.' He turned and looked directly into Louisa's eyes. 'She looks as though she might blow away in the wind if I don't capture her at once.'

He had recognised her of course. The sea-green dress, the piled curls, the emeralds – none was sufficient disguise. Jane had been wrong. Nicholas might only ever have seen her looking like a gipsy, but here in the glittering ballroom, dressed in finery such as he could never have imagined on her, she was still Louisa. Or Moll . . .

The music came to an end. For a few minutes there was chatter and laughter. Louisa sat in an agony of terror. In a few moments the music would start again. She would have to stand up with Nicholas, give him her hand, let him hold her in his arms. With the whole of Furness looking on, she would have to be close to him, as close as she had been on the beach at Bardsea or in the meadows at Broughton Beck, and all the while she must pretend that he was no different from any other partner. All the while she must pretend that they were strangers.

The band struck up the music for a quadrille. Shaking, Louisa stood up. Nicholas took her hand and led her on to the floor.

The set formed and they began the grand square, following the movements with the stately grace that the dance demanded. Forward and back, meeting and parting, circling, chaining from one to the other. Each time Nicholas took her hand and Louisa felt the heat of his skin, her heart trembled. Each time they met in the dance, she felt his eyes upon her face, and kept her own cast down, for fear of seeing what his expression might be.

The dance ended. Louisa made to go back to her chair, but Nicholas caught her arm.

'You look hot, Miss Sherwin. Let's get some fresh air.'

'It's cold outside,' she demurred, but he led her firmly over to the tall glass doors and slipped his own jacket round her shoulders. Outside, on the terrace, several couples were enjoying the night air but at the end it was dark and quiet, and Louisa, her wrist trapped in his strong fingers, was forced to follow him.

'And now,' he said, turning her so that she stood against the balustrade, 'tell me what a serving wench called Moll is doing at a ball, masquerading as Louisa Sherwin.'

Chapter Fifteen

The marriage of Louisa Sherwin to Nicholas Craven was a surprise to all Furness, and more than a surprise to her family. To Susannah, Jane and Martha, it was insulting as a slap in the face.

'How could he prefer *her*?' Jane raged. 'She must have cast a spell on him, the sly little minx. The handsomest, most eligible man in the district and he must set his eyes on Louisa. It isn't fair.'

'I understand it no more than you do,' snapped Susannah, who was as disappointed as Jane and reacted, as usual, with anger. 'After all the trouble and expense I've gone to to give you the accomplishments you needed. You've had everything a girl could wish for, yet still you can't catch a husband!'

Jane stared at her. Her face was drained of all colour save for two angry spots of red, burning on her cheekbones. She looked very like her mother. 'Perhaps Louisa was right all the time,' she said bitterly. 'Perhaps gentlemen aren't interested in *accomplishments* after all. Perhaps they were a waste of my time as well as yours.'

Martha, too, was disappointed, but since she was only seventeen and liable to fall in love with any young man who came within her sphere, she soon recovered and started instead to become excited about the wedding.

'It's so romantic,' she sighed to Louisa as she sat in the bedroom, watching her stepsister try on yet more new clothes. 'A whirlwind romance! Why, it's like a fairy tale.'

Louisa said nothing. In fact, she was as bemused as everyone else by the rapid turn of events; with the wedding date set for Easter she had scarcely had time to take it all in.

Her fears that Nicholas would be angry at the deception she had played on him had quickly been dispelled. Instead, he had been amused and intrigued; he still, when they were alone, called her 'Moll' and she sensed a certain excitement in him as he did so. What this meant she had no idea, except that it quickened a similar excitement in her.

Nicholas had only been able to dance one more dance with her at the Christmas ball, but that was enough to set tongues wagging. And Susannah was in the act of reprimanding Louisa for her shameful behaviour next morning when he was announced at Pennington Hall. There, he convinced an astounded and privately indignant Susannah that it was indeed Louisa to whom he wished to pay court, and later in the same day he found and spoke to Timothy as well. A short but discreet courtship was permitted, and the engagement announced in February. From then on it was all bustle, preparing for the wedding.

And now the day was here. Since early morning, the house had been astir. Servants who had been for the past week dusting, polishing, sweeping and brushing had disappeared into the kitchens where everyone's help was needed in mounting the wedding feast. Cook was in a frenzy of last-minute preparations. Cold meats and desserts were ready and the oven was filled with joints of beef and pies, while puddings on top of the range filled the air with steam. Maids were busy tammying the soup, pushing the thick mash of cooked vegetables through a large muslin cloth until their arms ached. In the great dining room, used only on special occasions, the table was laid with a long white cloth garlanded with ribbons and set with nosegays of spring flowers, with the bride cake as the centrepiece. Six tiers high and iced white as snow, it stood like a monument to virginity amongst the shimmering glasses and sparkling china.

Louisa went through the day in a dream. It was difficult to believe it was all really happening as she was helped into her bridal gown and went out of the front door, accompanied by her father. He handed her into the carriage and she sat rigid, her fingers cold and unresisting in his. She looked out of the window at the big house, made larger and finer since his marriage to Susannah. Louisa felt no regrets about the prospect of leaving it to set up her own home with Nicholas. It was no longer the rambling farmhouse she had grown up in; small rooms had been knocked together to form larger ones, and the great dining room had been added, together with several others, to provide the kind of accommodation the Mayor of Ulverston might be expected to offer his guests. The Lord Mayor of London, more likely, Timothy had commented and Louisa had sensed his unease in the grander rooms and thought that, like her, he still preferred the simplicity of the home he had shared with her mother. But Timothy had learned quickly that Susannah's wishes were best met if one wanted a peaceful life, and whatever his thoughts were he kept them to himself.

The hedges were bright with new green leaves as the carriage rolled between them, the banks thick with yellow patches of primroses and the taller pink clusters of ragged robin. Finches, tits and sparrows were twittering about their nests and the fields were busy with men and women beginning to sow oats; some, well ahead, were setting potatoes and one farmer had started on his barley.

Louisa loved to see these signs of a new season beginning. It had always seemed strange to her that the

258

year should 'begin' on the first of January, when it so clearly should have been in spring. Now was the time when the land woke from its sleep and began to live again; now was the time when the sun's rays uncurled buds that had been tight as fists all winter, when the breeze breathed life into earth that had been frozen hard. All around were the signs of new life, in the lambs that capered in the meadows, the ducklings already on the ponds, the spring flowers that coloured the cottage gardens.

The little church, too, was filled with flowers. Great sprays of magnolia and lilies adorned the altar, trailing blossom wound about the lectern. Every seat was taken, the pews on the left crowded with people from all over Furness, while the Craven family and their friends from Liverpool filled the groom's side. The servants were there at the back of the church, ready to slip out the moment the service was over. As Louisa entered on her father's arm she could see Nicholas, tall and fair, standing at the head of the aisle. She looked at him with the same disbelief that she had felt all morning. Could she really be marrying this man?

Afterwards, she remembered little of the service – nothing of her responses and promises, little of his save that his voice was unusually deep. And then it seemed that they were at once back in the house, greeting their guests, leading the way into the dining room, sitting down at table to begin the wedding breakfast.

Louisa was reminded sharply of that other wedding, seven years ago, when her father had remarried. She sat beside her new husband, trying unsuccessfully to eat, looking at the huge cake, and thought how she had sat with her stepsisters and seen her future as a cage from which there was no escape. Thinking it would be her last such opportunity, she had slipped away during the speeches and gone running over the meadows to see the gipsies.

That was the day when she had first met Kieran. And as she sat beside Nicholas, his fair head bright as the Easter sunshine, she saw in her mind's eye Kieran's dark curls and merry black eyes. And she felt again the same deep yearning that she had known as she had tramped over the Furness hills, waiting for the travellers to return.

The wedding breakfast was over. The guests had taken their leave at last, and Louisa and Nicholas were on their way to the house at Bardsea Green where Sir Stanley Craven had suggested they should live.

'You can oversee the building of Craven Hall for me,' he had remarked to his son, and Nicholas had readily agreed. The idea of spending his days riding around the countryside, checking on the progress of his father's house, was an appealing one. Until now, he had been forced to spend much of his time in Liverpool, learning the business of shipping and, as he told Louisa quite frankly, he found this tedious in the extreme.

'I shan't do anything, once it's mine,' he said. 'I'll employ good managers and expect them to do the work. Then we can just enjoy ourselves.'

'But don't you want to be involved with it?' Louisa asked. 'Don't you find it exciting to be sending ships all around the country, all over the world, to carry all those interesting cargoes from one place to another?'

'Oh, it's interesting enough, I suppose, just to talk about it,' Nicholas said carelessly. 'But to go into the offices and warehouses every day as Father does, having to study all those dull ledgers and accounts – ugh! I'd rather leave that to someone else, thank you very much.'

'But it's the way your money is made,' Louisa said. 'Aren't you interested in that?'

'The money? Of course I'm interested in it! I like spending it – and so will you.' He smiled at her. 'We'll have some good times, you and I. But you don't want me to waste my time going to stuffy offices in Liverpool, do you? Life's too short for that kind of nonsense.'

Louisa said no more. She thought of her father, going off day after day to the mines or working in his own office on the ledgers that so fascinated her. She thought of the satisfaction he obtained from knowing that every-thing in the house, every morsel of food eaten, every stitch of clothing was paid for by his efforts. Could one gain the same pleasure from comforts that had been earned by someone else?

The gig bringing them from Pennington Hall came to a stop in front of the house where she and Nicholas were to begin their married life. The Cravens had bought this a year or two ago, to accommodate them on their visits to Furness. These had begun as little more than occa-sional holidays with Sir Stanley's brother at Broughton Beck, but as Sir Stanley and his wife had grown more attracted to the area they had bought their own house at Bardsea Green and then, deciding that this was too small, had started to build Craven Hall.

Green House stood in a sheltered enclave, reached by a narrow lane from where the village of Bardsea clus-tered around its little hill. Here there was protection from the storms and gales that sometimes whipped the waters of the broad estuary into a white-capped fury, yet it was only a few minutes' walk to the beach. And no further, up a narrow, hedge-lined track, to the broad spaces of Birker Common from where one could gaze over the spine of Furness past Pennington and Lindal, across to the dark, whale-backed mound of Black Combe.

The servants were lined up to welcome the bridal pair and Louisa walked towards them with a confident smile, certain that she would soon be on the same friendly footing with them as she was with the servants at Pennington Hall.

To her surprise, however, their smiles were distant

and formal. The housekeeper, Mrs Jackson, stood stiff and unbending, giving little more than a nod of acknowledgement along with the customary bob – and that no more than was strictly necessary, Louisa thought. The cook looked as if she spent her life tasting unsweetened rhubarb. The other servants seemed to take their cue from these two and as soon as she and Nicholas had passed through the line and into the front hall, the servants scattered about their duties again, obviously relieved to have the brief introduction over with.

'Not a very warm welcome,' Louisa commented as she preceded Nicholas into the drawing room, but he looked surprised.

'It seemed perfectly adequate to me. They were polite, respectful – what more would you want? They're only servants, after all.'

'But –' Louisa began, and then stopped. *Only servants*. It was an expression she had heard often enough, on her stepmother's lips, from the mouths of other people, and had never been able to understand. The servants at Pennington Hall were her friends – sometimes, it seemed, the only ones she possessed. She had spent hours in the kitchen, out in the stables or in the gardens, and each time her companions had been one or more of the servants. From them, she thought, she had learned everything worth knowing; in fact, especially after her mother had died, they had brought her up.

Servants who gave her no more than a chilly smile or ducked their heads and refused even to meet her eyes made her feel uncomfortable. How could she ever feel at ease living in a home with such creatures?

She walked slowly to the window and stared out. The room looked down towards the Green – a broad space with just a few cottages scattered about its edge. A low ridge rose sharply from the far side of the little dell and a few cows were grazing there. Half a dozen trees – elm, oak and ash – grew about the edge of the grass, and the fresh, light green of buds about to break cast a hazy veil about their branches.

Nicholas came up behind her. She felt his hands on her shoulders, unfastening the clasp of her cloak. The tips of his fingers brushed against her neck.

Louisa shivered. Suddenly, she felt vulnerable, exposed. She knew that no longer could she put off the moment when her marriage must become reality. No longer could she hide behind the fuss of preparations, of entertaining, of writing invitations and consulting with her stepmother and Cook over menus. All that was over. From this moment, she was entering a new life.

Louisa had thrown herself wholeheartedly into the wedding preparations. She had surprised herself, and frankly astonished her stepmother, by the enthusiasm she had shown over even the smallest detail. And when Nicholas had complained that he seldom saw her these days, she had laughed gaily and told him that there would be plenty of time after the wedding.

Now that time had come. And by the sinking of her heart she knew that she had been hiding – hiding from Nicholas, the man with whom she had promised to spend her life.

'What a pretty view,' she said brightly, craning her neck as if to gaze further along the valley. 'Look, we can see the bay. I shall be able to tell when the tide is out.' Her words sounded inane and ridiculous even in her own ears. Nicholas only laughed and drew her close against him.

'We'll have an even better view from upstairs,' he murmured in her ear. 'Our bedroom window faces the same way.'

'So it does. But it will be dark when we're there. Except in the mornings, of course; it will be light then.' Why was her voice so high, so unnatural? Nicholas was stroking her neck now; her heart was beating fast and her hands trembled. She sought frantically for something

263

else to say, something that would distract him.

'Why not go for a walk?' she asked, moving sharply away from the window, away from those stroking hands. 'It seems so long since we walked on the shore. The tide's out now. We could walk for miles on the sands.'

'Tomorrow,' he said softly; she had not escaped him, he had followed her and his hands were on her shoulders again, turning her to face him. 'Tomorrow we will walk as far as you please. But it's late, the evening's already drawing in. And it's our wedding day, Louisa.'

'And is that any reason why we shouldn't go for a walk?' she asked, trying to make her voice light. But it came out as brittle as crazed glass.

'Every reason.' He took her face between his hands and tilted her head back so that she was forced to look up at him. She gazed into his eyes, feeling the kick of her heart against her ribs. 'We are married now, Louisa. There are certain duties we must perform. Pleasant duties.'

'D-duties?'

He smiled. 'Are you so innocent, little Louisa? You did not seem so when you told me your name was Moll and let me kiss you in the fields. When you looked at me with bold eyes and teased me: I would not have said you were innocent at all.'

'I wish you would forget that,' she said, but he laughed and shook his head.

'Forget little Moll? How could I do that? Why, do you suppose I never thought of you between our meetings? Do you suppose I never remembered you during those years I spent in Paris? Oh, Moll, my darling Molly, I've been burning for you these past six months and more, and thinking of you for longer. There was always something different about you. You were a puzzle, and I love puzzles. There was a mystery about you that I had to solve.' His mouth widened in a slow smile. 'I mean to solve that mystery tonight. Walks on the beach can wait. I've waited long enough.'

He bent his head and touched her mouth with his. Louisa trembled again and her lips grew stiff and unresponsive. Nicholas's arms tightened about her, the pressure of his mouth increased, and she cried out involuntarily, her cry muffled by his lips. His arms were crushing her against him and through her gown she could feel the hardness of his chest, his loins, his thighs.

He had never held her in this way before. His kisses had been sweeter, softer; tender and gentle. His sudden roughness startled her, and she laid her hands on his arms and pushed, trying to withdraw herself from his embrace.

'So you're not so innocent, little Moll,' he muttered, and opened his mouth against hers. 'You know enough to struggle a little. Enough to send a man wild when he holds you in his arms . . .' His arms were clenched about her, and her efforts at loosening his hold were no more than the struggles of a newborn kitten. So closely held was she that she could not even move her head, and was compelled to suffer the bruising of his mouth against her lips. She felt herself bend backwards, forced into an arch by the pressure of his body, and in an automatic attempt to save herself from falling she clutched his shoulders.

Nicolas gave a deep groan that she felt low in his chest, throbbing against her breasts, before she heard it issue from his throat. He dragged her hard against him, standing upright so that she was lifted off her feet. She stared at him, shocked by his roughness, shocked again by his expression.

His eyes were dark, almost black, the shimmering grey now no more than a rim of glinting silver round the wide pupils. The whites were suffused with red, flushed as his face, and his nostrils were flared like those of an angry stallion. His lips were full and red, drawn back a little from his teeth, and he was breathing quickly. There was an avid excitement about the tautness of his skin and muscles, and although he looked directly at her, Louisa felt as though she had become strangely invisible; as though he saw, not her, but an object he must possess, a creature he was compelled to subdue, a challenge he must conquer.

Desperate now, she struggled and he lowered her to the floor, standing her once again on her own feet. Fear invaded her heart. She could feel his fingers at her breast, tugging at her clothes. Frantically, she twisted in his arms, but he only laughed deep in his throat and murmured words she could not hear. He had her bodice open now and bent his head to lay his mouth on her breasts. He took her nipple between his lips and sucked, then bit it gently with his teeth. Louisa cried out and her body jerked, pulling the nipple painfully so that she cried out again. And Nicholas laughed again, as if with satisfaction and pleasure, and sucked the breast harder into his mouth.

'Please, Nicholas,' she whispered, 'please don't. The servants – someone may come in at any moment.'

'On our wedding evening?' He raised his head, laughing at her. 'They'll know better! Why should anyone come in, anyway? We need nothing more tonight, nothing more than each other.'

He bent again and Louisa felt the panic rise up, almost engulfing her. She put her hands on his shoulders, pushing him away, and he frowned.

'What is it? What's amiss?'

'I'm afraid,' she began in a whisper, but could not continue. What could she tell him? How could she say that she was afraid of what he would do, afraid of his lovemaking? Tilly had told her what would happen, and the thought of it repelled her. But it was a wife's duty to submit. Everyone who was married had to do it – it was the price of freedom, of escape. She had promised it in church that morning, before the whole of Furness.

Nicholas smiled slowly. 'You're afraid of one of those little maids coming in and catching us,' he said, and she sensed a certain excitement in his tone, as if he found the thought pleasurable. 'Well, perhaps you're right. And we'd be more comfortable upstairs, in our own bed.' His arm still tightly about her, he turned and steered her towards the door. 'But one day, little Moll, we'll take our pleasures here, on the floor if we like. Or out of doors, in the long grass – wherever we happen to be. Like the dairymaid you pretended to be, hmm?'

They were at the door and he opened it. Louisa dragged the edges of her bodice together, still terrified that they might meet a servant – the housemaid, perhaps, come to make up the fire, or a parlourmaid to ask if there was anything they would like to eat or drink. His arm still about her, the fingers stroking the side of her breast, Nicholas walked her up the stairs. At the top, he pushed open their bedroom door and drew her inside.

'There,' he said, turning the key. 'Now we are safe from any prying eyes. There is nothing more to fear.'

Louisa stared at him. Nothing more? But she had everything to fear now, for there was no further excuse, no more reason to prevent him taking his pleasure of her in any way that he pleased. There was no escape.

Nicholas kissed her again and Louisa closed her eyes. If she must suffer this, let it be over soon. Only let it be over soon.

She felt his mouth hard against hers, felt his tongue against her lips, her teeth, inside her mouth. One arm was round her now, holding her close against his body; the other hand was unfastening the rest of the buttons of her gown. Her breasts, the little breasts that had no need of a bust improver but had their own curving shape, were free of the restraint of lace and silk, and she heard his quick breath as he took them in both hands and buried his face in their whiteness.

This was not the wedding night Louisa had envisaged.

Although Tilly had given her an outline of what would happen, she had not been able to picture any details. Rather than this, she had thought of undressing alone or with the help of her maid; of donning the white nightgown, frilled with lace and threaded with thin satin ribbons, that Susannah had said was right for this occasion and Martha had sighed over; of waiting in the big bed, the room lit by candlelight, for Nicholas who would appear arrayed in his own nightshirt and slip into bed with her. She had imagined his kisses, gentle and tender as before, had expected him to caress her with an equal gentleness. And then what Tilly had told her to expect would have happened, quite quickly she supposed, and Nicholas would have given her a few more grateful kisses and they would have gone to sleep.

She had never imagined this hurly-burly, this rough wrenching off of clothes, this almost demented handling that must surely leave her bruised. She had never thought that Nicholas would strip first her and then himself naked, so that all the parts of her body which she had thought private and never even looked at herself were exposed to his view. She had never expected him to stare at her in that way, as if he wanted to devour her. And she had certainly never expected his appearance to be as it was.

Were all men like that? Did they all have this great protuberance, this jutting thing so dark a red it was almost purple, thrusting out of a nest of tangled hair? She stared at it, feeling sickened. Was it natural, or was it a deformity? And did he really mean to force it into her body, into a space that surely could never receive it? Why, it must be seven, eight inches long, and so thick she could barely close her fingers round it – not that she'd ever want to try. The thought of touching it, letting it touch her, was utterly repugnant.

'See how you excite me, little Moll,' he whispered, and came close, so close that it rubbed against her belly and she flinched and twisted sharply away. But Nicholas caught his hands under her buttocks and dragged her against him, so that she could feel the protuberance against her skin, and then working its way between her thighs. 'It's been so hard to wait,' he said against her ear, and lifted her again from her feet, carrying her over to the bed. 'All these months, I've been longing for this. And now it's here.' He looked into her eyes and she stared back, trembling. For a moment longer, he held her; then he laid her on the bed. He stood gazing down at her as she lay splayed beneath him. 'You're my wife at last . . .' And he lowered himself on top of her.

His body was heavy, but the softness of the bed dispersed most of his weight. Louisa felt his length against hers, skin against skin. Her body quivered. She could feel a succession of unfamiliar sensations, a tingling that ran through her blood, a terror that was in itself almost pleasurable, but a pleasure that brought fear rapidly in its wake. It was as if she were in several parts, some of them crying *yes*, others screaming *no*. As Nicholas touched her breasts, she gasped with something that might have been delight; but as he squeezed them in his hands she moaned with pain and discomfort.

The jutting thing was pressing against her now, forcing itself again between her legs, pushing hard against her groin. Her panic grew. It surely could not be right, this great weapon thrusting its way into the delicate recesses of her body. It was too big, too hard. It would tear her skin, wrench her flesh, damage her in ways she could barely imagine. She wanted to stop him, to plead with him, but her voice came in whimpers and he only laughed a little and renewed his thrusting.

'Moll,' he muttered against her throat, 'Moll, Moll, Moll . . . If you knew how you've tormented me these past months. But you've always known that, haven't you? With your saucy smiles and pert ways – you knew quite well what you were doing to me. And now it's my turn. Now, at last, I can enjoy you as I've wanted. You're mine! Mine to take whenever I will. Ah, Moll, Moll, there'll be no more teasing. No more torment.' He was pushing harder with each word, as if determined to force his way through a door that was locked, a door that was too small, as if he would tear down the walls in his efforts. 'Mine!' he muttered, intense and absorbed, as if each violent push took him nearer to his goal. 'Mine – mine – *mine* . . .'

Louisa screamed. With that last thrust, she felt her skin tear, felt the warmth of blood, felt the whole of his organ surge forward into her body and fill her so that his groin was pressed hard against hers. His hard thighs forced her legs wide apart and she found herself gripping his shoulders, though whether she wanted to hold him close or push him away she scarcely knew.

Nicholas's voice rose too in a series of loud groans that burst from his throat as again and again he pushed himself into her, oblivious of her pleadings. She felt the rasp of his skin against hers, the roughness of his hair against her belly, the violent friction of his movements in and out of her body. He drove himself into her, deeper and deeper so that she could feel him pressing hard inside, thumping against her, and she cried out again in fear, certain that he was killing her, certain that her body could withstand no more of his desperate insistence.

At her cry, Nicholas seemed to reach a climax of frenzy. He rose above her, head flung back so that the muscles of his neck stood out like ropes, eyes wide and staring, and gave one last mighty thrust that, if he had not grasped her shoulders to keep her there, would have sent Louisa sliding away from him across the bed. For a moment he stayed, thrusting no longer but squirming his groin against hers, as if there were still depths he had not reached, could not reach. And then he gave a great shudder and suddenly, unexpectedly, collapsed on her trembling body.

Louisa lay still. She felt dazed and shocked. Her mind went back to the things Tilly had told her, to the pictures she had conjured up in her thoughts. Why had none of it happened? Why had Nicholas not stroked and caressed her? Why had he attacked her in this brutal way instead? Where was the tenderness, the love, that she had hoped for?

Was it all a dream? A romantic fiction to make women marry? And if so, why did no one tell the truth? Why was it hidden, never spoken of? Why did women themselves pretend that it didn't happen?

Perhaps they are all too ashamed, Louisa thought, knowing that she could never speak of what had just happened to her.

She wondered what he was thinking. Was he as disappointed as she? Had it been as painful for him? She thought of the distorted, almost agonised expression on his face during those final moments. Perhaps the dreadful swelling had caused him some utterable torture, perhaps he had only continued because he felt it his duty. Was there something wrong with him, to cause such agony? Or was something wrong with her, something that made his body unable to function as it should so that he had strived and strived and finally collapsed with the effort?

She tried to move but Nicholas was too heavy upon her. He seemed to have gone to sleep. She wondered how long she must lie here, half crushed beneath the dead weight of his body, feeling the chill of the evening air upon her exposed skin. Suppose he stayed asleep on top of her all night, what would the maid think when she came in tomorrow morning to draw the curtains? Would she even be alive then, or would the breath have been crushed entirely from her body?

Or was he not merely asleep, but unconscious?

'Nicholas,' she whispered, and to her relief he turned his head.

'Humm? Louisa, my love.' He sounded sleepy, but not ill. Rather, he sounded almost content. And his next words confirmed the astounding notion. 'Louisa – Moll – that was all I dreamed of.'

All he'd *dreamed* of? She turned her head towards him in astonishment and he kissed her cheek. 'But—'

'Let's get into bed,' he said softly. 'Never mind your nightgown, sweet Moll. I want to feel you close to me. I want to feel your body, warm against mine.' He drew back the sheets and held her body between his hands, drawing her into the circle of his arms. He covered them both with the blankets and pulled her half across him so that she could feel every contour of his body. She stiffened, fearing a second assault, feeling her body already closing against the intruder, as if even without her wish it was determined not to be invaded again.

But the great jutting organ with which he had attacked and invaded her had gone. In its place was something much smaller, soft and flaccid, something that hung uselessly between his legs as he moved across the bed. It had no power of its own at all, though when she inadvertently touched it, it stirred a little as if coming to life. She withdrew her fingers quickly and Nicholas laughed.

'So insatiable, little Moll?' he murmured. 'Not yet, I fear. But I promise you that we'll play again before morning and I'll satisfy you as much next time as the last. Better, in fact, for we'll have no barrier to break through then; there'll be no need at all for delay.'

Louisa listened, not knowing what he meant but understanding that the night was not yet over. Having claimed his rights once, Nicholas would claim them again. And again and again. How often? Every night? Several times each night? She had no idea. She only knew that in his eyes everything that had happened was as he expected, what he had wanted and been waiting for.

It was what her father had wanted too, she thought with sudden clarity, on that July afternoon all those years ago. He too had wanted to lie with her like this, thrusting himself into her. But he had known it was wrong. He had withheld himself, had kept himself apart from her and turned instead to his wife, because only in marriage could a man safely unleash these dreadful passions. And this was the price a woman must pay for the security only a man could give, and for the children that a woman must have.

I must have children, she thought as Nicholas fell asleep beside her. I must have children, because if I don't none of this will be worthwhile. Because without them to give meaning to it all, life will be intolerable.

And as she lay, bruised and sore, staring wide-eyed into the darkness and listening to the breathing of her new husband, she saw that she had escaped from one cage only to walk into another.

Chapter Sixteen

In 1842, two years after Louisa and Nicholas were married, Parliament passed a law which made it illegal to employ children under ten years old in mines and factories. In the same year, the baby Prince of Wales was christened, the Anti-Corn Law League became even more vociferous despite the Government's attempt at compromise, and Chartist meetings became more frequent and more violent. In Sir Walter Peel's budget, income tax of sevenpence in the pound was introduced – the first time such a tax had been imposed in peacetime – and the Queen herself volunteered to pay, along with her subjects. Overseas, the uneasy peace in Afghanistan was broken as the British retreated from Kabul, but a peace treaty signed in China brought an end to the war there and a new acquisition to the Empire in the form of the island of Hong Kong.

Few of these events stirred the communities on Furness. The Children's Employment Act was of far greater moment than an island on the other side of the world, and although the introduction of income tax was received with little pleasure, it was agreed that there was nothing to be done about it. And Chartist riots in Manchester and strikes in Sheffield, where furnaces stood idle and men paraded the streets demanding 'a fair day's wage for a fair day's work', were more important than the fate of an army somewhere in Asia.

Louisa heard of the Children's Employment Act with

relief. She had grown more and more uneasy about the lives led by little children deep under the ground and had been firmly in support of the Royal Commission which had enquired into their conditions, reading every word reported in the newspapers and never letting pass an opportunity to speak of it to her father or the other mine owners.

'Really, it's most unladylike to take such an interest in these things,' Susannah had told her sharply. Louisa's marriage had made little difference to her stepmother's attitude; she still took it upon herself regularly to criticise Louisa's ways. 'People will begin to avoid you.'

'Only the ones I'd like to avoid myself,' Louisa retorted. 'Anyone who can believe it is right to send little children down into mines or make them work in noisy, dangerous factories for twelve or even eight hours a day is not the kind of person I want to know anyway.' She glanced at her father as she spoke. Timothy, who had once defended his right to employ children, had conceded that the new Act was right and now employed only those over ten years old. Even that seemed young to Louisa, but at least they had a few more years to spend in the fresh air. Not everyone shared her view, however.

'I don't see why you have to worry so much about them,' Nicholas observed. 'They're nothing to us. Anyway, I've been told that the miners themselves don't like it much – they needed the money their children could earn. Now they can only work on the land, and there are more of them than the farmers can employ. Will you be pleased when all the children you've been so anxious about starve to death?'

'Will you care at all?' Louisa's tone was sharp, as it so often was nowadays. She moved to the window and sighed. Two years married, and she and Nicholas seemed far apart. And in her own ears she often sounded as shrewish as her stepmother. Was this what marriage did to all women?

Perhaps it was not surprising if they all had to put up with what she endured night after night. Although it had never again been quite so terrifying as that first night, for at least she knew now what to expect, Louisa had never overcome her repugnance for Nicholas's lovemaking. Though little love was made between them, she thought, and indeed she could not see how it might be. To her, the whole procedure was no more than the satisfaction of her husband's animal lust, to be tolerated because it was her legal duty and because it was the only way of conceiving the children she now so ardently desired.

But it was still uncomfortable, even painful as Nicholas thrust himself into her body. The only good thing to be said for it, she thought as she lay and suffered the friction of flesh on dry flesh, was that it was quick. Within five minutes of getting into bed, he had penetrated her, and after only a few quick thrusts he had rolled away and fallen asleep. Indeed, if she concentrated hard on other things she could almost forget it was happening. And matters had certainly been better since she had confided in Tilly.

'It shouldn't be like that,' the maid declared. She had now left Pennington Hall and come to live at Green House as Louisa's own maid. 'You oughter get wet – it'd slide in easy enough then. Try some oil or some of that cream you put on your face.'

Louisa did so and found an immediate improvement. There were even times when she almost enjoyed the sensation, but no sooner had she begun to take pleasure in it than Nicholas uttered the grunt that meant for him it was complete and pulled himself away from her. And she would lie awake, staring into the darkness and wondering if that really was all; if there might not, sometimes, be more. If a woman could enjoy it as a man seemed to, if only she were kissed and caressed into desire, if only that brief hint of pleasure she sometimes glimpsed could somehow be prolonged. And then she

276

would feel shame creep over her, the shame she had always felt about the yearnings of her body. Such thoughts were sinful, wrong. They must be pushed away.

If only she could conceive a child. But as yet, nothing had happened. Her monthly bleeding occurred with depressing regularity and even Tilly couldn't offer much help.

'There's potions and stuff you could take,' she said doubtfully, 'but I don't set much store by them meself. Pity the gipsies ain't about. I've heard tell of folk going to them. But it's early days yet, Miss Louie. Plenty of folk take two, three years to fall.'

'Well, I wish I wasn't one of them,' Louisa said. The sooner she became pregnant, the sooner she could claim respite from Nicholas's attentions. The thought of months of undisturbed nights was like a vision of paradise.

It still seemed impossible to Louisa that the procedure which was such an ordeal to her could be a pleasure to Nicholas. Not that it was such a pleasure these days, she thought. Lately, he had been even more perfunctory, as if the act of love had become no more than a tiresome habit, as little enjoyed as brushing the teeth but without which it was impossible to sleep. And in the mornings, where once he had been ready to give her the tender kisses she had enjoyed, he now scarcely glanced at her. Instead, he rolled grumpily out of bed and dressed without a word. Louisa, remembering unhappy attempts at conversation in the early days, knew better than to speak.

'Moll,' he had whispered to her on waking together on that first morning of their marriage. 'Moll, my sweet little dairymaid. Have I made you as happy as you've made me?'

Louisa had turned in the bed and stared at him. His fair hair was tousled, his grey eyes sleepy but smiling. He did indeed look content and, feeling the bruises of her

277

body, the soreness, she felt a welling resentment.

'Happy?' she echoed. 'I've done my duty as a wife, should it make me happy too?'

'Why, of course.' He reached for her and moved his hands over her body. 'Ah, little Molly, did I hurt you? It's always like that the first time. It'll be better now, I promise you. Let me show you.'

'No, please!' She twisted away from him. 'Let me alone, Nicholas. I don't want—'

'You *don't want*? You don't want my love?' His eyes were wide awake now. 'Louisa, do you know what you're saying?'

She shook her head. 'Please. I'm so tired.'

Nicholas smiled. 'Naturally you are. It's been a new experience for you – and a very happy one, I'm sure. And it will be even better. But I know young women sometimes do feel a little tearful after the first time.' He drew her towards him and she was sharply aware of their nakedness. Something brushed against her belly and she gasped. Was it starting all over again? Had that – thing – grown again, was it even now stretching towards her like some greedy reptile? She shuddered and Nicholas gave a little laugh. 'You see? You're as excited as I am. Oh, my little Moll. There's never been anyone like you, so ready, so eager, so generous in your loving.' He moved his hands on her body, stroking the shivering flesh, his fingers now at her breasts, squeezing her nipples, now sliding over her belly and down to her thighs, probing the delicate creases and insinuating themselves into areas that were more sensitive than she had ever realised. 'Move against me, Moll,' he murmured in her ear and she felt him push hard against her. 'Let me feel you move – ah yes, yes . . .'

It was starting again – had already begun. And once more Nicholas was taking her involuntary struggles for compliance, for eager response. With each squirm his excitement grew, with each frantic plea he held her a little more tightly. Within a few minutes he was once again thrusting himself into her, driving deep into her body so that she lay helpless beneath him, any movement now causing her even greater discomfort. But once again, it was mercifully quick; after only a few quick stabs he was uttering his own loud groan and collapsing upon her, just as he had done the night before.

'Moll,' he whispered again, and Louisa's patience, so sorely tried, snapped.

'Don't call me that!' she exclaimed, trying to push him away. 'I'm not Moll, I never was, and you know it. And please get off me, you're heavy.'

Nicholas opened his eyes and stared at her in astonishment. 'Louisa? What's wrong, my love? What have I done?'

To that, Louisa could find no answer. Assaulted me, she wanted to say, hurt me, used violence on me. But none of these would have been true. For Nicholas, his actions had been no more than the simple consummation of their marriage and, for him, a pleasure too.

'Aren't you happy, Louisa?' he enquired when she made no reply. 'Have I not made you happy?'

His tone reminded her of a fawning puppy. She thought of a dog she had once had, which had been so attached to her that she had been unable to move without it, unable to sit down without finding its paw upon her knee, waiting to be stroked and patted. The dog had irritated her so much that she had in the end given it away.

Irritation threaded her voice now as she said, 'Happy? How should I be happy?'

'Why, through our loving,' he said. 'You wanted it when you were Moll, the dairymaid. You wanted my kisses then.'

'Your kisses, yes. But not – not *that*. Not to be hurt and forced and – and—' But she did not know the words

279

for what she felt. She only knew that there had been some kind of violation.

'*Forced*?' Nicholas echoed. 'Louisa, I never forced you. You wanted it. You held yourself against me, you cried out in pleasure. You opened yourself to me. It's always difficult the first time, you must know that. But once that's over—'

'How should I know that?' she broke in. 'I knew nothing, nothing. I thought you would kiss me and hold me, I thought you would make me feel beautiful. Instead, you pushed that – that *thing* into me and didn't care if I were hurt or not. Look,' she pushed back the bedcovers, showed him the blood on the sheets, 'look at that. Now can you say you didn't hurt me?'

Nicholas looked. His eyes moved over her body, taking in the whiteness of it, the silky smoothness. He said, 'But that always happens, Louisa, the first time. I told you, it will be better now, better every time.'

'Better?' she spat. 'How can such a humiliation ever become *better*? How can such a disgusting thing ever be a pleasure?' Tears came to her eyes, began to roll down her cheeks, and she turned away from him. 'It will never be better for me,' she whispered. 'I've been soiled all my life. Take your pleasures, Nicholas, if you must, but don't expect me to share them.'

There was a long silence. Louisa lay still, fighting her tears, fighting the bitterness of disappointment, the crashing of all her hopes. Then Nicholas spoke, his voice very quiet.

'I wanted only to love you, Louisa. I wanted only to show my pleasure in having you for my wife. If you prefer to look on it as a humiliation, a duty, then so be it. And now I'm getting up. I'll tell your maid to bring you tea.'

She felt the movement of the bed as he swung himself out of it, heard his movements as he dressed. And then the door opened and closed softly and she was alone.

Louisa rolled on to her back. She stared at the ceiling with its ornate plasterwork. And fresh tears came to her eyes and rolled down the sides of her face, into her ears and out again to soak the pillow.

And on that morning, the first of their marriage, the pattern had been set. At night, Nicholas would take her, quickly and with a kind of desperation, as if afraid that if it were not quick it would not happen at all. Louisa, accustomed by now to every movement, would lie silent and quiescent in his arms, distracting her mind with thoughts of household matters, of the mines, of her brother Walter – anything that might make these few minutes pass more quickly.

As soon as it was over, Nicholas would pull himself away; then they would both turn over, he to sleep and she to toss until the small hours.

In the morning, without even glancing at her, he would leave the bed and dress in silence. And when she next encountered him, downstairs, they would speak to each other politely, like strangers.

Night after night, for two long years. And still no sign of a child to compensate for their misery.

The gipsies, Tilly said, might be able to help her. But the gipsies had not been in Furness for several years now. In their place had come another group of travellers, a dirty, unkempt rabble who begged and stole food rather than hunted or earned it, who left rubbish and filth behind them where they had camped and brawled in the public houses of Marton and Lindal. Few people would go to them for potions and it was unlikely they even knew of such things, though no doubt they would be pleased to sell some concoction to anyone gullible enough to pay.

Throughout the summer and winter of 1842, Louisa waited and hungered for the child she craved. To ease her longing, she took to visiting her father's house where she spent hours with Walter, by now a well-grown child of seven.

'He reads well already,' she told Nicholas during one of their lonely dinners. 'And can recite several poems. But of course he really likes best to be in the open air.'

'And you with him, no doubt.' Nicholas looked at her with wistful eyes. 'You've never lost your liking for roaming the countryside, have you?'

Louisa glanced away immediately. She hated to be reminded of those days when she and Nicholas had wandered the fields and lanes together. More because of the effect such reminiscences had on him than on herself, it seemed best to keep the conversation in other channels. But occasionally it veered in that direction despite all her efforts, and Nicholas would look at her with hunger in his eyes, as if still reluctant to believe that she was not the pert dairymaid Moll he had thought her then.

Moll would have responded to him as he wanted, she thought sadly. Moll would have been saucy and eager, willing enough to satisfy any man. Moll would have enjoyed it too – known *how* to enjoy it.

And why can't I do the same? she wondered sometimes when Nicholas had rolled away from her into sleep and she still lay wakeful. Why do I feel as if I've taken part in something shameful? Why do I still remember my father and feel as if it were all my fault?

By the following summer, 1843, Jane was married, to a shipowner of fifty years, a friend of Sir Stanley Craven. The festivities were attended by a sense of relief – the family had begun to resign itself to the fact of Jane's remaining a spinster all her life. Jane herself was almost delirious with excitement and patronised her sister and stepsister unmercifully.

'Hubert will see to this,' she would say, as if nobody else in the world were capable of dealing with whatever situation had arisen. 'Hubert will look after it . . . Of course, Hubert knows all about *that* . . . I must see what Hubert thinks first . . .' And so on.

It had been easy enough to tolerate this, for, once married, Jane moved to Liverpool and only returned to Furness for short visits.

'I wonder if I'll ever get married,' Martha said wistfully. 'Here are you and Jane, both with husbands, and here am I, twenty-one years old and still single. I wonder if Jane will have any babies. Do you think you ever will, Louie?'

'How should I know?' Louisa said shortly. 'We have babies or not as God wills. There's nothing we can do about it if He doesn't.'

But is there? she wondered. And when Tilly told her that gipsies had been seen over on Duddon Sands, her heart stirred.

'Not the drunkards that've bin coming these past few years,' the maid said. 'It's the old uns, that used to come – Scarth's tribe. You remember 'em, Miss Louie.'

'Yes, I do. I do indeed.' Scarth's tribe. Kieran. And Kieran's grandmother, who had known all about babies who were born with lumpy heads, about how to help girls who didn't want babies – and perhaps also how to help those who did.

Kieran, she thought, and again her heart moved. What would he be like now? He must be about Nicholas's age, but he would be broad and well muscled where Nicholas was slender, dark where Nicholas was fair, strong in all the ways that Nicholas was weak . . . For Louisa knew now that her husband was a weak man, a man who was content to let others earn his bread, a man who would shelve any responsibility rather than disturb his own easy, indolent life.

Their life now had settled into an uneasy pattern. Louisa spent her days ordering her household, though apart from Tilly she had never gained a satisfactory footing with her servants and had resigned herself to the formal, distant relationship that they seemed to prefer. Always, she had the feeling that they were laughing at her behind her back, that the housemaid's expression stopped only just short of a sneer, the butler's of contempt. When she had finished with household duties, her day was free and as often as not she would take up her shawl and bonnet and go walking along the beach or up on the common. If Nicholas were not using the gig, she might get the stable boy to harness the horse and drive over to Lindal or Pennington to see the mines.

And at night, though not every night, Nicholas would demand his 'rights'. While Louisa lay still and silent in his arms, he would make desperate efforts to gain some response. Or not try at all, but simply thrust himself into her and out again so quickly that she almost wondered if it had really happened.

Once or twice he had suggested that she dress in dairymaid's rig – 'be my little Moll' – but Louisa would not agree. 'I'm not your little Moll,' she said. 'I'm your wife, no dairymaid, and if you can't love me as I am—'

'Do you love me as I am?' he demanded bitterly. 'Do you love me at all?' And she was silent.

Perhaps if they had not both so badly wanted a child, he would by now have taken a mistress, as so many husbands did, and left her alone. But a child could only be got one way and so, night after night, he would pound himself into her and Louisa would accept him, both in the hope that this might be the time they were successful, that from this unhappy union would come the son they both desired.

Now, three years after their marriage, there was still no sign of a child. So when Tilly told her that the gipsies were back at Ireleth, Louisa took the gig one July afternoon and drove herself across the moor.

She left the horse and trap at the mine – her own mine. Billy Rigg was there, working a jackroll. He had never been into a mine since the earthquake but was able to do a few tasks above ground. His father Jacob had died of his consumption a year earlier and Billy was now the eldest of the family, but not the breadwinner. Now, every member of the family had to work at whatever job could be found and the younger children were no longer able to tumble in the garden but instead must go out into the fields to gather stones or scare crows; Jacob's widow, wearing Jacob's old trousers and a thick cloth cap, now went down the mine herself to hurry with a barrow chained to her waist.

Louisa stopped for a word with Billy, but he was uncommunicative and she thought sadly of the days when they had chattered and laughed together like friends. Now he was surly and there was a bitterness about him, as if he blamed Louisa herself for his misfortunes. And perhaps he has cause, she thought as she set off on foot across the moor, for if it weren't for my family and the other mine owners, he might not have been in the mine that day. If miners had had better pay they would not have needed to send their children into the pits and wouldn't now have to send them into the fields.

But she did not spare many thoughts this afternoon for the miners or their children. Instead, she found herself thinking of the children she wanted herself, the family she longed for, that would make marriage worthwhile.

Would Kieran's grandmother still be alive? Would she have any potions that could help her conceive? And . . . would Kieran be there?

Louisa felt her heart bump at the thought. She thought of the last time they had met, the kisses he had given her, the way he had held and touched her. She had known only dimly then what he wanted; now she knew clearly, and she felt again the surging excitement that she had never felt with Nicholas, and the shame that had followed it. Shame, she was accustomed to; excitement, she feared. It would be a good deal better if Kieran were not there, she thought, and knew that if he were she would depart as quickly as she came, for she could not face him even after the years that had passed between.

The camp was in its usual place, in the hollow between the trees. She stood on the rim of the valley, her hand on the twisted trunk of a hawthorn, looking down. The tents were scattered about, the great fire in the middle with gipsies moving about it, some feeding it with sticks, others tending cooking or simply sitting nearby, working at some task.

There were several women, some with babies at their breasts. A tumble of children, darting between the tents. A few men and youths, lounging in the shade of the hawthorns, whittling at pieces of wood – making pegs, perhaps, or the dolls they would clothe in scraps of fabric to sell at the next fair.

There was no sign of Kieran.

Louisa gathered up her courage. Most of the gipsies had known her when she had been a regular visitor to their camp. At first wary, they had come to accept her friendship with Kieran and she had been given a cautious welcome. But would they remember her now? Would they even recognise her?

She let go of the tree, feeling as if she had let go of a comforting hand, and trod slowly, carefully, down the narrow path into the camp.

The men noticed her first. She saw their hands stop moving as they ceased their whittling. They did not otherwise stir, but their eyes were on her, dark and watchful.

The women noticed the men. They turned to look where the dark, watchful eyes were directed, and they saw Louisa.

Nobody spoke. They simply sat, quite still, and waited for her to approach.

Louisa walked steadily on. Her heart was quaking but she held her head high, refusing to be intimidated.

Perhaps, indeed, they did not want to intimidate her but were merely curious. But no one rose to welcome her, no one smiled, there was no flicker of warmth in any of those dark, wary faces.

She stopped a few yards from the fire. She could feel their hostility now, sweeping towards her in waves, and it formed a barrier, holding her back so that she could not go nearer. She looked at the men, who stared back unmoving. She looked at the women and held out her hands in appeal.

'Please,' she said, and her voice shook a little, 'I need your help.'

One of the men rose slowly and came towards her, and she saw with a tremor of fear that it was Scarth himself. An older Scarth, greying around the temples now, but as broad and powerful as ever, his shoulders like those of an ox, his thighs like the trunks of trees. She looked up at him, afraid but determined to stand her ground. What had she ever done to cause his hostility? What had he ever done to cause her to fear him?

Scarth stopped a yard or two away. He looked into her face and she saw that he knew her.

'It's Miss Louisa,' he said, and she realised that these were the first words he had ever spoken to her direct. 'Miss Sherwin – as was.'

Louisa gasped. They knew, then, of her marriage? But how? And why should they be interested?

'Mrs Craven now,' she said. 'But still Louisa. I used to come here, when I was a child.'

'And since you grew to be a woman too, I reckon,' he said. 'Or so Kieran would have us believe.' His eyes were black, piercing as knives. 'After that, we weren't good enough for you no more.'

'That's not true! I just – I—' But how could she explain why she had made no attempt to meet Kieran again, why she had avoided the moor? She glanced helplessly around and her eyes caught a movement on

the edge of the camp. A shadow was there, between two
of the tents, and as she watched, it resolved itself into the
figure of a man.

Kieran.

'I was so afraid. I always have been afraid.'

They were sitting in a hollow, a mile or more from the
camp. They had walked there rapidly, hardly speaking,
after Kieran had come forward and taken her away from
Scarth's hard gaze, from the hostility of the camp. His
face had been grim, his expression closed as if shutters
had come down over his eyes, but his hand on her arm
had been firm and warm. And when they were at a safe
distance, he had stopped suddenly and taken her in his
arms and kissed her.

Louisa, to her own astonishment, had kissed him
back. All her fears, all her shame, seemed to have
evaporated as she stood against him, feeling the warmth
and the strength of him. The hair at the back of his neck
curled tightly about her fingers, the muscles of his
shoulders flexed under her hands. His arms were tight
about her body, pressing her close so that her breasts
were crushed against his broad chest. She could smell the
good male smell of him, the smell of outdoors, of leaves
and grass and wood smoke. A smell so different from
Nicholas's smell of Macassar and tobacco, the smells of
indoors where the air was stuffy and used.

Kieran lifted his face away from hers and looked down
into her eyes. His own were black, their expression
grave, and she saw that he was as moved by this meeting
as she was herself, and as shaken by their kisses.

'Why?' he asked, his voice low. 'Why did you do it,
Louie? Why did you run away from me that day and
never come back?'

She could not answer then. Instead, their hands firmly
entwined, they walked on to the hollow and sank down
there upon the grass. Once more Kieran took her in his

arms, and again she returned his kisses, straining her body against his. This was what she had wanted all along, she thought, this passion that could only exist if shared by two people. Nicholas's passion, though real enough, had never touched her and that was why their lovemaking had been empty for them both. But between herself and Kieran . . .

She gasped and pulled herself away from him, staring at him with wide eyes.

'Kieran, I mustn't do this. I'm a married woman.'

'I know it. And why? Was he so much better than me, Louie? Is it because he's rich and I'm not?' He gazed sombrely at her. 'I would have wed you if it was what you wanted. I would have asked you to come away with me. I'd have stayed in Furness if it had been your wish, but you never gave me the chance to ask. You never came near me again, after that day.' He rolled away from her suddenly, staring at the sky. 'You and me were meant, Louie. Didn't you know that?'

Slowly, she nodded. She had known, deep inside her, that Kieran was the right man for her. Even though he was a gipsy, a traveller, even though there would have been enormous difficulties, she knew that they could have been overcome. Nothing could have stood in the way of their love – if only she had admitted it, if only she had possessed the courage.

'I was afraid,' she said then. 'I was so afraid.'

'Afraid of what? Of me? Of leaving your home? Living in a tent? But I've told you, I would have stayed here. I'd have done whatever you wanted.'

She shook her head, remembering how she had longed once to be kidnapped by the gipsies, to live their wild, roving life. 'I was afraid of love.'

He stared at her and she knew he was recalling those kisses, the way she had reacted. Her sudden terror, her panic-stricken flight.

'And now,' he said quietly, 'now that you're married

and know what love is, are you still afraid?'

Louisa shook her head. She moved closer to him and laid her hand on his arm. She looked up into his eyes and saw there all she had ever desired, all she had foresworn.

'I don't know what love is,' she whispered. 'But I no longer fear it . . .'

Chapter Seventeen

The country was rocked during the rest of that summer
by disturbances. Corn Law repeal agitators in Ireland,
Rebecca and Her Daughters in Wales – everywhere one
looked, it seemed, people were rising up and demanding
better conditions, fair pay, almost the right to live itself,
as if the iron hand of their masters had taken even that
away from them. Disraeli, in a speech about Ireland in
Parliament, declared that not only the Government but
the whole social state of Ireland needed to be reorgan-
ised. And in the new weekly paper *Punch*, which had
fast become a necessity in the homes of all thinking men,
Thomas Hood published a poem called 'The Song of the
Shirt'.

> With fingers weary and worn,
>   With eyelids heavy and red,
> A Woman sat, in unwomanly rags,
>   Plying her needle and thread—
>   Stitch! stitch! stitch!
> In poverty, hunger and dirt,
>   And still with a voice of
>   dolorous pitch
> She sang the 'Song of the Shirt!'
>
>   Work – work – work
> Till the brain begins to swim:
>   Work – work – work

291

Till the eyes are heavy and dim!
Seam and gusset and band,
    Band and gusset and seam,
        Till over the buttons I fall asleep,
And sew them on in a dream.

'O! Men, with Sisters dear!
'O! Men! with Mothers and Wives!
It is not linen you're wearing out,
    But human creatures' lives!
        Stitch – stitch – stitch,
    In poverty, hunger, and dirt,
Sewing at once, with a double thread,
    A shroud as well as a shirt.

Louisa read it with tears in her eyes, her heart going out to the women who sat and stitched all day in poverty and squalor so that gentlemen could dress in finest linen. But for the most part, her mind was taken up with other concerns, primarily her meetings with Kieran.

There was no question now of her avoiding the moor. Instead, she was there whenever she could safely escape, and because Nicholas himself seemed hardly to care where she was these days, escape was easy. Only on days when her stepmother was visiting or expected to be visited, or other engagements were arranged, did she not take the gig and drive it to the bottom of the slaters' road from where she would walk up the hill to meet the gipsy. And there, among the heather, they would lie together and he would teach her about love.

'Of course you like to be touched, Louie,' he said softly in her ear. 'Every woman does. It's natural.' And he would let his fingers move gently, softly, across her bare skin, his touch as light as a feather, brushing the tiny hairs so that each separate nerve quivered with delicate delight. She would think of Nicholas's clumsy caresses, more like the harsh rubbing Tilly had given her in the bath as a child, and stretch herself like a cat in Kieran's arms, purring with pleasure.

She loved to feel his fingers sliding down her spine, hovering over the small of her back so that she arched herself involuntarily and moved against him. She loved to feel him stroking gently the inside of her wrist, her elbows, the backs of her knees, everywhere where the skin was thin and sensitive. There was no part of her that was forbidden him, even though at first she felt a stab of anxiety as his hand slipped between her thighs and touched the sensitive areas that Nicholas had pinched and bruised. But Kieran soothed her fears by touching only gently, by stroking the patch of soft hair, letting his fingertips stray into the creases almost as if by accident, so that she moved again and twisted in his arms, wanting more, wanting she hardly knew what, until his touch became firmer, surer, and she gasped and moved again, twining herself round him, clinging to his body, kissing his face and neck and ears with an abandon that almost frightened her. And then, when it seemed there could be no more delight, she felt him push against her, as Nicholas had pushed yet so differently, and she opened herself to him and welcomed him into her body as she had never welcomed Nicholas, had never thought to welcome any man.

And even then, it was different. Kieran did not want to thrust to his own climax in moments, then roll away, spent and wanting only sleep. Instead, he stayed within her, moving gently, then with more urgency, then slowly again, so that Louisa felt herself transported. When she opened her eyes the sky reeled about her, small white clouds racing overhead; when she closed them, she had no knowledge of where she was or of any world outside their own two bodies.

And always there was the mounting force of those last moments, when Kieran's patience deserted him and he soared into his own world, his passion finally, gloriously, unleashed, taking Louisa with him. During those last few minutes, she knew that there was nothing, no power on earth, which could have stopped their wild flight. And when it was over, with their last cries mingling, they both lay spent and exhausted – but not apart. And if they slept, it was together, in each other's arms, still part of each other as the sky slowly stopped its spinning and the world crept gradually back to surround them.

'Come away with me, Louisa,' Kieran said.

Louisa sat up and combed her fingers through her hair. There was heather in it and she picked out a few pieces, then bent her head towards Kieran, for she could not go home with such signs still about her. Idly, he picked out the sprigs and made a tiny bunch of them, then kissed it.

Louisa reached for her shift and slipped it over her head. She looked down at Kieran's body. He was brown all over, as if he rarely wore clothes at all, his skin darker than hers just as his hair and eyes were darker. He was sturdier than Nicholas, his arms and legs thickened by muscle, and his torso was solid, tapering towards narrow hips.

Nicholas had started to thicken round his waist. His skin was pale, his limbs and muscles less developed. In a few years, he would begin to look flabby.

In a few years . . . Where would she be then? If she went away with Kieran, what would her life be like? And if she stayed with Nicholas?

'Come away with me,' Kieran repeated softly. 'You've no life here. You know we're meant to be together. We always have been.' He grinned suddenly. 'I should've kidnapped you that first day. You wanted it then, you'd have come, just to get away from your new stepma.'

Louisa laughed. 'Perhaps I would.' Her face grew grave again. 'Kieran, I don't know. I want to come, but—'

'You're afraid,' he said, and she nodded.

'I think I am.' She looked out over the purple hill, towards the smoking furnaces of Ulverston. Out there was the life she had always known, the mines, the bloomeries, the meadows and hills of Furness. Across the bay was the little harbour of Poulton-le-Fylde and on the low hills above it the ancient city of Lancaster. Further than that she had never been.

She thought of going with Kieran, with the travellers. They roamed far afield, sometimes north into Scotland, sometimes down into the southern parts of Lancashire, to Cheshire and even further. They followed the fairs, setting up their sideshows and stalls wherever they might find custom, knocking on the doorways of grand houses with their baskets of pegs, their sprigs of 'lucky' heather. They told fortunes and sold love potions and cough mixtures, asking always silver and gold as payment though as often as not they were given only copper. And when there was no money, they fed themselves with fish and game poached at night by men and boys who could move as silently as shadows through the woods.

Could she become a traveller too? Could she learn the skills and arts of the gipsies, become one of them? She seldom went into the camp, conscious of the suspicion with which they looked upon her. She knew now that it arose from the way she had treated Kieran in past years, that they believed her to be simply amusing herself with him. But if she abandoned her own life, if she joined them in theirs?

'We'll be wed,' he said, as if trying to read her thoughts. 'You'll jump over the broomstick with me, Louie.'

She smiled. 'But I'm married already, Kieran.'

'That!' he snorted. 'That's no real marriage. You and I are married more than you ever have been to him, and you know it.'

Louisa turned back and looked at him again. Yes, she

was closer to Kieran than she ever had been to Nicholas. In their bodies they were close, as husband and wife should be; in their minds they could reach out and touch each other almost as deeply. Between herself and Nicholas there had never been such rapport, never such desire, never such joy.

Not for the first time, she wondered why she had married Nicholas. Was it just because she had wanted to score over her stepsisters, to snatch away the prize that they coveted? Was it just to anger her stepmother? Was it for escape?

If so, she had been sadly mistaken, for marriage had proved a trap worse than the one she had escaped. At least, while she had been at Pennington Hall, unmarried, there had been the hope of a better life. Now, there was none – unless she ran away with Kieran and the gipsies.

'Come with me,' he urged, and sat up, taking her hands and gazing deep into her eyes. 'Come next week.'

'Next week? But—'

'We're leaving then,' he said, watching her. 'We're going south. You can come with us. I've already talked to Scarth—'

'You've talked to *Scarth*? About me?'

'Aye. Why not? He'd have to know. And I've talked to Grandma as well. She'd give us a tent of our own, Louie.' He moved a little nearer. 'I'd give you a good life, I swear it. I'd make you happy every day. Come with me.'

She stared at him. Her heart was beating fast. The thought had been in her mind often enough, but always as some dream of the future, scarcely likely to materialise. Now the moment of decision had come, and the day was suddenly charged with urgency. Yes or no. She must say yes or no. Which was it to be?

She met Kieran's eyes and her heart quivered. In their depths she could read passion, love, a strength that she needed, a need that she could satisfy. And something else, a message that he might not even have known he was sending.

If I don't go with him now, she thought, I shall never have the chance again. Kieran will never come back to Furness . . .

A week until the travellers departed. A week in which Louisa must make her preparations.

'You don't need to do anything,' Kieran had said. 'You don't need to bring anything. I'll give you all you need.' But she could not accept that. She had clothes, warm cloaks and mantles that would be needed in winter. If she had too many, could she not give them to the other gipsy women? It seemed ridiculous to leave them behind.

Restlessly, she paced about her room. How could she, in the middle of August, demand that her winter clothes be brought to her? If only she could confide in Tilly, but her maid, though she had always been her friend, had an unruly tongue and could never be trusted to keep a secret. And if she confessed later, as she surely would, that she had known of Louisa's plans, she would certainly be dismissed.

Louisa sat down at the window and gazed out across the bay. The tide was high and the estuary filled with ships beating up against the breeze to Ulverston or Greenodd. Their sails billowed in the sunshine, gleaming white or brown as bracken. Across the bay, buildings stood out sharp and white in the clear sunshine.

After next week, she would never sit and look at this view again.

The door opened and Tilly came in. She gave Louisa a strange look and came to stand beside her at the window.

'Did you ever go over to see the gippos?'

Louisa gasped and gave her a quick glance, then turned quickly back to the window.

'Why do you ask?'

'I just wondered,' Tilly said. 'I just wondered if you'd bin to see that old woman. I wondered if she'd given you owt – you know, what we talked about.'

'A – a potion, you mean?'

'That sorta thing, aye.'

Louisa said nothing. She stared out over the bay as if it were imperative to watch each ship, battling its separate way up the estuary. She had almost forgotten her original reason for going to the gipsies' camp. The desire for a child had been swamped, overwhelmed by her desire for Kieran. It was still there, no doubt, would surface again later, when she and Kieran had settled, when they began to want to raise their own family. But there would be time enough then to turn to his grandmother, to ask her help, if help could be given. Louisa had begun to suspect that she must be barren, as Nicholas had so often accused her. Their childlessness was her fault, he said, and she half believed him.

'No,' she said, 'I never did. I don't think potions can help in cases like mine.'

Tilly gave her another look.

'Well, summat has.'

For a moment or two, Louisa did not take in the meaning of her words. Then she turned and stared up at the maid's face. There was a suppressed excitement there, a secret look, as if Tilly had been granted some knowledge that was kept hidden from Louisa. . . .

'What do you mean? What are you saying?'

'When did you last see your monthlies?' Tilly asked, and Louisa felt a shock.

'I don't know, I haven't thought.' She gripped the arms of her chair and half rose to her feet. 'You don't think . . .?'

'You bin acting funny these past weeks,' Tilly stated, as if that were in itself a sign. 'Going out, roaming around, not eating proper. It takes some women that way. I started to wonder, and then I thought, you ain't given me no linen to wash these past two months. And I looked at the calendar.' She grinned suddenly, the secret knowledge breaking out at last in a wide smile. 'I reckon you're almost two months gone.'

'*Two months*?' Louisa echoed.

'Well, what's so strange about it?' Tilly asked. 'It's normal. And you know you bin frettin for it long enough.'

'I know. I know. I just – I just thought it would never happen.' Her mind was working furiously. Could it be true? Could she really be expecting a child? And if so, whose child was it?

All through the past tumultuous weeks, Nicholas had still been coming to her bed, though less often. And although she might have lain in rapture with Kieran only a few hours earlier, Louisa had been unable to refuse him. If she did, she knew it would end in a violence that was little short of rape, for Nicholas's petulance had grown to a simmering rage which needed little fuelling to make it erupt. She would lie supine beneath him, trying to believe that it was Kieran whose body was pressed to hers. But it was impossible, for every touch was different and there was no fire between them, no tenderness. After only a few minutes, Nicholas would roll away and begin to snore by her side.

Was it really so satisfactory for him? she wondered. Now that she knew how it could be for a man, could she really believe that Nicholas derived the same pleasure from her body as Kieran did? Did he even know that such pleasure could be found?

And now, had he finally succeeded in making her conceive? Or had it been Kieran?

Instinctively, she knew it must have been Kieran.

She stared at Tilly. 'You're sure? It couldn't be – I've missed before, sometimes. When I was younger.'

'When you first started, aye. But you ain't missed now

for years, regular as clockwork, you bin. That's why I reckon it's certain.' Tilly gave her a critical look. 'How you bin feelin' else? A bit faint sometimes? Sick in the morning?'

Sick in the morning. That very day, she had woken with a nauseous feeling, but it had soon disappeared. 'Is that a sign?'

'Oh aye. And it'd be startin' about now. Tain't nothing to worry about, mind. It don't mean there'll be owt wrong with t'babby.' Tilly grinned at her again. 'And there was me, thinkin' you'd bin to the gipsies and got summat from one o' them.'

Oh, I did, I did, Louisa thought wryly. A potion more vital than any an old gipsy woman could produce.

'Well, you'll be tellin' Mr Craven now, I suppose,' Tilly remarked. 'He'll be that pleased. Make all the difference, I reckon, that will.'

All the difference. Yes, it would. But when the child was born, would it look like its father? Would Nicholas see at once that it was not his?

She caught up her thoughts. Nicholas would not even see it! By then, she would be far away, living in a tent with Kieran, a gipsy herself and cut off for ever from her home and family.

'No,' she said, following Tilly's train of thought. 'I won't tell him yet. I – I'd rather be sure. And please, Tilly, don't mention it below stairs. Not until I give you word.'

The maid looked disappointed. 'Well, it's for you to say. But I reckon he oughter know soon. He'd know to take care of you then.'

He'd know to leave me alone at night, Louisa thought, and was tempted. And then reminded herself again – it was only another week. Only six or seven days. And then she would be away for ever, a new life beginning.

Two new lives. Her own and that of her child.

★ ★ ★

Timothy had been to the Louisa mine. Standing there at the head of the shaft, watching the kibbles rise slowly to the surface with their load of ore, his mind had gone back to the days when he had brought Louisa to the pits as a small girl, letting her run free among the men, delighting in her childish chatter, her increasing questions.

He sighed. What had happened to sour it all? If he had not lost control on that July day when she was a budding woman, if he had not suddenly been overwhelmed by her resemblance to Margaret, the wife he had loved so dearly and missed with such desolation . . . It had been a moment only, yet a moment which had changed their lives. He had lost his daughter and gained a son.

Walter was now eight years old. Still spurned by his mother, he had become almost uncontrollable. Intelligent enough, despite their early fears, he scorned his studies and escaped out of doors, much as his half-sister had done. But he did not go to the mines with his father; instead he disappeared over the moors for hours at a time. And if there were cattle let out to roam the lanes, sheep driven away from their territory or chickens terrified, you could be sure that Walter had had a hand in it. Caught at last and brought into his father's presence by an angry mother, he would admit his crimes with a cheerfulness that would have won Timothy over, but Susannah would have none of it. He must be punished, and if Timothy would not do it, she would carry it out herself. And Timothy, knowing that her hand would be the harsher, was forced to comply.

He hated beating his son for these petty crimes. Each time he did so, he was reminded of the day he had beaten Louisa, the day when he had felt those first stirrings of illicit feeling towards her. He remembered the torment he had suffered through the long, lonely nights and the pain of it was as sharp now as it had been then.

The sun beat down hot upon his bare head and he turned away from the pithead. He had completed his business there for the day. His mine captain, a man called Abe Ricketts, able enough but never the friend that Jacob Rigg had been, had shown him the latest samples of ore and they had agreed that the latest great sop was almost worked out. New levels would have to be dug, but it was Abe's opinion that it was hardly worth the effort. Louisa, he said, had had her day.

Timothy did not believe it. There was still a mass of ore down there, he was certain, and he suspected Abe of harbouring some devious motive of his own. But he had not the energy to pursue the matter today; he was tired and hot, and wanted only to go home.

Halfway along the Carrkettle track, his horse threw a shoe. Timothy sighed and dismounted. It would take him twice as long to walk but there was nothing else for it. He wondered if Susannah was having one of her 'At Homes' today; if so he would have to steer clear of the drawing room for it would be full of chattering women and he had no wish for small talk.

But when he reached the yard, he saw that Louisa's gig stood there and his heart lifted. Since her marriage, they had grown a little closer, distance somehow making it easier for them to be friends, and he had begun to hope for a return to that old, easy relationship. Louisa did not bother with small talk; she always had something interesting to say or could be relied upon to listen with attention.

Timothy paused at the door before taking off his boots. Even the smallest action seemed today to be an effort and he was breathless when he had on the shoes that Susannah insisted upon indoors. Even then he wasn't finished for he must go upstairs, hot and thirsty as he was, and change from his workaday clothes into something more appropriate for the drawing room. That quarrel between him and his wife, years ago at the beginning of their marriage, had left its mark.

By the time he was ready to present himself, Timothy felt hotter than ever.

It was strange to go to Pennington Hall again, Louisa thought, knowing that this would be one of the last times she would see it. She sat in the drawing room taking tea with her stepmother and Martha, looking around at the familiar furnishings, some that she had known all her life, others that had come with Susannah or been newly bought. The striped chairs Susannah had wanted soon after her marriage, the chaise-longue, the heavier arm-chairs that had been her most recent acquisition. Soon all these would be no more than a memory for Louisa, any kind of chair a luxury in the life she was about to begin.

'Of course, Jane's home will have everything of the best,' Susannah remarked, continuing her favourite theme. 'Hubert will spare no expense. A most generous husband.' She glanced at Louisa. 'Has Nicholas agreed to new carpets for your drawing room yet?'

'I haven't thought to ask,' Louisa answered. 'I don't really believe we need them.'

'Of course you need them! Why, that style has quite gone out of fashion.' Susannah patted her hair compla-cently. 'Jane, of course, doesn't need to ask. Hubert understands the necessity for keeping a nice home. I must say, I'm thankful she decided not to take Nicholas after all. An older husband is so much more satisfac-tory.'

Louisa bit her lip to prevent herself from making a retort. As usual, Susannah was distorting the facts to suit her own wishes. Everyone knew that Jane had never even had an opportunity to consider Nicholas as a husband, but if Susannah repeated it often enough, they would come to believe it. Not that it mattered any more, since in a few days it would all be in the past, part of another life . . .

The door opened and Timothy came in. He was red-faced and hot, and Louisa glanced at him in some alarm. Of late, she had several times thought that her father did not look well. Now he appeared out of breath, wheezing as if he had a cold. She reached forward and poured him a cup of tea.

'Here, Papa. Sit down and drink this. You've been walking too fast.'

'I think I have.' He took the cup and sat down on one of the striped chairs. 'It's hot today.' He sat for a moment, swallowing his tea, and Louisa caught Susannah's grimace of disapproval. She felt immediately indignant. Why shouldn't her father drink noisily if he was thirsty? Hadn't he been out in the heat, overseeing his mines, making the living that enabled Susannah to buy new furniture, to take her ease in this overstuffed room?

'You work too hard,' Louisa said. 'There's no need for you to go to the mines every day. You have a captain to do that for you.'

'Exactly what I've been telling him,' Susannah said triumphantly. 'He should leave the work to the men whose task it is. Perhaps then he could spend more time at home, behaving as a husband should.'

'And how's that?' Timothy demanded irritably. 'As a carpet knight, making chit-chat with a lot of women who have no other way of passing their time? As some kind of lapdog, to be dressed up and paraded about like a prize won at a fair?'

'Don't be ridiculous,' his wife said sharply. 'You know quite well what I mean. A little of your company is all I ask. And little enough I get. It's at least a fortnight since I saw you in this drawing room in the afternoon.'

'I have work to do. And I'm here now, am I not?'

'And easy enough to see why. I suppose you saw Louisa's gig in the yard. Otherwise you would not have dreamed of coming in. Simply drinking tea with me and my daughter would never be enough to tempt you.'

Timothy flushed and Louisa glanced at him with alarm. His face was almost scarlet now, his eyes bulging. He looked as if he were about to suffer some kind of seizure and she started up.

'Please, Stepmamma. Please don't quarrel. Can't you see, you're making him ill.'

'*I'm* making him ill!' Susannah exclaimed. 'Oh, of course, it's always *my* fault. My fault Walter was born almost an idiot, my fault that nothing ever goes right. I suppose it was *my* fault that Nicholas Craven took it into his head to marry you instead of Jane – not that she hasn't done a great deal better for herself. And my fault that you don't seem capable of bearing a child. Three years married and not a sign, and I'm quite sure it's all my fault. Whose else could it be?'

'Susannah,' Timothy began, but Louisa was on her feet now, white-faced.

'Not capable of bearing a child! What makes you think that?' She stared at her stepmother, seeing only dislike in the pasty face, seeing only the hatred that had grown between them over the years. During all this time, nothing Louisa could do had been right. There had always been something that Susannah could pick on to find fault, and although Louisa had thought herself a rebel, she could see now that she had never stopped striving for attention. Because she had no hope of gaining Susannah's love, she had sought her hatred instead.

Spite and the need for revenge had caused her to make a marriage that Susannah desired for her own daughters. It had set that hatred in stone, for ever. And it had proved a trap from which she was only now trying desperately to escape.

But Susannah's last cruel words were too much for her. She stood with her hands clenched together at her waist, staring at her stepmother, and told her the news that she had bid Tilly keep secret.

'I *am* capable of having a child,' she said, and her voice rang through the room. 'I am expecting one next spring. And it will be a son.' She turned to her father. 'I shall give you a grandson, Papa.'

Timothy's face turned so deep a red that she started towards him. He tried to speak, choked a little, reached up with his hands and clawed at the air. And then his face seemed to slip sideways, as if all his features tried to crowd together. His body sagged and he crashed from the striped chair to the floor, taking the small table and most of the teacups with him.

Louisa did not go with Kieran and the gipsies a few days later. Instead, she stayed by her father's bed, tending him as he lay in his paralysis. She stayed through all the months of her pregnancy and then, in giving birth to the grandson she had promised her father, she escaped at last from the cage in which she had lived.

JOANNA

Chapter Eighteen

I woke to find Mark sitting in the wicker chair beside me. He was leaning forward, his hand on my shoulder, and he looked concerned, even alarmed. I stared at him. My throat ached and when I put up my hand I found that my face was wet with tears.

'Joanna,' he said, 'what is it? What is upsetting you so much?'

I looked at him and then away, staring up from the long chair through the whispering leaves of the apple tree, at the feathered sky above. A great sadness washed over me, a grief for people I had never known yet knew more intimately than my own living family. A girl, bewildered and lost, finding love only to lose it again; an old man who had lost his love and sought it in the wrong places.

Had it all been a dream? Dreams could, I knew, leave one with a strong sense of emotion. But as powerful as this? I felt the tears begin to flow again and turned my head aside.

Mark leaned closer, drawing me against his shoulder. His fingers stroked my hair, pressing my face gently against him, and I could resist no longer. I let the tears come, great sobs rising in my breast, and all the suffering that had been endured all those years ago by Timothy, by Louisa, by Nicholas, poured out of me in a torrent. It shook me from head to foot, the sobs wrenching my body, tearing at my flesh. Mark held me close, not saying a word, and I clung to him, grateful for his silence.

At last the painful weeping subsided and I managed to gain a little control. I drew slightly away from him, fumbling for a handkerchief, and found one of his pressed into my hand.

'Yours won't be anywhere near big enough,' he said, and there was a smile in his voice.

I smiled back shakily and wiped my face, then looked ruefully at his shoulder.

'A towel might have been more use. I'm sorry, Mark, I've made you all wet.'

'I'll dry,' he said comfortably. 'I'm not made of sugar. Do you feel ready to talk about it now?'

I looked at him. He looked very solid, there in the orchard in the afternoon sunshine. Very real. But the others, the ghosts I had been living with for so long, had seemed just as solid. And their pain had been real, too. It was painful to remember. Could I talk about it to anyone? Even to Mark?

'Don't worry if you can't just yet,' he said gently. 'I'll wait. But you'll have to sometime, Joanna. You can't keep it all bottled up inside you for ever. And it would be a mistake to talk to the wrong person.'

Who would be the wrong person? I wondered, and thought of Julian. He had been to see me three times since my collapse and had once found me crying in my sleep, as Mark had done. He had been awkwardly comforting, patting me gently, telling me not to cry, it had been a bad dream, better not to think about it any more. He hadn't stayed long, and I overheard him telling Aunt Martha that I needed rest. 'She's overstrained and exhausted,' he said, as if he were a doctor. 'Better not to have too many visitors, I think. It seems to upset her.'

Aunt Martha had agreed, and in fact not many of the family had come to visit me. Elinor, Dora, Celia, Lilian – all these had made duty calls, bringing flowers or fruit and leaving messages with Martha. And I'd been glad enough to be left alone. But Mark, apparently, did not count as a visitor. My aunt let him in whenever he came and he would sit beside me for hours, not saying a word, just letting me rest.

It was easy, I found, to rest in Mark's company. As easy as it was to cry.

'I'm sorry to be so weepy,' I said, wiping my eyes again. 'I don't seem able to stop. It just keeps coming over me. Whenever I think—' I turned my head away, unable to say any more, and once again he drew my head down on to his shoulder.

'Perhaps you just need to do a lot of crying,' he said quietly. 'Who's to say that once is enough? If a wound is very bad it doesn't heal with one dressing. Don't try not to cry, Joanna. But talk as well – when you're ready. You need to share it with someone.'

I lay back again, my eyes closed, still clinging to his hand. I did not want to drift off again into sleep, into the dreams that haunted me. I tried to think of other things. The garden. The pictures I had been painting of Martha's flowers. The sketch of the sands at Dunner-holme . . .

And I was there again with Louisa, watching the gipsies come across the sands and thinking of Kieran.

It had been like this ever since I had been brought home, incoherent and shivering with shock, by a group of miners who had found me crouched on the old road as they came home from the pits. Thinking me seriously ill, they had wasted no time in calling for help but had removed a gate from a nearby field and laid me on it, on a pile of coats. Barely conscious, I had no thought for the indignity of such a return home, all I wanted was to be safely indoors, with familiar things about me and Martha fussing like a mother hen. I wanted to be taken care of, to creep into a burrow like a wounded animal and stay there until I felt ready to face the world again.

Mark was right, I knew. I could not keep such an experience shut up inside me. Already, like a great caged bird it was beating its wings against my ribs, demanding release. But how could I begin? And how did I know what was true and what merely my imagination?

I could not, surely, have imagined such horrors as Louisa's wedding night or such delights as the loving she had shared with Kieran? But again I reminded myself that in dreams one sometimes did seem to have a knowledge that came from somewhere outside experience, to feel emotional reactions one had never known yet were every bit as real as those that came during waking hours.

As if one had known them before, in another life.

'Aunt Martha,' I said, when Mark had gone, promising to call again soon, 'will you tell me about my Aunt Louisa? What was she like as a girl? What kind of things did she do?'

Martha gave me an odd look. She had always been a little reluctant to talk about Louisa, as if by doing so she would be giving away some family secret. But she seemed to realise that I needed an answer, and she sat down and thought for a few moments before speaking.

'I was only ten years old when I first came here,' she said at last. 'My sister Jane was fourteen and Louisa was twelve. I suppose they thought we'd get on well, but we didn't, of course. Louisa and her father were very close and I think dear Mamma was a little jealous, you know. Of course, she had no need to be, but she never felt quite secure somehow. She disliked seeing him pay attention to anyone, and he and Louisa had been alone together since her mother died, so . . .'

So they were closer than most fathers and daughters, I thought. And if what I had seen had been the truth, the closeness, allied to Susannah's coldness, had brought disaster and guilt to them both.

Had it been the truth?

'And were they always close?' I asked cautiously, hardly knowing what I wanted to hear. 'They never quarrelled at all? He never punished her?'

Martha sighed. 'It was rather sad. I never really knew what happened. But something went wrong between them. It might have started the day he beat her – she had been very rude about Mamma,' Martha went on quickly. 'And when Jane reproached her, well, I daresay there was fault on both sides and they were certainly both very angry. But to see them like that, rolling on the schoolroom floor, pulling each other's hair . . .'

I could see them only too well. And the aftermath. Louisa, recklessly defiant, certain that Timothy would never strike her. Jane, running to her mother with the tale, maliciously gleeful at the prospect of her stepsister's humiliation. And Susannah, grasping at the opportunity to drive a wedge between Timothy and his daughter.

'She was locked into her bedroom for the rest of the day,' Martha said, and I could have said the words with her. 'And when Papa came home, Mamma demanded that she be punished.'

'But it wasn't just that,' I said. 'The beating was a shock to them both, but what really came between them was much worse.'

Martha gave me a startled look and I realised that I had spoken as if I knew more than she about what had happened – as I was beginning to be miserably convinced I did. For neither Louisa nor Timothy would ever have spoken to Martha, or anyone else, about that day when he had stopped the pony beside the little bridge. About the fatherly caress that had gone too far.

'I never knew what really happened,' Martha said again. 'But something changed. For a long time, they scarcely spoke. Louisa would go off for hours at a time on her own, tramping the moors. Just as you do now, but it seems more acceptable these days for a young girl to go walking alone. When we were girls, it was very different, we were so much more sheltered.' She smiled. 'Of course you've had even more freedom in your life. Louisa would have envied you. I can just imagine you roaming the moors together, the two of you, so alike. But there was no one to go walking with Louisa, so she went alone. Why, she went on the very day Mamma and Papa were married. Slipped out from the wedding breakfast, if you please!' Martha gave me a sudden mischievous grin and was suddenly no longer an old woman, but a ten-year-old girl, envious of her new stepsister's daring. 'I longed to go with her, to be her friend. But Jane would never allow it. And by the time I was old enough to think for myself, it was almost too late.'

'And did she have no other friends?' I asked. I had heard enough to be certain that the vision I had seen, the life that I had lived, was as real as my own, that Louisa and Timothy had been estranged in just the way I had experienced. That in some strange way I *knew*.

'Other friends?' Martha considered. 'No one close, I think. It was more difficult then, you see. We had no cars or bicycles, no telephones. We had to walk everywhere or use horses. It was not so easy to meet friends, we were thrown much more on the family for company. Not that that's a bad thing,' she added hastily. 'Families should stay together and be friends. But many of them don't, of course.' She considered for a moment, as if trying to decide whether to say more, then added slowly, 'All the same, I did sometimes wonder, well, if Louisa *might* have a particular friend.' She hesitated slightly before using the word, and I knew at once that she meant lover. 'There were times – she used to go out much more in the summer. Well, that was understandable, the weather's better. Usually, anyway. But she was different then. She seemed happier. She looked prettier. Her eyes were bright, her skin glowed, even her hair seemed to shine more. And sometimes she seemed to be smiling at some private joke.'

No, I thought, it wasn't a joke. It was the memory of Kieran's lovemaking . . . Another memory that was as clear to me as any of my own, and again something I had never experienced.

So how could I have imagined it?

And how could I have imagined the fear of being left behind when Kieran went away? The panic, the excitement, when I – she – first realised that a child had been conceived? The shock of going to Pennington Hall on that last, hot day, believing that it was to bid a silent goodbye, and seeing Timothy collapse on the floor of the drawing room, spilling tea and cakes all over the striped red and gold chairs Susannah was so proud of, chairs that, I realised with a start, stood even now in the hallway, shabby and worn yet familiar to me from the first day I had arrived here from India.

Could I have imagined all that?

Could I have imagined the next seven months? The knowledge that I could not leave Papa now, when he needed me so desperately and when, at last, everything was as it should be between us . . . The bitter misery of knowing that Kieran had waited in vain, that he must have gone with the rest of the tribe, leaving me behind . . . The expression on Nicholas's face as he stared at the baby and then, accusingly, at me . . . The pain of knowing that I would not be able to protect my son and that he needed my protection, my love, above all else . . .

No. I could not have imagined these. Not all of them, and in such painful clarity. I could not have imagined such suffering in the time it took for me to walk up the old road and be found, not two hours later, lying half conscious on the grassy verge.

Nor, I thought, could I have lived through it in that short time. What I had experienced could only be memory. My own memory, seen through a lifting of the veil that so mercifully hides our past lives from us.

'But what does it mean?' I asked Mark a week or two later. I was stronger now, able to face the memories and discuss them with him, as I had known I must. He had called to take me for a drive in the Argyll. We had stopped down by the little church which stood almost on the beach at Aldingham. 'Why did it happen? Why must I go through it all, whether it's for the first time or not? What's the purpose of it?'

'You're sure there is a purpose? You don't think it was just—'

'Overstrain, as everyone seems to think? No, Mark, it was real, as real as today. Besides, I got so much right. I'm sure that every detail I could ask Martha, or anyone else who was there at the time, would turn out to be accurate. The earthquake the day my father was born—'

'He must have told you about that. It's the sort of thing parents do tell their children.'

'Yes, he did. But he didn't know just what it was like. Well, perhaps that wasn't a good example,' I conceded. 'After all, we did experience earthquakes in India, though never anything major, thank goodness. But other things, the lumps on his head, for instance. I don't think he ever knew about those. But Martha did. Apparently the whole family thought he was going to turn out to be an idiot. His mother wanted him put away in an asylum. Can you imagine that? His *mother*!'

Mark sat looking thoughtfully at the waves. The tide was high, a rare sight along the shores of Furness, for although the tide came in twice each day, as it did everywhere else, it did not stay long. Soon after reaching its height it was on the turn, running fast down the estuary, sweeping out to sea anything that stood in its path. That was why it was so dangerous to swim here, and why there were several tragic deaths each year.

'What would your Indian friends say, do you think?' he asked at last.

I had considered this point several times. 'I don't think they would be in any doubt about it. They would say that I'd seen into a past life. I don't think it's a common occurrence, but it does happen. For instance, when they look for a new incarnation, a Rimpoche or the Dalai Lama—'

'That's the chief of all lamas, didn't you say?'

'That's right. The leader of the Buddhist religion. A Rimpoche is a very high monk, often an incarnate.'

'An incarnate? But aren't we all, according to them, incarnates? Reincarnations?'

I tried to explain. 'Yes, but an incarnate is one who carries his knowledge with him into a new life so that he can start more or less where he left off – except that of course he starts off as a child again, so has to be found and taken back into the monastery. It takes a long time, sometimes, to find him and he needs to be found as early as possible because he'll need training. Though not as much as an ordinary child. The records are full of stories of children who recognise people and places from their previous incarnation, and can even quote passages from the *dharma*. That's one of the tests. The monks take along a selection of bits and pieces owned by the previous incarnate – the Dalai Lama or Rimpoche – along with similar items, and the child picks out the ones he is familiar with.' I paused. 'I don't know how much such a child would remember of his past life, but obviously the inference is that he remembers quite a lot.'

'But why should you—'

'Why indeed?' I broke in. 'Why *me*? None of my memories are very holy.' I thought again of Louisa's terror on her wedding night, and shuddered. 'I'd rather not have them, Mark. If it's true that we live over and over again, it's better to forget. There's enough suffering in one life without taking on the burdens of the past.

317

Whatever happened to Louisa, it's over. What can it have to do with me today?'

'What did you say about *karma*?' he asked. 'That it can follow you through several lives? Do you suppose there's a pattern in all this, Joanna? Something that Louisa, or Timothy, did that's found its way down to you? Something you're in danger of repeating? A lesson that still hasn't been learned?'

I stared at him, feeling cold. A pattern I might be repeating? More suffering in store to compound the unhappiness of the past? I would not be able to bear it.

'But what can the lesson be?' I asked miserably. 'What's the pattern? I can't see it, Mark.'

'No,' he said. 'I think it's like a jigsaw puzzle. You need all the pieces to see the pattern. There's still a piece, or pieces, missing.'

I stared at him. 'What are you saying?'

'If all this is true,' he said gravely, 'and like you I just don't know what to believe, except that obviously something's going on, I think you have some more to see yet. You told me before that Rupert seemed to be calling you, as well as Timothy and Louisa. Perhaps it's his life you need to understand before you can see what the pattern is.'

'No!' I said violently, pulling away from him. 'No! I can't, I won't. You don't understand, Mark, I saw it all, I *suffered* it all. I can't go through more of that. I won't, I tell you, I won't!'

He put his hand over mine but made no further attempt to touch me. He sat quite still, watching me, until I had calmed down a little. Then he spoke again.

'I don't pretend to understand all this, Joanna. I don't know what I believe about it. But it's quite clear that something very odd is happening, and I'm not sure you have any choice. Did anyone ask you if you wanted to follow Louisa on to the moor and watch her live her life? No. And do you suppose you are going to be asked if you want to follow Rupert, or anyone else?'

'I'll go away,' I said desperately. 'I'll go to South America. They can't follow me there. I'll get away from here and I'll never come back. I will *not* be ruled by ghosts!'

Mark was silent for a moment. Then he said quietly, 'But you might be ruled by your own *karma*. Joanna, if I've understood you aright, that's something you can't escape, no matter where you go. Whatever was done in those lives, whatever mistakes were made were – what did you call them once?'

'Throwing actions,' I said wearily. 'It's like throwing a stick into the future. A wrong or mistaken act committed now might show its consequences next week or not for a hundred years. But it will return sometime. There's no escape.'

'And the suffering is worse each time,' he said gently. 'Joanna, it has to be faced. And it may not be so dreadful a sin. Did Louisa kill anyone, for instance? Did Rupert? Perhaps it's no more than a mistake you may be about to make? If it warns you away from that, won't it be worth it? And you've told me that *karma* is the natural law of consequences. If you make the mistake again—'

'I may not get such a good chance next time,' I finished. 'For someone who doesn't think he believes it, you make out a very good case, Mark. But you don't know what it was like. I haven't told you half. I can't even think of some of it, let alone talk about it.'

'Then don't think,' he said, and slipped his arm round my shoulders. 'Perhaps Martha and the others are right. Perhaps it's no more than overstrain and tiredness. You had a bad dream, Joanna. It was no more than that. Forget it.'

We sat silently for a while, watching the birds at the edge of the tide. I was conscious of the warmth of his arm about me. I let my eyelids droop. For a little while, I felt totally at peace.

Why could it not always be like this? Why did I have to concern myself so much with the past?

For a few days, I felt better. The dreams and shadows seemed to recede, as dreams do. I absorbed myself in everyday activities, helping Martha in the garden, sketching and painting flowers to add to my collection, exploring the house and answering invitations to visit neighbours and friends. There were more tennis parties, with plenty of young people of my own age, swimming parties on the shore, and picnics among the mountains and fells of the Lake District. A group of us would take a train to Coniston and sail on the lake, or tramp up Old Man, the burly hill that loomed over the sparkling water. We lit fires to boil water and make tea, fried bacon on sticks and baked potatoes in the embers. I thought of days in the Himalayas, when making a fire had not been fun but a matter for survival with little fuel to be found, when we had walked ten or twelve miles day after day, with no chugging steam train to take us home, never knowing whether we would reach the end of our journey or whether we would starve or be set upon by bandits. But my thoughts were only fleeting; each time they drifted into my mind, I turned away from them and made a more determined effort to join in the fun. I was resolved that the past should not intrude on me again.

And if there was a lesson to be learned? I would learn it in my own way. Louisa, Rupert and the others had had their life, their chances. They must let me alone, and if there were mistakes to be made, they would be mine.

I pushed from my mind Mark's words. *But you might be ruled by your own* karma. *That's something you can't escape* . . . No, I said fiercely. No.

I saw little of Mark during those few weeks. He was occupied with work and although he appeared at several of the parties he seldom stayed long. Julian, who seemed to spend more time in Furness than he did in Millom, called him the Judge and said he was growing solemn and old before his time. And I, determined to forget the experience I had had and enjoy myself, veered away from serious talk and refused to discuss the past again. I even told myself I was thankful when he wasn't there, because without his presence I didn't have to think about it.

But when he was absent I found myself looking about for his tall figure, his black, curling hair and dark eyes. There was something about him that made me feel easier, more comfortable. It was nothing like the tingling excitement I felt when Julian was next to me. It was more like the restful contentment of being with a favourite brother. With Mark, I decided, I felt safe.

I did not feel safe with Julian. Every glance from his dark blue eyes, every touch of his long fingers, every word he spoke in that light, drawling voice, spelt danger. But it was a danger that attracted me, so that I was drawn to him like a moth to a candle flame. It was an exciting danger that lifted me out of myself, so that I talked and laughed more, my voice high, and I joined in all the foolish pursuits of the summer with a zest and vigour I would not have thought possible back in India. There, I had scorned such pastimes. I had been more interested in planning the next journey with my father or talking with Chanden Singh.

I had been more interested then in the adventures of the wilderness, the unknown tracks of Tibet, the lonely mountain passes. And in the adventures of the mind, of discovery and exploration of the spirit, which was so much a part of the East. Now, I was becoming engrossed in adventure of a different kind – adventure that bound up emotion and physical sensation together, that set my blood racing and my skin prickling, that kept me awake on moonlit nights and blinded me to all else.

Julian was in my mind, in my eyes, in my thoughts, day and night. I watched and listened to him, keeping every word he said in my mind to be taken out and heard again when I was alone. I savoured every glance, every touch, seeing and feeling them again as I lay in bed, staying awake late because remembering was better than sleep.

I knew that the rest of the family watched with varying degrees of disapproval. Julian had been earmarked, apparently with his willing consent, for Violet. His father and William had discussed their marriage, using it as a cement to bond their two businesses together. With Violet and Julian married, the Pennington Moor mines and the Millom steelworks would have made a formidable concern. With their joint assets, they could have bought out every small business in Furness, able to dictate the progress of iron and steel in the whole area. Julian would, in time, have inherited a powerful position as head of such a company.

But he seemed less interested in Violet these days. His attention was turned to me. And I felt flattered and excited that he could turn his back on such material wealth. Perhaps he was not, after all, as materialistic as I had at first thought; perhaps he too was more concerned with his heart.

'I've never known anyone like you, Joanna,' he said one day as we sat on the shores of Coniston Water, watching the others rowing some borrowed fishing boats across the rippling waves. 'You've seen so much, done so much. You make the girls around here seem pale and dull.' He turned and smiled into my eyes. 'Life with you could never be dull.'

'Doesn't it depend where you are rather than who you're with?' I asked a little teasingly, excited and disturbed as usual by his words. Each time we met, Julian seemed to edge a little nearer. His first joking suggestion that we should go exploring together had not been forgotten. He talked of it, still half jokingly, as if it were a fact, something we were definitely committed to doing. Sometimes I thought that, underneath the banter, he was serious. And I felt torn, half ready to say the words that would turn it from a joke to a serious proposition, half drawing back, afraid of what it would mean.

'One can be in an exciting place with an exciting person,' he said now. 'Don't you think that would be best of all, Joanna?' His fingers stole across the grass and found mine. 'You're an exciting person,' he murmured. 'A very exciting person . . .'

I stared at him. He was very close and I could see a pulse beating in his neck. His eyes were very dark.

'Julian, you mustn't talk like this,' I said desperately. 'Violet . . .'

'What about Violet?'

'You – she – you're almost engaged. Everyone's expecting—'

'Then everyone must be disappointed,' he said. 'I'm not engaged to Violet, nor ever will be. Silly, vain little flibbertigibbet. Why, she thinks a trip to Lancaster is a great expedition! I don't know why I allowed such an assumption to arise.'

'But I thought your father and William—'

'My father is too fond of trying to arrange my life. And William is more interested in the future of his mining company than that of his daughter. I felt sorry for her, I suppose. But I never intended to let her think . . .' He shook his head.

I looked at him doubtfully. Was that really all there was to it? I remembered that it had been a topic of discussion between Mark and Martha on the day I had arrived. And I recalled, too, Elinor's conversation on the day of the tennis party.

I had always known that any friendship between me and Julian would cause antagonism. But if he had already decided not to marry Violet . . .

'I was thinking,' he said, breaking in on my musing,

'that I might ask your Aunt Martha if I might stay at Pennington Hall next time I come over. I know it's your house really, but it would be polite, don't you think? And it would be so much easier for us, wouldn't it?' His eyes met mine and I could find nothing to say. It was very nearly a declaration. And would certainly be seen as such by everyone else in the family.

I thought of Elinor and Dora, who had been so condescending towards me. Violet, livid with jealousy. Celia, with her sweet smile that hid spite, and Lilian, looking down her long, sharp nose. And William, patronising me, treating me like a child, still trying to keep control of my income.

What would they say if Julian came to stay at Pennington Hall?

Martha, I thought, would be disturbed by it but would accept it. After all, as Julian said, it was my house now and it was I who should say who might visit there. And whatever she thought privately, Martha's prime concern would be my happiness.

I did not think of Mark at all. It was as if he stood for warmth and comfort, for stability. But my spirit was not yet ready for such things. Instead, it was disturbed and restless, dancing with danger.

My instincts knew that Julian was dangerous. But I could not keep away from him.

Chapter Nineteen

Summer ripened into autumn. The sun was still warm but there was a haze over the distant horizon and in the mornings a mother-of-pearl mist hung like cobwebs in the trees. The grass was wet with dew, mushrooms sprang in thick, creamy clusters over the fields and there was a bite of freshness in the air.

I had been in Furness for five months, and still I did not know what I wanted to do next. I had come with such clear ideas – to meet my family, sell my house and depart again on my travels. But once here, it was as if the past had caught me like a net, reaching out to me with tendrils so fine they were at first almost unnoticeable, but so strong that, like a fly in a spider's web, I was enmeshed. And nothing was as easy or as straightforward as it had seemed.

Mark had played his part in keeping me in Furness. He was the first Westerner, apart from my father, to treat me as a person in my own right. With him, I was able to have the discussions I needed, the purposeful thinking, the working out of thoughts that required more than one mind to bring them to a satisfying conclusion. I knew well enough that this was a rare quality in a man. I needed him to help and support me through the strange experiences that had forced themselves upon me in Furness. Without his presence, I thought I might have gone mad.

And then there was Julian. So tall, with that blond

sweep of hair flowing away from his forehead, those dark blue eyes that looked into mine and gave me such disturbing messages. His long, tapering hands with the sensitive fingers that had only to touch me to set my skin tingling, my blood racing. And his talk, half teasing, half serious, about exploring South America together. Yet there was a darkness about him, a shadow that seemed to stand at his shoulder, and like the moth and the candle flame, even as I was drawn towards him I was also repelled.

'You're very special, Joanna,' he said to me one day at Pennington Hall, his hands resting lightly on my shoulders as he looked down into my face. 'Very, very special . . .' And his eyes narrowed and darkened. I felt my heart thump and experienced that strange tingling deep inside that I could only recreate by thinking of moments like this.

And then, as I had feared and longed for him to do, he bent and kissed me. I felt his lips on mine, cool and firm, moving gently but purposefully so that my own parted in response. His arms slid about me, drawing me close against him, and I felt the hardness of his lean body, the taut muscles of his arms and thighs. Half afraid, half excited, I slid my arms round his neck and for a moment we held each other close. Then he loosened his clasp and stepped back slightly, smiling down at me.

'I'm sorry, Joanna. I forgot myself for a few minutes then.'

Forget yourself again, I wanted to say. But I was mute, gazing up at him, still trembling a little. It was the first time I had been kissed and I wanted it to happen again.

But Julian had moved away, smiling at me a little regretfully. What did he regret? That the kiss had happened, or that it had ended? What did a kiss mean, in this society where I still did not know all the rules? In India, strictness had alternated with laxity. Girls could dance and flirt, they could slip outside into the warm darkness of the night, presumably to kiss and perhaps a little more – but only, I thought, when there were serious intentions of marriage. The consequences of 'going too far' were too disastrous to risk for the sake of casual dalliance.

But there was plenty of flirtation among the married couples, the Army officers and their wives, the civil servants and the tea-planters who made up most of the European society of Darjeeling, Delhi and Calcutta, the cities I knew best. There was a great deal of banter, of innuendo, as if every woman had a lover and every man a mistress. No doubt some of them did.

To learn the secret rules of a society, one needed to have grown up in it. I moved in and out of Anglo-Indian society, learning the rules of independence instead, learning to think for myself and act as I thought best. I never quite fitted, nor wished to fit with what I saw as a shallow, empty way of life. But here in Furness I was even less at ease. I had come too late, and knew none of the rules.

Had Julian kissed me because he loved me? Or was it merely because I was there – and had shown him that I would welcome it?

My face scorched. I turned away quickly, moving over to the window and gazing down into the garden. The leaves were beginning to change colour. I loved their golds and browns and dark, glowing reds and had found fresh subjects to paint. But today I scarcely saw them.

Julian came across the room and stood behind me. His hands touched my arms lightly. I held myself stiffly, trying not to tremble again.

'Have I upset you, Joanna?' His voice was deep. 'I didn't mean to. But you look so beautiful this afternoon, and I've wanted to kiss you for so long.' His voice deepened even further. 'Ever since that first day when I came into the drawing room at Green House and saw you there.'

I gasped and turned to look at him. 'But that was months ago!'

'I know,' he said solemnly. 'Don't you think I've been exceptionally patient?'

We stared at each other and then began, spontaneously and simultaneously, to laugh. Julian caught me against him again and I wrapped my arms round him and leaned against his shoulder, feeling suddenly comfortable there. And this time, when he kissed me, I responded without fear. What did it matter what society decreed? It was a kiss between the two of us, and nothing to do with anyone else.

'Oh, Joanna,' he said at last, cradling me in his arms, 'what a wonderful girl you are. So different, so fresh. You care nothing for what people think or say, you go your own way, live your own life. Ah, lucky the man who goes with you, say I.' He looked down at me. 'Who will he be, Joanna? Who will you choose to share your life?'

'Surely it's as much a matter of who will choose me?' I said lightly. I was still recovering from the effects of his kisses, and the feel of his arms about my body, his hands stroking my hair . . . 'I still have to wait to be asked,' I said and wondered immediately if I had sounded coquettish. It was so much the kind of thing that Violet would have said. Hastily, I added, 'Not that I'm expecting to be asked to make any decisions on that. I don't really think many men would want to share my kind of life.'

'Oh, Joanna!' He pretended reproach. 'Haven't we discussed all this already? Africa, America – haven't we talked of visiting them both, seeing the world together? I thought it was understood.'

I looked searchingly at him but his dark eyes laughed at me and still I wasn't certain if he was teasing me or not. I knew too well what travelling in the wilds meant, I understood the weariness, the hardships that were so large a part of it. I could not quite believe that Julian was ready for that kind of travelling.

'We'll talk about it again,' he murmured, gathering me close again. 'Soon. In the meantime, let me tell you how delicious you look in that new dress. And how your hair and skin smell of flowers. And how good you feel in my arms. Kiss me again, Joanna . . .'

I lifted my lips to his. I was no longer worried about the meaning of a kiss or whether Julian was serious. I had entered a new world and I was eager to tread its paths further. This was the world I now most wanted to explore.

When Julian went back to Millom, I felt restless and unable to settle. Before leaving, he had suggested that I go to his home for a visit next, but something in me had drawn back from that idea. As far as the rest of the family was concerned, he was still courting Violet, and I felt a reluctance to appear to be stealing him too openly from her. For decency's sake, I thought, there should be a gap between his attentions to her and to me.

So far, we had met only socially – the odd call at Pennington Hall, ostensibly to visit Aunt Martha, the tennis party or picnic with a group of other young people. Julian had managed to make several opportunities to be alone with me, but he had not as yet severed himself completely from Green House, and I knew he was still considered to be Violet's suitor.

I wandered over to Birker Common and went into the old Quaker burial ground. Margaret Fell, wife of George Fox, the man who had founded the Society of Friends, was buried here but of course there was no headstone to denote where. There was an atmosphere of serenity and calm which soothed me a little and I sat on a rock, my eyes closed, resting my heart. No ghosts here to disturb me, no voices from the past to draw me back into the pain and suffering of those who had gone before.

Perhaps they had given up, I thought. Perhaps those strange experiences, the dreams or memories that had flooded my mind, were now over. Imagination or past life, perhaps I was free of them at last, free to live my own life again.

I got up from the rock and walked out of the burial ground. There was a new determination in my step and I strode fast across the common, back towards Pennington.

I had not been in the churchyard since I had been found on the Carrkettle road, half conscious and bewildered. I had not dared to go near those graves again. But now I meant to confront them. Running away was, I knew, no answer. If I wanted to have charge of my own life, I must lay their ghosts once and for all.

The churchyard was empty. I walked up the path and over to the corner where the Sherwins and Cravens lay buried. I passed the Ashburners, Jane and Thomas, who had died thirty-two years apart, and the Fells, James and his wife Dorothy who survived him by only fifteen months. Mary Dawson, sister of the vicar, and Robert Salthouse who was only thirty-one. And the twenty-one-year-old boy who had been killed by the tramway engine at Lindal Moor.

No voices yet. And, walking slowly, I reached at last the graves I had come to see.

I knelt down and reached out a hand to trace the names carved on the mossy stone. Under my hands, warmed by the October sun, it was almost as if I touched living flesh. I drew back, startled, and felt my heart kick. Were they still there after all, the ghosts? Were they still waiting to draw me back, to make me endure yet more pain?

I stood up abruptly and moved away, out of their reach, to look at some of the other stones. There were names there that meant nothing to me. Robert Marr, died 8 August 1839 aged 72 years. Elizabeth Pichall, died 9 July 1880, aged 74. William Hunter, aged 43, William Benson, 50. William Rigg, 48. Tess Goodwin, 18 . . .

I stopped suddenly. Those last two names – William Rigg and Tess Goodwin. Hadn't it been Billy Rigg who was Louisa's friend, hurt in the earthquake on the day my father was born and never the same again? And Tess . . .Who was Tess?

I knelt again and scratched at the moss that hid some of the lettering. But there was nothing more, only the date of her death: 1873. The year before Rupert and Nicholas died.

They had probably known her, I thought. Indeed, she must have been part of the family, surely, to be buried so close the rest of the graves. The others, including Billy Rigg, were all a little distance away, separated from the Sherwin plot. But Tess was close, as if she were important.

I stared at the small, plain headstone as if willing it to give up its secrets. Perhaps Tess had known and understood what it was that lay like a curse on the Sherwins and Cravens, a curse that followed them down through the generations and seemed now to be menacing my own life. If only she could speak to me.

I stood looking from her grave to the others. Louisa. Rupert. Timothy. Nicholas. Tess. What was it that lay between them? What was it I needed to know?

And I felt the earth shift a little and saw the stones blur as if the light had changed. From the corner of my eye I caught glimpses, as I had once before in the orchard, of people from another life. A funeral procession, making its way up the church path. And, like a dream, a vision of a man in a train, staring in horror at something he saw from the window . . .

I backed away, feeling suddenly faint and sick. The terrible distress, the appalled dismay, washed over me in great waves of dread. No! I screamed silently, putting out my hands as if to ward off some nameless evil. No, I can't. I *won't*. I can't be made to go through all this. I'll go away. I'll never come here again.

'Who was Tess?' I asked Martha.

For almost a week I had struggled with one question. The name had haunted my mind, driving away even thoughts of Julian. It had repeated itself insistently inside my head, until at last I had given in, knowing that I would have to find out.

'Tess?' Martha looked startled. 'Who told you about Tess?'

'Nobody told me. I saw her name on a headstone in the churchyard. It seemed as if she had some connection with the family.'

There was a short silence. I glanced at Martha and saw that her face was puckered, but whether it was distress or deep thought I found it hard to decide. Martha's skin was tanned and weathered, criss-crossed by tiny lines; and expressive though it usually was, I sometimes found it hard to read.

'Did she have some connection?' I asked eventually. 'I've never heard of any other Goodwins.'

'No, the Goodwins were no relations by blood or marriage,' Martha replied, as if glad to be able to give an honest answer. Then she looked at me and sighed. 'But you're right, she did have a connection. She was a nursemaid.'

'A nursemaid?' It was the last thing I had expected to hear. A cousin, a protégée, these ideas had circled in my mind with others more fanciful. But a servant? 'Why was she buried so close to the family? There are no other servants buried there, surely.'

'No. But I know it would have been his wish.' Suddenly, to my great surprise, Martha's face puckered even more and she began to cry. 'It was what he would have wanted. And that last day, when he came to see me, he was so shocked. And when I told him – he didn't know, you see, she'd never even hinted . . . I knew he would want her buried near him. They wouldn't let it be on the same day, of course. I didn't expect that. But I insisted . . .' And then she began to weep in earnest, her old body shaking with sobs and her face red and crumpled as a baby's and I felt ashamed of having brought back such distressing memories.

'Please, Aunt Martha, don't cry.' I rang the bell for the maid and put my arm round the shaking shoulders. 'I shouldn't have asked. I didn't realise it would upset you.' I held her close, wondering how long it was since she'd been held like this. Who comforted old ladies, who hugged them and warmed their sad old bones? 'Forget it now,' I whispered. 'It's all over a long time ago. They're at rest, all of them.'

But was it true? Or were their spirits still wandering the earth, bewildered and lost? Was I one of them, making the same mistakes, following the same bitter pattern? And if so, how was I to know the truth? Who was there to help me?

I couldn't ask Martha to tell me more. And although I realized that both Celia and Elinor must have known at least part of the story, I could not go to them for the answers. Nor to William.

Whose nursemaid was Tess? And who was the 'he' who would have wanted her to be buried near the family graves? Rupert? Nicholas? But she had died before them. Was it something to do with Louisa – with Kieran, the gipsy lover who was Rupert's father? Or was there someone else involved in this increasingly tangled family, some black sheep I had still not heard of?

That last day . . . he was so shocked . . . he didn't know, she'd never even hinted . . . Louisa had never told Kieran she was pregnant. Had he found out, years later, and come to see Martha? But what could that have to do

333

with Tess, a nursemaid who had not even been born then?

My head ached with the questions that filled it, tangling with each other like a mesh of coloured embroidery silks. I went out and walked for hours, hoping that the cool autumn air might clear my brain. But the questions refused to leave me. And the voices that I had sensed before, the presence of that other life, pressed ever more insistently upon me. I stared out across the estuary, the wind in my hair as it had been on that first afternoon when I had arrived here and Mark had met me from the train with his Argyll.

I knew there was no escape. Sooner or later, it would catch up with me. Whatever it was – call it *karma*, for want of a better word – it would force itself upon me. As Mark had suggested, there was still a lesson to be learned, a mistake about to be made. And until I knew what it was, I would go on making it, down through the lives ahead, suffering a little more each time.

All I had to do was let go of my doubts and believe it. Then perhaps I would be given the answer and there would be no more need for suffering.

But like a person visiting the dentist, even though I knew that subjecting myself to pain would result in freedom from worse agony, I was still reluctant, still afraid. And still I tried to avoid it.

When I saw Mark again, there was a constraint between us. It was as if a barrier had risen and we could no longer talk as easily as we once had. I felt angry with him, for I had grown used to the idea that he was there to share my problems and now we seemed to have grown apart.

'I suppose you're jealous of Julian,' I said at last, driven to pick a quarrel.

'Jealous? Of Julian? Do I have reason to be?' He turned to look at me, frowning. We had gone to look at the ruins of Furness Abbey and were wandering down what had once been the nave of the great church, no more than a few walls of red stone now, the roof gone centuries ago, but still impressive, and with a certain torn majesty among the weeds and undergrowth. How beautiful it would be, tidied up, with the grass mown and the old walls allowed to reveal their glory, I thought. And once I would have said so, but I didn't feel like sharing such thoughts with Mark that afternoon.

'Why should I be jealous?' he persisted and I felt embarrassed and annoyed. I had regretted the words the moment they were out of my mouth, but there was no calling them back now. I shrugged, as if it didn't matter.

'Oh, no reason. Just that he's been coming to see me quite a lot lately and I thought you might be a bit put out.'

He considered this, then shook his head. 'You're free to make whatever friends you choose, Joanna. And you know I've been busy. I hadn't actually realised that you were seeing so much of him.'

'Oh.' I felt deflated. 'Well, the rest of the family seem to think so. Violet is quite annoyed, I'm afraid.'

'Is she?' He sounded noncommittal, almost uninterested. We had reached the far end of the ruins and stopped to explore a building that still stood intact. It was about the size of a large house and we went inside and stood gazing up at the vaulted roof.

'I believe this used to be an infirmary,' Mark remarked. 'There's a great deal of it left – one doesn't realise from the outside. It must have been a beautiful abbey when it was in use.'

'I suppose so.' Exactly what I'd thought myself, but I didn't even want to feel in tune with Mark this afternoon. There was something I needed from him, something he wasn't giving me, but I didn't know what it was or how to ask for it. And I couldn't reach him across the barrier that had grown between us. Like a dog worrying a bone, I went back to the subject that had been occupying my thoughts. I wanted Mark to show some emotion, some reaction that would tell me he cared. He seemed too remote, too detached.

'I suppose it's natural that Violet should be upset,' I continued. 'She seems to have got the idea that Julian was more or less engaged to her. And her mother and grandmother seem to have thought so too.'

'I think it was assumed by everyone,' Mark said easily, examining a carving on one of the walls. 'Including Julian himself. You may remember Aunt Martha and I discussing it the day you arrived.'

I did remember. I felt uncomfortable, as if I'd been caught in some wrongdoing. But hadn't he said I was free to make my own friends? Didn't that apply to Julian as well?

'They've never been formally engaged,' I said defensively. 'Anyway, it was mostly a business arrangement between William and Julian's father. It was nothing to do with love.'

'And how would you know?' he asked, turning to look directly at me. 'Has Violet told you so?'

I was taken aback. It was Julian I had been talking about, not Violet. 'I've never discussed it with her.'

'Perhaps you should before making such statements. You might find that, to her, it was very much to do with love.' He paused as if to give me time to think about that, then added casually, 'Not that I applaud her taste. She could do a lot better than Julian.'

'So you *are* jealous!'

'Of Julian and Violet?' He looked bemused. 'Why ever should I be?'

'Not Julian and Violet. You know what I mean.' I stopped. I was saying too much, assuming too much. I looked at him miserably and felt my anger ebb away. 'Mark, I'm sorry. I didn't mean to quarrel. It's just that . . .'

'Just that what?' he asked after a moment or two.

336

'Joanna, what's wrong? You're upset and unhappy. Can't you tell me about it?'

He came closer and laid his hands on my shoulders. I looked up at him and felt the tears come to my eyes. He drew me closer and I laid my head on his shoulder and, with his arms round me, began to cry.

'I'm sorry,' I said after a while, mopping my face with his handkerchief. 'I always seem to be doing this to you.'

'Maybe it's because you haven't anyone else.' He led me to a low wall and we sat on the broken stones, looking down at a narrow stream. 'Tell me what's upsetting you. Is it Julian?'

'No!' But I said it too quickly, and he looked quizzically at me. 'Perhaps it is,' I said reluctantly. 'But there's no reason why we shouldn't be friends, is there, Mark? If he doesn't want to be engaged to Violet, surely there's nothing *wrong* in that? And if he and I . . .' But I couldn't go on. I couldn't say to Mark *If he and I are in love* . . . Not with those dark eyes looking into mine and those strong arms warm about my shoulders.

'You and Julian are free to make your own lives,' he said slowly. 'Nobody can deny that. But be very careful, Joanna. Be very sure that you're doing the right thing.'

'Do you think it's the wrong thing?' I asked, and he sighed and asked a question of his own.

'How am I to know?'

I felt a return of my misery. He still wasn't saying the things I wanted to hear. I felt confused, as if I had taken a wrong turning somewhere. I needed to go back, to find the right road.

'Let's talk about something else,' he said after a few minutes. 'How have you been, these past few weeks? You haven't had any more disturbing experiences?'

That was one of the questions I'd wanted to hear. Apart from my conversation with Martha, I had not mentioned Tess's grave or the strange sensations I'd had in the churchyard to anyone. Who could I have told? Not

Julian, that was certain. And there was no one else.

'Tell me,' he said gently, and the last of the barrier crumbled and fell away.

We had been invited to tea at Green House, and the visit to Furness Abbey had been a way of spending the afternoon first. Feeling better than I had for weeks, I climbed back into the Argyll and Mark started the motor and then jumped in beside me.

'I suppose you're feeling a little apprehensive about this tea party,' he remarked as we chugged through the lanes. The hedgerows were looking damp and bedraggled now, their heavy crop of blackberries stripped by local women and their leaves brown. 'I take it you're not very popular with Mother or Dora at the moment.'

I shook my head. 'But I haven't done anything to take Julian away from Violet. If he chooses—'

'If he chooses another girl, it's his right, of course. But he shouldn't continue to come and stay at Green House if his intentions have changed. *That's* not his right.'

'I know.' I didn't add that Julian had already hinted strongly for an invitation to stay at Pennington Hall, a hint I had so far not taken. That would have compromised me more strongly than I was prepared for. In fact, I was uncomfortably aware that Julian was really not behaving very well at all, and I was even more uncomfortable about my own part in this.

We drove along the shore towards Bardsea. The tide was on its way out and there was a fringe of birds wading along the edge of the water. Mark stopped the car and we sat for a moment watching the cockle-gatherers on the sands.

'Joanna,' he said, and stopped. I looked at him. His hands were on the steering wheel and he was frowning at them. He seemed to want to say something, something that was difficult to put into words.

338

'Yes?' I said at last. 'What is it, Mark?'

He sighed, then turned and looked into my face. I searched his eyes, trying to read his thoughts, but his mind was closed to me. I felt the barrier begin to grow between us again and reached for his hand, suddenly agonised. *Don't*, I wanted to cry, *don't go away from me again*. But I could not speak. We sat in silence, gazing at each other, both wanting to reach out, both unable to make the first move.

'We'd better go,' he said at last and turned away again. 'Mother doesn't like people to be late for her tea parties.'

He started the car again and I sat beside him feeling cold as we drove the last mile to Green House. I wished he had told me what was in his mind. And for the first time, it struck me that Mark, too, had feelings and thoughts that he needed to share. Mark also might, at times, need a shoulder to lean upon.

'Joanna dear, how nice to see you.' Elinor's voice was cool as she greeted us in the hall. Her sharp eyes moved over Mark and me. I took off my coat and handed it to the maid, then asked if I might go and wash my hands.

'We've been to Furness Abbey. I feel a little untidy.'

'Of course.' Elinor turned to the maid. 'Take Miss Sherwin up to the Blue Room, will you? You'll find everything you need there, Joanna.'

I followed the girl up the stairs. I felt exhausted, as if the emotion I had given way to in the Abbey had drained me of all energy. I touched my hand on the oak banister, thinking of all the hands that had touched it before me. Elinor, Nicholas, Rupert, Louisa.

Rupert.

I had barely formed the thought when I was swept with the most powerful sensation I had experienced yet. Of course, Rupert had lived here. This had been his home. He had been born here, spent most of his life here. One of these rooms had been his, perhaps the very room I was going to now, the Blue Room.

I drew back, but the maid was glancing at me curiously and I knew I would have to go in. I knew too that this was the moment I had been dreading, the moment I had tried to avoid. Once in that room, it would be upon me, and there was nothing I could do to prevent it.

The voices were all around me now, whispering, pleading, entreating. But whose voices were they? Voices from the past – but whose past? Louisa's? Rupert's? My own?

I passed the maid, who was standing in the doorway, and went into the room. I heard her murmuring voice as she showed me the washstand, I watched her pour water into the bowl, but it was as if we inhabited different worlds. I felt like a ghost, watching a mortal human being going about its business, yet if I reached out and touched her, there would be nothing there.

Who was the ghost? Who was real?

She was gone, with another curious glance. I stood quite still, looking around the room, waiting.

There was nothing ghostly about it, nothing to say that a young man had once slept here, a boy grown up with all his possessions. It had been cleared out long ago, refurnished and redecorated. It was bare, empty and impersonal.

But as I stood there by the window, looking at the bed, my vision blurred and shifted. And I seemed to see a movement, at first no more than a shimmering in the air, a thickening, as if something were beginning to form. And then I saw that there were two bodies on the bed; two people, lying in a close embrace. And even as I tried to turn my head away, I felt myself drawn closer and knew that I was merging into one of those bodies, that I was sliding into another life.

The past had reached out to me again and I could no longer resist its claim.

RUPERT

Chapter Twenty

Rupert Craven had just turned seventeen when his stepmother Elinor seduced him. It hardly came as a surprise, for she had been showing him marked attention for some time.

Rupert was barely eleven when Elinor married Nicholas. A quiet boy, he spent much of his time out of the house, roaming the fields and meadows of Furness or visiting the mines. And Elinor, almost twenty years younger than her new husband and with a four-year-old son of her own, had been happy enough for him to continue in his lonely way. She had certainly never, as far as he could see, felt any desire to be a mother to him.

Before then, Rupert scarcely knew what a mother was. He was only a few days old when his mother died, and throughout his childhood his father rarely mentioned her. When he did, it was with a bitterness that seemed to encompass both Rupert and the dead Louisa, as if they had been accomplices in some crime against him. But what it could have been, the boy had no idea until after Elinor had seduced him.

She told him that first afternoon as they lay together on his bed, the sunlight slanting through the half-drawn curtains to fall in soft bands on her pale flesh. The same stripes lay across his own darker skin, which had prompted Elinor to liken him to a tiger, striped in brown and gold. She leaned over him, her full breasts brushing

343

his chest, and ran her fingers through his black hair, and then she told him.

'A *bastard*?' Rupert raised himself on one elbow. He stared down at his stepmother's face, still flushed from their lovemaking. The room seemed to spin about him and there was a pounding through his body that had nothing to do with lust.

'You're saying that I'm a by-blow? That my mother—'

'Was a whore,' Elinor supplied softly, and then drew quickly back against the pillows as Rupert drew in a harsh breath. 'No! I didn't mean that, Rupert. It's simply what your father—'

'My *father* has called my mother a whore?' He spoke unbelievingly, his voice low and tense. '*He* told you this?'

'It's why he treats you as he does. Why he . . .' She seemed to search for the right words. But Rupert had no doubt as to what the right words were.

'Why he hates me. He always has hated me. But if – if what you say is true, why didn't he abandon me? Why call me his son and give me a home, send me to school as if I were his, and yet treat me all the time as if I were something that crawled out of one of Grandfather's mines?'

'Have you thought what it would mean if he had not acknowledged you?' she asked shrewdly. 'His wife dead in childbirth, a child just a few days old . . . Suppose he had rejected you then, what would people have said? That it wasn't possible to tell at so young an age, that he was deranged with grief. And if he had left it longer, what then? Besides,' Elinor added softly, 'your father is not a man to take humiliation lightly. To let it be known that he'd been cuckolded, and that it was he who was barren and not his wife—'

'Is that what he told you?'

She shrugged smooth, bare shoulders. 'I've been married to him for six years, Rupert. There are some things a wife doesn't need to be told.'

Rupert was silent for a few moments. 'But why blame me? Is it because my mother died when I was born? I've always thought that was the reason. But if she – if I—' He stopped. The words that he must use now refused to leave his tongue. 'Did he – does he – hate her too?' he asked numbly.

Elinor moved her cool body against his. 'Don't worry about it, Rupert. It all happened long ago. Let's just think about you and me. Have you really never made love to a woman before?'

He shook his head, but his mind was still occupied with what she had told him. He lay back on the bed, his arms behind his head, staring at the ceiling as the thoughts chased each other through his brain.

A bastard. Not his father's son. The child of some other man, unknown – or perhaps not unknown. A rapid procession of faces passed across his mind's vision, men he knew, friends of his father or his grandfather, relatives. Could one of them be his true father? Had any of them shown any signs of interest in him beyond what might be expected? If one was indeed his father, did he even know?

Did Nicholas know?

Rupert could think of no one, no one in the family or his acquaintances who treated him as anything other than Nicholas Craven's son, and no one whom Nicholas treated as other than a friend or acquaintance. No one who bore a resemblance to him.

He looked down at his body. His skin was brown, several shades darker than Elinor's, and tanned darker still where he had been exposed to the sun. Black hair had started to grow on his thighs and body, as black as that which curled over his head. His eyes were a dark brown that appeared nowhere else in the family.

Why had it never occurred to him before? Why had no one else given any sign of suspicion?

He thought of the portrait of his mother that hung in his grandfather's library, one of the few rooms at Pennington Hall not furnished entirely to Susannah's taste. Its walls were cluttered with remnants from his grandfather Timothy's life, much of it from the days before he married Susannah. His first wife, Louisa's mother Margaret, was represented by only one picture, a rather poorly executed portrait that showed her as a dark-haired eighteen-year-old. The artist had lacked technique and the general effect was oddly lopsided and gauche, but he had nevertheless captured a certain warmth, an eagerness about the eyes and a soft curve to the mouth that gave an allure to the portrait that other, better paintings might lack.

Louisa's portrait had been painted shortly before she was married. She wore a gown of sea-green silk that must have presented the artist with some challenge, for its colour changed with the light; the bodice, drawn close over her small breasts, gleamed with silvery colour, while the skirt which billowed like foam from her slender waist was alternately dark and bright, according to its folds. Above the low neckline, gleaming on her pale skin, lay a necklace of emeralds set in silver, their colour reflected in eyes which seemed to look questioningly from the frame, as if Louisa were uncertain of her place in the world.

Green eyes. Not dark brown like his own; chestnut hair, not black. Why had he never wondered before from whom he had inherited his wild colouring?

Elinor was moving lazy fingers across his skin, down the hard muscles of his chest and stomach. Only an hour earlier, her touch had been like fire and his body had responded with a flare of passion. Now he lay supine, scarcely noticing the languorous touch. He felt disoriented, as if the world had shifted suddenly, leaving him behind. He no longer knew his place. For the first time, he understood the question in his mother's painted eyes.

'He's not my father,' he said slowly. 'Nicholas Craven is not my father. All these years I've believed, never questioned . . . All these years he's known – and hated me for what my mother did and for who I am.' He sat up again, knees drawn up to his chin, thrusting Elinor's seeking hand aside, and held out both palms as if begging for enlightenment. 'So who am I? Who was my father? Does he know?'

Elinor laid her hand on his arm, trying to draw him back beside her. He resisted a little, then turned and looked down. Her bright hair lay like an aureole on the pillow, and her breasts swelled richly from the curving body. Her hip was twisted slightly so that one leg lay above the other, half crossed, not quite concealing the soft golden hair that had so excited him a little while ago.

'Rupert,' she said softly, 'why let it matter so much? All that was yesterday. This is today, this is what matters. You and me, here together and perhaps not much time left. Let's spend the time as best we can.' Her fingers stroked his arm, his waist, his buttock; slipped between his thighs and played gently there. He felt the heat of excitement begin again, slowly at first, then spreading more rapidly through his body, focusing in his loins. For a moment, he held on to his thoughts, knowing they must be pursued; then the sensations of his body drove them away and he let them go, lowering himself on to Elinor's body and fastening his mouth to hers with a kind of desperation.

She was soft and compliant beneath him, still damp from their previous lovemaking, and he thrust himself into her without preamble. Her mouth was open and her tongue alive in his, making its own small thrusting movements. She locked her legs round his body, holding him there, and lifted herself against him, squeezing him deeper inside, grasping him close. He felt the small, soft ridges and crannies deep inside her body and thrust again and again with a compulsive and irresistible vigour

347

that seemed to draw strength from his entire body, so that in the final moments he was wholly consumed by an urgent desire that swept all else from his mind. There was nothing but this, himself and Elinor, caught in a frenzy, and the sensations that tore through him.

He lay spent again, breathing as if he had just scaled a mountain at a run. He sprawled across Elinor, his head sunk on the pillow beside hers. Her hair was in his mouth, her arms and legs still wound about him, but he was scarcely aware of her presence. For what seemed an eternity, he was in his own world, still spinning, still dazed. He felt her warmth and softness, still had need of them; but he did not for the moment connect them with the woman who had been stepmother to him for the past six years.

Presently, she moved beneath him, laughing a little. Rupert completed his journey back to earth and lifted his head. He looked down into her eyes.

'Well!' Elinor said with a smile. 'You certainly are a surprise, Rupert. Did you speak truly when you said this was your first time?'

He felt himself blush. 'Well, there was a maid at school . . .'

'Aha!'

'But we never did this together,' he added quickly. 'Only a few kisses and – you know—'

'I'm sure she enjoyed it very much,' Elinor said gravely. 'And she certainly seems to have helped in your education. Unless you're a naturally good lover, of course, but so few men are, I'm afraid.'

Rupert looked at her. 'How many—'

'Rupert!' Elinor bridled, as much as any woman could bridle while lying naked beneath her lover. 'Don't you know that's a question you should never ask a lady? But I have been married twice, you know.'

Yes. And there was Curtis during the Easter holidays. And now himself. How many others? he wondered.

Since marrying Elinor, the reclusive Nicholas had been forced to do much more entertaining. People had come to dine with the Cravens, people had come to stay. How many of these had been Elinor's lovers?

Rupert lifted himself away from her body and rolled on to his back. Elinor must, he knew, have had many lovers. And would have others yet. And so, probably, would he. It didn't really matter. Yet he could not suppress the surge of jealousy that reddened his mind as he thought of other men lying with her as he was lying with her, their hands touching her body, their legs tangling with hers. Even his father . . .

His father! And with the words, reality rushed back and the spinning elation vanished.

'Elinor,' he said slowly, 'when my father – when he told you he was not my father, did he tell you who—'

'Who really is your father?' She was sitting up now, reaching for her clothes. 'I don't believe he ever knew for certain, Rupert. He talks of tinkers sometimes, gipsies, but I don't think he ever knew the truth. She died too soon, you see. Until you were born, he couldn't know. You could have been his.' She turned and her blue eyes moved over him, lingering on his tousled black hair, almost physically caressing his brown skin. 'Once you were born, of course, he knew. But it was too late to ask.'

Too late, because Louisa was dying. And no one else, save for his real father, could know the truth.

Unless Tilly . . .? But Tilly had a tongue like a runaway train. She could never, surely, have remained silent all these years.

Rupert watched as Elinor got up and began to dress again in the loose robe she had been wearing for her afternoon rest. Everyone was out of the house: William had been invited to spend the afternoon with a friend, Nicholas was off on some business of his own, the servants had been set to picking fruit in the

349

vegetable garden. Rupert, restless and overheated, had declined to go with any of them and had not even wanted to accompany his grandfather. Instead, nervously aware of his stepmother's presence, he had roamed from room to room, unable to settle, waiting while scarcely knowing what he awaited – until she came down the stairs clad in that same loose robe of grey silk, her golden hair loose upon her shoulders, and beckoned him.

He had gone with her as if bound by an invisible chain. She had led him to his own bedchamber – 'Safer than mine, I think' – and once inside had locked the door and begun to unfasten his shirt. And Rupert, shaking with nerves and anticipation, had let her undress him, had let her guide him on that first unfamiliar journey, until his own virility had been unleashed and taken them both by storm.

It seemed like a hundred years ago. It was little short of two hours.

'Elinor,' he said suddenly, hoarsely, 'you'll come again, won't you? You – we'll do this again?'

She turned and smiled at him. Her lips were full and red, as if bruised. Her eyes were sleepy, as if she now really needed that rest. Her hair was as tousled as his, a heavy tangle of burnished gold that hung past her shoulders.

'Oh, I'll come again, I'm sure,' she said in a low, husky voice. 'And we'll do it again, yes. For a little while, anyway.'

A little while? But the need was already beginning to rise in him again. It was as if the desire for her had been pent up behind floodgates for a long time – certainly for the months since Easter, perhaps longer than that. Now that those gates had been opened, the demand for satisfaction would come again and again. The gates could never be closed.

For a brief moment, Rupert had a clear vision of the

situation he and Elinor were in, and knew that it was an impossible one.

But his vision clouded almost at once. He rose from the bed, took Elinor in his arms and kissed her.

'Tomorrow?' he said. 'Tomorrow afternoon?' And waited anxiously for her answer.

Elinor smiled and touched his cheek with one finger-tip. 'Perhaps,' she whispered, and moved out of his arms and over to the door.

The slaters' road, leading up from Broughton Beck to Kirkby Moor, was rough and stony. Men trudged up here every day to the quarries that overlooked Duddon, to toil in the great holes that had been torn from the hill like bites gnawed out by a giant's teeth. But there were still quiet places among the heather that turned the slopes to amethyst, and it was here that Rupert came next day, to lie on his back and stare at the reeling sky, thinking of what Elinor had told him.

Now, at last, he was beginning to understand why his childhood had been as it was, and why his father hated him. He felt a surge of bitter hatred of his own towards Nicholas, thinking of the unhappiness of the child he had been, of the efforts he had made to win his father's love. All futile, all doomed, because everything had been false.

Nobody has the right to make a child's life a misery, he thought. Was it my fault I was born? Is it my fault I am who I am?

Was this also why Nicholas had, before his marriage to Elinor, such a dislike for women? Not many had come to Green House, but those who did – Rupert's grand-mother Susannah, his aunts Martha and Jane and the few others who were wives or daughters of their neigh-bours around Furness – were treated with patronising coolness, as if they were of some lesser breed than men. Perhaps Rupert himself would have learned to behave in the same way, save that he came in for like treatment from his father and so felt more akin to the women than to the men who visited Green House. And even those were few. Nicholas Craven was known as something of a recluse, though it seemed that he had not always been so.

'Oh, he used to be quite the blade,' Rupert's Aunt Martha told him when he was having tea with her one day. Rupert loved his aunt's teas. She seemed to know what a thirteen-year-old boy would enjoy, and there were no thin sandwiches or dainty *petits fours*; instead, she provided large fruit cakes that could be cut into thick chunks, piles of hot buttered muffins and Rupert's favourite biscuits, made by Martha herself and covered with chocolate. Teas such as this could only be eaten when his grandmother Susannah was out, visiting her own friends, and Rupert and Martha felt like conspirators as they sat by the fire or out in the orchard, consuming their feast.

'A blade?' he said. 'Father?'

'Oh yes. Caused quite a stir when he first came to Furness. All the young ladies in the district set their caps at him, including my own sister, your Aunt Jane – but don't ever tell her I said so!' She giggled a little. 'Oh, I remember the ball we all went to that evening. Your mother insisted on going too, though she normally hated such events. And she wore Jane's dress – a sea-green silk. It suited her better than it ever would have suited Jane. I remember Papa having a portrait painted of her in it – it must be in the house somewhere.' Her eyes took on a reminiscent look. 'It was such a lovely evening, and your father had eyes for nobody but Louisa. We could all see it immediately.' She smiled, but her smile was sad, and Rupert held back the questions he longed to ask.

What had she been like, the mother whose portrait hung in his grandfather's house but not in his own? Perhaps he should ask his grandparents. But Susannah, whom he had always called his grandmother though she was in fact his grandfather's second wife, clearly had no more time for Louisa than had Nicholas. And when Rupert asked his grandfather, Timothy's slightly twisted face simply twisted a little more with old grief and a tear welled up in the eye that never quite closed, so that Rupert wished he had not asked and did not do so again for a long time.

Perhaps she had been a wicked woman. Perhaps she had brought shame and disgrace on the family. That might be why his father treated him with such aloofness, as if he carried bad blood. Had she really been the faithless, deceiving whore that Nicholas had presented to Elinor. Or had she been no more than an unhappy woman, seeking comfort outside a bitter marriage?

Knowing his father now, it was easy to think of his mother, trapped in lovelessness, turning to another man. But Rupert had both Martha and Tilly's word for it that Nicholas had changed, that he had not always been the remote, forbidding figure that Rupert knew and feared. He had once been merry and full of life, an attractive and eligible bachelor, sought after by every young girl and her mother in Furness.

What was the truth? Did anyone know it, now that Louisa was dead? And who could tell him? Not his father, that was certain, nor his grandparents. His aunts? But his Aunt Jane was rarely in Furness these days, for her home in Liverpool kept her fully occupied. And Aunt Martha, small, dumpy and inquisitive, whose curiosity would surely have led her to know more than anyone else, would have wanted to know too much in return. Why was he asking? Who had told him, and why? In five minutes, he felt, she would have ferreted out the exact relationship between himself and his stepmother, and that he dared not risk. Instead, he looked into his childhood for clues.

It had been quite a long time before he realised he had

no mother. Tilly, his mother's maid, had taken over his care as soon as the monthly nurse had departed. There had been a wetnurse too, of course, but he remembered nothing of her, only a vague impression of soft warmth and sweet dampness that had been taken from him too soon. For a time, Tilly had held him on her lap and cuddled him, but Rupert could remember the day that Nicholas had come into the nursery and found her so, and his flesh still shrank at the memory of the fury in his father's eyes. Tilly, at first clutching Rupert close to her, had then let him go so suddenly that he had slipped to the rug where he lay crying with shock and fear. From the floor he looked up at his father towering over him, his tall body oddly distorted from this angle, his jaw and thick greying brows heavy as he stared down.

'I'll not have the boy brought up as a namby-pamby,' Nicholas roared, filling the nursery with his rage. 'Look at him, snivelling and grovelling there as if afraid of his own —' he paused suddenly, then went on – 'his own father. You're turning him into a milksop and you'd better change your ways if you want to stay in my employ, d'you hear?'

'Yes, sir.' Tilly was trembling and beginning to cry herself, which frightened Rupert all the more. Until now she had been his rock; without her, there was only an abyss. 'But sir, he's no more'n a babby still—'

'Baby? He's a good three years old, able to walk and talk and learn what it means to be a man.' Rupert felt his father's eyes on him, then the nudge of a foot against his body. 'Get up, sir, and look me in the eye.' And when he stayed still, afraid to move, he found himself suddenly scooped up by strong arms and set none too gently on his feet. 'There. Now tell me, what have you learned today?'

Rupert cast a helpless glance towards his nursemaid. If he had learned anything, he was not aware of it. New ideas, new manners, new words were absorbed into his consciousness every day, but he did not know that he had 'learned' them; the word meant nothing to him. He stared imploringly at Tilly, but she was sobbing quietly into her apron and did not meet his eye.

'No looking to her for help!' Nicholas snapped, jerking Rupert's head back with one large hand. 'Look me in the eye like a man, and answer up.'

'Please, sir,' Tilly began quaveringly, but was silenced by a furious glance before Nicholas turned his attention back to Rupert.

'Well? Have you nothing to say for yourself? You've learned nothing, is that it?'

'No, Papa.' He could only whisper the words, knowing they were the wrong ones but unable to make any other reply. His eyes filled with tears again and his lips trembled.

Nicholas stared at him. His eyes and hair were the colour of cold iron and there was a curl to his upper lip, a flare to his nostrils, that Rupert was to see over and over again during the coming years. As a three-year-old child, scorn was another word he did not yet know, but he sensed very clearly the meaning of his father's expression and understood that he was the cause of it. He learned later to bury his own feelings, but he could not do so then and his tears brought fresh disgust to Nicholas's face and a hardness to his hand as he slapped Rupert away.

'He needs a man to take care of him,' he declared, straightening up and striding to the door. 'Women have no idea how to bring up boys. But I suppose he'll have to stay in the nursery a few years yet – no man worth the name would want to take on a child not yet out of frocks. And by then there'll be a task to undertake and no mistake.' He turned at the door and glared back at Tilly, now mopping her eyes. 'But no more treating him like a doll, you understand? I'll not have it.'

'No, sir,' Tilly sniffed. 'I'm sorry, sir. I'll remember.'

And when the door had closed behind his father, although Rupert came and laid his small hand on her knee, she did not draw him close again. Instead, she looked sadly into his eyes and touched his cheek with her fingers.

'Poor little mite,' she said softly. 'Poor, poor little mite.'

There were times after that when Tilly would still take Rupert on her knee. But she never did so when Nicholas was in the house or when anyone else might see.

The only other person to touch Rupert was Martha, who would hug him whenever they met and whose comforting bosom gave him the only human warmth he knew. No one else touched him at all. It was only much later, when he saw other children with their families, that he understood what he had missed.

But in those early years, Rupert met few other children. Bardsea Green was a tiny hamlet of only a few houses, a short distance away from the coastal village of Bardsea and close under Birker Common. He would look out sometimes through the gates and see the children from the cottages nearby, playing on the grass or making mud pies in the trickle of water that ran down the edge of the green. But he was never allowed to join them. If he asked, Tilly would shake her head. 'It don't do to mix,' she said once. 'It only causes trouble, in the long run.' And she looked sad, just as she did when he asked about his mother, so that he gained the impression that the cottage children had something to do with whatever sin Louisa had committed – though what it could be, he could not imagine.

The nearest to him in age was Walter. As Louisa's half-brother, he was actually his uncle, but he was only nine years his senior. That nine years was enough to make him seem grown up to Rupert, though when he was six or seven and Walter about fifteen, the two spent more time together.

It was an idyllic summer when Tilly was confined to the house with an injured leg. She had fallen on a slippery rock while walking on Birker Common and cracked her shin, and it took a long time healing. Nicholas was away a good deal of the time and did not seem to realise how disabled she was, and the other servants did not enlighten him, knowing that he was capable of dismissing her without a thought. Rupert found himself, for the first time in his short life, free to do much as he wished.

At first, it was a little frightening. He had been accustomed to being looked after. He was not long out of dresses and still had difficulty with buttons and hooks. He could only just fasten his shoes. But he learned quickly, with help from the other servants when needed, and when Walter made a call with his father and took him out to the meadows, the sensation of freedom went straight to his head.

'We're going to build a dam today,' Walter would say. Or, 'We're going down to the beach to swim.' There was a flavour of danger and excitement, because swimming from either the Bardsea beach or the sands at Duddon could be dangerous. There were numerous stories of people who had been caught by the rapid tide or lost in the quicksands.

Walter cared little for such stories. There was a wildness in his eyes, almost as if he sought danger for its own sake, for the excitement it brought to life. Yet he never led Rupert into real peril, only along the edge of it, so that they could catch its flavour in the salt air, could sniff and taste it. Rupert put all his trust into his young uncle's hands, confident that nothing could happen to him so long as Walter was there.

For the rest of his life, he was to look back on that summer as the focus of his childhood. So much was happening in the district that there was always something new to see or do. The Furness Railway, started two years after Rupert's birth, was almost complete and, nearer at hand, the Lindal Tramway had been begun. The two boys would climb up the hill from Pennington Hall to see the long gash running from the open works up near Snipe Gill, down past Old Pit, along the road by the Harrison Ainslie offices to Old Gin and so to Lindal Bank, where the main railway would take ore to the furnaces of Ulverston or to the shipyard at Barrow.

There, too, industry was thriving. The first ship to be built at Barrow was due to be completed in a year or so, and two determined boys, taken to Barrow for a morning and left to amuse themselves, could easily enough find a way in to the docks to watch progress. Or they might spend a day down by the foot of the Ulverston Canal, near the blast furnace, watching the ships beat up the bay with their great sails billowing, bringing their cargoes of rope and tallow and such to be unloaded on the quays.

Behind Ulverston rose the dome of Hoad Hill where the monument to Sir John Barrow was erected that summer. It was a replica of the Eddystone lighthouse, off Plymouth in Devonshire, a county as seafaring as Lancashire itself, and Walter took Rupert to see the opening and join in the celebrations. They watched the lighting of the bonfire and looked down on the twinkling lamps of the town and out over the moonlit bay.

'I'd like to go out there,' Walter said as they sat on the grassy slopes and stared towards the dark, glimmering sea. 'I'd like to go on one of those tall ships, before the mast, and see all the different countries – India, China, Australia. They're all there, Rupert, waiting to be discovered.' He moved restlessly. 'I've read about them in my father's books. I want to see them.'

'Then you should go,' Rupert said. At six years old, life seemed straightforward enough to him. Grown-ups – and Walter was, in his eyes, a grown-up – could do whatever they liked. 'You could be a sailor.'

'Sometimes,' Walter said thoughtfully, 'I think I'll do exactly that.'

By the time the September evenings began to draw in, Tilly's leg had healed and Rupert found it less easy to join his uncle on his rambles. Nor did Walter seek his company so readily. He had drifted on to other pursuits and found other friends. The company of a small boy was no longer welcome and Rupert was thrown back on his nursemaid for companionship. But just as he was no longer enough for Walter, so Tilly was no longer enough for him. His mind had been stretched and broadened, he wanted to be out and about, he wanted to know more and more. He wanted to learn.

At last he understood what his father had asked him in the nursery that day, three or four years ago.

During Nicholas's lengthy absences, Rupert took his meals mostly in the kitchen, but when Nicholas was at home, supper was served in the dining room and Rupert was expected to be present, washed, brushed and tidy. He was also expected to be quiet. His father had made it clear that childish conversation was not required, and either perused the newspaper or some periodical; or, if he had nothing to read, sat in gloomy silence, masticating his food as if it were a penance, while Rupert sat in tremulous fear.

'And what have you been doing today?' Nicholas would ask abruptly, bending his glowering gaze upon his son. 'Learned anything?'

Rupert could have told his father how he had observed the tide going out at Duddon, how he had seen the wading birds along the edge of the water, probing with long bills for sea creatures burrowing in the sand. He could have described the cloud patterns that told him it would rain before evening, or the darkness of the mountains that told him it was raining already in the north. He could have told how the leaves were changing colour, growing dry and golden on the trees and how even now the buds of next year's canopy were appearing on some bare twigs. He could have talked of squirrels collecting nuts, of birds massing to fly somewhere warmer before the cold weather caught them, of hedgehogs fattened by good eating, searching for secluded spots to hibernate.

Or he could have talked of the mines, of his fascination with the lumpy red kidney ore, of how he loved to watch the kibbles being drawn up filled with bulging rock. He could have described the men and boys, the women and girls who went down the mines every day, faces and clothes permanently stained with the crimson ore. He could have practised some of the knowledge he had gleaned from his grandfather on trips to the furnace or the quays.

But he said nothing of all this. Instead, aware of that derisive curl of his father's lip, fearing his scorn, he merely shook his head and said, 'No.'

'Nothing at all?' The lip curled anyway, as he had known it would. 'My God, what have I got for a son, a dumb idiot?' His scathing glance raked Rupert up and down. 'What has she landed me with, she and her tinker?'

Rupert had no answer for him. He understood nothing of his father's references, and as he grew older he forgot that they had ever been made, for Nicholas grew yet more remote and ceased to ask what he had learned, or indeed to show any interest at all in his doings. It was only yesterday, when he lay in bed with Elinor and listened to what she had to tell him, that Rupert remembered.

She and her tinker . . .

Chapter Twenty-One

That autumn had a lasting effect on Rupert's life. With Walter spending more and more time with his own friends, disappearing for hours or even days at a time, Timothy turned instead to his grandson, calling for him when his morning lessons were over and taking him to the mines, the bloomeries or the furnaces, as once he had taken Rupert's mother. By the time Rupert was nine years old, the two were close companions, for Rupert had never known Timothy in the days before his stroke and accepted the twisted face and difficult speech as others apparently could not. 'It's not Grandpapa's fault he can't talk properly,' he said to Tilly. 'Anyway, I can understand him perfectly well. So why can't Grand-mamma?'

Tilly shrugged. 'Mebbe she don't want to understand. It ain't easy, when you've been used to someone strong, to see 'em so changed. You didn't know your grandad before.'

'Well, he's good enough for me now.' And Rupert snatched up his jacket and cap and ran out to the yard, where Timothy's trap was clattering to a stop. He grinned cheerfully up at the old man and was rewarded by a dragging movement of the distorted mouth, which showed a few teeth in a travesty of Timothy's old smile. To others, it still came as a small shock every time Timothy did this; to Rupert, it was a smile like any other, and warmed the boy who received so few.

'Where are we going today?' he asked, swinging himself up into the seat beside his grandfather. 'Up to Carrkettle?'

'No.' The speech, too, was slurred and sometimes unexpected words came out, making nonsense of the things Timothy said, but to Rupert it was just another dialect, like that used by the mineworkers. Everyone knew they had different words for some things – 'owt' for 'anything', 'nowt' for 'nothing' and 'l'al' for 'little'. Nobody thought these or any of the other dialect words odd, so why should his grandfather's words be any different? But today even Rupert was confused as Timothy went on, 'Going to Louisa.'

'Louisa?' Rupert looked doubtfully at the old man. 'You mean we're going to the churchyard?' Tilly took him every Sunday to visit his mother's grave. They laid flowers there and he knew that his grandfather did the same. But they had never gone together. Or perhaps Timothy didn't mean to say 'Louisa' at all, but something quite different.

'No, not the churchyard. Mine. Going to Louisa.' He showed an unusual hint of irritation as he stumbled on, trying to make Rupert understand. '*Louisa* mine.'

'The Louisa mine?' Rupert stared at him. 'You mean there's a mine called Louisa? After my mother?'

Timothy smiled and nodded. He flicked the reins on the horse's back and the trap moved forward, out of the yard, across the Green and up the track to Birker Common.

From here they could see over the whole area. It was a brilliant October afternoon, with a soft haze blurring the distant horizon. The sands of the bay gleamed in the sunshine, their pale gold ribbed by the outgoing tide. The narrow channel was busy with ships making for the little ports of Grange and Arnside, and on the far side the hills rose green behind Lancaster.

To the west, Rupert could see the smooth whaleback

362

of Black Combe on the far side of the Duddon estuary; nearer at hand were the mineworkings of Lindal Moor and Pennington. Many of these workings now had steam engines to ease the task of raising and lowering the ore and the men and boys who worked it, and the clear air was smudged with steam and smoke. There was a constant traffic of engines and trucks along the tramway too, bringing ore down to Lindal Station; since its opening two years ago, this had been one of Rupert's favourite places, where he loved to go and watch the engines, sometimes even begging a ride on the footplate.

But they were not heading for Lindal Station today. Instead, Timothy directed the trap high up on Pennington Moor, to a part where Rupert had never been. As the horse came to a stop, he stared around him, surprised by the size of the working. Was this really named after his mother?

'Now, where's Ricketts?' Timothy climbed awkwardly down and set off with his stick. He moved with a crablike gait that was nevertheless quick enough and soon had the mine captain out of the shed he used as an office and deep in conversation. Rupert caught up in time to hear it.

'. . . have to extend the railway,' Abe Ricketts was saying. Like all mineworkers, his skin was raddled with the rusty colour of haematite and his beard was stained as if it had been dyed red. His eyes, a startling blue against the ruddiness, passed over Rupert without much interest. 'Ought to have been standard gauge from the start – 'twas daft, building it narrow. Stands to reason workings like this are going to produce more than that l'al line can cope wi'.'

'Think it'll come soon,' Timothy said. His speech seemed easier when he was with the mineworkers and worst of all, Rupert had noticed, when he was at home with his wife. 'Heard the railway company's thinking of tendering. Have to widen the hole too.'

The 'hole' was the tunnel, four hundred feet long through the limestone ridge. It had caused some interest when it was first being blasted and the miners had followed the navvies in the hope of discovering new ore. Nothing of interest had been found, however.

It had taken three different companies to complete the project, and now it looked as if the work would have to start all over again.

'And all because the masters didn't look far enough ahead,' Abe Ricketts grumbled. He was a good mine captain but inclined to surliness. Sometimes, when leaving him, Rupert had heard his grandfather sigh and talk of an older captain called Jacob Rigg. He was dead now and it was as if Timothy had lost a friend rather than an employee.

'Is Billy about?' he asked now and Ricketts jerked his head in the direction of the shed. Rupert followed his grandfather over and found a small group of men engaged in minor maintenance tasks – splicing ropes, greasing tools, mending kibbles and chains. Most of them were either too old now to go down the mines or disabled in some way – one-armed or with a twisted leg.

Billy Rigg was in his middle thirties, though he looked much older. The injury he had received in the earth tremor eighteen years before had left him with a tremor of his own, a permanent shaking of his grey head. He had little to say to Timothy and Rupert hung back, obscurely uneasy. The blurred brown eyes rested on him once or twice in puzzled half-recognition but there was no friendliness in the wavering glance, more a dull hostility. Rupert was relieved when Timothy drew a few coins from his pocket and handed them to the men before turning away.

For the rest of the morning he showed Rupert the Louisa mine. He told him how one day he had descended the pit with Jacob Rigg and how they had gone through the workings, looking at the ginnels that were to produce such fine ore, and the great sop from which millions of tons had been dug out. He told Rupert about the pencil ore, a rarity that occurred only in the finest veins.

'Best mine we ever had,' he said in his terse, economical way; when words did not come easily, one used as few as possible. 'Thought it was worked out. Then Abe tried a new direction. Good as ever it was.'

That explained why his grandfather had never brought him here before – Timothy had no time or inclination to look at defunct pits. 'So it'll be working again?' Rupert looked around the pithead with the new engines in place, the kibbles already winding up and down, the narrow railtrack and bogies that transported the ore to the main tramway.

Louisa mine. His mother's mine. He felt a quickening of excitement and knew suddenly that this was his world.

He slipped his hand into his grandfather's, and they stood together in silence, watching as the mine came slowly back to life.

During the next few years, Rupert took more and more interest in the mines. Gradually, they became less a place to play and explore on the trips he made with his grandfather and more a place to learn, to watch and listen and absorb. Afterwards, jogging home in the trap, he would ply his grandfather with questions and Timothy would answer in his slightly slurred voice. Frequently, there was an expression in the sad eyes that Rupert didn't understand, as if Timothy were reliving old memories. But if he was, he never spoke of them and he seemed happy to talk about the mines and mining for as long as Rupert was happy to listen.

'Some say the Romans mined hereabouts,' he remarked, gazing out across the moor. 'No one knows for sure. Pits were sunk in Richard the Second's time, though, up Marton way. And monks at Abbey mined it, till Henry the Eighth destroyed the place.'

Rupert nodded. He had been to see Furness Abbey, a long-disused ruin of red sandstone with a few towering walls and cloisters still standing as a hint of the magnificent building it must once have been. It was strange to think of monks, whom he had always supposed to be holy figures more occupied with psalters and prayer than strenuous toil, labouring in the mines.

'Lands went to Duchy then,' Timothy went on. 'Lancaster, that was. Then it was the Albermarles, then the Montagues. Always a duke. Now it's Buccleuch we rent royalties from. But it's ironmasters do the work.'

He took Rupert to the bloomeries and blast furnaces too. These were scattered over the area and further afield into High Furness, on the shores of Coniston Water or even further to Cunsey, near Windermere. As the industry had prospered, other furnaces were built in Scotland where there was plenty of wood for charcoal, and Furness haematite was shipped there regularly for processing.

One of Rupert's favourite places was the forge at Duddon. He loved to go there with his grandfather, travelling over the fells and beside the swift-running river with its grassy banks and rocky falls. The forge was one of the largest in the area, massively constructed, and he would watch as the ore was smelted to make it workable.

'See,' Armstrong, the forge manager at Duddon, told him one day, 'when iron working started, a furnace needed three things – ore, timber an' watter. Timber for charcoal, watter for power. But charcoal needs trees and trees tak' time to grow. 'Tweren't too long afore trees were runnin' out in some parts. That's why a lot of our ore goes to Scotland.'

'But what about coal? Don't they use that now?'

'Aye, where there's plenty. But you can't use coal straight off for smelting. Coal has sulphur in it, see, an' sulphur combines with iron. Don't matter too much if 'tis to be used for casting, like, but it won't mak' good wrought iron – crumbles up at heat, see.' He paused and drew on his pipe. 'Make t'coal into coke and it works better. But coal's too far away for us to bother wi', and we still got a main of trees so we still use charcoal. Reckon it makes better iron anyway.'

The furnace was sending thick dark smoke billowing into the air above Duddon. Rupert watched the men tapping the molten iron from the hearth to run it into the sand pig-bed. Here it solidified in the long, narrow channels and was left to cool as cast iron.

'Most of it'll be takken ower to the finery to be made into wrought iron,' Armstrong said, jerking his head at the other part of the forge. 'Never bin a lot of use, has cast iron. But we get a few orders for it now an' then – graveslabs, cannons and such. And I reckon when they finds out how to mak' it stronger, it'll be used a lot more. Trouble is, it can't be worked, only moulded.'

This period, Rupert thought later, had been one of the happiest of his childhood. His father, having arranged for him to join the morning lessons given to a few local boys by the vicar, took little further notice of him. Most afternoons Timothy would call for him or, if he was too busy, Rupert would slip out on his own and go down to the beach or roam the fields and commons near his home. He rapidly grew familiar with every lane and byway and, like his mother, became a welcome visitor in many a small cottage. And if he lay awake at night, wondering why his father seemed to dislike him so, wondering what he had done to cause such dislike and feeling loneliness like a crushing layer of darkness all about him, he never gave a hint of it during the day. He had learned early that a miserable face was more likely to give rise to irritation than to sympathy.

Other events took place during those years, some happier than others. In 1851, the Great Exhibition was held in London and one of Rupert's fellow pupils at the vicarage was taken to see it. He came back glowing, with tales so fantastic – of huge glass fountains, trees growing indoors, stuffed elephants and displays of unimaginably exotic richness from all over the world, all contained within a huge cast-iron and glass canopy – that it was difficult to believe more than a quarter of them. The next day, in proof, he brought with him the official catalogue and the boys and their master pored over it, fascinated, not least by the statistics given for the exhibition building itself.

'Four thousand, five hundred tons of iron,' Rupert said in an awed tone.

'Why,' the vicar said, 'it's three times as long as St Paul's Cathedral.'

'Six hundred thousand cubic feet of timber,' read out another boy, whose father owned large stretches of woodland.

Clearly, it was a sight that should be seen by everyone in the land, and the other boys immediately persuaded their own fathers to take them to London to see it. Rupert said nothing. He listened to their tales and looked at the pictures they brought back, but he did not mention them to Nicholas at the silent meals they shared each evening. He did not even know whether Nicholas was aware that the exhibition existed.

The Great Exhibition was designed to show the world that Britain was in the forefront of design and manufacture, a leader of civilisation. But in less than three years she was at war with some of the very countries which had sent displays. On the Crimea, a place Rupert had never heard of, nearly three thousand men died, some killed in battle, many more of disease. The war was fought through several cruel winters and it was during this time that Walter, grown ever more rebellious, finally left home to join the army.

His departure left Timóthy sadder than ever and

increasingly inclined to turn to Rupert as his only companion. For a long time, the family feared Walter lost in the muddle of the war, but when it was over, they heard that he had been at the siege of Sebastopol and survived.

But he did not come home. It was as if, having finally broken away from Furness, he had severed a link that he did not intend to re-forge. He stayed abroad, wandering; they heard of him, through infrequent letters, from Greece, Italy, Persia. He wrote articles which were published in newspapers about his travels, and slowly, as the years passed, he became known as an explorer. His name, to everyone's surprise, became known and respected.

But before then, when Rupert was just eleven years old, Nicholas met and married Elinor Corney.

Elinor was a young widow from Grange-over-Sands. Her husband, Henry Corney, had moved in the same circles as Nicholas's father, Sir Stanley Craven; he had been a respected merchant from Liverpool before he retired with his young wife. Elinor had lived in innocence of the way that money was actually earned, and the inescapable prominence of iron-mining so near to her home came as a shock.

'You mean your father-in-law actually *goes down* the mines?' Rupert heard her say. 'And he takes Rupert with him? Well, I hope he doesn't intend to do the same with William!' She caught her son to her and he nestled his head against her breast. A pretty four-year-old with curly blond hair not yet cut short, dressed in velvet suits with lace collars, he looked a very unlikely candidate for a trip into a haematite mine. Rupert, however, still wearing the old clothes he normally used for jaunts with his grandfather, was as stained as any miner, his finger-nails ingrained with the red soil of the area and his dark hair turned auburn by the dust.

Elinor eyed him with distaste. 'Look at him,' she said

369

to Nicholas. 'He looks like a labourer. And his grandfather was no better – I saw him driving away, looking like a vagabond, filthy dirty. I wonder Susannah tolerates it.'

She doesn't, Rupert thought, remembering his grandmother's disapproval whenever Timothy entered the house. He had to wash thoroughly and change his clothes before daring to enter her presence, and even then it seemed that he spent no longer in it than necessity and good manners demanded. Susannah's tongue could be very sharp if she considered her husband was neglecting her, but his company seemed to make it no softer.

'He'll have to go to school,' Elinor declared, still staring at Rupert. 'It's the only way to civilise him. He'll never learn to be a gentleman in this place.'

'Certainly he'll go to school,' Nicholas said, to Rupert's surprise. 'It's been arranged for some time. I was merely waiting for his eleventh birthday.' His cold grey eyes moved over Rupert, showing as much distaste as Elinor, but he continued to speak as if Rupert were not there. 'He starts in September.'

September! That was only a few weeks away. Had this really been arranged, discussed, known about, for months, maybe even years? And where would he go? There were no schools in the Furness area.

'You'll go to Rugby,' Nicholas stated when he asked. 'Yes, of course you'll board. And perhaps there you'll learn a few more useful subjects than iron-mining. Your stepmother's right, you've run wild for too long. You need some sharp discipline.'

Run wild? But he had spent most of his time with his grandfather, learning the business of ironmining. What could be more useful than that?

Rupert went off to school feeling bewildered and rebellious, but unable to do anything about it. He was also acutely shy. He had known few other boys apart from his young uncle Walter and his fellow pupils at the

370

vicarage, and to be suddenly thrust among several hundred who all seemed larger, stronger and more confident than he was terrifying.

It took him two years to settle down, two years of bewilderment, of bullying and fagging. After that, he suddenly found his feet and began to make friends. Sometimes he stayed with them during the holidays. And during his last holiday, he brought Curtis Stratton home with him to spend Easter.

Curtis was a tall boy with the same blond good looks that William Corney, now ten years old, had inherited from his mother. Nicholas, too, had once had fair hair though his eyes had always been a cool grey, never the blue of Elinor's or of Curtis's. Perhaps it was the colouring that attracted Elinor. Perhaps it was just the youth and vitality that Curtis possessed, and the smooth urbanity of his manner which even six years at Rugby had never succeeded in imparting to Rupert. Or perhaps, after six years of marriage to Nicholas, she was simply bored.

Whatever the reason, it was quickly apparent that Elinor saw Curtis as more than a schoolboy.

'Oh, Curtis will escort me,' she would say when some minor expedition was proposed. 'It will be an opportunity for him to see the abbey ruins.' Or, 'Curtis and I are going for a walk. He wants me to show him the rocks at Bardsea.' Or, 'If you're going to be out with your grandfather all day, Rupert, I'll borrow Curtis. I want to take him to Peil Island and show him the castle.'

It was not long before Rupert noticed a sleek satisfaction about the two of them. There was a secretiveness in the glances they gave one another, an air of suppressed excitement that he only half understood. When they were together, it was as if the air quivered with tension, almost as if some quarrel had taken place, yet their smiles and laughter denied any possibility of a quarrel. When they were apart each one was restless, absent-minded, with eyes that continually strayed towards the door and ears that seemed to be listening for something.

The effect on Rupert was disturbing. For some time he had been aware of the restlessness of his own body, of unexpected and often unwelcome reactions. Life at Rugby had scarcely left him innocent, and the erections which, according to his fellow pupils, proved he was a man occurred at the least convenient times. They seemed to bear no relation to his thoughts or desires, but simply happened and were all too frequently observed and remarked upon by other boys. The fact that every boy suffered in the same way did not at all prevent their jibes; nor were the squeaky, cracking voices, the wet sheets or the growth of hair on both face and body allowed to pass unnoticed.

This period had more or less passed now; Rupert had greater control of his body and had learned to enjoy the sensations and reactions he could evoke, though his pleasure was invariably tainted with furtive guilt. But he was unprepared for the effect that the relationship between Elinor and Curtis Stratton had on him.

The tension between them communicated itself to him. He caught the heat in their eyes and felt it spread through his own body. He watched them during the day, observing every small nuance of expression, every private touch, and his pulse quickened. He saw Curtis's eyes rest on Elinor and realised with a shock that she was a beautiful woman, her hair still shimmering with gold, her figure enticingly curved. And he saw, too, that she was aware of her beauty and used it.

He felt then a surge of emotion he had never known before: jealousy. And as he stared first at her and then at Curtis, seeing their air of secret knowledge, of possession, the strength of his jealousy and his desire shook him with a force that left him breathless.

At that very moment, Elinor turned her head. Her blue eyes looked into his and he knew that she saw the truth. He saw the pupils widen and her brows rise, and then she smiled, slowly. After a long, speculative look, she turned away again.

Rupert was left with the discomfort of a reaction he had not experienced in company for some time. And Elinor knew that too; he could see it in the amused twitch of her lips, and he felt his face burn with embarrassment.

When she said goodbye to him on the last evening of the holiday, she let her fingers touch his cheek in a way she never had before.

'You've grown up, Rupert,' she observed, her voice soft. 'You're almost a man. Or perhaps not *almost?*' Her eyes regarded him questioningly while he stood speechless under her caressing fingers, and then she shook her head slightly and smiled. 'No, not quite, I think. Well, there's another holiday to come.' He said nothing and she added lightly, 'I like your friend Curtis. Will you be bringing him to stay again?'

'No.' Rupert's voice came in a croak. In fact, the matter had not been discussed but he knew he would not be bringing Curtis Stratton here again. Nor any of his other friends. This summer, this last long holiday with school and boyhood behind him and manhood about to begin, he wanted to be his.

'Well then, we must spend some time together, you and I.' Elinor smiled at him and he felt the now familiar heat spread through his body. 'We must get to know each other properly. Don't you think that's a good idea?' Her soft voice and silky, caressing fingertips left him in no doubt as to what the summer would bring.

He lived through the term in feverish anticipation and then, only a week or so into July, what he had simultaneously feared and longed for happened at last. And Elinor told him the truth about himself.

Mining talk that summer was all of steel, the new form of

iron that had been made possible by the invention of Henry Bessemer.

'It'll bring an end to wrought iron,' Timothy declared one evening as he and Susannah ate supper with the Cravens. 'Quarter the time to convert. Bigger furnace, make bigger pieces. Change the whole industry.'

Nicholas pursed his lips. 'D'you really think so? I mean, it all sounds very wonderful but the new Bessemer converter is expensive to install, it's huge and unwieldy. How many ironmakers are going to give up the blast furnaces they've only just completed in favour of this? Production of wrought iron in this country is the highest it's ever been, about three million tons a year, while steel is still hardly produced at all. Wrought iron has proved its worth – we've been using it now for three or four thousand years. It's not going to die out overnight.'

'Not overnight in our terms,' Timothy said. 'But in terms of thousands of years, doomed. Can't last. Steel's the coming thing.'

Rupert listened eagerly. He had already seen a Bessemer converter working and been impressed by its speed and efficiency. He had been impressed by the final product too. Steel could be used for all the tasks that had until now been accomplished by wrought iron, but because it came molten from the converter rather than in the balls produced by the puddling furnace – the largest of them no more than a hundredweight – it could be moulded into ingots of several tons. Rolling large items, such as plates for the iron – or steel – ships now being built, was therefore much easier. The shipyard at Barrow had already begun to use it and it was clear that demand would grow.

Nicholas, however, was still unconvinced. 'The converter hasn't proved itself yet,' he objected, reaching for the claret. 'I still think it's likely to cool the iron. And it's no use at all for most of the ores. No, it'll be like a good many other inventions, nothing but a passing fancy.'

'But it doesn't cool the iron,' Rupert said. 'I know some people thought it would, but what happens is that the oxygen being blown in actually burns out the carbon and raises the temperature. The metal ends up hotter than when it began. There's no problem with working it. As for the problems with some ores, they're working on them now and I'm sure they'll solve them all soon. I agree with Grandfather. I think steel is the coming thing.'

'And you, of course,' Nicholas said in the acid tone he reserved specially for Rupert, 'are an expert on the subject.'

Rupert flushed scarlet and fell silent. He bit his lip, staring at the table. He knew that he was right, for he had been with his grandfather to the mines and the furnaces and listened to the talk. He had also read most of the papers and journals that his grandfather received. Nicholas received some too but gave them only a cursory glance, for he had not been brought up in mining and took only enough interest to allow him to maintain a conversation.

But it was useless for Rupert to argue. Nicholas still treated him as if he were a child, and a particularly irritating one at that. If only you knew, Rupert thought, lifting his eyes to gaze at him. Your wife could tell you how much a man I am.

'And don't look at me like that, you insolent young pup,' Nicholas said sharply. 'You may have spent the past six years at Rugby learning to behave as a gentleman but that doesn't give you the right to come home and lord it over your elders and betters. If you've nothing worthwhile to say at table, you'd do better to keep quiet.'

Rupert opened his mouth but before he could give vent to the angry retort that rose to his lips, Elinor smoothly intervened.

'I'm sure Rupert had no intention of being insolent,'

she said peaceably. 'He was just interested in the conversation. And you know what the young are like, always enthusiastic about the latest developments. Now,' without giving Nicholas a chance to reply, she rose to her feet, 'shall we withdraw, Susannah? I expect the gentlemen would rather continue their interesting discussion alone.' She smiled at her husband. 'Rupert, of course, will stay with you. After all, he's not a schoolboy any longer, is he?'

The two women left the room. Rupert glanced at his father, then at his grandfather. Nicholas's face was a picture of baffled annoyance, while Timothy was looking secretly amused. Elinor, it seemed, had scored a point but only Rupert knew just how high her scoring was.

He looked at Nicholas and felt a sudden sensation of power. For the first time in his life, he felt he stood on equal terms with his father and knew himself to be the better man. For the first time in his life, he was unafraid.

It doesn't matter what you think of me, he told Nicholas silently. Your opinions are all founded on bitterness and hatred and have nothing to do with *me*. What matters is what I think of myself – and what I know to be true.

He met Nicholas's eyes steadily as he took the decanter and poured his own glass of port. But as he raised it to his lips, he knew that even this new confidence was not enough. There were things he still needed to know, questions he still wanted answered.

Was there anyone alive who could give him those answers?

Nicholas swung himself up into the saddle and turned his horse's head towards the yard gate. It was a hazy September morning, the fields frosted by a pearly mist and the first touch of autumn smouldering on the trees. The white caps of mushrooms gleamed in the dewy grass and the hedges were thick with blackberries.

He set Marquis to a trot down the lane and on to the beach. The tide was out and the sands firm, ideal for a canter. One could go for miles on these sands, either along the Conishead shore towards Ulverston or west in the direction of Piel Island and Walney. He supposed it would be possible to go right round the peninsula and back over the spine from Duddon, but he had never attempted it. He preferred an easier ride, no more than a mealtime away from home.

He had woken that morning with a headache. Not surprisingly, Elinor had pointed out spitefully, considering the amount he had drunk last night. Claret with the meat, a good Madeira with the dessert, port to follow and then a nightcap of malt whisky. No more than he was accustomed to drink at dinner, he had retorted with spirit.

'Perhaps not,' she had answered, 'but more than you can successfully hold. You wake with a headache more often than without one these days.'

'At least I don't have one at night, as you so conveniently contrive to do.'

'Do I?' Her eyes flashed. 'I don't recall having a headache at night for some considerable time. I haven't needed to.'

That barb had been a cruel one, he thought, savagely kicking the horse's sides. A man didn't mind so much having a reluctant wife – that was a common enough state, after all, and mere reluctance need be no bar to the rights of marriage – but to be reminded that reluctance wasn't even necessary was a reflection on his ability as a man, an attack on the very roots of his pride.

'Are you complaining that I don't come to your bed often enough?' They had always had adjoining rooms, but in the first year or two of their marriage Nicholas's had been seldom used. Now he slept more frequently alone, angrily aware of Elinor next door but knowing that if he went to her it was more likely than not to end in failure.

'I'm not complaining at all. Simply stating a fact.' She looked boldly at him, daring him to retaliate. He stood helpless, longing to strike the smugness from her face but aware that this was exactly what she wanted. She could then begin to weep, to recriminate, and everything she said would be undeniably true, and yet somehow twisted.

'You never loved me . . . You married me only to give you a son because your first wife cuckolded you, because you know you don't have a son of your own . . . You picked me because I already had a son, and you thought – you thought . . .' Her tears would overwhelm her, but if he attempted to interrupt or even offer comfort, she would go on with renewed energy. 'You thought you could prove yourself with me.' She would lift her wet face at this point and stare at him with accusation. 'You wanted to prove to yourself that it wasn't your fault you and Louisa never had a child. But it didn't work, did it? I never did conceive.' Here her voice would rise and she would begin to scream at him, so that he feared the servants would hear and knew he would be compelled to silence her by force. 'The truth is, you can't father children, Nicholas. You can't father sons or daughters, you never have been able to, and now you can't even try!'

And his patience would snap. He would clap his hand across her mouth, shake her by the shoulders, slap her face in an attempt to bring her out of her hysteria – and to hurt her too, he was forced to admit it – and it would end with Elinor weeping in his arms or lying on the bed sobbing uncontrollably. Or, more frighteningly, crouching on the floor while he rained blows on her from above.

Such scenes had become all too common until Nicholas learned to recognise the signs and avoid them. It was not always easy. Elinor seemed able to whip up the smallest disagreement into a furious quarrel, ending always in the same way. And unless Nicholas were on guard, his own emotions would become drawn in, so that he followed the same disastrous path, almost as if he were following the rules of some painful game. It was like being on a horse that had run wild and could end its mad career only by galloping over a cliff or dashing itself against a tree. As if Elinor and he were compelled to play this strange game and could gain their bizarre satisfaction only from following it to the end.

But slowly, over the years, the rules had changed. To begin with, satisfaction could be gained in bed, though their lovemaking was more release of anger than an expression of affection. Later, the pattern had become more frightening, with release possible only after Nicholas had lost control and struck his wife in a burst of temper that shocked and bewildered him. Then he must beg a forgiveness which Elinor would grant only when she was convinced of his remorse – each time, it seemed, requiring more proof, more begging, more humiliation.

Humiliation did not suit Nicholas's idea of himself. At first acknowledging his fault, he began gradually to resent the scenes which it seemed Elinor deliberately engineered. He would take himself away and walk for miles across the hills or gallop Marquis on the sands. And he would hide his impotence with drink. Wine, it was well known, could impair a man's abilities. A man whose wife consistently turned him away was entitled to take comfort from his wine, to drown his sorrows. And if that made him unable to come to the bed where she had so often rejected him, well, that was her fault. And she'd indicated clearly enough that she didn't care, anyway.

Cantering along the sands, as far from the shoreline as it was safe to venture, he wondered, as he had so often wondered in the past, why he had married her. Why had he felt the urge to marry again at all, especially after the way his first wife had treated him? With the evidence of her faithlessness constantly before his eyes, why had he allowed himself to believe that any woman could be trusted?

Perhaps Elinor was right; perhaps he had been trying to prove to himself that he was as potent as any other man, that he too could father sons. His life with Louisa had never been quite satisfactory, after all. How could she taint his love and desire for her by accusing him of attacking her, of taking his pleasures without thought for hers, by flinching when he touched her and weeping when she ought to have shown joy?

He had been hurt, disappointed, bewildered. Meeting Louisa the way he had, he had expected so much more. He had thought to find in her the pertness, the saucy willingness that her pose as a dairymaid had seemed to promise. Impudent 'Moll' had excited him, and the thought that Louisa, brought up as a young lady, shy and reluctant, was really the wild creature he had met tramping the hills, had led him to expect the same piquant lovemaking that he had experienced with other young serving girls. A sense of naughtiness, of secret complicity, had added spice to such encounters, and he had looked forward to the same spice in his marriage bed.

He had truly believed that Louisa had shared his desire. Didn't they all protest at first, didn't they all squirm in his arms and plead for mercy? Wasn't it all part of the game? How was a man supposed to know when the woman was serious, when she really was afraid or repulsed? And why should he expect to find such fear or repugnance in his own wife?

In Elinor, he had believed he had found a woman of experience, who could satisfy a man and make him believe he had satisfied her too. For didn't every man need that, the knowledge that his woman was happy in his arms, that she welcomed rather than feared his body, delighted in his caresses rather than simply endured?

And to begin with, it had seemed he was right. Elinor had shown no inhibitions in the bedchamber, had in fact startled him with her forwardness, her imagination. Things he had never dreamed of doing with Louisa, things he had thought only whores did. The first time such a thought had entered his head, he had turned quickly away from it. Elinor was no whore, she was his *wife*. But once admitted, it persisted. Where had she learned such things, where had she learned to touch a man in that way, to use her own body so? Surely not with Henry Corney, over thirty years her senior and by all accounts rigidly straitlaced.

Nicholas knew that such a public persona often concealed a very different character. Some of his own acquaintances, highly respected in the local community, parading on Sundays as men of God with their wives decked out in jewels and furs and their families neatly arrayed beside them, had a darker, more secret side to their lives. 'Business trips' to Liverpool or Manchester included visits to brothels or even to mistresses kept in small houses and given a regular allowance. But Henry Corney, he was sure, had not been one of these.

So where had Elinor learned so well what pleased a man?

He found himself growing uneasy with their relationship. Driven by his own needs, obsessed by the pleasure she could give him, he found his satisfaction marred by the thought of men who might have gone before him. How many and who? And it was not long before a second, even more disturbing thought followed the first: if she had cuckolded Henry Corney, might she not do the same to him?

To his dismay and Elinor's scorn, he found himself failing. More strenuous efforts brought about not only scorn but distaste. Elinor began to plead headaches. And then, as she had so spitefully told him that morning, to have no need for such excuses.

Nicholas slept and ached alone. He retired again to the shell he had lived in after Louisa had died, and the thought that obsessed him now was: where was Elinor gaining her satisfaction? For he felt certain that she must be finding it somewhere.

He began to watch her, to look for the signs that had once excited him. That light in her eye, the faint flush on her cheeks. The brightness in her voice, a certain archness, a sidelong look. A speculative expression when meeting a man for the first time, as if watching for certain signals.

Slowly, uncomfortably, he realised that Elinor gave these signs almost every time she spoke to a man. Servant, gamekeeper, ironmaster or landowner, it made no difference. Each one was worthy of assessment, if nothing else.

He tortured himself, imagining Elinor with the men he had thought to be his friends. James Harrison, Walter Unsworth, John Stead . . . Did she meet them when he was away on business? After years of indolence, he was called away more and more to deal with his father's business, for Sir Stanley was old now and very nearly helpless. There was plenty of time for an errant wife to follow her own way. And why else should she refuse so consistently to accompany him?

'It's so dull in Liverpool. I'd rather be at home.' Or, 'I promised your mother-in-law to help with a dinner party.' Or, 'The maids will be spring-cleaning and I must be here to oversee.'

And recently, 'Rupert's bringing a friend home for the holidays. I can't leave them alone.'

Rupert had brought his friend, a tall, handsome youth

who reminded Nicholas of himself at the same age. And he had seen the look on Elinor's face, the way her gaze rested on Curtis's fair face. He had seen the answering light in the boy's eyes.

He had tried to comfort himself with the thought that Rupert's friend was no more than a boy. And only staying for two or three weeks. Surely nothing could happen in that time. In the event, he had, in the famous words of Admiral Nelson, turned a blind eye, feeling relief when the two boys returned to school. But now Rupert had come home for good and he had seen the look again, and knew that this was the final humiliation.

To be cuckolded by his own son!

But Rupert wasn't his son, he reminded himself. He was the fruit of that union between his wife and some unknown man – a tinker, a gipsy, to judge by Rupert's looks. All the same, Nicholas had acknowledged him as his. He had brought him up, sent him to school, given him everything he would have given to his own son. No one but he knew the truth – except Elinor, of course. Now he regretted having trusted her with the knowledge in the early days of their marriage.

Had she told Rupert?

Marquis had begun to tire and Nicholas allowed him to slow to a walk. He stared out over the rippling sands to the edge of the tide. Soon it would be turning, the water spreading rapidly over the broad expanse, and anyone caught by it was likely to have a hard time getting back to shore. Only a few days ago two men, journeying across from Poulton, had found their cart caught in quicksand and overturned. One had been found yesterday, washed up near Ulverston; the other was still missing.

It would be easy enough to simply ignore that incoming tide, to stay here until it was too late . . .

But Marquis did not deserve such a fate, and Nicholas turned him and headed for the trees that fringed the beach. It was time to go home.

He wondered what would happen if he confronted his wife, if he took a horsewhip to Rupert. But he knew he could never do it. As long as he did nothing, nobody would ever know the humiliation that two successive wives had brought him.

Chapter Twenty-Two

'Need you ask where they are? Off jaunting about their precious mines, of course, where else?' Susannah's wrinkled fingers picked impatiently at her embroidery. Her eyes were failing now and Elinor could see several wrong stitches, but she knew better than to point them out. In any case, what did it signify? The tablecloth Susannah was making would, if it were ever finished, simply join the others in a drawer. They weren't needed; they served simply to provide Susannah with something to occupy her days.

'For myself, I'm glad enough to have Timothy out of the way,' Susannah continued, peering among the silks. 'Can you see a pink to match this one? I swear Martha tangles them up deliberately. He only brings mud and dirt into the house, and his voice is so loud these days – he shouts as if I were deaf. Ridiculous! It's his voice that's the problem. It's no better, you know, and he makes no effort to improve it.'

Elinor found a skein of pink silk and untangled enough of it to thread the needle for her mother-in-law. Then she rose and went to the window, staring out at the hills that rose soft and green towards the mine workings. Annoyance tightened her brow. She had been expecting Rupert to come to her this afternoon – Tuesdays had been a regular appointment for the past three years now – and instead he had gone off with his grandfather. Why? Couldn't he do that any day of the week? What was so important about this afternoon?

'Do you know where they went?' She tried to keep her voice casual. Disappointed and angry, she had waited for half an hour and then come to Pennington Hall, ostensibly to call on Susannah but really to see if her stepson had been delayed. But apparently he had absented himself quite willingly.

'Oh yes, I know.' Susannah sounded as annoyed as Elinor. 'They don't tell me, of course, I'm not supposed to be interested. But I can hear better than they think.' She raised faded eyes to Elinor's face. 'They've gone to Louisa.'

'Louisa?' For a moment, Elinor entertained a wild vision of Rupert and his grandfather conjuring up ghosts on some remote part of the moor.

'Louisa mine,' Susannah said bitterly. 'You know, of course, that they're sinking new boreholes there. Timothy says they've discovered yet another rich new vein.' She snorted. 'Iron! Always iron. Can't he leave it alone now? He's seventy-five years old, for heaven's sake. Isn't he old enough to retire and leave it all to some younger man? Aren't I entitled to a little of his company?'

Perhaps that's why he doesn't retire, Elinor thought, looking at the old woman with dislike. She had never been in Susannah's company without having to listen to a series of complaints, usually about either her husband or her son Walter. On the rare occasions she could find nothing to say about them, she was never short of other subjects. And as she grew older, she grew worse.

How old was she now? Sixty-five, seventy? Old enough, certainly, to expect her husband to stay at home a little more. Old enough to feel that she deserved some attention. But Timothy continued to go regularly to the mines, to manage them with the help of his mine captains, to keep the reins in his hands. And, more often than not, taking Rupert with him.

'Have you heard from Walter lately?' she asked, and was rewarded by another snort.

'Walter! A fine son *he's* turned out to be. Not that he ever was any good.' Even Elinor was shocked by this outburst. 'Jaunting about all over the world, without so much as a thought for his poor mother eking out her last few days alone. He's in India now, if you please. Exploring the Himalayas, if you ever heard such non-sense. And planning to go to China, or some such place.' Her tone dismissed China as if it were some tiny, little-known island somewhere in the Pacific. 'What good does he expect to do there? He ought to be at home, taking the burden from his father's shoulders and looking after his mother.'

Who never, by all accounts, looked after him, Elinor thought. Walter had left home soon after she had married Nicholas, and she had never known him well, but she had heard how he had been born with a misshapen head and his mother had rejected him, con-vinced she had borne an idiot. Walter was no idiot – Elinor remembered him as a tall, well-built young man and occasionally regretted his departure – but he had always been a rebel and no one had been surprised when he had finally left home to go to war.

She sipped the tea that had been brought, wondering whether it was worth waiting in the hope that Rupert and Timothy would return. But the thought of Rupert's knowing she had virtually followed him here was an unwelcome one, and she set the cup down, determined to leave at once. At that moment, however, the door opened.

Elinor looked up quickly, but it was only Martha bustling into the room, looking more like a robin than ever with her bright, inquisitive eyes, her drab brown dress enlivened only by a red scarf at her throat. And surely she was even dumpier, a round face above a round body. As plain as a pikestaff, but always nauseatingly

387

ready with a smile. She was smiling now.

'Elinor! How nice to see you. Have you had tea? Ah, I see Mamma's given you some.' She sat down and poured herself a cup. 'And how are you? It seems an age since we saw you.'

Elinor made conventional responses. She did not dislike Martha, who at forty-two had become the typical spinster daughter, accepting apparently without regret that her role in life was to care for her parents and home. Perhaps that was why she was so inquisitive, gaining all her small excitements from the lives of others. Not that it signified, Elinor thought, and at least her presence took a burden from herself and Nicholas. Without Martha, they might have been expected to do a good deal more for the Sherwins.

'Isn't Rupert a fine young man now!' Martha was saying fondly. 'I saw him before he and Papa left for the mine this afternoon. He had luncheon with us here, you know. He's changed so much since he left school – so tall and dark. I love to look at him. Such beautiful hands, such broad shoulders. He looks so strong, so *virile*.'

It was odd that Martha, the maiden aunt, could observe and draw attention to all the finer points of the male physiology. Possibly because maiden ladies weren't supposed to understand the implications, Elinor thought. To Martha, perhaps it was no different from exclaiming over the beauty of a baby boy kicking on a rug, his nakedness displayed for all to see.

'And his hair's really black, have you ever noticed that?' Martha went on with an almost unbelievable innocence. 'And so *curly*. One wonders just where he gets it from. It must be from the Dawson side, don't you think? Some relative nobody here has ever heard about. They had connections in Scotland, I believe,' she confided in a low voice, as if it were Outer Mongolia and a matter for some shame. Then she laughed and went on, 'He looks positively romantic. I wonder every young

388

woman in Furness isn't setting her cap at him.'

So do I, Elinor thought, playing with her teacup. And how long can it be before they do? He's twenty years old now and looks more. And he's becoming restless.

This was in fact the third Tuesday afternoon Rupert had missed in the past few weeks. For the other two, he had produced plausible excuses – his father had suddenly demanded his company on a trip to Liverpool, an old school friend (not Curtis, unfortunately) had called unexpectedly while journeying north. But this was different. Going to the mines with his grandfather was something he did every other day of the week. It could not have been imperative that he go today.

Was he growing tired of her?

Elinor set the cup down with a tiny crash. Never, never in her life had she found herself so dependent on a man. Always before, her lovers had passed through her life leaving very little trace, usually dismissed before they had a chance to tire. Part of the game, for Elinor, was to have a spurned lover begging to be allowed back into her favour. The sense of power it gave her to watch a man who had dominated her in bed now subjugated and reduced to grovelling at her feet was as heady as any sexual excitement; in fact, an affair which did not finish in this way left her as frustrated as a sexual encounter that ended without climax. It was as if the whole process of seduction, conspiracy and dangerous liaison was designed to build towards that end.

Well, every love affair must come to an end, she thought, tapping her fingers on the arm of her chair and listening with only half an ear to Martha's prattle. And if Rupert is indeed wandering, it's time he was sent packing. And *I* shall do the sending. I'll not have a young upstart of barely twenty, and a by-blow at that, showing me the door. And I'll make sure he's sorry about it, too.

All the same, she hadn't intended it to end just yet. Her liaison with Rupert had lasted longer than any other, partly because, under her tuition, he had become such a good lover, partly because of the added spice of excitement afforded her by the knowledge that she was committing adultery with her husband's son – even though he was son in name only. The danger that attended their assignations had become an essential ingredient, increased when it began to seem too safe by Elinor's insistence on using different meeting places. Thus Rupert's bedroom, where Nicholas was unlikely to come, was given up in favour of Elinor's, and that in turn to even more risky trysts such as the hayloft when all the servants were supposed to be occupied, or a secret valley or glade where almost anyone might chance upon them.

'It's so much better out of doors,' she urged, pressing her body against his, her breasts spilling from her low neckline as she moved so that they brushed provocatively against his chest through the thin cambric shirt he wore. 'Don't you find it so? So *exciting*.' And as she had known he would, Rupert had responded immediately to her words and forgotten his doubts and inhibitions. He had taken her there and then, under the trees and under the sky, with a rough passion that lifted her to a new pitch and left them stunned by sensations new to them both.

'Standing up . . .' Elinor said, when they had recovered their breath. And, with a little, excited laugh, 'Well, didn't I tell you?'

The thought of it now, in Susannah's parlour, brought a flush of memory to her cheeks and a tingle low down in her stomach. No. She could not let Rupert escape her yet. There was still a good deal of spice to be enjoyed. And besides, who could take his place?

Deep under Pennington Moor, walking with bent heads in the low tunnel, Rupert and Timothy raised their tallow candles to inspect the latest finds.

'See,' Abe Ricketts said, his lugubrious tone making it

sound like bad news, 'this here's about the richest vein we've struck yet. Reckon it goes back a fair way under the moor and all on the Buccleuch royalty. Means we can mine it no matter who owns t'land up top.'

'We'll need a new tramway,' Rupert observed. 'The best way is to run it down over to Lindal Station. I'll start work on the plans at once.'

'Aye, that's it.' Abe never sounded any more cheerful, whatever the occasion; the wonder was that he could ever summon up a deeper gloom. 'We'll need a main of transport. And more men, too.'

'Plenty around Lindal and Marton,' Timothy said. These days he was leaving more and more of the talking to Rupert, for his voice, as Susannah was saying at that very moment to Elinor, was no better. His words were slurred and indistinct, though Rupert still found him easy enough to understand. But his friends and acquaintances were finding him more difficult to converse with, and strangers often supposed he was drunk.

'Marton!' Abe said with the grunt that was his way of laughing. 'We'll be hard up before we employ men from there. L'al Hell, that's called these days, and folk saying you have to fight to get in and fight to get out. Aye, and that's just about the way of it. They're barbarians in Marton these days, what with all those pubs. Fifteen at the last count!'

'Still work in pit,' Timothy said. 'Don't care what they do in spare time.'

The three men turned and made their way back to the shaft. It had been dug on a steep slope so that it was possible to walk in and out of the mine. They passed several old workings on their way; the deep shafts disappeared into thick darkness, the flickering light of the candles showing the scored and pitted walls. Here and there great pits were fenced off, their black depths denoting where ore had been dug from a great sop, producing hundreds or even thousands of tons of haematite. Ginnels formed huge cracks in the walls, like the alleyways between high buildings. Ore had been scraped from these too, leaving only a rusty stain on the limestone host rock.

Rupert felt a deep sense of satisfaction. This mine had held a fascination for him ever since he had first heard its name – his mother's name.

He came up the steep slope of the adit ahead of his father and Abe, blinking in the sunlight. For a few moments as he waited for them, he stood looking at the old machinery. They would have to install better plant, he thought. More modern pumping engines, a more stoutly built headframe to wind the cage up and down, for it had been agreed that a new vertical shaft must be sunk as well, and Rupert had already decided he would have no kibble here, filled like a cannibal's cauldron with men and boys. Good seasoned oak would be needed for the shaft lining.

The new tramway, too, was already taking shape in his mind – more of a proper railway, he thought, narrow gauge but still well able to shift many tons of ore in a day. It could take a more or less direct line down to the Furness railway at Lindal. His fingers itched for pencil and paper; like his mother, he loved drawing but his preference was for designing something that would work, something that would be useful.

'All for today,' Timothy said, joining him. 'Home now. Tea.'

Lifting his hand in farewell to Abe, Rupert followed his grandfather to the trap and they set off in the direction of Pennington Hall. The afternoon was still warm with the humidity of early autumn, but Rupert, his mind still busy with the new mine, scarcely noticed his surroundings. It wasn't until Timothy drew rein in the stable yard that he noticed the little governess cart standing in one corner.

'Hullo,' Timothy said, spotting it at the same time. 'Elinor here?'

Elinor! Rupert stared at the little trap. He felt suddenly cold inside.

Tuesday afternoon. It was Tuesday afternoon, and he had forgotten it. He had been so wrapped up in the excitement of the new vein that Elinor had been pushed from his mind.

Had she come here seeking him? And if so, what was her mood? Anger, certainly. Elinor was not a woman to be let down lightly. She had been displeased on the two other occasions he had missed their regular Tuesday appointments, though in both those cases he had been able to make his excuses beforehand. But now . . .?

While Timothy stood with the stable boy, discussing one of the horses that had gone lame, Rupert examined the thought that Elinor might be so furious she would declare their association at an end.

It was an idea that had occurred to him more than once. In the early days, he had been unable to believe that she would continue to want him – she, a woman of restless desires, with several lovers already, while he was no more than a boy. He had thought that one or two experiences of his inept lovemaking would be enough for her, that she would toss him aside in favour of some more mature lover. Instead, she appeared to delight in his inexperience. He sometimes wondered what it would be like to try his newly acquired knowledge with another woman.

After a while, however, he had begun to suffer from guilt.

His feelings towards Nicholas were ambivalent. After a boyhood spent believing that Nicholas was his father, trying all the time to win his approval and living with the ache of failure and loneliness, it had been difficult to come to terms with the truth that Elinor had told him.

There had been so many different things to consider.

Nicholas had certainly acknowledged him as his son, had done all that a father should do – sheltered him, fed him, clothed and educated him. He had been cold and distant, but weren't a good many fathers remote from their children? He had never beaten him, never deprived him of the things he needed.

But he never loved me either, Rupert thought. He never showed me the slightest degree of affection, or even interest. He disliked me, even hated me, because of who I am, and he never saw that it wasn't my fault. He never tried to overcome his feelings.

He remembered the surge of bitter hatred he had felt when Elinor had first told him. In that moment, the world that had been his had slipped away from him, leaving him swinging helpless in a void. He had never known his mother; now it seemed he had never known his father either. Everything about him had shifted, and he felt as if he were crossing the bay and had suddenly encountered quicksands. Much that he had wondered about was suddenly made clear, but what he saw was frightening.

A cold, remote father whose nature made it difficult to show love was better than one who was no father at all and whose emotion was not love but hate.

What else was false about his life? he wondered. What other beliefs might be shattered? For a while he had walked as if on eggs, half afraid that the whole edifice of his life was about to tumble round his ears. He even wondered if he had really been Louisa's son. Couldn't he have come from somewhere else – be neither Sherwin nor Craven? Elinor had only Nicholas's word for what had happened, after all. There were tales that gipsies stole children. Did they sometimes sell them too?

It was his grandfather who finally convinced him. A year or so ago, they had been out together and, as they were doing today, had come back to Pennington Hall for tea. Tea at Pennington Hall was always an uneasy experience and he knew that Timothy himself avoided it as much as possible, but there were occasions when he felt it his duty to appear in the drawing room. And Rupert, who had clung to his grandfather as if to a rock during that time of turmoil, had come into the house with him.

He knew too, though he was reluctant to admit it, that he was relieved to have an excuse to stay away from home an hour or two longer. By that time, Elinor's attentions were beginning to be just a little too much for him.

'So it's you,' Susannah greeted them when they came in, having washed and changed their boots. She spoke as if Timothy had not been seen in the house for months and his return was a burden. 'I suppose I'd better ring for more cups.'

Timothy gave Rupert a glance of resignation which the slight distortion of his face rendered faintly comical. Rupert quickly smothered a grin and bent to give his grandmother a dutiful peck on the cheek.

'Don't let me be a nuisance,' he said. 'If you don't want visitors—'

'Nonsense,' Susannah said sharply. 'Of course you'll have tea. And you're not a visitor, you're family.'

He gave her a startled glance. Susannah did not usually volunteer such warm sentiments. But he decided that she was not so much expressing affection as stating a fact. He hesitated a moment, then said as casually as he could manage, 'One wouldn't think so, though – to look at me, I mean. I've often wondered who I take after.'

'Well, not your father, that's certain,' she said, clearly reading nothing untoward in his words. 'Your mother was darker, of course – like Timothy.' The maid came in with extra cups and fresh tea, and Susannah busied herself with pouring out. 'He could tell you more about her family. I know nothing of the Dawsons.'

You've never wanted to, Rupert thought, accepting a

cup. Understandably, perhaps, for Margaret Dawson seemed even now, over thirty years after her death, to have a hold on Timothy's heart and Susannah might well have had cause to be jealous during the early days of her marriage. But the Dawsons were Rupert's relatives and he felt a sudden irritation that he had never been encouraged to know them.

He glanced at his grandfather, but Timothy was standing at the window, sipping his tea, his eyes directed up towards the moor. Rupert had noticed that Timothy rarely sat down in this room and usually seemed only half there. Susannah seemed content enough with this, as if both of them acknowledged that it was only his physical presence that was required.

Susannah was chattering now about her daughter Jane, who lived in Liverpool. Jane, it seemed, was less than satisfied with her life. Her husband Hubert was a close-fisted man, who hated parting with his money, and their house had not been refurbished since their wedding. They could easily, Susannah declared, enjoy a very comfortable life, but instead poor Jane was forced to live in a home that lacked all modern conveniences and even had to scrimp on food.

'Martha is staying with them and has written home telling me all about it,' she said. 'Really, it's disgraceful. But I told your grandfather at the time, she should never have been allowed to marry him. I knew he wouldn't make a good husband.'

Rupert saw his grandfather give her a sharp glance, but he said nothing. It was only later, when he had taken Rupert to his study, that he made any remark.

'Moved heaven and earth to catch that man for Jane,' he said. 'Boasted all over Furness about him. Truth was, couldn't afford to let him slip – wanted your father but he wasn't interested. Not once he'd seen your mother.'

'Tilly told me that once. She said my father was the most eligible man in the district.'

'So he was, if looks and money and family count most. Never happy about it myself. Always thought Louie needed more than that.' He glanced up at the portrait of his first wife Margaret and Rupert caught the sadness in his expression. 'We all need more than that.'

'What happened,' Rupert asked, gathering up all his courage, 'when my mother died?'

Timothy transferred his gaze to the picture of Louisa. They looked at it together. Rupert saw the thick chestnut hair, the skin touched with gold by the sun. He saw, too, the character in the sensuous mouth and the firm jaw, the level brows and straight, almost challenging glance of the eyes that looked in some lights green, in others blue.

'Only a few months after my stroke,' Timothy said. 'Happened the day she told us you were on the way.' The sadness was in his face again and Rupert half wished he had avoided the subject. But he had to know.

He remained quiet, his eyes going back to the portrait. He sensed that if Timothy wanted to tell him anything more, he would do so now. There was no need for further questioning.

'Louie and I were close,' Timothy said, after a few minutes' silence. 'Especially after her mother died. Took her about with me.' He stopped again and seemed to find it difficult to go on. 'Then . . . things changed. Susannah . . .' Again, he paused. Rupert felt uncomfortable, as always, with his grandfather's emotion. Sadness, grief, these were among the emotions Nicholas openly despised, calling them 'women's vapours' and sneering when Rupert had displayed such feelings. He remembered when his pet rabbit had died and Nicholas had tossed the limp little body on to the waste heap and forbidden him to hold the small funeral he had planned, bidding him roughly to dry his tears and stop behaving like a girl. And again when he and Tilly had made their weekly pilgrimages to Louisa's grave in the little churchyard at Pennington. These Nicholas could scarcely forbid, but the tears on Rupert's cheeks could be and were remarked upon. 'I'll not have the boy upset by it. She's gone and there's nothing to be done about it, so what's the use of weeping and wailing? He never knew her, anyway. What does he have to cry for?' And Rupert knew that if he wanted to continue his visits, he must learn not to show his sadness.

Timothy had never made any secret of his sorrow over either his first wife's death or Louisa's. But he was the only man Rupert knew who showed his emotion so plainly. He supposed it was one of the results of the stroke but the sight of his grandfather apparently close to tears was no less disconcerting.

'Please,' he began, 'you don't have to—' But Timothy shook his head.

'Ought to talk about things. Get tangled up if you don't. Twisted in your mind.' He was talking almost to himself. 'Goes on for years, people growing apart because they don't talk. Nobody knows the truth. All hiding from each other.' He turned suddenly and looked directly into Rupert's eyes. 'Remember that. Don't hide. Important.'

'Yes,' Rupert said, barely understanding what Timothy meant. 'I'll remember.'

Timothy looked back at the portrait of Louisa. 'We hid,' he said sadly. 'Something . . . happened. We never talked about it. Couldn't. In the end, it killed her.'

'Killed her?' Rupert stared at him, shock running through his body. 'What do you mean? I thought she died—'

'When you were born. Aye. But would it have happened if – if we'd talked? Your father . . . did his best. But he didn't understand – couldn't. It was her problem and my fault. If we'd talked . . . things might have been different. She might not have been so frightened.'

'Frightened? Of my father?' Rupert searched for

words. Did his grandfather know the truth, that Nicholas wasn't in fact his father? Should he ask him, or would it upset him even more? He rubbed his hand across his face and decided it was better to say nothing. But perhaps this was what he meant by 'hiding'.

'Frightened of living,' Timothy said. 'Never lived her own life. Different as a girl. Wild and free. And then she changed. Still roamed about on her own. But more secret, somehow. Slipping out. Pretending. *Hiding*.' That word again. 'Marrying Nicholas – that was hiding. Or escaping.' He sighed. 'Not very happy for her, here.'

Rupert glanced up at the portrait. The wildness that Timothy spoke of – was that there in the haunted eyes? Or was it fear? And what was it that she feared? What was it that had happened?

He guessed that only Timothy knew. And if he didn't want to tell . . . But how could it have killed his mother?

'And when I was born?' he asked at last.

'Ah. Changed then.' The sadness went a little from Timothy's face. 'Those last few months back to her old self, at first. Looked alive again. Came here one day and told us – having a baby. Fire in her eyes.' His own eyes brightened with the memory. 'As if it was all she needed. All she'd ever wanted.' There was a pause. Then he went on, his voice quiet again, 'That was the day I had this.' He touched his distorted face. 'Hot day, tired, felt unwell all day. But Louie stayed with me. Came every day. Just like we'd always been.' He fell into a deep silence.

'And then?' Rupert prompted at last. 'When I was born?'

'Aye. Lived long enough to see you. Hold you. I was better then. Went over to Green House to see her.' He smiled. 'Remember her face looking at your black hair. Dark brown eyes, even then – they say babies all have blue eyes, but yours . . . Louie looked at you and she was happy. First time in years – really happy.'

Rupert felt an ache in his throat. He thought of his mother, holding him in her arms, looking down into his dark eyes, brushing his black hair back with a gentle forefinger. And looking happy.

She must have known he was not Nicholas's son. But whoever his father was, she was happy about it. And the fears he had had seemed now to have been foolish, irrational fears. Imagining that he was a gipsy child, a changeling! How could he have supposed such a wild notion?

Timothy got up from his chair and went over to the desk that stood in the corner of the room. He opened a drawer and took out a thin, flat package.

'Here,' he said, limping back, 'have this. Your mother's. Did a lot at one time, but this was the best.'

Rupert took the package and opened it. He lifted out a canvas, turned it over and laid it on his knee.

It was a painting of Duddon Sands executed, he guessed, from the Dunnerholme promontory where the old quarries had been. The broad expanse of sand, left in ripples by the outgoing tide, gleamed with a succession of soft colours – fawn and gold, the muted blue of sky reflected in shallow water, shadowed by the clouds that raced above. At the edge of the water was the fringe of long-legged wading birds that followed the waves in the hope of picking up small sea creatures and on the far side rose the dark whaleback shape of Black Combe with the little port of Millom huddled below.

Rupert gazed at the painting. Had his mother really done this? He had never seen any of her work before, never even known that she could do it. Why were there none at Green House?

'There are people crossing the sands,' he said, noticing the trail of small dark figures. 'A lot of them, with horses and carts. I wonder who they were.'

'Gipsies perhaps.' His grandfather glanced at them

without much interest. 'Or nobody at all. Put them in to make it look less empty.'

'Yes, she might have done.' But Rupert felt sure she hadn't. The people had been there, just as the sands and the birds and the clouds had been there. His mother had painted what she had seen. It had been important to her.

He had taken the picture home and hung it on his bedroom wall. Looking at it had brought him comfort. It was as if by gazing at the scene that his mother had seen and painted, long before he was born, gave him a share in her life, brought them somehow closer. As if the picture were telling him something about her.

Looking at those broad sands, empty save for the trail of figures slowly crossing, he felt that he no longer walked on quicksands of his own. The sensation that everything about him was false, that nothing was what it had seemed, was dispelled by the honesty of the picture his mother had painted when she was no older than he was.

Timothy finished his talk with the groom and turned towards the house. Rupert drew a deep breath.

He had still not decided what to say to Elinor; he was not even sure what he wanted. They had been meeting secretly for three years now; he had always known it would have to end sometime. And in the early days, confused, tormented by both guilt and anger towards his father, together with a raging desire that demanded incessant relief, he had often wished it would.

But he had been unable to finish it himself. Elinor obsessed him. He thought about her constantly, haunted by the image of her body, tortured by the sensations she aroused in his. He was possessed alternately by a driving need to be with her and a desperate impulse to escape. One moment adoring her, the next

401

loathing her, he was never free; he felt as if he were enmeshed in a spider's web, caught in strands as fine as silk yet with the strength of steel.

Desperately, he would plan the words to end their secret association, intending to tell her that he could no longer deceive Nicholas. But when she was with him, they died on his lips. As if knowing what was in his mind, she would wind her soft arms about his neck and press her body against his, and at the feel of her ripeness his body would respond, his mind swim and he would forget all his intentions. Or a small voice would whisper to him: wait till next time. Tell her then. For now, enjoy what is offered . . .

For three years he had enjoyed and suffered. For three years he had dreaded discovery. Sometimes, as the three of them ate supper together, he had wondered if Nicholas suspected what was going on. Looking up, catching his father's eye, he had felt a flush of guilt stain his cheeks and thought, *he must know*. How could he not know? But Nicholas never spoke, never hinted at any knowledge. His eye was sardonic, but then it always had been. His manner was cold, but it had never been warm. And if he was cold towards Elinor as well, it meant nothing for he had treated her coolly since the first year of their marriage. It was as if they were each as disappointed as the other. And Elinor's passion for Rupert suggested that there was little or none between her and her husband; indeed, hadn't she told him so?

But Rupert was no longer a naive seventeen-year-old. He was almost twenty-one now, a grown man. And he was aware that he would soon be expected to make a life of his own. He would have to make decisions about his career. He would be expected, after a while, to marry. He could not do that and keep his stepmother as a mistress. So perhaps it was just as well that he had forgotten this was a Tuesday. Perhaps it was the chance to escape at last from that silken web.

His grandfather was at the garden door now, turning to wait for him. Rupert took another deep breath and followed him into the house.

403

Chapter Twenty-Three

'The *Army*?' Rupert echoed. 'But . . . why?'

Nicholas strode to the window and looked out. Trees had grown up in the garden since he had first moved here with Louisa; they were just beginning to burst with new life but he could still see across the bay to Morecambe and Poulton-le-Fylde. The sands were a soft fawn, rippling away towards the narrow channel of low tide.

He turned. Rupert was staring at him. He felt a sense of satisfaction that his words had at least made some impact on the boy. So often he felt that when he spoke to him, Rupert was simply not there. As if he had abstracted himself from his body and drifted off, leaving nothing but a polite semblance of attention.

'Why the Army?' Rupert repeated.

'Do you really need to ask?' Nicholas waited for a moment, watching the flush rise and spread over Rupert's face, darkening it even further. So there was guilt there, he thought. He'd had little doubt of it, but the confirmation brought a fresh surge of anger. The little whipper-snapper! He had a sudden inclination to fetch a horsewhip to him, to slash the good looks from that dark face, but he contained himself. Better to let the little cur stew.

'It's time you thought about a career,' he said instead. 'You've done nothing since you left school. You're not interested in the shipping business—'

'You've never given me the chance!' Rupert had

recovered now and was on the attack. 'How many times have you taken me with you to Liverpool? Anyway, Cousin Daniel is going to inherit there, it's obvious. I'd never be more than a clerk.'

That was true enough, Nicholas thought. His elder brother's son had been toadying to Sir Stanley ever since he was a brat, and there would be little enough chance for Rupert to make a mark. Not that he was prepared to admit that.

'Besides,' Rupert added, before he could speak, 'I shall work with Grandfather.'

Nicholas had foreseen this. The boy had spent so much time with his grandfather, visiting the mines and planning the new tramway from Louisa mine, it was inevitable that his thoughts should have taken this direction.

'There's nobody else, after all,' Rupert continued. 'And Grandfather's getting old now. He needs someone ready to take over.'

'He has mine captains and managers,' Nicholas said sharply. 'None of whom would take the slightest notice of you.'

'I know them all—'

'And they know you, they know you are still a boy. You need age and experience to deal with men like that, Rupert, and the confidence that authority gives you. The Army would give you that confidence—'

'What use would it be to me, stuck out in some foreign country, thousands of miles away? Suppose Grandfather were to be taken ill again?'

'I've told you, his managers would run the business perfectly adequately. And you could be called home if necessary.' He paused. 'In any case, why should you expect to be given such responsibility? Your Uncle Walter will inherit the business.'

'But he's been abroad for the past ten years.'

'He has indeed. And look at what he's done.' Nicholas

held up his hand, counting on his fingers. 'He did exactly what I want you to do: he joined the Army, he saw action and survived, he went on to become a well-known explorer. He has the authority and experience to come home and run a business. When he left here, he was no more than a boy, just as you are today. I have no doubt that he has become a man who can command others.' He lowered his hand. 'Does that not seem a good example to follow?'

Rupert opened his mouth, hesitated, then closed it again. Nicholas watched him with satisfaction. He saw the mutinous set to the young mouth but discounted it. The boy had always had a tendency to sulk. It didn't matter. His arguments were unanswerable.

Walter, so long absent from the family, was inclined to be overlooked. He seemed unreal. But he would be real enough when Timothy died, for Nicholas had no doubt that he would inherit Pennington Hall and everything that went with it. Susannah would see to that. She might never have cared for her son as a mother should, but she would never allow him to be forgotten. Particularly, she would never allow him to be passed over in favour of Rupert.

Nicholas looked with satisfaction at Rupert. Yes, the Army was a good solution. He would be rid of the boy and would once again have his wife to himself, under his control. And Rupert should have some career. There was nothing for him here. Tagging around with his grandfather had been all very well when he was a child, but he was a man now and should be looking to his future. There was no future for him in Furness.

'I am thinking of your good,' Nicholas said, almost convinced of it himself. 'You're strong, independent, accustomed to the outdoor life – you'll make a fine officer. The Army is the right choice for you.' Never before had he praised Rupert so fulsomely. But if it helped get the boy to see sense . . .

'No.' Rupert lifted his head, looking Nicholas defiantly in the eye. 'I don't want to go into the Army. I'd rather stay here.'

Nicholas felt a spurt of anger. More and more, over the past three years, he had longed to have Rupert out of the house. He had been a thorn in his flesh ever since he was born.

Nicholas had known from the start that the baby was not his, that his wife had betrayed him, but his pride had prevented him from making the fact public. Other people might suspect, but he could not face the humiliation that their knowledge would have brought. He could not bear the looks of pity on the faces of his friends, still less the derision of his enemies. He preferred to live a lie, to pretend that Rupert was his son. He did it so well he almost convinced himself, and he was sure he had convinced Rupert – which made Rupert's behaviour with Elinor all the more reprehensible.

Even now, Nicholas was not quite certain that his suspicions were true. He believed they were, but he tried hard to believe they were not. Once again, his pride was at stake.

'I'm sorry,' he said coldly, 'but what you want is not really the issue here. I've decided that you're to go into the Army, and go into the Army you shall.'

'Oh, shall I?' Rupert came to his feet, his dark eyes suddenly blazing. 'It's my life, but *you'll* tell me how to live it. You expect me to meekly agree to whatever you want me to do. You say I'm to go into the Army, so I go, no matter what *I* want. And how do you propose to make me go? Are you going to use force?'

Nicholas realised suddenly how Rupert had grown. He had always been long-legged and could surely not have put on any more inches lately – he had been a good six feet since he was seventeen. But he had filled out, his shoulders were broader, his muscles well developed. Nicholas was not small but he felt dwarfed.

The sensation gave him fresh cause for anger.

'Force won't be necessary. You'll go because you'll no longer be welcome here. I won't have defiance in my house.'

Rupert stared at him. 'No longer welcome? You mean you're turning me out?'

'Only if you refuse to obey me.'

'And if I do obey you, I'll be leaving anyway. And that's all you really want, isn't it? Why not speak the truth, *Father*?' The name was bitterly emphasised. 'You've never wanted me here. I've always been in the way. But you always want people to think the best of you, so you've done whatever you thought necessary – and that's all. Now, all you want is to be rid of me but you still want people to believe you're acting as a father should, so you'll buy me a good commission and hope never to see me again. Well? Isn't that the truth?' He stared at Nicholas, challenging him with dark, scornful eyes. 'Why not admit it?'

Nicholas felt his anger rise further. Much more, and he would no longer be able to control it. His heart was pounding, filling his breast, making it difficult to breathe. He moved to stand behind a chair, gripping the back of it with both hands.

'I have never heard such ingratitude,' he said at last. 'Just what are you complaining about? That I've always acted as a father to you? What would you have me do? Should I have thrown you out as a puking newborn, sent you to the poorhouse or given you to some passing gipsy?' He stopped suddenly, then went on, 'Should I have neglected you, left you to the care of some cottager or a young girl barely out of napkins herself? Do you know what happens to children who are neglected like that? They fall into fires or pour boiling kettles over themselves, they eat berries and fall down wells. Have *you* ever been neglected?'

'I never said—'

'You could not. You've had good food, good clothes, good schooling. You've been allowed to ride around the countryside doing whatever you please long after many young men are working for a living. And when you're offered the chance of a career that could take you far and give you an interesting life, you turn on me like a dog who's been kicked. Like the ungrateful cur you really are. And you ask *me* to speak the truth.' He let go of the chair. 'Well, I have. Do you like it, when it stares you in the face?'

Rupert did not answer at once. Nicholas wondered what was in his mind and felt suddenly afraid. Would truths be spoken that neither of them wanted to hear?

'You've told me nothing I haven't always known,' Rupert said at last. 'Yes, you've done the things a father should. But all the same, you've never really treated me as your son.'

'And you,' Nicholas said in a low, trembling voice, 'have never behaved as my son.' He gripped the chair again, standing with bent head as he fought to control his anger. There was a long silence. At last, he said, 'You've been given all the freedom you could expect. You've been given a home. You've enjoyed and made free with whatever was in this home. But you will not make free with any more.' He raised his head and looked directly into Rupert's eyes. For a moment, Rupert held his gaze, then let his own drop. Yes, the boy knew what he meant right enough. 'You will go into the Army as soon as it can be arranged.' He turned and stalked out of the room. He was still trembling, but he kept himself rigidly under control until he was safely in his study where nobody ever disturbed him. Then he sat down and let the anger have its way.

It broke over him in waves, like a dam unleashed. It turned his body hot and cold in turns; it thundered through his head and through his veins. It was white-hot, burning his skin, and then it was a cold black abyss into which he was falling. It tore through him in great painful shudders and it left his muscles weak and shivering.

Twenty-one years of restraint, of iron control, passed through his memory. Twenty-one years of watching Rupert grow up, knowing that some other man had fathered him. And as if that were not enough, over three years of betrayal.

The sooner the boy was out of the house, the better. And pray God that, once out, he would never come back.

Rupert said nothing to his grandfather of what had happened. Both were too engrossed in the Louisa mine, which looked like being even more profitable than when it first opened.

'It's often the way with old workings,' Abe Ricketts said as the three of them inspected progress one afternoon. 'Leave 'em to stand for a while, let 'em fill up and you'll find a whole lot more ore come down with the muck and rubble. Do half the work for you, that will.'

They were in one of the new shafts. There had been a problem with the older shaft, directly above, which had begun to collapse while the miners were actually clearing it. Hastily, they had escaped back up the ladders and shortly afterwards had extended one of the others to come back beneath it.

'Aye, an' just as well we did too,' Abe remarked. 'We found this big chamber, worked out years ago and full of new ore. See here.'

The three men held up their lamps and Rupert gave a low whistle. The ore was lying in great mounds, huge chunks of rock that had fallen from the roof as the ground above, distorted by much mining, began to settle. All that needed was for it to be dug out, and already Abe's gang of miners were hard at work, wielding picks and shovels, filling up the trucks for the hurriers.

From this main chamber three roads had been opened at different levels, the lowest running steeply down to undercut other old workings. By the unsteady light of tallow candles, over a hundred and fifty men and boys had laboured here, hewing and blasting their way through the rubble of old workings to the new territory beyond. They could be heard now, still working far away to extend the mine further yet, but there was no sign of their lights and their voices echoed eerily, like those of forgotten ghosts, along the dark and dripping tunnels.

'Subsiding here, look,' Abe remarked, holding up his lamp. 'Should be a good few ginnels come to light in this lot.' The country rock, or limestone, was shattered and distorted by earlier workings and crumbling ground, and when the miners drove new levels through, they often found new seams of ore. 'Aye, it's a good rich pit, Louisa. Allus has been.'

'Problems there, all the same,' Timothy remarked as they made their way back to the cage. 'Landowner's objecting. Says we're going to damage his pasture.'

Rupert frowned. 'Does he? But there's never been a problem before with Louisa.'

'Different landowner. Extending further this time. Captain Parry.'

'Oh.' Rupert thought about it. Captain Parry lived near Coniston and had bought a large farm on the edge of Pennington Moor about a year ago. He had already threatened prosecution to several mine owners who had encroached under his land.

'Says he'll take me to court,' Timothy said indignantly. 'See him in Hell before I pull out of Louisa.'

'But we're not exceeding our royalty.'

'No. Every right to extend.'

The cage emerged at the surface and Rupert glanced about the meadows among which the mines were situated. It was true enough that the mineheads themselves made great scars on the landscape. Raw red earth scored the low hills, churned into seething mud by the constant ferrying of ore. Gins, gantries and tumbletrees stood in stark silhouette on the skyline. Around the pitheads were scattered wooden sheds and shacks and piles of machinery, some new and in use, some discarded and falling into decay. The new tramways, leading to the main railway at Lindal, clattered with trucks and bogies, and here and there an old pit was filling with red-stained water.

But away from the pitheads, the countryside remained intact. In the meadows, sheep grazed and their lambs skipped oblivious of the toiling men and women hundreds of feet below. There were places where the ground had fallen suddenly, as a pit far below collapsed, but for the most part this meant no more than a stretch of ground more hollowed and hummocky than the rest. Rupert had never heard that any animal had been injured in such mild subsidence, nor that pasture had been damaged for more than a season or two. Nevertheless, more than one farmer had objected to the mines tunnelling under pasture. They had little grounds for objection, for the land of all Furness was owned by the Duke who held the mineral rights and rented them out as he pleased. Farmers were rarely miners as well.

'Talks about subsidence,' Timothy said contemptuously. 'Risk farmers hereabouts have to take. Ought to have known when he took it on.'

'Perhaps if I go to see him,' Rupert suggested, 'he might listen to reason.'

'Reason!' Timothy snorted. 'Doesn't know what reason is. Still, nothing to lose. You talk better than me. Have to go to Coniston, though. Doesn't come down to Pennington much, for all his talk.'

'I'll go tomorrow. The sooner it's sorted out the better.' He would be glad of a trip away from home, he thought. The situation with Elinor was becoming more difficult each day.

'That's the third time you've not come to me,' she had accused him when they were at last alone that Tuesday afternoon when he'd forgotten her. 'Do you think you can play with me? I'm not a toy, Rupert, to be picked up and discarded at a whim. And I take quite a lot of risks to be with you.'

'So do I.' He was on the defensive, and angry with himself for being so. 'It isn't as easy as you think for me. If Father ever suspected—'

'You would be turned out,' she finished for him. 'So would I, and where could I go? What could I do? You are a man, but a woman alone in this world . . .' She shivered.

'Then perhaps you should never have taken the risk in the first place,' Rupert retorted, and was immediately ashamed. 'I'm sorry. I didn't mean that.' But perhaps, in truth, he had meant it. For hadn't it been Elinor all along who had pursued him with sly glances and secret touches, Elinor who had led him to his room that first day and made it so very clear what she wanted? An inexperienced seventeen, he had been unable to resist her then and unable to resist her since, though he had tried often enough. Whenever he had voiced his doubts, Elinor had answered him in the simplest and most conclusive way, by pressing her soft body close against him, lifting her mouth to his and running her fingers from the back of his neck and down the length of his spine in the way that always made him shudder with desire.

Yes, it was Elinor who had been the driving force in the whole affair. But he had had his choice too. Difficult, almost impossible, though it may have been, he could have said no. He could have drawn back when Elinor first began to look at him in that special way, when he knew after Curtis's visit what she was. He could have drawn back later, when it dawned on him that this was to be no brief *amour*, that Elinor would expect him to be

413

her private paramour, dancing attendance on her every whim. But by then it was too late.

'We've always known it couldn't last for ever,' he said now, facing his angry mistress. They were in her boudoir, a light, airy room facing the bay. It was a stormy afternoon, at first bright, then swiftly dark with the sudden showers of spring, and through the window he could see the wind tossing the waves into a white foam. 'It must end sometime, Elinor.'

'Why?' Her eyes burned. 'Why must it end?'

'Because . . .' He sought for the right words. 'Because I must have a career. I can't go on living on Father's money for ever.' Especially as he isn't my father, he thought, and has no obligation to keep me. 'And I'll marry—'

'Marry? Why should you marry?'

The question gave him a much-needed shot of anger. 'Why shouldn't I marry? Am I to live my life out dancing attendance on you? And you'll grow older—'

'And be of no further interest to you?' She was as angry as he. 'At what age will you decide I'm of no further interest? When I'm forty, fifty, sixty? When my skin begins to sag and my breasts to droop? You're fifteen years younger than I am after all – what interest can a sixty-year-old woman have for a man in the prime of his life? Easy to see how you see me, Rupert. A body to enjoy while it's still young, nothing more.'

'And isn't that exactly how you see me? You had no interest in me whatsoever before you realised I'd become a man. Bodies are all you're interested in, Elinor, and if I walked out of here now, you'd find another before the week was out. Shepherd, gamekeeper, one of Father's business friends, it wouldn't matter one jot to you so long as he was willing.' He looked her up and down, almost enjoying the anger that fuelled his tongue. 'I wonder only that you don't make use of the one man who is legitimately yours to enjoy.'

'And what makes you think,' Elinor said, her lips white, 'that I do not?'

Rupert stared at her. He thought of the afternoons he had spent lying with her in his arms, of the intimacies they had shared. *'I've thought of something new, Rupert. Let's try it now . . .'* He thought of her going, perhaps that same night, to Nicholas. *'I've thought of something new . . .'* And he felt suddenly sickened.

There was a long silence. To Rupert, there seemed nothing more to be said. He stared out of the window, at the racing clouds, at the sweeping darkness of rain over the Lancashire hills. He felt their coldness in his heart, the ugliness of regret heavy in his breast. He felt as if he had misused something valuable.

Behind him, Elinor moved closer. She laid her hand on his arm and he looked down at the white fingers, the glittering rings. Her engagement ring, with five diamonds, her wedding band, the emerald Nicholas had given her on their first anniversary, the sapphire for their fifth . . . And all the time, she had cuckolded him, shamelessly, with first one man, then another. With Rupert . . .

'Rupert, my sweet,' she murmured cajolingly, 'don't let's be angry with one another. I'm sorry I was cross. Of course you must go with your grandfather, whenever you like. He's an old man and may not be with us much longer. All I ask is a little of your company, a little of your loving, when you have the time.' She increased the pressure of her hand so that he turned to face her. 'All I want is your loving,' she said softly and gazed up into his eyes.

Not so long ago he would have melted. Not so long ago he would have been unable to resist. He would have taken her in his arms, kissed those soft, slightly parted lips, lifted her and carried her to the couch. All thought would have left his whirling mind and the urgent desires of his body would have taken their inexorable path.

And, once more, Elinor would have won.

But today, still strengthened by his anger, still heavy with his remorse, Rupert turned away. He stared again out of the window. The hills across the bay were now obliterated. Trees bowed and twisted in the wind and hail was rattling against the glass. A few crows, tossing like scraps of black paper, tumbled in the air.

'But it isn't loving,' he said at last, very quietly. 'Whatever it is, Elinor, it isn't loving.'

Captain Parry's home farm lay on the shores of Coniston Water, close to the village of Torver. Rupert approached it by a long, narrow track bordered with wild daffodils, which led from the road and brought him to the house, set low amidst its pasture. As he dismounted from his horse, the farmhouse door opened and a girl came out.

'Good morning.' She gave him a smile. She was, he guessed, a year or so younger than he was, wearing the clothes of a servant – a plain dress protected by a white apron, boots, and a plain white cap over her hair.

But if she were a servant, he thought, she was an uncommonly pretty one. The dark brown of her dress echoed the rich bronze of the hair that clustered in curls around her small, almost triangular face. Her features were neat, with soft lips and a nose that turned up slightly at its tip, her large eyes the colour of topaz, and her waist slender. She stood at about shoulder height to him.

'Good morning. I'm looking for Captain Parry. My name's Rupert Craven.'

She looked a little uncertain. 'I don't think Papa's in the house at the moment, Mr Craven.' So she was the captain's daughter, not a servant at all. 'He may be in the fields down by the lake. If you'd like to wait, I'll send someone to find him.'

Rupert hesitated. There was really no reason why he should not go and find Captain Parry for himself.

Sending someone to fetch him could easily annoy the man he'd come to appease. But the idea of waiting in the company of such pleasant and attractive company was tempting.

And look where temptation led you last time, he told himself sternly and, albeit with reluctance, shook his head.

'I'll walk down to the lake. I daresay I'll recognise him easily enough.'

'Oh yes. Well, probably.' She, too, was hesitating. Then, with a quick, half-shy glance, she offered, 'I'll walk down with you if you like, so you'll be sure not to miss him.'

'I'd be delighted,' Rupert said truthfully, 'as long as you can spare the time.'

'Oh yes,' she said again. 'There's always plenty of time here.'

There was an odd note in her voice and he wondered just what she meant. Was it a lonely life for her here, on the shore of the lake and away from the village? From the little Rupert had heard of Captain Parry, he didn't seem to be a very sociable man. Perhaps few visitors came here and this girl, so plainly dressed, was hungering for new faces.

They started to walk together down the track which led through the fields towards the quiet lake.

Not many boats used Coniston Water, for there were no towns along its banks, only the villages of Nibthwaite, Torver and the larger settlement of Coniston itself. A few boats plied between them and there was an occasional fisherman to be seen rowing his flat-bottomed craft, or a picnicking party making their way to one of the small islands, but often there was no one at all to be seen and the great sheet of water was left solely to the geese, ducks, divers and grebes who built their nests along the wild shores.

On the far side of the lake, the wooded hills above

417

Nibthwaite were quiet. Somewhere up there were the charcoal burners Rupert had sometimes come to see with his grandfather. He glanced along at the trees, wondering if he might see the thin spiral of smoke that meant they were burning now, but there was nothing.

'Do you enjoy living here, Miss Parry?' he inquired politely. 'You came quite recently, I believe.'

'Yes, we used to live in London.' Her accent, though certainly not local, was familiar enough, for there had been plenty of southerners at school with him. 'Then Papa left the Army and decided to become a farmer, and so we came here.' She glanced around and shivered a little. 'I don't know if I enjoy it or not. It's so wild and strange, yet at times it's very beautiful. Especially just now.'

The field they were walking through was filled with daffodils and the sky, washed clean by rain, showed no sign of yesterday's storms. Above them, to the south-west, reared the bulk of the Old Man of Coniston, one of the most imposing mountains. Rising so steeply almost from the shores, it could often look as dark and threatening as an avenging god; today, its bulk outlined against a soft blue sky, it was like a benign old patriarch, shoulders hunched against the westerly breeze.

'I never expected so many spring flowers,' she went on. 'People told me the north was too cold and hostile. But today, with all the daffodils and the primroses, it's as beautiful as anywhere in the south. Even the mountains don't look so forbidding this morning.'

'They're beautiful too,' Rupert said. 'Have you walked up them at all?'

'Oh, no!' The idea clearly shocked her and he laughed.

'You should. The views from the tops are magnificent. You can look down on the whole of the lake and right out to sea.' He hesitated, then said, 'I could take you one day, if you'd like it. We could have a picnic.'

He looked at her and caught her glance. She opened her mouth, but at that moment they heard a call from the neighbouring field.

'Oh, that's Papa. He must have seen us.' She walked quickly towards the gate which led between the two fields as if glad of the diversion. Rupert followed a little more slowly. For a moment, he had thought she was about to accept his invitation. He wondered if she would be as ready once he had spoken to her father.

Captain Parry was short and stocky, with a round head covered with straight black hair cut short, hard blue eyes and no whiskers. He carried a stout ash stick and looked as if he'd be prepared to lay about him with it if anyone displeased him. He stared at Rupert with suspicion, and looked at his daughter as if expecting to catch her out in some misdemeanour. When he spoke, his voice was like the sharp bark of a watchful guard dog.

'Yes? You wanted me?'

Rupert stepped forward, holding out his hand. This was not going to be easy. 'Good morning, sir. My name's Craven, Rupert Craven. I've come on behalf of my grandfather, Timothy Sherwin.'

'Sherwin? Sherwin?' The stare hardened further. 'Isn't that the miner, Pennington way?'

'My grandfather is a mine owner, yes. He mines a lot of the haematite in Low Furness.'

'A lot of it under my land.'

'That,' Rupert said quietly, 'is why I've come to see you. Perhaps we could talk about it.'

Captain Parry snorted. 'Nothing to talk about. Your grandfather's encroaching under my fields—'

'Which he has a perfect right to do. The Duke has granted him the royalty—'

'He has no right to cause damage. If he damages my pasture—'

'But he won't. The shafts are too deep.'

'– then I'll be entitled to compensation,' Captain Parry

419

went on, raising his voice to override Rupert's words. 'And in my view, prevention's better than cure. I can't graze my sheep on sovereigns. It's grass they need.'

'But there'll still be grass. We'll not cause any damage.'

'I've seen it all before.' The captain's voice had a carrying, stentorian quality that must have served him well on the parade ground. 'Fields torn to pieces by pit machinery, the ground ripped open, grass trampled away to shreds, nothing but a morass of useless mud. You can't deny it.' He fixed Rupert with an accusing glare. 'It happens every time a new pit is sunk.'

'But only around the pithead,' Rupert said. He glanced about him, at the smooth green fields running down to the lake shore. The water was blue, and as smooth as the fields, reflecting perfectly the hills above Nibthwaite. 'And no shafts are going to be sunk on your land. It's only levels running underneath it, and they'll be a hundred feet deep, perhaps more. Your grassland won't be affected at all.'

'Until it subsides.' Captain Parry said tersely. He gave Rupert a challenging glance, as if to state that the conversation was at an end.

But Rupert stood his ground. He glanced at the girl who had been standing quietly beside them all this time, and said, 'Perhaps we could talk about this at the house. I could come back another time, if you're busy now. There are a good many things to consider.'

'Don't know what they might be. Seems to me we've said all there is to be said. I've told your grandfather, I'll see him in court.'

'Where we'll simply say all that we could have said less expensively here,' Rupert answered. 'At least we could go over our arguments in private.' He shifted position slightly, settling his legs apart as if prepared to take root until he had the answer he wanted.

Captain Perry stared at him and then gave an abrupt,

unexpected laugh. 'Well, you're determined, I'll say that for you. All right, we'll have our talk. But it'll not make an iota of difference. I won't have mining under my land, not at any price. And that'll be my last word, whether you like to take it now or ten years hence. It's up to you if you want to waste your time.'

He glanced at his daughter, as if noticing her for the first time. 'What, Celia, you still here? Haven't you any tasks to do in the house? Go back and get some refreshments ready. I daresay Mr Craven's hungry and thirsty after his ride.' He watched as the girl turned and walked away, then added to Rupert, 'Daughters! They tell me they can be a comfort to a widowed man but precious little comfort I get from her. Silence and sulks, that's all she's good for, though she's a fair cook, I'll admit that.'

Rupert thought of the bronze hair, the topaz eyes, the quick glance that was half shy, half bold. What was life like for her here, so isolated after the busy whirl of London? He wondered if she were lonely and unhappy, removed from all her friends and with little chance of making new ones. Perhaps it was no wonder that she was silent; perhaps her sulks were really misery. He hadn't cared for the tone in which her father had spoken to her. There was an unfatherly abruptness there, more than a hint of dislike, which reminded him sharply of the way he was addressed by Nicholas. Perhaps Celia suffered too from a father who cared nothing for her.

He wondered if there would be another chance to talk to her. The captain was now showing him his fields, explaining how he farmed them – he seemed, for some reason, to have moderated his first hostility. If Rupert could only work on that, he might achieve both his objectives.

Both? When he had arrived here, not an hour earlier, he had come with only one idea in mind, that of persuading the captain not to go to law over the mines.

Now, he realised, he had two. And the other – to get to know Celia Parry better – was fast becoming uppermost.

'I missed London very much at first,' Celia said. 'All my friends are there, you see. And life was very gay. There were parties and balls to go to, any amount of theatres and concerts, and the art galleries and exhibitions – always something happening.'

'It must be very dull for you here after such a busy life.' Rupert turned to look at her. They had taken a small boat across to the island that lay opposite Nibthwaite and moored it in the tiny natural harbour, sheltered by long low ridges of rock. Celia had packed a picnic basket and they carried this up to the highest point of the island and now sat on a flat rock, looking down at the clear water.

'It wasn't dull at first. There was so much to do getting things straight in the house, making it nice for Papa. He does like everything just so, you see. And there's no one else to see to it all. And to speak the truth, I didn't go to so very many parties in London, not after Mamma died. Papa expected me to stay at home and take on her duties then.'

'Duties?'

'Keeping house. Cooking. That sort of thing.'

'But didn't you have servants? A cook?'

'Oh yes. But they never stayed long. Papa . . .' She hesitated, then went on, veering away from whatever she had been about to say, 'Anyway, Papa preferred his meals to be cooked by Mamma. And she taught me what he likes, so . . .'

So he treats you as a skivvy, Rupert thought. After several visits to the farm, he was aware that there was only one indoor servant, a whey-faced, half-witted girl who could be glimpsed on her knees scrubbing stone kitchen floors or hunched over the low sink in the scullery washing dishes or preparing vegetables.

'Do you have to do all the work?'

'Oh no. Annie does quite a lot.'

Celia opened the picnic basket. Inside were two glasses, a bottle of lemonade and some cheese, cold chicken and bread. Presumably Celia had made the bread as well as the lemonade and, of course, cooked the chicken.

'But the washing?' Rupert asked. 'The cleaning and polishing? All the other things that have to be done?' He was only hazily aware of most of them but knew there was enough in his own home to keep half a dozen servants occupied.

'We do them between us.' She looked up at him with her great topaz eyes. 'I know it seems a lot and I do get tired. And in London it did seem hard, when my friends were all going out and having good times. But here—' She gestured with one hand at the empty fells.

'– there's nothing else to do anyway,' Rupert supplied. 'But there should be. You should be going to parties and meeting people and having a good time. You shouldn't be buried here, slaving for your father. You're too young and too,' he hesitated then plunged on, 'too pretty.'

The colour deepened in Celia's cheeks. She busied herself with pouring lemonade. As she handed him his glass, their fingers touched and she glanced quickly up at him under her lashes and then as quickly away.

Rupert sipped his lemonade thoughtfully. This was his fourth visit to the Parry farm, and the first occasion Celia had come out with him. It was time, he thought, to assess the situation.

His talks with Captain Parry had progressed little. The older man's hostility towards the mines was as great as ever, though Rupert suspected that a good deal of his antagonism was rooted in envy. It was galling to think that what he made from the land via the wool and mutton from his sheep was being so much exceeded by those who worked below it. He was still threatening to

423

take Timothy to law over the supposed encroachment, and Rupert was inclined simply to allow him to proceed with his plan – but then he would not have been able to see Celia.

Their friendship had developed rapidly during these few visits. She was always in the yard to greet him when he arrived, and he usually contrived to arrive a little earlier than expected, in the hope that Captain Parry would be at some distance from the house. They seldom had more than a few minutes' snatched conversation, but twice she had invited him to stay for dinner and today, discovering that Captain Parry had gone away for the day to inspect a neighbouring farmer's sheep, Rupert had suggested a walk together.

'I have a better idea,' she said with that shy, upward glance. 'I've prepared a picnic. I thought we might row out on the lake and have our luncheon on the island. Unless you think you should hurry back home, of course,' she added demurely.

'No. Oh, no. There's no hurry at all.' He gazed at her. Was it correct behaviour for a young lady to invite a man, little more than a stranger, to spend several hours alone with her in such an isolated place? But Celia's eyes, meeting his, were limpid and innocent. Her trust was not misplaced; he had no intention of taking advantage of the situation.

Briefly, he wondered if the event had been planned with Captain Parry's connivance. Perhaps Celia had been deputed to bring him here and talk to him. Was it Celia's task to add her persuasions to her father's threats over the mine? But she showed no sign of wishing to discuss the matter; instead, she was gazing dreamily out over the water and nibbling at a piece of cold chicken.

'I don't really mind,' she said now, answering Rupert's last remark. 'About not going to parties, I mean. After all, I know no one here, so I should feel awkward anyway. And as for the work,' she shrugged, 'Papa says it's good training for when I get married. He says a man expects his wife to have all the housewifely skills.'

'But not to *use* them,' Rupert said, outraged. 'Only so that you can see that your servants are doing their job properly. I'd never allow my wife to make her hands rough with heavy work.' He looked down at Celia's hand, lying on the rock between them, and picked it up to examine it. 'These should be soft and smooth,' he said, stroking the chapped fingers. 'Look at your poor nails, all broken and split. What is he thinking of, to make you work so hard?'

The little hand lay cupped like a bird in his palm. He touched the lines of ingrained dirt, feeling a mixture of indignation and protectiveness. She was so small, so delicate, and her father was nothing but a bully. Retired from the Army, he had lost the men he could oppress and, his wife having died (from what? Rupert wondered), he had only his daughter to persecute. It was clear enough why he had never been able to keep servants; only the half-wit Annie, knowing no better, would stay with him, and his daughter who had nowhere else to go – unless she married. But what chance was there of Celia marrying anyone, living in this isolated place where she never had the chance to meet a man?

But she's met me, Rupert thought, and looked again at the small hand.

How would it be to place a wedding ring on that finger?

'I don't really mind the work,' Celia repeated. 'In fact, I quite enjoy cooking. I'd like more help, of course – sometimes I think I'll never get through. But I like to see the house looking polished and shining, and I like to see Papa enjoy his food. He's quite good to me really.'

'He is not good to you,' Rupert said forcefully. 'He should be taking you out and about, making sure you meet people. If he can't do it himself, he should be providing you with some lady companion who could do so. He should be inviting people to the house and not making you cook and clean for him. That's the least he should do. He's your father, Celia.'

There was a sudden pause. It was the first time, Rupert realised, that he had used her first name. He saw her blush rise and her lashes lower. Her fingers trembled a little in his.

'Celia,' he began, his heart thumping. 'Celia—' But before he could say more, there was a shout from the lake.

Startled, they glanced up and saw a rowing boat coming round the end of the island. Inside, bending clumsily to the oars, was one of the farmhands.

'Mr Craven! Mr Craven! Are you there, sir? Mr Craven!'

Rupert's heart sank. Captain Parry must have come back early and, asking for his daughter, discovered that she was on the island with him. He stood up and waved. 'Here, Jed – on the island. What is it? What's amiss?'

The man stopped rowing. He was close enough now for them to see the perspiration on his brow. He rubbed it with the back of his hand and looked up at them.

'You're wanted back at Pennington, sir. Message just came – been some sort of accident. Or mebbe it's an illness. Any road, they're sending for you to go back straightaway.'

'I'm coming at once.' Rupert bent and scrambled the picnic things back into the basket. With Celia beside him, he hurried down from the rocks, along the length of the little island and back to the harbour. He handed her into the boat, dropped the basket in after her, and settled himself at the oars.

'But who is it?' Celia asked. 'Who has had an accident? Who can it be?'

'It could be any of them.' He was rowing steadily now

across the lake. 'It could be Father, or Elinor – any of them.' But he knew who it was most likely to be. And it was probably not an accident at all. They had always known that Timothy was likely to suffer another stroke some day. And Rupert knew, from the clutching of his heart, that the day had almost certainly come.

Chapter Twenty-Four

In the year that Timothy's second stroke killed him, the great Civil War of America came to an end and President Lincoln was assassinated. Brunel's iron ship, the *Great Eastern*, made its first attempt at laying the first transatlantic telegraph cable and the death of Lord Palmerston, who had been in Parliament for nearly sixty years, was announced. From the mines on Pennington Moor, over forty thousand tons of haematite were dispatched to customers all over the country, and more stockpiled at the pitheads.

For the next few years, Rupert worked hard, for he was master of the mines now. On the death of his grandfather, a few days after he and Celia had been so urgently summoned from the lake, he had inherited the greater part of Timothy's business and full control of its management. His cousin Walter, who had been expected to inherit, received only an income – though enough at present to provide him with a reasonable living during his travels – and the house, in which Susannah was to be allowed to remain. There had been other bequests – a legacy for Jane, a lifetime's income for Martha – but Rupert had been the main heir. And, like everything else in his life, it had occasioned much discussion with his father and stepmother.

'You're far too young to have charge of such a large and complex business,' Nicholas stated, as if there were no question about the matter. 'You'll bring in a manager, of course. It needn't change your plans about going into the Army.'

'*My* plans? But I had no plans. I never intended to go into the Army and I certainly won't now.'

Nicholas had blustered but Rupert remained firm. With the security of his own business, he could afford to stand up to Nicholas. He did not even need Elinor's support; indeed, it was an embarrassment to him.

'You don't have to say anything,' he told her. 'In fact, I wish you wouldn't. It's making him very suspicious. And it would be foolish to ask for trouble now, just when—'

'Just when what?' she asked when he stopped. 'Just when we're about to finish our liaison? Is that what you want to say?'

'I wouldn't express it like that,' he began unhappily, but she interrupted.

'No, I don't suppose you would. But you can't deceive me, Rupert. I know you too well. I know you're trying to break away. And it's easy enough to see why, too. It's that little girl at Torver, isn't it? The Parry child. Don't trouble to deny it. I've seen your face when you come back from your visits there. It's not Captain Parry you keep going to see.'

Rupert had not denied it. With his new confidence, and his growing attachment for Celia, he had at last found the courage to break away from Elinor. He had set about taking over the mines, spending as much time as ever at Pennington Hall, in Timothy's study where he worked on his papers. And he had begun to build his own house, on the edge of Loppergarth.

'I don't have anywhere of my own,' he told Celia as he outlined his plans for the future. 'Green House is my father's and he'll probably leave it to William. Pennington Hall is my cousin Walter's and in any case my grandmother is to go on living there. So if I am to be independent, I must have my own house.'

'And live in it alone?' She gave him her half shy, half bold look and Rupert smiled.

'If I must. But I hope I won't be long alone.' He took the small hand, still roughened by work. 'I'd like you to come and live with me, Celia. I'd like you to be my wife.'

It was to be a long time, however, before this came about. First, Celia's father must be persuaded, and at that time he was still intent on his lawsuit against the mine. Timothy's death made little difference to this, and Parry's antagonism towards Rupert increased.

'He'll never let us marry,' Celia said despondently. 'Never.'

Their meetings were snatched and hurried. Rupert would arrive early at Torver and, if she could do so without being observed, Celia would meet him at the end of the drive. They would spend half an hour together in the little wood by the road before she must hurry back home and he linger for a while before riding down to the house. Or if that could not be managed, he would wait among the trees after his talk with Captain Parry and Celia would slip away when her father had gone out again about his own work.

She could not always manage to do this, and Rupert had many a wait in vain. But the difficulties lent spice to their meetings when they did occur and convinced them both that their love was real, for why otherwise would they take such risks?

'You're too useful to him,' Rupert said. 'If he loses you, he'll have to pay a servant. Several servants. And no guarantee they'll stay with him.'

'I know.' She sighed. 'I've tried burning his food, but he simply gets angry with me. He knows I can cook. It isn't easy, living with someone like Papa.'

In the end, in spite of all Rupert's efforts, the case came to court. But Captain Parry, so convinced of his rights, did not win. He came out of court with a bill for costs in his pocket and was at first in no mind to listen to any suggestions.

'Partnership!' he snorted. 'Why should you offer me a partnership? You've got what you want, haven't you? You've beaten me.'

'Only because you forced me to. Listen.' Quickly, he outlined his plan. It was not a true partnership that he was proposing – he had no intention of giving Captain Parry any authority in the mines – but more a disguised bribe: a percentage of the value of all ore taken from Louisa under the captain's fields. It was not a high percentage, but when he told Parry the amount of ore dug out so far and indicated how much there was to come, the older man's hard blue eyes widened.

'But why should you do this? You've won your case, cost me a mint of money. What interest is there for you?'

'I want,' Rupert said quietly, 'to marry your daughter.'

Captain Parry stared at him. His face reddened. 'Marry Celia? You?'

'Why not? I'm of good family –' he thrust away the knowledge that he had no claim to Craven blood, Sherwin was good enough surely – 'and I've a sound business. Isn't that what most fathers want for their daughters? Position and income?' He hated himself for setting the case in those terms, but there were no others that Captain Parry would understand.

'And what about me?' the Captain demanded. 'Celia's all I have. Am I to spend the rest of my life alone? Even supposing she'd take you, which you've no way of knowing she will.' He glanced sharply at Rupert and then said suspiciously, 'Or have you? Have the two of you been conniving behind my back?' His temper, always on a short tether, began to rise. 'If you've been toying with my daughter, Craven—'

'I've done no such thing!' Rupert was as angry as Parry at the suggestion. 'But you must know that we've

431

become friends during my visits here. She's a personable young woman and would have many more suitors if you ever allowed her off this farm.'

'So I'm a bad father now, am I?'

'Listen.' With an effort, Rupert controlled his anger. 'I'm saying no such thing. All I'm asking is your permission to court your daughter, and meanwhile I'm offering you a share in the royalties under your land.'

Parry's hard blue eyes took on a sly expression. 'And if she don't agree to marry you? What happens to my share then?'

'Nothing happens,' Rupert said, and added, 'I am not offering to *buy* your daughter, Captain Parry.'

Parry's flush deepened. He coughed and turned away. 'Well, I'll think on it,' he said. 'No more than that, mind. I'm only thinking.'

Rupert and Celia were married in the little church at Torver, with the fields as alive with daffodils as on the day when they had met, five years earlier.

There were plenty of people there to see them wed. Rupert's family, including a good many from Liverpool, filled one side of the church. The other, more sparsely occupied by the Parrys' few relatives up from London, was supplemented by friends and neighbours of both families. Outside there was a small crowd of villagers and miners who had been given the day off to come and see their master and his bride.

Rupert and Celia waved to them as they drove away in Rupert's new carriage, to the house he and Celia had built together. From the beginning, she had taken a considerable part in the design and furnishings, even though it was five years before she could walk into it as mistress. Captain Parry, reluctant to lose her services and pointing out Rupert's youth, had insisted on a long engagement. And then, when both had despaired of his ever agreeing, he had come in from the fields one morning and died in the act of removing his boots. Celia's mourning had been perfunctory and solely conventional, and the wedding was arranged at the earliest possible moment.

Those years had seen many changes. The reform of Parliament had taken place at last, and many of the miners who waved Rupert and Celia into their new life now had the vote. All children between the ages of five and twelve were to be educated. 'So that they know how to use their vote when they get it,' Nicholas said sardonically, and added a rare comment about Louisa. 'Your mother would have been pleased to see this. She always did think the working classes were hard done by.'

Rupert knew that the remark had been uncharitably meant, for Nicholas seldom mentioned his first wife and then only with bitterness. But he treasured it for the glimpse it gave him of his mother's character, and he made up his mind to support the new schools that were to be built.

Other events, in the wider world, caught his interest too. The Atlantic Telegraph Cable was successfully laid at last, and Queen Victoria and the President of the United States exchanged telegrams of congratulation. Italy, Austria and Prussia warred with each other and made peace; and the opening of the Suez Canal shortened voyages to India and the Far East.

At Pennington, the Louisa mine had been extended further than anyone had dared imagine and produced more ore than any other mine in Furness. And as Rupert carried his bride over the threshold of their home, he felt confident that his new life was securely on course.

'There you are, Mrs Craven,' he said, setting her down in the hallway. 'You're home.'

Celia glanced around. She knew it well already, of course, for together they had planned the decorations and she had herself chosen the dark brown carpets and the stained glass in the door. She had admired the new banisters when they were put in, and asked for the carving of the newel post at the bottom. The marble fireplace in the parlour, the elegant archways at one end of the dining room and the daintiness of the morning room had all been chosen either for or by her. Even though Rupert had been living here for the past two years, it was as much her home as his.

Now she gazed around and wrinkled her small nose. 'Do you know, I have never noticed before how shabby the wallpaper is becoming in here,' she said. 'We shall have to redecorate at once.'

Rupert looked at her in surprise. 'Redecorate? But, my love . . .'

'Yes?' she said when he paused.

'It's barely two years since it was done. It can't be shabby already.'

Celia inspected the walls closely. 'Not shabby, perhaps. Merely drab. Unfashionable. Not the kind of welcome one wishes to extend to one's visitors. You must know, Rupert, that the hallway is the first part of the house a visitor sees – it must be impressive.' She walked through to the morning room. 'And I'll need new hangings in here. The new lace that's become so popular. And some heavy drapes – these are positively flimsy.' She twitched the dark red velvet between her fingers. 'In fact, I think the whole house will need refurbishing.'

Rupert stared at her. This was a Celia he had never seen, a critical, exacting woman far removed from the shy, submissive girl he had known at Torver. He watched as she went from room to room, commenting as if she had never been inside the house before. 'This must be repainted, there ought to be portraits on this wall, we must have some good china to put on these shelves . . .' and his bewilderment increased. Where was the girl who had planned their home with him, who had shown such pleasure with the arrival of each new square of carpet, each freshly papered wall? Where was the Celia with whom he had fallen in love?

Even their bedroom did not escape.

'This toilet table,' Celia said in a dissatisfied tone when Rupert came in. She was brushing her hair at the dressing table, dressed in a white peignoir, frilled at the neck and embellished with pink ribbons and drawn thread embroidery. 'I shall have to make some muslin drapes for it, with calico underneath to make it stand out . . . Shall we have pink, or would you prefer blue?'

Rupert came across to bury his fingers in the fall of bronze hair, stroking the slender neck beneath. He glanced without much interest at the dressing table. It had been in place for only a month, for it had been the last room to be furnished and this was his first night in it; until now he had been sleeping in another room, on the far side of the house.

'I don't see why we need to hide it with muslin at all. I like the colour of the wood. And the legs have a nice shape.'

'It isn't the fashion,' Celia said coldly, 'for furniture legs to be on show. Except for chairs, of course, which can't easily be draped. But everything else – it looks so much prettier.'

'Does it?' Rupert bent to slip his arms round her, touching her breasts with his fingertips. His heart began to beat faster. 'I hadn't noticed. I think most things look prettier without the benefit of muslin and lace.' He inserted a finger into her bodice and pulled it gently so that he could bend his head to her breast. 'Let's stop thinking about furniture, my love,' he murmured. 'This is our wedding day.'

Celia sighed. She allowed him to kiss her, and for a few moments suffered his caresses. He lifted her to her feet and turned her to face him. Her lips were cool and soft beneath his and she stood quite still in his arms. Then she stepped back slightly.

435

'You may undo my buttons, Rupert.' Her voice was coolly practical but he felt his fingers tremble a little as he unfastened the row of tiny buttons, some of them half buried in lace. Since he had ended his liaison with Elinor, there had been no other woman in his life and he had not even had recourse to the doubtful delights offered by the bawdy houses of Barrow or Ulverston; nor, as some young men of his acquaintance did, had he gone further afield to Kendal where whores might easily be found. Such relief as he had managed had been a private, lonely affair, no more than a pale but still painful reminder of the pleasures Elinor had offered. Fantasy was a poor substitute for the feeling of warm, living flesh in his arms, and the momentary satisfaction his own hands could bring dissipated as rapidly as the fantasy itself when he was left with no body to hold close in the aftermath of loving. The release, purely physical, gave him no emotional comfort; instead, he suffered a guilt that tormented him until the next time, when the ache in his loins became too much to bear and he succumbed again, only to increase his guilt the more.

Celia stood quite still, only shivering a little as his fingers touched her bare flesh. He remembered how Elinor had shivered and he felt the tingle of pulsing blood. Suddenly his need became urgent, and he pulled the gown away from her with shaking fingers. Beneath it, she wore a nightgown very nearly as frilled and lacy as the peignoir, with a low neck that revealed her breasts almost to the nipples.

'Celia,' he breathed. 'Oh, my love . . .'

He buried his face in the warm, swelling breasts and then lifted her and carried her to the bed. She was limp and passive in his arms, but the stored passions of five years' celibacy had Rupert in a grip that needed no response. He laid her on the bed and gazed down at her for barely a minute before dragging off his own robe and dropping his naked body on hers.

His fingers tangled in the frills of her nightgown. He pulled it impatiently, and felt the lace tear slightly. Immediately, Celia tried to push his body away, but Rupert was beyond drawing back and pressed himself all the harder against her. He fumbled with lace and fine cotton that seemed to be everywhere, wrapping itself round his threshing body, tangling between his legs, and the feel of Celia's hands, fumbling with what seemed to be equal urgency, excited him all the more. The throbbing of his body increased to an almost unbearable intensity and he was suddenly afraid that all would be over before he had found the way past all these frills. He remembered once in the early days with Elinor when this had happened – although Elinor had never bothered with lacy nightgowns – and could still recall the painful humiliation. If it should happen now, on his first night with Celia . . .

His fingers touched the soft warmth of an inner thigh, the skin as thin and smooth as silk, and he realised that Celia was pulling the nightgown out of his way. With a surge of gratitude and passion that merged together as love, he moved into a better position, parting her legs with his. He felt her body against his, felt the swelling skin and secret crevices that excited him so much, and his body reacted with a surge of desire so that he groaned and thrust hard against her.

Celia gasped. With a tremendous effort, Rupert forced himself to pause. He knew, although he had never taken a virgin before, that this would not be as it had been with Elinor. Elinor's door had been opened many times and swung freely on its hinge; Celia's had until now remained locked and entry must be gently forced.

He pushed against her, tentatively at first, then with increased pressure, his urgency tempered by a touch of anxiety. With Elinor, it was as if she had been buttered; it had been so easy to slip inside and she had, as often as

437

not, drawn him in with legs locked round his buttocks. But Celia's body was dry and he could not find the entrance; as he pushed, he heard her whimper and felt his excitement rise again, but realised then that it was no sound of passion but rather of discomfort, and he recalled Elinor telling him once that if a woman was not ready, she would not be moist, and insistence could cause real pain.

He licked his fingers and slid them between Celia's legs to stroke her. She moved a little beneath him and then lay still again, submissive but breathing a little faster now. Encouraged, he found the right position and guided himself in, still trying to be gentle. But the door remained obstinately closed and his pushing grew more frenzied until at last, beyond all control, he thrust hard again and again. He felt her skin stretch, give a little, and finally tear. Celia's cry sounded in his ears but his body was now its own driving force and could not be restrained. He clung to her, feeling the surge of power, conscious of nothing but the overriding need to thrust himself into her, deep and hard. Beneath him, Celia was lying quite still, her knees slightly bent, and when he looked down at her face, her eyes were closed. He could tell nothing from her expression and once again he remembered Elinor, her features distorted with pleasure, her body writhing under his. With the memory he came to his final thrust, held it as the sensation washed over him in a great white wave of ecstasy, and then collapsed on to his wife's body.

For a few moments he lay spent, breathing rapidly. Celia was soft beneath him; he stroked her breast and began to feel slightly guilty. Elinor had said that a woman needed a great deal of stroking and caressing before the act itself, to make her ready and to help her enjoy it. Besides, she'd told him, the kisses and caresses themselves were to be enjoyed and savoured, not hurried over, and he had found she was right. Time spent in

438

these preliminary activities invariably resulted in a more satisfactory, not to say ecstatic, union for both. He knew that in his haste he had neglected this part of his lovemaking, and wondered if Celia had been disappointed. But even as the thought crossed his mind, she moved her head and her cheek rubbed against his.

'Celia . . .' he murmured, drawing her yet closer into his arms, but she shifted away, pushing his body so that he lifted himself away from her. 'My love?'

'Get off me now, please, Rupert. You're heavy.' Her voice was cool but she didn't sound disappointed. He rolled over, ready to pull her close again, but she moved away and when he opened his eyes he saw that she was sitting up and rearranging her nightgown. As he watched, she slipped off the bed and went over to the screen which concealed the washstand. He heard her pour warm water from the big jug into the bowl and a few moments later she came back and slipped into bed beside him.

'Celia,' he whispered again, and slipped his arms round her once more. But again, she pushed him away.

'I can't sleep like that, Rupert. Let's just say goodnight now.' She gave him another perfunctory kiss and turned away.

Rupert lay still, physically satisfied, half asleep yet slightly disconcerted. He was aware of Celia's body, warm in the wide bed, of the lace of her nightgown, slightly rough against his skin. He could hear her breathing, soft and steady. A stray hair lay against his cheek, tickling it slightly.

He wanted to touch her, to hold that warm body against his. He wanted to kiss her, to explore her breasts, her arms, her legs and waist, as he had not given himself the chance to do before. He wanted to feel her kisses on his skin, her hands on his shoulders, his back, his thighs. He wanted, in the aftermath of his frenzy, to make love to her in a different way – gently, softly, tenderly. He wanted their loving to be something between the two of them, rather than simply his own release.

Elinor would have come into his arms now, pressing the length of her body against him. He would have felt her full breasts against his chest, her head on his shoulder. Her hand would have rested on his stomach and, as often as not, after a little while it would have begun to move, making its own explorations, stroking him, rubbing him, bringing his dozing passions to life again. He remembered the weak protests of his half slumbering brain and then the slow arousal until finally his body was unable to resist and they began to make love with even greater frenzy. Elinor, sitting astride him, would gaze down in triumph at this renewed proof of her ability to rouse him; while Rupert, gripped by a response beyond his control, heaved and thrust his way to a climax he had thought out of his reach.

It must, he knew, be different with Celia. She was his wife and could not be expected to behave as a mistress would. And she had been, until tonight, a virgin and would never be as knowledgeable, as imaginative, as Elinor. Nor would he want her to be so; no man wanted a wife who behaved like a whore. But the gentleness, the tenderness, those he wanted, had looked for.

Had he been too rough, too hasty? He knew that the answer must be yes. But wasn't any bridegroom, long frustrated, likely to be so? And Celia hadn't seemed upset by his clumsiness.

Perhaps tomorrow would be better. After all, he thought, we have the rest of our lives.

Celia was asleep now. He slipped an arm across her body and moved closer, feeling her warmth through the cotton of her nightgown. In the morning, he would make love to her as she deserved.

Chapter Twenty-Five

Susannah Sherwin died suddenly shortly after Rupert and Celia's wedding; she never saw their first son, Thomas, born soon after Christmas the following year.

Celia had accepted her pregnancy with the cool practicality she brought to every event in her life. She said nothing to Rupert until she was certain, then presented him with the news over breakfast one morning. He stared at her, then got up and came round the table to kiss her.

'My darling, that's wonderful! But so soon – can you be sure?'

'We've been married for three months,' she said, lifting her cheek to his lips. 'It isn't so surprising. Marriage is for procreation, after all.'

'And other things.' As so often happened, Rupert found himself slightly disconcerted by his wife's outlook. On occasions when he felt sentimental, she was cool; when he was loving, she was dismissive; when he was passionate, she did no more than submit.

She never rejected him, as he knew some men's wives did, but neither did she ever react as Elinor had done, welcoming his body eagerly into hers. Nor did he expect it; but he had hoped, at the beginning, for an increase in warmth, for some sign of enjoyment. Instead, for Celia, her conjugal duties seemed to be just that – duties, carried out with neither more nor less pleasure than any of her other household tasks. In fact, he suspected that when he lay above her, striving ever more desperately to grasp at the delights he knew were possible, Celia's mind was more occupied with tomorrow's dinner than with him. Their couplings became just that, a physical mating rather than love making. For Rupert, they were little more satisfactory than his private stimulation, and Celia almost less real than the women of his fantasies.

But it was still early days, he reminded himself. For a girl as sheltered as Celia had been, it must take time. And perhaps the arrival of a baby would help her to relax, to cast off the coolness he had mistaken for shyness and bring her the warmth that had been as lacking in her life as in his.

'A baby!' he said now, returning to his chair and gazing at her. 'Oh, my dear . . . When do you think he'll be born?'

'It,' she corrected him. 'We can't know until it's born what sex it will be. I think in January.'

'In January! Then it must have happened almost at once.' Pride added itself to the emotions he was feeling. Fleetingly, he thought of Elinor. Thank heaven she had known how to protect herself . . . He brought his mind back to his wife and smiled at her across the table. 'But you must take care of yourself. Have you been feeling ill? Faint? Have you been resting enough? You mustn't take any risks – no more riding, I'm sure it's bad for you, and no gardening.'

'Nonsense,' Celia said impatiently. 'Having a child is a normal condition, Rupert, and nothing to make a fuss over.' She stopped suddenly and gave him a thoughtful glance. 'Although there's one precaution we should take. You'll sleep in the other bedroom now, of course.'

'In the other bedroom?' Again, he was disconcerted. He looked at her in dismay. Sleep apart from her for how many months? Six until the child was born, and for how long afterwards? He knew that some women did have their family quickly, sometimes as quickly as a year or less after each other, so presumably it needn't be more than a matter of weeks . . . But it was a long time for a man who had only just begun to be accustomed to having a wife. Even a wife as cool and unresponsive as Celia.

But that would have changed, he told himself, feeling disloyal. She only needed time. Now this has happened . . .

His first delight, his pride, were clouded slightly. He made an effort to pull himself together. It was Celia who mattered, after all, Celia and the baby – *their* baby. As he looked at her, seeing her slightness, her fragility, his disappointment vanished and he made up his mind to take the utmost care of her.

He went to the mines that morning feeling as though the world had suddenly turned to gold. A child. He and Celia were to have a child. The first, he hoped, of several. And then, at last, he would know for himself the warmth and joy of family life. A warmth and joy that had always eluded him; that he had only ever seen from outside, as if, like the little matchgirl in the Hans Andersen fairy tale, he had spent his life peering through a window at the warmth within.

Now, at last, he would come in from the cold.

Thomas was born on 18 January 1871, during the final weeks of the siege of Paris. All England had been following the story with fascinated horror. The tribulations of the citizens, made known to the world through dispatches flown out by balloon, were almost too horrible to contemplate. Almost no food, circus and zoo animals, including even the favourite elephant, used as dishes in restaurants while the poorer folk ate their own cats and dogs and even the rats that foraged among the increasing rubbish. Smallpox running rife, and a constant bombardment of the hastily built ramparts – all these seemed a world away from the peace of Furness.

Rupert, laying down his copy of the *Times* or the *Illustrated London News*, would sigh heavily and wonder why it was that countries had to go to war when all that most folk desired was to live their own lives peacefully.

'It's the family that's important,' he said to Celia as he sat by her bed, gazing into the little cradle at their newborn son. 'Bringing up a family, that's all that really matters. And if all these so-called leaders did just that and forgot about gaining more and more power, the world would be a better place. What good does power do a man? How can it compare with this?' He leaned over the crib and touched the petal-soft cheek with the tip of one finger. 'How can anyone want to leave home and go to war if he has a child at home? How can he contemplate killing other men's children?'

Celia looked up at him from her pillows. 'Wait until you hear him wailing all night long,' she advised him, 'and then you may understand why men go to war. Or wait until he's toddling and tips a bottle of ink all over your ledgers, or breaks your favourite pipe. Then you might wish you had indeed joined the Army, as your father wanted.'

But Rupert smiled and shook his head. He knew that Celia thought him over-sentimental, but he was still overwhelmed by the love he felt for this tiny scrap of life, born from their union. It still seemed incredible to him that this new existence could have come from one occasion of loving between himself and Celia. The baby was so *complete*, the little round head covered with black down, the tiny eyelids shut tightly over milky blue eyes, the minute fingers with their specks of fingernail. And all because one night, early in their marriage – perhaps the first night of all – he had taken Celia in his arms and lain over her and taken his pleasure of her. And given her pleasure too, he hoped, although he still could not be quite certain of that . . .

He tore his eyes away from the baby and bent to kiss

his wife. 'You've done well, my love. Very well indeed. And soon I'll be able to show you once again just how much I love you.'

But it had been the wrong thing to say. She turned her head away impatiently, avoiding his kiss, and there was an edge to her voice as she spoke. 'Oh, really Rupert! Can you think of nothing else but your – your conjugal rights? Am I to have no rest at all? Thomas is only three days old, for heaven's sake. Must I start another pregnancy within days of ending this one?'

'Of course not.' He felt hurt and misunderstood. 'My love, you can't say I've been anything but patient all these months.'

'But now your patience is running out, obviously.'

'Not at all. I'll give you all the time you require. All I'm saying is that once you're fit and strong again, I'll be happy to show you how much I love you – that's all.'

'You can show me best,' she returned, 'by staying where you are, in the other bedroom.'

There was a short silence. Rupert felt as if he had been kicked in the stomach. After a few moments, he said carefully, 'Are you saying that you don't want to risk having any more children at all?'

Celia sighed. 'Oh, I suppose I must eventually. I know my duty and I know what marriage is for. But a decent interval – is that too much to request?' There was a touch of bitterness in her voice now. 'You don't have to bear the child, Rupert. You don't have to endure months of sickness, of painful indigestion, of backache and tiredness and, worst of all, growing bigger and bigger. You don't have to carry that dreadful burden, day after day. And you don't have to face the birth.' She shuddered. 'Men have no idea of what pain is, Rupert. No idea at all. There can be nothing worse than giving birth, *nothing*.'

Rupert was silent. He knew that in this Celia was largely right. There might well be pain worse than that of giving birth, but most men did not have to suffer it. Most women did, not once, but many times. And with each time they risked their own lives as well as those of their babies.

He half bent again to kiss her, then straightened up and, instead, touched her cheek as he had touched the baby's.

'I promise I won't trouble you until you are ready, my love,' he said gently. 'And if you really don't want to face having any more children, there are things that can be done, I know . . .'

She gave him another bitter look. 'You mean well, Rupert, I know. But you're as selfish as any other man, thinking only of your own pleasure. You know very well what the Church would have to say about such a suggestion. Marriage is for procreation.' She turned and looked into the cradle where Thomas was beginning to stir. 'And I wish to be a mother. I want more sons. So if to endure what I have already endured is the only way to get them . . . Just give me a little time, that's all I ask. And now I'd like to sleep. Tell Nurse to take him away.' She turned her head away again, and Rupert left the room quietly. He went downstairs feeling half bemused, half comforted.

Celia had not banned him for ever from her bed, only for a while. And she was not averse to having more children – those last few words had wiped away a fear that had been growing in his mind for some time. But she had made it very clear that his loving was no more than the means by which to conceive them.

The warmth he had envisaged receded a little and once again he felt himself outside in the snow, watching family life through a cold, frosted window.

But it need not be like that, he told himself. Thomas is born and will grow up, and there will be others, brothers and sisters. The family has begun. The warmth and the magic will follow.

It was expected that when Susannah died, leaving only Martha in Pennington Hall, Walter Sherwin would come home to claim his inheritance. But he seemed no more interested than he had before. Letters telling him of events in Furness went a long time unanswered, and the replies that finally came told of a life that was very different from the quiet existence led by the family at home.

'This letter came from India,' Martha told them. The family was gathered in the drawing room at Garth House where they had come to admire the new baby. 'He says he's hoping to explore Tibet. Imagine, Tibet! It sounds so exciting, so *mysterious*.'

'He's a fool,' Nicholas stated unequivocally. 'Nobody's allowed into Tibet. It's like Nepal, closed to all foreigners. He'll be turned back or more probably murdered.'

'Ugh!' Martha shivered. 'Do you really think so? Poor Walter!'

'Why is he there?' Celia asked. 'What's he doing it for?'

Rupert answered her. He was sitting beside her on the sofa where she always, smilingly, insisted he sit when they were in company though when alone together she banished him to a separate chair, just as she banished him from her bed. They had been examining the daguerreotype portraits taken of themselves a few days earlier. The visit to the photographer had necessitated a good deal of preparation and no little expense but it was worth it, Rupert felt, to have such a memento of his firstborn. 'Why does Walter go exploring?' he said. 'Because he wants to know about the world. He was always curious about his surroundings. He used to take me for long walks over the hills, showing me rocks and plants, telling me the names of the birds we saw – it was always fascinating to go out with Walter. But he could never stay long in one place, he was always a roamer.'

'Humph! He was a wilful and difficult boy,' Nicholas snorted. 'Timothy never knew how to control him. He gave him far too much freedom. He ought to have been in charge of the mines – he should have inherited the whole business. It says a great deal about how Timothy felt that he left them to you instead.'

'Poor Walter,' Martha said. 'He wasn't an easy boy to understand, I agree, but he had a difficult life, you know, Nicholas. Dear Mamma never really took to him – she was so ill when he was born and he was such an odd-looking baby, with those huge lumps on his head. For a long time we all thought he'd be an imbecile.'

'Not sure you were far wrong,' Nicholas commented. 'Who but an imbecile would want to travel in Tibet?'

'I think it sounds fascinating,' Elinor observed. She had been saying little, sitting in a chair slightly outside the circle and watching Rupert as he looked first at the daguerreotypes and then at the baby on his wife's knee. He was aware of her gaze, but took care not to meet it. As always these days, there was a constraint between them, particularly when Celia was also present. It seemed to Rupert that his wife's public display of affection, so different from her behaviour when they were by themselves, was increased when Elinor was present, and he tortured himself by wondering whether his former mistress was deceived by it, or whether her sharp eyes saw through Celia's pretence to the cold truth of his marriage. But there was nothing he could do about it and when with the family they made only the smallest contact, for politeness' sake.

'I wish I had known him better,' she went on. 'He was such an interesting boy. So tall and strong. So *alive*. It was quite clear to me that Furness could never be enough for him. I was sorry when he left before we could get to know each other.' Her limpid gaze was transferred to her husband. 'We'd been married a very short time when he went, hadn't we?'

Rupert glanced at Nicholas and saw his skin redden. He felt at once a pang of the guilt that had never quite left him, and then a twinge of jealousy which he immediately tried to stifle. Why should it matter to him, after all this time, that Elinor found other men attractive? It was a long time now since their affair had been over. And although he was sure that there must have been other men during that time, she had been discreet and he had heard no gossip about her.

'But why is no one allowed into Tibet?' Martha asked. 'Why is it kept so secret?'

'It's never been easy to get into the country,' Rupert said. He had always taken an interest in Walter's travels. 'When it was under Chinese rule, the Chinese forbade people to enter – they've always kept people out of their own country, so it was to be expected. They're different from us, those Far Eastern races. They think differently. They don't want to explore and they don't like being explored. And of course when foreign powers like ourselves began to find their way into China and then take over, as we've done in so many other countries, especially India, the Tibetans, who were independent by that time, became frightened. They'd had enough oppression from the Chinese, they didn't want it starting all over again with Western powers. So they closed down once more, and now foreigners are strictly forbidden.'

'And that makes people like Walter want to go there all the more,' Nicholas added. 'As I said, he was always a wilful, obstinate boy. One had only to forbid something for him to be determined to have it.'

'But it sounds a horrid place,' said Celia, who had been reading the letter. 'Bitterly cold in winter, he says, or burning hot in summer. No trees, almost no water, hardly any food. Isn't there somewhere more comfortable he could explore? Nobody else is going to want to go there. He would be better off discovering places where people could go and live, like America.'

'I don't think there are many places like America left to discover,' Nicholas said dryly. 'But I doubt very much if he'll ever get there anyway. It's just a fashion at present – a good many explorers want to enter Tibet. It's a race to be first. And none of them will succeed.'

'Why not?' Elinor seemed unable to let anything Nicholas said go unchallenged. 'How can you know so much about it?'

'I take the trouble to keep myself informed,' her husband said shortly. 'Tibet is a hostile country in which it's almost impossible to survive secretly. As Walter's letter says, travel is almost impossible, and as a European he'll be instantly recognisable. Who is going to assist him in this harebrained idea? Who will hire him horses, or whatever those barbaric animals are that they use for transport.'

'Yaks,' Rupert said.

'Yaks. Who is going to give him accommodation? Anyone sheltering a foreigner risks instant punishment – and their punishments are far more ruthless than ours. Mutilation, torture, death. I tell you, it's a savage country. And as I said just now, only an imbecile would want to go there.'

There was a silence. Then Elinor said, 'So what is going to happen about the house? Will it be sold?'

They all glanced at Martha. She had lived at Pennington Hall ever since coming here as a child of ten with her mother, when Susannah and Timothy had married. The house had been left to Walter, with the condition that Susannah should live in it for her lifetime. But Martha had received nothing but a small income.

'Presumably she'll go and live with her sister,' Nicholas had said when he and Elinor had discussed the subject at home. 'It's the obvious thing to do. I don't

450

imagine the old man expected me to look after her in her old age.'

'She's only forty-eight,' Elinor protested. 'Hardly old.' Only seven years older than me, she thought, and shivered at the idea of becoming like Martha, so plump and plain, her life filled with triviality. Who was marrying whom, who had just died, who was in an 'interesting condition' – all these were the stuff of Martha's life, keeping her endlessly interested in her neighbours, a fund of local knowledge and gossip. And dull, Elinor thought contemptuously, dull, dull, *dull*.

'Well then, that's all the longer to be saddled with her,' Nicholas said. 'Why, she could live another thirty years or more, and probably will, with her appetite. No, she'll be off to Liverpool to live with Jane, and very welcome to each other they are.'

His eyes gleamed a little and Elinor knew he was thinking about Pennington Hall. He had always coveted the house and had feared that Rupert would inherit it. She knew too that he had already made plans to offer to buy it from Walter, and that now Susannah was dead he was only waiting for a decent period to elapse before doing that.

As she asked her question this afternoon, she glanced across at him to watch his reaction.

'No, the house won't be sold,' Martha said. 'Walter says he wants to keep it so that he can come back when he's too old to travel any more.' She folded the letter and looked round the room, a smile creasing her plump face. 'And he's asked me to stay on and look after it for him.'

Elinor saw Nicholas's face change and darken. 'You?' he exclaimed. 'But that's ridiculous!'

Martha's face paled and then flushed. Elinor saw her soft mouth tremble. A maid's mouth, Elinor thought, an unkissed mouth. Did she miss what she had never had? Did she even know she had missed it?

'Why is it—'

'It's not ridiculous,' Rupert intervened angrily. How like him, Elinor thought. He hardly ever stands up for himself, but let anyone attack his precious Aunt Martha and he's springing to her defence. 'It seems an eminently sensible suggestion to me. Aunt Martha's lived here since she was a child, she knows the house better than anyone else. She knows the servants and all their ways – in fact she's been running the house since before Grandfather died. You know how Grandmother was the last few years.'

'That's hardly the point,' Nicholas said loftily, but again Rupert broke in.

'Then what is the point? Aunt Martha is the best possible person to look after the house for Walter. Besides, she probably doesn't want to leave it anyway. It's her home.' Belatedly, he recalled that Martha herself might be the best person to answer this point, and he turned to her. 'Is that right, Aunt Martha? Would you rather stay here than go to Liverpool, say?'

'Well, I'd enjoy living with Jane, naturally,' Martha said unconvincingly. 'As a matter of fact, she's already invited me. She's such a busy person and there's always something I can do to help.' In fact, she usually came back from a visit to Liverpool exhausted. 'But I think it's my duty to stay here and look after dear Walter's inheritance. And he's been very kind about it.' She folded the letter and gave them all a look that from any less self-effacing person might have been described as triumphant.

'So,' Nicholas said as he and Elinor drove home, 'Martha stays at Pennington Hall and treats it as her own. Which means she'll allow it to fall to pieces. She has no idea how to look after a house like that.'

'Well, I daresay you can advise her.' Elinor was tired and disgruntled. She still found it upsetting to be in the same room with Rupert and this afternoon, watching him with his wife and their baby, had been particularly

452

galling. That insipid little thing, having the right to go to bed with Rupert every night for the rest of her life! I'll warrant she knows nothing of what makes a man happy, Elinor thought bitterly. She probably doesn't even know what makes herself happy.

Since Rupert had ended their liaison, Elinor had been unable to form a real attachment to anyone. It had been so easy, having him in the same house; the possibility of being able to slip away for half an hour at any time had kept her in a state of permanent excitement, while Tuesday afternoons had been delicious luxury. And Rupert, so young and virile, so untried when she had first seduced him, had learned well and quickly. He had soon been able to anticipate her every desire, and his passion was strong enough to sweep them both away.

She had not found any man who could satisfy her as well as Rupert had. And none of them had been as available. A snatched hour on the common or in a meadow with a local farmer, a tryst in the woods with a mine captain – none left her with the sense of fulfilment she had known after an afternoon's dalliance with her stepson.

But Rupert had abandoned her and Elinor must search endlessly for the fleeting pleasures of brief and invariably unsatisfactory affairs, while he and Celia . . .

'What did you think of the child?' Nicholas asked, as if reading her thoughts. 'A sturdy enough little fellow, by the look of him.'

'I suppose so.' The sight of Celia with Rupert's baby in her arms had turned the knife in the wound of her jealousy. 'I'm surprised she managed to bring it to term. She never looked strong enough to me.'

'Oh, I think Celia's stronger than she looks. She worked hard enough at Torver, by all accounts.' Nicholas gave his wife a sideways glance and added with some malice, 'He's very like his father.'

'He is,' Elinor agreed and, with equal maliciousness,

'but not a bit like his grandfather. But then Rupert doesn't take after you at all, does he? He's so very dark, not at all like a Craven . . .' Did Nicholas remember that confession, early on in their marriage, that he suspected he was not Rupert's father? Whether he did or not, the reminder brought a scowl to his face. She added innocently, gazing straight ahead, 'It must be such a comfort to a man, to see his children resemble him so strongly.'

Nicholas said nothing. But his face was dark and his frown heavy. He flicked the reins sharply on the horse's back and the animal broke into a startled trot.

The rest of the journey passed in silence. And when they arrived at Green House, Elinor went straight up to her room.

After such an afternoon, she desperately needed relief. But there was nobody to give it to her; least of all her husband.

Chapter Twenty-Six

Celia did, finally, allow Rupert back into her bed, but only for a brief interval. When she became pregnant again, he returned to the room he had occupied before they were married; and after Oliver was born, eighteen months after his brother, it seemed that she had the sons she desired and considered her family complete.

'But only two children!' Rupert protested. 'I looked forward to a large family. I'd like daughters too – or more sons, if God so wills. And the fashion now is for larger families. Why, even the Queen—'

'The Queen had all modern medicine to assist her,' Celia said sharply. 'And plenty of servants. All I have is a cook-housekeeper and a few maids. And a husband who is never at home.'

'That's not true. I'm at home more than a good many husbands. Do you know what it's like to be left at home alone from breakfast until late-evening dinner like some wives are? And I would be at home more if I had a better welcome here.'

'And do *you* know what it's like to see a sour face across the table at every meal? Perhaps if you were a little better tempered—'

'Yes, I do!' he retorted. 'Yours! And I would be better tempered if I were allowed the privileges, the *rights*, that other husbands take for granted. Am I to be treated as nothing but a stud stallion, to provide you with the sons you want and then remain celibate all my life?'

'There is no need to be coarse—'

'There is every need!' he exclaimed. 'Celia, since we were married you have never shown me the slightest warmth. You have never voluntarily kissed or touched me, you hardly even smile at me. You tolerated my love simply and solely in order to have these two children. And now you have them, I am of no further use to you other than to provide a home. And if telling you of my needs is "being coarse", then coarse I must be if I am to make you understand.'

'Oh, I understand very well,' she said. 'What you call love is no more than your animal desire, which I must tolerate because it is necessary for the production of children. But why I should tolerate it for any other reason, I simply cannot comprehend. The whole process is quite distasteful. And if you really loved me, you would respect my feelings. Your persistence merely serves to prove your selfishness.'

Rupert stared at her. She was cradling Oliver as she spoke; little Thomas, now almost two years old, was playing on the floor with a set of wooden bricks. Her hair, still the same rich bronze, was curled over her forehead and drawn back behind her head. She was wearing a gown of dark red, fitted tightly over her bodice and with a long full skirt. Her waist was as small as it had ever been, even after the birth of two children, and she looked very little older than on the day he had first encountered her at the door of the farmhouse at Torver.

He thought of the years he had courted her. Those shy, upward glances, the smiles, the secret touches when her father wasn't looking. The meetings in the woods or down by the lake. The picnics on the island . . .

Celia had loved him then, he was sure of it. There had been times when his desire had been almost too powerful to withstand, when he had longed to make love to her, times when he was sure he had sensed the same desire in her. Had it all been a mirage, a dream? A façade, to entice him into a marriage that had proved frigid and empty?

'I didn't get married to be a skivvy,' she had said sharply when he'd once expressed a desire for the jams and preserves he had enjoyed at the farmhouse in Torver. 'I spent some of the best years of my life slaving in a kitchen and I don't intend to do it now I'm married. I'm surprised you should even think of it.'

'But being married surely means doing things for the one you love,' he said, 'just as I do things for you. And plenty of married women make preserves and suchlike for their families, and take a pride in doing so.' He cast about for the words he wanted. 'It shows their affection.'

'And do I not show affection?' she demanded. 'Didn't I insist you sat by me at the Priors' soiree last Tuesday? Didn't I cling to your arm almost half the evening? Didn't I smile at you enough?'

Rupert stared at her helplessly. Didn't she understand how hollow these displays were? Didn't she realise that it was real affection he craved – the lightest touch in passing when they were alone, the unexpected kiss, the soft caress when nobody else could see?

If you really felt any love for me, you would do those things naturally, he thought. But all you want is to appear to other people as the perfect wife. To you, a husband and children are nothing but public proof of your own success, to be displayed like toys and then put away till next time.

But human beings could not be put away in cupboards like toys. And if this was to be the pattern of his life, how was he to survive? Again, he asked himself the question: Am I to remain celibate all my life?

If Celia's cool response had been all he had ever known, he might have borne it. But he had known Elinor. He had lain with her, had felt her body pulsate against his, had felt himself warmly enclosed within her, had felt her shuddering with him to a mutual peak of excitement and delight. He understood what passion could be. He had believed that love must surely enrich the experience.

Whether he believed it still, he did not know. But he hungered for it. More and more, he went to the mines for comfort, at least for occupation. There, amidst the noise and the clatter, with the red dust in his eyes and nostrils and the crimson mud beneath his boots, he could forget domestic cares and push aside the longings that, without diversion, might have overwhelmed him.

And there was plenty at the mines to divert him. Only a few months before, the men working Louisa mine had extended it in a new direction, intending to go to the boundary of the royalty where it bordered land mined by a neighbouring company, based in Barrow. But before reaching the boundary they had begun to break through into existing workings. They had seen at once that these were no old tunnels, hacked out years or even centuries before. The caverns were new, with timbers still fresh and ginnels gleaming with rich ore not yet dug out.

'Trespass!' Abe had said when reporting the discovery to Rupert. 'The bastards have been down there robbing out our ore for devil knows how long. Thousands of tons gone. Downright theft, that's what it is, and they ought to be brought to book.'

'They certainly should,' Rupert agreed. 'But I don't want to create unnecessary trouble. These things can usually be settled quite amicably. A meeting between you and their captain, perhaps, calculating the amount of ore gone, and simple reimbursement. It's been done before and all remained friends.'

'Friends!' Abe snorted. 'When they've shipped out something like twenty thousand tons of our ore! That'll tak' more than a chinwag between me and Bill Cropper – and he don't talk any straighter than he can see.'

Rupert frowned and pursed his lips. He knew Abe was right. Bill Cropper, mine captain of Rawlings, Insworth and Co., had a fearsome squint which was said to enable him to see round corners, and his tongue was as devious as his glance. If he had been robbing Louisa of ore he was never likely to admit it and even less likely to agree to a reimbursement. In any case, such admittance would almost certainly cost him his job, even if his employers had been – as they probably were – well aware of the trespass.

'Trouble is, folk have allus bin too soft over trespasses,' Abe went on. 'Gentlemen's agreements and such! Pity we don't go by the old laws. Time was when any man caught stealing ore was locked in his hut and the hut burnt down. That's the way to treat 'em.'

'Rather a barbaric way,' Rupert observed. 'Well, the first thing we must do is carry out a survey. I suppose they thought by the time we reached that boundary their workings would have been crushed and we'd never have noticed.'

'Aye, that'll be the size of it,' Abe agreed. 'But we're a bit quicker than they thought. Anyway, even if the shafts had subsided, we'd have found the timbers. You can allus tell when a trespass has bin going on.'

'How have they been getting it out, do you think?'

'Along to B45 pit, of course. See,' Abe's finger traced a line along the map of the workings, 'that's the boundary of Louisa and over here's their pitheads. B45 is in direct line – it must have bin there. And a tramway straight down to the sidings at Lindal. The ore's gone before we know it's out of the ground, and who's to prove how much?'

'Well,' Rupert said, getting to his feet, 'we'd better go down and see. We can judge by looking at the size of the workings. Maybe a claim against them will be sufficient.'

Abe snorted his doubts but followed Rupert willingly enough, and they went to the pithead and were lowered down the damp, dripping shaft.

It was clear that Abe was right and there had been a

trespass. Rupert, staring at the freshly stripped walls of the tunnels, felt the captain's anger burn in his own breast. This was no inadvertent encroachment, such as often happened and was usually sorted out in a friendly manner between captains or mine owners. This was, as Abe had said, deliberate robbery.

'I want to see what else they've been doing,' he said as they returned to the surface. 'I suspect there's more than we can reach through our own tunnels. We'll sink some new shafts, up on the moor.'

The work took time to organise and it was not until after Oliver was born that the new boreholes were finally completed. The area had so far not been mined, for Timothy had always taken the view that it was unlikely to be good ore, and in any case he had concentrated on Louisa and the other mines. But to Rupert's delight, three of the shafts struck through to good ore. No trespass was found, but the veins – thirty, forty and even sixty feet of solid haematite – made it well worthwhile proceeding and he almost forgot the trespass that had originally led him to work here. When Oliver had just begun to sit up and was even trying to crawl, a message came from Abe.

'They've found it!' he told Celia as he read the note at luncheon. 'They've found the trespass.'

'Indeed?' she said with indifference. 'You know, I'm sure that new housemaid has a follower. She's been extremely neglectful of her work lately and sometimes when I speak to her I could swear she doesn't hear a word I say. I hope she's not going to be foolish – you'll remember the scullery maid we had last year who ended up in trouble. I had to be very sharp with her before I dismissed her.'

'Yes, I remember.' Rupert spoke absently. 'I'll go along this afternoon – we must investigate this at once. Abe says it's enormous. And—'

'This afternoon?' Celia interrupted. 'But you were to

take me to Kirkby for tea with Mrs Lilly. I reminded you only this morning.'

'I know. But this is important. I have to see the extent of the trespass. If it's as much as Abe says, I shall start legal proceedings at once. Twenty thousand tons is one matter, but this could run into hundreds of thousands and—'

'But you *promised*!' Celia looked as if she had not made up her mind whether to be petulant or angry. 'Surely it can wait until tomorrow. It's waited months already, one day can't make any difference.'

'But it wouldn't be one day. Have you forgotten I have to go to Liverpool tomorrow? I'll be away until the middle of next week. No, I'm sorry, my love, but I have to go this afternoon. And you don't need me to take you to Kirkby, Bates can drive you just as well.'

'Bates,' Celia said coldly, 'is not my husband.'

Am I? Rupert thought, looking at her. She sat at the other end of the table, wearing dark blue today, her hair all the richer for the contrast. Her face was pale, for she took care never to let the sun colour it, and her topaz eyes were like a cat's. He had seen her look like this a hundred times or more since their marriage, yet she was less familiar now than she had been at the beginning and growing further from him with every day that passed.

I should insist that we live a proper married life, he thought. I should go into her room, her bed, as if I had a right. As if? I *do* have a right. And it was *our* bed, *our* room. I should never have allowed myself to be excluded. And now Oliver is eight months old and still she shows no sign of relenting. Nor, I believe, ever will.

But there was no time to think of that now. He gathered up Abe's note and rose to his feet.

'I'm sorry, Celia. I know I promised to take you to Kirkby this afternoon, but the mine must come before a tea party. Particularly one at which I'm to be displayed as a possession, like a monkey on a stick. Bates will drive you perfectly well.'

Celia tightened her lips. 'Very well. But next time you make me a promise, I shall expect you to keep it.'

As you have kept yours to me? he thought, but again said nothing. Arguments with Celia, particularly on this subject, were likely to become an unpleasant exchange of insults. It was better to remain silent.

'This is it,' Abe said as they descended the borehole. A cage had been fitted and crowded in with them were the miners who had made the discovery. By the glow of his lamp Rupert could see the raw scars of the rock as they passed its face. Water oozed from cracks in the red earth, gleaming in the flickering light like blood running from a fresh wound.

About sixty feet down, the cage stopped and he saw a hole in the wall of the shaft, a black space where there should have been rock. He lifted his lamp and stared at it.

'That's been dug some time,' he said at last. 'The face isn't fresh. And it's not a natural watercourse either, those are pick marks.'

'Aye.' Abe's voice was grim. 'Now you come along it and see what else we've found.'

They climbed out of the cage and began to walk along the tunnel, cautiously in case there had been any fresh rock falls. After a short distance, Rupert saw that ladders had been brought already and laid along the rough floor. After a few minutes Abe stopped and held up his lamp. Rupert peered over his shoulder.

Before them was a wide black pit. It descended into solid darkness but when all the lamps were held over it, the bottom could just be seen. It seemed to be a meeting point for several more tunnels.

'Fetch the ladders,' Abe ordered.

The ladders were brought and one was lowered over

the edge. It reached the bottom with a foot or two to spare and one of the men went down. The rest watched as his lamp slowly descended and became no more than a point of light in the darkness below.

'All right, Tom?' someone called down to him. 'Only we're knocking off now . . .'

His voice echoed around the walls, bouncing back and forth so that some of his words were almost lost while the last repeated itself, growing fainter with each repetition, '. . . *now*, *now*, now, ow, ow, ow-w-w . . .'

The men laughed as Tom shouted back something derisive, and then Capper, who had first shouted, began to climb down after him. Rupert watched as the two lamps moved about, far below, and then Tom called up again for the other ladders to be lowered.

'I'll go next,' Rupert said, and set his foot on the first rung. The blackness seemed to draw itself around him, as thick and suffocating as a heavy cloak. After a few moments the lamps of the men above were like Tom's down below, no more than small glimmers in the dark. The glow given out by his own lamp was feeble, lighting up no more than a few feet around him. He could see the rock face, dark and wet, a few inches from his face; beyond that, nothing.

He could hear them still, their voices talking and echoing, the odd cackle or boom of laughter magnified by the silent walls. But as he drew further away from them, the sound became less human, as if caused by other beings, as if the denizens of the mines themselves, strange creatures of a nether world, were discussing this new intrusion. As he descended, the level of noise varied, as if the voices were now close to him, now far away; once or twice he heard words spoken quite clearly in his ear, as if someone else were on the ladder with him and bidding him take care.

And then his lamp went out.

It was not an uncommon experience. Lamps frequently

ran out of oil or needed their wicks replacing. It was usually no more than an irritation when one light among many died. For a man alone in a tunnel, it was more serious, but even then most of the men knew their way around the mines as well as they knew the paths and lanes above. Seldom did anyone get lost. But to have your lamp fail when you were halfway down a ladder in an unknown system was a different matter.

Rupert looked down. Beneath him he could see the two small patches of light from Tom and Capper. One was almost directly below, its owner presumably holding the ladder so that it would not tip. The other was moving about, probably looking at the tunnels that led away from the central cavern. It must be a huge working.

Rupert could not keep looking down as he descended. He took his eyes away from those two small but comforting gleams, and felt for the next rung. It made no difference, after all, whether he had light or not. A ladder was a ladder, there was only one way to go. It wouldn't be long before he was at the bottom and standing once again on firm ground.

Nevertheless, he could not restrain himself from looking down again. To his dismay, there was no light to be seen. Both small glimmers had disappeared. There was only solid darkness beneath his feet.

Rupert stopped. What had happened? What were they doing down there? He listened to the voices echoing around him but could make out no words at all now; it was no more than noise, a tantalising reverberation of inhuman voices, an almost palpable menace on every side of him; and every now and then a burst of mocking laughter, as if he were being watched by alien beings who knew that he was descending into depths of unimaginable horror . . .

Rupert gripped the ladder hard in both hands. He stayed quite still for a few minutes, fighting for self-control. He had heard of men, missing their way underground, losing their senses; being brought out as lunatics, raving about ghosts and hell-creatures, talking incessantly about the voices of long-dead miners who still stalked the passages. It was easy now to understand what had happened to them. But it's not going to happen to me, he told himself fiercely. I'm not even alone here. There are friends above and below, though God knows why they've abandoned the ladder. I'll have something to say to Tom Bright and Capper when I get down there. But there's nothing to fear. Nothing.

He climbed down slowly, feeling for each rung. It was like being suspended over an abyss; despite his attempts to keep his imagination under control, he could not help feeling he was alone in an underworld that was more than just a mine, as if he had strayed into some primeval Hades. The darkness gathered close about him, dank and oppressive, and he strained his eyes to try to penetrate it. How far away were the walls? Half a dozen feet or a few hundred? He had no way of telling. He could only reach past the ladder with one hand and touch the rock for comfort.

But there was no rock there. He reached forward, groping, and found only empty space under his hand. At once he grabbed again at the side of the ladder and felt it quiver and shake. His heart kicked against his ribs. He felt a cold sweat break out on his brow.

Was the ladder still leaning against the rock or had it started to tip backwards, taking him with it into a void of unimaginable depth? With nothing to touch, nothing to see, he could not tell if he was moving or still. He turned his head, but the darkness was absolute. And for a moment the voices themselves ceased, as if leaving him alone in hollow desolation.

This is what death is like, he thought with sudden coldness. This is what happens. We leave our warm bodies and go into eternal darkness, with nothing above, below or around us. And Hell is hearing the voices mock and not being able to talk to them; and reaching out, with nothing to touch; and knowing that there may be something above or something below, but never knowing what. Or whom.

Perhaps he had died. Perhaps somewhere on the descent he had died and was doomed to stay here for eternity, in this solid darkness. Or perhaps he had never lived at all and this was existence and the rest no more than a dream, flickering through his mind and then, like his lamp, going out.

The silence was as solid as the darkness. And then, out of the void, came a voice he recognised.

'You all right, Mr Craven?'

Relief flooded through him and he was back in the real world again. The ladder was still in place, there were still friends about him.

He began the descent again. After a few moments he put one hand out and felt the rock, cold and damp but reassuring, under his fingertips. There must have been a hollow where he had felt before. He knew that he would not feel the rock after this, for the angle of the ladder was taking him too far out. But it mattered no longer, for he felt safe and secure and with every step he was nearer the floor of the cavern.

Almost before he expected it, he was there. He felt Tom's hand on his leg, warning him, and then he stepped off and stood on hard rock, breathing a little hard and laughing in his relief.

'You've lost your light, sir,' Capper said, as if Rupert might not have noticed.

'I know. And what the devil happened to yours? When I looked down there was nothing to be seen.'

They looked at him blankly. Then Tom grinned, his teeth shining in the darkness of his face. 'Oh, that must hev bin when Capper went off to look down one of the roads. And I was bent down here, trying to see if that were a vein. I never let go of the ladder, though. You were quite safe.'

Quite safe! Rupert thought. He shuddered slightly, knowing that he would have more sympathy now with those who came out gibbering, and then put the memory of his terror firmly aside.

The other men descended the ladder, with Abe coming last. They stood in a small group, looking around. One of them carried a sack of spare equipment and he gave Rupert a fresh lamp.

'Look at this,' Capper said, leading them into one of the tunnels. 'There's another horizon underneath this one. And I'll be surprised if some of the others don't lead to more.' He looked around at the ring of faces, raddled in the fitful light. 'This trespass has bin going on for a long time. I reckon they've had as much ore out o' this lot as we've had out of Louisa in all her years.'

Chapter Twenty-Seven

'Certainly we'll be taking legal action,' Rupert said. 'The extent of the trespass is unbelievable. We went down through one horizon after another – we were a hundred feet below surface at the finish. Great caverns, littered with boulders, high tunnels that must have been dug out time and time again, ginnels cleaned out – a drift mined entirely away, leaving a huge void. Why, they've wiped half our land out of existence. There's even a tunnel which we knew about, running close to one of our own. If you squeeze through the loose rocks, you can see the miners using it. We thought it was just a roadway from one working to another, and so it was, but the workings were inside our own boundaries!'

'The insolence of it,' Nicholas said. 'How much do you suppose they've taken? Must be hundreds of tons.'

'Thousands,' Rupert said bitterly. 'And when you think we count thirty-three hundredweight as a ton, rather than the Imperial twenty . . .'

'It's a great deal of ore,' Nicholas nodded.

The two men sat in silence for a few minutes. Of late, they had met frequently to discuss the trespass. Whatever his qualities as a father, even a nominal one, Nicholas had, over the years, become an astute business-man and Rupert respected his opinion. He also knew that it gave Nicholas a good deal of pleasure to be able to advise him, and in a complicated way this helped to assuage the guilt Rupert still felt over Elinor.

'So what action are you taking?' Nicholas asked, filling his pipe.

Rupert stretched out his legs. He had always liked the library at Green House and had spent many hours here as a boy, taking refuge in books. It was the room he felt most comfortable in; here he could talk to Nicholas with confidence, almost forgetting the uneasy relationship between them.

He held up his fingers, counting off the points as he spoke. 'First of all, I'm taking out a writ. It states that they've taken upwards of twenty thousand tons of ore and "furtively conveyed it away" – I rather like that phrase. I'm demanding that they should pay a wayleave on all the ore they've carried secretly through our royalty, even when it was theirs, plus interest. I want to know where the ore was sold and how much for, and I'm expecting payment of all that money, again with interest. I want an injunction to restrain them from any further trespass. And lastly, I want damages for trespass, and costs.'

'They'll try settling out of court,' Nicholas said.

'They can try,' Rupert laid his hands on the arms of his chair, 'but they'll have to offer something very substantial. There are our costs for the bores we sank to investigate – two thousand pounds. Five hundred to open up the trespass workings. Another two thousand for legal advice. Together with the wayleave and damages. No, I shan't settle for less than eight thousand.' He rose to his feet. 'And probably, by the time all's over, I'll want more. Time's money and I don't like wasting it on chasing what's rightfully mine.'

He was almost at the door when it opened suddenly and he had to step back. Elinor stood there, her hand still on the latch, looking up at him.

'Rupert. I didn't know you were here.'

Rupert returned her look, feeling conscious of Nicholas behind him. His heart thumped uncomfortably.

'I just called in to discuss the trespass with Father.'

Her eyes gleamed. 'Oh yes, the Great Trespass. It's fascinating, isn't it, to think of all those men toiling away underground and nobody knowing what they were doing. So secret, down there in their tunnels. Quite exciting, don't you think?' She gazed up under her lashes. 'I love secrets.'

'I don't,' Rupert said abruptly. 'Especially when they're about people being robbed of what's theirs. I'm sorry, Elinor, I have to go now. How's William?'

'He's well. He's enjoying his travels abroad.' William, now twenty-four, was rarely seen in Furness. Since going to university at Oxford he had spent most of his time with friends there. They had decided to take up the old idea of the Grand Tour and were currently travelling in Europe. 'What use it will be to him I don't know, but he'll certainly have some experiences to recount when he comes back.'

'I'll look forward to hearing about them.' Rupert wished she would move. He could not leave without pushing past her and he did not want to brush against the body he had once known so well. Her closeness was having the same effect on him that it had had in the past, and he was uncomfortably sure that she knew it.

I'll have to do something about this, he thought, when he had finally escaped. Either Celia accepts her duties as a wife, or I'll have to find a mistress. I can't go on like this.

And what better mistress, a voice in his head asked, than Elinor, who has given you such pleasure in the past and who is clearly not only willing but anxious to do so again?

Elinor . . .

He rode home, thoughts of the trespass driven from his head. His mind was filled with visions from the past. Elinor, that first afternoon, dressed only in a robe of thin, flowing silk. Elinor in his bed, teaching him the

470

ways of love – the places to touch and kiss, the parts as silken as her robe where she liked to be stroked, the sensuousness of caresses that lingered and teased. She had taught him, too, about his own body, caresses that could drive him wild, touches and kisses that sent him into ecstasy, none of which he had come close to feeling since the day their liaison had ended. Celia did not like to be touched, did not welcome his caresses, was shocked and disgusted by the things that Elinor most enjoyed. Nor would she touch him, or even look at him. In her mind, lovemaking had nothing to do with love.

If you loved me, you would leave me alone. How many times had she said that to him? How many times had he been forced to turn away from her, to find relief in some other way?

And if that made him feel guilty too, why not take what was so clearly offered and know again the delights he had known before? Better hung for a sheep than a lamb, he thought as his horse trotted across Birker Common. If I'm to suffer, I might as well suffer for something worthwhile.

But even as the heat spread through his body at the thought of holding Elinor in his arms again, he knew that it was not what he really wanted. He still hungered for the warmth and completeness that he felt instinctively must be possible between a man and a woman.

He was still, like the little matchgirl, standing on the outside looking in.

'Such news!' Martha arrived in a flurry of excitement, in her eagerness almost falling from the little dogcart in which she drove about the lanes. She waved a sheet of paper at them. 'Such news, you'll never guess what it is!'

'You'd better come in and tell us then.' Rupert was fond of his Aunt Martha, though he was never quite sure whether to envy her or feel sorry for her. For years she had crept about the place like a shadow, dominated by both her sister and her mother. All the less congenial tasks of the household had fallen to her and, as Susannah had grown older, Martha had taken over more and more responsibility, though without being given much credit for it. She had been hardly less imposed upon when visiting her sister in Liverpool; often enough, her visits had been used as an opportunity to give the children's nurse a holiday or even to engage a new one, so that Martha had the task of looking after her nephews and nieces as well as training a new nanny.

But since she had been living alone at Pennington Hall, she had blossomed. She could be seen jaunting about in her pony and trap, visiting the friends from whom she gleaned all her gossip, her plump face wreathed in smiles for one and all. She held frequent tea parties and sewing circles, and was often to be found in the garden, her hands covered in red earth as she dug and planted. The gardeners seemed to be on the same terms with her as the friends she visited in the larger houses of Ulverston and its surrounding villages, and the indoor servants treated her with a comfortable familiarity which caused Elinor and Celia to frown and purse their lips.

'It never does to allow servants to become familiar,' Elinor would comment. 'The next step is insolence and idleness. She'll regret it, mark my words.'

Celia agreed. She had little time for Martha anyway, disliking the older woman's effusive warmth and chatter. Even more, she disliked the affection that existed between Rupert and his aunt, and expressed this in her usual way by finding fault. Martha's housekeeping came in for much derisive comment, her teas – still the hearty ones that Rupert had always enjoyed – were sneered at, and her unfashionable way of dressing deplored. When Celia had looked out this afternoon to see the little trap rattling up the drive, she had given a sigh of exasperation.

'Your aunt's coming, Rupert. Heaven knows why, she knows I dislike visitors except on my At Home days. I've a mind to tell the maid to turn her away.'

'You'll do no such thing.' Rupert, who had been reading the latest reports on the Russian incursion into Turkestan in *Punch*, leapt to his feet. 'Aunt Martha's welcome to call here any day she chooses. She's one of the family, and we don't turn family away from our door.'

'Oh well, if you'd rather see her than me,' Celia sniffed, turning aside. Rupert ignored her and strode to the door, opening it before the maid could get there. He went out smiling and caught his aunt as she hurried from the cart and stumbled against a stone.

'Come inside and tell us all about it.' He led her through the door. 'Give Annie your wrap, that's right, and come and sit by the fire. It's cold today, even though it is May.'

'Yes, there's a spiteful little wind.' Martha hurried into the parlour. 'Celia dear, how well you're looking. And how are the dear babies? I'm longing to see them again. To think that Oliver is almost a year old!' She gave them both a coy glance. 'I daresay it won't be too long before they have a sister.'

Celia turned away sharply and Rupert sighed. Only he and his wife knew how little chance there was of Thomas and Oliver ever having a sister, or yet a brother.

'Tell us this wonderful news,' he said to his aunt. 'A moment ago you were all agog.'

'Oh, I still am!' She sat down, unwinding several yards of lacy scarf from round her neck. 'Such a lovely fire!' She felt in her reticule and the pockets of her skirt. 'Now, where is it? I had it a moment ago. Oh, in my coat.' She gave Rupert an appealing look. 'Would you mind, Rupert dear? The maid's taken it'.

He laughed and rang the bell. There were a few more minutes of flurry, explanation and apology and then

Martha had the sheet of paper once more in her hand. Now all she must do was find her lorgnette, but although Rupert offered to read the letter himself, she clung to it, obviously determined to impart the news in her own way. At last she was ready.

'I hope it's going to be worth all this fuss,' Celia commented.

'Oh, it is, it is,' Martha assured her and lifted the sheet of paper to her eyes. She scanned it rapidly, seemed about to read and then lowered it dramatically and gazed from Rupert to Celia and back again.

'It's from Walter,' she announced impressively, although both had recognised the paper he used and the large, flowing handwriting upon it. 'He's going to be married!'

Their reaction to the news was everything she had hoped for. They stared at her, then at each other. Celia, who had been standing by the fireplace as a hint that Martha need not expect to stay too long, sat down rather suddenly.

'Married? *Walter*?'

Martha nodded happily. There was nothing she enjoyed more than to be the first to bring news. 'Isn't it exciting?'

'Exciting?' Celia glanced at Rupert. 'Well, it's certainly a surprise.'

'I know. He's almost forty, after all, and he's been travelling about for so long. I confess I thought he would never marry. But I'm so happy for him.' She clasped her small, plump hands together and gazed at Rupert with shining eyes. 'It's such wonderful news!'

And there speaks one who has never been married, Rupert thought, and wondered if Celia were thinking the same. What did Martha expect from the state of marriage? The same as he had himself, perhaps: entry to that magical world of warmth and affection that had so disappointingly eluded him. The world he had glimpsed when his grandfather talked of Margaret. Perhaps Martha, too, had been influenced by Timothy's memories, by his longings.

Did she not realise as she looked about at her family and friends that such expectations were rarely realised? Did she not remember Timothy's second marriage, to her own mother, and see the difference?

'I just wonder who he found to marry in the benighted places he travels in,' Celia was saying. 'Does he say who she is, Martha? I hope he's not thinking of bringing some blackamoor home with him.'

'Oh, surely not!' Martha perused the letter again, though Rupert guessed she must have read it a dozen times already. 'No, he doesn't say much about her family. Just that her name is Josephine Manders and she's been living in Darjeeling with the family of an officer.'

'A servant?' Celia asked in scandalised tones.

'Oh, I'm sure not,' Martha said. 'Surely all the servants are natives. A companion, perhaps,' she added doubtfully, and Celia sniffed and twitched her shawl closer about her shoulders. 'Well, it's to be hoped he knows what he's doing. It will be extremely difficult for us all if she's someone nobody wishes to know.'

'Does he say he's coming home?' Rupert asked, and Martha gazed at the letter again and shook her head.

'No, he doesn't. He doesn't mention it at all.'

'Well, he surely will be coming home,' Celia stated. 'He can't continue his travels with a wife and family to consider.'

'Oh!' Martha laid the letter down and gazed at them both again, her eyes brighter than ever. 'Do you suppose there will be children? I hadn't thought – it was so exciting to hear about their marriage. And with Walter almost forty . . .'

'I don't think that's any bar,' Rupert said dryly. 'It depends rather on his wife – how old she is.' Martha blushed and he chastised himself for his indelicacy. 'Children normally do occur,' he added with a glance at Celia.

'Of course. Of course. Oh, how lovely it will be.' Her voice was rapturous. 'Walter home again – and children in the house. I must begin to think about preparations. Which bedroom will they want, do you think? And a nursery for the children, of course, with a room for Nurse. Those small rooms we had when Jane and Louisa and I were girls, they must all be refurbished. I wonder where the old rocking horse is?' She was on her feet, quivering with excitement. 'Rupert dear, please will you ring for my coat again? I must get back, there's so much to do, so much to think about. Children . . .' She fluttered about the room like an agitated thrush, clasping and unclasping her hands, her eyes bright and eager at the prospect of so much to do.

Poor Aunt Martha, Rupert thought, watching her. I hope she's not doomed to disappointment. He went over and laid his hands on her shoulders.

'Now sit down, Aunt. You can't leave without having some tea. And you mustn't get too excited, you know. We're not sure that Walter will be coming home at all. He may decide to settle down in India. If his wife has always lived there, she may not like the idea of coming to a country she doesn't know. And even if he does come—'

'– he may not want you to stay at Pennington Hall,' Celia put in nastily.

There was a long pause. Rupert felt a rush of anger. The thought had entered his own mind, but he would never have put it so baldly, saw no reason to mention it at all – at this stage, anyway. He gave his wife a murderous glance.

'Oh.' Martha's hand fluttered to her throat. She turned suddenly frightened eyes on Celia, then looked at her nephew. 'Do you really think—'

'No, I don't,' Rupert said robustly. 'I don't think so at all. You've looked after the house for years and Walter was happy for you to go on doing so. He'll never turn you out. Even if he were to come back here to live, which I doubt—'

'– he'll need a housekeeper,' Celia said, as if agreeing with her husband.

'Oh, I shan't mind that,' Martha assured them hastily. 'I shan't mind that at all. I'd be glad to help, only too glad.'

'And I'm sure they'll be grateful for all the help you can give.' Rupert flung another glance at his wife. 'Nobody knows more about Pennington Hall or the area than you, Aunt Martha. But they won't expect you to be a servant and they won't turn you out of your home, of that I'm certain.' He hoped devoutly that he was right. 'And as we've already said, there's no suggestion yet that they are coming home. So I think you should stop worrying and go back to being excited, as you were when you arrived.' The door opened and the maid came in with tea. 'And now let's celebrate a little, with muffins and chocolate cake!'

'Oh yes. Yes, let's.' However excited or upset she might be, Martha's plump little body could always accommodate a hearty tea of muffins and cakes. She smiled tremulously at her nephew and mopped her eyes with a lacy handkerchief. 'I'm sorry, it's all been a little overwhelming. Reading Walter's news and hurrying over here with it straightaway – you're the first people I've told, you know – and then when Celia said – I was really beginning to wonder . . . I was really quite frightened for a moment. But as you say, Rupert, there's no need to worry really. No need at all.'

'Of course not.' He gave her a hug and went to uncover the dish of muffins. 'It's splendid news, and we must all wish Walter and his bride well.' He poured a cup of tea and handed it to her. And you and I, Celia, he

477

thought grimly, will talk about this later. You may deprive me of my rights, you may be cold and unwelcoming to your own friends and family. But you do *not* treat an innocent creature like my Aunt Martha with the cruelty you've displayed this afternoon.

He did not talk to Celia immediately. After tea, she slipped out on the pretext of needing to talk to the cook. Rupert knew quite well that this was merely an excuse – Celia never went to the kitchen at this time of day, when the servants were snatching their only chance of a rest. But there was little he could do about it, so he merely nodded as if it did not matter and took his aunt up to the nursery to see the children.

They were just finishing their own tea. A fire burned brightly in the small grate, and the table was laid in front of it. Both were in high chairs, swathed in white napkins. They looked round as Rupert and Martha came in and smiles broke over their rosy faces.

'Oh, the little darlings!' Martha exclaimed and went over to kiss the two faces, crumbed and sticky as they were. 'Don't they look sweet. There, my loves, it's your Auntie Martie come to play with you. Are you going to show me your toys?'

Rupert paused for a moment in the doorway, watching them. Here in the nursery, as the boys grew from babies to toddlers, he had begun to find the warmth he had been seeking all his life. Their unquestioning, unconditional love wrapped itself round him as the warmth of the room enfolded him, and he sat down in the big armchair by the fire and held out his arms.

The nursemaid untied both napkins, wiped the crumbs from the cheerful faces, and released them from their chairs. They immediately made for their father, Thomas now walking confidently while Oliver scrambled across the floor on hands and knees.

'They're both looking very well, Tess,' Rupert said to

the nursemaid, rocking each on a knee. He felt their bodies under his hands, both firm and pliable. 'You're taking good care of them.'

Tess blushed. She was a slender scrap of a girl, scarcely more than a child herself – seventeen, had Celia said? She had come here only a month or two ago, after the previous nursemaid had left to take care of an ageing mother, and Rupert had not had much opportunity to speak to her. Now that the tedious business of investigating the trespass was over, he hoped to have more leisure, though he was gloomily aware that the processes of law were likely to take up even more time. But he was determined to have time to spend with his family. They would grow up all too soon, and there seemed little hope of more to follow them.

'They're lovely babies, sir,' Tess said shyly. 'I've got little brothers of me own, but these two are, well, they're sort of special, if you know what I mean, sir.'

'They are special,' Martha said fondly. 'They're the loveliest babies I've ever seen.'

Rupert smiled. 'They're special to me, too. But then I'm their father, so they would be.'

'Oh, but it ain't – I mean, it's not always that way.' Celia had decided that Tess must learn to speak well, to avoid the boys growing up with a local accent, and she was trying hard to remember her lessons. 'A lot of fathers never come near the nursery – wouldn't recognise their babies if they met them in the street. Not like you, sir.'

'They're fools then.' Oliver had his fingers in Rupert's hair, pulling it to look at it better. 'Yes, it's black, isn't it? Not like yours.' Both boys had the rich tawny hair of their mother. 'No, don't pull too hard, I'd like to keep it a little longer, if you don't mind.' He tickled Oliver's fat stomach and the baby laughed uproariously.

'Would you like a cup of tea, sir?' Tess asked diffidently. 'Miss Reid? The pot's still hot.'

Rupert opened his mouth to say no; he had already drunk three cups downstairs. But tea made a good excuse to linger in the nursery, playing with his boys and enjoying the company of his aunt, relaxed and happy now that she was away from Celia's critical presence. He was reluctant to leave the cosy warmth of the room and its cheerful occupants.

'Yes, I'd like a cup of tea,' he said and watched as Tess poured it. She set it on the small table by his side and he put the children on the floor while he drank it.

'Show Papa your bricks,' Tess said, and they fetched an assortment of coloured wooden blocks and began to pile them up haphazardly. 'No, build a house. Like you did when your auntie was here.' She knelt on the floor, her brown hair falling over her face as she bent to help the small fingers. Rupert looked at her, wondering what it was about her that gave him such a feeling of warmth. She was not beautiful, scarcely even pretty; her slim body was almost like a boy's, her hair and eyes quite an ordinary brown. But her cheeks were rosy and healthy, her lips smiled readily to show white teeth and there was an air of freshness about her that he found attractive. He felt glad she was in charge of his children and hoped she would stay a long time.

'Tell me about your family, Tess,' he said suddenly. 'Do they live far away? How many brothers and sisters do you have?'

'Oh, I lose count of them!' she said with a laugh. 'Ten of us, there are. I'm third – I've got two older brothers. So it was me had to help Mother with the little ones. And she lost a few too – you know the way things are.'

Rupert nodded. 'She's done well to keep ten living. How old are they?'

'Well, the youngest, little Bobby, he's the same age as Thomas here. And the oldest, Dick, he's near twenty now. He helps Father on the farm.'

'So you're a farmer's daughter.'

'That's right, sir. Grew up helping all over the place – in the dairy, in the fields, wherever I was wanted. But mostly with the children, till my sisters were old enough to help too.'

'And that's why you're so good with Thomas and Oliver.'

Tess blushed and cuddled Oliver against her. 'Oh, I love little ones, sir. I'd like a nursery full of 'em – me own. *My* own,' she corrected herself, and gave him a shy look.

Rupert smiled. 'Do you have a young man?' He hoped not. He wanted to keep her in his own home, looking after his children.

'No, sir, not yet. Mother says it's better to wait a while. And I haven't met anyone I like well enough anyway.'

'Very sensible of you,' Martha commented from the floor, where she was now sitting with Oliver. The pins were coming out of her hair and it fell around her face, making her look suddenly younger. Why, she's not much older than Elinor, Rupert thought in sudden surprise. Six years, seven? He wondered if she had ever loved a man, if she had known the torment and the delight, the ecstasy and the disillusionment. 'It's always a mistake to marry someone you don't really love,' she went on. 'That's the only real reason for marriage, in my belief. Otherwise it's better to stay single.'

'It's hard for a woman, though,' Tess said. 'Being single.' She seemed to realise suddenly what she had said, and blushed. 'I'm sorry, miss. I didn't mean—'

'It doesn't matter at all. I'm perfectly happy as I am. I can do as I like, live as I please.' Martha held Oliver against her. 'And if I can borrow a baby or two once in a while . . . You must bring them to see me, Tess. Often. Come on your afternoon walks sometimes.'

'I'd like to.' Tess's face glowed with pleasure and Rupert had the feeling that he was witnessing the beginning of a friendship. Martha being familiar with the servants again, he thought, and yet why not? Tess was a nice girl, warm-hearted and intelligent enough to make a friend worth having. And Martha would be a comfort to her when she missed her family, as she'd been a comfort to him when he was younger.

He looked at the two children, tumbling on the rug together. They were happy as he never remembered being happy himself. All he could recall of his early childhood was a few blurred memories of having to sit still, to eat food he disliked, and to remain silent when his father came to see him. There was none of this happy play, for he had no other child to play with. If it had not been for Tilly, he would never have known that there was warmth to seek.

Tilly herself had gone long since. She had been given a pension soon after Elinor and Nicholas had married and departed to live in a cottage near Arnside, with a sister. For a time, Rupert had visited her, but then the visits had become less frequent and one day he had heard she was dead. It was one more thing to feel guilty about.

Tess would, he thought, give his children the warmth that Tilly had given him, for although Celia had wanted sons and no doubt loved them in her own way, her way was cool. Rupert did not want his sons growing up as he did, gazing in through a frosty window.

The quarrel with Celia was all he had expected it to be – ugly, angry and ultimately frustrating. Her icy coolness was something he found almost impossible to deal with. The colder she grew, the more angry he became, even though he was aware that when angry he began to bluster and lose his temper, while Celia retained a maddening composure. In the end, as he always did, he flung out of the room and stormed out to the stable to fetch his horse. A gallop on the moor was the only thing that could soothe him after one of these furious encounters.

For Celia was as furious as he was. It was simply that she expressed it in a different way. And he knew that once again he had spoiled all chances of being allowed back into her bed.

Why should I want to go back anyway? he asked himself, digging his heels into his horse's sides. There's no love between me and Celia now, she no longer has any attraction for me. I doubt if I could satisfy myself, let alone her. I would simply make a fool of myself and give her yet more ammunition for saying what an ineffective husband I am.

So, the question rose once again in his mind: Must I live the rest of my life celibate?

He thought again of the alternatives. Whores in Barrow, Ulverston or Kendal. A kept mistress, tucked away in a little house in some back street. A series of seductions – housemaids, dairy girls.

Or Elinor.

Chapter Twenty-Eight

'I knew you'd come back,' she said, sitting up in bed. 'Eventually.'

Rupert gazed at her. Her back was as smooth as it had ever been, her spine and shoulder blades delicately outlined in the creamy skin below the mane of her hair. But her waist was a little thicker than he remembered it and her heavy breasts sagged a little more. And when she sat over him, he looked up at a face that now showed a few lines, and an abdomen that wrinkled oddly with the movement of the muscles inside.

But there was no ageing in the way Elinor made love, no lessening of her energy or enjoyment. Indeed, there was added pleasure in the discovery that he need no longer take the care that had always been necessary – Elinor told him that her childbearing days were over. They could now lie together without fear, and forget the need for an abrupt withdrawal when their bodies most wanted to stay together.

He lifted one hand and trailed his finger down her spine. The guilt would come, he knew, but for now he was able to luxuriate in the sensations that only making love with Elinor had ever given him. He wondered how he had managed to do without them for so long. The excitement of her body, the delight of her caresses, the ecstasy which seemed to take them both to some peak of sensation, as if they had suddenly arrived on the shining mountaintop of the world – all seemed essential, as if to lose them now would be to lose life itself.

And yet . . . there was always the aftermath, the feeling of something still missing, the emptiness that should have been filled – but with what? He knew that there was something he still sought, something that he needed, but he was beginning to doubt now that it could ever be found. Or even if he would recognise it if it came.

Elinor turned and looked down at him. Her face was still flushed, her hair dishevelled. She looked heavy-eyed and sated, and he felt a sudden repulsion.

'I'm sorry,' he said, sitting up and swinging his legs off the bed. 'I'm sorry, Elinor. This has been a mistake. I shouldn't have come here.'

She stared at him. 'What do you mean? Rupert, what's wrong? What have I done?'

'Nothing. It's not your fault.' But in his heart he despised her. 'It's just a mistake, that's all. We should have stayed away from each other.'

Her face was white now, her mouth half-open. She watched unbelievingly as he began to dress, and then jumped off the bed and flung her arms round him.

'Rupert! You can't go like this. Why, it's been so good. You don't know what these last two weeks have meant to me.' She pressed her naked body against him and he felt the softness of her breast, the curve of her hips. 'I need you, Rupert,' she whispered, pressing her mouth against his ear, probing with the tip of her tongue. 'You don't know what it's been like all this time, seeing you with *her* and knowing that you were really mine. You *are* mine, Rupert—'

'I'm married,' he interrupted, 'and so are you.'

'We belong together just the same. You're mine, I'm yours. It doesn't matter about anyone else. You know it's true, Rupert. You know we belong together.' She turned and looked at the bed. 'Haven't we just proved it?'

485

Rupert was silent for a moment. Then he said quietly, 'All we've proved, Elinor, is that we can enjoy each other's bodies. But I need more than that. And perhaps you do too. I don't even know exactly what it is but I know we'll never find it with each other.'

Elinor stared at him. Then her expression changed, grew hard and angry. She dropped her arms and stood quite still, facing him.

'I see. So you're leaving me again.'

'I'm afraid so.'

'Afraid?' she mocked him. 'Afraid! Yes, that's exactly what you are, Rupert, what you always have been. Ever since I first came to this house, you've been afraid. You were afraid that first afternoon, weren't you? And not just afraid, you were terrified! But I had patience with you then. Oh, you were so ignorant, so clumsy, not at all like your friend Curtis, but you learned well. Everything you know, you learned from me and I suppose *she*'s been reaping the benefit. And now something's gone wrong between you, or perhaps you're just tired of her, so you come running back to me. Only I'm not good enough any more, am I?' Rupert tried to interrupt her again, but she was past hearing him, her eyes flaming, her voice rising as the tirade went on. 'I'm too old. You see a difference between her body and mine. That's the truth of it, isn't it? You've decided to find someone younger, but I'll tell you this, Rupert. Youth isn't everything. Young girls don't know how to satisfy a man the way an older woman does. The way *I* do.'

'I've told you, it's nothing to do with that.'

'Then what is it?'

Rupert gazed at her. Then he said quietly, 'I can't tell you, Elinor. I only know that it's something I desperately need. And I won't find it here.'

He pulled on his jacket and then laid his hands on her bare shoulders, looking down into her eyes. He felt a great sadness for her, and for himself. And for Celia and

Nicholas too. The four of them, caught in this web, each needing something none of the others could give. Was this what happened in every marriage? Was everyone trapped like this?

'I really am sorry, Elinor,' he said. 'I know you've given me a lot, risked everything. But it's too late now for us.' Too late for any of us, he thought. 'Let's not have any bitterness between us.'

She met his eyes contemptuously, then twisted away from his hands. Her body was still a fine one, he thought, and felt sorry that it was not being fulfilled as it should be. He reached to touch her again, but she moved sharply out of reach.

'Very well, Rupert. Go if you must. But don't be mealy-mouthed about it. Don't try to soothe me as if I were a child.' Her voice was hard. 'And don't ask me not to be bitter, or to remain your friend. A woman's toleration has its limits, and you did this to me before.'

They stood silent for a moment, then Rupert made to speak again. But before the first word had left his mouth, she turned on him, her face working with fury, her eyes ablaze.

'Go! Go on, get out! Get back to your insipid little wife and see if she can give you what I gave you not an hour since. And when you find she can't, don't come running back to me for comfort, for there's none here for you any more. You've taken your last fill of me, and I don't want to see you again. Do you hear that? Never again!'

Her voice had risen to a scream and Rupert cast an anxious glance at the door. Surely the noise would bring servants running. He hesitated, hardly knowing what to do, reluctant even now to leave her in this condition. But Elinor was past all reason. She turned to the washstand and lifted the big blue jug in both hands. She raised it above her head.

He was outside the door before it smashed against the

wall, exactly where his head had been. He stood for a moment, quite still, waiting for the crash of the bowl which would surely follow it, waiting for the sound of running feet. But there was silence. And then he heard muffled sobbing.

Slowly, he opened the door again and peered in. Elinor was lying on the bed, face down, her shoulders shaking.

For a moment, he hesitated still, feeling that he should go and comfort her. But what comfort could he give? There was only one kind that Elinor understood, and he feared his own weakness. He turned and went softly down the stairs.

As he rode slowly home, trying to dissipate the horror and guilt that haunted his mind, he thought of the one place where he could find peace and comfort and the warmth he needed.

He would go to the nursery and play with his children. And talk a while with Tess, their nursemaid.

'We've evidence enough now,' Rupert said. 'Abe and I took three of our older men through the workings last week. They recognised several of the places in one of our own old diggings, where Rawlings' men have been robbing out. An old ginnel where they used to eat their bait, timbers they knew were the sort Grandfather used. And those tunnels led on to the new horizons where Rawlings has been taking ore. It's plain robbery and can't be denied.'

'So why don't they settle? Why let you take them to court?' Nicholas drew his horse level with Rupert's and came to a halt as they gazed out across the Duddon estuary. They had ridden over to Dunnerholme to give their horses some exercise. The early morning sun threw the broad shadow of Kirkby Moor across the shore in front of them and Rupert thought of the picture his mother had painted from this very spot, of wide, rippling sands. And as he thought of it, he looked across and saw what she had seen on the afternoon when she had painted it: the long, dark trail of a travelling fair on the move.

But there was a difference in the scene. Louisa's gipsies had used only horses and carts, pitching their camp in tents. These travellers making their way slowly across the sands towards him boasted wagons – small houses on wheels, in which whole families could sleep, cook and live. They were to be seen more and more now at fairs, gaily painted with yellow or blue sides and wheels of red. If his mother had seen them, he thought, what a picture she could have made. But probably she had never seen an encampment close to. Girls of her background would never have been allowed near the gipsies.

But by all accounts his mother had been wild and free, roaming where she liked across the windy moors. Wasn't it likely enough that she had met the gipsies? And he remembered what Elinor had told him about his real father: *Nicholas thought it might be a tinker or a gipsy*. He recalled, too, Nicholas's words, uttered in a moment of fury: *She and her tinker*. Had she not only met the gipsies but known them well – known one of them all too well?

He glanced sideways at Nicholas, wondering if he was remembering too, if he also gazed at this long trail of carts, horses and wagons, and thought of Louisa.

'Oh, they'll settle,' Rupert said, bringing his mind back to Nicholas's question. 'It's just a question of frightening them enough to get the best figure. I've no intention of letting them get away with it. It's not just ore they've stolen, it's the work my men would have had in mining it. Their men have lived well and grown fat on what mine should have been earning. In fact, I feel I ought really to be reimbursing the men for what they've lost.'

'Sentimental nonsense!' Nicholas snorted. 'And quite unworkable. How would you decide which men would have been employed in those mines had you opened them up yourself? And they've all been in full employment, haven't they? You haven't actually laid any off?'

'No,' Rupert admitted. 'But I might have taken more on.'

'And how would you reimburse them?' Nicholas demanded. 'Men who don't even work for you! Why, they'd probably have been the same ones who dug out the ore anyway. Consider the miners paid, whoever paid them, and take your profit. You've earned it. You're the one who's spent time and money investigating this affair. You're letting sentiment confuse you over this, Rupert.'

'Yes. You're probably right.' Rupert laid his hand on his horse's neck. He was still watching the gipsies. At first no more than black, distant figures, they were now becoming clearly discernible. Brightly painted wagons, their wheels making tracks in the sand. Horses drawing the wagons, horses being ridden or led. And people walking – women, men, children. A large family, extending beyond the usual limit of parents and children, uncles and aunts. A family that enfolded families, a travelling community that took its identity with it wherever it went. A community in which every person knew his place, every person belonged.

Did he belong? Was he one of them? He felt a sudden longing to join this secret group of families. To be done with the cares and anxieties of mining, to live life on the open road, moving leisurely from place to place, sleeping under the stars and making a living by his wits. Precarious it might be, but how little he would bow to any man, how petty would seem the worries that haunted him at night. The warmth of that community, that family of families, would enclose and comfort him, and that would be sufficient.

'Let's go back,' he said abruptly, and turned his

490

horse's head. 'It's a long ride and I've work to do. And we should get the beasts home before it gets too hot.' By the time he reached Garth House, he thought, the children would be up and about, perhaps at breakfast in the nursery or playing in the garden or out walking with Tess. He might just be in time to enjoy half an hour with them before starting the day's work.

They had become the focus of his life now, Thomas, Oliver – and Tess.

'You know how I feel about you,' he said to her that afternoon. They were sitting under the apple tree in the orchard. The two boys were asleep on a mattress spread under a nearby tree and Tess was in a wicker chair, her lap full of small garments to be mended. Rupert sat on the grass, his arms looped round drawn-up knees. He looked up at her and caught her startled glance and saw the blush rise in her cheek.

'Sir, you mustn't say such things.'

'I must. How can I not say them, when they are true?' He reached up and took her hand. She tried to draw it away, glancing anxiously about her, but he held it fast. 'No one can see us. We can hear if anyone comes through the gate. Tess, do you really not know how much you mean to me?'

'Sir, please. I'm just a nursemaid.'

'No,' he said, 'you are not just a nursemaid. You're a lovely young woman. You're warm and loving and honest and natural. You're—'

'*Sir!*' she protested.

'Everything about you pleases me,' he went on. 'The way you walk, the way you smile, the little frown on your forehead when you're thinking about something. The way you look after my children, the way you pick them up when they fall and soothe them with kisses . . . I should like to be soothed with kisses, Tess.'

She gazed at him and he saw distress in her eyes, but

the distress was mixed with joy and he knew that he could win her if he chose.

He hesitated. The temptation to take her in his arms and kiss her was almost overwhelming. But could he stop at a kiss? His longing had been suppressed for so long, he doubted whether it could be restrained once the barrier had been lifted. He let her hand go and clasped his hands tightly round his knees again. He wanted her badly – now. He wanted her so much, he dared not touch her.

'Oh, sir,' she whispered, and her voice trembled. She had dropped her mending in her lap and raised her hands to cheeks that burned scarlet. Her eyes were bright, her lashes glittering.

'It's all right, Tess,' he said quietly. 'I'll do nothing to hurt you, nothing to cause you harm. I know it's impossible for us. But I want you to know that for me you are the only woman in the world. I've never truly loved yet, but I love you. I wondered if I even knew what love meant, but I know it now. If I could marry you, I would.' He reached up again and touched her hand, and this time she let it lie, turning hers over so that the two palms lay together. 'I can't marry you, Tess. But I'll love you till the end of my life.'

A tear dropped from her eye and fell like a blessing on their clasped hands. For a few moments, both were silent, then she said in a shaking voice, 'I think I love you too, sir. Oh, I know I shouldn't say it—'

'Say it,' he urged her, almost losing possession of himself. 'Oh Tess, say it, say it! You don't know what it means to me, to hear those words spoken with truth, to hear them from your dear lips. Nobody has ever said them before, not from their heart. Oh Tess, Tess. My darling Tess . . .'

She was out of her chair and in his arms. He laid his palm under her cheek and began to cover her face with rapid kisses. He felt her shudder against him as she turned her head, kissing him in return. With a groan that seemed to force its way up from his very soul, he took her soft, trembling lips and held her close, straining his whole body against her in his desperate need to convey the depth, the strength, the infinity of his love.

A faint murmuring cry brought him back to reality. Dazed, he lifted his head and stared around him.

Were they really still in the orchard? Surely the sun was brighter now, the grass greener, the songs of the birds more tuneful? Perhaps time had slipped by without their noticing during those few rapturous kisses. Or perhaps time had been away and somewhere else, and they were now in some different world, where all was possible.

The murmur came again and this time Tess moved, slipping quickly from his arms and moving over to the blanket that lay spread on the ground only a few yards away.

'Oliver. It's all right, pet. Don't cry, Tess is here.' She picked the baby up and cradled him against her, holding his cheek against the cheek that Rupert had kissed only moments before, his body against the breast that Rupert had touched. 'It's all right, my lovey. It's all right.'

The baby stopped crying. He looked over Tess's shoulder at his father and smiled. And Rupert knew that the kisses he and Tess had just shared must be their last.

He could not, for the sake of his own desires, risk his children losing the nursemaid who was so much a mother to them. He could not risk Tess losing her job. For there was nothing else he could offer her. Nothing.

He held out his arms for his son, and Tess put Oliver into them. She met his eyes gravely and he knew that she understood.

It had begun again. Nicholas was certain of it. After almost twenty years of marriage, he knew when Elinor had begun a new attachment, and the signs were unmistakably there. The extra glow about her skin, the shine on her hair, the secret triumph that looked sideways out of her eyes. There was some subtle differences, too, in the way she stood and walked, the way her body was held upright, and the way she lifted her head. She looked like this whenever she embarked on a new love affair, but never so much as when she was cuckolding him with his own son. No, not his son, he reminded himself bitterly. The bastard his first wife had foisted upon him.

Had they started their liàison again? Had Rupert tired of his wife and turned back to Elinor? Did he slip into the house when Nicholas was absent and go to her bed? Nicholas tormented himself with thoughts of what they did there. He imagined Elinor, naked, clasped in Rupert's arms, her legs wound round his body. His own desire, for so long dormant, rose again at the thought and shocked him. How could he want her after all her faithlessness? Why should the thought of her and Rupert together rouse his own passion? But the treacherous heat spread through his loins and he twisted uncomfortably in his bed at night, thinking of her in the next room.

Over the years a tenuous relationship, based almost entirely on their interest in business, had formed between himself and Rupert. As a young man, Nicholas had felt little interest in business affairs; he had been spoiled at home, allowed to have his own way and given whatever he desired without being taught where the money came from to pay for his whims. But after Louisa's death, he had felt in need of occupation and had developed an interest in his father's business.

He had never wished to move to Liverpool and take it over completely but had taken an active part in its management. Rather to his own surprise, he had begun to enjoy it. And although at first he had been contemptuous of Rupert's ability to manage the mines, he had soon been forced to admit that the boy was making a

494

good job of it and had been more willing to treat him as an equal in discussion. The result had been that Rupert had been more inclined to talk to him, and both had felt the gain.

Now that relationship was under threat once more. Since Rupert's marriage, Nicholas had been able to suppress his jealous anger over Rupert's suspected affair with Elinor, as he had been forced to suppress so much anger and so many jealousies. But now . . .

It was all happening again! He was sure of it. The way Elinor was looking and behaving could only mean that she had a lover. It need not, he knew, be Rupert, but his instinct told him that it was. And when he saw them together, he was certain.

The look in Rupert's eyes, the heightened colour in his cheeks, the quality of his very voice – it all added up to guilt and fuelled Nicholas's silent rage.

But it was short-lived. No sooner had Nicholas begun to suspect than it seemed it was over. Elinor's over-bright eyes and brittle tension implied anger rather than passion. She was distant and irritable. Rupert came less to the house, and when he did he behaved with an awkwardness that was as guilty as his former evasiveness.

Clearly, for some reason their affair had not been a success this time. Perhaps Elinor was at last becoming too old, her attractions fading. Perhaps now, realising this, she would turn back to him.

Again the old passion stirred within him, and Nicholas wondered whether it might yet grow to its former strength. To hold Elinor in his arms again, to feel her skin warm against his, to know once more the burgeoning excitement, the crescendo, the soaring climax . . .

He watched her for signs. He let his fingers brush hers when passing her a glass of wine, or a dish at supper. He came into the room where she was sitting and stayed with her rather than retiring to the library. He looked directly into her eyes when he talked to her, and he complimented her on her clothes, her hair, her jewels.

It did not occur to him that he was courting her. And perhaps it did not occur to Elinor either. But slowly, very slowly, she began to respond.

At the same time, Rupert had begun to pay court to his own wife.

With Tess in the house and always present when he visited his children, it was impossible to forget his love for her even for a moment. But if he could not do that, he could conceal it from all others, and the person from whom it was most important to hide it was Celia. For Celia held Tess's livelihood in her hands. At her whim, the nursemaid could be dismissed from the house, sent penniless and without a reference into the world, and Rupert would never see her again.

But he was finding his enforced celibacy more and more difficult to tolerate. Somehow, with someone, he must find relief. And if it could not be with Tess, it must be with his wife. There was, for Rupert, no alternative.

Whatever he did, he knew it would bring guilt. Whichever woman he lay with, he would feel faithless. If he went to Tess, he was in the eyes of the law and, presumably, God, betraying his wife. If he went to his wife's bed, he was in his own eyes betraying the woman he truly loved. Guilt would find new reason to haunt him; but guilt had been his most steadfast companion since he was a child and he scarcely knew what life would be like without it.

Besides, he wanted more children. He wanted more sons to grow into men, and he wanted daughters. If he could not have the warmth he craved with Tess, then he would seek it in children. And the only person who could give him those children was Celia.

Like Nicholas, he started to make the little signals of courtship. The tiny, almost accidental touches, the slightly lingering glances, the small courtesies and attentions. Celia's response was exactly as he had expected – she took them all as her right, as the least a husband should do, without making any overtures of her own. But since their marriage, she had never been any different; and, thinking back to the days of their long engagement, he had to admit that she had never been very forthcoming, accepting his kisses rather than sharing them, submitting to his caresses rather than returning them.

All the same, she was his wife. He had his legal rights and if he must not betray her, then neither must she keep herself aloof.

At last his longings became too much for him. It was a night of full moon, the harvest moon, full and golden in the dark sky. It had been shining across his bed for the past three nights, keeping him awake with its brilliance, his mind tormented by thoughts of Tess in her small room up in the nursery. His body burned as if with a fever and he knew that there would be no peace for him until he had broken his long fast. He went to the door and stood hesitating. A few yards along the passage was the door to Celia's room. And not much further than that were the stairs which would take him to Tess.

He stood wrestling with his desire. The stairs stretched above him, their darkness half lit by the moon which streamed in through a landing window. Was she, too, lying awake, watching the moon and yearning for him? Did she listen for his steps on the stairs, imagining that every creak might be made by his feet? Was she aching, burning, for something she hardly knew, as he burned for what he knew all too well? Would she welcome him if he came to her now?

It would take only a minute to climb silently up those

half-lit stairs, a minute to slip into her bed. And then she would be in his arms, her body close against his, her lips whispering against his and her fingers in his hair.

He stood a full minute, his hand on the newel post at the bottom of the stairs. And then he turned and went into his wife's bedroom.

Chapter Twenty-Nine

With fury in every step, Elinor strode along the shore at Bardsea. The tide had recently dropped, leaving a wave of huge, translucent jellyfish stranded on the beach. Distastefully, she picked her way past them and down to the firm wet sands. Her boots left angry prints on the ripples, the heels dug firmly in and little jabbing arrowheads left by the toes.

Why did this have to happen to her? Why, after all these years, must she be caught unawares? She, who had taken so many risks yet always been careful in this respect. She had been so certain she was safe. And it had been so good not to have to take precautions.

Perhaps she was wrong. Perhaps the signs she had noticed were not what she had thought at all. Perhaps she was simply panicking over nothing.

But her instincts told her that this was no empty panic. She might not have the most positive sign of all to guide her, but there were plenty of others. The fullness in her breasts. The burning indigestion that came each evening. The odd little fainting attack only a few days ago. And, most of all, the nausea that washed over her every morning as soon as she stepped out of bed.

Elinor had only been pregnant once in her life, but she knew the signs as well as any mother of ten. And she could not, dared not, ignore them.

What could she do? She stared unseeingly across the sands towards Lancaster and the hills beyond. It was a clear, sunny morning and the sun would soon be hot. But there were no answers for her in the cry of the seabirds and the ripple of the tide. It's your problem, they seemed to say. Deal with it yourself.

What were the alternatives? She played with the idea of ridding herself of her burden. There were ways and means. Potions one could take. She had heard that the gipsies were back again – hadn't Nicholas told her he and Rupert had seen them only a short time ago, coming across Duddon Sands? Gipsies could often help with such things and, staying so short a time, would not pass on gossip as a local woman might. In any case, she knew of no local potion-mixer, though undoubtedly they existed. And who could she ask? Who could she trust?

Besides, it was dangerous. Elinor had heard of more than one woman who had taken such a potion and died from it. And others whose attempts to rid themselves of an unwelcome pregnancy had resulted in a maimed child. She had no wish for either of those things to happen to her.

No. She would have to bear the child. And she must make Nicholas believe it was his.

The sticky mass of the jellyfish had come to an end. Elinor walked up the beach again and sat down on a flat rock. She rested her elbows on her knees and her chin on her clenched fists and stared moodily across the bay.

Nicholas had been impotent for years. It was a long time since he had come to her bed, and long before that since he had been successful in it. She remembered seemingly endless nights of struggling attempts to penetrate her with an organ so limp that it seemed remarkable that it had ever been capable of functioning. Would it be possible, after all this time, to rouse Nicholas sufficiently to convince him that he was the father of her child? It must be done quickly, too. She must be almost two months' pregnant now. Another month and it would be too late, for how could she convince him, even if she went to full term, that the baby was his? Six-month children seldom lived and were small in any case. And if she gave birth early, and the child survived . . . No, if Nicholas were to believe he was the father, it must be soon.

Tonight.

She turned and walked back along the beach, scarcely noticing the jellyfish now. For the past few weeks, Nicholas had been more friendly, even affectionate. Several times she had noticed his fingers brushing hers as he passed her something, more than once she had caught him watching her in a way he had not since early in their marriage, and occasionally he had even made some flattering remark about her appearance. Perhaps it would be less difficult than she had feared to entice him back to her bed. But, once in it, would he be able to perform?

And if not, what then?

There was no moon on the night when Rupert finally relinquished his last scrap of control and let himself into Tess's bedroom.

She was waiting for him, cool and trembling as he slipped into bed beside her. Her body was as sweet as he had known it would be, slim as a boy's yet with breasts that were firm in spite of their smallness. Like little ripe apples, he thought, touching them with his lips, and more delicious than many a fuller fruit. He leaned over her, cradling her in his arms, and stroked her hair back from her forehead. The light from the candle showed the glow of her wide eyes, the pale softness of her skin. She lifted her lips towards him and he bent and kissed them tenderly, almost reverently.

For Tess, he knew, this was the first time. It was a special time, the time no one ever forgot, good or bad. And for her it must be good. It must be a memory ever sweet, a treasure to keep in her mind into old age and beyond. The first time of making love could never come again; it was not to be thrown lightly away. And he knew a moment of regret that it was not the first time for him also, a memory they could share in full. But, failing that, he could make it a night of magic. He could love Tess with all the tenderness she deserved, with all the passion he felt, holding back his own desires until he knew she was ready.

His joy surpassed anything he had known before. Even as he touched and kissed Tess's silky skin, he could feel the difference, in both her and himself. This was no lustful search for gratification; this was the coming together of two people who loved each other. This was a generous giving on both sides, a sensitivity to each other's responses. As he let his fingers move gently over her shoulders, her belly, her waist, he could feel the quiver that meant he had found a spot which gave her especial delight. And when he slid his hands down her spine, barely touching the fragile bones, and felt her shiver against him, he knew that she had cast aside her fears and was as eager for their loving as he himself.

But it must not be too quick. He was ready now, but forced himself to wait. And in waiting, took pleasure in the shape of her, the feel and the smell of her. He stroked her body, her thighs, the inner side of her knees, and her small, quivering feet; and then his lips followed where his fingers had led, seeking out the hollow places, the places where thin skin gave extra sensation, laying his lips on the softness of her and brushing his mouth across her ankles, her insteps, each separate toe.

For a while he avoided that most secret, most sensitive area where he most longed to be. His own passion running high, he knew that to touch her there would be almost unbearable. And yet he must, for she needed that last touch to set her afire. She was luxuriating in his kisses now, but he wanted her ablaze and he thanked all his experience now for the fact that this was not his first time and that he knew how to set her alight.

He let his fingers slip between her thighs. For a moment, she stiffened against him and then relaxed with a small whimper. His fingertips moved against her, feeling the soft, moist warmth of her, finding the shape he sought. She was lying quite still, only gasping a little; but as he continued his stroking, she began to move against him, twisting a little and clinging to him. The fire was beginning, he thought with a leap of excitement, and knew that he could not wait much longer. Yet wait he must, for it would be inhuman to stop now and take his own pleasure; and again the waiting proved worthwhile, for in a few moments Tess gave a little cry and quivered violently in his arms and, with a swift movement, he had raised himself over her and was making his first thrust.

Even now, he thought amidst the whirling of his brain, he must be careful lest he hurt or frighten her. But the fragile barrier parted as if waiting only for his touch, and Tess cried out again and gripped his shoulders. And then there was no barrier at all, no pain, no fear, and he knew from her whispers, from her touch, from her movements beneath and around him that this, at last, was what he had always sought. This was the loving that would bring him the fulfilment and the warmth that he needed. This was the woman he had been born to love.

The next day, strolling along the shore where Elinor had walked so furiously only a day or two before, Rupert was still bemused. It had been so perfect, so exactly right. In trying to make it magical for her, he had made it an enchantment for them both. In taking time, he had been given ecstasy; in exploring her whole body with tenderness, he had discovered more than he had suspected. In holding back, he had multiplied both her desires and his own, until that final moment when he had thrown away all restraint and allowed his body at last to have its way. And Tess, clinging to his shoulders, had begun to move

503

with him, sharing the rhythm so that together they swung high in shared emotion, shared delight. And the rapture between them had become a force of its own, lifting them to a height he had never reached before. The world and time were nowhere. There was only this enchantment, which could have lasted an eternity and yet still have been all too brief.

Nothing had prepared him for this. Certainly not that disastrous night with Celia . . .

Rupert shuddered a little as he remembered that moonlit night. He thought of the long moments he had stood at the foot of the stairs, longing to go to Tess. And of how he had turned, instead, and entered his wife's room.

Celia had been in bed. The candle was out and the moonlight lay across her quilt, broken into squares by the panes of the window. As he came in she lifted herself in the bed and he saw her face, white in the glimmering darkness, and her eyes staring across the room.

'Rupert? Is it you?'

'Who else would it be?' But his attempt at a joke fell flat in the chilly room. He came to stand beside the bed, looking down at her.

'What do you want? Why have you come?'

He felt a flash of irritation. 'What do you think I want? Why does a husband come to his wife's room?' He bent and pulled back the covers, revealing her in a long nightgown of white cambric, frilled with lace and ribbons. 'A pretty sight,' he said, 'but for whom is it intended?' He began to unfasten the ribbons that tied her neck. 'You might as well be dressed in sackcloth for all the pleasure you give with your frills and flounces.'

'And am I not allowed to give myself pleasure?' she asked coldly, making no move either to assist or prevent him. 'May I ask you not to do that, Rupert? I've told you, I want no more children.'

'But I do. And even if we had no more, I am not

prepared to lie alone, night after night. I'm a young man still, Celia, with years of life before me. Am I to spend them like a monk? Or do you wish me to take a mistress, or go to whores?' He stared down at her, hoping to have shocked her, hoping for anger, even disgust, any response that would show she had feelings. But Celia merely stared icily back.

'You must do whatever you wish about that, Rupert. I've told you, two sons are enough for me. Yes, I know I said I'd like more, but that was before Oliver was born. You do not know what it is like to have children. Oliver nearly killed me. And I am not prepared to endure it again.'

'Then I will ensure you don't have to,' he said, his voice shaking a little. 'But I will have my rights, Celia. I *must*.'

'At risk of my life?'

'At risk of my sanity,' he said, and threw himself upon her.

Thinking of it afterwards had turned him cold. Even with Celia, even with the desperation he had been feeling for so long, he would never have dreamed he could be so brutal. And if she had resisted him he feared he might have killed her. But instead she simply lay there while he carried out his assault, for assault it was, he thought, even though in the eyes of the law he had every right to do as he had done. Every right to kiss her with a roughness that amounted to biting, every right to squeeze her breasts between his fingers, every right to thrust himself into her without care.

It was over very quickly. With Celia so cold and quiescent, there was no incentive to stroke and caress her into life. From past experience, he knew such efforts would merely bring sighs of exasperation rather than pleasure, and a hand which would push his away rather than urge him on. And his own body, starved for the love he so desperately needed, would not let him linger.

In anger as well as need, he thrust rapidly to a climax that left him shuddering.

He rose and dressed, aware of Celia's face looking up at him, cold and still as marble. And when he left her room, he knew that it was for the last time. He would never go to her again.

For the rest of that summer, he and Tess met whenever they could. Forgotten were the reasons why they could never be together; sitting on the rocks as Thomas and Oliver played with sea shells, they planned a future they knew must be impossible. Running away together – 'We'll take the children, of course' – living in a tiny cottage somewhere, going abroad, all these and other, even wilder schemes, presented themselves. Rupert began to believe that it would happen, that he would leave everything behind, all that he had ever known, and take Tess away with him to live as people should live, in closeness and harmony, with the rest of the world well lost.

'We'll have our own family,' he said, wishing that he dared slip his arm round her waist and hold her close. But who knew what eyes might be watching? 'Tom and Olly will come with us, of course, but they'll be our eldest sons. There'll be others, sons and daughters of our own.' He remembered Celia's words and gave her an anxious glance. 'Unless you don't want – I know it can be painful, even dangerous, having babies—'

'Not for me,' Tess said confidently. 'We have babies easy in our family. Just like shelling peas, my mum says. Anyway,' she gave him a smiling glance, ''tis soon over, and worth it.'

Rupert looked at her. He felt a swelling within him, as if his heart were about to burst, and then, no longer caring who might be watching, he drew her close and kissed her. For a moment, he held her against him, feeling her heart pound under his, and as he rested his cheek against hers he felt her hand lightly stroke his face.

And he knew that in that touch he had found all the love and warmth he had been seeking for so long. No longer was he standing in the cold, looking through a frosty window at the merriment within. Because of Tess, he had come inside, drawn near the fire and could never be excluded again.

'Tess,' he said, his voice trembling, 'we'll make it all come true. We *will* go away together. We'll live together for the rest of our lives, and I'll make you happy. I swear it.'

She looked up at him and smiled, and he wondered how he had ever thought her ordinary. Had she grown in beauty, or had his eyes been closed? If so, they were open now.

'I'll make you happy too,' she said, but there was a tiny hesitation in her voice and a shadow in her eyes. She doubts it still, he thought, and drew her into his arms again. She still thinks it's make-believe. But for me, it has always been real.

I'll make it real for her too. And very, very soon.

It was difficult to know how to start planning it. For one thing, there was the business. Rupert could not abandon his mines without making certain that they would be worked as efficiently without him. Too many men's livelihoods were at stake, too many women and children depended on him. Who would be ready to take over when he had gone? It would be impossible to stay in Furness. He and Tess – especially Tess – would be ostracised. They would have to go far away where they were not known and where their past could not follow them.

Could William take over? He would be coming home soon. He had the intelligence and the education to be able to make a success of any business, and he had accompanied Rupert to the mines often enough. But was he sufficiently interested? His education had taken him beyond the needs of a simple mine-owner. Rupert doubted if he would ever be willing to settle in Furness again.

Besides, he was Elinor's son, no kin to either Sherwin or Craven, and Rupert wanted his own sons to inherit some day, sons who carried his blood, and that of his mother and grandfather. He would have to find a manager. And that might take time.

Then there were the boys. He did not want to leave them, knowing that in one stroke they would lose both him and Tess. A new nursemaid would have to be found and how would they fare meanwhile? Celia wanted them, he knew, but only so that they could be shown off as her sons, as she liked to show him off as her husband. Perhaps it was a result of all those years at her father's beck and call, thinking she might never have a husband or sons. Or perhaps it was just vanity. Whatever it was, she was little warmer as a mother than as a wife.

He thought of his Aunt Martha who often visited the boys and frequently invited Tess to bring them to see her. She and Tess had become good friends and he sometimes wondered whether to confide in her. She would take care of the children, and love them too, as they needed to be loved. But would Celia even allow her into the house once he had gone? Besides, he and Tess both wanted the boys. They were a family as he and Celia had never been. Together, the four of them radiated the warmth he had sought for so long, and that was something he could not lose.

But how to start again, with two small children. He realised he had no idea how to begin life anew in another place. How did one find a house? How could he earn a living for them all? Could he continue to draw money from the mine, or must it all be left to support Celia? How would they choose where to go? The whole scheme seemed impossible.

Shall we be forced to go on as we are now? he

wondered. Living in the same house, able only to snatch moments together during the day, never able to share our lives fully? Is that all we shall ever be able to have? And when the children grow a little older and we have no more need for a nursemaid, what then?

'Rupert!' Celia's sharp voice interrupted the thoughts that circled constantly in his head. 'I've been speaking to you for the past ten minutes and I don't believe you've heard a word.'

Rupert looked across the breakfast table. He had been so far away in his mind that for a moment he did not even recognise her. Then his vision cleared and he felt the bitter dislike that Celia always aroused in him now; a dislike made all the worse for being combined with guilt.

Guilt! Was he never to be free of its nagging?

'I'm sorry,' he said. 'What were you saying?'

She stared at him. 'You really haven't heard a word, have you? I sit here, trying to make conversation, and you can't even be bothered to listen to me. I might as well not be here at all.'

If only that were true, Rupert thought. If only it could be Tess facing me across this table. Instead, she's at the top of the house with the children, while I . . .

'I was saying,' Celia said with the exaggerated patience of one who has already repeated herself more than once, 'that Elinor is keeping remarkably well, considering her age.'

Rupert stared at her. She was watching him with an odd look on her face. He racked his brain to discover what she might be referring to but could think of nothing that made sense.

'Age?' he said stupidly. 'But Elinor's no more than forty-four or -five. She's not old.'

'Oh no,' Celia said with a casualness that did not deceive him. 'Not old at all, in usual terms.'

'In usual—? What do you mean, Celia?'

509

'But quite old,' she went on as if he had not spoken, 'for having a baby.'

'Having a—?' His voice dried in his throat. He swallowed, cleared his throat and began again. 'Having a *baby*? *Elinor*?'

'Why, yes,' she said innocently. 'Didn't you know?'

Rupert took a deep breath. Of course he had not known and of course Celia knew it. He wondered how long she had known.

'When did she tell you this?'

'Oh, a little while ago.' Celia furrowed her brow, still pretty but to him not nearly as beautiful as Tess's more homely countenance. 'I really thought you knew.'

'Don't you think I would have mentioned it if I had?'

'Oh, not necessarily.' She smiled at him with a sweetness he had learned to distrust even more than her malice. 'After all, you don't tell me all you hear or see.' She paused. 'Or do.'

Rupert looked at her sharply. 'What do you mean by that?'

'Why, only what I say. What else should I mean?' She smiled again with a dreadful coquettishness. 'Perhaps you have a guilty conscience, Rupert.'

Rupert got up abruptly and strode to the door. In the hall, he took two or three deep breaths and then went outside. He stood for a moment or two in the garden, drawing the sharp autumn air into his lungs, and then set off for the moor.

Good brisk exercise was what he needed while he allowed his brain to assimilate this latest news and while he waited for his racing, heated blood to simmer into coolness. Then he would be able to think rationally about this new development, and about Celia's malicious hints.

Elinor pregnant! As he climbed the sloping meadows, the implications crowded his brain. Was it his child? He recalled her assurances that care was no longer necessary, that she was past childbearing. Had she been mistaken, or had she been deceiving him? Had she intended this to happen? And if so, why? And why had she not told him?

Perhaps she had tried, he thought, remembering how he had avoided her for the past few weeks, how he had stayed away from Green House. He had not seen her for a month or more. And he had found business to keep him from the house on the afternoons when Celia was At Home, so as not to have to make polite talk with her. Yes, she might have tried. But Elinor was not a woman to be easily dissuaded. If she had wanted to tell him, she would have found a way.

And it may not be my child at all, he tried to comfort himself. God knows, she's never been one to remain chaste. She's had more lovers that most women have children. Why, she may not even know herself who the father is. It might even be Nicholas.

Nicholas! It was almost funny that Nicholas should be the last person to come to mind, he who should have been first. But Rupert did not waste much time in thinking of Nicholas. He was more concerned with Celia and her words.

You don't tell me all you do . . . Perhaps you have a guilty conscience.

What did she know? What did she suspect?

'Your child?' Elinor's eyes were opaque, unreadable. 'And what would you do if it were?'

Rupert shrugged helplessly. 'I don't know. What would you have me do?' He had come to Green House straight from the moor, unable to think of anything else until he knew the truth. 'I just want to know if – if it's possible.'

'Oh, it's *possible*, certainly.' Her eyes taunted him now. 'After all, you've proved your capability, haven't you? You already have two sons. And you've carried out

511

the necessary function. Let me see, it was in May, wasn't it, that we had our little dalliance? May and June. And now we're in October. And I judge that the child will be born sometime in March. So, yes, it's possible.'

He stared at her. 'Only possible? You mean you don't really know?'

'Oh, *I* know,' she said. 'But you see your father also thinks it's possible it may be his. And who am I to spoil his pleasure?'

Rupert felt disgust spread like a stain through his body. 'Haven't you been spoiling his pleasure for years?' he said bitterly. 'And are he and I the only two candidates for the honour of fathering your child?'

Elinor laughed harshly and he wondered how he had ever found her beautiful. There was beauty there, certainly, in her colouring and the arrangement of her features but, like Celia's prettiness, it was soiled and contaminated, a superficial beauty only, with no clue to the real nature that lay beneath. There was something disturbing in a beauty that went no deeper than the skin, and his knowledge of the callous self-interest that lay beneath made his skin crawl. He remembered Tess's freshness and generous warmth and felt his heart ache at the thought of how it could have been had he only met her first.

Nursemaid or not, he would have married her. Together, they would have built a life of love and truth, and he would never have become enmeshed in this tangle of pretence.

'Don't look at me as if I were beneath contempt, Rupert,' Elinor said with acid in her voice. 'You are as guilty as I am in this. We both lay together in that bed upstairs, not once but many times. A woman can't do it alone, you know.'

'But she can warn a man when he still needs to be careful. You told me all danger was past. There was no risk any more.'

512

'I thought it was so. It's been over a year . . . I didn't dream I could still conceive.' She turned on him. 'Do you think I *wanted* this to happen? Another child at my time of life? Don't you realise it can be dangerous at my age? And even if I survive, do you think I want to have another brat tagging on my apron-strings?'

'Then you shouldn't have taken the risk,' he told her brutally. 'If I'd known there was any possibility—'

'You'd have come to bed with me just the same. You were pleased enough to do so.'

'Pleased? My God, if you knew how I fought against it.'

'*Fought* against it? Surely, Rupert, you jest. I was hardly forced to drag you to my room. And you never protested before –' her eyes gleamed suddenly – 'before you fell in love with that skinny little nursemaid.'

He gasped. It was as if she had kicked him in the stomach. For a moment he was too breathless to speak, and then he said hoarsely, 'How did you know? How *can* you know?'

Elinor laughed again. 'So it's true! I didn't know, Rupert, not certainly. But I suspected, and I can't be the only one. Do you imagine you're invisible, walking on the shore, sitting on rocks together? Do you think it is common for a father to go on children's outings with their nursemaid? Do you really suppose that it hasn't been noticed, talked about?' Once more her laugh rang out, as pretty and tinkling as a bell yet to him ugly with malicious glee. 'But you don't have to tell people it's the truth, any more than I have to tell you whether you're my child's father or not. Unless they know without a doubt, they will always wonder – although only a few will give you the benefit of their doubt.'

Rupert was silent, furious with himself. He had fallen neatly into Elinor's trap and now the secret of his love for Tess was a secret no more. What would Elinor do with her knowledge? It was as if he had handed her a

513

weapon that could destroy both him and Tess.

'So,' he said at last, 'you won't tell me the truth about your child. It may be mine, or it may be Father's. Or it may belong to neither of us. Perhaps the fact is that you don't even know yourself.'

'Perhaps it is,' she said coolly. 'We shall have to wait and see, shan't we? All of us. After all,' her glanced moved over his black hair and brown skin that looked always as if it were tanned by the sun, 'a great deal can be deduced from colouring, can't it?'

Again, Rupert was silenced. For wasn't it his own colouring that had led Nicholas to believe that he was not his son? And wasn't it that realisation that had brought about the coldness, the bitter hatred, that Rupert had endured throughout his childhood, so that he had spent his life searching for the warmth he should have known?

Had his mother, too, been driven by the same need? Had she too looked for warmth and love outside her marriage?

If so, he thought, still staring at Elinor's face where bitterness and malice lay only partially hidden by the deceiving beauty, I hope she found it, wherever it was she looked.

On the second and fourth Wednesday of every month, Tess had an afternoon off.

It always meant a tussle with Mabel, the housemaid who was supposed to take charge of the children during that time. Mabel was as experienced as Tess in the care of small children, having five or six brothers and sisters of her own, but unlike Tess she did not enjoy it. Nor did Thomas and Oliver enjoy being looked after by her and often enough Tess had given in and foregone her afternoon off or come back early. But for the past few months every second and fourth Wednesday afternoon had been an opportunity to spend time with Rupert, and this she was less willing to give up.

This week, however, Rupert had been forced to go to Liverpool on business and since it would have appeared strange if she had not gone out, she set off alone through the fields. The path she took was one of the children's favourite walks, leading eventually to the ruined castle and watermill at Gleaston, but today she saw few of the many small landmarks they always looked out for. Her feet took her the accustomed way, but if she had been asked where she was, she would scarcely have known the answer.

The fields were full of rabbits. They scattered before her as she came along the hedge, scampering away with white tails bobbing, and dived into the burrows that pocked the banks. The children would have been delighted, but Tess barely noticed them. Her thoughts were like the rabbits, scurrying this way and that, but with no safe refuge to dive into. Instead, she saw herself cornered, crouching like an animal at bay, with no escape.

So Mrs Nicholas was pregnant. Well, she was not the only one.

Tess had suspected her own condition for some time. It had first occurred to her only two weeks after that first night when Rupert had come to her room, that night of magic and entrancement when she had discovered what love could be when shared with a man whose tenderness and consideration surpassed his own desires. It had been so different from what she had expected; so different from the tales she had heard in the kitchen, in the cottages where she had grown up, even from her own mother.

'Men! they're all the same. Takes what they wants and leaves you stranded.' So often that was the tenor of their words. 'All over you till you gives in and then it's bang, bang, ta very much – if you're lucky – and roll over and go to sleep. That's when they're not in too much of a hurry to get home to the missis. Never mind if you wanted it or if you liked it, and never mind if you wants it when they don't, either. No, 'tis all their own way and if you gets caught, you're the one with the problem.'

That was true enough, Tess thought as she sat down on a rock and contemplated the view before her. There were fewer mines on this side of the peninsula and the low hills rolled gently away to the shore. She and Rupert had often walked along that shore with the children, sitting down to watch as they played on the firm sands. What could she do? Who could she tell? Who would help her?

Of course she must tell Rupert. He had a right to know – he would know, as would everyone else, soon enough. But he ought to know first. It was his child – their child. The child they had made together from a night of loving, the child that ought to have been greeted with joy. Yet each time they were together, she let the chance go by. They had so little time of happiness, how could she destroy it? For destroy it she would once the words were out of her mouth. How could she lie in his arms, lost in the world they conjured up around them, and shatter that fragile cocoon for ever?

Once I tell him, it'll all be over, she thought. He'll be as sick with worry as I am. He'll come to my room just the same, for a while, and he might even try to go on loving me. But it'll never be the same again. It'll change everything once he knows.

And there won't be a thing he can do about it.

Tess had never believed Rupert's promises, never believed that he would leave Celia and take her away. She didn't even suppose he expected her to believe it – all their plans were just make-believe, fairy tales. Dreams of something that could never be. Men like Rupert did not leave their wives and run away with nursemaids. They did not leave their livelihood and go to

516

live in some tiny cottage, like farm labourers. They did not risk poverty, or throw away the respect of their friends and neighbours for love of a girl who wasn't even beautiful.

No, all that was just play, like children who promise to marry when they grow up. Rupert might have thought he believed it, but when faced with reality, he would realise that he was never really serious. He might be racked with guilt, but he would never leave his wife and children. His love for her, which she never doubted, would come second to his sense of duty. He would want to help her, but what could he do?

Tess knew exactly what was likely to happen to her, once her pregnancy became obvious. She would be dismissed without a reference and turned out of Garth House to make her way as best she could. Where could she go? Not back to her family – the cottage was crowded with younger brothers and sisters, with no room for her let alone another child.

In any case, she dared not take her shame back home. Hadn't her mother always warned her daughters against such a happening? 'Don't none of you never bring trouble back here,' she would say. 'We're a respectable family, and don't you forget it.'

No, there would be no welcome there.

Nor would she be able to get another job. Who would take on a pregnant, unmarried girl? The most she could expect was some menial task in a tavern or public house, washing dishes or scrubbing floors. And again, no respectable house would take her, she could only look at the lowest of public houses with the roughest customers, and what kind of life could she expect there?

It was like looking into a long, dark tunnel. The end of her bright, sunlit life and, worst pain of all, the end of her loving with Rupert.

I shall never see him again, she thought sadly. I shall have to go away from here, away from him, and I shall

517

never even know how he is faring. Whether he's well or ill; whether he is alive or dead. It is the end of everything.

But it doesn't have to be, a small voice said inside her head. It doesn't have to be the end. There are things that can be done . . .

The thought brought her up short and she repudiated it violently. She had known other girls who had found themselves in this predicament and had 'done something' about it. Elsie, who had jumped off chairs in an effort to bring about a miscarriage, until one day she'd fallen too hard, broken her leg and had the baby in the Free Hospital. Janet, who had known an old women who could 'help', and had lain in her bed racked with the most terrible pains for three days before she finally expelled her little son. Betsy, who had gone to the same old woman and bled to death.

And Milly, who had gone to the gipsies and come back with a potion. She had suffered pain too, but no worse than that of childbirth itself, she declared, and no little bundle to drag through life after it. And they said that the earlier you went the more effective it would be, and the less painful.

But it was still a baby you were killing. And, in her case, Rupert's baby.

She could not kill Rupert's baby. It was all she would ever have of him. She would never totally lose him if she had his child. If she could look into eyes as dark as his, touch hair as black. If she could watch his son growing up straight and handsome, or his daughter beautiful.

But how could she have his baby? What could she do? Where could she go?

The thoughts spun round and round in her head. There seemed to be no answer. With every turn they took, she was faced with the same dreadful end. Penniless, homeless, fit for nothing but the lowliest of tasks, until eventually she gave birth to her child in some squalid room, perhaps even under a hedge or, worst of all, in the poorhouse. And what chance was there for the child? What chance of life, of decency, for Rupert's beautiful daughter or handsome son?

No. Better dead, both of them – she and her child – than face such a fate.

Rupert came home from Liverpool as fast as the train would carry him, taking little note of the sights to be seen along the track. As a boy he had always enjoyed this journey, his morbid schoolboy's imagination revelling in the fact that it was on this line that the first fatal railway accident had occurred. And in such a way! At the very opening of the line, at Parkside, the local Member of Parliament had been run down by the *Rocket*, no less. Further on, Rupert used to crane his neck to catch the first glimpse of the sea and as the train trundled slowly across the viaduct towards Ulverston he had felt a mounting excitement at the thought of being home again, among all that was familiar. Invariably he had been disappointed. The welcome he never ceased to hope for was never as warm as in his imagination.

Today, he took little notice of the corrugated sands, turned amber by the setting sun. The herons and wading birds he usually watched with such interest passed unseen. His eyes were fixed instead on the dome of Hoad Hill with the lighthouse memorial that stood on its summit, a landmark for miles around. He remembered the day he had gone with Walter to see its opening, and the bonfire celebrations that night. They had sat there and looked out over the dark, glimmering sea and talked of the future. Of going to sea; of exploration.

The slowness of the train over the viaduct, usually such a pleasure to him, was today infuriating. With every mile he drew nearer to his home, the minutes seemed to stretch longer and longer.

He was worried about Tess. Just lately, the brightness of her face and voice seemed to have dimmed a little. And although her love had been given as generously as always, lying in his arms at night, she had been quieter than usual, a little slower to respond. He had asked if she felt ill or tired but she had shaken her head and smiled and kissed him, and he had been warmed as usual and forgotten his anxiety.

But during these few days away from her his worries had returned. He thought of all the small signs he had noticed – the glitter of a tear on her lashes, hastily wiped away and declared to be 'something in my eye', a pallor she had not had before, a boniness about a body that had been merely slim the first time he had held her in his arms.

Was she working too hard? Was she ill, though she denied it? Perhaps she was worrying about her family, her mother. She had told him she sent money home each month, leaving little for herself. Did she need anything that he could provide?

He made up his mind that tonight, when he went to her room, there would be no lovemaking, much though he desired it, until she had told him what ailed her. It gave him little pleasure to take from her what he needed while giving nothing back. And although he knew that Tess found as much joy in their loving as he did himself, he sensed that she now had a deeper need. For understanding; for comfort; for help.

But he was given no chance to go to Tess's room that night. When he finally arrived back at Garth House, Celia was waiting for him.

He knew at once, by the glitter in her eyes, that something was wrong. His heart sank. Possibilities ran through his mind. The children? No, she was angry, not distressed; in any case, she took only the barest notice of them. A servant, perhaps. No, Celia would have dealt with any problem of that kind herself, ruthlessly and efficiently, and told him about it only in order to display to him her power.

It must be Tess. Somehow, she had found out about Tess.

'Come into the drawing room,' she said, her voice barely controlled. 'I have something to say to you.'

Rupert followed her into the stuffy, over-furnished room. Every surface was covered in the small ornaments Celia loved; ruby-coloured glass vases, grotesquely shaped and bristling with spiky decoration; porcelain figurines of shepherdesses and angel-faced little boys, painted with bright, gaudy colours; large Staffordshire dogs guarding the fireplace. They all struck at the eye and created an atmosphere of restlessness. Although the furniture itself, large and substantial, was comfortable enough (a great deal more comfortable than the old-fashioned spindly striped chairs his grandmother Susannah had favoured), there was just too much of it. Every time he came in, Rupert was afraid of knocking over some small table and setting the whole lot crashing to the floor, like a set of dominoes.

'What is it?' He crossed to the fireplace and stood there, warming himself. October was turning into November, raw and damp, and he was tired from the journey. 'Has something happened?'

'Something most certainly has.' The edge of anger in her voice was unmistakable. She was like a keg of explosives, ready to go off. He gave her a wary look. It must be Tess. Nothing else could make her look and sound like this.

'Tell me then,' he said, and heard the edge in his own voice. How had Celia found out? And what had she done? Had she already sent Tess away? '*Tell* me, for God's sake!'

Celia faced him across the room. She was clearly furious, more angry than he had ever seen her before.

But there was something else, a shadow in her over-bright eyes that had nothing to do with anger. At any other time, he would have identified it as fear. But what had Celia to fear? Even if she had found out . . .

'I'll tell you,' she said in a low, bitter tone. 'I'll tell you what's wrong, Rupert Craven. You've done the one thing I begged you not to do, the thing you swore you'd never do. I had to give in, didn't I? I'm your wife, after all, and therefore have no rights. But you have rights, you reminded me of them, you were determined to have them, whatever it might cost me. And now I have to take the consequences of your brute desires, your selfishness.'

Rupert stared at her. For a few moments her words made no sense at all. What had all this to do with Tess? And then a dreadful suspicion began to form in his mind.

'Are you saying . . . Celia, for God's sake—'

'I think it's quite clear what I'm telling you,' she said with cold anger. 'I am expecting your child, Rupert. Just as you wanted. And I hope you're satisfied with your work that night.'

Chapter Thirty

Rupert went to the mines next morning with his head still reeling.

Celia and Elinor, both pregnant and both by him! At least, more than probably, for although Elinor had refused to tell him the truth, he thought it was almost certainly his child. Hadn't Nicholas been impotent for years? Or so she had said. He hardly knew what to believe any more.

How could this have happened? After being so long celibate, and then to make two women pregnant almost simultaneously, it seemed. And neither of them the woman he loved. He groaned and reined in his horse at the top of the hill, looking down at the pits, his heart heavy.

As he approached the engine shed at the pithead, his mine captain came out to greet him. They stood for a moment discussing the work of the day, and then Abe motioned him to come into the shed where he had a small office.

'Reckon there might be trouble brewing,' he said when the door was closed. 'Have you heard owt of t'Slunk Club?'

'The Slunk Club? No, what is it?' Rupert spoke without much interest. His mind was still occupied with Celia and her fury. And with Tess. What would happen to their plans now? It would have been difficult enough leaving Celia before, but now, with another baby on the way . . .

'. . . sort of like the Freemasons' Lodges,' Abe was saying, and Rupert brought back his attention with a start. 'Story is that it's been going for years, handed down from time immemorial, they reckon.' He snorted his disbelief. 'All a lot o' nonsense, of course. It's just some newfangled way of getting extra time off. A week at Whitsuntide, that's their main aim in life, that and getting themselves drunk. They reckon they're going to parade on Whit Monday – got themselves "regalia" and a few musical instruments. Fat lot any of them know about music! They claim they should have the same rights as the Salvation Army. Lot o' nonsense,' he snorted again.

'But why do you suppose it will cause trouble?' Rupert asked. 'I've heard of this claim to a week's holiday at Whitsun, of course, and I don't really see why we shouldn't allow it. And it seems inevitable that a number of the men will get drunk. But I don't see why it should cause any further trouble.'

'That's because you've not thought it out,' Abe said. 'Look, it's not just a club. Working men have had clubs for years, there's nowt wrong with that. But this is summat different. There's a sort of insolence about it, saying they're as good as their masters, with their Lodges and so forth. There's been trouble in other industries with unions and strikes and all that. If we do nowt about this Slunk Club, we'll be having it here.' He paused. 'They give a belt to the biggest slunk every year, did you know that? It's considered an honour to wear it.'

Rupert was hardly listening. It seemed all too petty beside his own problems. Let the men have Whitsun off if that was what they wanted. He still felt uneasy about the wages they had lost through the trespass. But Abe was waiting, so he said, 'No, I didn't know it. I hardly could, since I'd never heard of Slunks until today. Why do they present this belt? And what is a Slunk anyway?'

'A Slunk,' Abe said, 'is a man who loses labour through malingerering – a dodger. The belt goes to the man who loses most in a year. Now perhaps you'll see why I don't like it. The club's full of all the worst characters in the pit and it's a bad influence on the rest. And in my opinion it's going to lead to trouble.'

'Well, you may be right. But we can't do much about it until it happens. Where do they meet, anyway?'

'In Marton. I could say one of the pubs, but I reckon they aim to meet in 'em all, and on the same night too. And you know how many pubs Marton's got.'

'Fifteen, sixteen?' Rupert shrugged. 'Well, there's still little we can do about it, Abe. Men are entitled to spend their free time, and their wages, as they like. Now, is that all?'

'No, it's not.' Abe hesitated. 'There's one other matter – I don't know if you'll reckon it's owt to do with you. But it's Billy Rigg, him whose dad was mine captain afore me.'

'Billy Rigg? He was injured, wasn't he, some time ago?'

'Aye, in the earthquake back in thirty-five. Turned him simple, like. But just lately he's bin acting funny.'

'Funny? In what way?'

Abe looked embarrassed. 'Well, seems he's allus had a down on Sherwins, even though your granddad treated him proper all along – give him work when no one else would have took him on, let him do jobs like picking ore when most of the time they has to be done over again. But he reckoned t'whole family suffered through Sherwins – father died of consumption, mother went down the pit as a hurrier. No worse'n any other family, but there you are. He've allus carried a chip on his shoulder and being simple he wasn't likely to put it down. But now it's got to be more'n just a chip.'

'So what exactly is he doing?' Rupert glanced at the

door. He wanted to get out of the shed, get away from the mine and go back to the house. He might meet Tess taking the boys out for a walk. He needed desperately to see her.

'He's not doing owt – not yet. But he's turned surly. Allus bin a bit that way, like I said, but he never actually lifted his hand against anyone. But lately—'

'You mean he's become violent?'

'It's nothing you can put your finger on. Just . . . things falling near folk, bogies running a bit faster'n they should, that sort o' thing. And Billy Rigg allus around when it happens. Nothing much, but I just don't trust him any more. And he's bin talking a lot about the old days, about his dad and some little brother who got hurt when he was a baby – died long since, but Billy don't forget. And the blame's allus laid at Sherwins' door.' Abe hesitated. 'I think the way he's going he could turn nasty, and it could be when you're about.'

'And what do you think we should do about it?'

'Only one thing to do. Turn him off. He don't do much use anyway, he's only employed because your granddad insisted. Said Billy Rigg had allus got to have a job, so he was kept on when better men were laid off.'

'And must be still,' Rupert said. 'If Grandfather wanted him employed, employed he must be.'

Abe stared at him. 'But the man's useless, not far from being an idiot. And he's got it in for you, he could be dangerous. I tell you, you'll get no thanks.'

'I don't want thanks. It doesn't matter that he doesn't understand what's being done for him, what matters is that it should be done, as my grandfather wanted it to be. As for his being dangerous, I don't imagine he can do much to hurt me, and the other men can look after themselves, I'm sure. But there's to be no bullying, understand that. I won't have them setting on him.'

'As to that,' Abe said in a dissatisfied tone, 'there's a

good many of 'em like to encourage him. They've got him in the Slunk Club now – that's why I wanted to talk to you about it.'

'Well, we've talked. And I don't think either Billy Rigg or the Slunk Club are much of a threat to us at present. The mines are prosperous and the men are all in work. They'll not cause trouble while that's the case. And if they get their week at Whitsuntide—'

'They'll want more,' Abe said, but he spoke as if he knew there was no further point in arguing. 'Well, if that's what you want.'

'That's what I want.' Rupert hesitated. 'It's the last of my grandfather's wishes that I can carry out, the last thing I can do for him. Billy's father, Jacob, was more like a friend to my grandfather than an employee, and for that reason, I think, Billy Rigg was important to him. Now, have there been any more signs of trespass? Or do you think we've frightened them all off?'

'Oh, I reckon so.' Abe sounded more cheerful. 'That court action scared off anyone who might be thinking of encroaching on our royalties. No one wants to be faced with that kind of bill to settle.'

'Then if that's all we have to discuss, I'll be on my way.' For a few minutes he had forgotten about Celia and Tess, but now the urgency flooded back. He might still be in time to catch Tess on her morning walk. 'I'll call in again tomorrow.'

'Aye.' Abe came with him to the door of the engine house. The men had finished their morning break now and gone back to work, some of them below ground, others sorting ore and loading it on to the wagons, ready to be trammed down to Lindal. Rupert walked across to where his horse was tethered, glancing around for Billy Rigg as he did so. He knew the man vaguely by sight and soon caught sight of him, trudging across the waste ground near a spoil heap.

As he stopped and looked, Billy Rigg turned his head.

527

For a moment, their glances met. And Rupert felt a small shock.

He did not expect all his men to like him. Miners were a tough breed and could be sullen if things were not going their way. But few of them had ever looked at him like this, with black hatred. Even though he knew Billy Rigg was not responsible for his moods, the shock was still an unpleasant one.

But he couldn't worry about it now. There were more urgent matters to see to. He *must* find Tess.

Tess packed both children into the basinette that Rupert had brought back from one of his visits to Liverpool and set off along the lane from Loppergarth. It was clear that she was not going to see Rupert that day. Perhaps not even that night.

Why hadn't he come to her room the night before? Knowing he was home again, she had waited until her candle had burned to a stub, longing to feel the comforting warmth of his arms round her. She needed to know he was still there, that he loved her just as well.

The rawness of November had given way again to the softness of autumn and the morning was bright, full of glowing colours and mild breezes. There were mushrooms in the fields, like pearls in the grass, and she gathered a few for the kitchen. But her heart was not in it. All the time, she found herself glancing around, in the hope that she might see Rupert coming towards her. But it was not until she was on her way home, her heart heavy with fear, that she finally saw him.

'Tess!' He drew up his horse beside her and leapt off, pulling her into his arms. 'I've been looking everywhere for you.'

'Oh, *Rupert*!' Her usual caution was forgotten as she buried her face in his shoulder. 'I thought – I thought—'

'Thought what?' He lifted her head and looked into her eyes. 'Tess, what's the matter? You look pale.'

'Nothing's the matter.' She smiled at him through the tears that brightened her eyes. She could not tell him yet. 'I've just missed you. Oh,' her voice shook, 'I've missed you so much!'

He gathered her close again. 'And I've missed you. It seemed an age.' He bent his head and kissed her, then recollected himself and glanced hastily around. But there was no one in sight. 'Tess, I have to talk to you.'

There was an odd note in his voice; she looked at him and saw the lines of worry on his brow, the shadow in his eyes. 'What is it, Rupert? What's happened?'

'I can't tell you now. You'll be expected back soon with the children and I—' He stopped and his face seemed to draw in upon itself, like a purse being drawn tight. 'I'll come to you tonight, Tess. We'll talk then.'

The children were clamouring for his attention and he bent and gave them both a hasty kiss, then swung himself back on his horse. Tess watched as he galloped up the field, and her anxiety redoubled. What had happened that he needed to talk to her about? And again, why had he not come to her last night?

A nameless fear crawled into her soul and she felt the darkness of approaching shadows.

He came late, so late that she was afraid he was not coming at all. But by now she knew that there was trouble of some kind in the house, serious trouble. The servants had been talking about it when she went down to the kitchen with the children's dishes, though nobody seemed to know just what it was.

'The mistress has bin in a paddy this past week,' Peg, the housemaid, said. 'Nowt's right for her. If I've dusted the drawing room once I've dusted it a dozen times and still she's finding specks.'

'Same with the meals,' Cook agreed. 'Sent back her food hardly touched every day this week. Says it's got no taste or it's overcooked or underdone – whatever she can

529

think of. It's like she's got it in for everybody.'

'Reckon it's the master she's got it in for most,' Peg observed. 'She was like a cat on hot bricks yesterday, waiting for him to come home. And he hadn't been in five minutes before I heard her going at him hammer and tongs. Dunno what he's done, but she means to make him suffer for it. I felt right sorry for him.'

Tess crept away unnoticed. There was a slight constraint between her and the other servants these days and she had wondered several times if they suspected what was happening between her and Rupert. She did not want them seeing her now and making the connection in their minds between herself and Celia's behaviour.

Was there any connection to make? Had Mrs Craven somehow found out? Was that why she was so angry, and why Rupert had been so distracted?

She lay in her narrow bed, watching the candlelight flicker on the walls. What would Rupert do? Would he take his courage in both hands and leave Garth House, leave his wife, his business and perhaps even his children and take her away with him? Or would he choose the easier course – stay where he was, tell her that it had all been a mistake, and let his wife turn her out.

For that's what Mrs Craven would do. There'd be no mercy there. And then what happens to me? Tess thought. What happens to our baby?

Better dead . . .

There was a soft sound at the door and she turned her head quickly. It opened slowly, and Rupert slipped into the room. He stood looking down at her, his shadow huge and distorted on the wall behind him, and then he threw off his robe and slid naked into bed beside her.

'Tess, my darling Tess.'

'Oh, Rupert.' She clung to him, pressing her body against his, trembling at the touch of his skin against hers. 'Rupert, I thought you weren't coming.'

'I almost thought so myself. It's been so – so difficult.' He was covering her face with kisses, the small biting kisses that never failed to arouse her. But although he was tense with passion, his hands urgent on her body, she sensed that he was not going to make love to her now. This was simply the reaction of having been apart and having her once again in his arms. He wanted her, she knew that, but there were other matters on his mind too, matters that must be spoken about before they could lose themselves in love.

'Tess.' He stopped kissing her and slid his arms round her shoulders, leaning up slightly so that he could look down into her eyes. 'Tess, we have to talk.'

'I know. And I've got something to tell you too.' She met his glance for a moment then touched his cheek with her fingers. 'But you tell me first. It's something bad, isn't it? Has she found out about us?'

Rupert shook his head. 'No. It's not that.' He paused. 'It's difficult,' he said again. 'Difficult to explain to you. I don't really know where to start.'

Tess felt cold. She was sure now she knew what he was going to say. He loved her, would always love her, but he'd decided he had to stay with his marriage. She'd been expecting it all along. Men like Rupert did not run away with nursemaids – hadn't she told herself that a hundred times? Hadn't she reminded herself of it, warned herself against raising her hopes? Hadn't she known that one day Rupert would come to her and say all these things? And perhaps offer her a cottage somewhere – for she wouldn't be able to stay here once that happened – or money? Either of which, of course, she would refuse. She hadn't loved him for that.

But now, with the baby on the way, wouldn't she have to change her mind about that? There was no room for pride in the predicament in which she found herself.

'If she hasn't found out,' she began, but again he shook his head.

531

'It's nothing to do with us, Tess. And yet it has everything to do with us. In a way, it was because of you—' He stopped again. 'No, that sounds as if I'm blaming you. And it was not your fault. Never your fault.'

'Please,' she said, 'tell me. Just tell me and then we can talk about it.'

'Yes,' he said, 'that's best.' But it was still a long time before he spoke again, and when he did it was as if the world had fallen about her ears and she was spinning in a dark, bottomless void.

She lay shaking in the flickering candlelight. Rupert's arms were about her, but in those first moments of shock she was barely conscious of them. She felt sick and clung to him, waiting for the world to steady itself about her, wondering if it ever would.

'A . . . baby?' she said at last in a queer, croaking voice. 'Your *wife's* having a . . . baby?'

'Yes,' he said and then, seeing her stricken expression, 'My love, I'm sorry. It was before you and I – before we . . .' He groaned and buried his face against her quivering shoulder. 'I swear it was only the once.'

'But she isn't even showing yet. It *can't* have been more than a few weeks ago.'

'Two months, a little more.'

'But you told me—'

'I told me our marriage was over in that sense, yes, and it was true. We haven't been together – Celia wouldn't allow it – since before Oliver was born. As soon as she knew . . . It was the same with Thomas. You see, she hates the whole business and sees it only as a means to have babies. Without that, she has no wish for it at all.'

'So she wanted another baby,' Tess said dully. 'And you?'

'No,' he said. 'She didn't want another baby.' He lifted his head and looked directly into her eyes, and she saw the shame there but also the truth. 'I was afraid, Tess. I wanted you so much but I was afraid to take the risk of loving you. I didn't want to put you into jeopardy. And it wasn't just your body I wanted, it was your love. Yourself. All of you. I knew that if I once began to love you, and you loved me in return, I wouldn't be satisfied with the little we could have.'

Tess stared at him, bewildered. 'But if you felt like that, how could you—'

'It isn't always love that drives a man into a woman's bed,' he said quietly. 'There are other factors too. It's a need, a pressure that builds up daily. A desperation if it isn't satisfied. It can torment a man day and night until he must find relief. If there's a woman he desires but can't have, the torment is increased a hundredfold. And if there's a woman he doesn't desire but can have – well, what do you think? And Celia is my wife. Darling, I was afraid I would come here and take you, whatever the risks. I thought it would help.'

'But it didn't,' she said, and he shook his head. 'You came anyway.'

'I couldn't stay away,' he said simply. 'That night with Celia – it was disastrous. She hated me for it, but no more than I hated myself. I felt as if I'd been unfaithful to you, even though we'd done nothing but talk and play with the children then. I could never, never do it again.'

'You should have come to me at once,' Tess said. 'You know I wouldn't have turned you away.'

'But what could I offer you? Nothing but worry and fear, the fear of an unwanted pregnancy – how ironic that is! – and dismissal. Well, at least we've avoided that, thank God. Such a complication would be too much to endure.' He recollected himself and gave her a hug. 'Oh my love, I would be so happy if it were you who were expecting my child. And one day you will. One day we'll be together. But it can't be yet. Not until this is over.'

This is the moment to tell him, Tess thought. If I don't

tell him now it will never be possible. But how, when he has just said he could not endure it? How, when he has such trouble? And when Mrs Craven has first claim?

'No,' she said. 'I can see that.'

'It will happen,' he promised her. 'And we can still meet, still make our plans. Once the child is born and Celia well again – it's not so long to wait, is it? A year, no more. And then we can start again. You and I. And forget all this.'

Forget it? she thought. Forget a wife and three children, a moor full of mines, a way of life that's been yours for thirty years? No, it will never be forgotten. It will always be there to haunt us, and your guilt will never let you rest.

And a year was too long to wait. Even a few weeks were too long. Soon both she and Celia would begin to show their condition, and what then?

'What was it you wanted to tell me?' he asked after a few moments, and Tess hesitated. If she told him now, what would he do? What could he do? She thought of Celia, the boys, the mine, and knew that the scales were weighted heavily against her.

She did not doubt Rupert's love for her. But she doubted his strength. He would share her despair, he would swear his love, but there would never be a time when he could leave his wife. Tess knew that the child she bore within her body was a burden she must bear alone.

She turned her head away. 'Nothing,' she said. 'Nothing that mattered.' And then her love for him swept over her in a great wave of longing. She hugged him fiercely against her and wound her legs about his. She felt the stirring of his response and the tightening of his arms about her body.

'Don't think about it any more,' she begged him. 'Just love me, love me. It's all we can do.'

He turned his lips to hers and his hand moved over her

breast. Surely he would notice the extra fullness. Surely he would suspect . . . But he said nothing, only increased the pressure of his arms and the weight of his body on hers. And Tess let go of her fears and met him with her own caresses, her own burning passion.

Once again they were lost in their own private world of enchantment. But it was a bitter enchantment now, for one of them was aware that this must be the last time, and the other was stepping unknowingly into a new hell.

Chapter Thirty-One

Nicholas strode across Birker Common. He felt the need for exercise, to put his thoughts in order and try to come to terms with what Elinor had told him.

Could it be true? Even at the beginning of their marriage, when he and Elinor had been sharing a bed, there had never been any sign of a pregnancy. He remembered how he and Louisa had waited four years, until he had decided that she must be barren, and then Rupert had been born and he had no further opportunity to prove himself. Was it possible that, after all these years, he had managed at last to father a child?

Or was there a more likely explanation?

He sat down on a slab of limestone, staring north towards the mountains. They were a dark blue frieze against the afternoon sky, shadowed as if rain were falling. Nearer at hand, he could see Hoad Hill with its monument, and the scattered cottages of Swarthmoor and Urswick. A few masts showed at the foot of the canal at Ulverston and even from here he could hear the clatter of machinery from the pits on Lindal Moor and Pennington.

He thought of the night when Elinor had taken him back into her bed. For several weeks he had noticed a softening in her attitude, a gradual return to the coquettishness that had first attracted him, a kind of serving-girl sauciness that he had always found appealing. It sat a little oddly on Elinor who was well past girlhood, but it served to increase his renewed desire for her.

He had gone apprehensively to her bed at first, afraid of being humiliated, but Elinor had been patient, encouraging him and using all her considerable skills to help.

It hadn't happened easily, but at last he had known that moment of climax, that soaring release, and after a few moments' frenzy and the inevitable collapse, he had opened his eyes to find Elinor smiling at him. A secret, satisfied smile. And he had felt once again as he had not done in years – virile, proud, a man once more.

Why had it not lasted? A few more nights and Elinor had begun to avoid him again, making excuses – she had a headache, she was particularly tired, she felt slightly ill. And then she had told him she was pregnant.

'No wonder you've felt ill.' He was all concern. 'But surely – I thought . . .'

'I know. That I was too old. So did I.' She was disturbed, he could see. 'But it can happen, even at my age. And there's nothing to be done about it.'

'Indeed not!' He was outraged at the very idea. 'But we must take care of you. Is there anything you need? Anything I can do for you?'

She smiled at him and touched his cheek. 'Only one thing, Nicholas. And I am sorry to ask it. But I think you must go back to your own bed. It could be dangerous to the child.'

'Of course.' He agreed at once, but not without regret. Those few nights, with Elinor showing him all the care of an attentively loving wife, had been like a return to youth, though there had been more than one anxious moment. But Elinor had seemed as eager as he for a satisfactory conclusion, and had urged him on, her hands excitingly skilful, until the difficulty had passed and he was once more able to take control. It was a pity indeed that this had happened and brought their new life to an end.

But it need not be for long, he comforted himself. A few months only and then, with the child safely born, he could return to his wife and be sure of his welcome.

Or could he?

Perhaps it was her condition. He tried to believe that it must be. But as the months drew on he had to admit that Elinor had returned to behaving as she had behaved towards him for years – coldly, with no pretence of love, as though she not only disliked but loathed him.

So why that brief period of loving? And why, after years of barrenness, had it ended in pregnancy?

There was no turning away from the answer. The truth was that his brief respite with Elinor hadn't ended in pregnancy at all. It had begun with one.

Rupert, he thought. The cuckolding bastard. He's made my wife pregnant and left me to pick the fruit he's sown. Just as his mother did. And Elinor enticed me deliberately so that I would never know.

But I shall know, he thought. I shall know the moment the child is born, the moment I look at its face. Because it will look like Rupert. His colouring will always show – his darkness is bound to win over Elinor's fairness. And when I know . . .

When he knew, he would be ready to commit murder.

At Garth House, the situation was equally strained. Celia was making no secret of her condition, nor the fact that she bitterly resented it. She was suffering from constant sickness, sleeping badly and liable to come to Rupert's room at any hour of the night to demand that he sit up with her. Not that she enjoyed his company, but it gave her a new excuse to harangue him, and this itself seemed to give her some relief.

It meant that Rupert could no longer go to Tess's room. Nor could he spend much time with her during the day, for there were new problems at the mines. Work on the new levels was not going as well as expected; there was less ore than had been thought. Several men had to be laid off and this was causing trouble among those remaining, who were afraid that it would be their turn next. And the Slunk Club was proving as great a nuisance as Abe had predicted.

On the few occasions that he saw Tess, Rupert noticed that she was looking white, her eyes dark hollows in a face that was becoming pinched. Yet she did not look thinner; in fact she seemed to be putting on weight. No, she said when he asked her, she wasn't ill. Just sleeping badly. Missing him. And he assured her that it was the same for him.

'I want you so much,' he said during a snatched moment when he met her out with the children. 'If only there were some way . . .'

But she shook her head. 'There is no way. I know it as well as you.' She hesitated as if she wanted to say more, then shook her head again and he saw the glitter of tears on her lashes. 'I'm sorry, sir. I'll have to go now.'

'Sir? Tess, why do you call me "sir"? You've not done that in a long time.'

'No,' she said, 'but things are different now, aren't they?'

'No! Not that different. Tess, this is only for a while. Once the baby's born—'

'The baby,' she said quietly and looked down at the grass beneath her feet. 'Aye, the baby.' And then she looked up at him again and shook her head. 'It's not going to happen, is it?'

'What's not going to happen? Our plans, do you mean? You think I'll abandon you?' Desperately, he tried to convince her. 'Tess, never! I love you, I swear it.' He stared at her, frustrated in his longing to take her in his arms. If only they could be alone together. 'Tess, you have only to wait. I promise you, it will all come right in the end. Just have patience. That's all I ask.'

'No,' she said, 'it isn't all you ask. But you don't know

that.' She bent and covered Oliver with his blanket. 'I'll have to go now. The children are getting cold.' She gave him one last look from eyes that seemed to be trying to convey a knowledge he could not have, a message he could not read. 'Goodbye, sir.' She bit her lip and added in a trembling voice, 'Goodbye . . . Rupert.'

He watched her walk away, disappearing over the crest of the hill. He felt as if she was walking out of his life. As if he would never see her again.

She spoke as if everything were over. But it wasn't. It couldn't be. Only have patience, he thought. Just patience . . .

But for Tess, time was running out. As she looked at herself that evening in the darkened window that was her only mirror, she saw that the outline of her body was changing. Her breasts were fuller, her waistline thickening. And her dress that morning had been more difficult to fasten and felt tighter through the day.

She stood staring at her reflection. It would not be long before her condition was obvious to everyone. And then she would be dismissed.

She thought of herself and Rupert living out their lives apart. She, spurned by her family, eking out a living for herself and her child, living poorly in some hovel, unable to feed or clothe either of them properly; having to apply to the workhouse for help, having to scrub, beg, or worse. And Rupert, trapped in a loveless marriage with a wife who would become more shrewlike than ever, sentencing him to lifelong punishment for the sin she had driven him into. Who would be the worse off? She and her child, starving and abused, or he in the prison that Celia would make of his home, cold and alone, racked with guilt and with never a chance to feel the warmth of love again?

Better if he never knew the truth, she thought. Better if I'm gone, quietly and secretly so that he never knows. And the voice came into her head again. *Better dead . . .*

With a swift movement, she pulled open the drawer where she kept her few personal belongings and took out the dress she had been wearing when she first came to the house. Rapidly, she pulled it on and fastened the buttons, leaving those that would not meet round her waist undone. With shaking fingers, she found a scrap of paper and the pencil stub she used for writing to her mother. She scribbled two notes and left them on her washstand.

Dared she leave one for Rupert? Could she trust Mabel to give it to him without the mistress seeing? She wrote again, then paused and stared at the words. Then she tore them into shreds and thrust them into her pocket.

'The ungrateful minx!' Celia was white with fury. 'The selfish little hussy! After all that's been done for her. She's had a good position here, a good home, comfortable accommodation, a wage that was obviously far more than she was worth, and what does she do? She just ups and leaves without a word. Can you imagine it? She's left me completely in the lurch, but does she care? Obviously not one whit. And—'

'Celia!' Rupert had been eating his breakfast alone, as he usually did these days for Celia liked to lie late in bed. 'What are you talking about? Who has left? One of the servants?'

'Of course it's one of the servants. It's the nursemaid. She was here yesterday, brought the children down to me for their half-hour after tea, saying nothing, *nothing*, mark you, and this morning she's gone! Left a note for Mabel and—'

'The nursemaid?' Rupert paused, a fork halfway to his mouth. 'You mean *Tess*?'

'Who else would I be talking about?' Celia snapped. 'How many nursemaids do we have? Yes, Tess. Little innocent butter-wouldn't-melt-in-her-mouth Tess. God knows why or where – presumably she has a follower and has run off with him. But why she couldn't give notice in the proper way as any decent girl would—'

'Tess has disappeared?'

'I've been telling you! And a fine state she's left us in. I've been dragged out of my bed early by Rose telling me Mabel's having hysterics in the kitchen, the children haven't been washed or dressed – though she did manage to bring herself to give them some breakfast – and here I am with half a dozen ladies coming to luncheon, two screaming babies, one servant gone and another threatening to give notice. And you needn't sit there with your mouth open, Rupert. Do something about it!'

'Do something?' All he could think of was Tess, gone. Gone from his life . . . 'But where has she gone?'

'I've told you, I don't know! Nobody knows. She simply left a note, one for Mabel, who can barely read anyway, and one for me.' She produced a scrap of paper from her pocket. 'It tells one nothing. I told you, she's an ungrateful hussy and I wish I had never taken her on.'

Rupert snatched the note out of her hand. It was crumpled, as if it had been screwed up and then smoothed out again. He read it quickly:

Dear Missis,
I'm sorry but I have to leave at once. I've got family trouble that must be seen to. I've asked Mabel to look after the boys till you get someone else. Please tell the master I'm sorry.
       Tess

'Why she should want me to apologise to you on her behalf I've no idea,' Celia said tartly. '*I'm* the one who's been given all the trouble. Advertising for a new nursemaid, training her to my ways, and just at a time when I feel least able to deal with such matters. I just cannot understand it. Why she should go, just like that—'

'She says she has family trouble,' Rupert said, struggling to believe it. Perhaps it was true. But Tess had said nothing to him about any trouble. And how could she have heard about it? Had there been a letter, a message? Wouldn't Celia be aware of it if there had?

And why, if that were the case, did she not say she was coming back? Why had she not simply asked Celia to be allowed to go home until the 'trouble' was resolved? Why tell him she was sorry?

'Has she taken her belongings?' Tess had few things of her own: the dress she'd been wearing when she arrived, a daguerreotype of her parents and younger brothers and sisters, a shell he'd picked up on the beach one day and given her . . .

'Her belongings? How should I know? I haven't been to look. Presumably if she's left she'll have taken anything that was hers. And probably a few things that weren't as well!' Celia turned and hurried from the room, with Rupert close behind her. Her last words had infuriated him, Tess would never have stolen anything! He was not going to let Celia make any false accusations out of sheer spite. And he wanted to see for himself just what Tess had done.

In the nursery, it seemed that she had done nothing at all. Mabel had been persuaded out of her hysterics and was washing and dressing the two boys, though with an ill grace. As Celia and Rupert entered, she stood up and said sullenly, 'I'm doing it for now, madam, for the little boys' sake, but I can't take it on permanent. I wasn't engaged as a nursemaid, nor ever wanted to be. You'll have to find someone else or I'll have to look for another position.'

'Yes, Mabel, you've already made that clear.' Celia spoke coldly, barely looking at either the girl or her children. She walked across the room to the night nursery where the children slept, and then to Tess's own small room.

Rupert followed her. He looked down at the narrow bed where he and Tess had so often lain entwined in love. It was neatly made, with its cotton quilt drawn up. A plain white nightdress lay folded on the pillow. On the washstand next to it there was the stub of a candle, and on the small chest of drawers which was the only other piece of furniture in the room he saw a daguerreotype and a shell.

'Well, it seems she's taken nothing,' Celia said, opening drawers and banging them shut again. 'She's even left the clothes I provided for her – she must have gone off in that dreadful little print frock she arrived in. Well, she'll have difficulty getting another post in that, it was little more than a rag when she came here.'

Rupert knew the dress she referred to. Tess had worn it sometimes on her afternoons off, when they had met secretly in the meadows and the woods. It was poor and shabby, but it had always been clean and fresh, and the gaudy pattern of flowers had faded to a gentle softness. To him, that shabby little frock had been the essence of the Tess he knew: simple, unpretentious, unashamed.

'. . . needn't apply to me for a reference, either,' Celia was continuing. 'Not after this piece of barefaced ingratitude!'

Rupert stared round the bare little room. He had seen it so many times by moonlight or in the dancing flame of a candle. Then it had been alive because Tess was in it and because it was here that they shared their love. Now, it seemed dead, a stark and cheerless place. Was it really in this kind of room that girls like Tess and Mabel were condemned to spend their leisure moments?

But the thought was only fleeting. He was more concerned with the implications of what he saw.

The daguerreotype. The shell. Tess had left them behind. But her note had said she wasn't coming back. *I've asked Mabel to look after the boys till you get someone else.* She had left, not just for 'family trouble', which he did not believe anyway, but for good.

For good, or for ill?

Where had she gone? And why?

The full moon poked long, shining fingers across the bay and touched Tess's shivering body, huddled on the rocks at Bardsea. She had walked all night, trudging through the fields, finding her way by moonlight yet hardly knowing where she went. The paths she followed were familiar but she barely saw them. Her feet knew every stone, every twist and turn, and they led her steadily, surely, towards the beach.

What was she to do? Where was she to go? The pale sky gave no answers. The tide was high, rippling softly on the shingle, and the moon threw a glimmering path of light towards her across the pewter surface. She stared at it, remembering her childhood wonder at seeing it for the first time, when the path had seemed to lead to some magic land. One had only to take a step from the shingly beach to set foot upon its glittering surface; she imagined it, cold and metallic beneath her toes yet firm enough to tread, leading her out into the bay, towards the brilliant white sphere of the full moon; away from pain and into comfort, away from the dark shadows of despair and into cool, clear light . . .

The rocks where she sat were overhung by trees, their branches bare of leaves, reaching twisted, skeletal fingers towards the sky. Occasionally, in the undergrowth, she could heard the rustling of some small animal, while overhead she glimpsed the silent waft of the broad white wings of an owl. The whistling lament of a wading bird sounded eerily through the air and she thought of souls lost in the sea, of those who had wandered into quicksands and been sucked into shifting mud, of those who had been swept out into the bay and never seen again.

The rock was cold beneath her and she got up and moved restlessly about on the rocks. The tide was falling now and the path of moonlight glowed on sands of rippled iron grey, all colour washed away by the dark and silver shades of night. Tess stared at it, mesmerised. Slowly, she walked down the beach towards it and stood in the full beam of light, looking up at the cold white sphere so high above. She reached out both hands, lifting them high, and walked along the glimmering path slowly, almost daintily, stepping as if in a stately dance with each foot held high a moment, then lowered on to the toes.

The wet sand was soft and yielding beneath her feet, but she sank in no more than an inch or two before the underlying firmness resisted. The water was cold about her ankles, but she scarcely noticed. Her eyes were on the silver path, the path that led to enchantment and ease, the path that would take her away from despair. As she moved on, the water rose to her knees and she could feel the tug of the tide, but it was gentle, no more than a soft swirl about her thighs. The path stretched before her, luring her on, enticing her with its faint gleaming promise. All will be well, it seemed to say; trust me.

Once, she turned and looked back towards the shore. But she could see only darkness and shadows behind her. The trees were outlined against the sky, their gnarled fingers reaching up as if to echo her own despair, and behind them the hills rose in menacing blackness.

The tide had her in its grip now, drawing her more and more strongly out into the bay. She hesitated at last and tried once more to turn away from the beguiling light. But the sand beneath her feet grew suddenly softer and the water tugged her legs and eddied about her waist. She stumbled, half fell and managed to right herself. In sudden terror, she turned again and looked across the bay. The moon still flung its silver path before her. And as she gazed at it and felt the irresistible lure of its terrible magic, it was as if she had known all her life that

546

this was the path she must one day follow; that this had always been her destiny.

November deepened into December. Elinor's pregnancy progressed with a rapidity that to other people seemed almost alarming. She must surely be expecting twins, they commented on seeing her size; that big at only six months! Nicholas watched with bitter cynicism. Six months? he wondered. Or seven, or eight? And how would she manage a 'premature' birth – a fall on the stairs, perhaps, when no one else was in the house? And a child miraculously large, able to survive even though it came early?

Rupert wondered too. Elinor had never admitted the truth to him and he had not asked again. He had trouble enough, after all, with his own wife's pregnancy and his gnawing anxiety about Tess.

Nothing had been heard of her. She had not gone back to her family, nobody had heard from her. Her mother had written several times enquiring if Tess had returned, and Rupert felt anxious and guilty. Where had she gone? And why, *why* had she run away?

'I've told you. The hussy had a follower and has run off with him,' Celia said sharply. 'I can't imagine why you're so interested, Rupert. She was nothing but a cottage girl, after all. Good enough with the children, I suppose, but so are a hundred others. I'm perfectly satisfied with the one Mrs Bracknell has found me and don't much care what happened to Tess. I wouldn't be at all surprised if she ran off with the gipsies. They were here again recently.'

Gipsies. Could she have done so? Rupert remembered the morning when he and Nicholas had ridden over to Dunnerholme and watched them coming across the sands. He had thought of his mother, watching the same scene years before and setting it down in paint. Could Tess have gone to the gipsies? Or – he remembered their

547

reputation and shuddered – could they have taken her away against her will?

No. She had left notes. Wherever Tess had gone, she had gone knowingly.

But still he did not know why.

Christmas came. Celia, like Elinor, grew larger and more bitter. Even when she felt the child kick inside her, she did not soften towards her pregnancy, though only Rupert knew of her anger. To her friends she was the perfect mother, displaying baby clothes and chatting about names. To him she complained constantly, bewailing the condition that kept her indoors and shut her away from the world.

'You'd hardly have gone out much in this weather anyway,' he said, looking out at the raw grey afternoon. 'Much better in here by the fire.'

'That's not the point. I'd like to be able to go out on fine afternoons.'

'Well, so you can.'

'To walk down the lane, yes. But what else? I can't go visiting, I can't even ride in the dog-cart because of the shaking. And only my closest friends can visit me. We can't do any entertaining while I'm like this. What sort of life is it for me, do you suppose? What can I *do*?'

'You could spend more time with your children,' he retorted. He still tried to do so himself, though the new nursemaid was less congenial than Tess. Not that he expected or wanted to find anyone like Tess, but he was disappointed by the lumpy, rather stupid girl who had taken her place. The children seemed to like her well enough, it was true. But they seemed less lively these days, as if without Tess's bright presence they had slumped into lethargy. The only interest they showed was when Martha came to visit them, when they seemed to wake from their listlessness and regain their former energy.

Martha would firmly brush aside the nursemaid's

protests and wrap them in scarves and hoods to take them into the garden, throwing a ball for them to chase or filling a bucket with apples from the trees. Rupert too would often join these small expeditions. The only comfort he could find these days was in his children or with his aunt, and more than once he wished he could confide in her. But although she looked at him with a soft, almost compassionate glance, he could not bring himself to say the words. She would be shocked. She would turn away from him. He dared not take the risk.

'The children need attention,' he said to his wife now. 'They need someone to play games with them, teach them a little. Meg looks after them well enough, I agree. She keeps them washed and fed and sees that they're in bed at the proper time. But she doesn't seem to talk to them much. She doesn't take them on interesting walks. They need such things, to help them develop their minds.'

'What nonsense! They're babies still, what minds have they to develop? If you ask me, Tess was bad for them. She over-excited them. Meg is a much better type.'

For want of other company, Elinor came to Garth House and the two women would drink tea together and discuss their condition. But after Christmas, Elinor stopped coming. She was feeling a good deal of discomfort, Nicholas said, and the doctor was worried about her. Celia was welcome to go to Green House, but Elinor really could not travel now.

'Apparently the confinement might be earlier than expected,' Nicholas added. 'The doctor thinks she must have mistaken her dates, but Elinor is confident there was no mistake.' He looked directly at Rupert as he spoke. 'And of course she must know.'

'But at her age . . .' Rupert said. 'It's possible to be mistaken, surely.'

'Oh yes. It's always possible. Anyway, we shall all know once the baby's born.'

He departed then, and Rupert was left to wonder what Nicholas knew or suspected. Did he really believe he was the father of Elinor's child? Did he have *cause* to believe it? Or did he know that it was impossible? If he did, he knew more than Rupert. It would certainly account for the coolness of his manner these past few months. Gone was the tenuous respect, almost friendship, that had begun to grow between the two of them, gone the early-morning rides, the business discussions. Nicholas rarely came to Garth House now and since Rupert avoided Green House, there was little contact between them. When they did meet, it was with coldness on Nicholas's part, a coldness that seemed to mask an underlying rage.

But hadn't it always been so? Hadn't Nicholas always treated him with that same chill resentment? Was there really any difference, or was it no more than his guilty conscience that made him see anger where none existed?

Rupert went daily to the mines, more to take his mind off his domestic worries than because he was needed there. Abe had taken over more and more of the management, and on most days all Rupert did was collect a report from him and come home again. But the busy atmosphere, the clatter of machinery, the hurly-burly of carts and trams being loaded with ore, and the sight of men filling the cages to go down the deep shafts were all a welcome change from the anxieties that beset him. At the mine, he could forget for a while the tight bitterness of his wife's face, the cold anger of his father, the contempt of the woman who had been his mistress.

But even at the mine, he could never forget Tess. Her face rose constantly before him, her warm and generous nature lending it a beauty more enduring than Elinor's fair colouring, which was fast fading now, or Celia's prettiness, spoiled by resentment.

Tess, Tess, Tess. Where was she? Why had she gone? Why hadn't she told him, or at least left him some message? The questions circled endlessly in his brain, giving him no peace. They taunted him throughout the day, haunted him at night. Would he ever know the answer? Would he ever see or hear from her again?

February came, and still there was no word. Celia was within a month of her confinement now and Elinor, if she was to be believed, within two months. Rupert was tense, waiting to see if the doctor was right and Elinor would have an early confinement. And when he saw Nicholas he realised that he too was waiting.

What will Nicholas do if the baby resembles me? Rupert wondered anxiously.

The days and nights crawled by, and it seemed that there would never be relief.

For Nicholas, too, the waiting was becoming intolerable.

Daily, he watched his wife for signs that the birth was imminent. He was certain it must happen soon. She was surely too large to be only seven months pregnant, and the doctor and midwife both declared that there was only one baby there. Mistakes could be made, of course, but Elinor herself said that there did not seem to be more than the usual quantity of arms and legs. 'Though he kicks enough for two,' she added. 'He must just be a particularly large baby.'

He. She seemed certain that it was a son. Sitting alone in his library, sipping the whisky that had become a constant companion, Nicholas thought morosely how he would have welcomed a son of his own. It had been a dream for so long, relegated to the place in his mind kept for dreams. During the years of his celibacy he had accepted the fact that it could never be. The fact that he was now to be forced to father a second bastard, and that this second one was the child of the first, seemed particularly cruel. He didn't know for certain, of course. But he expected to know the moment he first looked at the child's face.

★ ★ ★

March came in like a lamb. Wild daffodils tossed at the foot of every hedge and in the woods; primroses were already lifting their pale, buttercream faces to the sun. The sky was a tender blue, skimmed by a gauze of high, thin cloud, and the winter gales had softened to a mild breeze.

For the first few days it was as if Nature held her breath, waiting to be certain that this was indeed spring and not some teasing joke. Birds sang but seemed uncertain about building their nests. Frogs croaked in the ponds but had not yet laid their spawn. A few lambs skipped in the meadows, but for the most part the sheep were still bulky, waiting to give birth.

So, too, did Elinor and Celia, Nicholas and Rupert, restless with their own frustrations and fears. It was as if the four of them circled round each other, never meeting each other's eyes but never losing sight of each other, as if their destinies were too closely linked for them to be parted and they must wait together for whatever truth might emerge.

It was with some relief that Rupert found reason to journey to Liverpool at the end of the first week of the month. By now, the mild weather had ceased to be a surprise and the world had caught its breath and begun to work again. The bushes were thick with birds busy about their nests, the ponds were suddenly filled with spawn and along the hedgerows a faint dusting of green appeared as buds shook themselves and began to open. Across Morecambe Bay, the sand shone soft and gold in the new, gentle sunlight.

The train trundled slowly along the coast, taking the route Rupert had always loved. From his seat he could look out to the left towards the mountains of Westmorland. To the right, he could see across the salty marshes and stretching sands, far down the estuary towards the open sea. Soon the tide would begin to come in, racing across the flat, rippled mud, driven by a rising breeze and reaching up to the marshes to fill the channels between each small, grassy islet. Rapidly, they too would be covered, for this was a spring tide and one of the highest of the year, and the beachcombers would be out to see what could be found along the beach when it began to fall again.

The train took its leisurely way, pausing at each small station. People got on and off, the driver leaned out for a chat, the guard waved his flag. The engine puffed and sent up clouds of smoke and billowing steam. At each stop there were meetings and greetings, partings and departures. And each moment was filled, for Rupert, with visions of Tess.

He had never for a minute ceased to think of her. He had never ceased to hope that she would return. Each morning he looked for a letter, though he knew she would scarcely dare write to him. But to one of the maids, perhaps? To Mabel or to the cook?

He wondered if she might write to his aunt. But Martha shook her head. No, Tess had not written. And then she would hesitate and glance at him, her eyes troubled.

If anyone knew what Tess's trouble was, he thought, it would be his Aunt Martha, the collector of gossip. But Martha was not necessarily a gossip herself. She liked to know, but she could keep a secret, her own and other people's.

But what secret could Tess have had that Martha might have known?

'I would have given her a home here,' she said once. 'She could have stayed with me.' But she had immediately closed her mouth tightly, as if regretting her words, and when Rupert pressed her, she shook her head and turned away.

What had she meant? What did she know?

The train was making its way slowly across the long

viaduct that spanned the head of the estuary of the River Kent, from Grange to Arnside. There had been a good deal of discontent when this viaduct was built, for it had destroyed the shipping trade for Milnthorpe and the other small ports that lay above it. Rupert stared out of the window, thinking absently of the sails that must have thronged the river before that time. Ships bound for Liverpool with slate, limestone and Sedgewick gunpowder. Ships arriving with coal from Whitehaven, slaves from Liverpool. Where were they now, those ships?

Above the viaduct lay the old saltpans also, used in medieval times. Disused for centuries, they were now a grazing ground for sheep at low tide. But the farmers kept careful watch to see that the animals were back safely on higher ground as the tide turned, for it rose so quickly here that it was easy to be caught in the swift waters.

Looking seawards now, Rupert could see the race of the tide, surging up the estuary. It came in a wave, waist-high above the bare mud, a wall of water powerful enough to sweep a man off his feet, fast enough to outpace any runner. And with it, the sea came deep and dominant, claiming the naked shores for its own. For an hour or more it would rule the sands, and woe betide any who stood in its way. Its retreat would be just as swift and perilous.

It was a dramatic sight, and one Rupert had rarely witnessed. He sat fascinated, gazing at the rippling waves. Already the beach was filled with people, eager to see what the tide might have brought with it. A wreck somewhere down the coast might yield treasure, and it was no uncommon sight to see kegs and barrels floating on the water. First come, first served, was the rule, and if you could get it home quickly before the Customs men spotted you, who was to know?

But today something else was drawing the crowd. As

the train drew nearer to the village of Arnside which had grown so much since the coming of the railway, Rupert saw a knot of men and women gathering to stare at something that floated and bobbed on the incoming tide. Something that looked very like a bundle of old clothes, drifting here and there at the mercy of the waves – until a stronger ripple turned it over and he saw the white, bloated face looking directly up at him as the train passed over it.

He sat back in his seat, sick with shock. The apparition had been before his eyes for less than a minute but the horror of it was stamped upon his mind for ever.

He closed his eyes and turned his head, trying to blot out the image, but it was there before him, inescapable, inexorable, demanding that he acknowledge it. Look at me, it seemed to say as it spread its dreadful whiteness across his mind, look at me and *know*.

The whiteness was perhaps the worst part. No human body should have that almost luminous pallor, that greenish tinge of rottenness. And the puffed and bloated look of the skin, so grotesquely swollen yet laid bare to the bone here and there by the gnawing of sea creatures. He had seen a crab, still crawling on the staring face . . .

The hair was like weed, draggled over the empty eyes. Hair that had once been soft to the fingers, eyes that had once been merry, soft and loving . . . Sickened again, he turned his head this way and that, trying desperately to escape the vision, trying to deny the ultimate knowledge. But it was useless. He had seen it. He knew. And there was no way back.

Worst of all had been the clothes. The shabby print frock, its colours bleached by the months in the sea, its seams strained and torn by the swelling flesh beneath, but still recognisable to one who had known it well. And the body, so briefly yet so vividly seen, so distorted yet so familiar to one who had held it in love, stroked and caressed the skin now white and bloated, kissed those lips now white and swollen.

Tess. *Tess* . . .

Rupert recalled little of his journey home. He knew that he had left the train at Arnside, almost carried from it by anxious fellow passengers. He had been taken into the station master's office, snug with its coal fire burning in the grate, and given strong, sweet tea. Someone had produced a hip flask and his throat had burned with brandy. But nothing could warm him. Shivering and sick, he had crouched beside the fire, muttering her name over and over again. Tess. Tess. Tess . . .

They had brought her body to the station too, her pathetic body, so bloated and white, with the shabby print frock no more now than a few tattered remnants and the crabs still crawling over her skin. Thinking at first that he had been shocked simply by the sight from the train, they had not allowed him to see it; but then the local constable had arrived and when it was realised that Rupert believed he knew the dead girl, he had been asked to confirm her identity. And so he had looked again at that dreadful face and into those empty eyes, and knew that he would never, never be able to forget.

Tess, why did you do it? he cried silently in his mind. Was it deliberate, that night when you disappeared? Did you know, when you left the house, that you would be dead before the sun rose? Or did you just wander in despair on the shore and find yourself caught by the tide?

And why were you so despairing? Did you believe I would abandon you, that I'd never leave Celia, that all our love was an illusion?

His journey to Liverpool was abandoned. A man was found to accompany him back to Lindal, for it was agreed he wasn't fit to travel alone. And Tess's body was laid in a separate compartment so that she too could go home, to be buried at Pennington where at least he could be near her.

Little welcome she would receive from Celia. But Celia was nothing to him any more. He would never call her wife again, for in truth she had never been wife to him. Tess had been his wife, in everything but name, and it was from Tess that he had been widowed.

Chapter Thirty-Two

On the day that Rupert brought Tess home, Elinor
Craven gave birth to her second son.

For the past two or three days she had feared that the
birth was imminent. The child inside her had suddenly
begun to indulge in frenzied activity, kicking and squirming until she was exhausted by its movements. From
riding high in her womb it had dropped, so that the
bump lay low, almost resting on her thighs and making it
uncomfortable both to walk and to sit. And yet she
suddenly felt filled with a need to do something, to
occupy herself. She sorted through her wardrobe, resting
every few minutes on the bed. She went out into the
garden and gathered daffodils, arranging some of them
in vases and then leaving the rest for the maid to deal
with. She went into the kitchen and cross-examined
Cook on the meals she was preparing, and inspected all
the cupboards.

It was behaviour she recognised, although it was
almost a quarter of a century since she had given birth to
William, and she paced about the rooms, unable to rest,
afraid not only of the birth itself but of what must surely
follow. The baby should not be born until May; would
anyone believe that it was a full-term child? Would
Nicholas believe?

She must make it appear a premature birth, brought
about by some shock. A fall on the stairs? But that could
be dangerous, not only for the child but for herself.

What else? Her thoughts ran this way and that, like mice scurrying at the approach of a cat. What else, what else, what else . . . And then, suddenly, it was too late.

When the housemaid came into the room to answer the jangling summons of the bell, she found her mistress on the floor. She took one look at the writhing figure and ran, screaming, to the kitchen. Within minutes, the whole staff was assembled and staring in equal dismay.

'It's the babby!' Cook exclaimed, though everyone could see that. 'It's coming. Here, you,' she reached out a muscular arm and grabbed the boot boy who was wide-eyed with fascination, 'run for the doctor. No, go and fetch old Mother Ward first, she's bin midwife to hundreds, and then go for the doctor. Don't stand there staring, boy, *run*. The mistress could die at our feet if we don't get a move on.'

The boy took one last look and ran. Elinor, released for a few moments from pain, clawed her way to a sofa and tried to raise herself on to it. The cook and one of the maids immediately began to help her.

'I won't have that Ward woman,' Elinor said through her teeth. 'She's dirty and slovenly. I engaged Mrs Rigby to come in.'

'But she ain't coming till next month,' Cook pointed out. 'Don't reckon you can wait that long, missis. This babby wants to be born now and I can't take no responsibility for it. I'm a cook, not a midwife.'

Elinor groaned and lay back as a fresh wave of pain rolled over her. She had known when engaging the monthly nurse that the baby would be born before the woman would come. But what else could she have done? She had been forced to go through the motions of anticipating her confinement in May.

The pain gripped her like some huge preying bird, boring into the small of her back and clamping its vicious talons round her body. Its squeeze was slow but inexorable, crushing her tightly, so that she felt as if she were encased in an iron vice operated by some machine that, once set in motion, could not be stopped. And that's just what it is, she thought as the agony began slowly to abate. A machine that Rupert and I set in motion when we lay together in my bed, a machine that can't be stopped until this baby is born. And then?

The next wave of pain was worse, the talons gripping even more viciously, the iron vice wound tighter still. Elinor screamed and clung to the hands that reached out to her – whose hands, she neither knew nor cared. Her body writhed and thrashed on the sofa, taking no instructions from her brain now, for this business was purely that of the body. No use to try to control it, no use to try to lie still. Her muscles knew what to do and did it. She was not even aware of the midwife's voice telling her to bear down; she had no need of it. Instinct and the power of the process that was now in motion took her over completely. Thought played no further part.

For three hours more she lay on the sofa, racked by the pains that tore through her body. Relief came after each pain, but it was short-lived and gave her only time to sip some water or, more often, to be sick. Faces swam before her eyes. The old midwife, Mother Ward, hastily summoned and still in the clothes she had been gardening in. Cook, the housemaid and once, to her shame, the boot boy who had slipped back into the room. And Nicholas.

Nicholas had been summoned from the stables where he had been discussing a new mare with the groom. He came striding in, his face grim. She saw the heavy grey brows drawn over his steely eyes and knew at once what he was thinking. He was waiting to see the baby, waiting to see who the baby resembled. I hope it's me, she thought with sudden savagery. I hope it looks like me and then he'll never know . . . And then pain washed over her again, and she closed her eyes and screamed.

They did not try to take her upstairs and put her on the

bed, for the midwife declared it would be dangerous to move her. She must give birth here, in the drawing room, on a bed hastily made of old sheets and cushions, pushed under and around her. Her clothes were loosened and then partially removed by Cook and the midwife, and for modesty's sake a sheet laid over her. But Elinor was still, even through the red haze of pain, aware of the indignity and knew that she would suffer the shame of it later. At least Mother Ward had sent the boot boy and Nicholas out of the room.

With one final, tremendous thrust, the baby tore its way into the world, almost elbowing her aside in its haste to be free. Elinor let out a screech that sounded right through the house, the force of her thrust sending her almost off the end of the sofa. Cook caught her, holding her thrashing body by the shoulders, using all her strength to keep her still; and a yard away, the midwife eased the shuddering and slippery baby away from its mother's body, turned it upside down and gave its small buttocks a slap.

The baby let out a furious scream. It hung for a moment by its ankles in the midwife's hand. And then she turned it expertly right way up and laid it down on the blood-spattered sheets beside Elinor's limp, panting body.

'It's a boy,' she said. 'A fine, healthy boy. And a big 'un, too. You must have got your dates mixed after all, missis.'

A fine healthy boy. No seven-month child, but one who had gone full term. Elinor lifted her head weakly and stared at the black, curling hair. At the eyes, so dark as to be almost black. At the face, red and crumpled as that of any newborn baby, yet with an unmistakable resemblance to Rupert.

There would be no gossip, of course, no queer looks. There was nothing strange in mixing one's dates, especially at her age, when confusion could so easily take place. Only Nicholas would know the truth. And he had already acknowledged one child not his, a child moreover who must also have been born with black hair, dark eyes and a skin that looked as if it had already been out in the sun. Nobody else would think it strange. 'Look at that,' they'd say, 'just like his big brother,' and think only that the colouring must be somewhere in the Craven family.

But Nicholas would know. He would know at once. Elinor lay back on the sofa, her eyes closed, waiting and dreading the moment when he came in to see his wife and new son.

Rupert waited at Lindal station. He was still dazed, still reliving in his mind that terrible moment when he had looked down from the train and seen Tess's body floating beneath him in the water.

The vision filled his thoughts, leaving room for little else, but there was still one small part of his brain operating with precise clarity. With this part, he sent for the undertaker in Ulverston. He ordered that Tess should be laid out decently and put in a coffin, not the most expensive but not the cheapest either. There on the station platform, he arranged her funeral, simple and unpretentious as Tess herself had been, with a few spring flowers to accompany her. And then he watched as the undertaker's trap bore her slowly away.

None of it seemed real. It was as if he walked in a dream, seeing himself and his own actions through the small end of a telescope. He was just one of a group of tiny figures, moving about at the station, lifting Tess's body into the trap. He saw the group pause momentarily as his own small self stood making a last, silent farewell to the woman he had loved so dearly and so disastrously. And then he turned away and set his footsteps towards home.

But he did not go to Garth House. Instead, he crossed

the fields to Pennington Hall and went to visit his Aunt Martha.

'So, my lady,' Nicholas said grimly when he and his wife were alone at last. He stood at the side of the bed, staring down at her; staring too at the baby who lay swathed in blankets beside her, only the fuzz of dark hair showing. 'So, how are you going to explain this?'

Elinor looked up at him. She felt weak from the birth, and her heart shook with trepidation, but she had not lost her spirit and she did not intend to let him see her fear. She lifted her chin a little in her old, defiant manner.

'Explain what, Nicholas? You have a son. You can be proud—'

'*Proud*?' His temper snapped and he started forwards. In sudden terror, Elinor covered the baby with her arms and caught him close against her. Her heart thudded and the baby, startled by the abrupt movement, began to cry. Immediately she began to stroke the back of his still damp head, and lifted him against her cheek.

'Don't touch him, Nicholas,' she ordered in a voice that, although weak, was firm enough to give him pause. 'Don't you dare to touch him, or me. He's your son in the eyes of the world. And if you hurt either of us, what do you suppose the world will say?'

'The world will say nothing in blame of me,' he retorted. 'The world will know what you've done and no one will blame me—'

'Is that what you really want? Do you want the world to know what I've done?' She paused, taunting him with her eyes. 'And what you could not do?'

Nicholas caught his breath. She saw the colour come and go in his face, dark red ebbing to marble white. For a moment, she thought he would have an apoplexy, then he gathered himself together again and spoke, his voice dry and husky.

'Is this what you mean to do? Foist another bastard on me, and expect me to say nothing? Do you really expect me to bring up this brat as I brought up his father, and let everyone believe he's mine?'

'If you don't,' she said coolly, 'they will realise that not only is this child a bastard, but Rupert also. Do you really want them to know that you let this happen twice, and with different wives? Can you imagine the feast of gossip that Furness will gorge itself upon? And not only Furness. Both you and Rupert are well enough known in Liverpool too. No, Nicholas, better to remain silent and keep what pride you have.' She watched him carefully. The baby had been soothed back to sleep by the gentle rocking that she had automatically given him. She felt his warmth against her breast and, almost at once, the tingling desire to suckle. There would be no milk yet, but she had always believed that those three days before the milk came in were designed for teaching the baby to feed. She wished that Nicholas would go away and leave her alone.

The strength of the feeling that had flooded through her on first sight of the baby's dark, downy head had taken her by surprise. Not for one moment during her pregnancy had she expected such a reaction. The baby had been a burden, an imposition, an embarrassment; even a danger. Yet with his birth she had experienced a surge of love that had warmed her entire body. For the first time in her life, she felt fulfilled.

Nicholas was standing very still. His eyes were fixed upon her. She saw his glance move to the baby and shrank away a little, holding him more closely. There was a mad look about her husband now, a look she had never seen before in even the worst of his rages. She was reminded abruptly of the times when he had struck her, and she trembled in the bed.

'I see,' he said slowly. 'So I am to stand by and let you betray me and never utter a word of the truth. And I am to bear the consequences of your actions. Well, we shall see.'

He turned abruptly on his heel and strode out of the room. Elinor heard his feet tramping heavily down the stairs. A few moments later, the front door slammed and she could have sworn the whole house shook.

With a relief that weakened every limb, she bent her lips to the baby's head. She slipped down lower in the bed, still holding him against her. She looked at him, feeling love for every tiny pore, every eyelash, every curling hair. And then her eyes began to close with exhaustion, and the two of them fell asleep.

'You mean poor Tess *drowned* herself?' Martha stopped, her teacup halfway to her lips, and stared at Rupert. Her face whitened and her eyes grew dark and wide. She set the cup down as carefully as if it were made of spun sugar and felt in her pocket for a handkerchief. 'Oh, surely not . . .'

Rupert sat opposite her, his tea untouched. It was Martha's habit to offer refreshment whatever time a caller should arrive, and normally he enjoyed her fluttering attentions. But today he had barely noticed them, had been almost brusque in his anxiety to tell her the news and receive her comfort. Only the necessity to wait until the parlour maid was out of the room had kept him silent until now.

'It can't be true,' Martha said. 'There must be some mistake.' But he recognised her tone as that of one who wishes it were not true rather than of disbelief. 'Tell me it isn't true,' she begged, but already the knowledge was in her eyes, the grief in the working of her mouth.

'I wish I could. I wish to God I could.' He lifted his hands towards her. 'Why? Why did she do it? What thoughts were in her mind, that last night when she went down to the shore . . . she must have walked into the water, knowing what would happen, knowing the tide would be too strong for her.' He bent his head and covered his face with his hands. 'I saw her, all white . . . the *crabs* . . .' The horror was too great to put into words and he fell silent. He felt Martha's touch on his shoulder and shook his head. 'I'm sorry. It was so horrible.'

'Of course it was. Horrible.' With surprise, he realised that she was not as shocked as he had expected. But perhaps she had always thought that this might be an answer to Tess's disappearance. And although she had been fond of Tess, it was no more than the fondness of any kindly woman for a servant. She had not loved Tess, nor, he thought, suspected that he had loved her. 'You've had a dreadful shock. Now, drink some tea. It'll help you. I daresay you've neither eaten nor drunk since breakfast this morning, have you?'

He thought for a moment, though nothing seemed less important. 'No. Nothing. Some tea and brandy at the station, that's all.'

Memory flooded over him again and his body shook.

Martha lifted the cup and held it against his lips, as if feeding a child. 'Come along, while it's hot. It'll make you feel better.' She waited while he took a sip and then, feeling the comforting heat of it, took the cup in his own hands and drained it. 'Poor girl,' she said softly, 'Poor, poor girl.' And then, bafflingly, 'I wonder if he ever knew.'

'He?' Rupert lowered the cup and stared at her. 'Who do you mean?'

'Why, the young man of course. Didn't Celia say that Tess had one – wasn't that why she was believed to have run away, to be with him?' Martha shook her head. 'Why ladies like Celia expect girls not to have followers passes my comprehension. Of course they will. It's natural, and not the least use forbidding it. It only leads to trouble.'

'But Tess didn't –' Rupert began, and stopped. His

aunt was looking at him oddly. 'Tess didn't have a follower,' he said more firmly. 'I'm quite sure she didn't.'

'I'm afraid you're mistaken,' Martha said, shaking her head sadly. 'Quite mistaken. I suppose the young man, whoever he was, let her down. And that was why she did it.' She looked at him again, shy about the turn in the conversation. But she had never minced her words with Rupert; they had been friends for too long. 'Poor, poor Tess. She must have been in complete despair. Let down by her young man and with a baby on the way.'

'A . . . *baby*?'

The words seemed to come from a long way away, like an echo distantly heard. Rupert was never conscious of having spoken them himself. But someone did, and using his voice. 'A baby?'

'I'm afraid so,' Martha said with a sigh. 'I saw the signs a week or two before she disappeared. Oh, she denied it at first, as one would expect, but Tess and I were friends, you know, and she confessed it eventually. Poor child, she was almost at her wits' end. She wouldn't tell me who he was or why he couldn't help her, but it was clear she loved him.' She shook her head sadly. 'So tragic, two young lives, lost and wasted. And she was such a lovely girl, such a beautiful, sweet nature.'

Her voice went on, extolling Tess's goodness, excusing her for her sins. But Rupert heard little more. He rose to his feet, tipping over his cup as he did so. Without apology, he walked from the room. He brushed the parlour maid aside as she offered him his coat and walked out of the house, through the garden and up on to Pennington Moor.

There was only one place to go now, only one place where he could find comfort. The mine which had been named after his mother.

Louisa mine.

★ ★ ★

567

The pithead was busy. Men were changing shifts, some spilling out of the cages as they came to the surface, others waiting to cram into them to descend. Rupert saw Abe Ricketts talking to Billy Rigg and a few others, but he did not go over to speak to him. Instead, he lifted one hand in greeting and turned away, making for the path that led to the old working.

Here, all was quiet. This shaft, one of the earliest dug, had been abandoned long ago. Over the years, water had seeped in and formed a dank, reddened pool at the bottom. Rusting machinery lay in broken heaps, all the useful parts removed. Even the fence round the head of the pit, put there to stop animals straying in and falling to the murky depths, was rusty and giving way in places. It ought to be mended, Rupert thought absently. Something is going to fall in there some day and be drowned.

He sat down on a stone and stared at the deep hole. It was about twelve feet across and vegetation had begun to fill the gap, gorse and hawthorn bushing out from the sides. Soon the depths would be hidden from above and any animal pushing through the fence would step unwarily, thinking itself on solid ground. It would probably fall right through, leaving no sign.

Any animal. Or any man.

Rupert wrapped his arms over his body, rubbing his hands on his shoulders. He was still cold from shock, shivering and occasionally giving way to great shudders as the vision of Tess's white face rose once again in his mind. Had she known that this was how it would be? Had she even thought of it? Or had her despair been so great that nothing mattered but to end it?

A baby, Martha had said. *His* baby. And she had never told him.

Why had she never told him? Why had she borne her knowledge, her despair, alone?

He began slowly to rock back and forth. He tried to imagine what it must have been like for her, at first suspecting, waking each day to the hope that she was mistaken; then, gradually, facing the fact that it was true, that she must believe it. A child, growing in her womb. A truth that could not be denied, could not be hidden.

For a girl in Tess's position, it was disaster. He had known of more than one maid turned summarily away from the house where she had lived and worked for the same reason. What happened to them then? Ostracised, stigmatised, they wandered from one place to another, doing menial tasks, sometimes reduced to begging for food, and more often than not ending in the workhouse, starved, ill, near death. And if they survived, what then? What life was there for a girl with a child and no husband? How could she care for a baby and earn a living for them both?

He could feel Tess's despair, her fear. It crept cold through his veins, turning each limb to ice. The sickness of it burned in his throat.

Why had she not turned to him?

But he knew the answer. Celia had reached him first.

He thought of the day his wife had told him she was pregnant. There had been something in Tess's eyes then. Had she already known? Was she about to tell him of her own condition? And when he told her that he must stay until after the baby was born, had she lost faith in him then, believed he would never support her, felt herself alone?

He recalled the night when he had told her about Celia. She'd been going to tell him something then, but she'd shrugged it off, saying it was of no importance. And then made love to him, fiercely, hungrily, as if knowing it must be for the last time. As indeed it had proved to be.

He thought of the nights when he had been unable to go to Tess because of Celia's demands. Had she lain

569

alone in her bed, longing for his comfort, his strength, his help?

I would have given it, he thought. You had no cause to worry, Tess, my love. I would have given you all you needed.

But he had not . . .

How could she believe in him when already he was putting Celia before her? How could she believe that with a third child born he would abandon them all? The despair coursed more strongly through his veins and he felt the depths of it in his heart and glimpsed the abyss she had faced.

I failed her, he thought. I failed her when she needed me most. I saw the need in her eyes that day and turned away from it, and who is to say I would ever have turned back? Who is to say that I would not always have found some excuse – the baby is too young, Celia is sickly, Thomas and Oliver need their father . . . I thought I meant my promises, but how can I know now, for I broke them without even realising it.

I killed her, he thought. I killed my love, through not recognising her need.

A terrible groan burst from him at the thought and he rocked forward, burying his head in his arms, feeling her despair and his wash over him in a great flood, as the tide had washed up through Arnside that morning. His body shook as if with an ague, and the sweat broke out over his brow in cold, heavy droplets. Sickness rose again in his throat and he turned his head and retched painfully, but there was nothing to vomit but sour bile, and his stomach felt wrenched and bruised.

Tess, his heart cried out in agony. Tess, Tess, Tess . . .

In his mind he heard her calling his name. *Rupert, Rupert* . . . It was as if somewhere she still waited for him; somewhere, in whichever world her soul had gone, she waited for him to join her. He saw her, dressed in the print frock, but not as she had been in death; instead, fresh and smiling, standing in a field of buttercups, lifting her hands towards him, beckoning. Her brown hair was smooth and shining, her eyes merry and her mouth ready for kissing. And her voice was calling him sweetly. *Rupert, Rupert, Rupert . . .*

He lifted his head. Surely it was real, that voice. It seemed to come from all around him, but it was deepening now, unlike Tess's light tones, as if it echoed up from the earth at his feet, from the dark yawning gap of the mine below him. He stood up, took an uncertain step, stared down into the murky depths. Was it there that he might find peace? Was it there that he might end his troubles and be once again with Tess?

He took another step. The voice was louder now, more insistent. And not Tess's at all. Dazed, he turned his head and looked back across the meadow.

Nicholas was striding across the broken ground towards him. His face was thunderous.

'Rupert! So you're here.' He came to a halt about a yard away. His brows were drawn together in a scowl like an iron bar. His mouth was thin and savage, lips pulled back like a dog's from his teeth. A muscle twitched in his cheek and his hands were clenched into fists at his sides. He breathed heavily, like a bull about to charge.

Rupert stared at him. 'Father, what's amiss?'

'*Father*? You dare to call me that? When you know full well what you've done to me, you and your whorish mother! You and my whorish wife!'

Rupert took a step back. He felt the ground give a little beneath his feet. He came forward again, watching Nicholas warily.

Never in his life had he seen his father look so angry. Never had he seen the lips curled like that, the nostrils widened, the eyes black. Always before, Nicholas had expressed his anger coldly, with sarcasm and contempt.

571

He had never allowed rage to take possession of him as it seemed to have done now, with heat and fire and the quiver of violence.

'Please,' Rupert said, though his mind told him already what had happened, 'tell me what's the matter.'

He saw Nicholas gather himself together, saw the effort that such control required. He heard the strain in the harsh, shaking voice, and knew that the control was slipping. He glanced uneasily at the chasm at his feet.

Nicholas drew a deep breath and spoke the words Rupert had known must be coming.

'Elinor has had her child. A boy.' He paused, drew a deep, ragged breath. 'I don't need to tell you who he resembles, do I?'

The air stood still. There was no sound; no cry of a curlew over the moor, no cackling lament from a passing seagull; no bleat of a lamb, newly born. All Rupert could hear was the beating of his own heart and the harsh breath of the man who stood so near him.

Nicholas spoke again, his voice low, as if it were difficult to force it from his throat. 'You've been a thorn in my side ever since you were born. I knew the first moment I saw you, but I kept you, gave you my name, did all a father should for you. And were you ever grateful? No. You took it all as your right. As if you were my true son instead of a tinker's bastard foisted on me by a wife who slept in ditches. All you ever had came from me. And this is the way you repay me. By dumping another bastard on me. Well, you'll deceive me no more, you swine, nor any other man.'

He was coming closer and Rupert backed away again. He looked into Nicholas's eyes and saw the wide black pupils, the glitter of madness. Beneath his feet, he could feel the crumbling rim of the shaft. Below him, he knew, was a chasm of darkness, a bottomless pool of murky red water.

He knew a moment's blind terror. And then he

thought of Tess, of what had happened to her. Of what she had done and what he had been about to do.

'Well?' Nicholas demanded hoarsely. 'Have you nothing to say before I throw you in to the rats as you deserve? Aren't you going to beg for your life, like the cur you are? You've got two minutes!'

Rupert stared at him. He thought briefly of the old tale that a drowning man sees his whole life pass before his eyes in the last few moments. Was it true? Had Tess seen her life as the waves washed over her face, had she seen him and their loving, had she regretted it?

He had no regrets for those nights of love, only for their consequences. But as he looked at Nicholas and saw the fury, the frustrated madness, the bewilderment of his rage, he had no more thought for Tess.

It wasn't fair, he thought. Whatever Nicholas was, whatever faults he might have, he had the right to feel the rage of betrayal. He had the right to reject Rupert as his son, and to reject Elinor's child in the same way. Yet he had not done so. Cold as he was, he had brought Rupert up as his own. And would doubtless do the same again, trapped, living a lie, knowing that both his wives had followed the same pattern, that both his sons were bastards.

Must he be allowed to add the sin of murder to his burdens?

'No!' Rupert cried. 'Father, don't do this. Think what it means. You'll be tried for murder, you'll hang—'

'And be pleased to, if it gets you out of my life!' He was coming slowly closer, hands outstretched, his face distorted, nostrils wide, lips stretched back over his teeth. 'Swinging will be a pleasure if it's for you.'

'You don't mean it,' Rupert said desperately. It was the only thing he could do now for Nicholas, this one act to save him from the terrible charge of murder. 'You can't mean it. You're angry, and you've every right to be angry, but you don't mean to kill me. You don't—'

'*Don't mean it?*' Nicholas was almost upon him now, his fingers clawing the air only inches from Rupert's throat. 'It's the best moment of my life, the moment I've been waiting for. Don't mean it? I'm going to enjoy every moment, every second of watching you choke away your life.'

Rupert glanced wildly about him. There was no escape. On either side grew bushes thick with thorns. Behind him lay the old mine shaft. And Nicholas barred the way forward.

Briefly, he caught a glimpse of figures in the background. Men coming this way. But they were too late. He felt the crumbling edge of the shaft, felt it give way beneath his feet. He cried out, threw up his hands and felt himself begin to topple backwards. The sky reeled above him.

At the same moment, Nicholas lunged forwards, his hands reaching out for Rupert's throat. As the younger man's body fell before him, he too lost his balance. His foot slipped on the greasy red mud. He staggered, tried to regain his footing and failed.

His clutching hands found Rupert's shoulders as they fell. They met their end together, joined in death as they had never been in life.

JOANNA

Chapter Thirty-Three

Once again, I came to myself crying and shivering with shock as I huddled in a corner of the Blue Room. Once again, I had to be taken home to Pennington Hall and put to bed, to sleep and wake as if in a fever until slowly the terror abated and I was able to think and talk clearly again.

The local doctor poked and prodded me, passed his stethoscope over my chest and back, and declared that I was physically quite fit though a little thin. He asked if I had been banting but Martha assured him that my appetite was normally good and that I had shown no signs of wanting to reduce my weight. He stared at me for a while and finally suggested consulting a specialist.

'She's only recently come here from India,' he said to my aunt. 'There's no knowing what she might have picked up there. You can catch some very strange diseases in the tropics.'

The specialist came, a man from Liverpool with a small goatee beard and horn-rimmed spectacles. He made more or less the same examination as Dr Horner and gave it as his opinion that I had no disease, tropical or otherwise.

'However, she's obviously very highly strung,' he observed, packing away his equipment and talking as if I were not there. 'And she's been through some distressing experiences in the past year. It's all taken a toll on her nerves. She needs complete rest for at least six months, and I would advise you to engage an alienist to treat her.'

'An alienist!' my aunt said in dismay. 'But surely you don't think she's mad!'

'Not mad, no. I know many doctors don't approve of alienists, but I believe Professor Freud's work is invaluable in cases like this. His *Interpretation of Dreams* which was published last year throws a whole new light on the workings of the mind.' He seemed to remember that I was capable of speech. 'Do you have many dreams, Miss Sherwin?'

I stared at him. Dreams? Were they nothing but dreams, the terrible events I had lived through? Could even the most fevered imagination conjure up such nightmare visions?

'You do think I'm mad,' I said. I turned my eyes to Martha, standing beside him and looking frightened. 'You all do, don't you? You and Elinor and Dora and William. And Celia.' I thought of how they had all stared at me when I'd come down from the Blue Room, shaking and incoherent. They'd thought I'd had some kind of fit. I remembered their embarrassment and fear, the way they'd looked at me as if they'd expected me suddenly to run amok with the cake knife. Dora had screamed and run from the room, closely followed by Violet. Celia had turned away in disgust, as if faced with a gibbering idiot, and Lilian, predictably, had looked down her long nose and said nothing. Only Elinor had behaved practically, ringing the bell sharply for a maid and sending the boot boy for Dr Horner. Only Martha, fluttering and anxious, and Mark, who offered to drive me home in the Argyll, showed any sympathy at all.

They all thought me mad. And I could hardly blame them. This was the second attack I'd had since arriving in Furness. How could they know that it wasn't a regular occurrence? How could they know that I had not always suffered from such fits?

But a doctor for sick minds . . .

I had read a little of the work of Professor Freud and the alienists who followed his teachings. Did I really want some foreign doctor to come and sit beside my bed, probing into my mind and writing down my experiences in his notebook? Calling them dreams and analysing them? Making something entirely different out of what I knew to be the truth?

I thought of Rupert's last hours, the pain and suffering, the agony he had endured. Of Tess, walking out into the waves. Of Nicholas, twice a cuckold, his crimes no more than those of ignorance and clumsiness. Did any of them deserve to have their lives recorded in some analyst's notebook, treated as 'dreams' and dissected as sexual fantasy?

Did I deserve it?

'I won't have an alienist,' I said. 'There's nothing wrong with me. Dr Horner was right, I just need rest.' I looked at my aunt, silently imploring her to make this man with the goatee and owlish spectacles go away. 'I want to see Mark.'

He came a day or two later. I was out of bed, as I should have been from the start, but still sleeping a great deal. I lay for most of the day on the sofa, dragged up in front of the drawing-room fire. Outside, it had turned bitterly cold, with a raw north-easterly wind which threatened snow, and I was glad to be indoors.

Mark came just as my aunt and I were settling down to a tea of muffins and hot buttered scones. He drew up a chair and joined us, holding out his hands to the blaze. I looked at him, drawing strength from his comforting presence. Julian had not been near me since my last collapse; no doubt Violet had told him all about it on the telephone. Presumably he too thought I was mad.

'It's so nice to see you again, Mark,' Martha said, licking buttery fingers in her comfortable way. 'It seems a long time since we had tea together. Are you still as busy?'

'No. I've finished the big case I've been working on.' He smiled cheerfully at her. 'Back to the humdrum world of house conveyancing and petty litigation. I can't say I'm sorry, though. It was interesting enough, but I prefer a quiet life.'

'You should be married,' she advised him. 'You're a home-loving man. You need a wife to welcome you in the evening and look after you.'

Mark smiled and looked at the fire. I watched him, wondering what it was that made him look so sad. He seemed especially quiet this afternoon, as if he had something on his mind. I wondered suddenly if he agreed with Martha that he ought to be married, if perhaps he even had some young woman in mind. He had been away a good deal these past few weeks. There might be someone he was missing.

Soon after tea, Martha disappeared, saying she had something to attend to in the kitchen. Mark and I were left alone. We sat in silence for a while, both gazing into the fire, each busy with our own thoughts.

'Do you want to talk about it, Joanna?' he asked at last.

I looked at him. He had realised at once what had caused my collapse. He must be eaten up with curiosity, I thought, wondering what had happened, whose life I had lived this time. Yet although he was ready to hear about it, I knew he would not press me. He would leave me to talk about it in my own time and my own way or, if I wished, not at all.

But I had to talk about it to Mark, he was as closely concerned as I was.

'I'm afraid some of it will shock you,' I said, choosing my words carefully. 'Some of it concerns you – and your father.'

'I thought it might,' he said with a smile. 'My father's

death on the day I was born has always had some mystery attached to it, just as Rupert's death has. Why are their headstones so stark and plain, for instance? It's as if no one cared enough about them to mark their passing with a proper inscription, and yet they both left widows and children. And why will no one talk about it?' He gave me a sudden glance and stopped. 'I'm sorry, Joanna. This must be more painful for you than it is for me. I'm talking of things I've always known, or won= dered about. You've lived through them. At least, I assume you did.'

'Yes. I did.' I paused. It was not easy to say what had to come next. 'Mark, I know what happened between you and your father. I was there. I was part of it.' I shuddered, thinking again of the scene that still haunted me. The terror of the dark chasm that lay beneath my feet, made all the more horrifying by an older memory, of the day when Rupert and some of the miners had gone down into the old pits. Those moments on the ladder when the light had failed and he had thought himself in Hell. It was as if he had always known he would die that way. 'Your father,' I said hesitantly. 'He – he wasn't—' I stopped again.

Mark moved from his chair and came to sit beside me on the sofa. He stretched his arm behind me and I leant back against it, feeling its comforting warmth about my shoulders. In another moment, it might be he who needed comforting.

'He wasn't what, Joanna?' he asked quietly. 'Tell me.'

'He wasn't your father,' I said, letting the words come out too quickly in my desire to have them said and over with. 'Nicholas Craven wasn't your father, Mark. Rupert was.'

There was a long silence. Then he said, '*Rupert* was my father?'

'Yes.'

'Rupert? My mother and – *Rupert*?'

I nodded. I could barely imagine what this meant to him. To discover that he was a bastard, his mother a faithless wife . . . But Mark's thoughts were running on different lines.

'But Rupert was my half-brother! How *could* he—'

'No,' I said miserably, 'he wasn't. Don't forget, he wasn't Nicholas's son, either.'

He stared at me. Then he shook his head, as if trying to get the relationships straight in his mind. I watched with some sympathy. It had been hard enough to understand living through it. For Mark, suddenly jerked from the niche he had always occupied, it must be doubly hard.

'Of course,' he said slowly. 'Louisa and the gipsy. Kieran. *He* was Rupert's father. So that makes me—'

'Kieran's grandson.' I nodded. 'Didn't it ever seem strange to you, Mark, that you have different colouring from the rest of the family? Didn't it seem odd to anyone else?'

He shook his head. 'I knew I was like Rupert, and just assumed that it was part of the Craven family colouring. Martha used to say that.' He frowned. 'Martha . . . Joanna, do you suppose she knows anything?'

I turned my head to look up into his face. The question had bothered me a lot, but after Martha's reaction when I asked her about Tess, I hadn't wanted to upset her again. Now, I was afraid I must.

'I think she does,' I said slowly. 'And I think we have to ask her. Otherwise . . . we'll never be quite sure who we are, Mark. You and I – and the rest of the family. We have to find out the truth.'

It took much talking over several days to tell Mark the whole story. It was not merely a matter of giving him facts, I had also been given an insight into the minds of many people, more than either Rupert or Louisa could ever have seen. I had been granted the knowledge of men and women's hearts and I needed time to assimilate it all. We spent hours trying to understand the motives that had driven the previous generations, and the more we searched, the more we pitied them for the tragedy of their lives.

'None of them was really to blame,' Mark said at last, soberly. 'They did their best, in the light of their times and their own experience. It wasn't Louisa's fault she was ignorant about love and afraid of Nicholas, and it wasn't his fault that he didn't know about her fears. It wasn't even Rupert's fault that he was seduced by my mother—' He stopped. It had been a bitter pill to swallow, facing up to the kind of woman Elinor had been. 'But who's to know what made her like that? I know nothing of her first husband, William's father, or anything else about her early life. If the others can be excused, why not her as well? Why not everyone?'

I nodded. I had found it hard at first to forgive Timothy what he had done to Louisa. But now, with my knowledge of Rupert's feelings, of what it was like to be married to a cold and unloving wife, I could understand and sympathise with the frustration that had overwhelmed him.

The whole saga was a tragedy of errors. Mistakes made over and over again, marriages entered into for the wrong reasons . . . The phrase chimed a note in my mind. Hadn't someone said that not long ago? Louisa, Rupert, Mark, myself – a quartet joined together in a dance that went down the years, a slow and tragic saraband.

Mistakes made over and over again. A pattern of errors.

Was this what I was being shown? Was this the purpose behind my journeys into the past?

'I know,' Martha said. 'I've known all the time that

something was happening to you.' She looked at me with eyes filled with pity. 'I had no idea what it was, of course, but I knew there was something important. It's to do with the family, isn't it? You've been seeing ghosts.'

I shook my head. 'Not quite ghosts, Aunt Martha, but something rather like that. But we don't want to upset you.'

'You won't do that now,' she said quietly. 'I buried it all for years, you know, refused to face up to what had happened. I wouldn't think about it. I kept busy all the time, to stop the thoughts crowding in, and eventually I suppose I succeeded. I hadn't thought about it all for years, until you came home and started to ask questions. I realised then that something was happening, and that it couldn't be hidden any longer. And when you started to ask about Tess . . .'

I reached out and touched her hand. 'Don't talk about it if it makes you unhappy.'

She shook her head. 'I told you, it's all right. I made myself think about it then. Poor Tess, nobody ever really knew what happened to her.'

'I think I know,' I said. 'She was expecting Rupert's baby, wasn't she? They were in love, they planned to go away together. And then Celia told him she was pregnant and he couldn't leave her. He never knew Tess was pregnant too.'

'That's right. I knew of her condition – I noticed it quite soon and she confided in me. But I didn't know it was Rupert's child. And that last afternoon, the day you were born,' she turned to Mark, 'he came to tell me her body had been found. And I told him then.' She looked at me piteously and I saw that for all her brave words, she still had doubts. 'I always wondered if that was why he died,' she whispered. 'I always wondered if it was my fault . . .'

'No!' I had to scotch that immediately. What use for

Martha to go to her own grave believing she had driven Rupert to his? 'No, it was between Rupert and Nicholas. They met on the moors and fell into an old shaft. It was an accident, no more than that.'

She stared at me. 'An accident? You're sure?'

I knew it was not. I knew that Rupert had been about to commit suicide, that Nicholas had come along and tried to kill him. Whether in the end their deaths had been accidental even I could not tell. My memories of that moment were too confused, too desperate, too overshadowed by terror and that final fall into silence. But there was so much I could not tell Martha.

'Billy Rigg saw them,' I said. 'What did he say?'

'Oh, Billy Rigg. He said so many things. He said they were fighting. He said that Nicholas tried to push Rupert in and Rupert clung to him and pulled him down. But everyone knew that Billy Rigg couldn't be relied on. He had hated the Sherwins and everyone to do with them ever since he was a boy. His father had died of consumption, his brother had been injured in the head and the family were almost penniless. He blamed poor Papa, and went on blaming for the rest of his life. And there was his own injury in the earthquake.' She sighed. 'There were a good many people who thought that Billy pushed them in himself. But I never thought that. Anyway, he died too, not long afterwards, so no one ever knew the truth.'

Until now, I thought. I had been shown the truth. But still I didn't fully understand why.

'The pattern,' I said to Mark after Martha had left us alone. 'I can see the pattern but I still don't quite understand it. And what does it mean to the family? So many people are not who they believe. You—'

'I'm no Craven at all,' he said slowly. 'I'm part Sherwin – Timothy was my grandfather – and part gipsy. And if Rupert was my father, Lilian must be my sister. And Tom and Oliver my brothers.'

585

'Half-sister and -brothers,' I said. 'More half-relations! This family is full of them. And what am I to you?'

He gave me a quick look, as if about to speak, then changed his mind. After a moment's thought, he said, 'I think we're second cousins. Or half-cousins once removed if there is such a thing! In any case, we're not at all closely related.' The thought seemed to give him some satisfaction but he went on quickly, 'Mother must have known the relationship between Lilian and me. I wonder if Celia knew or suspected.'

'I expect so.' It would have accounted for some of the tensions in the family. I thought of the two women, watching their children grow, knowing the truth. Suppose Mark and Lilian . . . But it was scarcely likely. Marriages between cousins were generally unpopular, though they did happen. And surely either Elinor or Celia would have taken steps to prevent any such thing taking place.

We sat quietly for a while. I let my mind drift back again to the events I had witnessed, the memories that were still fresh in my mind. Why had it all happened? And why did I have to understand?

'Let's go back to the idea of reincarnation,' Mark said at last. 'Would the theories account for this? What would they say?'

'I think they would say that I am a reincarnation,' I answered. 'A reincarnation of a spirit that's gone through several lives, making the same mistake. These visions, or memories, have been a chance for me to understand the mistakes and put them right in this life.'

'So you were Louisa. And Rupert?'

'I must have been.' I had certainly felt their emotions strongly enough. I had known the sensation of living inside their skins, their minds. 'I told you, reincarnations don't have to be the same sex.'

586

'Louisa died as Rupert was born,' he said thoughtfully. 'But Rupert was dead for several years before you were born.'

'That doesn't matter. When a body dies, the spirit goes into a state called *bardo*. It hovers around for as long as is necessary to find the right body to inhabit – the body it needs, with the parents it needs, to bring about the right circumstances for its next life. It all follows strict natural laws, you see. Everyone is on their own particular ladder and the rungs must come in the right place. I can't step off my natural path, or ladder, and climb yours instead. I have to stay on mine and learn the right lessons for me.' I sighed. 'I don't seem to be very good at learning them.'

'Well, you've never had such help before. Neither Louisa nor Rupert saw what you've seen. Neither of them knew all this. It's as if you had to be born in India to gain the knowledge you needed before coming here and—' He stopped. 'That's exactly what you're saying, isn't it? You needed to be born in India. You needed your particular father. So when you came here, you were ready.'

'It all fits in, doesn't it?' I said. 'But what is the lesson I'm supposed to learn? Why do I still not understand?'

Mark took my hand. He looked at my fingers and then lifted his eyes to my face.

'I think you do understand,' he said simply. 'I think you are just still a little afraid to face it.' He waited a moment and then said, 'What caused all Louisa and Rupert's problems? What was the root of their unhappiness?'

'For Louisa,' I said, 'it was surely when Timothy lost control of himself.'

'Very well. Let's begin with Timothy. Why did that happen?'

'Because he was unhappy in his marriage,' I said.

'Because he had married the wrong woman, for the wrong reasons.'

'And Louisa?'

'She married the wrong man. She never loved Nicholas, but she saw him as a way to escape from her home and from Susannah. But what Timothy did had frightened her. She needed gentle loving, and Nicholas didn't know that. He couldn't give it to her.' I thought again of the bewilderment between them, the expectations so cruelly shattered on both sides. 'If only they could have said . . . And Rupert married Celia for her pretty face, and because he wanted to escape from Elinor.' I gave Mark an apologetic look. It was difficult to reconcile the seductress of Rupert's story with the stiff, elderly lady who was Mark's mother. 'And then they both found people they really loved, and betrayed them.'

'And do you still not think there is a message there for you?' Mark asked quietly.

I stared at him. Then I turned my head away sharply. 'You mean Julian, don't you?'

'Only you can answer that, Joanna.'

I twisted back towards him. 'I've never said I was going to marry Julian! He hasn't even asked me.' But he very nearly had, and I'd very nearly said yes. 'And would it be so terrible if I did? There's nothing mercenary about it, I don't care about his money. Who's to say it would be for the wrong reasons? What *are* the wrong reasons for getting married?'

'Any, except for love, I'd say. And you may not care about Julian's money, Joanna, but I think he cares a good deal about yours.' He got to his feet. 'I must go now. But think about it, try to see if the pattern could apply to you too. And if I might ask one favour?'

'Yes?' I was disturbed and, as always, showed it in irritation. But Mark had done so much for me, listening, helping me to work it out – even if I didn't like his conclusions. I softened and smiled at him. 'Of course you may. What is it?'

'Before you go rushing off to Peru or Chile or wherever you mean to go next,' he said with a wry look, 'will you help me find my own particular answer? Will you come with me to see the gipsies and find out if my grandfather is still alive?'

'Your grandfather . . .?' I stared at him. 'Kieran? But he'd be—'

'Over eighty. I know. But they're a long-lived race, and they're at Broughton now, camped there for the winter.' He gave me an odd look, half pleading. 'I'd like to go and see them, Joanna. But I need you with me. I have a feeling that Kieran would understand the things you've been telling me.'

Chapter Thirty-Four

It was on the first day of December that Mark and I made our journey to Broughton to visit the gipsies.

The raw, damp weather of November had given way to a soft mildness, with blurred sunshine glowing gently from a hazy sky. The last of the leaves still hung like bright flames on trees and hedges, and the holly was covered in brilliant red berries. I noticed them as we drove through the lanes in Martha's trap and determined to paint them before the birds stripped the bushes bare.

'I'm sorry about the Argyll,' Mark said, flicking the reins over the pony's back. 'I don't know exactly what's wrong with it. It just coughed and spluttered a bit and then died. There's a mechanic coming out from Barrow, but I think it's going to need a special part. If he can't make it himself, I may have to wait some time.'

'So you're demoted to old-fashioned horse-power,' I remarked teasingly. 'Well, it's probably good for you to see how the rest of us live. And to be honest, I'm quite happy to travel more slowly and quietly on a day like this. There's so much to see. And I love the smell of autumn – wet leaves and wood smoke. I've never known anything quite like it.'

We jogged on through the lanes. Coming back, Mark said, we would be able to use the route across the sands, which was much shorter, but the tide was too high just now. I was pleased enough to have the chance of seeing two different ways. The narrow roads which wound across Furness were always a pleasure with their unexpected views across the two estuaries, far across the sea to the south and west, and bordered by the craggy outlines of the mountains to the north. And the sands never ceased to fascinate me. I had wanted to make the strange, perilous journey across their hidden tracks for a long time.

I watched a kestrel hovering in the sky above the fields and my thoughts drifted back to the subject that had occupied them so much during the past few weeks. I had been able to discuss much of what had happened to me with Mark, but there were still some sides of the story that I hid from him. And I could not talk to him about Julian.

Julian. I shifted restlessly in my seat and stared out at the passing hedgerows. Julian still occupied a part of my mind, but my thoughts and feelings about him were confused. I needed to sort them out, but only Mark had ever been able to help me untangle my confused emotions, and this was one subject I could not discuss with Mark.

Why this should be, I did not know. Or perhaps the truth was that I didn't want to face it.

The experiences I had been through, first in Louisa's life and then in Rupert's, had caused me to be wary. I understood what Mark and I had been saying a few days earlier, about patterns and wrong marriages. Louisa and Rupert had both married for the wrong reasons, though they had scarcely realised it at the time. But both had experienced doubts, small worries at the outset. Both had been uncertain, then dismissed their doubts and gone on, plunging blindly down the wrong track.

Was this what I was in danger of doing?

It might be nothing at all to do with reincarnation, I thought. It might be no more than a family tendency, a propensity to take the wrong path, to be swayed by the wrong considerations. Getting away from home, stealing the man your stepsister wanted, as revenge for years of humiliation, escaping the attentions of a mistress who had become too demanding – none of these were good reasons for marrying. As Mark had said, no reason but love was likely to bring success to such an intimate relationship.

Had I been about to follow the family tradition? Was Julian the wrong man for me to marry?

'The gipsies are camped down near Foxfield,' Mark said as we came up to the road which linked Broughton with Ulverston. 'We don't need to go into the village itself.' He swung the trap to the left, heading towards the estuary again. Here, the land was low-lying and marshy – not very attractive for winter camping, I thought. But there were small hills and clusters of trees that provided dryer spots and gave shelter, and I thought the gipsies would be more easily tolerated here than on the pastures further inland.

We rattled along a wide track, the pony picking its way across mud and stones. Peewits wheeled overhead, uttering their plaintive cry, and gulls screamed and cackled. It was pleasant enough down here on a day like this, so mild and sunny, but what would it be like later when the raw winds blew from the north and the marshes were thick with ice? I shivered and wondered if I was becoming soft. I had camped in many worse places myself, after all, and thought little of it.

'Soon be there,' Mark said. He pointed with his whip. 'See, there's the smoke from their camp fires.' I saw the thin grey spirals winding up from a clump of trees, and smelt the aroma of cooking.

I felt my heart beat suddenly faster. Until now, it had not seemed quite real; within a few minutes I would meet the man who had walked with Louisa on the moors nearly seventy years ago; who had lain in the grass and talked to her; who had made love to her, had asked her to go away with him and finally been forced to leave her, pregnant with his child. If he was still alive. He might, after all, have died years ago. We might have come on this strange quest for nothing.

We were close to the camp now. I could hear voices, the sound of wood being chopped, the laughter of children. I felt almost sick with nervousness. And, as we came closer still, an overpowering sense of familiarity.

I had been here before. Not to this particular camp; Louisa had never travelled so far afield by herself. But to a camp like this, with tents and fires, with women sitting in groups on the dewy grass making wreaths of holly and ivy to sell in the villages, and men coming in with a string of rabbits dangling from their shoulders. I had seen them before, the swarthy faces, the rough clothes, the bright scarves. I knew them, better than I knew my own family.

It had not been quite like this though, I thought as Mark reined in the pony and we stopped at the edge of the camp, gazing around. Kieran's people had never had these brightly painted wagons when Louisa knew them.

We sat for perhaps a minute, staring around us, before we were noticed. And then the camp fell silent, the travellers pausing in their work to stare. After a few minutes, one of the men detached himself from the group and came over to us.

'Were you wantin' something?' He spoke with the odd accent I remembered – not the local dialect, nor any other that I had known since arriving in England, but an accent peculiar to the travellers, collected over years of roaming and merged into a tongue that had become almost a language of its own. I remembered some of Kieran's words – *chavvy* for child, *dinilow* for daft, *trashed* for afraid. And, when he wanted to express amusement or concern, *dordy me*!

Mark glanced at me. I shook my head. I wasn't ready to speak yet. I could not bring myself to ask for Kieran. It was as if I were Louisa again, come to look for him. But I was sixty years too late.

Mark sensed my confusion, and spoke for me. 'Do you have man here called Kieran Matthews?'

The gipsy turned his head slightly sideways, as if to look at us out of the corners of his eyes. He stared at Mark, then turned his attention to me. His black brows were drawn together and he seemed to be weighing up something in his mind.

I wondered if he were part of Kieran's family. A son, even a grandson. Would he sense that he was related to Mark? Would he know, without being told, that we had a special purpose in coming here?

'Kieran Matthews is an old man,' he said at last, and my heart leapt.

So he was still alive! Kieran, who had run and laughed on the hills of Furness, who had known how to make love with tender passion, who had roused a frightened body to willing response and ecstasy – he was still alive and in this very camp.

'I know,' Mark said quietly. 'I'd like to see him, if I may.' He paused, then added, 'I'm his grandson.'

There was a sudden stir and I realised that the other men had got up from their work and gathered behind him. And behind them were the women, silent and watchful, the children held close against their skirts.

'Would ye like to say that again?' the gipsy said, his voice deep in his throat.

'I would not. You heard me well enough.' Mark spoke quietly but his voice was strong and uncompromising. He did not intend to be bullied by these men. I shivered a little and moved closer. I knew that the travellers were not violent people, but I knew too how proud and independent they were. If they thought a *gauje* was trying to make mock of them . . .

'Kieran Matthews has seven grandsons, and they're all before ye now,' the traveller said. 'Tell us what ye want with him.'

'He has eight,' Mark replied, 'and my business is with

him alone, if he's fit to listen to me.'

There was another movement through the little crowd that had collected, and a murmuring sound. I gave Mark a glance and touched his arm, silently begging him not to anger them, but he was looking straight into the other man's eyes and took no notice.

'Kieran Matthews is fit to listen to any man. It's a question of whether he wants to hear.'

'Then why not let him decide?' Mark said. 'Go to him and tell him I'm here.'

'And how is he to know who you are?'

At last, Mark turned his head and looked at me. His eyes met mine and I read the question in them. I felt a tremor run through me and an instant withdrawal. No, I thought, no. That's too much. I can't . . . But I nodded, and he turned back to the gipsy.

'Tell him Louisa has brought me . . .'

The wagon was the largest and brightest in the camp. Its body was dark green, its wheels red and the carving around its door and windows picked out in yellow. It stood a little apart and on top of its steps sat a young woman of about my age, with hair that hung loose about her face in a cloud of black curls and eyes as bright and dark as a squirrel's.

She stared curiously at us as we approached, but at a word from the gipsy slipped down from the step and stood waiting as he climbed up and went inside. I saw her eyes on my clothes and smiled at her, but she did not return my smile and when the gipsy came out and motioned us to go inside, she looked sullen and angry.

'She's Kieran's granddaughter,' the man said. 'She looks after him and she'll not forgive you if you do him any ill. Nor will the rest of us.'

'We don't mean him any harm,' Mark answered, ducking his head to go through the little doorway. He stood just inside, accustoming his eyes to the darkness, and then motioned me to follow him.

But I could not. I stood on the step, gripped by the most powerful emotion I had yet known. I was scarcely aware of who I was – Joanna or Louisa. Or perhaps both, for in that moment I *was* Louisa. I had all her memories, I knew all her fears and pleasures, all her desires and all her suffering. I could not go in and face the old man who had been my youthful lover and know that he had gone through life believing himself betrayed.

'Joanna,' Mark said. He came out of the wagon and looked at my face. He took my arm, gently but firmly. 'Joanna, you can't stop now. You've come so far. Don't you see, this is the final part of the story. This is where you can lay your ghosts and look your *karma* in the face. You can't run away from it. You've never been able to run away from it.'

I tore my eyes away from the dark doorway and looked at him. My heart was thudding with fear. He looked back at me, and I saw his resemblance to Kieran. The colour of his hair, his eyes, the darkness of his skin – all these were outward resemblances and might have come from any family. But there was now something more in his eyes, a look, an understanding, that came directly from his grandfather. And I thought of the afternoons on the hills, when Kieran had made gentle, passionate love to Louisa and taught her what life was for.

It's for loving, I thought. That's all it is, for loving. And if we don't love, we do an injury to life itself, not simply to ourselves. We damage the very fabric of the world. Without enough loving, the world will degenerate into a chaos of war and pestilence and famine. And each of us has a duty to maintain it.

Perhaps that's what the Buddhists were trying to do, with their compassion for all living things. And the Christians, the Moslems, all the religions that preached love and honour. But it gets twisted and distorted. We think of material things, of power and riches and land. And we forget to love.

Kieran had known about love and taught it to Louisa, but it had been too late for her. Because of her mistake, Rupert had been born as Nicholas's son instead of Kieran's. And Mark, who carried Kieran's wisdom within him, was standing here now, waiting for me to recognise the pattern and go with him to meet his grandfather.

I have recognised it, I said to him silently. I know now where to find real love. And I put my hand into his and went with him through the door.

Kieran lay in a narrow bed along one wall of the wagon. A single lamp burned in a niche, and by its light I could see that he was very old. I went forward, suddenly overcome, and knelt beside the bed. His hand lay, thin and gnarled, on the blanket and I took it in mine and pressed it against my lips.

His eyes stared at me wonderingly. He lifted his other hand and passed it tremblingly over my head. I felt the cool, dry, papery skin on mine and wept inside for the young Kieran, leaping like a stag up the hills, lying with Louisa in the heather, vigorous and powerful, with his life before him.

'Louisa,' he said, and his voice was cracked and old, but still Kieran's voice. 'Louisa. They said it was Louisa . . . Louie . . . my Louie . . .'

'Kieran,' I said, swallowing my tears. 'I'm not Louisa. My name is Joanna. Louisa died.'

'You're Louisa.' He stated it positively, as if there could be no argument. 'My Louie, come back to me.' His eyes moved over me, as if remembering every detail of my face. I stayed quite still, letting him look his fill, wondering what memories stirred in his mind. Memories I knew we shared.

'I've brought someone to see you,' I said at last, and

Mark came forward out of the gloom. 'When you left Louisa she was expecting your child. You didn't know, she never had a chance to tell you, but she meant to come to you, until her father was taken ill. She couldn't leave him then, and when the baby was born, she died.' I tried to keep my voice calm. Had he known of her death? He must have done, the travellers came back year after year. He must have returned the following year, ready to ask her again to come with him, and discovered that she was dead and had left a living child. But he had not known that child was his.

'Louisa gave birth to your son,' I said, and took Mark's hand. 'And this is his son – your grandson, Kieran. He wanted to meet you.'

The old eyes moved over us both, taking in Mark's dark, curling hair, his deep brown eyes. A flash of recognition passed between them and I gave a little sigh of relief.

'Mark,' he said. 'A good name. Strong and simple. Mark.' He nodded and then turned back to me. 'And you've brought him to me. It took a long time, but you brought him at last. You came back, Louie, after all this time.'

I had not come back, I thought. Louisa was part of my past, but I was not Louisa. I was Joanna, who had taken on the torch of the spirit that lived within us both. But we were different beings, in different times.

We stayed a long time in the wagon, Mark and I, talking to the old man of times almost forgotten, of memories almost lost. Mark had been right, Kieran did understand the things I told him. He had never heard of Buddhists or of their beliefs, but he knew about the world of the spirit, he knew of the truth of the universe, and he knew about love. It was he who had saved the Sherwins from their tragic pattern of mistakes; for without his loving, Louisa would never have come to life, nor given life to Rupert. And Mark would not be here now, the right man for me to marry. It was Kieran's loving that had lived on, for Mark and me to fulfil.

We came out at last into a cold, frosty sunset. The travellers let us go without hindrance, understanding that something strange and vital had taken place in their camp that day. And we jogged home across the perilous sands of Duddon, safe in the knowledge that our way lay plain before us.

Through two lives, I had known what it was to founder in quicksand. But now I walked on rock, with my hand in Mark's. The pattern which had been so tragic had been woven with a different thread and shone with gold across the rippling shore as we left the gipsy camp behind and made our way home to Furness.

A selection of bestsellers from Headline

THE LADYKILLER	Martina Cole	£5.99 ☐
JESSICA'S GIRL	Josephine Cox	£5.99 ☐
NICE GIRLS	Claudia Crawford	£4.99 ☐
HER HUNGRY HEART	Roberta Latow	£5.99 ☐
FLOOD WATER	Peter Ling	£4.99 ☐
THE OTHER MOTHER	Seth Margolis	£4.99 ☐
ACT OF PASSION	Rosalind Miles	£4.99 ☐
A NEST OF SINGING BIRDS	Elizabeth Murphy	£5.99 ☐
THE COCKNEY GIRL	Gilda O'Neill	£4.99 ☐
FORBIDDEN FEELINGS	Una-Mary Parker	£5.99 ☐
OUR STREET	Victor Pemberton	£5.99 ☐
GREEN GROW THE RUSHES	Harriet Smart	£5.99 ☐
BLUE DRESS GIRL	E V Thompson	£5.99 ☐
DAYDREAMS	Elizabeth Walker	£5.99 ☐

All Headline books are available at your local bookshop or newsagent, or can be ordered direct from the publisher. Just tick the titles you want and fill in the form below. Prices and availability subject to change without notice.

Headline Book Publishing PLC, Cash Sales Department, Bookpoint, 39 Milton Park, Abingdon, OXON, OX14 4TD, UK. If you have a credit card you may order by telephone – 0235 831700.

Please enclose a cheque or postal order made payable to Bookpoint Ltd to the value of the cover price and allow the following for postage and packing:
UK & BFPO: £1.00 for the first book, 50p for the second book and 30p for each additional book ordered up to a maximum charge of £3.00.
OVERSEAS & EIRE: £2.00 for the first book, £1.00 for the second book and 50p for each additional book.

Name ....

Address ....

....

....

If you would prefer to pay by credit card, please complete:
Please debit my Visa/Access/Diner's Card/American Express (delete as applicable) card no:

Signature .... Expiry Date ....